AF522640

BHARATAVARSHA
THE
INDIA NARRATIVE

as told in

INDRAVIJAYAH

PANDIT

MADHUSUDAN OJHA

Translated by

Prof. Kapil Kapoor

Edited by

Wilson John

Shri Shankar Shikshayatan

RUPA

Published by
Rupa Publications India Pvt. Ltd 2017
7/16, Ansari Road, Daryaganj
New Delhi 110002

Sales centres:
Allahabad Bengaluru Chennai
Hyderabad Jaipur Kathmandu
Kolkata Mumbai

ISBN: 978-81-291-4913-8

First impression 2017

10 9 8 7 6 5 4 3 2 1

Printed at Replika Press Pvt. Ltd, India.

Contents

Preface

Shri Shankar Shikshayatan Trust is happy to present its first publication, *Bharatavarsha: The India Narrative*, an English translation of *Indravijayah*, an extraordinary work of Vedic scholarship, by an eminent scholar of the Vedas, Pandit Madhusudan Ojha (1866–1939).

The credit for making Pandit Ojha and his works (sixty-six published volumes in all) known to the English-speaking world should go to Rishi Kumar Mishra (1932–2009), a man of letters and learning in his own right. Shri Shankar Shikshayatan was set up by him to fulfil the promise he made to his guru, Pandit Motilal Shastri (1908–1960), to propagate Veda Vijnana, which can be broadly translated as Vedic Science. Shastriji was an illustrious disciple of Pandit Madhusudan Ojha.

Mishraji, the author of five illuminating volumes on the Vedas, chose *Indravijayah* as the first work by Ojhaji to be translated into English. There were a few important reasons for this decision. The most persuasive one was Pandit Ojha's reaffirmation of the Vedas and other related ancient texts as convincing reference points of history and geography. His lucid portrayal of the erstwhile Bharatavarsha and the progress made in the fields of science, linguistics, and other forms of knowledge based on a wide variety of sources, including the Vedas, Puranas, Ramayana, Mahabharata and other ancient texts, is remarkable.

There are indeed brave and contentious assertions made in this volume which will open up discussions which, if done in a spirit of free enquiry, can offer an insight into several facets of those ancient times. It is equally important to keep in mind the era covered in the book and the period in which Pandit Ojhaji wrote *Indravijayah*.

No word of thanks would suffice in expressing our gratitude to Professor Kapil Kapoor, an eminent scholar of linguistics, for translating *Indravijayah*. It has been a task requiring passion, patience and rigour.

Work of this character and magnitude would not have been possible without the help of countless people. Shri Shankar Shikshayatan Trust acknowledges with gratitude all those who gave their time and advice generously in the making of this volume. Three persons need to be specifically acknowledged and thanked—Dr Santosh Kumar Shukla, an Associate Professor of Sanskrit Studies at Jawaharlal Nehru University, a scholar who is wise beyond his years; Dr Lakshmi Kant Vimal at Shri Shankar Shikshayatan, who shepherded the tedious and tiresome process of putting such a complex work to print; and Dr Mani Shankar Dwivedi who helped with the bibliography.

No less grateful are we to Rupa Publications, Mr R.K. Mehra and Mr Kapish Mehra, and their team of editors for their unstinting support in the publication of *Bharatavarsha: The India Narrative.*

A last word for the discerning seeker—you will find several published works of Pandit Madhusudan Ojha, Pandit Motilal Shastri and Rishi Kumar Mishra on our website, www.shankarshikshayatan.org

Bharat Goenka
Chairman
Shri Shankar Shikshayatan Trust
New Delhi

Introduction

Bharatavarsha: The India Narrative is the English translation of an extraordinary work of scholarship in Sanskrit, *Indravijayah* or 'Indra's victory', authored by an equally remarkable Vedic scholar and orator, Pandit Madhusudan Ojha.

Pandit Madhusudan Ojha (1866–1939) was in many senses a pioneering man of words and wisdom, reigniting an interest in the study of Vedas and other Pauranic texts at a time when western mode of education had swept aside traditional learning and teaching in India.

Blessed with worthy teachers in Pandit Rajiv Lochan Ojha, his uncle, and Pandit Shiv Kumar Shastri, a renowned Vedic scholar of Kashi, Pandit Ojha recognized that the reading and understanding of Vedas would require rediscovering the meaning and context of the Vedic language, lost due to neglect and disaffection over the centuries. Distortions and misinterpretations had besmirched the true meaning of Vedic terminologies. These had to be corrected, he realized, to revive a deeper study of the Vedas in India. This became his life's mission.

A lifelong study of the Vedas along with other Pauranic texts made Pandit Ojha aware of an exceptional blend of reasoning based on natural principles and introspective insight in these texts. He discovered in the Vedas a living science, Vedic Vijnana, the key to unlock the profound mysteries of Creation, and life.

Indravijayah is one of his over 228 volumes written on various aspects of Vedic Vijnana which evidently has survived decades of neglect. The present volume is an endeavour by Shri Shankar Shikshayatan to foreground not only the extraordinary interpretive talent and scholarship of Pandit Madhusudan Ojha but also his remarkable contribution towards reviving an interest in the study of the Vedas.

Bharatavarsha: The India Narrative may not capture in entirety the magnificence and depth of knowledge contained in the original work of Pandit Madhusudan Ojha, but it certainly does open a beguiling window to the mysteries of life and Creation through the absorbing tale of Indra, a divine personification of a supraphysical energy, and his exploits of courage and dominance.

At the surface level, this book is a simple tale of Indra, a mighty and brave warrior armed with a vajra, who is also the lord of the heavens and light, and the devas.

Located within this adventurous tale of Indra's war and peace is the story of Bharatavarsha, a playground of the devas and asuras, where new cultures, new languages and the manushyaloka itihasa (history of the human world) took seed and flourished.

A substantial part of this book deals with the geographical contours of Bharatavarsha and its many facets which have hitherto remained undiscovered. Herein, Pandit Ojha, digging deep into the Vedas, Puranas and other important texts, has constructed a vigorously argued framework of reference points that steadily build the story of Bharatavarsha.

More important than the range and extant of information are the remarkably 'new' definitions and interpretations that Pandit Ojha has laid down in *Indravijayah* to dispel what he calls the numerous bhrantiyan (mistaken assumptions) about Bharata, which in fact is an entity much larger than what we understand today.

Bharatavarsha: The India Narrative is not limited to mapping the contours of a country—it constructs a composite image of the people and their culture in the Vedic period. It expounds on the principles of dharma, a way of life governed by ethics and duty, points to the origin of script and the evolution of languages, elucidates on the development of a solarium or observatory to study various facets of the sun, and enumerates in some detail various arts, skills, and accomplishments of the people.

Pandit Ojha's reliance on Rigveda as a principle source of history of Bharatavarsha has been a bold and controversial pursuit. There has been a traditional divide among scholars about Rigveda—majority of them believe that it is a work of divinity and cannot therefore be used as a reference point for studying mundane subjects like history or geography. They believe that names mentioned in the Vedas have to be read as pratik-s (symbols); their contention is that any resemblance to real people, places, and events is coincidence. Others, in minority, aver that each hymn is attributed to a rishi and hence is not 'divine' in nature but very human, and therefore contain narratives of what actually happened or had existed.

Pandit Ojha, on his part, has adopted a unique position—a middle path, arguing that while Rigveda is apaurusheya (not of human origin) but its epistemology is alaukika-pratyaksha (extraordinary direct perception) of drashta-s (seers), and therefore its encryption and expression, is human. Rigveda, he argued, could hence be used as a valuable reference point to map the history and geography of the land in ancient times.

It is evidently not an easy task to decode the complex nature of language, the sandhya-bhasha as it is called, or its encoded knowledge which Adi Shankaracharya called apara vidya, and draw out information about people, places, and events of an ancient age. The language of the Vedas is metaphoric, on the authority of Samkhya Darshana, and replete with symbols and allusions. It is Pandit Ojha's astounding scholarship and sharp reasoning which made it possible for him to interpret in human terms a repository of brahma-jnana (transcendental knowledge), beginning with the knowledge of Creation itself.

The English version of the work, *Bharatavarsha: The India Narrative*, follows the same structure as laid down by Pandit Ojha in *Indravijayah* where he articulated his findings about various aspects of Creation, cosmos, nature, human history, and geographical details. The book has five prakarana-s (chapters). These are further divided into prasanga-s (sub-sections).

The book opens with a grand sweep of Creation, illuminating in the process the existence of three triadic worlds representing Creation in all its manifestations. These worlds transcend barriers of time and space, existing as much within as outside. The prithvi (earth) is a part of these triadic worlds and within prithvi, similar triadic worlds exist.

The three geographic regions on prithvi have three presiding deities—Indra, the god of light, Vayu, the god of wind, and Agni, the god of fire. These distinctions are a classic mode of marking the climate of the three regions from north to south—the ice cold Siberian and Tundra regions, the windswept central Asia that includes Mongolia and China and the hot plains of Bharatavarsha.

Pandit Ojha applies these three divisions to the sharira (physical body) as well—from the head to the heart is denoted as divya (divine), from heart to the navel is antariksha (interspace) and from the navel to the lower organs constitute bhauma (earthly). Construction of this powerful ontology must be counted as one of Pandit Ojha's stellar achievements in this book.

This section is followed by a detailed presentation of proofs to establish the territorial boundaries of Bharatavarsha and the etymology of its name as found in the Vedas and Puranas. These sections are descriptive and make a convincing argument about the expanse of Bharatavarsha—'From the Eastern China Sea to the Red Sea in the West'. This almost approximates the dimensions in Ptolemy's First century CE map of India.

The fifth section offers a new interpretation of the names given to Sri Lanka, Maldives, and Lakshadweep Islands. Citing references from the Ramayana, and corroborating it with the latitudes and longitudes of given places, the book argues that 'Sinhaladvipa' and 'Lankadvipa' referred to the present day Lakshadweep and Maldives and not to Sri Lanka. It is 'Sinhala' which is the modern Sri Lanka, whose language is still known as the 'Sinhalese'. These assertions, cogently argued, call for serious reflection.

The next sections on the languages and script offer thought-provoking observations and assertions. Pandit Ojha has asserted that the Vedic metric language was the source language for all Indian languages. On the question of script, he has countered the common belief that there were no scripts during the Vedic period. He argues with interesting illustrations from ancient texts that lipi (scripts) existed in the Vedic period. This section on languages and scripts should pique the interest of modern linguists.

The tenth section discusses the question of dharma which is defined as an ethical way of life, and not as a religion. The section offers a rational definition of the much-misunderstood, and abused, term and lays out various principles of living governed by its embedded ethics and spirituality.

The last section is devoted to India's knowledge systems, including what are today identified in the Anglo-American world as 'the sciences'. Pandit Ojha has lucidly explained how the taxonomy of ancient knowledge was very different from what we today conventionally know. All vidya-s (disciplines), in the Vedic period, were divided into: (i) prakritvidya—knowledge that arises from or is available in nature and can be gathered by observation; (ii) laukika vijnana or knowledge of material arts and crafts; (iii) knowledge of separate, quantifiable objects such as herbal medicine; (iv) Vedic sciences such as Rasayana (Chemistry) and Ganita (Mathematics); and (v) solar energy.

This brings us to the end of what is not only the largest sequence, prakarana, but also one that is conceptually the most complex and dense. This is the Arya-Dasyu narrative. This sequence contradicts the theory that the Arya came to India from outside and that the narratives of wars between the Arya and Dasyus, for example, are the wars between natives and the invaders. This theory has been elaborately refuted on the ground that territorial boundaries have shifted over the centuries and no such boundaries existed in the past. If we look at Ptolemy's map of Asia, there are no recognizable political boundaries and a large mainland is simply a cauldron of races fighting each other for control of land (as depicted in the present work).

Pandit Ojha cites Vedic testimony to show that five kinds of battles were recorded in the Vedas. These were ethnic wars between the Arya and other Asian ethnic groups that came in search of food and wealth. Then the war between the devas and asuras was waged for the knowledge of solar energy and for cows, land, and water. The war with the dasas was fought for knowledge useful to the community, with the panis for cows, with the daityas for the secret of Soma and the rights over mountains where Soma grew, with the danavas for land and with fellow Arya for other reasons such as hegemony.

These narratives are followed by a fairly descriptive and fascinating account of the rishis [seer-scientists] establishing a solar observatory and carrying out studies of various cosmic phenomenon. Subsequently, many such observatories were built. These surya bhavan-s were of two kinds—a temple for worship of the sun and a laboratory for solar-energy research. These observatories had instruments in the form of brilliantly integrated separate discs or chakras. Their use and power have also been described. In these facilities, seer-scientists studied Nature and dimensions of Time and Cosmos. This 'laboratory', however, became a bone of contention between the devas and dasyus with the latter launching a series of attacks to capture the laboratory. Responding to these attacks, Indra and the rishis pooled their physical prowess and extraordinary powers to defeat the dasyus and protect the surya bhavan.

These developments are followed by another important narrative about how Indra finally freed the Arya from the repeated scourge of dasas in the resumed wars between the Arya and dasas that ended with 50,000 dasyus taken prisoners and entrusted to the care of a powerful deva king Ayu with the responsibility of 'civilizing' them.

With the final defeat of the dasyus, Indra brought peace upon earth. It is this victory of Indra that is celebrated in the last prakarana, the fifth and final sequence titled 'Indravijaya-abhinandana', the honouring of Indra on his victory. In this final sequence, we are given to understand how the communities grew into a holistic civilization in this land and how the cultural entity called Bharata evolved.

The original title of this work, *Indravijayah*, is inspired by this momentous event.

But the narrative does not end here. It concludes in fact in dayaniya-parishishta that may be read as 'a sad appendix' which records the subsequent defeat and decline of a grand ancient civilization, rich in wealth and knowledge. After a long, peaceful interlude when the arts and sciences flourished, the dasyus from the west again attacked the solar observatory and destroyed it or took away everything. Such observatories had been established elsewhere also, including one in Gandhara. The asuras attacked and destroyed those too and the surya bhavan set up in Syria that had brilliant pillars but not the chakra or disc-instruments was also razed to the ground by the attacking asuras and 'thus that age of knowledge, courage, purity, and wealth came to an end.'

Bharatavarsha: The India Narrative, undoubtedly, presents a grand narrative of an ancient era. But its assertions are contingent upon the right interpretation of Vedic terms and therefore offer further avenues of scrutiny and debate. Dismissing the averments, made herein, which are indeed substantial, would be tantamount to negating a freer, robust, and innovative pursuit of knowledge.

The importance of this book cannot be underestimated. It has, in its original Sanskrit edition, initiated a new stream of Vedic interpretation, an affirmative stream that reads the Vedas as texts of knowledge and not only as works of metaphysics. It was the first work to draw attention to the body of scientific knowledge in the Vedas and initiated research in ancient Indian sciences. This research has really expanded and now many institutes and scholars are actively developing a corpus of work on ancient Indian sciences. This work has also inspired students and scholars of sciences and engineering to rework Vedic geography and as a result, in 1964, a major full-length study, *The Geography of Rigvedic India*, authored by Manohar Lal Bhargava, was published from Lucknow.

The English translation of Pandit Madhusudan Ojha's book, under the aegis of Shri Shankar Shikshayatan, comes out at a time when there is a greater need to restore the sanctity of Veda Vijnana and free the pursuit of Vedic knowledge from distortions and bhrantiyans (misconceptions).

This work, the product of a magnificent obsession and determination on the part of Pandit Madhusudan Ojha, it is hoped, will ignite interest among students, teachers, and lay readers about the collective sacred legacy, the Vedas, and the little-known history of this ancient land.

Kapil Kapoor
New Delhi
July 2017

प्रक्रम: प्रथम:

भारतपरिचय:

CHAPTER FIRST

INTRODUCTION TO BHARATAVARSHA

1.1. त्रैलोक्यप्रसङ्ग:

1.1. SECTION ON TRIADIC WORLDS

1.1.1 त्रिविधं त्रैलोक्यम्

1.1.1 Three triadic worlds

देवयुगे त्रैलोक्यं त्रिविधमिदं ब्रह्मणाऽऽदिष्टम् ।
अधिदैवतमध्यात्मं तत्साम्येनाधिभूतं च ॥1॥

In the beginning, Brahma the Creator, created three distinct *trailokya*-s (triadic-worlds), named as *divya* (divine), *sharira* (bodily) and *bhauma* (earthly) in this very sequence. These divisions are based on three principles—*adhidaivika* (supraphysical), *adhyatmic* (spiritual), and *adhibhuta* (material).

	अग्निलोक: पृथ्वी 1	वायुलोक: अन्तरिक्षम् 2	इन्द्रलोक: द्यौ: 3
अधिदैवम्	6 त्रिवृत् (21स्तोम:) शिव: 9.15.21	15 पञ्चदश: (33 स्तोम:) विष्णु: 11.22.33	21 एकविंश: (48 स्तोम:) ब्रह्मा 16.32.48

अध्यात्मम्	वस्तिगुहा उदरगुहा	उदरगुहा उरोगुहा	उरोगुहा शिरोगुहा
अधिभूतम्	भारतीया: 1–32 शर्य्यणावत हिमालयपर्यन्त:	तैर्य्यग्योना: 32–40 निषध: अलतायिपर्यन्त:	वायंभुवा: 38–48 चन्द्रगिरि: भद्रगिरि: उत्तरसमुद्रपर्यन्त:

	AGNILOKA Prithvi	**VAYULOKA Antariksha**	**INDRALOKA Dyauloka**
Adhidaivam	6 Trivrtta (21 Stoma) Shiva	5 Panchadasa (33 Stoma) Vishnu	**21 Ekavimsa (48 Stoma) Brahma**
Adhyatam	Vastiguha (from rectum to navel)	Udarguha (stomach - from navel to heart)	**Uroguha (from heart to throat) Siroguha (from throat to top of head)**
Adhibhutam	**Bharatiya Shayyanavat Up to Himalayas**	**Tairyyagyona Nishada Up to Altaic Mountains**	**Vayambhuva Chandragiri Bhadragiri Up to the North Sea**

1.1.1.1 दिव्यत्रैलोक्यम्

1.1.1.1 Divine triadic world

तद्दिव्यं शारीरं भौमं चेति क्रमादुक्तम् ।
अग्निर्वायुश्चेन्द्रश्चेति त्रैलोक्यमिष्यते दिव्यम् ।।2।।

The *divya trailokya* (divine triadic world) is made up of Agni (fire), Vayu (air) and Indra (energy).

पृथ्वीयमग्निलोक: सूर्यो द्यौरिन्द्रलोक: स: ।
अनयोर्मध्ये वायोर्लोक: स्यादन्तरिक्षमिदम् ।।3।।

This earth is Agniloka (domain of fire), the domain of the sun or light is Dyauloka and Indraloka is the domain of sky, energy, and consciousness. The domain of winds, Vayuloka, lies in between these two and this is also the *antariksha* (interspace).

एतेऽतिष्ठावानो देवास्तेषु त्रयस्त्रिंशत् ।
वसुरुद्रादित्याख्या द्वावन्यावश्विनौ चेति ।।4।।

Thirty-three gods dominate these three *loka*-s (domains)—eight vasus, eleven rudras, twelve adityas and two ashvin kumars.

Divya trailokya

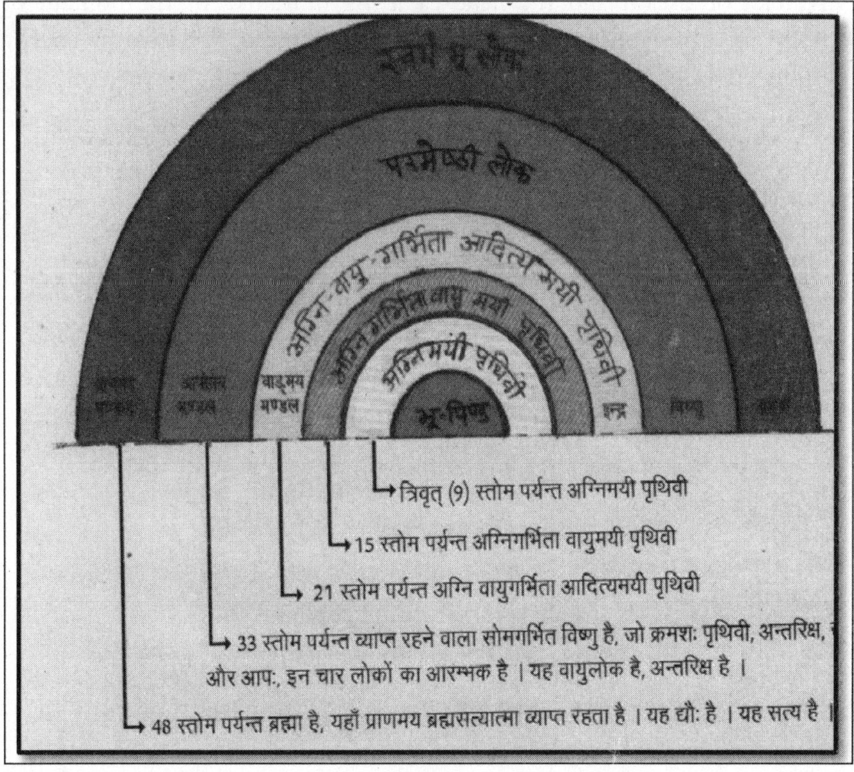

1.1.1.2 शारीरिकत्रैलोक्यम्

1.1.1.2 Bodily trailokya

गुदनाभ्यन्तः पृथ्वीर्द्यौर्हृत्कण्ठान्तरन्तरे व्योम ।
उदरमुरश्च शिरश्चेत्यथवा देहे त्रिलोकी स्यात् ।।5।।

From the rectum to the navel is Prithviloka (earth), from the heart to the throat is Dyauloka (domain of light), and between the two, the stomach part, is the *vyoma* (space). In this manner, in the form of stomach-domain, heart-domain and head-domain, three worlds are said to exist in the human body as well.

उदरगुहाऽग्नेर्लोको लोको वायोरुरोगुहाऽध्यात्मम् ।
लोकः शिरोगुहेन्द्रः सर्वे प्राणास्तदायत्ताः ।।6।।

In this human world, the stomach-cavity is Agniloka, the chest-cavity is Vayuloka or breath and the head-cavity is Indraloka or the domain of energy and consciousness. The entire life principle is governed by energy designated as *Indra* or *indra-prana* located in the head cavity.

Sharira trailokya

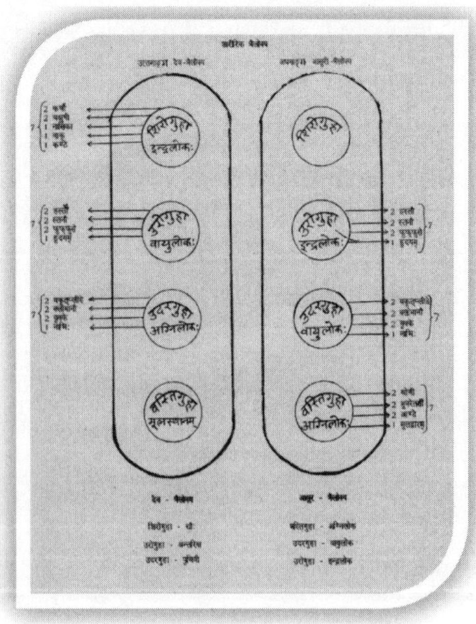

1.1.1.3 भौमत्रैलोक्यम्

1.1.1.3 Earthly triadic world

एवं कृतमधिभूतं भूमौ त्रैलोक्यमत्र देवयुगे ।
अधिदैवतवत् तत्र च विहितानि हि नामरूपकर्माणि ।।7।।

In the same manner, the earthly triadic world is of three kinds. As in the divine world, in the physical world too, name, form, and function are classified separately.

मनुजास्तैर्यग्योना देवा भौमत्रिलोकीति ।
वैवस्वतमनुविट्त्वं व्यवस्थितं त्वत्र मनुजत्वम् ।।8।।

This physical world is home to human beings, *tiryagayoni* (animals, birds and other creatures) and *devas* (deities). Human beings are the descendants of Manu, the son of Vivasvana.

मानुषलोक: पृथ्वी तैर्यग्योनाऽन्तरिक्षं स्यात् ।
दैवो लोको द्यौरिति भौमं त्रैलोक्यमाख्यातम् ।।9।।

The land inhabited by human beings is the earth; the domain of tiryagayoni is antariksha; the northern world of light is *devaloka* (the world of deities). All this has been designated as the earthly triadic world.

अधिपतिरग्नि: पृथ्व्या वायुरधीशोऽन्तरिक्षस्य ।
इन्द्रो दिवस्पतिश्चाध्यक्षा दिव्यवत् कल्प्या: ।।10।।

Just like in the divine triadic world, the presiding deities of the earthly triadic world have also been determined: Agni is the deity of the southern land, Vayu rules over the interspace and Indra is the presiding deity of the northern world of light.

दक्षिणसमुद्रतोऽग्नेर्लोकोऽस्ति हिमालयं यावत् ।
अलतायिगिरैरैन्द्रो लोकश्चोत्तरसमुद्रान्त: ।।11।।

यस्तु हिमाचलशैलादलताय्यचलान्त आन्तरो देश: ।
वायोर्लोक: स इदं त्रैलोक्यं भूतले विद्यात् ।।12।।

The expanse from the southern sea to the Himalayas is the Agniloka; the expanse from the Altai mountains to the northern seas is the Indraloka and the middle expanse between the Himalayas and the Altai mountains is the Vayuloka. This is how we have to understand the triadic world on this earth.

भारतमग्नेर्लोकोऽस्त्यैरावतवर्षमिन्द्रलोकोऽन्यः ।
अनयोर्मध्ये मरुतां लोको देवाः स्थितास्तेषु ।।13।।

Bharatavarsha is Agniloka and Airavatavarsha is the second Indraloka and in between the two is the Vayuloka where the devas live.

उत्तरकुरवः कथिताः शृङ्गगिरेरुत्तराः पुराणेषु ।
नीलगिरेरुत्तरस्तूक्तास्ते भारते भैष्मे ।।14।।

In the Puranas, the land to the north of the Shringa mountain is called Uttara Kuru, whereas in the Mahabharata, this name has been given to the land north of the Nilgiri mountains.

Further, sharira trailokya is of two kinds—*daiva* and *asuri*.

भारतवर्षस्थानमासीत् क्लृप्तं मनुष्यदेवत्वम् ।
उत्तरकुरुस्थितानां देवत्वं वा मरुत्त्वमन्येषाम् ।।15।।

Bharatavarsha was a land blessed with human divinity. Those who inhabited Uttara Kuru came to be called the devas. They were descendants of Indra. All others came to be called the Marut.

अग्नेः प्रजा मनुष्या भारतवर्षे नियन्त्रिता मनुना ।
ऐन्द्री प्रजा तु देवा उत्तरकुरुषु स्थिता अभवन्। ।16।।

The descendants of Agnideva, the humans, were settled in Bharatavarsha by Manu, the first ruler of the human world. Indra's descendants were the devas, who dwelt in the northern regions.

1.1.2 एशियादेशे त्रैलोक्यविभागाभासः

1.1.2 Asia in earthly triadic world

भौमं यत् त्रैलोक्यं तदिदानीमेशियानाम्ना ।
ख्यातं तत्र च देवासुरसन्ताना वसन्त्यद्य ।।17।।

The ancient bhauma trailokya is known today as Asia and the descendants of the devas and *asuras* (those who were not divine) live here even today.

अद्याप्येते देशास्त्रिधा विभक्ताः प्रदृश्यन्ते ।
ते च त्रयोऽपि लोकाः प्रत्येकं स्युर्द्विधा भिन्नाः ।।18।।

This land mass, even today, is divisible into three divisions, each with two sub-divisions.

हिन्दुस्तानं पारस्तानं चेत्यस्ति दक्षिणतः ।
चीनस्तातारो वा मध्ये रूसो द्विधोत्तरतः ॥19॥

Hindustan and Parasthan lie to the south of Asia; China, and Tatar in the middle; and Russia is divided into two parts in the north.

1.1.3. तातारस्य रूसदेशस्य च भौमस्वर्गत्वम्

1.1.3 Tatar and Russia known as earthly heaven

क्षुद्रैशियान्ततः प्राक् चीनात् प्रत्यक् तु विष्टपं ब्राह्मम् ।
सकैंशियादिपश्चिमरूसप्रान्तोऽत्र विष्टपं विष्णोः ॥20॥

The land mass east of Asia Minor and west of China was accepted as the *vishtapa* (seat) of Brahma. The land west of Korea up to Russia was the abode of Vishnu.

आसीद् विष्टपमैन्द्रं प्राग् रूसः सायिवीर्याख्यः ।
इत्थं प्रसिध्यति स्म त्रिविष्टपं स्वर्गलोकोऽसौ ॥21॥

In ancient times, the part of Russia known as Siberia was called Indra's vishtapa. In this way, this land mass being the abode of three gods was well-known as the trivishtapa and this was svargaloka.

1.1.4 सायिवीरियोत्तरीयकतिचिद्भागस्य समुद्रमग्नत्वम्

1.1.4 Submersion of some northern parts of Siberia in ocean

यावानद्य स रूसस्तावानखिलः पुराऽभवत् स्वर्गः ।
अपराजिता दिगेषा यो देशः सायिवीरिया नाम ॥22॥

All the land that constitutes Russia today was svarga in ancient times. The region of Siberia was in its north-east direction.

इह सायिवीरियासौ यद्यप्यद्यास्त्यसभ्यजनताढ्या ।
कृच्छ्रप्रधानभूमिः किन्त्वासीत् सा न चेदृशी पूर्वम् ॥23॥

This Siberia, which is today uninhabitable, very difficult climatically, and where today uncivilized (nomadic) people live, was not like this in ancient days.

इह सायिवीरियातो यदुदक्प्रान्ते समुद्रतटम् ।
यश्च समुद्रप्रान्तो भूरितुषारावृतोऽद्यास्ति ।।24।।

The ocean and coastal areas, north of Siberia, are today covered with thick layers of ice.

न्यू सायिवीरिया या प्रसिध्यति म्लेच्छभाषायाम् ।
तत्र पुराऽसीन्नगरं सोद्यानं विबुधजनताढ्यम् ।।25।।

But in the past, in the area called New Siberia in the *mleccha* (non-Sanskrit) language, there were populous towns and forested areas.

अपि वनमासीन्नानावृक्षचितं पशुभिरावृतं बहुभिः ।
कालेन तत् तुषारप्रवर्षणाद् भ्रंशमायातम् ।।26।।

Extreme weather destroyed the forests and its people, leaving the place uninhabitable.

अत एव तत्र कूले समुद्रगर्भे कदा च लभ्यन्ते ।
मेमाथनामकरिणां दन्ता बहुधाऽस्थिपञ्जरा अपि वा ।।27।।

Even to this day, tusks and skeletons of mammoths (huge prehistoric elephants) can be found in the coastal areas and in the surrounding waters.

सपादषड्ढस्तमितः स उच्चः पादोनितैकादशहस्तदीर्घः ।
सपादषड्ढस्तमितेन दन्तद्वयेन मेमाथकरी युतोऽभूत् ।।28।।

These mammoths were about nine-and-a-half feet high, fifteen-and-a-half feet long and had two huge tusks, each nine feet long.

दन्तोऽस्य वक्रो महिषस्य शृङ्गवत् कृष्णानि लोमानि तनौ तथोर्णवत् ।
न चेदृशः सम्प्रति दृश्यते करी यथा स मेमाथकरी पुराऽभवत् ।।29।।

The tusks of the mammoths were bent like the horns of a buffalo and their body covered with black hair. At present no such elephant survives.

एकोदराश्च द्विशिरोधराः पुरा भेरुण्डनामान इहाभवन् खगाः ।
न चेदृशाः सम्प्रति पक्षिणः क्वचिद् दृश्यन्त आद्ये तु युगे यथा श्रुताः ।।30।।

A strange bird with one stomach and two heads called Bherunda used to live there but it too became extinct over the years.

विज्ञायते तेन पुरा युगेऽभवद् वनं पशुक्रान्तमिहोत्तराम्बुधेः ।
स्थाने जनानां च पुराणि भूयसा तत्रैव सन्ति स्म च तर्हि देवताः ।।31।।

All these facts suggest that in ancient times, there were massive forests full of diverse, rich animal life in these northern oceanic lands.

Bhauma trailokya

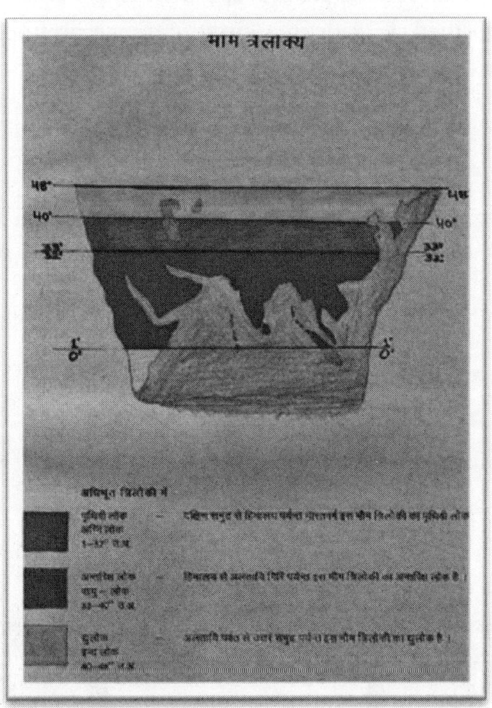

1.1.5 स्वर्गीयविष्टपत्रयविध्वंसे दैवो हेतुः

1.1.5 Divine forces responsible for the destruction of svarga

नाकस्थविष्णोः परितस्तु वेद दृग् व्यासार्धजे सञ्चरति ध्रुवं ध्रुवः ।
वृत्ते ध्रुवस्तत्र तथा पुरा युगे प्राग्मेरुखस्वस्तिकगोभिजित्यभूत् ।।32।।

The Pole Star (Dhruva) moves in the radius of 24 degrees latitude, around the firmament-point (a flower[1]-shaped point located in the centre of the

[1]Kadam is an evergreen, flowering tree found in south and south-east Asia. Its common English name is Burflower tree. The flower of this tree finds mention in the Vedas.

circumference of Pole Star's revolution, the point around it revolves) on which *Vishnupada* (the feet of Vishnu) is situated. For this reason, in ancient days, Dhruva occupied a position in the Abhijita-nakshatra (one of the lunar asterisms) on Kha-svastika (the svastika) formed by the movement of 24 degrees in all four directions around the firmament point. When reversed or inverted, it formed a 24-degree circumference around the svastika of Pamir mountains.

ध्रुवादधस्तादतिशय्य शैत्यं प्रवर्तते तेन तदा पुरात्वे ।
प्राग्मेरुदेशे बहुशैत्यमासीत् नतूत्तराम्भोधितटप्रदेशे ।।33।।

Since deep, freezing cold occurs directly below the Pole Star, the Pamirs became extremely cold, much colder than the northern Tundra lands of Asia.

Svastika-khasvastika

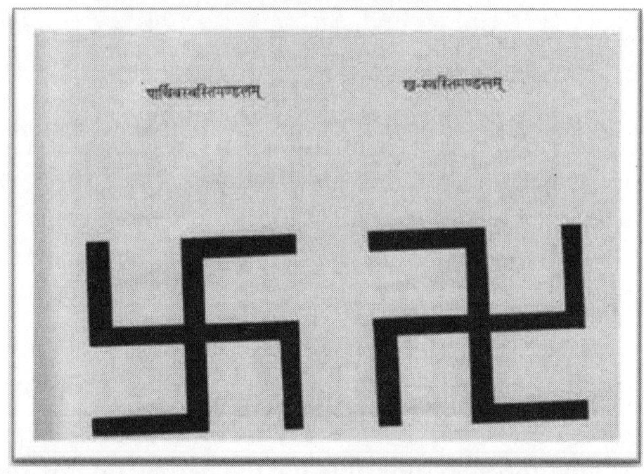

एष ध्रुवो जनयते च तुषारवर्षा विभ्रंशयत्यपि पुरातनवासिलोकान् ।
तौषारवर्षणवशादिव नाशमायन् प्राग् मेरुगाः क्वचिदुदक्कुरुभूमिपिण्डाः ।।34।।

With the movement of the Pole Star heralding extreme cold weather, the ancient people of Siberia were destroyed by frost, ice and snow. Because of this frost, ice and snow, the polar regions of the North and parts of Uttara Kuru too were destroyed.

1.1.6 विज्ञाने दिव्यत्रिलोकी इतिहासे भौमत्रिलोकी

1.1.6 Scientific history of earthly triadic world

इत्थं त्रिलोकी त्रिविधा निरुक्ता दिव्या च भौमी च शरीरगा च ।
त्रिधाग्निभिः सा शवसोनपाद्भिर्धृता पृथग् देवनिकायपूर्णा ॥35॥

In this way, three kinds of trailokya have been enjoined—divya, sharira, and bhauma. This perceptible, physical habitation that does not allow the strength [of dwellers] to decline, supported by the sacrificial fire of three kinds—*garhapatya, ahavniya* and *dakshina*—is populated with different devas.

विज्ञानभाषासु यदि त्रिलोकीप्रसङ्ग आयाति स दिव्य एव ।
ऐतिह्यभाषासु यदि त्रिलोकीप्रसङ्ग आयाति स भौम एव ॥36॥

Wherever the triadic world or trailokya is mentioned in the context of science, it is to be understood as the divya trailokya. In the context of *itihasa* (history), it has to be understood as the bhauma trailokya.

दिव्यत्रिलोकीमनु दिव्यदेवा भौमत्रिलोकीमनु भौमदेवाः ।
ऐतिह्यमत्र प्रवदामि तस्माद् भौमा हि भाव्या इह लोकदेवाः ॥37॥

The devas are associated with the divya trailokya. The bhauma trailokya is associated with earthly, ordinary devas. Here, when we give their history, by loka-devas, we understand the earthly, ordinary devas, who dwell here in this world.

ब्रह्मा गुरुः शिक्षयतीह विद्यया शक्रः प्रभुः शास्त्यनुगृह्य वा बलैः ।
विष्णुः सुहृद् यज्ञजसम्पदाऽवति त्रयोऽपि भौमा इतिहासगा इह ॥38॥

In this world, Brahma in the form of a teacher educates; Indra, with his power and valour, rules over people; Vishnu, like a friend, sustains us with wealth produced righteously. In this way, in the course of retelling history, we accept that these three are the divine beings of the earthly triadic world.

विज्ञानेऽस्ति यथैतेषु त्रिषु सर्वं प्रतिष्ठितम् ।
तथेह भौमस्वर्गेऽपि त्रिषु तेष्ववलम्बितम् ॥39॥

As in *vijnana* (science), everything has three as the substratum, likewise on this bhauma svarga also, everything depends on these three devas.

1.1.7 भारतवर्षस्य भौमत्रैलोक्यान्तर्गत-पृथ्वीलोकत्वम्

1.1.7 Bharatavarsha in Prithviloka in the context of bhauma trailokya

दिवमधिजगुर्बुधा यां पूर्वयुगे सा बभूव वसुधायाम् ।
उत्तरमेरौ स्वर्गस्तत्र स वसति स्म देवतावर्गः ॥40॥

In ancient times, the place known as svarga where the great seers and sages went, was on this earth itself. It was in the northern polar region of this earth where the devas dwelt.

दक्षिणतः प्राग् मेरोरिरावतीनिर्गमाद् गिरेस्तूदक् ।
अयमन्तरिक्षलोको वसतिः सा देवयोनीनाम् ॥41॥

These devas lived in the Antarikshaloka, between the south of Pamir mountains and north of the source of river Iravati.

देशो य उदग् विषुवत इरावतीनिर्गमाद् गिरेस्त्वर्वाक् ।
तदिदं भारतवर्षं पृथ्वीलोकस्त्रिलोक्यां सः ॥42॥

The area north of the equinoctial line and south of the source of origin of Iravati river, a part of the bhauma trailokya, which is called Prithviloka, is Bharatavarsha.

भारतवर्षं मानुषदेशः शिखिशशिरविकुलजोऽत्र नरेशः ।
धेनुभिरन्नधनैरपि धन्यः स हि देशानामिह मूर्द्धन्यः ॥43॥

This Bharatavarsha is that abode of human beings which was ruled by the kings of solar and lunar dynasties. This country was rich in grain, wealth, and cattle and therefore it occupied the highest place among all the countries.

यावान् मनुष्यलोकः सा पृथ्वी तच्च भारतं वर्षम् ।
तत्र च मनुष्यशब्दः पृथ्वीशब्दश्च लाक्षणिकः ॥44॥

The part that is *manushyaloka* (world of human beings) is Prithviloka, and is Bharatavarsha. Here the terms 'manushya' and 'prithvi' are indicative terms.

इति भारतपरिचये त्रैलोक्यप्रसङ्गः सम्पूर्णः ।

The trailokya section in the Introduction to Bharata is concluded.

1.2. नामधेयप्रसङ्गः

1.2 SECTION ON NOMENCLATURE

1.2.1. भारतवर्षस्य नामानि

1.2.1 Names of Bharatavarsha

यदिदं भारतवर्षं स्कान्दे तन्नभिवर्षमप्युक्तम् ।
आर्षभवर्षं चान्यैर्हैमवतं वर्षमप्यन्यैः ॥45॥

भरतस्यायं देशस्तस्माद् भारत इति प्रथितः ।
भरतं त्वेतमनेकं स्मरन्ति पौराणिकाः सर्वे ॥46॥

Bharatavarsha is known as Nabhivarsha (nabhi means navel and also centre point) in the Skanda Purana. Some people have named it as Arshabhavarsha and others have called it Haimavatvarsha (land along the Himalayas). It, however, became popular as Bharata as it was the land which belonged to Bharata. All *Pauranikas* (collection of Puranas) recall more than one individual by the name Bharata.

1.2.2. भारतशब्दव्यपदेशे मतचतुष्टयम्

1.2.2. Four views on the use of word Bharata

1.2.2.1 पौराणिकं प्रथमं मतम्

1.2.2.1 First view in the Puranas

स्वायंभुवस्य हि मनोराग्नीध्रः सूनुरस्य नाभिस्तु ।
नाभेर्ऋषयस्तस्माद् भरतस्तस्यैष देशोऽभूत् ॥47॥

According to the first pauranic view, Agnidhra was born to Svayambhuva Manu, Nabhi was born to Agnidhra, Rishabha to Nabhi and Bharata to Rishabha to whom this land belongs to, and named Bharata after him.

आग्नीध्रसूनोर्नाभेस्तु ऋषभोऽभूत् सुतो द्विजः ।
ऋषभाद् भरतो जज्ञे वीरः पुत्रशताद्वरः ॥
(मार्कण्डेयपुराणम्, 50.38-39)

O Brahmins, Nabhi was born to Agnidhra, Rishabha to Nabhi, Bharata to

Rishabha who was best among all hundred sons.

हिमाह्वं दक्षिणं वर्षं भरताय पिता ददौ ।
तस्मात्तु भारतं वर्षं तस्य नाम्ना महात्मनः ॥
(मार्कण्डेयपुराणम्, 50.40-41)

The father gave Bharata the southern country called 'Himahvam'. This came to be called Bharatavarsha after that great soul, Bharata.

ततश्च भारतं वर्षमेतल्लोकेषु गीयते ।
भरताय यतः पित्रा दत्तं प्रातिष्ठता वनम् ॥
(विष्णुपुराणम्, 2.1.32)

This Bharatavarsha was known in the three worlds after this Bharata. The Vishnu Purana records: 'While leaving for *vanaprastha* (exile into the forest), Bharata's father had given this land to him.'

नाभेः पुत्रश्च ऋषभ ऋषभाद् भरतोऽभवत् ।
तस्य नाम्ना त्विदं वर्षं भारतं चेति कीर्त्यते ॥
(स्कन्दपुराणम्, माहेश्वर-कौमारिकाखण्डः, 37.57)

In the Skanda Purana, it is said: 'Nabhi's son was Rishabha and Rishabha's son was Bharata, and hence the land came to be known as Bharatavarsha by his name.'

1.2.2.2 पौराणिकं द्वितीयं मतम्

1.2.2.2 The second view of the Puranas

विदुरपरे दौष्यन्तिर्भरतः शाकुन्तलेयो यः ।
वीरः स सर्वदमनस्तन्नाम्ना देश एषोऽस्ति ॥48॥

तंसुरोधाच्च दुष्यन्तो दुष्यन्ताद् भरतोऽभवत् ।
शकुन्तलायां तु बली यस्य नाम्ना तु भारताः ॥
(अग्निपुराणम्, 278.6-7)

In the second pauranic view, this land was named Bharata after the Bharata who was the son of Dushyanta and Shakuntala, and who was the destroyer of all the enemies. In the Agni Purana, it is said that Bharata was born to Tansurodha's son Dushyanta and this land was named Bharata after him.

एष जगद्विजयीति प्रथितो वेदे पुराणे च ।
काण्डे त्रयोदशे सोऽश्वमेधकृच्छतपथश्रुतावुक्तः ।।49।।

The Vedas and Puranas have stated that this Bharata was *chakravarti* (conqueror of the world).

अष्टा सप्ततिं भरतो दौष्यन्तिर्यमुनामनु ।
गङ्गायां वृत्रघ्नेऽबध्नात्पञ्चपञ्चाशतं हयान् ।।
(शतपथब्राह्मणम्, 13.5.4.11)

शकुन्तला नाडपित्त्यप्सरा भरतं दधे ।
पुरा सहस्रानिन्द्रायाश्वान् मेध्यान् य आहरत् ।
विजित्य पृथ्वीं सर्वाम् ।।
(शतपथब्राह्मणम्, 13.5.4.13)

In the thirteenth chapter of Shatapatha Brahmana, this Bharata has been stated as the performer of the *ashvamedha-yajna* (yajna involving horses carried out by ambitious kings to capture new territories). It is recorded–'Dushyanta's son Bharata tied seventy-eight horses on the banks of Yamuna and fifty-five horses on the banks of Ganga for the slayer of Vritra, that is, Indra. This means that he had performed ashvamedha-yajna many times. After conquering the whole earth, Bharata performed one thousand ashvamedha-yajnas.'

महदद्य भरतस्य न पूर्वे नापरे जनाः ।
दिवं मर्त्य इव बाहुभ्यां नोदापुः पञ्चमानवाः ।।
(शतपथब्राह्मणम्, 13.5.4.14)

Today or in times to come, no one can achieve the glory of Bharata and no one, whether of the mortal world or the one who belongs to 'seven cycles of Manu' (*manvantara*), can conquer Dyauloka with his hands or feet.

स्कान्दे प्रभासखण्डे द्वासप्ततिशततमेऽध्याये ।
यत्वार्षभभरतस्याश्वमेधकर्तृत्वमित्थमाख्यातम् ।।50।।

In the 172nd chapter of Prabhasa-khanda of Skanda Purana, the ashvamedha-yajna performed by Bharata, the son of Rishabha, has been described like this.

तत इह भिन्नं मन्ये तमश्वमेधं यमाहरद् भरतः ।
दौष्यन्तिः संख्याया भेदाद् वेदे पुराणे च ।।51।।

Because of the difference in the number of the Vedas and Puranas, I believe that Bharata, the son of Dushyanta, who performed the ashvamedha-yajna, is different from the one cited in the Skanda Purana.

भरतो नाम राजाऽऽसीदाग्नीध्रः प्रथितः क्षितौ ।
यस्येदं भारतं वर्षं नाम्ना लोकेषु गीयते ।।
(स्कन्दपुराणम्, प्रभासखण्डः 172.2)

On this earth, there was born a celebrated king Bharata, who was also known as Agnidhra, the performer of holy yajna. By his name, the glory of Bharatavarsha is sung throughout the world.

षट्पञ्चाशदश्वमेधान् गङ्गामनु चकार यः ।
त्रयस्त्रिंशद् यमुनाप्रान्ते भरतो लोकपूजितः ।।
(स्कन्दपुराणम्, प्रभासखण्डः 172.12)

This Bharata, having performed fifty-six ashvamedha-yajnas on the banks of Ganga and thirty-three ashvamedha-yajnas on the banks of Yamuna, earned honour in the world.

भरतस्यैताः कीर्तेर्गाथाः पूर्वैः पुरा गीताः ।
भरतो हीमां पृथिवी मनुष्यलोकं शशास चिरमेतम् ।।52।।

In ancient times, people had sung the glory of this Bharata. This Bharata ruled for a long time in the manushyaloka.

तन्नाम्नायं देशो भारत इति विश्रुतो लोके ।
पौराणिकमतमेतत्सा भरताय प्रशस्तिचाटूक्तिः ।।53।।

It is known in the world that this land was called Bharata after that Bharata. There are numerous statements in praise of Bharata in the Puranas.

भरतेनैतेनैते न भारता इति किल श्रुता देशाः ।
कुलमेव तेन भारतमस्योक्तं भारताख्याने ।।54।।

But, according to the Mahabharata, this land was not called Bharata after this Bharata. It was the descendants (born in the clan) of Bharata who were called Bharata.

दुष्यन्तस्तु ततो राजा पुत्रं शाकुन्तलं तदा ।
भरतं नामतः कृत्वा यौवराज्येऽभ्यषेचयत् ।।
(महाभारतम्, आदिपर्व, 69.44)

स राजा चक्रवर्त्यासीत् सार्वभौमः प्रतापवान् ।
भरताद्भारती कीर्तिर्येनेदं भारतं कुलम् ॥
(महाभारतम्, आदिपर्व, 69.47, 49)

The Adi Parva of Mahabharata records—'Then the King Dushyanta, having called Shakuntala's son Bharata as Bharata, conferred on him the title *yuvaraja* (prince or heir to the throne). That king was all-mighty, glorious, and an emperor and whose dominion extended as far as the ocean. The glory of Bharatavarsha extended throughout the world due to this Bharata and this dynasty of Bharata was called Bharata.'

1.2.2.3. वैदिकमतम्

1.2.2.3. Examination of the Vedic view-point

ब्रूमो वयं तु पूर्वं देवयुगेऽप्यत्र मानुषो लोके ।
अग्निर्भरतोऽधिपतिर्नियुक्त इन्द्रेण मनुरासीत् ॥55॥

In the vaidikas, it is stated, 'In ancient *devayuga* (age of devas), Indra deputed Agni in the form of Bharata as the custodian of the human world. There Agni was Manu.'

आसीद् व्यवस्थितं तु त्रैलोक्यं यत्र देवयुगे ।
तत्र च भारतवर्षं पृथ्वीमाहुर्मनुष्यलोकः स ॥56॥

Of the earthly triadic world which was settled in the devayuga, Bharatavarsha was called Prithvi; it was the manushyaloka.

स्वर्गेश्वरो यथेन्द्रो यथान्तरिक्षेश्वरो वायुः ।
पृथ्वीश्वरस्तथाऽग्निर्भरतः इति ह्यस्य नामासीत् ॥57॥

देवेश्वरो यथेन्द्रो वायुरयं देवयोनीशः ।
अग्निस्तथा मनुष्येश्वरो मतो भारतो नाम्ना ॥58॥

As the king of deities is Indra and Vayu is the lord of *devayoni* (demi-gods such as Yaksha, Gandharva, and other human beings), similarly this Agni is the lord of human beings and the name Bharata is believed to have derived from it.

शवसोनपात एते दिवि मरुतो वायुरन्तरिक्षेऽस्मिन् ।
भूमावग्निर्भारत एवं वरुणः समुद्रेऽप्सु ॥59॥

All these devas are the lord of their worlds and protectors of energy. The Marut travels through Dyauloka, Vayu flows through Antarikshaloka; similarly Agni permeates Prithviloka and Varuna walks through the waters of the oceans.

दिवा यान्ति मरुतो भूम्याऽग्निरयं वाते अन्तरिक्षेण याति ।
अद्भिर्याति वरुणः समुद्रेर्युष्मानिच्छन्तः शवसोनपातः ॥
(ऋग्वेदः, 1.161.14)

It is said in the Rigveda, 'O protector of energy, seeking you, all-illumined *devganas* travel from Dyauloka, Agni travels from Bhuloka, Vayu from Antarikshaloka and Varuna moves in the flow of water!'

ऋग्वेदस्य तुरीयकमण्डलसूक्ते हि पञ्चविंशतिके ।
भारत इत्याख्यातं नामाग्नेर्भूमनुष्यलोकपतेः ॥60॥

In the twenty-fifth *sukta* (a hymn) of the fourth *mandala* (section) of Rigveda, it is written that Agni, the lord of this Prithviloka, which is the manushyaloka, is named as Bharata.

तस्मा अग्निर्भारतः शर्म यं सज्योक् पश्यात्सूर्यमुच्चरन्तम् ।
य इन्द्राय सुनवामेत्याह नरे नर्य्याय नृतमाय नृणाम् ॥
(ऋग्वेदः, 4.25.4)

'One who is concerned with the welfare of the human beings, supreme among the leaders, for such Indra we extract Soma-rasa. May the all-nourishing and bestower of all desires, Agni offer happiness, and may the human beings witness the rising sun for a longer time.'

अपि च यजुर्वेदस्यावृति चोक्तो दर्शपूर्णमासेष्टौ ।
अपि सामिधेन्यकर्मणि उपमदनं भारतस्याग्नेः ॥61॥

In the description of 'darshapurnamash-ishti' in the Yajurveda, Bharata as the form of Agni is evoked in the yajna relating to wood and other materials in which ceremonial fire is evoked or manifested.

अग्ने महां असि ब्राह्मण भारतेति । (शतपथब्राह्मणम्, 1.4.2.2)
अस्मिन्निगदे मन्त्रे भरतोऽग्निः पठ्यते स देवेभ्यः ।
हव्यं भरति स्मेति ब्राह्मणवाग् भारतं ततः प्रथितम् ॥62॥

'O Agni! You are majestic, you are Brahmana, you are Bharata.' In this cited mantra, Agni is designated as Bharata, this Agni ensures that the sacred offerings reach the gods. Hence in the Brahmana texts or in the language of the Brahmana texts, this Agni is stated as Bharata.

अग्निर्वै भरतः । स वै देवेभ्यो हव्यं भरति । (कौषीतकिब्राह्मणम्, 3.2)
एष हि देवेभ्यो हव्यं भरति तस्माद् भरतोऽग्निरित्याहुः ।।

एष उ वा इमाः प्रजाः प्राणो
भूत्वा बिभर्ति तस्माद्वेवाह-भारतेति-तस्माद्वेवाहुः भरतवदिति ।।
(शतपथब्राह्मणम्, 1.5.1.8)

This Agni, transforming itself as the essence of life, nourishes its subjects and so it is called Bharata. That is why it is also called *Bharatavat* (identical with Bharata).

वैवश्वतमनुभिन्नो मनुरग्निरयं मनुष्यलोकेशः ।
भरतो नाम्ना तस्य च भवनानि त्रिषु समुद्रकूलेषु ।।63।।

विवस्वद्दूतत्वमस्याग्नेः श्रूयते ।

This *manushya* (human) Agni is different from vaivashvata Manu (Manu who is the progeny of the sun and considered to be the forefather of humankind). This manushya is the lord of the world. This Manu bears the name Bharata, by his name there are his dwelling places on the coasts of three seas. This Agni is said to be the messenger of vivasvan or the sun in the Vedic hymns.

अग्निर्जातो अथर्वणा विदद्विश्वा न काव्या ।
भुवद्दूतो विवस्वतः ।।
(ऋग्वेदः, 10.21.5)

This Agni is manifested by sage Atharva. He knows all kinds of devotional hymns and compositions. This Agni is also the messenger of the sacrificial performer for inviting the desired deities.

एतं भारतवर्षाधीश्वरमग्निं मनुष्यलोकपतिम् ।
शवसोनपातमैन्द्रं महर्षयो वर्णयन्ति स्म ।।64।।

The lord of manushyaloka, Agni, is said to be the lord of this Bharatavarsha also. Great sages and seers have hailed [in the Rigveda] Indra as the protector of energy of this manushyaloka thus:

त्वमग्ने यज्ञानां होता विश्वेषां हित: ।
देवेभिर्मानुषे जने ।।

(ऋग्वेद:, 6.16.1)

O Agni! You accomplish all kinds of sacrificial acts for the human beings. Hence you have been established here by the learned.

यो अग्नि: सप्तमानुष: श्रितो विश्वेषु सन्धिषु ।
तमागन्मत्रिपस्त्यं मन्धातुर्दस्युहन्तममग्निं यज्ञेषु पूर्व्यम् ।।

(ऋग्वेद:, 8.39.8)

The Agni that permeates in all the seven *hota*-s (sacrificial performers), including all the rivers and the three worlds, protects the learned, and sustains them. O! Destroyer of the wicked, doer of auspicious acts, may we obtain that absolute Agni so that all our enemies may be destroyed.

त्वां दूतमग्ने अमृतं युगे युगे हव्यवाहं दधिरे पायुमीड्यम् ।
देवासश्च मर्तास जागृविं विभुं विश्पतिं नमसा निषेदिरे ।।

(ऋग्वेद:, 6.15.8)

O god Agni! Devas and human beings make you their messenger. O! Immortal, bearer of *havya* (sacred offerings) across all the ages and worthy of worship, while being awakened and all-pervasive, nourisher of all the subjects. O Agni! We serve you while prostrating.

विभूषयन्नग्न उभयां अनुव्रता दूतो देवानां रजसी समीयसे ।
यत्तेधीति सुमतिमावृणीमहेऽध मा नस्त्रिवरूथ: शिवो भव ।।

(ऋग्वेद:, 6.15.9)

O Agni! Having adorned devas and humans, being the messenger of devas, you travel in space and on earth. We pray to you, and may we be protected in three ways (in mind, intellect, and body). May you be the benefactor of happiness.

अग्निर्होता गृहपति: स राजा विश्वा वेद जनिमा जातवेदा: ।

(ऋग्वेद:, 6.15.13)

That Agni, the king, who invites devas, is the lord of households, he is the knower and knows all the beings. May that Agni, who is the most respectable for devas and human beings, the follower of truth, satisfy the devas by yajna.

आग्निरगामि भारतो वृत्रहा पुरुचेतनः ।
दिवोदासस्य सत्पतिः ॥

(ऋग्वेदः, 6.16.19)

The Agni, protector of all the Bharatas, destroyer of Vritra and other asuras, extremely knowledgeable, knower of everything, follower of the path of truth, protector of good human beings has come.

उदग्ने भारत द्युमदजस्त्रेणदविद्युतत् ।
शोचा विभाह्यजर ॥

(ऋग्वेदः, 6.16.45)

O the nourisher, Agni! You are lit by the upward moving flame. O the immortal! Evershining! May you be blessed with infinite illumination.

त्वामीडे अधद्विता भरतो वाजिभिःशुनम् ।
ईजे यज्ञेषु यज्ञियम् ॥

(ऋग्वेदः, 6.16.4)

O illumined deva Agni! Bharata along with the other powerful human beings offer hymns to you and offer prayers to the god worthy of worship in your yajna that yield spiritual and worldly happiness.

इत्थं बहुधा बहवो महर्षयो भारतं वदन्त्यग्निम् ।
तत्समयो भरतः सः स दिवोदासः स मान्धाता ॥65॥

The seers have likewise equated Bharata with Agni many times. In that period when Bharata was *divodosa* (keeper of the heaven), he alone was also *mandhata* (a king of the Solar dynasty).

मत्स्यपुराणाध्याये चतुर्दशाधिकशतप्रमिते ।
मनुसम्बन्धाद् भारतमुक्तं स मनुस्तु लोकपालोऽग्निः ॥66॥

भरणात्प्रजनाच्चैष मनुर्भरत उच्यते ।
एतन्निरुक्तवचनाद् वर्षं तद् भारतं स्मृतम् ॥

(मत्स्यपुराणम्, 114.5-6)

In the 114th chapter of Matsya Purana, Bharata has been exemplified as Manu: 'The *lokapala* (protector of the world) Manu is Agni himself. This Manu is called Bharata as he nourishes and produces.'

यस्त्वयं मानवो द्वीपस्तिर्यग्यामः प्रकीर्तितः ।
य एनं जयते कृत्स्नं स सम्राडिति कीर्तितः ॥
(मत्स्यपुराणम् 114.15)

One who conquers the island of humans, which is said to be triangular in shape, shall be designated as samrat, the mighty emperor.

1.2.2.4. लोकमतम्

1.2.2.4. The popular belief

भूमौ क्षेत्रीयाग्निः सस्यं भरते नरस्य देहेऽपि ।
अग्निर्विश्वजनानां भरणप्रवणां मतिं धत्ते ॥67॥

The fire makes the land produce crops and the same fire present in the human body nourishes it. Therefore, this fire provides the vital nourishment for all human beings.

दातारो नोऽभिवर्द्धन्तां वेदाः सन्ततिरेव च ।
श्रद्धा च नो मा व्यगमद् बहुदेयं च नोऽस्त्विति ॥
(विष्णुस्मृतिः, 73.28)

अन्नं च नो बहु भवेदतिथींश्च लभेमहि ।
याचितारश्च नः सन्तु मा च याचिष्म कञ्चन ॥
(विष्णुस्मृतिः, 73.30)

May we grow and prosper as donor, may our ability increase, may our knowledge and progeny expand. May our reverence never get exhausted and may we have numerous means to donate. May we have ample grains, may many *atithi*-s (guests) visit us. May others ask favours of us. May we not ask favours from anyone.

एता आशिष एषामपेक्षिता भारतीयानाम् ।
व्यवहारे मन्तव्या नीतिरियं भारतस्यास्य ॥68॥

अन्नैर्धनैर्यतोऽयं देशस्त्वेषां परेषां च ।
उदरं भरति ततोऽयं देशो भारत इति प्रथितः ॥69॥

We, in India, have always aspired for this blessing. It is accepted as part of the cultural norms of Bharata. This land feeds and nourishes its own people and people of other countries. That is why this land is reputed as Bharata.

1.2.3. हिन्दुस्तानशब्दस्य भारतैकदेशसंज्ञात्वव्यवस्था

1.2.3. The word Hindustan denotes only one part of Bharata

हिन्दुपदेन च हिन्दुस्तानपदेन च यदाहुरद्यतनाः ।
भारतवर्षं तत् खलु नामार्द्धस्यास्य जानीयात् ।।70।।

The part which is addressed by the word Hindu or Hindustan is only half of Bharatavarsha.

सिन्धुनदोऽयं यद्दिशि तद्दिश्यं भारतं पूर्व्यम् ।
सिन्धुस्थानपदेन व्यवजह्रुः सिन्धुपश्चिमगाः ।।71।।

The direction in which river Sindhu is located is the eastern part of Bharatavarsha. This area was called Sindhusthana by the inhabitants of the west of Sindhu.

अपि पारसीकजातेरस्ति दसातीरनामके ग्रन्थे ।
पौरस्त्यभारतार्थं हिन्दपदं सर्वतः पूर्वम् ।।72।।

The word Hind was used for the first time for the eastern part of Bharatavarsha in the book titled *Dasatir* of the Parsis.

जरथुस्तस्य यदायतमस्त्यस्मिन् पञ्चषष्टितमम् ।
तत्र व्यासो हिन्दुस्तानादागत उदीरितो भक्त्या ।।73।।

व्यासो नाम ब्राह्मण आयातो ह्निन्ददेशाद् यः ।
तत्सदृशो धीमानिह कश्चिन्नास्तीति तस्यार्थः ।।74।।

It is recorded with reverence in the 65th *ayat* (verse) of the book of Zarathustra (referred to as *Jaradasti* in the Vedas) that Vyasa came from Hindustan. 'The brahmin named Vyasa came from the country, Hind. Here, no one was equal to his wisdom.'

अपि च त्रिषष्टिशततम आयत उक्तं पुनस्तत्र ।
व्यासमुनेर्बाह्लीके गमनं गस्तास्पनृपसमये ।।75।।

स प्रेत्यभावविषये व्यासात् संवदितुमेव गस्तास्पः ।
जरथुस्तमाजुहाव च धर्माचार्यं स्वदेशस्थम् ।।76।।

गुप्ताश्वापभ्रंशो गस्तास्पः क्षितिप ईराने ।
व्यासात् स पुनर्जन्मनि सन्देहं स्वं निराचक्रे ।।77।।

गस्तास्पेन तु पृष्टस्तद्व्यवहारानुसारतो व्यासः ।
हिन्दुस्तानाभिजनं विज्ञापयामास चात्मानम् ॥78॥

In the 163rd ayat of the book of Zarathustra, it is recorded that Vyasa muni went to Bahlika in the reign of the Iranian king Gastaspa. When Gastaspa or Guptashva enquired about his home, Vyasa answered that he was an inhabitant of Hindustan. The Iranian king wanted to resolve his doubts about rebirth with sage Vyasa. He invited the guru of his country, Zarathustra, to discuss matters of *atma* (soul) with sage Vyasa.

इति भारतपरिचये नामधेयप्रसङ्गः सम्पूर्णः ।

The section on naming in the context of Introduction to Bharata is concluded.

1.3. सीमाप्रसङ्गः

1.3 SECTION ON TERRITORIAL LIMITS

1.3.1 पौरस्त्यपाश्चात्यभेदात् भारतवर्षद्वैविध्ये चतुर्दशप्रमाणानि

1.3.1 Fourteen proofs of Bharatavarsha's division into east and west

पौरस्त्यं पाश्चात्यं भारतवर्षं द्विधाकृतं भवति ।
अनयोरस्तिविभाजक एष नदः सिन्धुरिति विद्यात् ॥79॥

प्राच्यां दिशि तु समुद्रे यो देशः फारमोसाख्यः ।
भारतवर्षस्यैषा सीमा पूर्वास्ति पूर्वस्य ॥80॥

यच्च विलूचिस्तानं ह्यपगानस्तानमद्य यद् ब्रुवते ।
ईरानदेश एवं मेसोपोटेमिया देशः ॥81॥

अर्बप्रान्ते यवनास्तपश्चाल्लोहिताम्भोधिः ।
एतावत्खलु पश्चिमभारवर्षं विजानीयात् ॥82॥

चीनसमुद्रारब्धं रक्तसमुद्रान्तमिष्यते यदिदम् ।
भारतवर्षं तत्र च हेतव एते प्रदर्श्यन्ते ॥83॥

Bharatavarsha is divided into two parts—eastern and western, with the river Sindhu as the dividing line. In ancient times, the country that was located on the eastern sea coast till Formosa was the eastern boundary of Bharatavarsha. On the west was Baluchistana (Baluchistan), known at various times as Afghanistan, Iran, and, Mesopotamia, the Yavana country in Arab, and the Red Sea which was located beyond that.

Thus it can be said that Bharatavarsha extended from South China Sea to the Red Sea.

1.3.1.1 प्रथमं प्रमाणम्- पुरायुगीयाः संज्ञाशब्दविशेषाः

1.3.1.1 First Evidence—specific names of ancient regions

सिन्धोः पश्चिमतो यः प्रदेश आलोहिताम्भोधेः ।
तस्य च संज्ञाशब्दाः प्रमाणमस्यार्यदेशत्वे ॥84॥

The region from the west of Sindhu river to the Red Sea is evidently known as Aryadesha, land of the Arya.

1.3.1.1.1 सिन्धुस्थान-पारस्थानौ प्रान्तवचनौ

1.3.1.1.1 States of Sindhusthana and Parasthana

अद्यत्वे यद् ब्रुवते भारतवर्षस्य सीमानम् ।
सिन्धुनदं सा हिन्दुस्थानस्यैतस्य सीमा स्यात् ।।85।।

These days the boundary of Bharatavarsha that is stated to be the Sindhu river is in fact the boundary of this Hindustan.

पूर्व्यं भारतवर्षं सिन्धुस्थानाख्यया ब्रुवते ।
पश्चिमभारतवर्षं पारस्थानं पुरातना ऊचुः ।।86।।

ईरानमात्रमद्य तु पारस्थानं ब्रवीति किन्त्वासीत् ।
निखिलं परस्थानं सिन्धोरालोहिताम्भोधेः ।।87।।

In ancient times, Bharatavarsha was known as Sindhusthana and western India as Parasthana (the area beyond or on the other side). Today only Iran is known as Parasthana but in those days the entire region extending from Sindhu river to the Red Sea was known as Parasthana.

1.3.1.1.2 पौरस्त्यभारते आर्यावर्तशब्दः पश्चिमभारते आर्यायणशब्दः

1.3.1.1.2 Use of words Aryavarta for east Bharat and Aryayana for west Bharat

आर्यावर्तः शब्दो भवति यथा भारते पूर्व्ये ।
पाश्चात्येऽपि तथास्मिन् आर्यायण शब्द ईराने ।।88।।

Likewise, as the term Aryavarta is popular in the eastern parts of Bharata, in the same way Aryayana is popular in Iran for western parts of Bharata.

1.3.1.1.3 पश्चिमभारतस्य आर्यवंशनिवासमूलः औरियंसशब्दः

1.3.1.1.3 Use of the word Oriyan for Arya, the original inhabitants of western Bharata

रक्तसमुद्रात्प्रागथ सिन्धुनदात् प्रत्यगर्णवात्तूदक् ।
आरालकाश्यपीयनजलधिभ्यां दक्षिणान् देशान् ।।89।।

प्रागोरियंस नाम्नाऽनार्याः पूर्वे वदन्ति स्म ।
तेन च पश्चिमभारतमार्यनिकेतनमिति प्रतीतं नः ।।90।।

The ancient Arya (not to be confused with the term 'Aryans') used to name the countries that were located in the east of the Red Sea, in the north from the Indian Ocean and in the south from the Caspian Sea as 'Oriyans'. That is why it appears that western India (Bharata) was where the Arya lived.

मतान्तरेण ओरियंसशब्दाभिधानेऽन्यहेतूपन्यासः ।

Analysis of other reasons in the designation of the word 'oriyans' from a different view-point.

ऋज्राश्वो नामासीत् पश्चिमभारत ऋषिः कश्चित् ।
जरथुस्त्रस्तस्याभूद्दौहित्रो ब्राह्मणद्वेषी ।।91।।

ब्राह्मणविद्वेषात् स हि तेषां ब्राह्मीं लिपिं त्यक्त्वा ।
विपरीतां तु खरोष्ठीं लिपिमन्यां कल्पयामास ।।92।।

In ancient Bharatavarsha, there was a seer named Rijrashva whose daughter's son was Zarathustra. He was opposed to the brahmins and discarded the Brahmi script and in its place created Kharoshti script which was written in the opposite direction, from left to right.

ऐन्द्रं देवाराधनधर्मं त्यक्त्वा स वारुणं विद्वान् ।
असुराराधनधर्मं लोके बलवत् प्रचारयामास ।।93।।

This Zarathustra, discarding the god-worship associated with Indra, forcibly popularized the alternative asura dharma associated with Varuna in the world.

विपरीताचरणात् ते मगा इति ख्यातिमायाताः ।
शाकद्वीपाभिजना मगा इमे ब्राह्मणा अभवन् ।।94।।

Being the followers of rival conduct they were called *Maga* (the one who does not follow the brahmin path). The brahmin followers of this sect born in Shakadvipa were also called Maga.

बाह्लीकानुप्रान्तः शाकद्वीपः प्रसिद्ध आसीत् प्राक् ।
शाकद्वीपाध्यक्षाः शका इति क्षत्रियाः प्रथिताः ।।95।।

ते मलेच्छभाषयोक्ताः स्कीथीया स्कीदिया देशाः ।
शकबलदृप्तास्तु मगा युध्वा धर्मं प्रचारयामासुः ।।96।।

The region adjacent to Bahlika was known as Shakadvipa in ancient times. The kshatriya rulers of Shakadvipa later came to be known as Shaka. They were called Skithiya or Skidiya in mlechha language. The inhabitants of these regions were called Maga, who were full of arrogance, boasted about their strength, and popularized their belief [religion] through warfare.

आर्ज्राश्वो जरथुस्त्रस्त्वसुरैरुक्तः स आरियस्प इति ।
तन्मतधराश्च लोकास्तन्नानावारियस्पनाम्नोक्ताः ।।97।।

एषां यावान् देशो युद्धजितस्तन्मतानुगतः ।
सोऽप्यारियस्प उक्तः कालेनाभूत् स ओरियंस इति ।।98।।

This land was designated as Ariyaspa by the asura descendants of Rijrashva such as Zarathustra and others. The land conquered by these asuras also adopted their faith and that conquered land was called Ariyaspa. Later, it changed phonetically to Oriyan.

इत्थं केचिद् ब्रुवते तथापि नैतावतः प्रदेशस्य ।
आर्यक्षितिता हीयत ऋज्राश्वादेरिहार्यत्वात् ।।99।।

Although some learned men support this theory, it does not weaken the argument that this land is the land of Arya because Rijrashva and others were themselves Arya.

ऋज्राश्ववंशजातैरार्यैर्धृत आसुरो धर्मः ।
तेन च पश्चिमभारतमार्यनिकेतनमिति ब्रूमः ।।100।।

The Arya born in the clan of Rijrashva followed the asura dharma (the belief systems of the asuras). The western Bharat (where they lived) therefore is part of the Arya land.

1.3.1.1.4 आर्यवंशनिवासमूलः एरियानाशब्दः

1.3.1.1.4 About the word Ariyana for Arya, the original inhabitants

प्रान्तोऽस्ति मार्गियाना तदधो हिन्दूकुशस्य दक्षिणतः ।
निर्गत्य पश्चिमां प्रागथोत्तरां या शरीफिशैलस्य ।।101।।

पश्चिमलग्ना वहते तामाहुर्वैदिका नदीं सरयूम् ।
तस्याः प्रान्तो दक्षिण उक्तोऽनार्यैः पुरैरियानेति ।।102।।

The term Ariyana also means the habitation of the Arya. In the south of the region called Margiyana, the river that flows from the Hindukush ranges, touching the western, northern, and eastern sides of the Sharipiya mountain, was called Sarayu by the Vedic people. The southern region of that Sarayu was called Ariyana by the ancient Arya.

1.3.1.1.5 आर्यवंशनिवासमूलः इण्डिया-वामनियादिशब्दाः

1.3.1.1.5 Words India and Vamaniya for Arya, the original inhabitants

प्राच्यां तदेरियानाप्रान्तात्प्रत्यग्गिरेः सुलेमानात् ।
प्रान्तोऽयमिण्डियाख्यः कथितोऽनार्यैः स आर्यवसतित्वात् ॥103॥

अत एव वेदमन्त्रश्चतुर्थमण्डलगते त्रिंशे ।
सूक्तेऽष्टादश आर्यान् सरयोः पारे समामनति ॥104॥

उत त्या सद्य आर्य्या सरयोरिन्द्र पारतः ।
अर्णाचित्ररथावधीः ॥

(ऋग्वेदः, 4.03.18)

From the east of the Ariyana province to the western part of the Suleman mountain was called India by the non-Arya (the British) as this was the land inhabited by the Arya. A verse in Rigveda mentions the Arya living beyond Sarayu: ' Indra! Those Arya killed Arna and Chitraratha, inhabitants of the area beyond Sarayu, instantly.'

1.3.1.2 द्वितीयं प्रमाणम्-अवरयुगीयाः संज्ञाशब्दविशेषाः

1.3.1.2 Second Evidence—Naming in the later ages

1.3.1.2.1 **पश्चिमभारते औरियंसशब्दवत् खुरासानशब्दः**

1.3.1.2.1 Like Oriyan term, use of Khurasan for western Bharata

विश्वामित्रः पूर्वं राजासीत् कान्यकुब्जदेशस्य ।
स वसिष्ठस्य कदाचिद्धर्तुं गां नन्दिनीमैच्छत् ॥105॥

सा नन्दिनी तु नैच्छत् तं विश्वामित्रमनुगन्तुम् ।
क्रोधात्सा बहुबारं खुरतो भूमिं तदा व्यखनत् ॥106॥

In the ancient age, there was a king in the country of Kanyakubja whose name was Vishvamitra. Once he desired to abduct sage Vasishta's cow Nandini. But the cow, Nandini, refused to go along with Vishvamitra and dug the earth at several places.

तत्र वसिष्ठो वरुणादैच्छत् साहाय्यमात्मकुलसुहृद: ।
उक्तं वेदे सख्यं वरुणेन हि तद्वसिष्ठस्य ।।107।।

बाह्लीकदेशराजो वरुणोऽयं देवयुग आसीत् ।
पारस्थानाधीश: सप्तसमुद्रेश्वरोऽसुराधीश: ।।108।।

Sage Vasishta sought help from his clan-friend Varuna. This friendship of Vasishta and Varuna has been stated in the Vedas. Varuna was the king of Bahlika country in the devayuga. He was the ruler of Parasthana and was also the lord of seven seas and asuras.

जग्मुर्वरुणाज्ञप्ता: पारस्थानाधिवासिपञ्चगणा: ।
पह्लव-पारद-यवना:, शककाम्बोजौ परे च दरदाद्या: ।।109।।

नन्दिन्यास्तु खुरं ते मूर्द्धन्यादाय प्रणम्य तां भक्त्या ।
वैश्वामित्रं सैन्यं व्यमर्दयन्नञ्जसा निखिलम् ।।110।।

After obtaining the order from Varuna, the five clans of the inhabitants of Parasthana namely Pahlava, Parada, Yavana, Shaka, Kamboja, and others like Darada offered obeisance to the hoofs of Nandini, paid homage to her and then destroyed completely the whole army of Vishvamitra.

तदवधि ते किल कथिता: खुरधा: खुरदास्तथा कुर्दा: ।
तेषां जनपदसङ्घ: खुर्दस्थानं खुरासानम् ।।111।।

Since then they have been called *Khuradha* (holders of hoofs), Khurda and Khursa, their republic was called Khurdasthana or Khurasan.

मोगलसम्राड् बाबर आह खुरासानमात्मजीवन्याम् ।
अफगानाश्च बलूचिन एकेऽद्याप्याहुरेवमिव ।।112।।

Mughal emperor Babar has referred to Khurasan in his autobiography. Even today, inhabitants of Afghanistan and Baluchistan call their region by the same name.

भारतवर्षीया अपि चक्रुस्तावत्प्रदेशस्य ।
तच्छब्दव्यपदेशं यथोदितं शक्तिसङ्गमे तन्त्रे ।।113।।

हिङ्गुपीठं समासाद्य मक्केशान्तं सुरेश्वरि ।
खुरासानाभिधो देशो म्लेच्छमार्गपरायण: ।।114।।

As stated in the Shaktisangama Tantra, people of India have also referred to that region by this name: 'O Devesvari! From Hingupitha [located at Balochistan, in present day Pakistan] to Makkesa [Mecca] there is a region called Khurasan which is occupied by the mleccha people.'

1.3.1.2.2 पश्चिमभारते आर्यनिवासमूल: ईरानशब्द:

1.3.1.2.2 Word 'Iran' indicative of Arya inhabitation in west Bharata

एवं पुनरिदमखिलं जनपदवृन्दं च सिन्धुत: पश्चात् ।
भूमध्यसागरात् प्रागासीदीराननाम्नैकम् ।।115।।

The group of nations beyond river Sindhu and up to the east of the Mediterranean is known as Iran.

ईरानव्यपदेशे त्वार्यायणतेरणत्वमरणत्वम् ।
मूलमथर्वणि तदरणमुक्तं त्वार्यद्विषां वासात् ।।116।।

In the word 'Irana', the words Aryanata, Iranata, and Aranata are implicit. As this was the habitation of the enemies of Arya, the Atharvaveda records the origin of these words as *arana* (enemy).

आर्यद्वेषिजनानामरणानां बाह्लिका देशा: ।
अपि मूजवन्त एवं महावृषा वा विशिष्यासन् ।।117।।

People envious of the Arya and the inhabitants of the land of their enemies, Bahlika, were called Mujavana and Mahavrisha.

अथवा कम्पनशीले प्रयुज्यते शब्द ईराण: ।
भीतानां चानियताभिजनानां देश ईराण: ।।118।।

The word Irana is also used in the sense of vibration. That is why Iran is said to be the land of the people who are scared and whose land is undefined and whose army retreats in fear.

द्वादशकाण्डे प्रथमे सूक्तेऽष्टाविंशके मन्त्रे ।
आथर्वणे स शब्द: प्रयुक्त आन्दोलितेऽर्थेऽस्ति ।।119।।

उदीराणा उतासीनास्तिष्ठन्त: प्रक्रामन्त: ।
पद्भ्यां दक्षिणसव्ययाभ्यां मा व्यथिष्म हि भूम्याम् ।।
(अथर्ववेद:, 12.1.28)

The word Irana is used in the sense of trembling as in the twenty-eighth mantra of the first sukta of the twelvth khanda of Atharvaveda: 'Let us not cause suffering to anyone on this land while disturbed, moving, seated, standing, and walking on right and left legs.'

पश्चिमभारते ओरियंस-पारस्थान-खुरासानादि-शब्दानां शासन-भेदेन भिन्नकाले प्रयोगः ।

Use of Oriyan-Parasthana-Khurasan terms for western India during different ages

इत्थं पश्चिमभारतमुक्तं क्वचिदोरियंसनाम्ना प्राक् ।
पारस्थानं क्वचन क्वचन खुरासानमीरानम् ।।120।।

Thus in ancient times, western Bharata was designated by words like Oriyan, Parasthana, Khurasan, and Irana. Today these countries neither form one region nor define any specific country. On the contrary, these terms have come to signify broad regions of Parasthana, Khurasan, and Iran.

ईरान-खुरासान-पर्सियादि-शब्दानां महादेशवाचिनाम् अपि कालभेदेन तत्प्रान्तमात्राभिधायित्वम् ।

Terms Iran-Khurasan-Persia which once meant vast regions reduced to indicate provinces.

अद्य तु नैवं ब्रुवते नायं देशः समग्र एकोऽस्ति ।
प्रान्तः पारस्थानं प्रान्त ईरानं खुरासानम् ।।121।।

राज्ञां शासनभेदाद् व्यवहर्तॄणां च भेदतोऽज्ञानात् ।
प्रान्तं हिरातसंज्ञं केवलमाहुः खुरासानम् ।।122।।

शासनभेदात् पश्चादफगानस्तानतः खुरासानम् ।
तत ईरानमिराको रोमकासामोऽथ पश्चिमाम्भोधिः ।।123।।

अपि सीरियेति रोमकसामप्रान्तं विदुस्तथेराकम् ।
कैलडिया चासुर्या मेसोपोटेमिया चेति ।।124।।

Due to frequent change of rulers, the word Khurasan, which was once referred to as a continent, today signifies, due to ignorance, only a small area called Herat [in the present day Afghanistan]. In subsequent periods, due to these regime changes, the western part was variously named from Afghanistan to Khurasan and again Iraq, Iran, Rome and Sam. The asura community called the present-day Syria as Romak and Sam, and Iraq as Caladia and Mesopotamia.

मिडिया नाम्नाऽप्यासीदा च खुरासानमन्वितः प्रान्तः ।
अद्यत्वे पर्यायादीरानं पर्सियेत्याहुः ॥125॥

The region adjoining Khurasan was also designated as 'Midia' which today is known as Iran and Persia.

अपि वास्ति काश्यपीयनसिन्धोराग्नेयतः खुरासानम् ।
तद्दक्षिणत ईराकं तद्दक्षिणतस्तु पारस्यम् ॥126॥

In the south east of the Caspian Sea is the Khurasan region, on its south is Iraq and to the south of Iraq is located Paras (Persia) region.

क्रान्तिप्रधान एषोऽस्त्यापृथिवीजन्मतो देशः ।
इह परचक्रक्रान्तिर्यथाऽभवन्न हि तथाऽन्यत्र ॥127॥

तस्मादनेकसीमा नामविभागाश्च दृश्यन्ते ।
क्षुद्रैशियाप्रदेशादासिन्धोरस्य देशस्य ॥128॥

This area has been entrenched with unrest and struggle from early times. The invasions that took place in this area led by other countries have not been witnessed elsewhere. Because of the continuous dominance of war in this land stretching from Kshudraisia [Asia Minor] to the Red Sea, many boundaries, names and divisions have since changed.

नियत-संज्ञाव्यवस्थापक-भारतीयानां भुवनकोश-शास्त्रे शासनमूलक-संज्ञाप्रभेदानाम् अनादरः ।

In Bharata's *bhuvanakosha* (geo-lexicology of world), no importance is given to the changes made in the definite names by successive rulers.

अस्तु तु यद्वा तद्वा शासनभेदात्तु देशभेदोऽयम् ।
न च तच्छास्त्रं वक्तुं शक्यं तस्याव्यवस्थानात् ॥129॥

तस्मादिह भूगोलग्रन्थो वैदेशिको नितराम् ।
शास्त्रं तथा यथेदं व्यवस्थितं भारतं शास्त्रम् ॥130॥

The names of countries or regions should not change with every new ruler. This leads to confusion. That is why the geography of the non-natives is not as organized and authentic as that of the Indians.

शासनदेशविभागो नियतो न भवति हि तेन तमुपेक्ष्य ।
आर्या व्यवस्थितं प्राग् देशविभागं निसर्गजं ददृशुः ॥131॥

The division of a country cannot be determined on the basis of regime changes. That is why, the Arya, right from the beginning, thought it proper to posit division of the country on the basis of a relatively stable nature.

देशप्रकृतिः शास्ता न तु शास्तृप्रकृतिको देशः ।
अस्तु च शास्ताऽन्योऽन्यो मुञ्चति देशो न चात्मनः प्रकृतिम् ॥132॥

Ideally the rule should be that the names of the countries should be decided by their geographical location and not by who ruled them. This is because the nature of the country does not change with the rulers.

तस्मात् सिन्धोः पश्चिमदेशोऽद्य तु शास्तृभेदेन ।
यद्यपि पृथगिव दृष्टो वस्तुत इदमस्ति भारतं वर्षम् ॥133॥

Therefore, even though the southern part of Sindhu river has had different rulers, it has remained in essence Bharatavarsha.

1.3.1.3 तृतीयं प्रमाणम्-इन्द्रवरुणनिमित्ते ब्राह्मणानां वैज्ञानिकं वाग्युद्धम्

1.3.1.3 The Third Evidence —Scientific debate among brahmins on Indra and Varuna

भारतवर्षविभागद्वयहेतुर्ब्राह्मणानां प्राक् ।
वैज्ञानिकवाक्समरस्तृतीयमस्ति प्रमाणमिह ॥134॥

The third evidence is the scientific debate among the brahmins on the division of Bharatavarsha in two parts.

आसुरधर्मे प्रविशतो जरथुस्त्रस्य देवेन्द्रनिन्दकत्वं विरोधहेतुः ।

बाह्लीके यो जज्ञे जरथुस्त्रस्तस्य समये प्राक् ।
सौत्रामण्यामिष्टौ ब्राह्मणवृन्दे विरोधोऽभूत् ॥135॥

After embracing the path of the asuras, Zarathustra became critical of devaraja Indra and this led to an altercation between them. In the sautramani yajna performed by Zarathustra, at Bahlika, a fierce debate broke out among the group of brahmins attending the yajna.

आर्ज्राश्वो जरदष्टिर्ब्राह्मण आसीत् तथाप्ययं धृष्टः ।
विद्विष्य देवमिन्द्रं वरुणस्तुद् धर्ममासुरं दध्रे ॥136॥

येऽसून् प्राणान् दधते तेऽमी असुरा महाप्राणाः ।
असुरत्वं तु न येषां तेऽमी देवाः 'सुराः स्म' इत्यूचुः ॥137॥

A progeny of Rijrashva, Zarathustra was a brahmin, but he was also rude and impolite. After his quarrel with Indra, he became an admirer of Varuna and adopted his asura dharma. Zarathustra believed that those who held *asu* (power of life breath) were asuras and they were immensely powerful and those who were bereft of this *asuratva* (power of life breath) only such devas called themselves as 'surah smah', that is, 'we are suras'. This meant they had no power and only asuras were powerful.

1.3.1.3.1 वरुणेन सुरानिर्माणम्

1.3.1.3.1 Preparation of sura by Varuna

असुरा विनाश्य सोमं जनयामासुस्तु वारुणीं मदिराम् ।
तां च सुरामिति जगदुः पीतामनु तां सुरान् पिबाम इति ।।138।।

It was also the time when asuras destroyed the favourite drink of the devas, Soma, and prepared a special wine *Varuni* and designated it as *sura* or *madira* (intoxicant drink). While drinking sura, they used to recite, 'We take the drink of sura'. [This meant two things: One, it meant drinking sura and the other implied meaning was that 'we drink the devas'.]

असुरवदेव त्वार्या अपि तां पातुं क्रमात् क्रमन्ते स्म ।
अपि देवेन्द्रः सौत्रामण्यामिष्टौ सुरामपिबत् ।।139।।

Like the asuras, devas too started drinking sura. Indra too started drinking sura during the sautramani yajna. It became a regular practice.

गुरुरसुराणामार्याऽनार्याणां यो न्युवास बाह्लीके ।
आर्यैः सुरा न पेया बुद्धिहरीत्युपदिदेश तान् स भृगुः ।।140।।

Seeing this, the teacher of the *anarya* (non-Arya), Arya Bhrigu (Shukracharya), who used to live in Bahlika, advised the Arya that they should not indulge in drinking madira—it weakened and destroyed the intellect.

सुरां वै मलमन्नानां पाप्मा च मलमुच्यते ।
तस्माद् ब्राह्मणराजन्यौ वश्यश्च न सुरां पिबेत् ।।
(मनुस्मृतिः, 11.93)

The Manusmriti records: Sura is the impurity of *atra*, which means it is prepared from defiled/fermented grains. Impurity has been stated as *paapa* (inauspicious act) and object of hatred. Hence brahmins, kshatriyas, vaishyas, should not drink sura.

1.3.1.3.2 आर्ज्राश्वैरिन्द्राधिक्षेप:

1.3.1.3.2 Insult of Indra by Rijrashva's followers

इन्द्रस्याधिक्षेपं कर्तुमिवैतेऽसुराः सुरायज्ञम् ।
सौत्रामणीं विधातुं वृषाकपिं प्रेरयामासुः ।।141।।

With a motive to insult Indra, these asuras instigated asura Vrishakapi to perform a surya-yajna named sautramani.

एष वृषाकपिरासीदसुरेन्द्रः प्राक् प्रियः सखेन्द्रस्य ।
पुत्रत्वेन तमिन्द्रः प्रेम्णा ह स्मानुगृह्णाति ।।142।।

This king of the asuras, Vrishakapi, was a dear friend of Indra and enjoyed his patronage and love.

वैकुण्ठस्य विकुण्ठागर्भोत्पन्नस्य दैवतेन्द्रस्य ।
नाम वृषाकपिरासीत् नामैक्यात् सख्यमेतयोरभवत् ।।143।।

Their friendship was also strengthened by their shared name—Vrishakapi (one who causes rain and thunder). Born of the womb of Vaikunta, Indra was also known as Vrishakapi because of his power to cause rain and thunder.

देवेन्द्रः स वृषाकपिरसुरवृषाकपिकृते यज्ञे ।
सोमं पातुमिहागादिन्द्राण्या सह तु सञ्जयाभिधया ।।144।।

In the yajna performed by Vrishakapi, Indra came with an Indrani named 'Sanjaya' to drink Soma.

एष वृषाकपिरसुरस्तेने सौत्रामणीयज्ञम् ।
तत्र सुरामपि सोमं देवेन्द्राय न्यवेदयत् पातुम् ।।145।।

The asura Vrishakapi offered sura along with Soma to devaraja Vrishakapi during the yajna.

इन्द्रः पिबति सुरामिति पारस्थानाः प्रचक्रिरे निन्दाम् ।
सौत्रामण्यामिष्टौ घोरविरोधं प्रचक्रिरेऽनिन्द्राः ।।146।।

On this, the inhabitants of Parasthana began criticising Indra by spreading the news that 'Indra is drinking sura'. Thus in that sautramani yajna, the opponents of Indra caused great ruckus.

मन्त्रेष्वनिन्द्रशब्द: षट्स्वाम्नात: पुरा वरुणम् ।
आराधयन्त एते नेन्द्रं देवं त्वमंसत हि ।।147।।

In those days, Indra was not accepted as a devata by the asuras and hence did not give him any importance. In some mantras, Indra is referred to by the term 'anindra'.

इन्द्र: पिबति सुरामिति हन्त पिबामो वयं सोमम् ।
इत्युक्त्वा तेऽनिन्द्रा असुरा: सोमं बलादहरन् ।।148।।

'Indra is drinking sura and we are drinking Soma', saying this the opponents of Devendra, the asuras took Soma in their possession by force.

इन्द्रनिवेदितसोमं यज्ञादपहृत्य तं पातुम् ।
तत्र वृषाकपिमसुरं न्ययुञ्जतासौ पपौ सोमम् ।।149।।

After taking away the Soma offered to Indra, asura Vrishakapi was asked to drink Soma by force, and finally he drank the Soma meant for Indra.

सोमं तत्र पिबन्तं द्रष्ट्वेन्द्राणी वृषाकपिं पुत्रम् ।
क्रोधादपगतचेता: स्वामिनमेवोपधर्षयामास ।।150।।

When Indrani saw son-like Vrishakapi drinking the soma-rasa [meant for Indra], she became furious and turned against her husband.

1.3.1.3.3 इन्द्राणीकृत: क्रोध:

1.3.1.3.3 Anger of Indrani

हन्त न किन्तेऽन्यत्रोपलभ्यते पीतये सोम: ।
यदतिव्यथितो धावसि वृषाकपेरत्र यज्ञमिमम् ।।151।।

This is a matter of great grief. Can you not get Soma elsewhere to drink? Why have you come so impatiently to drink Soma at this sacrifice of Vrishakapi?

किमनेनोपकृतं ते पुष्टमृगेणेति यस्मै त्वम् ।
वितरसि सोमसदृक्षं बहुमूल्यं धनमनुग्रहात् क्षमसे ।।152।।

What good has this 'stout animal' done to you that you gave him the precious Soma in return? Why are you so merciful in forgiving him?

यत्त्वं प्रियमिव रक्षसि तं शूकरभक्षक: इवाऽद्य ।
कर्णेऽपिगृह्य भक्षतु मा जीवतु दुष्टजीवोऽयम् ।।153।।

Why do you defend this dog, this pig-eater, like a dear one? May this wicked not be left alive!

अहमस्मि वीरपत्नी वीरवती तामवीरावत् ।
अवमनुतेऽयं धृष्टस्तदिदं क्षमसे कथं दृष्ट्वा ।।154।।

I am the wife of a warrior hero and mother of heroic sons. This rude [Vrishakapi] is hurting my self-respect. Having seen all this insult, you are still forgiving him!

इत्थं वृषाकपे: खल्वपराधान् क्षाम्यते तदेन्द्राय ।
क्रोधादधिक्षिपन्तीमिन्द्राणीं तामुवाचेन्द्र: ।।155।।

Indra spoke to Indrani, who was infuriated with him because he had forgiven the rude Vrishakapi despite his insulting behaviour.

1.3.1.3.4 इन्द्राणीं प्रति इन्द्रकृता परिसान्त्वना

1.3.1.3.4 Indra consoling Indrani

एष वृषाकपिरीजे सोमं सोतुं मयाज्ञप्त: ।
अन्ये त्वसुरा नेदं मन्वत इति तद्भयात्स सोममपात् ।।156।।

This Vrishakapi prepared Soma on my orders. Other asuras do not give him any importance. So he drank Soma out of their fear.

अयि भद्रकेशपाशे न त्वपराध्यति वृषाकपिस्तत्र ।
किमभिक्रुध्यसि सहसा वृषाकपिं वीरपत्नी त्वम् ।।157।।

O Indrani, adorned with beautiful hair! This Vrishakapi has not committed any offence here. O heroic wife! You are angry with this Vrishakapi without any reason.

न वृषाकपिं सखायं विना रमे देवि यद्द्वारा ।
इदमासुरकुलतोऽप्यां प्रियं हविर्याति देवेषु ।।158।।

O devi! This Vrishakapi is my friend, I can never be displeased with him, for through him the havya, dear to the gods, reached them.

सोमं पातुमिहाहं नायात: किन्तु तन्मिषत: ।
एमि समीक्षितुमेव त्वार्यं दासं विचेतुमिव ।।159।।

O Indrani! I have not come here to drink Soma but to discuss and appraise the issues relating to Arya and dasa.

1.3.1.3.5 इन्द्राणीं प्रति वृषाकपिकृता परिसान्त्वना

1.3.1.3.5 Vrishakapi consoling Indrani

अथ च वृषाकपिरपि तामिन्द्राणीं प्रत्युवाच विनयेन ।
इन्द्राणि नित्यसुभगे जरया म्रियते न जातु ते दयित: ।।160।।

Meanwhile, Vrishakapi also spoke politely to Indrani in response. He said—O Indrani! O eternally blessed one! Your husband neither attains old age nor does he die.

पञ्चत्रिंशन्मम मयानुक्ष्ण: संप्रति पचन्ति भुक्तिकृते ।
यानहमद्मि स्थूलो याभ्यां कुक्षी उभौ पृणन्ति मम ।।161।।

ऐन्द्रं सोमं पिबतो मम पुरनेतान् पशून् भक्ष्यान् ।
काचित्करं हवि: प्रियमेष नवेन्द्र: स्वतन्त्रमश्नातु ।।162।।

Those nourishments are being prepared for me which I will eat and become stout and strong; while drinking the Soma of Indra, these eatables are like offerings and it is upto Indra whether he eats them or not.

इन्द्रोऽयमसुरकन्यागर्भज एतस्य पत्नी च ।
अस्ति पुलोमासुरजा तत इन्द्रोऽश्नातु गोमांसम् ।।163।।

This Indra was born of an asura woman and his wife too is the daughter of an asura Puloma. So Indra can decide what to eat.

अयमिन्द्रो विश्वस्मादुत्तर इति हि प्रतिज्ञातम् ।
इन्द्राण्यपीन्द्रेणापि वृषाकपिनाऽसुरेन्द्रेण ।।164।।

Then, Vrishakapi, in front of Indra and Indrani, vowed that Indra was supreme in the entire world.

एतदाख्यानस्य ऋग्वेदसंहितायामुल्लेखः ।

Reference to the above narrative in the Rigveda samhita.

ऋग्वेदसंहितायां दशमे तन्मण्डले तदा सूक्ते ।
आख्यानमेतदुक्तं तन्मन्त्रा अत्र दर्श्यन्ते ॥165॥

This narrative is described in the forty-sixth sukta of tenth mandala of the Rigveda samhita of which the relevant mantras are illustrated here.

इन्द्राणीक्रोधविषया वेदमन्त्र यथा

Mantras relating to the anger of Indrani.

पराहीन्द्र धावसि वृषाकपेरति व्यथिः ।
नो अह प्रविन्दस्यन्यत्र सोमपीतये
विश्वस्मादिन्द्र उत्तरः ॥

(ऋग्वेदः, 10.86.2)

O Indra, I am deeply distressed that you are running after Vrishakapi. Why don't you go elsewhere to drink Soma? Because Indra is supreme among all.

किमयं त्वां वृषाकपिश्चकार हरितो मृगः ।
यस्मा इरस्यसी दुन्वर्यों वा पुष्टिमद्वसु
विश्वस्मादिन्द्र उत्तरः ॥

(ऋग्वेदः, 10.86.3)

What good has this stout, green-coloured, deer-like Vrishakapi done for you that you freely shower upon him prosperity? Indra is definitely supreme.

यमियं त्वं वृषाकपिं प्रियमिन्द्राभिरक्षसि ।
श्वान्वस्य जम्भिषदपि कर्णे वराहयुः ।
विश्वस्मादिन्द्र उत्तरः ॥

(ऋग्वेदः, 10.86.4)

O Indra, Vrishakapi, whom you defend, is like the dog desirous of eating pig by its ears. Definitely Indra is supreme.

अवीरामिव मामयं शरारुरभि मन्यते ।
उताहमस्मि वीरिणीन्द्रपत्नी मरुत्सखा
विश्वस्मादिन्द्र उत्तरः ॥

(ऋग्वेदः, 10.86.9)

This dangerous and lowly Vrishakapi calls me bereft of a valiant husband and sons and denies that I'm wife to Indra and mother of powerful sons. Definitely Indra is supreme.

देवेन्द्रवृषाकपिकृतपरिसान्त्वनामन्त्रा यथा

Devendra Vrishakapi's words of consolation.

वि हि सोतोरसृक्षत नेन्द्रं देवममंसत ।
यत्रामदद् वृषाकपिरर्यः पुष्टेषु मत्सखा विश्वस्मादिन्द्र उत्तरः ॥
(ऋग्वेदः, 10.86.1)

I (Indra) had asked the priests to perform Soma yajna, but they did not offer prayers to me. On the contrary they prayed to asura Vrishakapi, my best friend, who drank Soma and was pleased. But beyond all these, I, Indra, am supreme.

किं सुबाहो स्वङ्गुरे पृथुष्टो पृथुजाङ्घने ।
किं शूरपत्नि नस्त्वमभ्यमीषि वृषाकपिं
विश्वस्मादिन्द्र उत्तरः ॥
(ऋग्वेदः, 10.86.8)

O woman of beautiful arms! O lady of beautiful fingers! O Sukesi (having beautiful long hairs)! O lady of heavy sculptured thighs! O wife of hero, Indrani! Why are you getting angry with my Vrishakapi? Indra is still unsurpassable in the world.

नाहमिन्द्राणि रारण सख्युर्वृषाकपेर्ऋते ।
यस्येदनप्यं हविः प्रियं देवेषु गच्छति
विश्वास्मादिन्द्र उत्तरः ॥
(ऋग्वेदः, 10.86.12)

Never Indrani have I enjoyed without my friend Vrishakapi whose welcome offering here, made pure with water, goes to the gods. Indra remains supreme.

अयमेमि विचाकशद्विचिन्वन् दासमार्य्यम् ।
पिबामि पाकसुत्वनोऽभि धीरमचाकशं
विश्वास्मादिन्द्र उत्तरः ॥
(ऋग्वेदः, 10.86.19)

I came to the yajna on seeing the priests, to drive away the enemies and search for the Arya. I drank the Soma offered by those who extracted Soma with determined and pure minds and defended the wise, worshipping priests. Indra is supreme.

असुरेन्द्रवृषाकपिकृतपरिसान्त्वनामन्त्रा यथा

Mantras of consolation by asura Vrishakapi.

इन्द्राणीमासु नारिषु सुभगामहमश्रवम् ।
न ह्यस्या अपरं च न जरसा मरते पतिः
विश्वस्मादिन्द्र उत्तरः ॥

(ऋग्वेदः, 10.86.11)

I have been listening to Indrani, the most auspicious one among all the women. Unlike the husbands of other women, the husband of Indrani is ever young and immortal. Indra is supreme in the whole world.

उक्ष्णो हि मे पञ्चदश साकं पचन्ति विंशतिम् ।
उताहमद्मि पीव इदुभा कुक्षी पृणन्ति मे
विश्वास्मादिन्द्र उत्तरः ॥

(ऋग्वेदः, 10.86.14)

The worshippers bring for me nourishment so that I can become stout and powerful. They fill up my belly with Soma. Indra is supreme in the whole world.

1.3.1.3.6 देवेन्द्रासुरेन्द्रयोर्वृषाकप्योः सन्धिशान्तिः

1.3.1.3.6 Truce between devendra and asurendra Vrishakapi

अपिबत् सुरां सुरेन्द्रः स चासुरेन्द्रोऽपिबत् सोमम् ।
तत्रेन्द्रयोर्विवादोऽशाम्यत्कथमपि तयोर्नीत्या ॥166॥

Devendra Vrishakapi drank sura and then asurendra Vrishakapi drank Soma and thus the dispute that had surfaced in the yajna got settled.

1.3.1.3.7 ब्राह्मणानां विप्रतिपत्तिः

1.3.1.3.7 Difference of opinion among brahmins

क्रमशस्तत्रैव ब्राह्मणानां वैज्ञानिक-विप्रतिपत्ति-प्रारम्भः।

That was the beginning of gradual differences among the brahmins.

वरुणस्य राजधानीनगरेऽस्मिन् किन्तु बाह्लीके ।
यज्ञे समवेतानां विप्राणां विग्रहोऽत्यभवत् ॥167॥

But, in the capital city Bahlika of Varuna, where the dispute had first broken out among the brahmins assembled at the yajna (organized by Zarathustra), the debate became more contentious.

अग्निर्वसुभिः क्रमते सोमो रुद्रैर्मरुद्भिरिन्द्रोऽयम् ।
आदित्यैरथ वरुणो विश्वेदेवैर्बृहस्पतिः क्रान्तः ॥168॥

In this debate, three contesting views emerged. The first view held that Agni was permeated by eight vasus; Soma was moved by rudras and Indra by marudganas: Varuna was permeated by adityas and vishvadevas pervaded Brihaspati.

अग्निर्वसुभिः क्रमते, रुद्रैरिन्द्रोऽथ वरुण आदित्यैः ।
सोमः पितृभिः क्रमते विश्वेदेवैर्बृहस्पतिः क्रान्तः ॥169॥

The second view held that Agni moved with eight vasus, Indra by eleven rudras and Soma by *pitragana*-s (ancestors). Twelve adityas permeated Varuna and Brihaspati was pervaded by vishvadevas.

अग्निर्वसुभिः क्रमते वायू रुद्रैरथेन्द्र आदित्यैः ।
सोमः पितृभिर्वरुणास्त्वद्भिर्विश्वैर्बृहस्पतिर्देवैः ॥170॥

According to the third view, Agni was moved by vasus, Vayu by marudgana, Indra was permeated by adityas, Soma was permeated by pitraganas, Varuna by water and Brihaspati by vishvadevas.

इत्थं त्रयः प्रवादा अभन् वैज्ञानिके समरे ।
असुराः प्रथमं पक्षं जगृहुस्तत्रोत्तमं त्वैन्द्राः ॥171॥

Thus in this methodological dispute, three viewpoints emerged, of which the asuras supported the first view and the followers of Indra supported the third [best] view.

परमर्षयस्त्वपश्यन् न विसंवादावकाशमिह ।
शवसोनपात एते युञ्जन्त्यधिदैवतैस्तैस्तैः ॥172॥

But the great sages found no substance in this dispute as this was not a [ontological] dispute at all. Instead it was an exercise in deciding the presiding deities of the ontological objects.

अग्निर्वायुश्चेन्द्रो रोदस्यां क्रन्दसी देवाः ।
सन्ति बृहस्पतिसोमौ वरुणः स्वस्तेऽधिदैवतैः सयुजः ॥173॥

Agni, Vayu, and Indra are the devas of Rodasi (of the three triadic worlds comprising the earth, the sun, and interspace between the two, one is called Rodasi, and the other two are Krandasi and Samyati), Brihaspati, Soma, and Varuna are the devas of Krandasi. In heaven, they are all associated with their respective presiding deities.

पूर्वेषामयमुत्तम एष बृहस्पतिरथेन्द्रस्तु ।
प्रथमोऽयमुत्तरेषामित्यृषिभिर्हि स्थितिर्दृष्टा ।।174।।

In the upper worlds, Brihaspati is the first and in the lower worlds Indra is the first one. Such a state of the world has been witnessed by the seers.

इत्याह संयतीतोऽर्वाक् क्रमतो रोदसीदृष्ट्या ।
पृथ्वीक्रमतस्त्वग्निः प्रथमस्तुर्यो बृहस्पतिः सोऽस्ति ।।175।।

Thus according to the descending order of Samyati, it was stated from the point of view of Rodasi and according to the order of prithvi, Agni is the first god and Brihaspati is the fourth.

अग्निश्च वायुसोमौ सहेन्द्रवरुणौ बृहस्पतिश्चान्ते ।
लोकचतुष्टयदेवा इत्थं क्रमसंनिविष्टास्ते ।।176।।

The order is that of Agni, Vayu, Soma, Indra, and Varuna with Brihaspati coming at the end. Thus the presiding gods of all the four worlds (earth, interspace, *dyau*, and *divaprishta*) are located accordingly.

अग्निर्वसुभिः प्रथमो विश्वदेवैर्बृहस्पतिः क्रमते ।
वायू रुद्रैः सोमो रुद्रैः पितृभिश्च संयुङ्क्ते ।।177।।

आदित्यैरपि रुद्रैर्मरुद्भिरिन्द्रः सजूर्भवति ।
वरुणोऽद्भिश्चादित्यैर्युनक्ति नान्यैरिति ज्ञेयम् ।।178।।

Agni is pervaded by the vasus and is the first, Brihaspati is pervaded by the vishvadevas, Vayu moves by the rudras and Soma is jointly pervaded by rudras and adityas. The adityas, rudras and the marudganas jointly surpass Indra and Varuna is jointly permeated by waters and adityas. There is nothing other than these, so it is to be known.

इत्थं कृतसिद्धान्ते विज्ञाने निर्विवादेऽपि ।
अधिकृत्येन्द्रं वरुणं विप्रा विप्रोदिरे तत्र ।।179।।

But even after this undisputed cosmological principle was settled, a fresh dispute broke out among the brahmins over Indra and Varuna.

असुरो वरुणो मान्यो न त्विन्द्रो देव इत्यन्ये ।
इन्द्रो देवो मान्यो नत्वसुरो वरुण इत्यन्ये।।180।।

Some brahmins held that asura Varuna should be accepted as a deva and not Indra. Others held that Indra should be considered a deva and not Varuna.

जरदष्ट्यादयः केचिन्नेन्द्रं देवममंसत ।
बृहद्दिवादयस्त्विन्द्रमाराध्यं निरधारयन् ।।181।।

Zarathustra was among those who did not accept Indra as a deva while *Brihaddevata* and brahmins established Indra as a deva worth worshipping.

1.3.1.3.8 वरुणपरमासुरविज्ञानम्

1.3.1.3.8 The asura arguments in favour of Varuna

वरुणेऽध्याहितमिन्द्रं पश्यन्तश्चक्षते त्वमी असुराः ।
वरुणो भवतुस्वाराडिन्द्रः सम्राट् तथा हि विज्ञानम् ।।182।।

Indra is located in Varuna. According to the cosmic principle, Indra is the *samrat* (the master presiding deity) and Varuna is *svarat* (the presiding deity) of all the worlds including the heaven.

भूयस्य आप एताः कनीय एवात्र चेतना ज्योतिः ।
अप्स्वेव तु चैतन्यं बुध्यति वरुणः परस्ततो हीन्द्रात् ।।183।।

The asuras argued that since water was more pervasive on this earth than the principle of Indra which was the light of consciousness and since the principle of consciousness emerged in water itself, Varuna was superior to Indra.

भूतानि दैवतानि च जातान्यद्भ्योऽत एव ता आपः ।
प्राणः प्रज्ञा चेन्द्रो भूतान्यालम्बते तानि ।।184।।

All beings and devas originated from the element of water. Life breath, intellect, and consciousness (principle of Indra) that is inherent in all beings and objects ultimately depend on water. ['Water is the source of life,' according to this principle the element of water is supreme.]

देहेऽप्यधिका आपो लवणं चाधिकमिदं द्वयं वरुणः ।
प्राणप्रज्ञाचेष्टावहः स इन्द्रोऽप्सु संश्रितो भाति ।।185।।

In the gross physical body, water, and saline are dominant elements and both these elements are Varuna. Indra is the holder of life-breath and intellect and these depend on water [Varuna].

अन्नमभुक्त्वा जीवति नापीत्वापस्तदाप एवात्मा ।
अन्नैरपीह भुक्तैस्तद्रस एवात्मनि ध्रियते ।।186।।

A living being can survive without grain but not without water. Hence water is the essence or *atma* (soul) of all beings. Even on consuming food grain, its *rasa* (the essence or liquid) is retained in the body, its gross remains are excreted from the body.

परमेष्ठ्यपां समुद्रः प्रतिपत् तत्रानुचरवद् द्यौः ।
योऽसाविन्द्रो द्युस्थः स वारुणीस्वप्सु संश्रितस्तपति ।।187।।

This *parameshti-mandala* (one dimension of the five-dimensional universe, the other four being Svayambhu, surya, chandra and prithvi) is the sea of water. To reach over there, this Dyauloka is present at every step and Indra resides in this Dyauloka which draws its luminosity from water.

1.3.1.3.9 इन्द्रपरं दैवविज्ञानम्

1.3.1.3.9 Arguments in support of Indra

इन्द्राध्याहितवरुणं पश्चन्तश्चक्षतेऽथ देवास्तु ।
इन्द्रः स्वाराड् वरुणं सम्राडेवं हि विज्ञानम् ।।188।।

Then the devas, accepting the dependence of Varuna on Indra, said that Indra is the *svarat* whereas Varuna is *samrat* of this loka.

भूयस्यो विश एता एकः स्वाराट् प्रशास्त्यधिष्ठाय ।
स्वाराड् विक्ष्वनुबुद्धो विभवति तास्वेक उद्रिक्तः ।।189।

There are many subjects and the *svarat*, held in high esteem, rules over them. This deity, being awakened in the subjects, is endowed with intellect and prosperity.

		अग्निः	वायुः	इन्द्रः	बृहस्पतिः	सोमः	वरुणः	शवसोनपातः
प्रथममते	1.	वसुभिः 8	0	मरुद्भिः 7	विश्वैर्देवैः	पितृभिः 8	आदित्यैः 12	आसुरमतेऽधिदेवाः
मध्यममते	2.	वसुभिः 8	0	रुद्रैः 11	विश्वैर्देवैः	पितृभिः 8	आदित्यैः 12	ऐन्द्रमतेऽधिदेवाः
उत्तममते	3.	वसुभिः 8	रुद्रैः 11	आदित्यैः 12	विश्वैर्देवैः	पितृभिः 8	अद्भिः 4	
रोदसीदेवाः					क्रन्दसीदेवाः			द्यावापृथिव्यौ

	Agni	Vayu	Indra	Brihaspati	Soma	Varuna	shavasonpath
First Opinion	8 vasus		7 marutas	From vishvadevas	11 rudras	8 adityas	Presiding deity in the opinion of the Asuras
Second Opinion	8 vasus		11 rudras	From vishvadevas	8 pitrgana	8 from adityas	
Third Opinion	8 vasus	One rudra	12 adityas	From vishvadevas		4 from water	Presiding deity according to the devas

Deities of rodasi	Deities of krandasi	dyau-prithvi

आत्मनः

3. द्यौः संयत्याम् द्यौः-अन्तर्यामी-अभ्वम् = कर्मरूपनामानि।
अं.- सूत्रात्मा-सूत्रम् = ऋतं सत्यम् ।
पृ.- वाचस्पतिः-वेदाः = ऋक्, साम, यजूंषि ।

2. अं क्रन्दस्याम् द्यौः- वरुणः-आपः = अम्भः मरीचिः मरः श्रद्धा।
अं. सोमः पितरः = भृगवः अङ्गिरसः अथर्वाणः ।
पृ.- बृहस्पतिः विश्वेदेवाः = 2।

1. पृ. रोदस्याम् द्यौः- इन्द्रः- आदित्याः = 12
अं-वायुः- रुद्राः = 12
पृ.-अग्निः-वसवः = 8

Atma

Dyauloka in samyanti	:	Dyau—antaryami-abhva—action, form and name
	:	Antariksha—sutratma-sutram—rit and satya
	:	Prithvi—vachaspati-ved—rik, sama, yanjushi
Antariksha in krandasi	:	Dyau—varuna-apa—ambha, marichi, mara, Shraddha
	:	Antariksha—soma-pitr—bhargava, angirasa and atharva
	:	Prithvi—Brihaspati-vishvadeva
Prithvi in rodasi	:	Indra-aditya
	:	vayu-rudra
	:	agni-vasava

हिरण्यगर्भमते

पृथ्वी	रोदस्याम्	द्यौः	बृहस्पतिः-विश्वेदेवाः
			इन्द्रः-आदित्याः रुद्राः मरुतः
			वरुणः-आदित्याः आपः
			सोमः-रुद्राः पितरः
		अं.	वायुः रुद्राः
		पृ.	अग्निः-वसवः

AS PER HIRANYAGARBHA

Shavasonpath in rodasi (presiding deity)	Dyauloka	Brihaspati	Vishvadeva
		Indra	Aditya-rudra-marut
		Varuna	Aditya-apatatva
	Antariksha	Soma	Rudra-pitragana
		Vayu	rudra
	Prithvi	Agni	vasu

आत्मेन्द्रो ह्यधितिष्ठति रक्षति वा दैवतानि ।
नश्यन्ति तानि सद्यो यदात्मना तानि हीयन्ते ।।190।।

This Indra is atma, and he is ever present; while being the substratum, he defends and the devas cease to exist when they are discarded by Indra, the atma.

आपः शरीरमेतद्भोगाधिष्ठानमात्मनस्तदिन्द्रस्य ।
आलोम चानखाग्रं विभवत्यात्मा स देहऽस्मिन् ।।191।।

This water or body is the sphere of *bhoga* (experience) of Indra [identical with atma]. In this gross body, atma alone permeates from *loma* (hair) to the tip of the nail.

आत्मा शरीरयष्टिं धत्ते तेनोत्थितेऽत्र चेष्टास्ति ।
अथात्मना विहीनं निपतति सद्योऽथ पूयते श्वयति ।।192।।

This atma holds the frame of the body; the body is active only when atma inhabits the body. As soon as this body is deprived of atma, it starts decaying and stinking.

आपः सोमः सोमं भुनक्ति हीन्द्रः पिबन्ति तेनापः ।
रोगा जलोदराद्या दृष्टा नात्मास्ति तेनापः ।।193।।

This *apa-tatva* (water produced by a special yajna) is Soma and Indra relishes this Soma and when this compound is transformed into water, the world drinks it. This water causes *jalodara* (diseases) because this water is not self-sustaining, and is bereft of atma.

अपि च भवन्ति द्यावाभूम्यस्तिस्रो मिथोऽनुगताः ।
अर्वागहीयस्यः परावरीयस्य आम्नाताः ।।194।।

This Dyauloka is of three types—Rodasi, Krandasi and Samyati. These three exist in continuity. Rodasi and Krandasi are called *ahayasi* (lower in order) and Samyati is called *variyasi* (the top-most).

प्रथमा तु रोदसीयं तद्गर्भा क्रन्दसी मध्या ।
तदुभयगर्भा सान्या या संयत्युत्तमा महती ।।195।।

This Rodasi is the first ether sky and the ether sky that holds it is called Krandasi which is located in the middle. The third ether sky that holds both of them is Samyati. This is supreme and great.

प्रतिपद् द्यौरथ भूम्योऽनुचरन्त्यस्ताश्च बह्व्यः स्युः ।
एकैकस्यां द्यावाभूम्यां द्यौरेकधैव स्यात् ।।196।।

The earth follows *dyau* (sphere of light). These spheres are multiple but in each ether sky there is only one Dyauloka.

एकैकस्यां द्यावाभूम्यां ब्रह्मेन्द्रविष्णवो हृदये ।
सयुजोऽध्यक्षाः कुर्वत एते विश्वानि कर्माणि ॥197॥

Brahma, Vishnu, and Indra dwell in the heart of each ether sky. They are collectively the presiding gods and determine all the actions.

रोदस्यामिह सूर्यो हिरण्यगर्भोऽस्ति स ब्रह्मा ।
क्रन्दस्यां तु परमेष्ठी संयत्यां तु स्वयंभूः सः ॥198॥

In Rodasi, the sun is the Hiranyagarbha or the whole as well as the core. In Krandasi, Parameshti is the core and in Samyati, Svayambhu is the core.

त्रिविधं च वैश्वरूप्यं संयत्यां व्योममण्डलं परमम् ।
क्रन्दस्यां तु समुद्रो ब्रह्माण्डं रोदसीविषयम् ॥199॥

Thus there are three abstract forms of the world. Among them, in Samyati the vyoma-mandala is supreme, in Krandasi, the sea is dominant and in Rodasi, the egg-shaped cosmos brahmanda, is the core.

इन्द्रोऽस्ति विश्वकर्मा व्योम्नि स वाचस्पतिस्तु वेदमयः ।
वरुणस्तु विश्वकर्मा स समुद्रेऽपाम्पतिर्मध्यः ॥200॥

Indra is the *vishvakarma* (master) of Dyauloka (vyoma-mandala), he is the *vachaspati* (master of the spoken word) and is infused with the Veda. The master of water, Varuna is the vishvakarma of the oceans.

ब्रह्माण्डविश्वकर्मा त्विन्द्रः सोऽग्निक्लृप्तः ।
वेदा आपोऽग्नय इति तेषामहि कर्मयोनयस्त्रिविधाः ॥201॥

Indra is the master of the cosmos. He is supported by the three fires (Surya, Vayu, and Indra) and the Vedas, *apah* (water) and agni are their three sources of action.

पृष्ठे दिवस्तु वरुणः समुद्रनाथोऽस्ति पारमेष्ठ्यो यः ।
ऊर्ध्वं ततोऽन्य इन्द्रस्तपति तपोलोकनायकश्चेता ॥202॥

Behind the Dyauloka resides Varuna, the presiding deity of the oceans and the master of Parameshti. Above him is Indra, the master of Tapoloka (one of the seven worlds—bhur, bhuvah, svaha, maha, jana, tapa and satya) bestower of consciousness, and is ever illumined.

दिव्यादित्यास्त्विन्द्रो दिव्यादित्यं प्रशास्ति यं वरुणम् ।
वरुणस्ततः स भिन्नः स्वायंभुव इन्द्र एष यं शास्ति ॥203॥

The sun of Dyauloka is Indra and one who rules the divyaditya is Varuna. But that Varuna is different from this Varuna who is ruled by Indra, the master of svayambhu-mandala.

दिव्यादित्यं त्विन्द्रं शास्ति स वरुणः स्वमण्डलान्तस्थम् ।
परमे व्योम्नि स्वाराडिन्द्रः शास्ति स समुद्रमात्मगतम् ॥204॥

Located in its own sphere, Varuna rules the divyaditya Indra. But in that ultimate ether-space, Indra rules Varuna, located in his own self.

वाग् वै स इन्द्रोऽस्ति स सत्यलोके वाग्लोकतोऽपोऽसृजदत्र पश्चात् ।
अपा समुद्रो जनदस्ति लोकः स सत्यलोकादवरः प्रतीतः ॥205॥

Indra is the master of speech (*veda*), he alone has created water in Satyaloka (world of truth) from Vagloka. Beyond this Vagloka, there is ocean (of water) called Jandastiloka which is visible below Satyaloka.

परमं तु वैश्वरूप्यं स्वायंभुवमस्ति पारमेष्ठ्यं तु ।
तदवरमथ पुनरवरं सौरं भौमं ततोऽप्यवरम् ॥206॥

Beyond all these and all-pervading is the svayambhu mandala; parameshtiloka is below this, smaller than this is the suryaloka and the smallest one is (still below) bhaumaloka.

प्रति वैश्वरूप्यमिन्द्रो ब्रह्मा विष्णुर्नियम्यन्ते ।
वरुणस्तु पारमेष्ठ्ये सौरे वा वैश्वरूप्येऽस्ति ॥207॥

इत्थं परावतीन्द्रो वरुणादर्वावतीन्द्र आभाति ।
अन्तर्बहिरुभयेन तु वरुणोऽनुगृहीत इन्द्रेण ॥208॥

Brahma, Vishnu, and Indra control every world but Varuna is located in Parameshti or in the other world. Thus from the view of svayambhu, even the highest Indra appears lower. Thus both internally and externally Varuna is permeated by Indra.

तस्मादिन्द्रः स्वाराड् वरुणः सम्राडिदं हि विज्ञानम् ।
विज्ञानादनपेतो योऽर्थः स ब्राह्मणैर्ग्राह्यः ॥209॥

This Indra is the supreme presiding deity and Varuna is the ruler of a specific sphere. This is the cosmic principle, established by science and this meaning is accepted by the brahmins.

1.3.1.3.10 इन्द्रपक्ष्यैः ब्राह्मणैः उद्घोषितं देवेन्द्रमहत्त्वम्

1.3.1.3.10 Pro-Indra brahmins declare Devendra's importance

तत्र प्रक्रान्ते ब्राह्मणानां विचारयुद्धे प्रथमं तावत् काण्वो देवेन्द्रपक्षपाती स्ववर्ग्यानार्यानभ्यादिदेश ।

The brahmins unanimously declared Indra to be superior. Sage Kanva, who supported Indra, was the first sage to instruct his pupils thus:

मा चिदन्यद् वि शंसत सखायो मा रिषण्यत ।
इन्द्रमित्स्तोता वृषणं सचा सुते मुहुरुक्था च शंसत ।।
(ऋग्वेदः, 8.1.1)

'O friends, Do not pray to any other deity. Do not get distressed for having worshipped the other gods. In the sacrifice of extracting the Soma rasa, pray only to the mighty Indra. Recite again and again the hymns of Indra.'

नृमेधा आह–
इन्द्राय साम गायत विप्राय बृहते बृहत् ।
धर्मकृते विपश्चिते पनस्यवे ।।
(ऋग्वेदः, 8.87.1)

Sage Nrimedha said, 'O human beings, sing the expanded psalm (*sama*) for wise, dharma-oriented actions, knowledgeable and praise worthy Indra.'

हिरण्यस्तूप आह–
सूर्यस्येव रश्मयो द्रावयित्नवो मत्सरासः प्रसुपः साकमीरते ।
तन्तुं ततं परि सर्गास आशवो नेन्द्रादृते पवते धाम किञ्चन ।।
(ऋग्वेदः, 9.69.6)

Hiranyastupa said, 'Like the rays of the sun, bestower of bliss, destroyer of enemies, the Soma filtered through the taut threads does not go anywhere but to Indra.'

वामदेव आह–
नकिरिन्द्र त्वदुत्तरो न ज्यायां अस्ति वृत्रहन् ।
नकिरेवा यथा त्वम् ।।
(ऋग्वेदः, 4.30.1)

त्वोतासो मघवन्निन्द्र विप्रा वयं ते स्याम सूरयो गृणन्तः ।
भेजानासो बृहद्दिवस्य राय आकाय्यस्य दावने पुरुक्षोः ॥
(ऋग्वेदः, 4.29.5)

Vamadeva said, 'O destroyer of Vritra Indra! No one is superior to you. No one is greater than you. No one is like you. O prosperous Indra! Let us, the knowledgeable ones, protected by you, reciters of hymns and wise ones, praised by all the directions and replete with food grains, participate in your offering of riches.'

रेणुर्वैश्वामित्र आह–
इन्द्रो दिव इन्द्र ईशे पृथिव्या इन्द्रो अपामिन्द्र इत् पर्वतानाम् ।
इन्द्रो वृधामिन्द्र इन्मेधिराणामिन्द्रः क्षेमे योगे हव्य इन्द्रः ॥
(ऋग्वेद 10.89.10)

Renu Vishvamitra said, 'Indra is the master of Dyauloka; he is also the master of earth, water, and mountains. Indra is the master of intellect and wise people. To attain *yoga* (attaining what is non-attainable), and *kshema* (protecting whatever is achieved), one should pray to Indra.'

पूरणो वैश्वामित्र इन्द्रं संबोध्याह–
तुभ्यं सुतास्तुभ्यमु सोत्वासस्त्वां गिरः श्वात्र्या आह्वयन्ति ।
इन्द्रेदमद्य सवनं जुषाणो विश्वस्य विद्वाँ इह पाहि सोमम् ॥
(ऋग्वेदः, 10.60.2)

Purno, a friend of Vishvamitra, addressing Indra said, 'O Indra! This soma-rasa is extracted only for you. Henceforth too, it will be extracted for you alone. Pleasant, sacred chanting of hymns, full of praise, are always calling you. Having accepted this morning *savanna* (process of extracting Soma), you drink the Soma in our sacrifice.'

अथ स स्ववर्गेभ्य इन्द्रं प्रशंसति–
अनुस्पष्टो भवत्येषो अस्य यो अस्मै रेवान्न सुनोति सोमम् ।
निररत्नौ मघवा तं दधाति ब्रह्मद्विषो हन्त्यनानुदिष्टः ॥
(ऋग्वेदः, 10.160. 4)

Then praising Indra, he says to his class, 'Be like the person who by offering soma-rasa, is blessed with the sight of Indra appearing before him. That rich Indra makes him free of fear, holding him by the shoulders. Even without asking any favour, he destroys the enemies of the scholars.'

अथ गर्ग आह-
तस्य वयं सुमतौ यज्ञियस्यापि भद्रे सौमनसे स्याम ।
स सुत्रामा स्ववाँ इन्द्रो अस्मे आराच्चिदद्वेषः सनुतर्युयोतु ।।
(ऋग्वेदः, 6.47.13)

In the meanwhile, Garga said, 'Let us live with the highest intellect of a respectable being. Let us all be helpful and be associated with noble minds. Let that Indra, the great rich sustainer, drive away all our enemies hiding in remote countries forever.

इन्द्रः सुत्रमा स्ववाँ अवोभिः सुमृळीको भवतु विश्ववेदाः ।
बाधतां द्वेषो अभयं कृणोतु सुवीर्य्यस्य पतयः स्याम ।।
(ऋग्वेदः, 6.47.12)

'Let Indra, a great protector, endowed with spiritual powers, be bestower of happiness by his act of defending. Let him make us courageous. May we all be masters of the highest power.'

1.3.1.3.11 देवेन्द्रेणासुरनिहननम्

1.3.1.3.11 Motivated by prayers, Indra attacks asuras

तत्र विवादावसरे गर्गाहूतः क्षणादुपस्थाय ।
इन्द्रोऽनिन्द्रानेतान् क्षिपन्नुवाच स्वयं घृष्णवन् ।।210।।

On the invitation of Garg, Indra reached the place where the debate was taking place. He was upset by the asuras questioning him and hurling insults at him. Rejecting the asura claims, he declared:

अभीदमेकमेको अस्मि निष्षाळभी द्वा किमु त्रयः करन्ति ।
खले न पर्षान् प्रति हन्मि भूरि किं मा निन्दन्ति शत्रवोऽनिन्द्राः ।।
(ऋग्वेदः, 10.48.7)

'Even now I can defeat one enemy, I, who has no enemy left, can defeat two powerful enemies. I can even defeat three and they can cause me no harm. As the farmer presses the plant to separate the grain (paddy), I can crush all those who defame Indra.'

एवं क्रुध्यन्निन्द्रोऽभिव्लङ्गायाभिचक्रमे सद्यः ।
युद्धाभिशङ्कया प्राक् संनद्धामासुरीं सेनाम् ।।211।।

An angry Indra then decided to launch an attack on the asura army, which had anticipated such a war and was prepared.

क्षुद्रे युद्धे तस्मिन्निन्द्रभटा एकविंशतिर्निहताः ।
निहतास्तु यातुमत्यां तिस्रः पञ्चाशतोऽरिसेनायाम् ।।212।।

In this short war, twenty-one warriors from Indra's side and one-hundred-and-fifty warriors of the asura army were killed.

येऽत्रानिन्द्रा आर्यास्तेषां दाहः प्रमीतानाम् ।
असुराणां मृतदेहा नादह्यन्त क्षितौ त्वधीयन्त ।।213।।

Even those Arya who attacked this army of Indra were cremated after their death, but the dead bodies of the asuras were not cremated, but buried in the ground.

मृतदेहा असुराणां यत्र गृहे शेरते निहिताः ।
तद्गृहमर्मकमुक्तं वैलस्थानेऽर्मकाणि कल्प्यन्ते ।।214।।

The stretch of land in which the dead asuras were buried was called the *armaka*-s and the place where these armakas were made was called the Vailasthana.

आर्मीनियेति नाम्ना प्रथितं प्रान्तं तदर्मकं मन्ये ।
देवासुरसंग्रामे हतासुराणां श्मशानं तत् ।।215।।

I believe the province named Armenia might have possibly been an armaka or the cremation ground of the asuras who were killed in the battle between the devas and asuras.

असुरश्मशानभूमिं वैलस्थानाख्यया स्म ते ब्रुवते ।
राज्ञां महाश्मशानं तथैव कथितं महावैलम् ।।216।।

The cremation grounds of the asuras were known as the Vailasthana and the grand cremation grounds of the kings came to be known as the Mahavaila.

बहवोऽनिन्द्रा युद्धे निहता निहिताश्च ते महावैले ।
एतच्च परुच्छेपो युद्धान्ते वर्णयामास ।।217।।

Many asuras who were killed in the war were placed in the Mahavaila. An event of this sort has been described by rishi Parucchepa at the end of the war.

1.3.1.3.12 परुच्छेपेण वर्णितं इन्द्रमाहात्म्यम्

1.3.1.3.11 Parucchepa's account of Indra's victory

उभे पुनामि रोदसी ऋतेन द्रुहो दहामि सं महीरनिन्द्राः ।
अभिव्लग्य यत्र हता अमित्रा वैलस्थानं परि तृह्ला अशेरन् ॥
(ऋग्वेदः, 1.133.1)

I purify both the loka by the power of yajna. I burn down all the major enemies who are hostile to Indra. Where the warring enemies were killed and went into deep slumber, it became the cremation ground.

अभिव्लग्या चिदद्रिवः शीर्षा यातुमतीनाम् ।
छिन्धि वटूरिणा पदा महावटूरिणा पदा ॥
(ऋग्वेदः, 1.133.2)

O *Vajradhari* (the bearer of vajra, a weapon which is said to have been formed out of the bones of the sage Dadhichi) Indra! Rise above your violent enemies and crush them under your large and mighty feet.

अवासां मघवञ्जहि शर्धो यातुमतीनाम् ।
वैलस्थानके अर्मके महावैलस्थे अर्मके॥
(ऋग्वेदः, 1.133.3)

O wealthy Indra! Destroy the strength of these violent armies in the despicable, big cremation grounds where the pain-struck dead people lie.

यासां तिस्रः पञ्चाशतोऽभिव्लङ्गैरपावपः ।
तत् सु ते मनायति तकत्सु ते मनायति ॥
(ऋग्वेदः, 1.133.4)

O Indra! Bhaktas praise you for killing one hundred and fifty enemies by employing your tactics of siege.

इन्द्राय हि द्यौरसुरो अनम्नतेन्द्राय मही पृथिवी वीरमभिर्द्युम्नसाता वरीमभिः ।
इन्द्रं विश्वे सजोषसो देवासो दधिरे पुरः ।
इन्द्राय विश्वा सवनानि मानुषा रातानि सन्तु मानुषा ॥
(ऋग्वेदः, 1.131.1)

The powerful army of the asuras was destroyed in the fight with Indra. The vast earth, with all its finest objects, was destroyed before Indra. In the battle for acquisition of grains, the enemies, though well-equipped with optimum resources, were also destroyed. Elated by this victory, the devas honoured Indra. All the sacrifices performed by human beings, and the alms given by them, were offered as obeisance to Indra.

अथ पुरुहन्मा आह

The narration of Puruhanma

अत्यन्तं क्रुध्यन्तं तमिन्द्रमुपशान्तयंश्च पुरुहन्मा ।
अस्येन्द्रस्यात्मानं महयत्यधिदैवतं चेन्द्रम् ।।218।।

To pacify an angry Indra, sage Puruhanma praised him and invoked his godliness.

यद् द्याव इन्द्र ते शतं शतं भूमीरुत स्युः ।
न त्वा वज्रिन्त्सहस्रं सूर्या अनु न जातमष्ट रोदसी ।।

(ऋग्वेदः, 8.59.5)

O Indra! Even if this heaven multiplies and becomes hundred in number, or the sun becomes a thousand in count, they cannot, even together, become equal to you in your stature. Even the heaven and earth can never flourish enough to be equal to your might.

अथ श्रुतकक्ष आह-
The narration of Srutakaksha.

श्रुतकक्षोऽपि ब्रूते न त्वामतिरिच्यते कश्चित् ।
अर्हसि सोमं पातुं त्वमेव नैषोऽसुरोन्यो वा ।।219।।

Srutakaksha also had said that no one was as powerful as you. Only you were eligible for drinking Soma. This or any other asura was not fit for the same.

त्वे सुपुत्र शवसोऽवृत्रन् कामकातयः ।
न त्वामिन्द्राति रिच्यते ।।

(ऋग्वेदः, 8.81.11)

O son of might, Indra! Even immodest people behave well before you. O Indra! Nobody is greater than you.

आ त्वा विशन्त्विन्दवः समुद्रमिव सिन्धवः ।
न त्वामिन्द्राति रिच्यते ।।

(ऋग्वेदः, 8.81.22)

O Indra! May the soma-rasa which you drink, invigorate you just like the rivers which enter the sea. Nobody is as venerable as you.

पराकात्ताच्चिदद्रिवस्त्वां नक्षन्त नो गिरः ।
अरं गमाम ते वयम् ॥

(ऋग्वेदः, 8.81.27)

O Vajradhari Indra! You acknowledge our prayers even from a distance. O Indra! It may be so that we become the objects of your endearment and affection.

एवा ह्यसि वीरयुरेवा शूर उत स्थिरः ।
एवा ते राध्यं मनः ॥

(ऋग्वेदः, 8.81.28)

O Indra! You desire valiant people. You yourself are a hero, a great warrior. O Indra! You remain calm and steadfast even in the midst of a war. Your disposition is worthy of reverence.

त्वयेदिन्द्र युजा वयं प्रति ब्रुवीमहि स्पृधः ।
त्वमस्माकं तव स्मसि ॥

(ऋग्वेदः, 8.81.32)

O Indra! From you, we get the courage to face enemies. You are close to us and we are your people.

अथ हैमवर्चिः प्राह -

The narration of Haimavarchi.

एतावद्रूपं यज्ञस्य यद्देवैर्ब्रह्मणा कृतम् ।
तदेतत् सर्वमाप्नोति यज्ञे सौत्रामणीसुते ॥
सुरावन्तं वर्हिषदं सुवीरं यज्ञं हिन्वन्ति महिषा नमोभिः ।
दधानाः सोमं दिवि देवतासु मदेमेन्द्रं यजमानाः स्वर्काः ॥

(यजुर्वेदः 19.31-32)

The gods and Brahma have described the excellent form and nature of the sacrificial rites. If soma-rasa is churned out in the sautramani yajna, then the person who performs the rites becomes one with the yajna. Great priests who hold Soma for the gods, who dwell with all foods in the heavens, reinforce the leading priest who prepares superior Soma with the gods seated on sacred *kusha* (grass). We wish we could also draw happiness and contentment from this yajna, since we are performing it to please Indra, the bestower of the best food.

1.3.1.3.13 बृहद्दिवस्य ब्रह्मनप्तृत्वम्

1.3.1.3.13 Brihaddiva becomes Brahma's grandson

वरुणतनूजोऽथर्वा बृहद्दिवोऽथर्वणः पुत्रः ।
सोऽथर्वा, स बृहद्दिव, एतौ पक्षं विनिन्यतुर्दैवम् ।।220।।

Atharva was Varuna's son and Brihaddiva was born as Atharva's son. Both of them [Brihaddiva and Atharva] became supporters of the deities.

ब्रह्मण एषोऽथर्वा बभूव कालेन मानसः पुत्रः ।
पुत्रत्वेन स मनसाऽनुभावितः कृत्रिमः पुत्रः ।।221।।

Brahma adopted Atharva as his foster son. He started loving him as if he were his own son.

अत एवैषोऽथर्वा तस्य च पुत्रे बृहद्दिवो नाम ।
बाह्लीके प्रागास्तां पश्चात् तौ पुष्करेऽस्थाताम् ।।222।।

Therefore, both Atharva and his son Brihaddiva moved to Pushkara from Bahlika and settled there.

ब्रह्मपुरं यत्पुष्करमद्य बुखारेति गद्यते यच्च ।
तत्रत्य इन्द्रमूचे बृहद्दिवोऽथर्वणः पुत्रः ।।223।।

This Brahmapura [abode of Brahma] is known as Bukhara in present times. Brihaddiva, who lived there, praised and adored Indra.

बृहद्दिव आथर्वण आह–

Statement of Atharva's son Brihaddiva

तदिदास भुवनेषु ज्येष्ठं यतो जज्ञ उग्रस्त्वेषनृम्णः ।
सद्यो जज्ञानो नि रिणाति शत्रूननु यं विश्वे मदन्त्यूमाः ।।
(ऋग्वेदः, 10.120.1)

In all the loka, *Parambrahma* (the Supreme Self) is also the *adibhuta* (the first being) from whom emanated the fierce, radical, and splendid sun. He destroys enemies soon as soon as he assumes form. He is the one whom living beings are delighted to see.

वावृधानः शवसा भूर्योजाः शत्रुर्दासाय भियसं दधाति ।
अव्यनच्च व्यनच्च सस्नि सं ते नवन्त प्रभृता मदेषु ।।
(ऋग्वेदः, 10.120.2)

Aroused by strength, the brilliant one and the destroyer of enemies, Indra creates fear in the minds of *dasa*-s (slaves). By his grace, manifest as well as indistinct, immovable, and movable objects are happy and tranquil. Thus, O Indra! We pray for the endless mercy of that Supreme Being, who is responsible for the well-being of all.

इति चिद्धि त्वा धना जयन्तं मदे मदे अनुमदन्ति विप्राः ।
ओजीयो धृष्णो स्थिरमा तनुष्व मा त्वा दभन्यातुधाना दुरेवाः ।।
(ऋग्वेदः, 10.120.4)

In this way, O Indra, when after drinking Soma, you are delighted and win wealth and riches, wise folk eulogize you. O Indra, the one who defeats the enemies! You are mighty! Grant us wealth that is long-lasting. We wish that the vicious rakshasas may never succeed in harming you.

त्वया वयं शाशद्महे रणेषु प्रपश्यन्तो युधोन्यानि भूरि ।
चोदयामि त आयुधा वचोभिः सं ते शिशामि ब्रह्मणा वयांसि ।।
(ऋग्वेदः, 10.120.5)

O Indra! By your grace, we succeed in destroying enemies in battles. Bless us so that we may be able to discern the means they use in war. I pray to you to arouse your weapons, Vajrayodha [an epithet for Indra]. For arousing you, I purify havya and other food materials by chanting Vedic hymns in your praise.

इमा ब्रह्म बृहद्दिवो विवक्तीन्द्राय शूषमग्रियः स्वर्षाः ।
महो गोत्रस्य क्षयति स्वराजो दुरश्च विश्वा अवृणोदप स्वाः ।।
(ऋग्वेदः, 10.120.8)

Rishi Brihaddiva, the foremost among all the rishis and who desired heaven, chanted these Vedic hymns to please Indra: 'May he become the master of bright, brilliant, and great cows. He opens all the gateways to heaven.'

एवा महान्बृहद्दिवो अथर्वावोचत्स्वां तन्वमिन्द्रमेव ।
स्वसारो मातरिभ्वरीररिप्रा हिन्वन्ति च शवसा वर्धयन्ति च ।।
(ऋग्वेद:, 10.120.9)

In this way, the great son of Atharva, Brihaddiva recited his hymns for pleasing Indra. Born of mother earth, the pious rivers become equal to Bhagini and please Indra. They replenish his heaven with water and add to his valour.

1.3.1.3.14 औतथ्यकुत्साभ्यां वरुणस्य अग्नित्वप्रतिपादनम्

1.3.1.3.14 Autathya and Kutsa proclaim Varuna as Agni

मैत्रमहस्तु निशीथान्मध्यदिनान्तं, ततो निशीथान्ता ।
रात्रिर्हि वारुणी सा मित्रवरुणौ तदादित्यौ ।।224।।

The duration from midnight to midday is considered as day and it is Mitra's day. The duration from midday to midnight is night and it is considered to be Varuna's time. Thus, both Mitra and Varuna are Aditya.

ऐन्द्रमहश्चाग्नेयी रात्रि: प्रतिपद्यते तस्मात् ।
इन्द्रो मित्रादित्यो वरुणस्त्वग्नि: स्थितोऽप्सु यो निहित: ।।225।।

A day is considered to be *aindra* (belonging to or sacred to Indra), the time of Indra and a night is believed to be *agneyi* (belonging to Agni). Therefore, Mitra and Aditya are themselves Indra in a way. Varuna is Agni, who pervades all through the water element and is steady.

वरुणस्याग्नित्वाख्या तैत्तिरकब्राह्मणस्य के सेके ।
अपि शतपथस्य मेखे लेख्ये दृष्टा च राजसूयविधौ ।।226।।

In the seventh chapter of the first part of Taittiriya Brahmana, the *agnitatva* (energy) state of Varuna has been described, and in *rajasuya-yajnavidhi* (the method of performing rajasuya-yajna) given in Shatapatha Brahmana also we find a similar description.

इह राजसूययज्ञे इन्द्रतुरीय: प्रचर्यते याग: ।
तत्राग्निवरुणारुद्रा इन्द्रात्पूर्व्यास्त्रयोऽग्निभागा: स्यु: ।।227।।

In this rajasuya-yajna, Indra is considered to be the fourth part. Therein, the *agnibhaga* of Agni, Varuna and Rudra have been established before that of Indra.

पिण्डेऽग्निरग्निरुक्तो वरुणो नामाग्निरुच्यतेऽप्स्वन्तः ।
अग्निर्वायौ रुद्रो भूमिरसत्वात्त्रयोऽग्नयस्तेऽमी ।।228।।

The element of warmth found in every human being is also Agni. The agnitatva in water is known as Varuna. The agnitatva in wind is called rudra. Therefore, since Agni, Vayu, and rudra are the essence of land, they can be called Agni.

निविडे तरले विरले ध्रुवे च धर्त्रे च धरुणे च ।
अग्निर्वरुणो रुद्रः प्रथते त्रेधाऽयमग्निरेकाऽपि ।।229।।

In all dense states (solid), liquid states (water) and sparse states (air), and in cosmic bodies also, this Agni is known as Agni, Varuna, and rudra respectively.

सोऽग्निर्भूमेश्चापामथान्तरिक्षस्य चाधिपतिः ।
इन्द्रस्त्वेष दिवस्पतिरिन्द्राग्नी रोदसीनाथौ ।।230।।

The Agni referred to here is the master of land, water, and sky, and Indra is the lord of heaven. Thus, Indra and Agni are the masters of heaven and earth.

तौ सत्तमौ वरिष्ठौ ओजिष्ठौ पारयिष्णुतमौ ।
सममेनयोर्महत्त्वं न तयोरवरः परो वा स्यात् ।।231।।

Both of them are excellent, experienced, and powerful, and have the competence to accomplish tasks. Their importance is almost comparable. Among the two, no one can be thought of greater than the other.

अग्निः स्थानविभेदाद्धत्ते नामानि भिन्नानि ।
सोऽस्ति सुपर्णः स यमः स मातरिश्वा स वरुणोऽयम् ।।232।।

Agni takes on different names at different places. This Agni is *suparna* (sun), *yama* (god of death), *mathrishva* (air) and Varuna.

इत्थं दीर्घतमा अपि कुत्सोऽप्याङि्गरस ऊचतुस्तत्र ।
इन्द्रावरुणौ मित्रावरुणौ तौ रोदसीविषयौ ।।233।।

In this way, in a debate, Dirghatama Autathya and Kutsa Angirasa also said that Indra and Varuna, and Mitra and Varuna—all are subjects of this heaven and earth.

इन्द्रं मित्रं, वरुणमग्निमाहुरथो दिव्यः स सुपर्णो गरुत्मान् ।
एकं सद्विप्रा बहुधा वदन्ति अग्निं यमं मातरिश्वानमाहुः ।।
(ऋग्वेदः, 10.164.46)

It is mentioned in the Rigveda that intelligent and knowledgeable people of all the worlds retell the same singular *sat vastu* (wise statements) in myriad ways. That sat is pronounced by Indra, Mitra, Varuna and Agni. It is divya, suparna and *garutmana* (winged).

इन्द्रं मित्रं, वरुणमग्निमूतये मारुतं शर्द्धो अदितिं हवामहे ।
रथं न दुर्गाद्वसवः सुदानवो विश्वस्मान्नो अंहसो निष्पिपर्तन ।।
(ऋग्वेदः, 10.106.1)

All of us pray to Indra, Mitra, Varuna, Agni, the group of maruts and aditis (the earth, the mother of the gods) for our security and well-being—'O Vasus, bestowers of exquisite grants! Steer us clear of all difficulties just as you cautiously drive the chariot on a path full of obstacles.'

1.3.1.3.15 वरुणपक्ष्यैः ब्राह्मणैः उद्घोषितं वरुणमहत्त्वम्

1.3.1.3.15 Pro-Varuna brahmins assert Varuna's importance

तत्र ब्राह्मणा ऋग्भिर्वरुणमहिमानं श्रावयन्ति स्म ।

The praise of Varuṇa's glory by the brahmins through Rig-mantras.

इत्थं बहुभिरपीन्द्रः परमाराध्यस्तदा विनिर्णीतः ।
किन्तु तदानीमपरे व्याचख्युर्वरुणमाराध्यम् ।।234।।

Many brahmins chose to worship Indra as their only god, but some other brahmins chose Varuna as their *paramaradhya* (supreme deity).

यावादित्यौ मित्रावरुणौ तत एष भिद्यते वरुणः ।
एष समुद्रस्येशो यद्गर्भेऽयं दिवस्पतिस्त्विन्द्रः ।।235।।

The reference to Varuna here, is different from aditya and mitravaruna. He is the lord of the sea, in whose belly is found Indra, the master of heaven.

अत्रिस्तावद् वरुणं व्याचष्टे ब्राह्मणो देवम् ।
पञ्चममण्डलसूक्ते पञ्चाशीते त्वृचस्ताहि ।।236।।

There are several verses in the eighty-fifth sukta in the fifth mandala of Rigveda, where Varuna alone is considered worthy of worship. One such verse refers to a brahmin named Atri who said:

प्र सम्राजे बृहदर्चा गभीरं ब्रह्म प्रियं वरुणाय श्रुताय ।
वि यो जघान शमितेव चर्मोपस्तिरे पृथिवीं सूर्याय ।।
(ऋग्वेद:, 5.85.1)

Just as a hunter skins the hunted animal, Varuna enlarged the already vast heaven for the movement of the sun. So, we should sing an exhaustive and ceremonial praise for the extremely bright and famous Varuna, one that would be appreciated by him.

वनेषु व्यन्तरिक्षं ततान वाजमर्वत्सु, पय उस्रियासु ।
हृत्सु क्रतुं वरुणो अप्स्वग्निं दिवि सूर्यमदधात्सोममद्रौ ।।
(ऋग्वेद:, 5.85.2)

Varuna has filled the sea of space with the timber of woods and trees. (Here, woods may also mean clouds, according to which Varuna has filled the sea of space with clouds). He has given energy to horses, filled cows with milk, offered our hearts to accomplish tasks, placed Agni in waters, placed the sun in heaven and implanted Soma on the mountain.

नीचीनवारं वरुण: कबन्धं प्र ससर्ज रोदसी अन्तरिक्षम् ।
तेन विश्वस्य भुवनस्य राजा यवं न दृष्टिर्व्युनत्ति भूम ।।
(ऋग्वेद:, 5.85.3)

Varuna released the clouds for the benefit of the earth and space. By those rains, Varuna, the lord of the entire earth, renders the land fertile for a good yield.

उनत्ति भूमिं पृथिवीमुत द्यां यदा दुग्धं वरुणो वष्ट्यादित् ।
समभ्रेण वसत पर्वतासस्तविषीयन्त: श्रथयन्त वीरा: ।।
(ऋग्वेद:, 5.85.4)

When Varuna wishes it to rain, he waters land, sky, and heaven. As a result, the mountains are covered with clouds, and immediately after that, the powerful and brave marudagana, gods of winds and rain, let the clouds free, and cause rain.

इमामू ष्वासुरस्य श्रुतस्य महीं मायां वरुणस्य प्र वोचम् ।
मानेनेव तस्थिवाँ अन्तरिक्षे वि यो ममे पृथिवीं सूर्येण ॥
(ऋग्वेदः, 5.85.5)

Although stationed in space, Varuna measured the earth with the sun, using it as a measuring stick. I praise the intellect of the bestower of life, Varuna.

इमामू नु कवितमस्य मायां महीं देवस्य न किरा दधर्ष ।
एकं यदुद्ना न पृणन्त्येनीरासिञ्चन्तीरवनयः समुद्रम् ॥
(ऋग्वेदः, 5.85.6)

No one can harm or destroy the maya, the wonderful construction of this world that the extremely knowledgeable Varuna deva has cast upon us, because of whom the rivers, which water the earth, can never fill a sea up to the brim.

अर्यम्यं वरुण मित्र्यं वा सखायं वा सदमिद् भ्रातरं वा ।
वेशं वा नित्यं वरुणारणं वा यत्सीमागश्चकृमा शिश्रथस्तत् ॥
(ऋग्वेदः, 5.85.7)

Worthy of worship, Varuna deva! Please absolve us of any crime that we may have committed towards a good and virtuous man, a friend or an associate, one who is like a brotherly person, a close one or our leader.

कितवासो यद्रिरिपुर्न दीवि यद्वा घा सत्यमुतयन्न विद्म ।
सर्वा ता विष्य शिथिरेव देवाधा ते स्याम वरुण प्रियासः ॥
(ऋग्वेदः, 5.85.8)

We pray to you to absolve us of the false allegations levelled against us by people, just as gamblers unreasonably blame each other in a gamble, and also of such mistakes that we might have inadvertently committed. O Varuna deva! Loosen our bondages, set us free, so that we may continue to remain your dear ones.

1.3.1.3.16 अपरैः ब्राह्मणैः उद्घोषितं इन्द्रवरुणयोः माहात्म्यम्

1.3.1.3.16 Other brahmins agreed to the importance of both

अत्र विवादे पश्चान्मध्यस्थाः केचिदासाद्य ।
उभयोरेव महत्त्वं समानमास्थापयामासुः ।।237।।

After this debate, some of the brahmins came around to accept that both Indra and Varuna were equal in importance.

तपसो लोकाज्जाते ऋतसत्ये द्वे इमे नेत्रे ।
सा क्रन्दसी ऋतेन तु सत्येन तु रोदसी विधृता ।।238।।

Rita (universal truth) and *Satya* (truth) originated from Tapoloka. Both of them are like two eyes of this Tapoloka. One is prevailed on by Krandasi rita, another is enveloped by Rodasi satya.

ऋतमित्यपां त्रयं स्यादापो वायुश्च सोमश्च ।
अग्नित्रयं तु सत्यं स्यादग्निर्वायुरादित्यः ।।239।।

By Rita, one means all the three types of water, which are Apah, Vayu, and Soma. Similarly, three kinds of Agni are believed to be true. They are—Agni, Vayu, and Aditya.

ऋतमधिकुरुते वरुणः सोऽपां नाथः समुद्रनाथश्च ।
इन्द्रस्तु सत्यमीष्टे स वासवो वायुरादित्यः ।।240।।

Varuna is the presiding deity of water, the master of all waters, and the governor of seas. Indra is the presiding deity of truth; he is Vasava [one of the names of Indra], and he himself is Vayu and Aditya.

न ऋताद् ऋतेऽग्नयस्ते सत्येनापश्च गर्भिण्यः ।
नैकस्तयोर्विनाऽन्यं कदापि वा रूपमादध्यात् ।।241।।

Without water, Agni cannot acquire its form, and apah is filled with Satya also. Thus, both of them cannot acquire their forms without each other.

उभयोरनयोरेकः कः प्रवरः कोऽवरः कल्प्यः ।
इन्द्रात्प्रवरो वरुणो वरुणात्प्रवरः स इन्द्रोऽस्ति ।।242।।

If we try to assess who is superior among the two, we find that Varuna is superior to Indra stationed in Rodasi, and that Indra stationed in Samyati is superior to Varuna.

काण्वः सुपर्ण एव स भरद्वाजश्च वामदेवश्च ।
इन्द्रावरुणौ स्वाराट् सम्राजौ तुल्यमस्तौषुः ।।243।।

In this way, Kanva's son Suparna, Bharadvaja, and Vamadeva praised svarat and samrat, Indra and Varuna, on equal grounds.

सुपर्णः काण्वः

Kanva's son Suparna

अवोचाम महते सौभगाय सत्यं त्वेषाभ्यां महिमानमिन्द्रियम् ।
अस्मान्त्स्विन्द्रावरुणा घृतश्चुतस्त्रिभिः साप्तेभिरवतं शुभस्पती ।।
(ऋग्वेदः, 8.59.5)

O guardians of auspicious events, Indra and Varuna! Both of us praise your greatness whereby you augment the strength of people, and we also pray for our good fortune. You are an imparter of fortitude and we call upon you to protect us.

इन्द्रावरुणा यदृषिभ्यो मनीषां वाचो मतिं श्रुतमदत्तमग्रे ।
यानि स्थानान्यसृजन्त धीरा यज्ञं तन्वानास्तपसाभ्यपश्यम् ।।
(ऋग्वेदः, 8.59.6)

O Indra and Varuna! Through penance, I have acquainted myself with intellect, reason, oratory skills and knowledge that you bestowed on ascetics in ancient times, and also with the places built by people who performed yajna with perseverance.

इन्द्रावरुणा सौमनसमदृप्तं रायस्पोषं यजमानेषु धत्तम् ।
प्रजां पुष्टिम्भूतिमस्मासु धत्तं दीर्घायुत्वाय प्रतिरतं न आयुः ।।
(ऋग्वेदः, 8.59.7)

O Indra and Varuna! Bless both the hosts with politeness, generosity and invigorating fame; also bless us with long lives so that we may appreciate our people, nourishment, and other gifts that a long life affords.

भरद्वाजः

Bharadvaja

ता हि श्रेष्ठा देवताता तुजा शूराणां शविष्ठा ता हि भूतम् ।
मघोनां मंहिष्ठा तुविशुष्म ऋतेन वृत्रतुरा सर्वसेना ।।
(ऋग्वेदः, 6.68.2)

He is supreme among the two gods; He is wealthy, stronger among the two warriors, chief among the respectable, and possessed with immense strength. He is the one who kills enemies by righteous means and has all kinds of armies.

ग्नाश्च यन्नरश्च वावृधन्त विश्वे देवासो नरां स्वगूर्त्ताः ।
प्रैभ्य इन्द्रावरुणा महित्वा द्यौश्च पृथिवि भूतमुर्वी ॥
(ऋग्वेदः, 6.68.4)

No matter how much men and women could multiply, or how high the wise might rise through their hard work, or how vast could heaven and earth become, Indra and Varuna will be above all of these because of their worth.

यं युवं दाश्वध्वराय देवा रयिं धत्थो वसुमन्तं पुरुक्षुम् ।
अस्मे स इन्द्रावरुणावपि ष्यात् प्र यो भनक्ति वनुषामशस्तीः ॥
(ऋग्वेदः, 6.68.6)

O Indra and Varuna! You both bestow wealth that brings good name and prosperity to *purusha*-s (men) who are generous enough to give alms and are non-violent. Provide that wealth to us so that we can counter our detractors.

प्र सम्राजे बृहते मन्म नु प्रियमर्च देवाय वरुणाय सप्रथः ।
अयं य उर्वी महिना महिव्रतः क्रत्वा विभात्यजरो न शोचिषा ॥
(ऋग्वेदः, 6.68.9)

O my fellow-mortals! Praise the great samrat Varuna deva by singing his famous and favourite hymns; praise the one who accomplishes huge tasks, and who, through his great capacity undiminished by age, brightens up this vast earth with his ardour and his sense of duty.

इन्द्रावरुणा सुतपाविमं सुतं सोमं पिबतं मद्यं धृतव्रता ।
युवो रथो अध्वरं देववीतये प्रति स्वसरमुपयाति पीतये ॥
(ऋग्वेदः, 5.68.10)

O Indra and Varuna, both of you drink Soma! O great observers of fasts! We request both of you to drink this [freshly] extracted and pleasing Soma rasa. For drinking Soma and for acquiring godliness, your chariot goes to each *yajna-sthana* (place of yajna) to partake the nectar during the serene yajna.

1.3.1.3.17 पक्षत्रयवतां ब्राह्मणानां विज्ञानविरोधे विचारसमितिः

1.3.1.3.17 A council set up to mediate between three different brahmin groups

इन्द्रस्य पक्षे कतिचिद्बभूवुर्बभूवुरन्ये वरुणस्य पक्षे ।
परे बभूवुर्द्विसमत्वपक्षे मिथस्त्रिपक्ष्या ऋषयः समूदुः ।।244।।

Even after these exhortations, there was no consensus among the brahmins. Some brahmins continued to favour Indra while others supported Varuna. There were other brahmins who were in favour of according equal status to the two. Hence, the sages of these three groups decided to set up a council to mediate.

1.3.1.3.18 इन्द्रपक्ष्याणां ब्राह्मणानाम् इन्द्राय सोमाभिषवार्थं हिरण्यगर्भनियोगः

1.3.1.3.18 Pro-Indra brahmins in the council appointed Hiranyagarbha to extract Soma

अथेन्द्रपक्ष्या ऋषयोऽत्र सर्वे पुनर्विचाराय पृथक् समीयुः ।
विशिष्य कण्वा अपरेऽपि केचिद् बृहद्दिवाद्या व्यदधुर्विमर्शम् ।।245।।

The sages on Indra's side assembled separately for a review. Present in the meeting were Kanva and other sages like Brihaddiva who deliberated on the issue at hand.

सोमं सुरेन्द्र एवार्हति पातुं नासुरेन्द्रोऽपि ।
हन्तेन्द्राय सुतोऽयं सोमः पीतोऽनयाद् वृषाकपिना ।।246।।

Indra, the king of devas, is the only one who could partake Soma and other gods are not fit for this honour. It is unfortunate that Soma, which was extracted for Indra, was unlawfully drunk by other gods.

तस्मादिह पुनरन्यः सोमः सोतव्य इन्द्राय ।
इति निर्धार्य विधातुं हविषा प्रोचुर्हिरण्यगर्भमृषिम् ।।247।।

Therefore, Soma should be extracted anew by havi, and as decided, Hiranyagarbha rishi was asked to perform the rites.

1.3.1.3.19 हरिण्यगर्भेण इन्द्राय हविर्विधान-प्रत्याख्यानम्

1.3.1.3.19 Hiranyagarbha opposes havya for Indra

एष तु हिरण्यगर्भो मार्गं वैज्ञानिकं परं जगृहे ।
इन्द्राद्वा वरुणाद्वा हिरण्यगर्भं निरूपयन् प्रवरम् ।।248।।

Considering Hiranyagarbha tatva to be superior to that of Indra or Varuna, Hiranyagarbha rishi affirmed that it was the ideal and scientific way.

वज्री च पाशी च परश्च देवो हिरण्यगर्भस्य वशेऽस्ति सर्वः ।
हिरण्यगर्भं प्रथमं विदन्तः कस्मै देवायं हविषा विधेम ।।249।।

Vajradhari Indra and bearer of *pasha* (a noose used by Varuna as a weapon) are both influenced by Hiranyagarbha. Considering Hiranyagarbha as superior, it has been noted: 'For whom should havya be offered?' [Here, in the word *kasmai* (whom) lie both the question and answer. It is called *Vakyovakya pranali.* The word *kah* stands for both 'who' as well as Brahma.] Hence, the havya should be offered to Brahma.

यदेतदण्डं समन्तात् समुद्रस्तावान् स इन्द्रोऽपि हिरण्मयत्वात् ।
आपोमयत्वाद्वरुणश्च तावानेतौ हि नाण्डं तदतिक्रमेते ।।250।।

The expanse of sea all around this cosmic egg (the primordial egg of Brahma) is Indra, owing to the fact that it is Hiranyagarbha (of Brahma as born from a golden, celestial egg). On account of it being water, Varuna is also equally present. Thus, both of them are not superior to this cosmic egg.

हिरण्मयं त्वण्डमिदं समस्तं यस्यास्ति गर्भे परमस्य पुंसः ।
हिरण्यगर्भं तमनुव्रजन्तः कस्मै देवाय हविषा विधेम ।।251।।

Now, inferring that Hiranyagarbha is the Supreme (Brahma) in whose belly the entire Hiranyagarbha or the Cosmic Egg is located, to which god should we offer the havya? That is to say, should we perform that *havya-vidhana* (the rite of havya) for that *Prajapati* (the god presiding over the Creation, an epithet for Brahma)?

अपां पतिः स वरुणस्त्रीन् भृगूनधितिष्ठति ।
असुराणां पतिर्लोकं चतुर्थं चाधितिष्ठति ।।252।।

That presiding deity of waters, Varuna, presides over the three Bhrigu (primary elements)—Apah, Vayu, and Soma. He is the master of asuras and presides over the fourth loka in all resplendence.

मरुतां पतिरिन्द्रोऽधितिष्ठत्यङ्गिरसां त्रयम् ।
देवानां स पतिर्लोकं चाधितिष्ठत्यमूं दिवम् ।।253।।

The master of the marudganas, Indra, presides over the three agniras (Agni, Vayu and Aditya) with radiance. He is the king of devas and lords over Dyauloka.

देवो हीन्द्रः शास्ति सुरान् देवः स वरुणोऽसुरान् ।
नैवावरो न प्रवरोऽनयोरेकोऽपि कल्पते ।।254।।

Indra reigns over devas, and Varuna, also a deva, reigns over asuras. Of the two, we cannot judge who is superior or inferior to each other.

हिरण्यगर्भस्तु परः सर्वतः प्रवरो मतः ।
य एष चतुरो लोकानेक एवाधितिष्ठति ।।255।।

But Hiranyagarbha is the most distinguished one among them; he is superior to all and is supreme. This entity alone reigns over all these four worlds—Agni, Vayu, Aditya and Apah.

अप्सु वीर्यं क्षिपन्नग्निरमृतोऽद्भिः स संभवन् ।
हिरण्यं जनयत्येष सोऽमृताऽग्निर्हिरण्मयः ।।256।।

Hiranyagarbha is born from *amritagni* (immortal fire). This immortal fire, while being born in water, gives birth to Hiranyagarbha and therefore this immortal fire itself is Hiranyagarbha.

त्रिषु लोकेषु पर्याप्तश्चतुर्थेऽप्युपपद्यते ।
प्रजापतिस्त्रिलोकीस्थापः परिचरन्ति तम् ।।257।।

He already rules the three worlds (Agni, Vayu, and Soma) and he takes birth in the fourth world in the form of Prajapati.

इत्थं हिण्यगर्भेण कल्पितात्मा महानृषिः ।
हिरण्यगर्भ उत्थाय स्वं विज्ञानमदर्शयत् ।।258।।

In this manner, rising from the soul of Hiranyagarbha, the great sage Hiranyagarbha represents the wisdom of the four worlds.

1.3.1.3.20 हिरण्यगर्भ:

1.3.1.3.20 Hiranyagarbha

हिरण्यगर्भ: समवर्तताग्रे भूतस्य जात: पतिरेक आसीत् ।
स दाधार पृथिवीं द्यामुतेमां कस्मै देवाय हविषा विधेम ।।
(ऋग्वेद:, 10.121.1)

Even before the universe was created, this Hiranyagarbha had existed. He is the only peerless master of all those living beings who take birth. He sustains earth, heaven, and the outer space. We worship that Prajapati by making sacred offerings.

य आत्मदा बलदा यस्य विश्व उपासते प्रशिषं यस्य देवा: ।
यस्यच्छायामृतं यस्य मृत्यु: कस्मै देवाय हविषा विधेम ।।
(ऋग्वेद:, 10.121.2)

He also gives self-knowledge, grants power and vigour, he is the one whose orders are maintained by all men as well as devas, he is the one whose image is like *amrita* (ambrosia) and a denial of his shelter is like death. We worship that Supreme Being, an incarnation of welfare, by making sacred offerings.

य: प्राणतो निमिषतो महित्वैक इद्राजा जगतो बभूव ।
य ईशे अस्य द्विपदश्चतुष्पद: कस्मै देवाय हविषा विधेम ।।
(ऋग्वेद:, 10.121.3)

By making sacred offerings, we worship that Supreme Being, who, on account of his great acumen and dignity, is the only invincible lord of the mortal and transitory Creation.

यस्येमे हिमवन्तो महित्वा यस्य समुद्रं रसया सहाहु: ।
यस्येमा: प्रदिशो यस्य बाहू कस्मै देवाय हविषा विधेम ।।
(ऋग्वेद:, 10.121.4)

Again, by making sacred offerings, we call upon that Supreme Being because of whose solemnity these snow-clad mountains have sprung up, whose great vigour these mountains represent, whose great potential is being proclaimed by rivers, earth, and seas, whose power the arm-like directions manifest.

येन द्यौरुग्रा पृथिवी च दृह्ला येन स्वः स्तभितं येन नाकः ।
यो अन्तरिक्षे रजसो विमानः कस्मै देवाय हविषा विधेम ॥
(ऋग्वेदः, 10.121.5)

We praise that Supreme Being with sacred offerings, who was instrumental in rendering this sky as well as the outer space; because of whom this earth became substantial; he who stabilized the heaven, who stationed sun in the outer space and who created water in the sky.

यं क्रन्दसी अवसा तस्तभाने अभ्यैक्षेतां मनसा रेजमाने ।
यत्राधिसूर उदितो विभाति कस्मै देवाय हविषा विधेम ॥
(ऋग्वेदः, 10.121.6)

We make sacred offerings and sing praises of that radiant Supreme Being whose refuge the sun seeks, by shining bright in the sky.

आपो ह यद् बृहतीर्विश्वमायन् गर्भं दधाना जनयन्तीरग्निम् ।
ततो देवानां समवर्ततासुरेकः कस्मै देवाय हविषा विधेम ॥
(ऋग्वेदः, 10.121.7)

When the vast and mighty waters for the first time gave birth to the glorious Agni and the entire universe, and gave life to the devas, which is that life force that made these possible; for such a giver of life, we offer all our devotion.

यश्चिदापो महिना पर्यपश्यद्दक्षं दधाना जनयन्तीर्यज्ञम् ।
यो देवेष्वधि देव एक आसीत्कस्मै देवाय हविषा विधेम ॥
(ऋग्वेदः, 10.121.8)

He, who by his might, surveys the waters all around containing creative powers and giving birth to cosmic sacrifice, he who among the divine bounties was the one most supreme; who else, besides that giver of happiness, can we offer all our devotion?

मा नो हिंसीज्जनिता यः पृथिव्या यो वा दिवं सत्यधर्मा जजान ।
यश्चापश्चन्द्रा बृहतीर्जजान कस्मै देवाय हविषा विधेम ॥
(ऋग्वेदः, 10.121.9)

With the best of means and rites, we worship that Supreme Being, who is an incarnation of welfare. We expect that he who gave birth to the earth, the creator of the universe, who bears the religion of truth and the world itself, who is the architect of heaven, who produced an enormous amount of water that is a source of pleasure for all, will not punish us or inflict suffering on us.

प्रजापते न त्वदेतान्यन्यो विश्वा जातानि परि ता बभूव ।
यत्कामास्ते जुहुमस्तन्नो अस्तु वयं स्याम पतयो रयीणाम् ।।
(ऋग्वेद:, 10.121.10)

O Prajapati! Nobody but you can understand and accept [whole-heartedly] all the objects born in the past, present and future. We wish that we are granted what we desire, by offering you havya. Bless us so that we may become masters of all kinds of fortune and opulence.

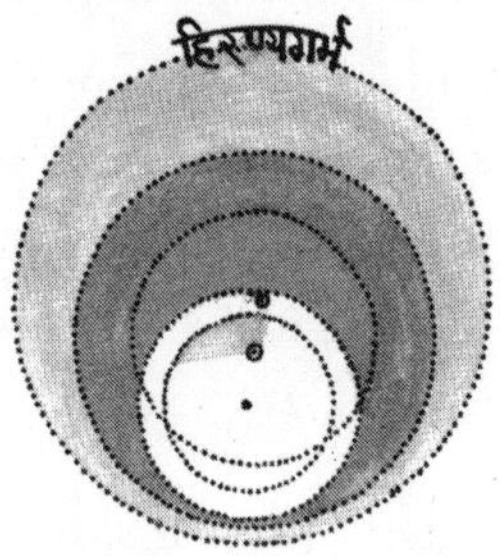

1.3.1.3.21 हिरण्यगर्भतात्पर्य:

1.3.1.3.21 Importance of Hiranyagarbha

हिरण्यगर्भो वरुणेन्द्रपृथ्वीचन्द्रैकबल्शामधितिष्ठतीति ।
प्रजापतिं तं परमं विदन्त: कस्मै देवाय हविषा विधेम ।।259।।

The Hiranyagarbha referred to here presides over Varuna, Indra, earth and moon. Hiranyagarbha is the supreme Prajapati. Who else can we worship by means of havya but him? Hence we call upon the supreme Prajapati.

प्रजापते: प्राण उदेति भूतान्यद्भ्य: समुद्राद्वरुणाद् भवन्ति ।
प्रज्ञेन्द्र इत्याहुरथाग्निसीमारब्धास्त्रिमात्रा इदमस्ति विश्वम् ।।260।।

The life-forces spring from this Prajapati and living beings arise from water or Varuna. All living beings form the core. The entire world, which begins from Agni, is made up of three parts—*prana*, *bhuta,* and *prajna* (life force, life, and intellect, respectively).

प्रजा प्राणो भूतान्येषां मात्राभिराचितं विश्वम् ।
ज्ञानं क्रियाऽर्थ एतद्व्यतिरिक्तं न क्वचित् किञ्चित् ॥261॥

Prajna, prana, and bhuta make up the entire world. *Jnana* (knowledge), *kriya* (action) and *artha* (purpose) are the entities beyond which nothing is meaningful.

इन्द्रः प्रज्ञा तस्मात् प्रज्ञामात्राभिराचितं ज्ञानम् ।
प्राणो हिरण्यगर्भः क्रिया इमाः प्राणमात्राभिः ॥262॥

Indra is prajna and is the epitome of knowledge. Likewise, prana is Hiranyagarbha. Thus all actions originate in these elements.

भूतान्यापो वरुणः सर्वेऽर्था भूतमात्राभिः ।
त्रिभिरेवैभिर्देवैरारब्धं विश्वमस्तीदम् ॥263॥

Bhuta (an epithet for Shiva), Apah and Varuna are the *artha*-s (objects) which arise from *bhutamatra*-s (the subtle elements). The entire world is initiated by these three elements.

अधिदेवास्त्रय एते तानितरे नातितिष्ठन्ति ।
एषां हिरण्यगर्भोऽधिदेव एकः क्रियाहेतुः ॥264॥

These three are the supreme gods and nothing lies beyond them. Among these, Hiranyagarbha is the presiding deity, and he is responsible for all actions.

सर्वक्रियैकमलं न विना क्रिययाऽर्थ उद्भवति ।
न विना क्रियया ज्ञाने सोऽर्थः प्रविशेन्न चेष्टेत ॥265॥

तस्माद्धिरण्यगर्भं प्रवरं मन्ये क्रियाहेतुम् ।
तमुपेक्ष्य सकमलं कस्मै देवाय हविषा विधेम ॥266॥

Without Hiranyagarbha, the sole cause of all actions, the world has no meaning. Knowledge combined with action creates meaning. Without action, knowledge cannot have any meaning, nor can any movement take place. Since Hiranyagarbha causes all actions, it is the Supreme God. How can we overlook this root cause of all actions and perform the sacred rites for some other god?

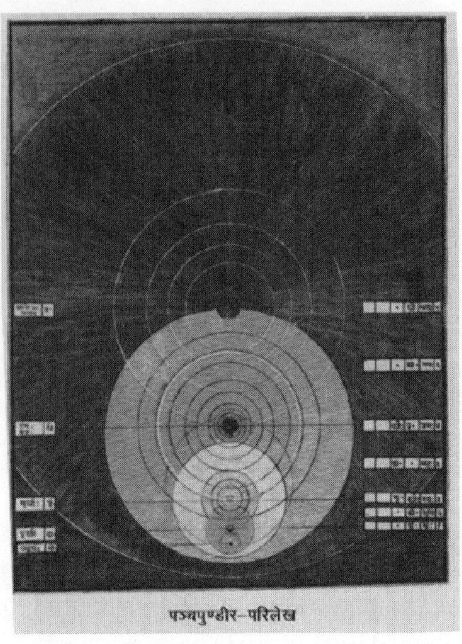

पञ्चपुण्डीर–परिलेख

1.3.1.3.22 इन्द्राय सोमाभिषवार्थं वसिष्ठविनियोगः

1.3.1.3.22 Vasishta invited to make Soma for Indra

इन्द्रायेत्थं सोतं हिरण्यगर्भे प्रजापतेः पुत्रे ।
अस्वीकुर्वति विप्रा वसिष्ठमृषिमार्थयां चक्रुः ।।267।।

After Hiranyagarbha, son of Prajapati, refused to extract Soma for Indra, the brahmins called upon Vasishta to prepare Soma for Indra.

1.3.1.3.23 वसिष्ठेन इन्द्रपरितोषार्थं सोमयज्ञकरणम्

1.3.1.3.23 Soma yajna by Vasishta for pleasing Indra

वसिष्ठ आसीद् वरुणस्य मित्रं बहूपचक्रे वरुणः पुराऽस्मै ।
किन्त्वेष वैज्ञानिकविग्रहेऽस्मिन् इन्द्रस्य पक्षे जगृहे विशिष्य ।।268।।

Vasishta was a friend of Varuna. Varuna had extended many favours to him in the past, but in the scientific debate over who was supreme, Vasishta chose to support Indra.

दृष्ट्वा तत्र स सोमं धाष्ट्र्यात् पीतं वृषाकपिना ।
अनयात्क्रुद्धः सद्यः स्वगृहे सोमं सुषाव चेन्द्राय ।।269।।

When Vasishta witnessed an imprudent Vrishakapi forcibly drinking Soma meant for Indra, he was enraged and quickly extracted Soma for Indra in his house and hailed Indra thus.

1.3.1.3.24 वसिष्ठकृता इन्द्रस्तुतिः

1.3.1.3.24 Vasishta praises Indra

पराणुदस्व मघवन्नमित्रान्त्सुवेदा नो वसू कृधि ।
अस्माकं बोध्यविता महाधने भवा वृधः सखीनाम् ।।
(ऋग्वेदः, 7.32.25)

O Indra! We request you to eliminate our enemies. See to it that we amass wealth with ease. Act as the protector of our friends in times of war. We request you to bless us with an increase in our wealth.

इन्द्र क्रतुं न आ भर पिता पुत्रेभ्यो यथा ।
शिक्षाणो अस्मिन् पुरुहूत यामनि जीवा ज्योतिरशीमहि ।।
(ऋग्वेदः, 7.32.26)

O Indra! Bestow us with intelligence. Just as a father gives instructions and wealth to his sons, enlighten us with wisdom and supplement us with wealth. O Indra! Bless us so that we succeed in this yajna and attain strength.

रायस्कामो वज्रहस्तं सुदक्षिणं पुत्रे न पितरं हुवे ।
(ऋग्वेदः, 7.32.3)

As a son turns to his father for the fulfilment of his requirements, similarly, I, in my aspiration for wealth and prosperity, pray to Vajradhari Indra, who is known for his benevolence.

इम इन्द्राय सुन्विरे सोमासो दध्याशिरः ।
ताँ आ मदाय वज्रहस्त पीतये हरिभ्यां याह्योक आ ।।
(ऋग्वेदः, 7.32.4)

O Vajradhari Indra! Mixed with curd, this Soma drink is being prepared only for you. To happily consume this Soma drink, come galloping to this site of yajna on your mighty horses.

न त्वावाँ अन्यो दिव्यो न पार्थिवो न जातो न जनिष्यते ।
अश्वायन्तो मघवन्निन्द्र वाजिनो गव्यन्तस्त्वा हवामहे ।।
(ऋग्वेदः, 7.32.23)

O Indra! Nobody can ever equal you in this heaven. No one on this earth, nor anyone born in the future, can surpass you. We, who desire prosperity in the form of horses, cows and grains, pray to you.

अथ च वसिष्ठः स्वगृहे सोमं सुत्व समानयन्निन्द्रम् ।
सम्मानयंस्तमस्तौन्निपीतसोमं स्वराजमभ्यर्हम् ।।270।।

Thus, after extracting Soma in his house, as a gesture of reverence towards Indra, Vasishta praised the holy, radiant form of venerable Indra after he drank the extracted Soma.

इन्द्रोऽस्ति राजा जगतो जनानां यच्चास्ति पृथ्व्यामखिलस्य तस्य ।
पितेव बन्धुः सममेति मन्ये तस्योपकारं न च विस्मरेयम् ।।271।।

Indra is the king of menfolk, overseer of the universe, and everything on the earth belongs to him. He is a guardian and a protector like a father and a well-wisher as friends are. I believe we should not forget the assistance that he has extended to us.

एभिर्दिनैरिन्द्र सभाजयाऽस्मान् दुर्मित्रलोका हि परिक्रमन्ते ।
कुर्यादनिष्टं वरुणोऽर्थवद्वा निर्हेतु वा तद् द्वयमप्यपैतु ।।272।।

O Indra! We request you to grace our assembly. These days, foes (like rakshasas) surround us on all sides. Varuna, advertently or inadvertently, cause us harm. Therefore, safeguard us from these two nuisances.

पुनर्वसिष्ठः इन्द्रं स्तौति

Vasishta praises Indra again.

इन्द्रो राजा जगतश्चर्षणीनामधि क्षमि विषुरूपं यदस्ति ।
ततो ददाति दाशुषे वसूनि चोदद्राध उपस्तुतश्चिदर्वाक् ।।
(ऋग्वेदः, 7.27.3)

Indra is the only lord of all the human beings and all the movable and immovable objects. Indra is also the proprietor of all those things on earth which have different forms. Therefore, he bestows wealth on all those who offer Soma. He directs prosperity in our direction if we pray to him.

उतो घा ते पुरुष्या इदासन्येषां पूर्वेषामशृणोर्ऋषीणाम् ।
अधाहं त्वा मघवञ्जोहवीमि त्वं न इन्द्रासि प्रमतिः पितेव ॥
(ऋग्वेदः, 7.29.4)

O master of wealth, the ancient rishis whose praises you have heard, be benevolent towards them. Thus, I pray to you. O Indra! You are like our father in giving us good moral lessons.

एभिर्न इन्द्राहभिर्दशस्य दुर्मित्रासो हि क्षितयः पवन्ते ।
प्रति यच्चष्टे अनृतमनेना अव द्विता वरुणो मायी नः सात् ॥
(ऋग्वेदः, 7.28.4)

O Indra, subjugate those who harm us. Let the falsehood, which the honest and capable Varuna can detect in us, be removed.

वोचेमेदिन्द्रं मघवानमेनं महो रायो राधसो यद्ददन्नः ।
यो अर्चतो ब्रह्मकृतिमविष्ठो यूयं पात स्वस्तिभिः सदा नः ॥
(ऋग्वेदः, 7.28.5)

We praise that rich Indra who gives us wealth, and who safeguards the hymns and verses of the people who pray to him. O Indra! Please protect us and shower on us the best of your benedictions.

1.3.1.3.25 वरुणेन वसिष्ठनिग्रहः

1.3.1.3.25 Vasishta's restraint before angry Varuna

वरुणसखे तु वसिष्ठे तथेन्द्रपक्षं तदा गृहीतवति ।
वरुणः क्रुद्धः काले तं स वसिष्ठं निजग्राह ॥273॥

Vasishta's obeisance to Indra angered his friend, Varuna and he imprisoned Vasishta.

निगृहीतः स वसिष्ठः क्षमापयन् वरुणमर्थयामास ।
सुरया कृतमपराधं क्षमस्व तेऽहं वशंवदः स्वजनः ॥274॥

On being detained, Vasishta prayed to Varuna thus: O Varuna, forgive any wrong done by me because of the inebriating drink. I am in your protection and I am yours.

पृच्छे तदेनो वरुण दिद्दक्षूपो एमि चिकितुषो विपृच्छम् ।
समानमिन्मे कवयश्चिदाहुरयं ह तुभ्यं वरुणो त्दृणीते ।।

(ऋग्वेद:, 7.86.3)

O Varuna! Eager to know about my misdeeds, I have come to you. I ask you. Curious to know the answer, I went up to the learned men, but those wise people gave me the same answer. They said that Varuna was indeed infuriated with you.

किमाग आस वरुण ज्येष्ठं यत्स्तोतारं जिघांससि सखायम् ।
प्र तन्मे वोचो दूळभ स्वधावोऽव त्वानेना नमसा तुर इयाम् ।।

(ऋग्वेद:, 7.86.4)

O Varuna! Have I committed such a grave offence that you have to punish me, although I have sung praises in your honour? O noble and steadfast Varuna! If I have committed a sin, then make it known to me, so that I may come to you in a modest manner, as a person who has committed no sin.

न स स्वो दक्षो वरुण ध्रुतिः सा सुरा मन्युर्विभीदको अचित्तिः ।
अस्ति ज्यायान्कनीयस उपारे स्वप्नश्चनेदनृतस्य प्रयोता ।।

(ऋग्वेद:, 7.86.6)

O Varuna! An action performed with one's knowledge does not lead to a wrong act. A hindrance in one's progress leads to a tendency to sin. Alcoholic drinks, anger, gambling and ignorance are the propensities that lead to a sinful act. A superior person, who induces or forces his subordinate to do wrong, promotes sin; so does slumber or laziness.

अरं दासो न मीह्लुषे कराण्यहं देवाय भूर्णयेऽनागाः ।
अचेतयदचितो देवो अर्यो गृत्सं राये कवितरो जुनाति ।।

(ऋग्वेद:, 7.86.7)

I serve Varuna deva with a clean and sinless mind. He is the one who fulfils all desires and is the sustainer of the world. I am his vassal. He is the supreme deva who inspires ignorant people like us. He is the most learned of all and he directs the people who praise him towards wealth and prosperity.

अयं सु तुभ्यं वरुण स्वधावो हृदि स्तोम उपश्रितश्चिदस्तु ।
शं नः क्षेमे शमु योगे नो अस्तु यूयं पात स्वस्तिभिः सदा नः ।।
(ऋग्वेदः, 7.86.8)

O Varuna, the one who has grains at his disposal. I hope this praise stirs your heart and this hymn finds a place in your heart. Bless us with the fulfilment of unfulfilled desires, and preserve all that has been given by you. I request you to protect us and look after our welfare.

1.3.1.3.26 वसिष्ठेन इन्द्रावरुणयोः साम्योद्घोषः

1.3.1.3.26 Declaration of Varuna and Indra as equals

निगडमुक्तेन वसिष्ठेन मेधातिथिवामदेवसहायेन इन्द्रावरुणयोः साम्योद्घोषः ।

The announcement, with the help of Medhatithi and Vamadeva, of the parity of Indra and Varuna by Vasishta, who is released from imprisonment.

अथ मुक्तः स वसिष्ठः समत्वपक्षानुमोदकः समभूत् ।
अपि वामदेवमेधातिथी व्यधातां तयोः सख्यम् ।।275।।

Thus freed, Vasishta became the one to approve the equal status of Indra and Varuna. Vamadeva and Medhatithi also joined him in reinforcing the friendship between the two.

इन्द्रस्य च वरुणस्य च परस्परं सख्यतासिद्धौ ।
सह तुष्टुवुर्वसिष्ठो मेधातिथि-वामदेवौ च ।।276।।

When the friendship between Indra and Varuna was established, all, including, Vasishta, Medhatithi, and Vamadeva, were pleased.

1.3.1.3.27 वामदेवेन इन्द्रावरुणयोः स्तुतिः

1.3.1.3.27 Vamadeva prays to Indra and Varuna

इन्द्रा को वां वरुणा सुम्नमाप स्तोमो हविष्माँ अमृतो न होता ।
यो वां हृदि क्रतुमाँ अस्मदुक्तः पस्पर्शदिन्द्रावरुणा नमस्वान् ।।
(ऋग्वेदः, 4.41.1)

O Indravaruna [Indra and Varuna]! We hope that the hymn that we sing modestly touches your hearts. O Indra and Varuna! Which hymn, brilliant, laden with elixir and sacred offerings, can delight you?

इन्द्रा ह यो वरुणा चक्र आपी देवौ मर्तः सख्याय प्रयस्वान् ।
स हन्ति वृत्रा समिथेषु शत्रूनवोभिर्वा महद्भिः स प्र शृण्वे ॥
(ऋग्वेदः, 4.41.2)

The person who, by making sacred offerings, befriends Indra and Varuna and wins their support, makes up for all his wrong-doings. He succeeds in defeating enemies in wars, and, watched over by Indra and Varuna, earns great fame and glory.

इन्द्रा ह रत्नं वरुणा धेष्ठेत्था नृभ्यः शशमानेभ्यस्ता ।
यदी सखाया सख्याय सौमैः सुतेभिः सुप्रयसा मादयैते ॥
(ऋग्वेदः, 4.41.3)

If the now-friendly Indra and Varuna are delighted by the Soma extracted on account of their friendship, and also by the best of grains, then Indra and Varuna endow these admirers, who praise them, with gems and riches.

युवामिद्ध्यवसे पूर्व्याय परि प्रभूती गविषः स्वापी ।
वृणीमहे सख्याय प्रियाय शूरा मंहिष्ठा पितरेव शंभू ॥
(ऋग्वेदः, 4.41.7)

O Indra and Varuna! We, who are desirous of cows, that is prosperity, desire the venerable protection of both of you, since both of you are majestic and the best of our well-wishers. Both of you are heroic, respectable, and providers of happiness like our parents. We affectionately invite both of you to befriend us.

ता वां धियोऽवसे वाजयन्तीराजिं न जग्मुर्युवयूः सुदानू ।
श्रिये न गाव उपसोममस्थुरिन्द्रं गिरो वरुणं मे मनीषाः ॥
(ऋग्वेदः, 4.41.8)

O bestowers of good fortune, Indravaruna! Just as your devotees come to you for tutelage during battles, our senses seek you in their desire for grandeur and glory. We wish that our prayers, offered sincerely, reach Indra and Varuna in the same way as cows flock to the site of extraction of Soma to intensify its essence.

इमा इन्द्रं वरुणं मे मनीषा अग्मन्नुप द्रविणमिच्छमानाः ।
उपेमस्थुर्जोष्टार इव वस्वो रघ्वीरिव श्रवसो भिक्षमाणाः ॥
(ऋग्वेदः, 4.41.9)

In pursuit of wealth, my senses go to Indra and Varuna in the same way as people aspiring to amass wealth go to the wealthy, and as a beggar who begs grains goes to the benefactors. Similarly, my prayers aim towards reaching Indra and Varuna.

1.3.1.3.28 मेधातिथिना इन्द्रावरुणयोः स्तुतिः

1.3.1.3.28 Medhatithi, son of sage Kanva, offered a similar prayer to Varuna and Indra

इन्द्रावरुणयोरहं सम्राजोरव आ वृणे। ता नो मृळात ईदृशे ॥
(ऋग्वेदः, 1.17.1)

I pray to both the samrat-s, Indra and Varuna, for providing me with the power to defend myself. In difficult situations, I wish they keep us tranquil and happy.

गन्तारा हिं स्थोऽवसे हवं विप्रस्य मावतः । धर्त्तारा चर्षणीनाम् ॥
(ऋग्वेदः, 1.17.2)

Both of them look after the well-being and sustenance of humankind. I wish both of them come to the place where the prayers are being offered for protecting brahmins like me as soon as possible.

अनुकामं तर्पयेथामिन्द्रावरुण राय आ । ता वां नेदिष्ठमीमहे ॥
(ऋग्वेदः, 1.17.3)

O Indra and Varuna! Provide us with wealth that can fulfil our desires. Satiate us. We wish to be close to both of you in spirit.

युवाकु हि शचीनां युवाकु सुमतीनाम् । भूयाम वाजदाव्नाम् ॥
(ऋग्वेदः, 1.17.4)

Let us be endowed with superior power, and empowered with good sense. Bless us so that we may become generous and give grains and alms to the needy.

इन्द्रः सहस्रदाव्नां वरुणः शंस्यानाम् । क्रतुर्भवत्युक्थ्यः ॥
(ऋग्वेदः, 1.17.5)

O Indra! You are the one accomplishing vital tasks among thousands of generous and benevolent ones. O Varuna! You are the most praise-worthy among thousands of commendable gods.

तयोरिदवसा वयं सनेम नि च धीमहि । स्यादुत प्ररेचनम् ॥
(ऋग्वेदः, 1.17.6)

Sheltered by the protection of Indra and Varuna, we want to secure a lot of wealth, even if we already have huge assets.

इन्द्रावरुण वामहं हुवे चित्राय राधसे । अस्मान्त्सु जिग्युषस्कृतम् ॥
(ऋग्वेदः, 1.17.7)

O Indra and Varuna! I heartily pray to both of you. Please bestow me with the choicest success and fulfilment. I pray to both of you to make me emerge victorious.

इन्द्रावरुण नू नु वां सिषासन्तीषु धीष्वा । अस्मभ्यं शर्म्म यच्छतम् ॥
(ऋग्वेदः, 1.17.8)

O Indra and Varuna! Our senses are acting in accordance with your designs. So gift us pleasure and a sense of achievement.

प्र वामश्नोतु सुष्टुतिरिन्द्रावरुण यां हुवे । यामृधाथे सधस्तुतिम् ॥
(ऋग्वेदः, 1.17.9)

O Indra and Varuna! We wish that this excellent prayer which we sing together in this assembly may reach you.

1.3.1.3.29 वसिष्ठेन इन्द्रावरुणयोः स्तुतिः

1.3.1.3.29 Vasishta's prayer hailing Indra and Varuna

सम्राडन्यः स्वराडन्य उच्यते वां महान्ताविन्द्रावरुणा महावसू ।
विश्वे देवासः परमे व्योमनि सं वामोजो वृषणा सं बलं दधुः ॥
(ऋग्वेदः, 7.82.2)

O Indra and Varuna! It is said that one of you is a samrat and other is a svarat. Both of you are great and majestic. O Indravaruna! Both of you are brimming with vigour! All the other gods have assumed strength and splendour in the high sky for serving both of you.

अन्वपां खान्यतृन्तमोजसा सूर्यमैरयतं दिवि प्रभुम् ।
इन्द्रावरुणा मदे अस्य मायिनोऽपिन्वतमपितः पिन्वतं धियः ॥
(ऋग्वेदः, 7.82.3)

Indravaruna! You have opened up the paths of water by your strength, that is to say, you have released the flow of rivers. You have inspired the sun by appointing him as the god of the sky. Elated after drinking this powerful Soma, you have replenished these waterless rivers with water and accomplished all the tasks wisely.

युवामिद्युत्सु पृतनासु बह्नयो युवां क्षेमस्य प्रसवे मितज्ञवः ।
ईशान वस्व उभयस्य कारव इन्द्रावरुणा सुहवा हवामहे ॥
(ऋग्वेदः, 7.82.4)

O Indravaruna! Even the most valiant, as bright as fire, call upon you when surrounded by enemies in a battleground. They kneel down and request you to safeguard them. O master of earth and heaven, we craftsmen, knowers of arts, also pray to you for help!

अर्वाङ्नरा दैव्येनावसा गतं शृणुतं हवं यदि मे जुजोषथः ।
युवोर्हि सख्यमुत वा यदाप्यं मार्डीकमिन्द्रावरुणा नि यच्छतम् ॥
(ऋग्नेदः, 7.82.8)

O Indravaruna! You are our leader. We request both of you to come to us with divine weapons of protection. Pay heed to our prayers, O Indravaruna! If you are affectionate towards us, see to it that we obtain your friendship, your brotherhood and your blessings whereby you bless us with plenty.

1.3.1.3.30 इन्द्रावरुणयोः समत्वोपपादकम्

1.3.1.3.30 Scientific principles that support the friendship between Indra and Varuna

वैज्ञानिकास्ते कतिचिन्महर्षयः समत्वविज्ञानमिहान्वमोदयन् ।
देवेश्वरो योऽस्त्यसुरेश्वरोऽस्ति यस्तयोः परः कोन्ववरश्च को नु वा ॥277॥

Other sages also similarly appealed to both Indra and Varuna. They said they were both alike and it was difficult to decide which one of them was greater.

तेजोविभागं स यथैक ईष्टे तथाऽपरः स्नेहविभागमीष्टे ।
सर्वं यथेदं व्यतिरिच्य नाग्निं नापस्तथेदं व्यतिरिच्य किञ्चित् ।।278।।

Indra is the chief of Dyauloka, and Varuna is the presiding deity of water. Just as nothing lives without fire, similarly without you too nothing can exist.

देहे च नापः क्व ममास्ति जीवनं देहे च नाग्निः क्व ममास्ति जीवनम् ।
अग्नेरिहापोऽग्निरपां तु गर्भजो विज्ञानमिन्द्राद्वरुणाद्बलं भवेत् ।।279।।

How will I have life if my body does not have water? Then again, how is life possible if there is no fire in my body. Therefore, we can conclude that fire emanated from the womb of water. Thus we receive intelligence from Indra and strength from Varuna.

एकस्तयोः सत्यहितो यथाऽयं परस्तथाऽसावृतसत्प्रतीतः ।
यथाऽङ्गिरा एष ऋषिः सुरस्यासुरस्य निर्भाति भृगुस्तथर्षिः ।।280।।

Out of the two, one is an incarnation of Satya and the other of Rita. Just as Angira is the sage of devas, Bhrigu is the sage of asuras.

अर्वाक् च सूर्याद्वरुणोऽस्ति रोदसीगतः स देवेन्द्रमनुव्रजन् स्थितः ।
यः क्रन्दसीस्थः परतोऽस्ति सूर्यतः स पञ्चविंशे वरुणं श्रयत्ययम् ।।281।।

In heaven and on earth, *Suryadeva* (Sun-god) appears below Varuna, and Varuna stationed in Krandasi, who comes after Devendra situated in Rodasi, is on the other side of the sun, and Indra takes the place of Varuna at the twenty-fifth stoma.

समुद्रगर्भे भुवनं हिरण्मयं तदण्डमद्भिः परितः समाप्लुतम् ।
समुद्र आकाशगतः स वाङ्मयो वागिन्द्र आकाश इयं हि संयती ।।282।।

The world inside the ocean is the core of Creation, the cosmic egg, and is surrounded by water on all sides. The ocean is situated in the sky and that sky is sound and that sound is Indra. Therefore, that supreme sky is the zenith.

सा क्रन्दसीतो ह्यवरास्ति रोदसी सा क्रन्दसीतोऽपि परास्ति संयती ।
द्यावापृथिव्यौ विविधौ इमे स्थिते अश्वत्थवल्शामनु ते निरीक्षयेत् ।।283।।

This Rodasi is below Krandasi, while Samyati is above the two—these are the three worlds that can be visualized in the layers of the Peepal tree (ficus religiousa) or ashvatthabalsa.

इत्थं स इन्द्रो वरुणं समाश्रितस्तथा तमिन्द्रं वरुणः समाश्रितः ।
नान्योन्यतोऽन्योन्यमिह प्रहीयते तेनायमिन्द्रो वरुणश्च तुल्यवत् ।।284।।

Thus, Indra is dependent on Varuna, and Varuna on Indra. Therefore, both of them, when viewed side by side, are not different from each other. Thus, both Indra and Varuna are similar.

1.3.1.3.31 ऐन्द्र-वारुण-भारतयोः मध्ये वसिष्ठनिवासः

1.3.1.3.31 Vasishta takes up residence

सुरेश्वरस्यैष ततः स्वराजः सम्राज एवं त्वसुरेश्वरस्य ।
सखा वसिष्ठः समभूत् तयोश्च द्वयोः प्रियं वर्तयति स्म नित्यम् ।।285।।

Vasishta became a dear friend of both Indra, the supreme god of devas, and Varuna, the god of asuras. He served both of them.

द्वयोस्तदा सोऽनुमते वसिष्ठश्चक्रे स्थितिं भारतवर्षमध्ये ।
ऐन्द्रं तथा वारुणमन्तराऽर्द्धं सरस्वतीं नाम पुरं व्यधत्त ।।286।।

Then with the permission of both Indra and Varuna, Vasishta made an abode for himself in the heart of Bharatavarsha. He established a place named Sarasvati in between Aindra and Varuna Bharata.

तत्रैष सूर्यसदनं चकार विज्ञानभवनं तत् ।
वैज्ञानिकीं परीक्षां कुर्वाणस्तत्र वसति स्म ।।287।

Then Vasishta constructed the *surya-sadhana* (solar house or a solar observatory) there, an abode of knowledge, where he began studying and examining scientific principles.

1.3.1.3.32 जरथुस्त्राभिज्ञानम्

1.3.1.3.32 Introduction to Zarathustra

आख्यानमेतदुक्तं जरथुस्त्रमतानुगामिनां ग्रन्थे ।
अपि च भविष्यपुराणे कथंचिदुक्तस्तदाभासः ।।288।।

This description is given in the religious text of the followers of Zarathustra and the same can also be found in the Bhavishya Purana.

जरथुस्त्रा इह बहवः प्रागभवन् किन्तु सर्वतः प्रथमः ।
दौहित्रः स ऋजिश्वन आसीत् स मगः स इन्द्रद्विट् ।।289।।

In ancient times, there happened to be many people named Zarathustra, but the first Zarathustra was the son of Rijrashva's daughter, who belonged to the Maga ethnic community, and was a critic of Indra.

अस्ति भविष्यपुराणे नभयाध्याये च धूलिकाध्याये ।
मन्त्रद्रष्टुर्ऋजिश्वन उल्लेखः प्राक्तनः सततः ।।290।।

In the 139-140 chapter of Bhavishya Purana, we get an ancient and competent description of a *mantradrashta* (a man of extraordinary knowledge, Rijrashva).

वैदिकमन्त्रकृदासीदृषिर्भरद्वाजवंशधरः ।
स ऋजिश्वा तस्यायं दौहित्रोऽन्यस्य वेति संदेहः ।।291।।

ऋज्राश्वो वा कश्चित् तस्य भवेदेष दौहित्रः ।
किन्तु पुरातन आसीदेष मगो नाम देवद्विट् ।।292।।

Sage Rijrashva was born in the family of sage Bharadvaja and was well versed in Vedic hymns. Even if we do not exactly know who Rijrashva was, whose daughter's son Zarathustra was, it can be said with certainty that Zarathustra was a man of ancient times, belonging to the Maga tribe and was an adversary of the devas.

मैत्रो धर्मः पूर्वं प्रचरित आसीच्छकेष्वेषु ।
ब्राह्मं व्रतं च गोत्रं मिहिरं जरथुस्त्रपूर्वेषाम् ।।293।।

उत्पद्य तु जरथुस्त्रो विदविस्परदविदाद आङ्गिरसः ।
इति वेदान् रचयित्वा मैत्रं धर्मं निपातयामास ।।294।।

In those times, worship of Mitra was prevalent among the people of the Shaka tribe. The ancestors of Zarathustra were from the Brahmin lineage and their clan was Mihira. Zarathustra was a great scholar and he composed four Vedas named Vida, Visparada, Vivada and Angirasa and thus rejected the Maitra faith.

जरथुस्त्रवंशजाता: सर्वे जरथुस्त्रनामान: ।
धर्माचार्या एते शकगुरुवर्या महामान्या: ।।295।।

All those born in the lineage of Zarathustra were known by the name Zarathustra. All of them were religious preceptors, great teachers of the Shaka and were very respectable.

काले कालेऽन्याऽन्यो जरथुस्त्रोऽभूत् प्रभावशाली स: ।
शाकद्वीपनिवासिषु मगेषु धर्मं स्वमप्रथयत् ।।296।।

At that time, there happened to be many influential people by the name of Zarathustra, who preached their ideology among the people of Maga tribe, the inhabitants of Shakadvipa.

जरथुस्त्रधिष्ण्यगा अपि जरथुस्त्रा एव कथ्यन्ते ।
तेषामेव तु कश्चिल्लिपिं खरोष्ठीं प्रवर्तयाञ्चक्रे ।।297।।

The followers of Zarathustra's preaching were also called Zarathustra. It is said that someone from among them invented the Kharoshti *lipi* (script).

अद्यत्वे त्वितिहासग्रन्था वैदेशिकानां ये ।
तेषु तु चतु:सहस्रादर्वाचां सन्ति वृत्तानि ।।298।।

Till date, we have the chronicle of around four thousand years in all the historical tracts discovered so far.

अत एव तु जरथुस्त्रो यो राजा बाबिलोननगरस्य ।
आहुश्चतु:सहस्रप्राये काले तमुत्पन्नम् ।।299।।

Thus it is believed that Zarathustra, who as the king of a place called Babilona, was born within this period of four thousand years.

किन्त्वसुरो जरथुस्त्र: सोऽर्वाचीनो भवेत्कश्चित् ।
तस्मात्त्विह बहुपूर्व: देवयुगेऽन्यो बभूव जरथुस्त्र: ।।300।।

But the asura named Zarathustra must have been a person of recent origin, and someone else named Zarathustra must have existed before him in ancient times in the devayuga.

देवयुगीय: सोऽयं जरथुस्त्रो निवसति स्म बाह्लीके ।
ब्राह्मण एषोऽनिन्द्रानसुरांस्तान् वर्द्धयाञ्चक्रे ।।301।।

That Zarathustra, who was born in the devayuga, used to live in Bahlika and was a brahmin. But he used to support and promote the asuras who were hostile to Indra.

अरणानां मूजवतां महावृषाणां बाह्लिकानां च जरथुस्त्रमतानुयायित्वम् ।

Arana, Mujavana, Mahavrasha and Bahlika becoming the followers of Zarathustra.

ये तेऽनिन्द्रा इन्द्रं निन्दन्तश्चेन्द्रभक्तानाम् ।
ऐन्द्राणामार्याणां विद्वेषिण आसुरा आसन् ॥302॥

All those who opposed Indra were called Anindras and they became resentful of the Aindra Arya, the followers of Indra.

अरणास्त एव कथितास्तेषामीरानदेशोऽयम् ।
अप्योरियंसवासिषु भूयांसश्चाभवन्नरणाः ॥303॥

These asuras were known as Arana, and their territory was Irana (Iran). Many people who were from 'Oriyana' desha became Arana.

आथर्वणे तु पञ्चमकाण्डे द्वाविंशकेऽरणाः सूक्ते ।
अपि मूजवन्त उक्ता महावृषा बाह्लिकाश्चैते ॥304॥

In the twenty-second Arana hymn of the fifth khanda of Atharvaveda, they have been referred to by names such as Mujvan, Bahlika, and Mahavrasha.

तक्मन् भ्रात्रा बलासेन स्वस्रा कासिकया सह ।
पाप्मा भ्रातृव्येण सह गच्छामुमरणं जनम् ॥
(अथर्ववेदः, 5.22.12)

ओको अस्य मूजवन्त ओको अस्य महावृषाः ।
यावज्जातस्तक्मंस्तावानसि बह्लिकेषु न्योचरः ॥
(अथर्ववेदः, 5.22.5)

तक्मन् मूजवतो गच्छ बह्लिकान् वा परस्तराम् ।
शूद्रामिच्छ प्रफर्व्यं तां तक्मन् वीव धूनुहि ॥
(अथर्ववेदः, 5.22.7)

अन्यक्षेत्रे न रमसे वशी सन् मृडयासि नः ।
अभूदु प्रार्थस्तक्मा स गमिष्यति बाह्लिकान् ॥
(अथर्ववेदः, 5.22.9)

It is written in the Atharvaveda—O *takman jvara* (a fever called takman)! Go accompanied by phlegm, cough and consumption, and infect that foul man. [The disease *takman* is usually seen infecting filthy people in areas where there is heavy downpour of rain, and excessive breeding of weeds, grass, and moss. In Bahlika, because of excessive rainfall, a grass named *munja* grows profusely. In this region, therefore, a fever called *takman* infects the people.]

विद्वेषाग्निर्ज्वलितः प्रतीयतेऽनेन वाक्येन ।
गन्धारादिस्थानां बाह्लीकादिस्थितैर्विरोधः सः ।।305।।

ब्राह्मणराजन्यानामन्योन्यं यो विरोधोऽयम् ।
तत्र च देवा ऐन्द्रानन्वसुरा वारुणानभवन् ।।306।।

From this statement, we can infer that there was an air of hostility between the inhabitants of Gandhara and the nearby areas, and the inhabitants of Bahlika and adjoining areas. In this mutual hostility between the brahmin kings, the devas sided with the supporters of Indra, and the asuras chose to support Varuna.

देवानामिदवो महत् तदा वृणीमहे वयम् ।
वृष्णामस्मभ्यमूतये ।।
(सामवेदः,पूर्वार्चिकः, ऐन्द्रपर्व, द्वितीयाध्यायः, तृतीयखण्डः मन्त्रः, 4)

This Agni is certainly eminent among the devas. That is why we choose him from among the devas. Like a mighty person, this Agni is always eager and ready for our protection.

1.3.1.3.33 पूर्वपश्चिमभेदेन भारतवर्षस्य द्वेधा विभागः

1.3.1.3.33 Division of Bharatavarsha into east and west

देवा इत्थं देवानेवाराध्यानपश्यंस्ते ।
बलदानसुरान्मेध्यान् पश्यन्तस्त्वासुरा अभवन् ।।307।।

While those devas in this way acknowledged that only devas were worthy of worship, those who held that powerful asuras alone were divine became asuras.

उभयेषां तु विरोधे भूयसि देशो विभक्तोऽभूत् ।
ब्रह्मा गुरुर्विरोधं जहार भारतविभागेन ।।308।।

With no sign of hostility between the two groups abating, Brahma decided to end the conflict by apportioning the country.

प्राच्यं भारतमैन्द्रं सिन्धुस्थानं तदेतदाख्यातम् ।
पश्चिमभारतमुक्तं पारस्थानं तु वारुणं तदभूत् ।।309।।

Eastern Aindra (belonging to Indra) was Bharata which became popular by the name Sindhusthana; Western Bharata came to be known as Parasthana, and this became Varuna Bharata.

वारुणपारस्थानं सिन्धोरालोहिताम्भोधेः ।
तत्रान्ये तु विभागाः शासनभेदात् पुनर्जाताः ।।310।।

Varuna Bharata named as Parasthana was the area which stretched from river Sindhu to the area up to Red Sea. It was later divided into many secondary parts because of different rulers.

कालेन राजशासनभेदात् सीमा हि देशानाम् ।
संज्ञा च तत्र प्रभिद्यते हीति तच्चिन्त्यम् ।।311।।

It is not relevant to discuss the different changes that took place on the territorial limits and names of the regions due to changes in the rulers.

1.3.1.4. चतुर्थं प्रमाणम्-भारतवर्षस्य भूवृत्तचतुर्थांशत्वाख्यानम्

1.3.1.4. The Fourth Evidence—Narrative of the fourth geographic part of Bharatavarsha

1.3.1.4.1 पृथिवीमण्डलस्य पद्मत्वाभ्युपगमः

1.3.1.4.1 Earth like a lotus

पद्मपुराणमत्स्यपुराणादिषु तावदिदं पृथ्वीमण्डलं पद्मत्वेन व्याख्यातम्। तथाहि-

This earth has been described in the form of a lotus in the Padma Purana and Matsya Purana. In these texts, we find descriptions such as—

पद्मं नाभ्युद्भवं चैकं समुत्पादित्वाँस्ततः ।
सहस्रवर्णं विरजं भास्कराभं हिरण्मयम् ।।

(मत्स्यपुराणम्, 168.15)

पद्मे हिरण्मये तस्मिन्नसृजद् भूरि वर्चसम् ।
स्रष्टारं सर्वलोकानां ब्रह्माणं सर्वतोमुखम् ।।

(मत्स्यपुराणम्, 169.1)

तच्च पद्मं पुराभूतं पृथिवीरूपमुत्तमम् ।
यत्पद्मं सा रसादेवी पृथिवी परिकथ्यते ।।

(पद्मपुराणम्, सृष्टिखण्ड:, 40.34)

एवं नारायणस्यार्थे मही पुष्करसंभवा ।
प्रादुर्भावोऽप्ययं तस्मान्नाम्ना पुष्करसंज्ञित: ।।

(मत्स्यपुराणम्, 169.15)

Lord Narayana produced a lotus from his navel, which was of different hues, absolute, pure, splendid like the sun and lustrous like gold. In this golden lotus, Lord Narayana created *Chaturmukha Brahma* (Brahma with four faces), the Supreme Creator. This first-born splendid lotus was a form of the earth. This very lotus came to be known as Rasadevi and Prithvi. Therefore, because of Narayana, this earth is *pushkarasambhava* (born out of a lotus). Thus, because it was born out of a lotus, this earth has also been called Prithvi.

1.3.1.4.2 भूपद्मस्य चतु:पत्रत्वप्रतिपत्ति:

1.3.1.4.2 Discourse on Prithvi sporting four petals

चतुष्पत्रं चेदं पद्मपुराणेषु निरूपितम्। यथा मार्कण्डेये-

This lotus with four leaves has been described in the Markandeya Purana:

तदेतत्पार्थिवं पद्मं चतुष्पत्रं मयोदितम् ।
भद्राश्वभारताद्यानि पत्राण्यस्य चतुर्दिशम् ।।

(मार्कण्डेयपुराणम्, 52.20-21)

'This worldly lotus has been declared as having four leaves by me. Bhadrashva and Bharatavarsha are its four leaves pointing in all the four directions.'

भारता: केतुमालाश्च भ्रदाश्वा: कुरवस्तथा ।
पत्राणि लोकपद्मस्य मर्यादा शैलबाह्यत: ।।

(ब्रह्मपुराणम्, 16.45-46)

This world, according to the Brahma Purana, has as its four leaves—Bharata, Ketumala, Bhadrashva and Kuruvastha, demarcated by mountains.

इत्थं चास्य पृथिवीमण्डलस्य चतुष्पत्रत्वे भद्राश्वभारतकेतुमालोत्तरकुरूणां पत्रभूतानां समानैरंशैर्विभक्तानां एकैकस्य नवत्यंशावच्छिन्नत्वमुपपद्यते। तथा चोक्तं सूर्यसिद्धान्ते भूगोलाध्याये-

Thus, it becomes clear how Bhadrashva, Bharata, Ketumala and Uttara Kuru are in the shape of four leaves of the earth and how each is equally divided by 90°.

भूवृत्तपादे पूर्वस्यां यमकोटीति विश्रुता ।
भद्राश्ववर्षे नगरी स्वर्णप्राकारतोरणा ।।

(सूर्यसिद्धान्तः, 12.38)

As it has also been described in 'bhugoladhyaya' (chapter on geography) of *Suryasiddhanta* (an early Indian treatise on astronomy): 'A village of the name Yamakoti is famous in the eastern quarter of this earth. This village is situated in Bhadrashvavarsha and is known by the name Svarna Prakara Torana.'

याम्यायां भारते वर्षे लङ्का तद्वन्महापुरी ।
पश्चिमे केतुमालाख्ये रोमकाख्या प्रकीर्तिता ।।

(सूर्यसिद्धान्तः, 12.39)

Similarly, to the south of Bharatavarsha is a famous region named Lanka. On the western quarter in Ketumala is a famous village named Romaka.

उदक् सिद्धपुरी नाम कुरुवर्षे प्रकीर्तिता ।
भूवृत्तपादविवरास्ताश्चान्योन्यं प्रतिष्ठिता ।।

(सूर्यसिद्धान्तः, 12.40–41)

On the northern quarter in Kuruvarsha, there is a village named Siddhapura. In this way, in all four quarters of this earth, the pillars of Kuruvarsha are erected in a manner where all of them form angles of 90° around a single point, and are to be found in all the four directions.

तासामुपरिगो याति विषुवस्थो दिवाकरः ।
न तासु विषुवच्छाया नाक्षस्योन्नतिरिष्यते ।।

(सूर्यसिद्धान्तः, 12.42)

The sun wanders above them along *vishuvata-rekha* (the line of Equator). But the line of Equator does not touch these four angles anywhere, nor is there any increase in the degree of the latitudes [as stated in the Suryasiddhanta].

तत्र च लङ्कासुमेरुप्रोतरेखाया भारतवर्षीयमध्यरेखात्वव्यवस्थानात् ततः प्राच्यां पञ्चचत्वारिंशदंशैः प्रतीच्यां च तावदंशैरवच्छिन्नस्य भूभागस्य भारतवर्षत्वं सिद्ध्यति । भारतवर्षात्प्राच्यां नवत्यंशं भ्रदाश्वं वर्षम् तत उत्तरतस्तावदंशं कुरुवर्षम्, ततः पश्चात्तावदंशं केतुमालवर्षमिति। एतानि भूपद्मस्य चतुर्दिक्षु चत्वारि पत्राणि। भारतवर्षीयमध्यरेखा चोज्जयिनीस्था निगद्यते।

यल्लङ्कोज्जयिनीपुरोपरि कुरुक्षेत्रादिदेशान् स्पृशत्-
सूत्रं मेरुगतं बुधैर्निगदिता सा मध्यरेखा भुवः ॥
(सिद्धान्तशिरोमणिः, गोलाध्यायः, मध्यगतिवासना, 24)

इत्युक्तेः । उज्जयिनी चेयं नगरी नवकलाधिकत्रयोविंशे उत्तरेऽक्षांशे स्थिता। ग्रीनवीचमध्यरेखापेक्षया त्रिचत्वारिंशत्कलाधिकपञ्चसप्ततिपरिमितात् पूर्वीयदेशान्तरांशादारभ्यते । तेन ग्रीनवीचमध्यरेखा-भारतीयमध्यरेखयोः षट्सप्ततिरन्तरांशाः सिध्यन्ति। अन्तरांशेषु पञ्चचत्वारिंशदंशैर्हीनेषु ग्रीनवीचतः एकत्रिंशे पूर्वीयदेशान्तरांशे नीलनदीसागरसंगमप्रदेशोपलक्षिते भारतवर्षस्य पश्चिमा सीमेति प्रतीमः । एवं भारतीयमध्यरेखातः प्राच्यां पञ्चत्वारिंशदंशाः फारमूसाद्वीपोपलक्षिते प्रशान्तसागरे पर्याप्नुवन्तीत्येष प्रशान्तसागरः पूर्वा सीमा संपद्यते ।

A straight line stretches here from Lanka to Sumeru, which has also been designated as the line running through the middle of Bharatavarsha. The entire region which stretches from 45° east to 45° west happens to be Bharatavarsha.

Bharatavarsha is Bhadrashva at 90° north, and Ketumalavarsha at 90° west. These are the four leaves of this earth situated in four directions. The central line running through Bharatavarsha has been informed as being situated in Ujjaini. It has been said that the line that stretches above Ujjaini, and the one that stretches till Meru [a mountain], touching places like Kurukshetra, and in between is the central line of Bharatavarsha.

This Ujjaini region is situated at 23° and 9 *kala* (a measure of time) (23/ 9) north latitude. As compared to the Prime Meridian passing through Greenwich, this standard meridian passing through Ujjaini begins at 75° and 43 kala east longitude. Thus, the clear difference between the central line located at Greenwich and the Indian standard meridian is around 76°. In this difference of degrees, the region that is meant to be situated at 45° less, i.e., at 31° east longitude at the mouth of the river Nile (Mediterranean

Sea), seems to be the western boundary of Bharatavarsha. Similarly, to the east of the central line, Bharatavarsha stretches to a region, apparently Farmosa [Formosa], situated at 45° in the Pacific Ocean. This Pacific Ocean appears to be the eastern boundary of Bharatavarsha.

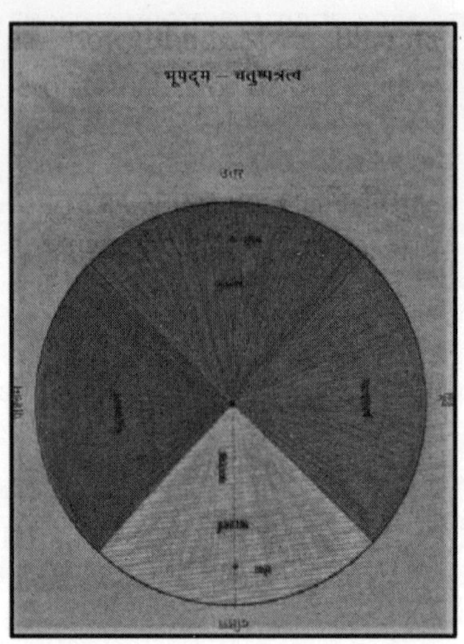

1.3.1.5 पञ्चमं प्रमाणम्-भारतवर्षस्य बहुविस्तृतप्रदेशत्वम्

1.3.1.5 The Fifth Evidence—Vast extension of Bharatavarsha

The islands situated in the far east are called *Bharatiya-upadvipa* (the Indian sub-continent) and this fact further supports the name Bharatavarsha given to a vast area which later came to be known as the Indian subcontinent.

अपि च भारतवर्षाद् बहुपूर्वस्थानाम् उपद्वीपानां भारतीयत्वाख्यानं भारतवर्षस्य बहुविस्तृतप्रदेशत्वे पञ्चमं प्रमाणम् ।

The fifth evidence of the wide expansion of Bharatavarsha is proved by the name of Bharatiyadvipa given to the islands situated in the far-east.

तथा हि ब्राह्मसप्तदशे, मार्कण्डेयचतु:पञ्चाशे, मात्स्ये तु चतुर्दशाधिकशततमे भारतवर्षस्यैतस्य नवोपद्वीपा: पौराणिकैराख्यान्ते।

Similarly, in the seventeenth chapter of Brahma Purana, the fifty-fourth chapter of Markandeya Purana, the one-hundred-and-fourteenth chapter of the Matsya Purana and other Puranas, there is a description of the nine islands of Bharatavarsha.

उत्तरेण समुद्रस्य हिमाद्रेश्चैव दक्षिणे ।
वर्षं तद् भारतं नाम भारती यत्र सन्ततिः ।।
(ब्रह्मपुराणम्, 17.1, विष्णुपुराणम्, 2.3.1)

It is written that the country to the north of the sea and to the south of the Himalayas is Bharatavarsha, and its inhabitants are Bharatiya.

भारतस्यास्य वर्षस्य नव भेदान्निशामय ।
इन्द्रद्वीपः कशेरुमाँस्ताम्रपर्णो गभस्तिमान् ।।
नागद्वीपस्तथा सौम्यो गान्धर्वस्त्वथ वारुणः ।
अयं तु नवमस्तेषां द्वीपः सागरसंवृतः ।।
(ब्रह्मपुराणम्, 17.6-7, विष्णुपुराणम्, 2.3.6-7,
मार्कण्डेयपुराणम्, 54.5-7, मत्स्यपुराणम्, 114.7-9)

Listen to the names of the nine islands of Bharatavarsha: Indradvipa, Kaserumana, Tamraparna, Gabhastiman, Nagadvipa, Saumya, Gandharva, Varuna and this island (where we live, Kumarika) is the ninth island, which is surrounded by water on all four sides.

स्कान्देऽप्याह माहेश्वरखण्डस्योनचत्वारिंशे ।
इन्द्रद्वीपः कसेरुश्च ताम्रद्वीपो गभस्तिमान् ।
नागः सौम्यश्च गान्धर्वो वरुणश्च कुमारिका ।।
(स्कन्दपुराणम्, माहेश्वरखण्डः-कौमारिकाखण्डः, 39.69)

In the thirty-ninth chapter of the 'Maheswarakhanda' of Skanda Purana also, it is written that Indradvipa, Kaserumana, Tamraparna, Gabhastiman, Naga, Saumya, Gandharva, Varuna and Kumarika are islands.

एषां चाद्यत्वे प्रचलितभाषायां नामानि यथा-

सं.	नामानि	पर्यायाः	भाषानामानि	इंग्लिशनामानि
1.	इन्द्रद्वीपः	इन्द्रद्युम्नः	इन्द्रमन	= एंडमन
2.	नागद्वीपः		निकोबार	= निकोबार
3.	सौम्यः	सोमत्रा	सुमात्रा	= यवद्वीप-बलिद्वीप
4.	गान्धर्वः		फलीपायिन	= लुम्बक सुम्बापलोरीन

5.	वारुण:		द्वीपसंघ:	= प्रभृतिजावाद्वीपसंघोप्यत्रैव
6.	कशेरुमान्	कसेरु:	बोर्नियो	संनिविशते।
7.	गभस्तिमान्		सेलेवीस	= बुनाई = ब्रूणी
8.	ताम्रपर्ण:-सिंहल:	ताम्रपर्णी	मलूक्का	= सीलोन् सरन्
9.	कुमारिका	कुमारी	टापूरोवेनसीलोन भारतखण्ड:	

The names of these islands are as follows:—

Name	Synonym	Name in Popular Language	English Name
Indradvipa	Indradyumna	Indramana	Andaman
Nagadvipa	—	Nicobara	Nicobar
Saumya	Somatra	Sumatra	Java and Bali
Gandhara	—	Philipayina-dvipasamuha	The Philippines
Varuna	—	Borniyo	Brunei (Bruni)
Kasheruman	Kaseru	Selevisa	—
Gabhastiman	—	Malukka	Malacca
Tamraparna	Tamraparna	Taparovena	Ceylon (Sri Lanka)
Kumarika	Kumaro	Bharata-khanda	India

1.3.1.5.1 इन्द्रद्वीप:

1.3.1.5.1 Indradvipa (Andaman)

पुरात्वे कदाचिदोड्रदेशीयपुरुषोत्तमक्षेत्रे इन्द्रद्युम्नो नाम राजाऽऽसीत् ।
पुराकृतयुगे कश्चिन्मालवेऽवन्तिकापुरे ।।

बभूव नृपति: श्रीमानिन्द्रद्युम्न इति श्रुत: ।
स गत्वा नृपति: क्षेत्रं मुक्तिदं पुरुषोत्तमम् ।।

तत्र संकर्षणं कृष्णं सुभद्रां चान्वसादयत् ।
मार्कण्डेयं वटं कृष्णं दृष्ट्वा रामं च सुव्रत: ।।
सागरे चेन्द्रद्युम्नाख्ये स्नात्वा मोक्षं लभेद्ध्रुवम्।

(ब्रह्मपुराणम्, 41.10–14)

एवं गत्वा स नृपतिर्दक्षिणस्योदधेस्तटम् ।
निवासमकरोत् तत्र वेलामासाद्य सागरीम् ॥
(ब्रह्मपुराणम्, 42.48, 59)

तेनाधिकृतत्वादस्योपद्वीपस्य ऐन्द्रद्युम्नसंज्ञा जाता। तदपभ्रंशादयम् 'ऐन्द्रमन' शब्दः प्रवृत्त इति प्रतीयते। चत्वारिंशदधिकदशोत्तराक्षांशात् पञ्चादशाधिकत्रयोदशाक्षांशपर्यन्ते प्रदेशे तथा षट्त्रिंशदधिकद्वानवत्यंशात् त्रिणवत्यंशपर्यन्ते पूर्वदेशान्तरे संनिविष्टोऽयमिन्द्रद्युम्नः ।

It is popularly believed that in ancient times, there was a king named Indradyumna in Avantikapura of Malava region, who was mighty and glorious.

He went as a *muktidayaka* (liberator) to a place named Purushottama in Audra desha [Orissa] where he came to know of Balarama, Krishna, and Subhadra. The king went to the shore of the southern sea and started living by the side of the sea (Brahma Purana 42, 48, 59). The *dvipa* in which the king lived came to be known as Indradyumna. It is said that a pious person who sees the *vatavriksha* (Banyan tree) named Markandeya, Krishna, and Balarama and the one who bathes in the sea named Indradyumna is sure to attain moksha. Corrupted by usage over the years, the island came to be known as Aindraman. This island Indradyumna is situated between 10° and 40 kala north latitude, and 13 and 15 kala, and spreads between 92°and 36' kala, and 93° east longitude [Brahma Purana].

1.3.1.5.2 नागद्वीपः

1.3.1.5.2 Nagadvipa (Nikobara)

अथ पुरायुगे नागवंश्याः केचन क्षत्रियाः स्वर्गे भूमौ 'तासकन्द' प्रदेशादौ राज्यमकुर्वन्। ते च काश्मीरप्रदेशं पश्चादधितिष्ठन्तोऽस्मिन् भारतवर्षे यत्र तत्रोपनिविष्टा बभूवः । तेषामेवाधिकारे यो द्वीप आसीत् स नागेश्वर इति प्रसिद्धो म्लेच्छभाषायामपभ्रंशात् 'नीकोवर' इति संभवति। सपञ्चाशषष्ठांशादष्टमांशं यावदुत्तरेऽक्षांशे त्रिनवत्यंशात् सपञ्चाशत्रिनवत्यंशं यावत्पूर्वदेशान्तरेनागेश्वराख्यो नीकोबरः ।

In ancient times, some kshatriyas of *nagavamsha* (Naga clan) reigned over the Tashkanda region situated in the bhauma svarga. With the passage of time, they expanded their kingdom up to Kashmir region and started living in various places in Bharatavarsha. The island that was under their kingdom was famous by the name Nageshvara, and it is possible that this name got corrupted in vernacular language and became Nicobar. The Nicobar island, same as Nageshvara, is located between 6° and 50° kala, and 8° north latitude, and between 90° and 50° kala, and 93° east longitude.

1.3.1.5.3 सौम्यद्वीपः

1.3.1.5.3 Saumyadvipa (Sumatra)

अथ सोमो राजा गन्धर्वेष्वासीद् गन्धर्वाणामधिपतिर्लोकपाल इति वेदे महाभारते पुराणादौ च प्रसिद्धम्। गन्धर्वदेशो गान्धारदेशः संप्रति 'अफगानिस्तान'-इति प्रसिद्धः । तस्याधिपत्येनायं द्वीपः सौम्य उच्यते। अधीने च त्राप्रत्ययो वेदभाषायामनुशिष्यते। तेनैतस्य पुरात्वे सोमत्रा इति नाम संभाव्यते। तदपभ्रंशादयं "सुमात्रा" शब्दः प्रवर्तते। निरक्षवृत्ते द्वियुतशततमे पूर्वदेशान्तरे सोमत्रा द्वीपः । यवद्वीप-बलिद्वीप-लुम्बक-सुम्वावा-सुम्बा-फ्लोरीनप्रभृतिर्जावाद्वीपसंघोऽपि सुमात्रासान्निध्यात् सौम्यशब्देनैव संगृह्यते। अत एव जावाद्वीपसंघस्य दक्षिणाष्टमाद्यक्षांशवृत्तित्वेऽपि भारतीयत्वं नोपहन्यते। षडधिकशतांशाद्दशाधिकशतांशपर्यन्ते पूर्वदेशान्तरेऽयं जावाद्वीपसङ्घः ।

According to the Vedas, Mahabharata, and the Puranas, there used to be a king named Soma who was the monarch and guardian of the Gandharvas. The Gandharavadesa is Gandharadesa, which is known in present times as Afghanistan. Because this island was under the sovereignty of their king Soma, this island is known as Saumyadvipa. In the language of the Vedas, the suffix 'tra' is used when one intends to mean 'under the authority of'. It is highly possible that because of this reason, this island came to be known as Somatra. This word later became corrupted to Sumatra. This island, Sumatra, is situated between 0°and 102° east longitude. Because of their proximity to this Sumatra, the Java group of islands such as Yavadvipa, Balidvipa, Lumbaka, Sumvava, Sumva and Phlorana have come to be known as part of this Saumyadvipa. Thus it is not illogical to consider Java as part of Bharata even if it is situated 8° south of Equator. This Java group of islands extends between 106° and 110° east longitude.

1.3.1.5.4 गान्धर्वद्वीपः

1.3.1.5.4 Gandharvadvipa (The Philippines)

अस्यैव सोमस्य सामन्तप्राया विश्वावसुप्रभृतयो गन्धर्वराजाः प्रसिद्धाः । तदधीनो द्वीपो गान्धर्वः । स चायं गान्धर्वद्वीपसंघः फीलीपायिनशब्देनाख्यायते। तत्र मनिल्लादयः प्रदेशा अन्तर्भवन्ति। द्वादशे उत्तराक्षांशे त्रयोविंशशते पूर्व-देशान्तरेऽयं द्वीपः स्थितः ।

The feudal lords known as Visvavasus, under the reign of this king Soma, were famous Gandharvas. The island that was under them came to be known as Gandharvadvipa. [Today, this archipelago (Gandharva-dvipasamuha) is known as The Philippines]. In these islands lie regions like Manilla [Manila]. This island is spread up to 12° north latitude and 123° east longitude.

1.3.1.5.5 वारुणद्वीप:

1.3.1.5.5 Varunadvipa (Borneo)

अथ वरुणोऽसुराणां राजासील्लोकपाल: । तदधिकृतो द्वीपो वारुण: । तदपभ्रंशादयं बोर्नियो शब्द उच्यते। द्व्यधिकपञ्चमे उत्तराक्षांशे द्वापञ्चाशत्कलोपेते चतुर्दशशते देशान्तरेऽयं वारुणद्वीप: ।

Varuna, the king of asuras, was like a custodian. The island under his control was Varuna-dvipa. This word Varuna got corrupted to form the word Borneo. This island is located between 52° kala north latitude, and 52° kala east longitude.

1.3.1.5.6 कशेरुमान् द्वीप:

1.3.1.5.6 Kasherumandvipa (Selevisa)

अथ कशेरु: कन्दविशेष: । तस्याधिक्येन कदाचिदत्रोत्पत्तिर्भवेदिति कशेरुमानित्ययमाख्यात: स्यात्। ककारलोपे सेलुवाशब्दोपपत्तिक्रमेणायं द्वीप: सेलेवीस इत्युक्त इत्यनुमीयते। बोर्नियो द्वीपादयं प्राच्यां संनिविशते। चतुर्थे दक्षिणाक्षांशे एकविंशशते पूर्वदेशान्तरे कसेरुमान् ।

There was a unique bulbous root named Kasheru which was largely found on this land in the past, which was why this island came to be known as Kasheruman. It can be inferred that with the loss of initial 'k', in the natural evolution of the residual form of the word, the word Selevisa came into being. This island is located to the east of Borneo. It is situated between 4° south latitude and 121° east longitude.

1.3.1.5.7 गभस्तिमान् द्वीप:

1.3.1.5.7 Gabhastimandvipa (Malukka)

सेलवीसात् प्राच्यां निरक्षवृत्ते मलक्कोपद्वीपो गभस्तिमान्। केचित्तु मलुक्वातोऽग्निकोणस्थमासन्नप्रायं पपुवाद्वीपं गभस्तिमच्छब्देनेच्छन्ति। अद्यतनास्तु पपुवोपद्वीपमाष्ट्रेलियाद्वीपानुबन्धिनमाहु:। अत एवेदानीं भारतीयोपद्वीपत्वाभावात् तत्परित्याग:। वस्तुतस्तु संभाव्यते पुरा युगे तस्यापि भारतीयत्वमिति मलुक्कामारभ्य पपुवापर्यन्तस्य द्वीपसंघस्य गभस्तिमच्छब्देन शक्यते व्यवहार: कर्तुं निरक्षवृत्ते सार्द्धे सप्तविंशशते देशान्तरे गभस्तिमानस्ति ।

The island named Malukka, located at 0° to the east of Selevisa island, was known as Gabhastiman. Some people prefer calling Papuadvipa, located in the south-east corner and ruled by Agni near Malukka, as Gabhastiman. [These days, people consider Papua to be the main island of Australia. Therefore, Gabhastiman has been dropped, because it is not an island of Bharat.] Actually, Gabhastiman was also an island of Bharatavarsha in ancient times, and the archipelago from Malukka to Papua was known as Gabhastiman. This island spreads up to 0° north latitude and 127½° longitude.

1.3.1.5.8 ताम्रपर्णद्वीप:

1.3.1.5.8 Tamraparnadvipa (Taparovena or Ceylon)

अथ सिंहलद्वीप एव ताम्रपर्णीद्वीपः । बौद्धग्रन्थे भारतवर्षीयदेशविभागप्रकरणे ताम्रपर्णीशब्देन सिंहलद्वीपस्योपदिष्टत्वात्। यूनानदेशीयग्रन्थे चायं सिंहलद्वीपः"टापरोवेन" शब्देनाख्यायते। तावताऽप्यस्य ताम्रपर्णसंज्ञोपपद्यते। टापरोवेनशब्दस्य ताम्रपर्णशब्दापभ्रंशतया संभाव्यमानत्वात्। यत्तु टापूरावणशब्दापभ्रंशतया टापरोवेनशब्दं केचित् संभवायन्ति तदयुक्तम्। टापूशब्दस्य भारतीयग्राम्यशब्दतया यूनानदेशे तदपभ्रंशस्य प्रयोगायोगात्। सिंहलस्य रावणटापूत्वाभावाच्च। चत्वारिंशदधिकसप्तमे उत्तराक्षाशें पञ्चाशदधिकाशीतिदेशान्तरे चायं सिहलद्वीपः ।

Sinhaladvipa is Tamraparna-dvipa because in the Buddhists texts, referring to the division of Bharatavarsha, the word *tamrapanu* is used to denote Sinhaladvipa. In the Greek texts, this Sinhaladvipa is called Taparovena. It seems fitting to call Taparovena as Tamraparna, because the word 'parovena' can possibly be the corrupted form of the word 'tamraparna'. It is not correct to infer the word 'taparovena' as being the corrupted version of the word *Tapu Ravana* (island of Ravana) as some people tend to do. The reason for this is that the word 'tapu' is a word used in north India which means 'island'. It is unlikely that a corrupted form of this word could have been used in Greek. Moreover, Sinhaladvipa could not have ever been the island of Ravana. This Sinhaladvipa stretches between 7° and 40' kala north latitude, and 80° and 50' kala longitude.

1.3.1.5.9 कुमारिकाद्वीप:

1.3.1.5.9 Kumarikadvipa (Indian archipelago)

सर्वोऽप्ययं भारतीयोपद्वीपसंघः संप्रति म्लेच्छभाषायामेकेन शब्देन 'इंडियन आर्किपैलैगो'- इत्याख्यायते। यस्तु कुमारिकाक्षेत्रादारभ्य काश्मीरपर्यन्तः प्रवितती महाद्वीपः सोऽत्र प्रधानो नवमो द्वीपः। एते चेन्द्रद्वीपादयः सिंहलातिरिक्ताः सर्वेऽप्युपद्वीपाः प्रचलितभाषायां वर्माशब्देन प्रसिद्धात् कृतवर्मणो राज्ञो राष्ट्राद् दक्षिणपूर्वस्यां दिश्येव संनिविष्टा दृश्यन्ते। तत्र वारुणकसेरुगान्धर्वादीनामुपद्वीपानां भारतीयोपद्वीपत्वाख्यानं नत्वेवोपपद्यते, यावता फारमोसाप्रदेशोप लक्षितप्रशान्तसागरस्य भारतवर्षसीमान्तर्भुक्तत्वं नाभ्युपगम्येत। तस्माद् भारतीयमध्यरेखातः प्राच्यां पञ्चत्वारिंशदंशा भारतस्यास्य पूर्वा सीमेति सिद्धम् ।

This is the Indian archipelago. The island that stretches from Kanyakumari to Kashmir is the main island and also the ninth one. Except Sinhaladvipa, Indradvipa and all the other islands are famous in modern-day language as Verma (Burma). They expanded upto south-east of the country ruled by king Kritavarma. It is not correct to call the islands such as Varuna, Kaseru and Gandharva as part of the Indian archipelago unless we acknowledge that the Pacific Ocean, implied by the Formosa region, as being within the periphery of Bharatavarsha. Thus, it is evident that the eastern limit of Bharatavarsha extended up to 45° to the east of the Indian meridien line.

अपि च शक्तिसङ्गमतन्त्रादौ चीनप्रदेशानामपि केषांचिद् भारतीयत्वेनाख्यानात् चीनसम्बन्धि फारमूसोपद्वीपपर्यन्तं भारतवर्षमासीदिति विज्ञायते। तथा चेदं भारतवर्षस्य नवत्यंशपरिमितत्त्वे पञ्चमं प्रमाणम्। हिन्दुस्तानशब्देन प्रसिद्धस्य कुमारीद्वीपस्य भारतीयत्वाख्यानं भारतवर्षस्य बहुविस्तृतप्रदेशत्वं गमयति।

Moreover, owing to the fact that some parts of China are also included within Bharata in Shaktisangama-tantra, it becomes clear that the limits of Bharatavarsha extend up to the Formosa islands, which is connected to China. Thus, the latitude of Bharatavarsha is up to 90°, such is the fifth proof. The fact that Kumarika was famous by the word Bharatiya proves that Bharatavarsha was an extensive territory.

1.3.1.6 षष्ठं प्रमाणम्- सिन्धोः पश्चिमस्थानां देशानां भारतीयदेशत्वाख्यानम्

1.3.1.6 The Sixth Evidence—The bharatiya character of the countries situated to the west of river Sindhu

तथाहि-पौराणिके भुवनकोशे भारतवर्षीयावान्तरदेशपरिगणनासूदीच्यदेशतया गान्धार-मद्र-पारद-पह्लव-कम्बोज-शक-यवनादि-देशानामुल्लेखादेषां देशानां पुरायुगे भारतीयत्वमासीदित्युपगम्यते। बृहत्संहितायां च भारतवर्षे मध्यात् प्रागादिविभाजिता देशाः । (बृहत्संहिता, 14.1)

इति प्रतिज्ञाय पश्चिमायां हैहय-पारद-शकदेशानां पश्चिमोत्तरस्यां च तुखारमद्रादिदेशानामाख्यानात् तत्कालेऽप्येषां भारतवर्षीयत्वं सुप्रसिद्धमिति गम्यते।

In the enumeration of northern countries, the puranic Bhuvanakosha includes Gandhara, Madra, Parada, Pahlava, Kamboja, Shaka, and Yavana among others; these references suggest that in ancient times these states were considered as Bharatavarsha. The Brihada Samhita records under the general section titled 'Countries radiating in easterly and other directions from the centre of Bharatavarsha', that inclusion of Haihaya-Paradah-Shaka in the west and of Tukhar-Madra in the north-west indicate that they were known widely as part of Bharatavarsha in those days.

1.3.1.6.1 गान्धारमद्रौ

1.3.1.6.1 Gandhara and Madra

तत्रायमफगानस्ताननाम्ना संप्रति प्रसिद्धः संपूर्णो देशः पुरात्वे गान्धारशब्देन, संपूर्णश्चामीरानदेशः पुरात्वे मद्रशब्देन व्यवहृतावास्ताम्। इत्थमेतत् पश्चिमं भारतवर्षं गान्धारमद्राभ्यां द्वेधा विभक्तं द्रष्टव्यम्। गान्धारमद्रौ चैतौ प्रत्येकं द्वेधा विभक्तावास्ताम्। तत्रैते गान्धाराः कन्दहारनगरोपलक्षितास्तावत्सिन्धोः पूर्वतः पश्चिमतश्च प्रसिद्धाः । रामभ्रातृभरतपुत्राभ्यां तक्षकपुष्कराभ्यां तक्षशिलां पुष्करावतीं च राजधानीं पृथगधितिष्ठद्भ्यां स्व-स्वराष्ट्रतयैषां गान्धाराणां द्वेधा विभज्यमानत्वात्। तथा च भारतीयराजशासनाधीनतयैषामुभयेषां भारतीयत्वं सुनिश्चितम् ।

The country, famous as Afghanistan today, was known as Gandhara in ancient times while the entire expanse of ancient Iran was called Madra in popular parlance. Thus, it seems that northern India was divided into two parts: Gandhara and Madra, each of which, in turn, was further divided into two parts.

The people of Gandhara belonged to two distinct parts: to the east of the river Sindhu which flowed by the city of Kandahar, and to its west. The sons of King Bharata, the brother of Sri Rama—Takshak and Pushkar—established the noted cities of Takshashila and Pushkaravati respectively, and made them their capitals, dividing the people of Gandhara accordingly into two kingdoms. Since the two parts of Gandhara were governed by kings from Bharatavarsha, their innate *bharatiyata* (Indian-ness) was beyond dispute.

काबुलतोऽनतिदूरे वायव्ये वामियानाख्याः ।
प्रान्तोऽस्ति तत्र पूर्वं राजा लोकाश्च वैदिका अभवन् ।।312।।

In the north-west direction from Kabul there is a place called Bamiyan. In ancient times, the kings and commoners of Bamiyan were all Vedic practitioners.

ईरानेऽपि तथासीत्पुरा युगे पार्सिपोलिसेत्याख्या ।
पारस्यपुरीयायां विदुरद्यत्वे त्विस्तखरनाम्ना ।।313।।

In ancient Iran, there was a city called Parsipolis in Parasyapuri, which was known across the world as 'Tvistkhar'.

प्राक्तनपारस्यलिपिप्रोल्लिखितास्तत्र ये शिलालेखाः ।
तेभ्यस्तत्रत्यानां भारतवर्षार्यसंस्रवोऽधिगतः ।।314।।

Epigraphs recorded in the ancient Parsi script record that its inhabitants were of Arya descent.

अथौत्तरमद्रा दक्षिणमद्रा इत्येवं मद्रदेशस्यापि द्वैविध्यं प्रसिद्धम्। तथा च द्विधा गान्धारा द्विधा मद्रा इत्येवमेते चत्वारो विभागा, भौगोलिका नित्या भवन्ति।

It is widely known that Madra was divided into two parts—northern Madra and southern Madra. Thus, from a geographical perspective, the two parts of Gandhara and the two parts of Madra together make four divisions.

1.3.1.6.2 पञ्चगणा:

1.3.1.6.2 Panchaganas

अथैतयोरेव गान्धारमद्रयोर्जनताविभागनिबन्धना: पुनरन्ये पारदपह्लवकाम्बोजादय: पञ्चधावान्तरविभागा इष्यन्ते। तथा हि यदुवंशीयहैहयसाम्राज्यकाले तन्मित्रराष्ट्रत्वेन तदधीनराष्ट्रत्वेन चैते पारदा:-पह्लवा:-कम्बोजा: शका: यवना इति पञ्चगणा: सिन्धो: पश्चिमतो राज्यं कुर्वन्ति स्म। ते चाणुवंश्या द्रुह्युवंश्या वा चन्द्रवंशीया: क्षत्रियापसदा: सम्राजमेतं हैहयमनुवर्तन्ते स्म। हैहयकुलशत्रु: सूर्यवंशीयो महाराज: सगर: स्वपितृविद्वेषिणं हैहयराजं विनिर्जित्य चक्रवर्तित्वं लेभे। स एषां हैहयानुगामिनां पह्लवादीनां पराजयचिह्नतया वैकृतं चक्रे। तदुक्तं ब्राह्मादिषु

After describing the divisions in the population of Gandhara and Madra in detail, the divisions of Paradah, Pahlava and Kamboja are elaborated.

During the time of the Haihaya empire of the Yadu clan, their allies and vassals have been enumerated as Paradah, Pahlava, Kamboja, Shaka and Yavana—the five lineages which had their kingdoms west of the river Sindhu. The kshatriyas, belonging to the Anuvanshi, Durvanshi and Chandravanshi clans, paid tribute to the Haihaya empire. The enemy of the Haihaya clan, King Sagara of the Suryavanshi kshatriyas, defeated his father's jealous rival, the Haihaya emperor, and took the title of chakravarty.

It is recorded thus in the Brahma Purana:

रुरुकस्य वृक: पुत्रो वृकाद् बाहुस्तु जज्ञिवान् ।
हैहयास्तालजंङ्घाश्च निरस्यन्ति स्म तं नृपा: ।।

(ब्रह्मपुराणम्, 6.28-29)

Ruruku's son was Vrik, and after Vrik, Bahu was born. The Haihaya and Talajangha kings defeated Bahu and banished him.

बाहोर्व्यसनिनः सर्वं हृतं राज्यमभूत्किल ।
हैहयैस्तालजङ्घैश्च शकैः सार्द्धं द्विजोत्तमाः ।।

(ब्रह्मपुराणम्, 6.35)

Bahu was weak and the most powerful brahmins in alliance with the Haihayas, Talajanghas and Shakas, snatched everything from him.

यवनाः पारदाश्चैव काम्बोजाः पह्लवास्तथाः ।
एते ह्यपि गणाः पञ्च हैहयार्थे पराक्रमन् ।।

(ब्रह्मपुराणम्, 6.36)

Yavana, Parada, Kamboja, Pahlava and others among the panchaganas attacked the Haihayas, and on occasions, defeated them.

सगरस्तु सुतो बाहोर्जज्ञे सह गरेण वै ।
और्वस्याश्रममासाद्य भार्गवेणाभिरक्षितः ।।

(ब्रह्मपुराणम्, 6.30–31)

Bahu's son was Sagara, and he was born with a poisonous urge for revenge. He sought refuge in the hermitage of sage Urva and gained the powerful protection of sage Bhargava.

आग्नेयमस्त्रं लब्ध्वा च भार्गवात्सगरो नृपः ।
हैहयान् विजघानाशु क्रुद्धो रुद्रः पशूनिव ।।

(ब्रह्मपुराणम्, 6. 31, 35)

King Sagara obtained a weapon called Agneya from Bhargava, and used it to attack and kill the Haihayas in a manner similar to what Rudra had adopted to kill animals.

ततः शकाँश्च यवनान् काम्बोजान् पारदाँस्तथा ।
पह्लवाँश्चैव निःशेषान् कर्तुं व्यवसितोऽभवत् ।।

(ब्रह्मपुराणम्, 6.44)

Then King Sagara decided to completely annihilate all Shakas, Yavanas, Paradas, Kambojas and Pahlavas, and began to duly prepare for it.

ते बध्यमाना वीरेण सगरेण महात्मना ।
वशिष्ठं शरणं गत्वा प्रणिपेतुर्मनीषिणम् ।।

(ब्रह्मपुराणम्, 6.45)

All those who were in fear of the brave King Sagara, as well as those who had been incarcerated by him, sought protection humbly at the feet of *maharshi* (great sage) Vasishta.

वसिष्ठस्त्वथ तान् दृष्ट्वा समयेन महाद्युतिः ।
सगरं वारयामास तेषां दत्वाऽभयं तदा ॥

(ब्रह्मपुराणम्, 6.46)

Subsequently, the great fiery maharshi Vasishta stopped King Sagara's rampage by extracting a vow from him, and enabled these people to overcome their fears.

सगरस्तां प्रतिज्ञां च गुरोर्वाक्यं निशम्य च ।
धर्मं जघान तेषां च वेषानन्यांश्चकार ह ॥

(ब्रह्मपुराणम्, 6.47)

The king, after taking the vow and attending to the discourses of maharshi Vasishta, instead attacked the religion—the beliefs and practices—of the panchaganas, and made them change even their attire.

अर्द्धं शकानां शिरसो मुण्डयित्वा व्यसर्जयत् ।
यवनानां शिरः सर्वं काम्बोजानां तथैव च ॥

(ब्रह्मपुराणम्, 6.48)

Though he left the Shakas after forcing them to shave half their heads, he compelled the Yavanas and Kambojas to shave their heads completely.

पारदा मुक्तकेशाश्च पह्लवाः श्मश्रुधारिणः ।
सर्वे ते क्षत्रिया विप्रा धर्मस्तेषां निराकृतः ॥ इत्यादिः

(ब्रह्मपुराणम्, 6.49, 51)

Likewise, the Paradahs were also divested of their hair and the Pahlavas were compelled to keep beards. These were all brahmins and kshatriyas whose religion was attacked and completely ruined.

1.3.1.6.3 पारदाः

1.3.1.6.3 Paradah

पञ्चाप्येते क्षत्रियापसदा भारतीयार्यधर्माद्विच्च्याविताः कालेन कैलडियादेशनिवासिकालकेयासुरधर्मे दीक्षिता भूत्वा क्रमेणाऽसुरवेषभूषां तद्भाषां चागृह्णन्। अहंमन्येषु पूर्णाभिमानिषु तेषु केचिदात्मनो धनुर्धरवीरत्वं प्रख्यापयन्तः पारदा इत्यात्मनो राजोपाधिं जगृहुः। तच्छब्दस्यासुरभाषायां धनुर्धरार्थत्वात्। ते चैते पारदाः उत्तरकाले म्लेच्छभाषया पार्थिया इत्युक्ताः। ऐषां च निवासप्रदेशः

काश्यपीयसागराद्दक्षिणपूर्वदिश्युत्तरमद्रोऽभवत्। तमिदानीं युगे खुरासानदेशमाहुः ।

These five kshatriya clans, after being excommunicated from the Arya traditions, had veered towards the asura practices of the kalakeyas of Kaladeya [Caldea]; they adopted their attire and ways of speech. These people soon became rather full of pride and self-adulation, declared themselves to be brave archers, and took upon themselves the royal title of Paradah. In the asura terminology, *paradah* means an archer. In later years, Paradah began to be called Parthia. Their land was the northern Madra region, south of the Caspian Sea. This is known as the Khorasan province today.

1.3.1.6.4 पह्लवा:

1.3.1.6.4 Pahlava

अथान्ये केचिन्महाबलिष्ठार्थकमासुरभाषया पह्लवान् शब्दं स्वोपाधिं जगृहुः। ते पह्लवाः इति आख्यान्त। पह्लवास्तु पार्थवाः पार्थिवा इति कालेनाख्याताः शासनीनाम्ना पश्चात् प्रसिद्धा अभवन्। इस्पहाननगरोपलक्षितो दक्षिणमद्रप्रान्तस्तेषां निवासभूमिः। यत्तु केचित् पाश्चात्यविद्वांसोऽद्यत्वे पारदानामेव पह्लवत्वमुपतर्कयन्ति पार्थिवा एव त्वपभ्रंशात् पार्थिया उच्यन्ते इति चाहुः। तन्न युक्तम्। पौराणिकेऽतिप्राचीने भुवनकोशे पारदानां पह्लवानां च भेदेन सर्वत्राख्याततत्वात् । यथा मार्कण्डेयः ।

बाह्लीका वाटधानाश्च पह्लवाश्चर्मखण्डिकाः ।
गान्धारा यवनाश्चैव पारदा हारभूषिकाः ।।
कम्बोजा दरदाश्चैव काश्मीरानुगुणास्तथा ।।
(मार्कण्डेयपुराणम्, 54.35-38)

जेन्दावस्ताग्रन्थोऽप्यादितः पह्लवीभाषायामासीत्। तेनैते तद्ग्रन्थानुयायिनामग्नि-पूजकानां पारसीकानां पुरात्वे चन्द्रवंशीयक्षत्रियत्वानुमानेऽपि कालेन पह्लवसंज्ञाप्रसिद्धजातिमुक्तत्वमनुमीयते। जेन्दावस्ताग्रन्थनिर्माता जरथुस्त्रो यद्यपि मगजातीयतया शक आसीत्। तथापि जेन्दावस्ताग्रन्थस्य पह्लवीभाषायां निर्माणात् पह्लवशकयोः परस्परतः संस्रवाधिक्यमासीदित्यवगम्यते।

Certain other people adopted a powerful asura title *pahalvan* meaning 'the one who is extremely strong' as their title. That is how they began to be called Pahlavas. These Pahlavas were, from time to time, called Parthavs or Parthivs, and afterwards they gained fame as Sashanis. They belonged to a place called Isfahan in the southern part of Madra. Some western scholars who regarded the Paradahs to be the same as Pahlavas argued that Parthiv was a synonym of Parthia. However, this is inaccurate as the ancient puranic Bhuvanakosha describes the Paradahs and Pahlavas as distinct from each other.

Likewise, the Bactrians, Vatdhanas, Pahlavas, Charmakhandikas, Gandharas, Yavanas, Paradahs, Harbhushiks, Kambojas and Dards of Kashmir share many traits and features.

The Zendavesta—the sacred text of the fire-worshipping Parsis—is recorded in the Pahlavi language. The Pahlavas were sometimes considered to be kshatriyas of the Chandravanshi clan. The author of Zendavesta, Zarathustra, belonged to the Maga clan [the Magas were the learned section among the Shakas]. It thus becomes clear that the Avesta was composed in Pahlavi and that the Shakas and the Pahlavis were on terms of familiarity, if not intimacy.

1.3.1.6.5 कम्बोजा:

1.3.1.6.5 Kamboja

कामभोजा: यथेच्छभोगप्रवणा: सर्वस्वतन्त्रा: वयमित्यात्मानं प्रथयन्तोऽपरे कालेन काम्भोजा: काम्बोजा उच्यन्ते स्म। त एव कम्बोडिया इत्याख्याता: । ते चैते काम्बोजा निषधपर्वताद्दक्षिणस्था अपि भारतीया एवासन्। "शवतिर्गतिकर्मा कम्बोजेष्वेत भाष्यते"-(महाभाष्यम्,पश्पशाह्निकम्) इति व्याकरणमहाभाष्योक्त्या तत्रत्यानामपि संस्कृतभाषाभाषित्वेनार्यत्वोपगमात्। ये त्विदानीं भारतवर्षस्य पूर्वप्रान्तेऽपि नूनं वर्माख्यप्रदेशपूर्वभागस्थात् स्यामदेशात् प्राच्यां कोचीनत: प्रतीच्यां तयोर्देशयोर्मध्येऽष्टमाक्षांशात् पञ्चादशाक्षांशपर्यन्तं केचित् कम्बोजा: प्रसिद्धयन्ति। याँश्च कम्बोडियाशब्देनैवेदानीन्तना: पाश्चात्या: व्यपदिशन्ति ते खल्वेभ्यो भारतपश्चिमप्रान्तवासिभ्य: काम्बोजेभ्यो भिन्ना: स्यु: । पुरा युगे भारतीयसर्वग्रन्थे कम्बोजानां भारतपश्चिमत्वेनैवाख्यानात्तेषां गारस्तानप्रान्तवासित्वं नापलपितुं शक्यते ।

The term 'Kam-bhoja' means 'those who indulge wilfully in pleasurable activities in the belief that each is separate and independent'; such people later came to be known as Kambojas. Though there is no connection, over time, this became the source for the name of the land called Cambodia. The Kamboja land, though located in the southern part of the Nishadh mountains, was Indian in character. The Sanskrit phrase '*gatyarthak shavti dhatu*' may be employed to describe Kamboja in this context. This meant that the inhabitants of Kamboja, by virtue of speaking Sanskrit, may said to be of Arya descent. The people who live to the east of India today—in Burma—and further east, in Siam and to the west of Cochin, about 8 to 14 per cent of the population, are also called Kambojas. Western scholars often mistakenly use the word Cambodia synonymously with Kamboja but that is entirely inaccurate. The Kambojas, who were found in the north-western regions of greater India, were different from them.

1.3.1.6.6 शकाः

1.3.1.6.6 Shaka

अथ शक्ताः समर्था वयमित्यावेदयन्तः केचन शका अभवन्। ते चैते शका उत्तरयुगे स्कीथीया नाम्नोच्यन्ते स्म। समर्था एते पूर्वभारतेऽपि चिरमागत्य राज्यं कुर्वाणा विक्रमादित्येनोज्जयिनीमहाराजेन पराजिता अभवन्निति वदन्त्यैहासिकाः शकानामेषां निवासप्रान्तविशेष एव शाकद्वीपः । शकजातीयानां ये ब्राह्मणविद्यावृत्तयस्ते मगा आख्याताः ।

एभिर्यजन्ति भूयिष्ठं तस्मिन् (शाक) द्वीपे मगाधिपाः ।
विद्यावन्तं कुलश्रेष्ठां: शौचाचारसमविन्ताः ।।
(भविष्यपुराणम्, ब्राह्मपर्व, 140.42–43)

The Shaka believed themselves to be strong and able. In later years they called themselves Scythians. Historians point out that the Shakas entered ancient India only to be defeated by King Vikramaditya of Ujjaini, whose clan had been ruling since time immemorial. The place they inhabited began to be called Shakadvipa. The brahmins among the Shakas, who made a living through their learning, began to be called the Magas.

It is recorded in the Bhavishya Purana: It is thus that the learned, aristocratic kings of the Maga clan with their pure practices would perform yajna alongside the Shaka brahmins of Shakadvipa.

पारसीकानां मतप्रवर्तको बाह्लीकजन्मा ऋजिश्वर्षिकन्यागर्भजो जरथुस्त्रोऽपि मगजातीय एवसीत् ।

वेदोक्तं विधिमुत्सृज्य यतोऽहं लङ्घितस्त्वया ।
तस्मान्मत्तः समुत्पन्नस्तव पुत्रो भविष्यति ।।

जरथुस्त्र इति ख्यातो वंशकीर्तिविवर्द्धनः ।
अग्निजात्या मगाः प्रोक्ताः सोमजात्या द्विजातयः ।।
(भविष्यपुराणम्, ब्राह्मपर्व, 139. 42–44)

Born in Bahlika, the founder of the Parsi faith, offspring of sage Rijrashva's daughter, Zarathustra was also of the Maga clan. The Bhavishya Purana records: By transgressing the ways of the Vedas, you have defied me; thus, my son will be the Maga, his name will be Zarathustra, he will make the name of the clan immortal. Those born of fire will be called the Magas and those born of Soma will be called dvijas.

एते च जरथुस्त्रमतावलम्बिनो वैदिकधर्मविरोधाद्विपरीतमतानुगामिनो बभूवुः । लिपिरपि जरथुस्त्रेण दक्षिणतो वामानुगा नवीना प्राकल्प्यत । देवाराधनावैपरीत्येनासुराराधना चानने प्रकल्पितेत्याहुः ।

विपर्यस्तेन वेदेन मगा गायन्त्यतो मगाः ।
ऋग्वेदोऽथ यजुर्वेदः समावेदस्त्वथर्वणः ।।

ब्राह्मणोक्तास्तथा वेदा मगानामपि सुव्रत ।
त एव विपरीतास्तु तेषां वेदाः प्रकीर्त्तिताः ।।

(भविष्यपुराणम्, 140.36-37)

In due course, the followers of Zarathustra began to follow the tradition propounded by him in opposition to Vedic practices and the Vedic religion. Zarathustra composed a new script that was read from the right to the left. It is said that this was used to introduce the idea of the worship of asuras over the worship of devas. As the Bhavishya Purana records—Those who sing the Vedas in the reverse order are called Magas. The Rigveda, Yajurveda, Samaveda, and Atharvaveda were composed by the brahmins and in a similar way the Magas composed four Vedas in reverse order.

तेषां वैदिकब्राह्मणविरोधिताया उक्तवान्। मगानामेषां चत्वारो वेदाः क्रमेण विद विस्परद (विश्वरद) विदाद, आङ्गिरस इत्युच्यन्ते। शाकद्वीपिनोऽप्येते भारतवर्षं पूर्वमागत्य मगधप्रान्तं स्वनाम्ना वासयामासुः ।

In this way, the Bhavishya Purana records the dispute between the Magas and Vedic brahmins. The Vedas composed by the Magas subsequently came to be known as Vid, Visperad, Vendidad and Adiras. In ancient times, the inhabitants of Shakadvipa came to India and established Magadha—which derives from the root 'Maga'—naming it after themselves.

1.3.1.6.7 यवनदेशाभिज्ञानम्

1.3.1.6.7 Identifying the Yavana country

अथ ये खल्वेतेषां सर्वधर्माणां मिश्रणामिश्रणाभ्यां प्रतीतास्ते यवनाः ते चैते संप्रति यहूदिया इत्याख्यायन्ते। यहूदियनामेषां प्रधानभूता काचिन्नगरी यहूदीयाशब्देनैवाख्यायते स्म। तां पाश्चात्या अपभ्रंशाद् यूडियाशब्देनाहुः । तुरुष्कास्त्वेतां नगरीं "वै तूलहम" इत्याहुः । तत्रैव च सन्निधाने वैतूलमुकद्दसनामा नगरी वर्त्तते। ताभ्यामुपलक्षितः फिलिस्तानप्रान्त एव चैषां यवनानां प्रधानभूतो देशोऽवगन्तव्यः । यद्यप्यत्र देवयुगे पणयो नामासुरा वसन्ति स्म। पणिस्थानस्यैव चापभ्रंशेनाऽयं फिलिस्तानशब्दः पश्चात्प्रसिद्धोऽभूत्। किन्तु नैतावता पणीनां यवनत्वमास्थेयम्। पणीनां वाणिज्यप्रधानासुरतया यवनानां तु यहूदियानां पश्चादसुराणां भारतीयक्षत्रियापसदतया भेदस्य भारतीयप्रामाणिकशास्त्रसिद्धत्वात् । पणीनां कालेन विनाशे यवनानां तत्रोपनिवेशस्य कालप्राप्तत्वाच्च । यत्तु यवनशब्दो ग्रीकजातिपरो न

तु यहूदियावचनः यूनानियानगर्या यवनानी शब्दापभ्रंशत्वोपपत्तेरित्याहुः । तत्र विप्रतिपद्यामहे। द्विधा हि यवनाः स्युः । किलातत्रैतन-शैलाभ-यवनाख्यया संस्कृतशास्त्रोक्तानां कैल्ट-ट्यूटन-स्लाव-ग्रीकनामभिर्म्लेच्छभाषाशब्दैः सांप्रतं प्रसिद्धानां स्वर्णरजातिविशेषाणामन्यतमभेदा एके यवना ग्रीकनाम्ना प्रसिद्ध्यन्ति। अपरे पुनः पह्लवपारदादिक्षत्रियापसदानां भारतीयानामन्यतमभेदा यहूदियाः संभवन्ति। तथा च नास्ति विरोधः इत्यवगन्तव्यम् ।

The ones who were created through intermingling and subsequent distillation of the faiths and practices came to be known as the Yavanas. They are called 'Yehudi' today. The main city of this tribe was known to the western world by the colloquial term Judea. The Turkic people call this region 'Vytulaham' (Bethlehem). In close proximity to this place lies the town of Baitul Muqaddas. The land where these two cities lie is the homeland of the Yavanas—Philistine or the modern-day Palestine. However, in the devayuga, an asura clan known as Pani used to live here. Subsequently Panistan, the land of Panis, became Philistan due to linguistic changes. This alone, however, should not be considered sufficient to establish Panis as Yavanas. They were primarily a trading community. The Indian *Pramanic Shastra* [a text of evidence] states that these Yavana-Yehudiya asuras were basically from a lower kshatriya clan. After the time of Panis, the place became a seat of the Yavanas.

However, the term 'Yavana' is neither synonymous with 'Greek' nor with 'Yehudi'. Many believe this is so by assuming that the word Yunaniya, denoting a city, was a derivative of 'Yavana'. This is not accurate. There were two different sub-groups within the Yavana tribe: the first was the swarnar tribe of contemporary times constituting the ethnic Greeks; the names of Kilat, Trainat and Shailabh quoted in Sanskrit texts actually refer to the tribes who were known to the western world as Celts, Teutons, and Slavs. The other group might be the outcaste tribes of kshatriyas (such as the Paradah) from Bharatavarsha, who were categorized as the Yehudiya. There can hardly be any dispute in this matter.

यूनानदेशीयेषु यवनशब्दप्रचारस्य अर्वाचीनत्वम् ।

The ambiguity of designating the people of Yunan as Yavanas.

अथवा विपर्यस्तमिदमुच्यते यवनशब्दो ग्रीकजातिवचनो न तु यहूदियावचन इति। वस्तुतस्तु यहूदियावचन एवायं शब्दः पुरात्वे व्यवह्रियमाण आसीन्न तु ग्रीकजातिवचन इति निभृतं प्रत्येतव्यम्। भारतीयेतिहासप्रचारकाले ग्रीसदेशेतिहासस्यान्धकारमयत्वात् तदभिप्रायेण भारतीयार्यशास्त्रे यवनशब्दप्रयोगयोगात्। उक्तं पूर्वम्। दक्षिणभारतस्थहैहयसाम्राज्यकाले तद्बन्धवः पश्चिमभारतवासिनः

पञ्चगणाः सगरसाम्राज्यकाले पूर्वभारतादस्मान्निर्वासिता धर्मभ्रष्टा असुरा अभवन्निति। तेष्वेके यवना एव क्रोधादार्यैर्नित्यं विद्विषन्तः सर्वदा योधितुमुद्यताः सन्तो युद्धधीत्वात् कालेन युद्धधीशब्दैनैवाख्याता अभवन्। युद्धधिय एवैते वीरा अपभ्रंशान्म्लेच्छैर्भूयसा युहदीशब्देन व्यपदिष्टा व्यवहारप्राचुर्येण यहूदीसंज्ञया प्रसिद्धा अभवन्। पारस्थानाख्ये पश्चिमभारते पृथक्-पृथक् संनिविष्टानामेषां पञ्चगणानामन्यतमा ह्येते यवनास्तदात्त्वे लोहितसागरीयपूर्वदक्षिणकूलस्थानाद् अदनप्रदेशादारभ्य आसीरिया प्रदेशान्तान् लोहितसागरपूर्वकूलप्रान्तदेशानधिवसन्ति स्म। अत एव भारतसीमाचतुष्टयीं निर्दिशन्तो भारतीयार्याः 'पश्चिमे यवनाः स्थिताः' इत्याहुः। अद्यत्वे तु यवनशब्दापभ्रंशेन यवनशब्दः केवलमर्वदेशस्य दक्षिणपश्चिमप्रान्तमात्रे संकुचितोऽवशिष्यते। अन्यप्रान्तेभ्यः क्रमेण यवनानामाधिपत्यविच्छेदाद्वा हेत्वन्तराद्वा यवनशब्दप्रयोगस्योच्छिन्नत्वात् यहूदीशब्दव्यवहारप्राचुर्येण च तेष्वयं यवनशब्दप्रयोगः सर्वतो विलुप्त एवाभूदिति नेदानीं वैदेशिकास्तेष्वमुं शब्दं प्रयुञ्जाना दृश्यन्ते। तदित्थमेतेषु यहूदीषु विलुप्तप्रयोगोऽयं यवनशब्दः कालगतेरद्भुतसामर्थ्यादतिदूरं गिरीशदेशमभ्याक्रान्तो भूयसा व्यवह्रियमाणो दृश्यते। सोऽयमर्वाचीनयुगे खल्वभवद् ग्रीसदेशे यवनशब्दप्रचारो न पुरात्वे तत्रासीत् ग्रीसदेशेतिहासस्य खीष्टजन्मनः प्रागष्टदशशतवत्सरेभ्य एव प्रवर्तमानतया तदभिप्रायेण यवनशब्दप्रयोगस्यापि तदवान्तरकालिकत्वेनार्वाचीनत्वोपपत्तेः।

The opposite of the above may also be stated: neither is the word Yavana suggestive of Greeks, nor of Yehudis. This was true of ancient times, and should be understood correctly. When the ancient history of Bharatavarsha was being disseminated, the history of the Greeks was yet to be known fully and therefore the word Yavana was used in the specific context of the intentions of the Yehudiya people. Some among these Yavana tribes were aggressive and were always ready for war. As they showed an uncanny talent for warfare, they began to be referred to as 'Yuddha-dhi'—that is, 'those who display great aptitude in the art of warfare'. In barbarian tongues, this became Yehudi over time.

In Parasthana, one of the leading tribes among the panchaganas were the Yavanas. In those times, they were inhabitants of the area, extending from Aden in the south of the Red Sea to Assyria in the east of the Red Sea. Thus, taking into account the entire scope of greater Bharatavarsha, the Arya of Bharatavarsha used to say that the Yavanas lived in the western border of Bharatavarsha. Today, the use of the word Yavana, a derivative of the Yavanas of the past, has shrunk considerably and is now limited to the south-western part of Arabia. Perhaps owing to the fall in the number of Yavanas in other parts of the world or the increased currency of the word Yehudi over time, the word Yavana is no longer used to denote Yehudis.

Nowadays, even westerners are not found using this word anymore. As this word was no longer representative of the Yehudis, 'Yavana' came to be associated with the people across the borders of Greece. However, neither was the word 'yavana' used in the context of Greece for the first time in contemporary times, nor was it popular in the pre-historic past. Owing to the fact that the Greek civilization dates back to 1800 BCE, the word 'yavana' must have been used retroactively on the asura tribe of Hellas that resided there.

1.3.1.6.8 ग्रीसशब्दयवनशब्दोपचारारम्भकालविचार:

1.3.1.6.8 Discussion on words Greek and Yavana

हैलेयासुरजातीनां ग्रीकायिनाम्ना पुराप्रसिद्धानां निवासाभिजनदेशविशेषे ग्रीसशब्दयवनशब्दोपचाराम-कालविचार: ।

ग्रीसदेशे चायं यवनशब्दोपचार: कस्मात् कालादारब्ध इति जिज्ञासायामुच्यते एष तावद् ग्रीसदेश: प्राचीनतमकाले पेलासगीनाम्ना प्रसिद्धै: वन्यैरसभ्यजातिविशेषै: पर्वतगुहानिवासिभिरेवाक्रान्त आसीत्। तत्र काले स्याम-सीरिया-केल्डिया-यमनादिप्रान्तवासिनो युद्धवीरा हैलेया आक्रममाणा: पेलासगीजातिविशेषान् पराभाव्य तत्र देशे स्वयं समुपनिवेशं चक्रु: । मध्यैशियाप्रदेशात्त्वेते हैलेया ग्रीसप्रदेशमागत्य वन्यान् पराजिग्यिरे इति पाश्चात्या आहु: तद् भ्रान्तम्। मध्यैशियाप्रदेशस्य देवलोकतया तदात्वे व्यवस्थितत्वे तत्र देशे हैलेयनामासुरविशेषाणां कदाप्यवस्थातुमशक्यत्वात्। 'हेलयो हेलय इति कुर्वन्त: पराबभूवु:' इति श्रुतेर्हैलिरयं पुरायुगे सीरियाप्रान्तवासी युद्धप्रिय: कश्चिदसुराणां संघविशेष आसीत्। तंद्वशधरा: सर्वे हैलेया: स्यु। तेषां विजयिनामावासप्रभावादयं ग्रीसदेश: पुरात्वे हैलेयावास: सन् कालक्रमेण व्यवहारविशेषानुरोधाद् 'हेलास' इत्याख्यायते स्म। वर्तमानग्रीसदेशापेक्षया बहुविस्तृतोऽयं हेलासप्रदेश आसीत्। तत्र वसन्त: पुनरिमे हैलेया निशि युद्धप्रवणतया निश्या: सन्त: क्रमेण हैलेनिसनाम्ना प्रसिद्धा अभवन्। हैलेयनिश्यशब्दापभ्रंशेन हैलेनिशा शब्दोपपत्ते: संभवात्। पेलासगीजातीयमनुष्याणामप्येषु सहयोगसंस्रवाधिक्यप्रभावमिश्रणे तन्मिश्रितहैलेया एवोत्तरकाले हैलेनिसशब्देनाख्याता: पुरायुगे ग्रीसदेशसवासिन: प्रधान्येनाभूवन्। अत्रैते श्लोका रच्यन्ते -

If we were to examine the use of the term 'Yavana' in Greece for the first time, the answer would be that in very ancient times Greece was surrounded by the barbaric and wild Pelasgi tribe which lived in the mountains. The inhabitants of Siam, Syria, Caldea and Yemen—the Hellas—a tribe of brave warriors who attacked Greece, defeated the Pelasgi tribe and established Greece as their seat of power.

Some Western scholars hold that the Hellas tribe descended from Central Asia and defeated the barbarians. However, this notion is erroneous; Central Asia was populated by the people of the deva tribes and was well-organized. There is no evidence of asura tribes called Hellas having come from there. There is an old song—'While chanting Hellas, they faced defeat' and we can use it to infer the origins of the word Hellas. Hellas coupled with the term 'nisya' gave rise to the word Hellenes which attained popular currency. The derivative of Hellas and nisya became a new term 'Hellenes'. The intermingling of the Pelasgi tribe with the Hellas gave rise to the Hellenes tribe which is now said to populate Greece.

On this subject, the following hymns were composed—

हैलेयवासः क्रमतोऽपशब्दो हेलास इत्येष बभूव काले ।
तत्र स्म हेलेनिसजात्यलोका वसन्ति नीवृत्यसुरप्रवीराः ।।315।।

The word Haileyavas over time became Hellas and it was there—in Hellas—that the leader of the then-Hellenes clan, a warrior asura, resided.

निश्याक्रमन्ते स्म विशिष्य युद्धे घ्नन्ति स्म सुप्तानिति कारणात्ते ।
हैलेयनिश्या अभवन् प्रसिद्धा हैलेनिसा इत्यपशब्दतः स्युः ।।316।।

During wars these people would attack the enemy at night and slaughter them while they were asleep which is why these people got the name Hellenic, the derivative of which became Hellenes.

हैलेनिसानां प्रथमस्तु देशः स्वः सामदेशः सहि सीरियाख्यः ।
जिगीषया पश्चिमदिग्गतास्ते यूनानदेशानधिचक्र रुग्राः ।।317।।

Originally, the Hellenes people were from what is the modern-day Syria. However, hunger for conquest took them westward towards the land called Yunan, the modern-day Greece, where they defeated the barbaric and aggressive incumbents and established their supremacy.

हैलेयलोका गिरिकायवत्त्वात् ख्याता बभूवुर्गिरिकायिनोऽपि ।
ग्रीकायिनामान इमेऽपशब्दादासन्नरस्तूवचनात् प्रतीमः ।।318।।

The Haileyavas were large in structure and thus referred to as *girikai* (large in size). According to Aristotle, this gives the etymology of the word 'Greek' through its derivative 'greekai'.

ग्रीकायिलोकोपनिवेशहेतोर्ग्रीसः स देशः कथितः पुरात्वे ।
तच्चेटलीवासिभिरस्य नाम ग्रीसेति क्लृप्तं खलु रोमकाख्यैः ।।319।।

Thus in ancient times, Greece derived its name as the place of the Greekai people. The inhabitants of Italy who went by the name of Romak christened Greek with its modern name.

कालेनास्मिन् ग्रीसदेशे 'आर्थेस' - राजधानीपतेः कोद्रसनामकस्य महाराजस्य कश्चित् पुत्रस्ततो ग्रीसदेशाद् एशियामाइनरप्रदेशमागत्य तत्र द्वादशनगरीः प्रतिष्ठापयामास। द्वादशनगरोपलक्षितस्य च तस्य प्रदेशस्य 'आइयोन' - इति नामकरणं कृतम्। अयमेव खल्वाइयोनशब्दो यवनशब्दयूनानशब्दयोः प्रत्युत्पत्तिहेतुरवगम्यते। न ततः प्रागेतद्दशपरतया यवनशब्दः प्रयुक्त आसीदित्यतस्त्रयं यवन-शब्दोऽर्वाचीनोऽस्तीति ब्रूमः। तस्य चैतस्य ग्रीसयूनानादिनामकरणस्याद्यप्रभृति प्राक्तनचतुःसहस्रवर्षपूर्वावधिकालावान्तरकालविषयकतया ततः प्राचीनेषु भारतवर्षीयशास्त्रग्रन्थेषु पुराणेतिहासभुवनकोशेषु प्रयुक्तस्य यवनशब्दस्य तत्परतया प्रयोगासंभवादवश्यं युहूदीपरत्वमेवास्तीति सिद्धम्। यहूदीनां चोपनिवेशोऽयं भारतचश्चिमसमुद्रकूलस्थो यूडियाप्रदेश एवास्तीति युक्तं यवनदेशस्य भारतीयप्रत्यन्तदेशत्वम्। इत्थं चैते क्षत्रिया भारतीयार्यधर्मात्परिभ्रंशिताः पञ्चगणा असुरधर्माणोऽयोध्याधिपतिसगरमहाराजसमयादूर्ध्वं प्रसिद्धा अभवन्। तेषां गान्धारकम्बोजादीनां भारतीय-भुवनकोशे भारतीयत्वेनाख्यानादवश्यमेषां निवासभूमयो भारतवर्षस्य प्रान्तविशेषा आसिन्नत्यवगच्छामः।

During this time, the king of Athens was Codrus; one of his sons travelled to Asia Minor and established twelve cities. The region around the twelve cities was known as Ion. Thus the word 'ion' re-established the use of the words 'Yunan' and 'Yavana' retrospectively. Before this, the word Yavana had not been used for Greece. It is actually neither very recent nor very ancient.

In this way, the panchaganas, the kshatriyas from Bharatavarsha, became outcastes from the Arya way of life in the time of King Sagara. Indeed, these references to Kamboja and Gandhara in the ancient geographic encyclopaedia emphasise their innate *Bharatiya* character and their inclusion within the scope of the greater Bharatavarsha subcontinent.

1.3.1.7 सप्तं प्रमाणम्-यज्ञवेदाध्यापकस्य काप्यमहर्षेर्निवास

1.3.1.7 The Seventh Evidence—residence of maharishi Kapya in Madra

1.3.1.7.1 काप्यमहर्षेर्मद्रदेशवासित्वाख्यानम्

1.3.1.7.1 Reference to the great sage Kapya as a citizen of Madra in Vajsaneya Shruti

अपि च गान्धारतः पश्चिमोत्तरेषु मद्रेषु यज्ञवेदाधयापकस्य काप्यमहेर्षेः निवासः सप्तं प्रमाणम् ।

The seventh evidence is related to the abode of Kapya Maharshi, preceptor of yajna-vedas, in the Madra country to the north-west of Gandhara.

वाजसनेयश्रुतौकाप्यमहर्षेः मद्रदेशवासित्वाख्यानम् ।

Addressing the great sage Kapya as a citizen of Madra in Vajsaneya shruti.

तथाहि - वाजसनेयश्रुतौ उद्दालक आरुणिर्याज्ञवल्क्यं प्रति सूत्रात्मानमन्तर्यामिणं च पृच्छन्नाह-

As Uddalak Aruni told Yajnavalkaya about Sutratma and Antaryami in Vajsaneya Samhita:

मद्रेष्ववसाम पतञ्जलस्य काप्यस्य गृहेषु यज्ञमधीयाना: । (बृहदारण्यकोपनिषद्, 3.7.1) इति। ते हीमे यज्ञ-वेदाध्यापकस्य काप्यस्यर्षेर्निवासप्रदेशा मद्रा: पञ्चत्रिंशे खलूत्तरेऽक्षांशेऽष्टाचत्वारिंशे तु ग्रीनवीचमध्यरेखात: पूर्वदेशान्तरे उज्जयिनी मध्यरेखातस्तु अष्टाविंशे पश्चिमदेशान्तरे सन्निविष्टा अध्यवसीयन्ते यथा हि दक्षिणोत्तरा विहारा: । दक्षिणोत्तरा: कोशला: । पूर्वोत्तरा: पञ्चाला: । दक्षिणोत्तरा: कुरव: । इत्येवमेते सिन्धो: प्राच्यदेशा द्वेधा विभक्ता आसन् एवमेवैते सिन्धो: पश्चिमभागस्था मद्रा अपि दक्षिणोत्तराभ्यां विभक्ता: स्मर्यन्ते। तांश्चैतान् मद्रान् पूर्वकाले मेडियाशब्देन म्लेच्छा व्यवहरन्ति स्म। किन्त्विदानीमुत्तरमद्रा: खुरासानशब्देन दक्षिणमद्रास्तु परसियाशब्देन व्यवह्रियन्ते। कालेन देशविशेषाणां सीमाभेदस्य संज्ञाभेदस्य च प्रकृतिनियमसिद्धत्वात् ।

'We resided in the house of Kapiya Patanjal learning yajna in Madra. Sage Kapya, the teacher of yajna and veda, lived in Madra, which seems to have been situated at 35° north axis, 48° east from Greenwich meridien and 28° west from Ujjaini. Moreover, the eastern regions of Sindhu like south-north Bihar, south-north Kosala, north-east Panchal and south-north Kuru were divided into two parts. Similarly, Madra, situated in the western region of Sindhu, was divided into two—south and north. These Madra regions were called Midia by the non-Sanskrit speaking people in ancient times. But in present times, north Madra is referred to as Parasia (Persia) because it is the rule of nature that time makes an impact on the name and boundaries of a nation.'

1.3.1.7.2 मद्रदेशाभिज्ञाने वीनमतप्रत्याख्यानाम्

1.3.1.7.2 New opinion on the names of Madra countries

केचित्तु पाश्चात्या नयपालचीनान्तरालस्थं भूटानदेशं मद्रदेशत्वेन कल्पयन्ति। तेषां नितान्तमनभिज्ञानां कल्पनाया: नि:सारत्वादुपेक्षामात्रं सत्कार:। यच्च पुनरद्यत्वे केचिदन्ये पाश्चात्यानुगामिन: पण्डिता इरावतीचन्द्रभागाप्रान्ते मद्रदेशं मन्यन्ते तद्विभ्रान्तम्। सिन्धुनदस्य भारतीयपश्चिमसीमात्वभ्रमेणोपकल्पिताना मीदृशप्रवादानामनादेयत्वात्। भारतीयोदीच्यदेशगणनासु गान्धार-बाह्लीक-पह्लव-शक-यवन-पारद-कम्बोजादिसहकारेण मद्राणामप्युक्ततया तेषामिवैषां मद्राणामापि सिन्धो: पश्चिमप्रान्तीयत्वेनोपगम्यत्वाच्च। दृश्यते च सिन्धुनदात् पश्चिमतो विंशत्यंशान्तरेण मेदियाशब्दप्रसिद्धो देश: तस्योत्तरमद्रत्वेऽध्यवसिते ततो दक्षिणपूर्वस्यां गान्धार-संलग्नतया दक्षिणमद्रत्वमुपक्लृप्तं भवति। तथा हि सर्वोप्यद्यतनोफगानदेश: पुरात्वे गान्धारदेश आसीत्। सर्वश्चायमद्यतन: पर्सियादेश: पुरा मद्रदेश आसीदार्याणाम्। विस्तृतौ हीमौ देशौ गान्धारो मद्रश्च पुराणभारतादिभ्योऽवगम्येते। तत्रैते मद्रा गान्धारत: संलग्नप्राया: पश्चिमोत्तरदेशा: स्यु:। तथा चैतस्य मद्रस्याद्यतनयोरिस्पहान-तिहरानयोर्नगरयो: प्रदेशे पुरात्वे सन्निविष्टतया

तावत्प्रदेशपर्यन्तं भारत-वर्षमासीदिति विज्ञायते। तत्र च काप्यस्य यज्ञवेदाध्यापकस्य निवासस्तेषां देशानामार्यनिवासभूमित्वं चोपपद्यते।

Some ancient people use the term Madra mistakenly for Bhutan, situated between Nepal and China. Some contemporary scholars, erroneously, also call the regions of Iravati and Chandrabhaga rivers as the Madra region. This is a figment of their imagination. These imaginations have risen due to the mistaken notion of Sindhu river being situated at the western border of Bharatavarsha; it is not correct. The Madra countries should be considered along with other countries like Gandhara, Bisapik, Pisanav, Shaka, Yavana, Parada and Kamboja, which are located to the north of Bharatavarsha. The Madra countries are also, like those countries, proven to be situated in the western region of Sindhu. The famous country named Midiya situated to the 20° west of river Sindhu is North Madra. Gandhara, situated at its south-west, is attached to South Madra. Afghanistan of present times was Gandhara in ancient times and Persia of today was Madra of ancient Arya.

In ancient times, both these grand countries were known as Madra and Gandhara by the people who lived in Bharatavarsha. To the north-west of this Gandhara was Madra. In ancient times, this Madra was situated in the regions of Orispahan and Tiharan cities and that is why it is clear that the boundaries of ancient India had spread to that country. Since there lived a great scholar of yajnaveda named maharshi Kapya there, it is proven that those countries were part of the Arya land.

1.3.1.8 अष्टमं प्रमाणम्-यवनदेशस्य भारतवर्षीयपश्चिमसीमात्वाख्यानम्

1.3.1.8 The Eighth Evidence—Yaman was the western border of Bharatavarsha

अद्यत्वे यवनशब्दस्य अर्वदेशप्रान्तविशेषे यमनदेशे संकोचः । किरातानां पूर्वसीमात्वं यवनानां पश्चिमसीमात्वं भारतवर्षस्य पुराणेष्वाख्यायते। यथा मात्स्ये-

Today the word Yavana is limited to identifying one particular region named Yemen. The ancient Puranas locate Kirats in the eastern border and Yavanas on the western borders of the country.

योजनानां सहस्रं वै द्वीपोऽयं दक्षिणोत्तरः ।
आयतस्तु कुमारीतो, गङ्गायाः प्रवहावधिः ।।

(मत्स्यपुराणम्, 114.9-10)

As it is mentioned in the 114th chapter of Matsya Purana—This island from south to north is spread over one thousand yojana (about 8000 miles) from Kanyakumari to the Ganges.

द्वीपो ह्युपनिविष्टोऽयं म्लेच्छैरन्तेषु सर्वशः ।
यवनाश्च किराताश्च तस्यान्ते पूर्वपश्चिमे ।।
(मत्स्यपुराणम्, 114.9.11)

The tip of this island was colonized by the mlecchas while Kirats lived on the eastern side and Yavanas lived on the western part of the island.

योजनानां सहस्रं वै द्वीपोऽयं दक्षिणोत्तरम् ।
पूर्वे किराता यस्यान्ते पश्चिमे यवनास्तथा ।।
(मार्कण्डेयपुराणम्, 54.7-8)

In the fifty-fourth chapter of Markandeya Purana, it is said: This island is spread over 1000 yojana from south to east. On the far east, it is populated by Kirats and the Yavanas live on its western side.

Situated in Arab country, Yaman is a place near the Red Sea. It is divided into five parts—Yaman, Hejaj, Tihama, Nejad, and Emama. The people of Bharatavarsha call the region Yaman. The region situated on the coastal boundary of the Mediterranean Sea, and with common borders, are also known as Yavana region. Secondly, the word Yavana refers not only to the people of Yunan (Parak) Greece but is also used in the *aryagrantha* (Arya texts) for the Yahudi community which lived in the Yahudiya region, a city near Jerusalem.

1.3.1.8.1 यवनशब्दस्य मुसलमानजातिपरत्वप्रत्याख्यानम्

1.3.1.8.1 Yavana is not connected to Muslim community

यत्तु यवनशब्दोऽयं मुसलमानजातिपरः । सन्ति हि सिन्धोरत्यासन्ने काबुलादिप्रदेशे पठानजातीयानां भूयांसः सन्निप्रवेशाः । तदभिप्रायेणैव च 'पश्चिमे यवनाः स्थिताः' - इत्यादि वचनोपपत्तिरिति सिन्धुनद एवैतस्य भारतवर्षस्य पश्चिमसीमा निष्कृष्यत इति केचिदाहुः-तत्तुच्छम्। मुसलमानानां चतुर्दशशताब्द्या अर्वाचीनतया पुराण-निर्माणकालस्य च चतुःसहस्राब्द्या अप्यधिकप्राचीनतया पौराणिकभुवनकोशे मुसलमानाभिप्रायेण यवनशब्दप्रयोगासंभवात्। पुराणनिर्माणकाले च गान्धारमद्रादिदिशे आर्याध्युषिता एवासन्निति महाभारतादिप्राचीनग्रन्थेऽवसीयते। तस्मात्सिन्धुनदोपलक्षितप्रान्तस्य भारतसीमात्वं नोपपद्यते।

Sometimes the word Yavana is used for Muslims. People of Pathan community lived in Kabul and other regions near river Sindhu. The statements about Yavanas that they live in the west were in reference to these communities. But it was an erroneous concept because the Puranas were created more than 2000 years ago and Islam came into existence only 1400 years ago and it was therefore impossible that the term Yavana could have been used for Muslims in the ancient dictionaries.

1.3.1.8.2 यवनशब्दस्य युहूदियाप्रान्ते निरुढ़िः

1.3.1.8.2 Yavana referred to Yehudiya region

पुरायुगे यवनशब्दस्य कैलडियापश्चिमतो युहूदियाप्रान्ते निरूढिः

अवश्यं चास्मिन् पश्चिमे भारते इराकदेशापरपर्यायः कैलडियाप्रदेशः कालकेयासुरगणाध्युषितः पुराकालादेवैतन्मद्रदेशात् पश्चिमतोऽनार्यगणाध्युषित आसीदतिप्राचीनग्रन्थेभ्योऽवगच्छामः । लङ्कावासिरावणकुम्भकर्णसोदरभगिन्याः शूर्पणखाया अस्मिन्नेव कैलडियाप्रदेशे कालकेयासुरतो विवाहसंबन्धस्य रामायणे व्याख्यायतत्वात्। ततोऽपि पश्चिमतोऽयं यहूदियाप्रदेशः प्रतिपद्यते। त ऐवैते यहूदीसंज्ञयाऽद्यत्वे प्रसिद्धा जातिविशेषा आर्यग्रन्थेषु यवना इत्युच्यन्ते स्म। यत्तु –

म्लेच्छा हि यवनास्तेषु सम्यक् शास्त्रमिदं स्थितम् ।
ऋषिवत् तेऽपि पूज्यन्ते किम्पुनर्दैवविद् द्विजः ।।

(बृहत्संहिता, 2.32)

After reading ancient books, it seems that people called Sur from the Kalkey community populated the Calidea region, which is synonymous with Iraq located west of Bharatavarsha. Therefore it could be surmised that the Anaryas lived in the western part of Madra country in ancient times. It is depicted in the Ramayana that Shurpanakha, the sister of Ravana and Kumbhakarna of Lanka, got married to an asura from Kalkey community of Calidea region. It also proves that Yehudiya region is situated in the west. In the Arya texts, people of Yehudiya community were called the Yavanas.

It is described in the Brihat Samhita, quoting sage Garga: Yavanas reside in mlechha country where this *shastra* (*jyotisha* or astrology) is known in *samyaka* form. Therefore, if those people could be respected like sages, what should be the status of the jyotisha-knowing brahmins!

इति गर्गोक्तेर्ग्रीसापरपर्याययूनानदेशवासिवचनोऽयं यवनशब्द इति केचिदाहुः, तत्रोच्यते। संभवति हि ग्रीकजातीयानामिवैतेषां यहूदीजातीयानामपि ज्योतिर्विद्यायां नैपुण्यमिति नैतावता यवनशब्दस्य यहूदीवचनत्वं शक्यमपवदितुम्। वराहमिहिरहस्याप्यत्रैव देशे ज्योतिर्विद्यालाभस्यानुमानात्।

अथवा सिकन्दरराज्यकाले तत्कर्मचारितया बहवो यवना इह निवसन्ति स्म। तेभ्य एवास्य वराहमिहिरस्य ज्योतिर्विद्यालाभः संभाव्यते। कालनेमिनामा यवनोऽपि कृष्णद्वेषी मथुरावरोधको न ग्रीसदेशीयो यवनः। किन्तु यहूदीय एवायं स्यादिति संभाव्यते। अस्या एवं जातेः परिवर्तेन मोहम्मदजन्मोत्तरकाले मोहम्मदमतग्रहणनिबन्धो मुसलमानकुल-प्रादुर्भाव इति प्रतीयते। त इमे यवना लोहितसागरभूमध्यसागरयोः प्राक्कूलोपलक्षितप्रान्ते प्रायेण पुरात्वे वसन्ति स्मेति यवनानां भारतवर्षीयपश्चिमसीमास्थत्वं साधूपपद्यते। यत्तु-अद्यत्वे अर्वदेशस्य दक्षिणपश्चिमप्रान्तमात्रे कनीयसि प्रदेशे यमनशब्दो व्यवहृतो दृश्यते तदिदमन्यान्यजातीयपरराजक्रान्तिनिबन्धनादेषां यवनानां पराभवादस्य यवनदेशस्य संकोचमात्रं प्रतिपद्यते ।

Following this statement of Garga, some people say that the word 'Yavana' is used for the people of Yunan country. In this context, it is said that: It seems that Yahudi people were as perfect in astrological study as the Greeks. But it does not mean that the word 'Yavana' is connected with the Yahudi people. It is believed that Varahmihira studied astrology here. It may be right. Many Yavanas lived here during the reign of Alexander. Varahmihira might have had the opportunity to study astrology from them.

During ancient times, the Yavanas lived in the eastern part of the Red Sea and the Mediterranean Sea. From this, it is clear that they lived on the western boundary of Bharatavarsha. Presently, the country called Yemen is situated on the south-west boundary of Arab country. The word Yavana seems to be a distortion of the original word due to invasions by rulers of different lineage.

1.3.1.9 नवमं प्रमाणम् - तूरसपर्वताभिप्रायेण आदर्शपर्वतस्य भारतीयपश्चिमसीमात्वाख्यानम्

1.3.1.9 The Ninth Evidence—Turas and Adarsh mountains as the western limits of Bharatavarsha

अपि चार्यावर्तस्य चतुःसीमानिर्देशं कुर्वता भगवता व्याकरणमहाभाष्याकारेण 'प्रागादर्शात्, प्रत्यक् कालकवनात्, दक्षिणेन हिमवन्तमुत्तरेण पारियात्रम्'-इत्युक्तम्। तत्रायमार्यावर्तशब्द उपलक्षणमार्यायणस्यापि। आर्योपनिवेशस्याभिप्रेतत्वेन दाक्षिणात्यभागरहितयोः पौरस्त्यपाश्चात्ययोर्भारत विभागयोः सहैवात्र विवक्षितत्वात्। तथा च-तत्रादर्शशब्दस्य भूमध्यसागरोत्तरप्रान्तस्थतारसपर्वतवाचितया, सिनाइपर्वतापरपर्याय-तूरसपर्वताभिप्रायतया वा प्रतिपत्तिः कार्या। समुद्रेण यहूदियाख्ययवनदेशेन च तस्यादर्शस्य तुल्यदेशत्वात्। यत्तु आदर्शशब्देन सिन्धु-नददक्षिणकूलस्थं सुलेमानपर्वतं केचित्कल्पयन्ति तन्न युक्तम्। पश्चिमसीमात्वेनोपदिष्टयोः समुद्रयवनदेशयोस्तत्रोपसत्त्यभावात्। अक्षरसाम्येन तारसस्य तूरसस्य वा सिनायिपर्वतस्यऽऽदर्शत्वेन प्रतिपत्तुं युक्तत्वाच्चेति दिक्।

In *Vyakarana Mahabhashya*, the profound commentator and linguist, Panini says: 'The *Aryavarta* (land of the Arya) had four boundaries. On its east was Adarsh Parvat, on the west was Kalak *vana* (forest), in the south was the Himalayan mountains and in its north, Pariyatra. Here the word Aryavarta signifies the sub-feature of the word called Aryayan. Since the Arya dominated the eastern and western parts of Bharatavarsha, the far southern part is not referred to here. And the word Adarsh may mean to be the name of Taras (Turas) mountain as well as the other name for the Sinai mountains. It is useful to understand that Adarsh Parvat is far from the sea and the Yaman country named Yehudiya. Some people believe that Suleiman mountain is on the southern coast of the Sindhu river but it is not right because the sea described in the western boundary and the Yavana country are not near to each other. Thus, it is reasonable to refer to the Sinai mountains as Adarsh Parvat due to the similarity of the letters of Taras and Turas Parvat.

1.3.1.10 दशमं प्रमाणम्-लौहपुरस्य पृथ्वीलोकस्थत्वाख्यानम्

1.3.1.10 The Tenth Evidence—Lauhpur in Prithiviloka

1.3.1.10.1 त्रैपुराख्यानम्

1.3.1.10.1 On Tripura

श्रौतग्रन्थे ब्राह्मणाख्ये पुराणे, मत्स्यादौ वा त्रैपुराख्यानमुक्तम् ।
तत्रैकस्याः सामदेशस्थपुर्याः पृथ्वीत्वोक्तिर्विद्यतेऽन्यत्प्रमाणम् ।।320।।

There is a reference in the Brahmana Purana and Matsya Purana to Tripurakhyan or discourse on Tripur. Here, a city situated in Samadesha is described as Prithvi. This is also an evidence.

1.3.1.10.2 असुरविभागविशेषस्य मयसंज्ञा

1.3.1.10.2 Different classes of asura and Maya

अनेकधा प्रागसुरा बभूवुर्वर्गैर्विभक्ता भुवि तेषु कश्चित् ।
वर्गो मयो नाम गतः प्रसिद्धिं मायाव्ययं भूरि चकार मायाम् ।।321।।

In ancient times, the asuras residing on the earth were divided into many classes. One of the classes was Maya, which was famous for its power of magic and illusion. They performed many magical and illusionary tricks.

बहूनि वीर्याणि कलाश्च बह्व्यो, बह्व्योऽत्र विद्याश्च विभूतयश्च ।
आसीन्मयानामिह संनिवेशः समुद्रकूले यवनप्रदेशे ।।322।।

Living in the Yavana region near the sea, this strong Maya class had many wonderful skills. It had learnt various arts and pursued different studies.

मयसोपोटेमीति प्रसिद्ध एषोऽस्ति वो देशः ।
तत्र मयानामेषां वसतिः संभाव्यते पूर्वम् ।।323।।

मयेषु कश्चित् त्रिपुरासुरोऽभूत् पुरत्रयं तेन विनिर्मितं प्राक् ।
त्रिष्वेषु लोकेषु पुरैस्त्रिभिस्तैर्देवानबाधन्त पुराऽसुरास्ते ।।324।।

There is also a possibility that Maysopotemia [Mesopotamia] could have been the residence of the Maya asuras. Among them, there was an asura named Tripur who was the first to establish Tripura—three cities. The asuras, who lived in these three cities, harassed the devas.

1.3.1.10.3 मयसम्बन्धित्रिपुरनिर्माणोत्तरं देवासुरेषु त्रिपुरनिर्माणप्रचारः

1.3.1.10.3 Maya-created Tripur attract devas and asuras

आसीत्सुराणां च पुरत्रयं पुरा यथासुराणां त्रिपुरं व्यधीयत् ।
कुतः स एकस्त्रिपुरासुरोऽभवत्, प्रसिद्ध इत्यत्र न वेद्मि कारणम् ।।325।।

In ancient times, like the asuras had *puratraya* (synonym for Tripura), the devas too had puratraya made. We don't know how Tripurasura became famous and how he got his fame.

मन्येऽसुराः सीम्नि सुरत्रिलोक्या दुर्गस्वरूपाणि पुराण्यमूनि ।
व्यधुः सुरैर्योद्धुममीषु वीरा आसन्निति ख्यातिविशेषहेतुः ।।326।।

I believe that cities in the form of forts were constructed [by the asuras] within the boundaries of the Divya trailokya with a purpose to wage war with the devas. Many warriors lived there and it was one of the main reasons for its popularity.

यतोऽथवा सर्वत एव पूर्वं मयासुरेण त्रिपुरं प्रणीतम् ।
ख्यातस्ततोऽभूत् त्रिपुरासुरोऽसौ पश्चात्परे त्रीणि पुराणि चक्रुः ।।327।।

It could also be possible that Tripur was constructed by an asura called Maya who then became famous as Tripurasura. Afterwards, many others constructed similar Tripuras.

राज्ञां तिस्रस्तिस्र आसंस्तदात्वे स्वर्गस्थानां चासुराणां च पुर्यः ।
तासामेकं धाम तन्मुख्यमन्यद्वैहारं स्यादत्रोपसत्स्यात् ।।328।।

At that time, the deva and asura kings ruled over their respective three cities. The first of these cities was used as their residence, the second as a place of pleasure and the third as a court.

किन्तु त्रेधा पूर्विधानप्रचारो यावन्नास्ति स्मासुराणां सुराणाम् ।
तस्मिन्पूर्वे काल एव प्रणीता दुर्गास्तिस्रः पुर्य एता मयेन ।।329।।

It is quite possible that only these three magical cities were constructed by an asura called Maya and the idea of constructing Tripurs did not attract either devas or asuras.

1.3.1.10.4 तारकस्य त्रयः पुत्राः

1.3.1.10.4 Three sons of Taraka

वज्राङ्गोऽभूद् वर्गपालो मयानां तारेत्याख्यां सोदधात् स्वान्वयस्य ।
युद्धे जित्वा दैवतेन्द्रं स तारस्तारस्याद्रौ स्वर्गसीम्नि न्युवास ।।330।।

There was another asura named Vajrang, born in the class of Maya, who named his son Tar. He defeated Indra and lived on the mountain of Taras.

तारो यस्मिन्पर्वते स्वयं निवासं कर्तुं राजा निर्ममे राजधानीम् ।
तारस्येति ख्यातिमागात्स शैलः शार्वे तीर्थेऽसौ महीसागरोदक् ।।331।।

As King Tar had set up his capital on this mountain, it became famous as Tarasya or Taras mountain. It is situated at a place called Sharva on the northern shores of the Mediterranean Sea.

वज्राङ्गस्यैतस्य तारस्य पुत्रो जज्ञे ख्यातस्तारकाख्यो वराङ्ग्याम् ।
पुत्रस्तस्याप्युद्बभूवुस्त्रयोऽग्र्या विद्युन्माली तारकाक्षोऽम्बुजाक्षः ।।332।।

King Tar had a queen named Varangi (a woman with beautiful limbs). She gave birth to three brave sons namely Vidyunmali, Ambujaksha and Tarakaksha.

संप्रत्यैश्यामायिनर्नामतो यो देशस्तस्मिन् शार्विकं नाम तीर्थम् ।
आसीत्कुले यन्महीसागरस्य क्षेत्रं प्राहुस्तत्पुरा तारकस्य ।।333।।

In a place known today as Asia Minor, there is a pilgrim site called Shavika. In ancient times, this region near the coast of Mediterranean Sea was known as Taraka's area.

स्कान्दमहेश्वरखण्डे द्वाविंशे यः कुमारिकाध्याये ।
उक्तो महीसमुद्रस्तमिमं भूमध्यसागरं विद्यात् ।।334।।

One should know that Mediterranean Sea is referred to as Mahi Samudra in the twenty-second Kumarika Adhyaya of Maheshvara Khanda in the Skanda Purana.

1.3.1.10.5 सामनाम्ना मयेन दैवत्रैलोक्ये त्रिपुरनिर्माणम्

1.3.1.10.5 Maya named Sam built Tripur in divya trailokya

तारः स्वर्गं जेतुकामोऽन्यमेकं शिल्पिश्रेष्ठं स व्यनैषीन्मयं प्राक् ।
वज्राङ्गेणाभ्यर्थितो निर्ममेऽसौ त्रैलोक्यान्ते त्रीणि मायापुराणि ।।335।।

With an objective to conquer svarga, King Tar asked his best architect Maya to construct three magical cities at the end of the triadic world.

नास्य त्रिपुरविधातुः स्मरन्ति नामेतिहासविदः ।
मन्ये सामेत्याख्यां देशस्यैतस्य सामत्वात् ।।336।।

Historians do not know about the creator of Tripur, but I believe that his name was Sam and that is why there is a country named after him.

पृथ्व्यामासीदायसी पूरथासीन्मध्ये लोके राजतीपूरमीषाम् ।
सौवर्णी पूः स्वर्गलोके कृतोऽऽसीन्मायादुर्गास्ते त्रयोऽयैरजय्याः ।।337।।

There was an iron city on the earth, in the middle was a silver city and a city of gold was constructed in the heaven. These cities were impregnable and could not be conquered by anyone.

तूरस्यार्देर्द्रक्षिणोपत्यकायां पृथ्व्यामासीदायसी पूरभेद्या ।
सौवर्णी पूस्तारसे तारशृङ्गे दैवस्वर्गप्रातिकृत्येन क्लृप्ता ।।338।।

On earth, at the southern base of the Turasya mountains was an invincible city of iron. On the peak of the Taras mountain, a city of gold was constructed to compete with the one created by the devas in heaven.

1.3.1.10.6 महीसागरकूले मध्यमा राजती पुरी

1.3.1.10.6 City of silver in the middle of Mediterranean Sea

तासामासीन्मध्यमा त्रैपुरीयं यामद्यत्वे प्राहुरेके त्रिपूलीम् ।
भूमध्याब्धेः पूर्वकुलेऽन्तरिक्षे द्यावाभूमिस्पृक्पुरी राजती सा ।।339।।

चतुस्त्रिंशोदगक्षांशे चतुर्विंशतिसाधिके ।
त्रिपुरी द्वादशोनेंऽशे षट्त्रिंशे ग्रीनवीचतः ।।340।।

Between these two cities was the city of silver, Rajatinagari, which is presently known as Tripuli. This silver city which touched Dyauloka and Prithviloka was situated on the eastern coast of the Mediterranean Sea in the space located between Dyauloka and Prithviloka. This tripuri is situated at 34° north latitude from Ujjaini and at 34° and 48 kala (a measurement of time or 60 in number) north latitude from Greenwich.

देशान्तरांशके चत्वारिंशे पञ्चकलोनके । (उज्जैनत: पश्चिमे ।।)
उज्जयिन्या: पश्चिमतोऽस्त्यासुरी त्रिपुरी पुरी ।।341।।

It is situated at 39° and 55 kala from the west of Ujjaini.

1.3.1.10.7 प्रतिपुष्यं त्रिपुरसमागम:

1.3.1.10.7 Merger of three cities at Pushya nakshatra

मध्यमपुरे पञ्चत्रिंशे त्रिपुरसमागम:

पुर्यस्तिस्रोऽप्यन्तरिक्षेन्तरिक्षे पुष्ये पुष्येऽन्योन्यसंयोगमाप्ता: ।
एकीभूता: संभवन्ति स्म तस्मादेकाप्येषा त्रैपुरीति प्रसिद्धा ।।342।।

At the time of Pushya nakshatra, these cities merged with one another and formed one city in space. This combined city was known as Tripuri.

चित्रं मध्या राजती सान्तरिक्षेऽप्यन्तर्भूम्यां लीयते गुह्यलक्ष्म्या ।
स्वैरं सद्य: सा निराधारमूर्ध्वं स्थातुं शक्याऽऽश्चर्यशिल्पप्रणीता ।।343।।

Surprisingly, the city of silver situated in the middle of antariksha could become invisible through *gudhh laksmi vidya* (a mysterious art of camouflage). It was created with such a unique technique that it could exist independently in the sky.

तस्या एवोपह्वरे दक्षिणस्यामायस्यन्या संनिधत्ते क्वचित्पू: ।
अन्या हैमी चोत्तरस्यामुपैतीत्याश्चर्यं तास्तिस्र एका पुरी स्यात् ।।344।।

On the southern side of this city of silver was the city of iron; the city of gold was located on its northern side. Surprisingly, these three cities could transform into one city called Tripuri during Pushya nakshatra.

यस्मात्ताभि: पूर्भिरेका पुरीयं पुष्ये पुष्ये जायते तेन सैका ।
मध्यस्थैव स्यात् त्रिपुर्याख्ययोक्ता देवैरस्यां युद्धमासीत् त्रिपुर्याम् ।।345।।

During Pushya nakshatra, the city which formed with the merger of these three cities was called Tripuri and here the asuras fought with the devas.

सेयं मुख्या त्रैपुरी नाम या पूस्तस्यामासीदम्बुजाक्षे मयः प्राक् ।
विद्युन्माली तारकाक्षोऽस्य दक्षे वामे पार्श्वे चोपपन्नो सहायौ ।।346।।

King Tar's son Ambujaksha is believed to have lived in Tripuri along with his two brothers, Vidhyunmali and Tarakaksha, who were also his close confidantes.

1.3.1.10.8 तारसादिशृङ्गे उत्तमा काञ्चनी पुरी

1.3.1.10.8 The fine city of Kanchani on top of Taras mountain

अस्यास्तूदक् पश्चिमे तारसाख्यो योऽद्रिस्तस्मिंस्तारकाख्यो मयोऽभूत् ।
कूटे हैमी तारकस्याभवत् पूः पामीराद्रेः पश्चिमे स्वर्गरूपा ।।347।।

In the north-west of Tripuri was the Taras mountain where lived a Maya named Taraka. The city of gold was situated on the Hemkut mountain, to the west of the Pamir mountains.

सप्तत्रिंशोत्तराऽक्षांशे तारसाख्योऽस्ति पर्वतः ।
त्रयस्त्रिंशे पूर्वदेशान्तरांशे ग्रीनवीचतः ।।348।।

This Taras mountain was situated at 36° north latitude and 33° east from Greenwich.

त्रिचत्वारिंशदधिके द्वाचत्वारिंशभागके ।
उज्जयिन्याः पश्चिमतस्तारसस्तत्र सा पुरी ।।349।।

The city called Taras was situated at 42° and 43 kala to the west of Ujjaini.

1.3.1.10.9 तूराद्रि-दक्षिणोपत्यकायां प्रथमा आयसी पुरी

1.3.1.10.9 First city of iron on the southern side of Tura

मध्या येयं त्रैपुरी पूरसूर्या दिश्येतस्या दक्षिणस्यामदूरे ।
पश्यामोऽन्यं पर्वतं तूरसंज्ञं लोका आहुर्यं सिनायीति नाम्ना ।।350।।

To the south of the asura city Tripuri was another mountain known as Tur, popularly known as Sinai.

अष्टाविंशोदगक्षांशे सार्द्धेऽयं तूरपर्वतः ।
चतुस्त्रिंशे दशोपेते पूर्व्यांशे ग्रीनवीचतः ।।351।।

This mountain is situated at 28-30° north latitude and 34° and 10 kala east from Greenwich.

त्रयस्त्रिंशत्कालाढ्यैकचत्वारिंशांशके स्थितः । (उज्जयिनीपश्चिमे)
उज्जयिन्याः पश्चिमतः सिनायी तूरपर्वतः ।।352।।

The Sinai mountain is situated at 41° and 33 kala to the west of Ujjaini.

1.3.1.10.10 पुरत्रयाध्यक्षाः त्रयस्त्रिपुरासुराः

1.3.1.10.10 Masters of Tripur

विद्युन्माली तूरशैलेयपुर्यामेकोऽध्यक्षो वीर आसीत्पृथिव्याम् ।
मध्ये सिन्धूपह्वरेत्वम्बुजाक्षः सर्वाध्यक्षोऽन्यश्च सामो मयोऽस्मिन् ।।353।।

Vidhyunmali was the head of the city of Turshail on earth. He was a strong warrior. In the middle, in the antarikshaloka near Sindhu river, Ambujaksha was the supreme head. A Maya named Sam lived there.

स्वर्गे त्वासंस्तारसाद्रिस्थपुर्यां धीरास्तारस्तारकस्तारकाक्षः ।
मुख्याध्यक्षास्तासु पूःर्षु त्रयोऽमी विद्युन्माली तारकोक्षोऽम्बुजाक्षः ।।354।।

Taras, Taraka, and Tarkaksha lived in a city on the Taras mountain in svarga. They were the chiefs of these three cities.

काञ्चनं तारकक्षस्य चित्रमासीन्महात्मनः ।
राजतं कमलाक्षस्य विद्युन्मालिन आयसम् ।।
(महाभारतम्, कर्णपर्व, 24.18)

This is clearly described in the twentyfourth chapter of 'Karna Parva' in Mahabharata. Tarakaksha was a superior warrior and he ruled the mysterious city of gold; Kamlaksha ruled over the silver city and the city of iron was ruled by Vidhyunmali.

मात्स्ये सूक्तं तारकाक्षोऽधिराजः कार्ष्णायस्यां रौप्यमयामधीशः ।
विद्युन्माली, हैमपुर्यां मयोऽस्थाद् यद्वा सर्वाधीश्वराः सर्व एते ।।355।।

In the Matsya Purana also, it is clearly mentioned that the ruler of city of iron was Tarakaksha, Vidhyunmali headed the city of silver and the asura named Maya owned the city of gold. It was believed that all of them were the heads of these cities.

1.3.1.10.11 पुरत्रयस्य देशान्तरसंचारित्वम्

1.3.1.10.11 All three cities were mobile

अन्तर्भूम्योऽन्तश्छदिभित्तयो वा शालाः सर्वा आयसैर्लोहपुर्याम् ।
हैम्यां हैमै राजते रौप्यामय्यां पट्टैः क्लृप्ता आशुयोज्यैर्वियोज्यैः ॥356॥

In the city of iron, all the rooms, the inner courtyard and the ceiling and walls were made of iron. In the golden city, they were made from the golden trees and in the city of silver, they were made from silver trees. These could be joined or separated quickly.

सर्वैरेतैरुद्धतैर्धातुपट्टैरेताः पुर्यो यत्र तत्रोपनेतुम् ।
शक्यन्ते स्मानेकधात्वं च नेतुं युद्धे वीरैरप्रधृष्या अभेद्याः ॥357॥

As these could be uprooted and de-assembled easily, these cities could be easily moved from one place to another and they were therefore indestructible. They could not be destroyed in wars.

पुष्ये पुष्ये चान्तरीक्षे त्रिपुर्यां विद्युन्माली स्वां पुरीं भूमिलोकात् ।
स्वर्गाल्लोकात् तारकाक्षः पुरीं स्वां नीत्वैकास्यां पुर्यवस्थानामेताम् ॥358॥

During the time of Pushya nakshatra, Vidhyunmali shifted his city from bhuloka and Tarakaksha moved his city from *svarnaloka* (the golden world) to Tripuri set up in the antarikshaloka.

ये वा भौमा आन्तरिक्ष्याश्च दिव्याः सर्वे वीराः संघशो ध्वंसयेयुः ।
सर्वैर्वीर्यैरेकहेलाप्रवृत्ताः न स्यादासामण्वपि क्वापि वृक्णम् ॥359॥

These cities thus became indestructible and even the combined might of divine warriors from all three worlds could not destroy them.

1.3.1.10.12 त्रिपुरस्य त्रिदुर्गतया तत्प्रजानां वीरत्वभाव:

1.3.1.10.12 The three forts made the citizens brave

आसन्नासु प्रायशो ये युवानो ये वृद्धा बालकाः याः स्त्रियो वा ।
योद्धारस्ते सर्वदा योद्धुकामा वाणिज्यार्थे शौर्यमेवात्र पण्यम् ॥360॥

All the residents of the city, whether young or old, men, women, or children, all were gifted with valour and they were always ready to fight.

नार्हन्त्येषामन्यदेशीयलोकाः पूर्दुर्गाणां गोपुरान्तः प्रवेशम् ।
अन्तस्तेषां राजमार्गे प्रतोल्यां बेत्याखड्गस्येव धारावगाहः ।।361।।

Outsiders were barred from entering the city. Entering the highways or lanes within the city was as dangerous as walking on the sword's edge.

1.3.1.10.13 पुरत्रयभङ्गहेतुश्छिद्रम्

1.3.1.10.13 Ways to destroy these three cities

आसीत् त्वासां छित्तये छिद्रमेकं यस्मिन्काले जायते पुष्ययोगः ।
तस्मिन्काले तिस्र एतास्तु पुर्यः संयुक्ताः स्युस्तत्र चैकापुरी स्यात् ।।362।।

There was only one way to destroy these three cities. These cities merged into one city during the time of Pushya nakshatra.

तस्मिन्पुष्ये वीर एकः पुरीस्तास्तिस्रोऽप्येकेनेषुणाऽवारपारम् ।
भेत्तुं सद्यः शक्नुयाच्चेत् ततस्ता विध्वस्ताः स्युर्नान्यथा ध्वंस आसाम् ।।363।।

During this period, at a specific moment, if a warrior were to pierce an arrow through them, these cities could be destroyed. There was no other way to destroy these cities.

देवा एतद् ध्वंसनोद्योगिनोऽपि च्छिद्राज्ञानान्नात्र शक्ता बभूवुः ।
इन्द्रं तारस्तारकस्त्वेष विष्णुं युद्धे सार्द्धं सर्वदेवैर्न्यगृह्णात् ।।364।।

Though the deities made every effort to destroy the cities but in vain as they lacked the know-how of using a single arrow to pierce all three cities at once. In this war, asura Tar imprisoned Indra and another asura named Tarak imprisoned Vishnu along with all other gods.

1.3.1.10.14 असुराणां स्वर्गविजये ब्रह्मविष्टपस्य तातारतूरानादिनामभिर्व्यपदेशः

1.3.1.10.14 On asura victory over svarga, Brahma-vishtapa became Tatar and Turan

तारास्तूरैः साकमेकीभवन्तो देवान् जित्वा संनिवेशं स्वमापुः ।
ते तं देशं तारतूरेति नाम्ना ख्यातं चक्रुश्चोभयेषां स देशः ।।365।।

The asuras of Tar joined hands with the Turs and returned home victorious after defeating the devas. The country became famous by the name of Tar Tur because both these classes ruled there.

तारतुरस्तारतरस्तातार: स: क्रमात् प्रसिद्धोऽभूत् ।
तूरास्तत्र तुरुष्कास्तुर्कीतूरांश्च तत्प्रान्ता: ।।366।।

Eventually, the country came to be known as Tar, Tur, Tartar, and Tatar. People named Tur and Turushk resided in the regions called Turan and Turki respectively.

स्वर्गे त्रिविष्टिपेऽस्मिन् यावदिव ब्रह्मविष्टपं प्रथितम् ।
तत्तूरानिति कथितं संप्रति तातारदेशश्च ।।367।।

The part known as Brahmavishtapa in Svarga Chitravishtapa came to be known as Turan. This country is presently known as Tatar.

तारोऽत्युच्च: पृथ्व्यां यो देश: सर्वथोच्चतर आसीत् ।
तारतर: स प्रथितस्तातारं तं विदुर्म्लेच्छा: ।।368।।

A higher place on the earth was known as Tar and the place even higher than that was called Tartar. The mlechha people call this place Tatar.

तातारोऽयं दिव्यलोक: पुरासीद् देवान् जित्वा तत्र चोषुस्तुरुष्का: ।
चीनात् प्रत्यक् प्राग् महीसागरान्तात् तारैस्तूरैर्देश आक्रान्त एष: ।।369।।

In ancient times, there was a divyaloka called Tatar where people named Turushk came to live after they defeated the deities. The people named Tar and Tur dominated this country which was situated across west of China and east of the Mediterranean Sea.

तारासुरवंशधरैस्तारातम्बोलनाम्नेयम् ।
नगरी विनिर्मिता प्राक् साद्यापि तु राजधान्यस्ति ।।370।।

In ancient times, the successors of Tarasur established a city called Tara Thambol, which continues to be a capital city even today.

प्राग्मेरुर्यो ब्राह्मो देश: पामीर उच्यतेऽद्यत्वे ।
तत्रेदानीं म्लेच्छा वसन्ति देवानितो विनिष्कास्य ।।371।।

The abode of Brahma, Pragmeru, is known today as Pamir. The mleccha people threw out the deities and live there today.

य: प्राक् सुमेरुखण्ड: स समरकन्दोऽथ तक्षखण्डो य: ।
यश्चार्यखण्ड आसीत् स तासकन्दश्च यारकन्दश्च ।।372।।

Sumerukhand of the past is today known as Samarkand, and like Takshkhand has become Tashkant and Aryakhand as Yarkand.

मन्दरगिरिर्य आसीद् विलूरताग: स कथ्यतेऽद्यत्वे ।
य: शृङ्गवान् गिरि: प्रागलतायीत्युच्यते सोऽद्य ।।373।।

Vilurtag is the new name of Mandar and Alatayi is of Shringvan-giri.

इनशान् खिनधान् शैल: शैलोऽन्यो यावलोनोई ।
विरखोईयनस्कोई, स्तानोवोईति माल्यवच्छाखा: ।।374।।

Inshan, Khindan and other mountains like Yavlonoi, Virkhoi, Yanskhoi and Stanovoi are the branches of Malyavan ranges.

यो गन्धमादनाद्रि: पश्चिमसीमैशियाभूमे: ।
अद्यत्वे तं शैलं लोका यूरालनाम्नाऽऽहु: ।।375।।

The Gandhmadana mountain, situated on the western boundary of the Asian land, is presently known as Ural.

इत्थं तारास्तूरा अप्रथयन्नत्र तातारे ।
शेषाणां तु मयानां मयसोपोटेमियादेश: ।।376।।

In this way, Tar and Tur became famous as a country called Tatar. Remaining asuras lived in a country called Maysopotemia.

आसुरवर्ग उपोत्तमनाम्ना संभाव्यते पुरा कश्चित् ।
तत्सहवासादुक्तो मयसोपोत्तम इति बूम: ।।377।।

Possibly, there was another class of asuras known as Upotham. The place where they lived therefore came to be called Maysopotam.

1.3.1.10.15 पश्चिमभारतेऽसुरप्रवेश:

1.3.1.10.15 The asuras invade western India

कालकदौर्हृदमौर्याद्यसुरविभागास्तु यत्र देशेऽस्थु: ।
सोऽसीरियाप्रदेश: कैलडिया कालकेयानाम् ।।378।।

अन्यान्यराजसमये मेशोपोटेमिया इराको वा ।
प्रथित: स एव देशो मयराष्ट्रं सामदेशस्तु ।379।।

The place where three classes of asuras namely Kalaka, Dauhridh and Maurya lived was called the Assiriya region. Keladiya [Caledia] was the place where the asuras of Kalaka class lived. Mesopotamia and Iraq gained fame during different regimes and these countries came to be called Mayarashtra or Samadesha.

1.3.1.10.16 देवैः उपसन्नामकपुरत्रयनिर्माणम्

1.3.1.10.16 Creation of three forts called 'Upasat'

इत्थं स्वर्गे चान्तरिक्षे च पृथ्व्यां काँश्चिद्देशान् देवतादायभूतान् ।
धृष्टैरुग्रैश्चासुरैः संगृहीतान् दृष्ट्वा देवा व्यग्रचित्ता बभूवुः ।।380।।

The devas were upset by their misfortune of seeing the insolent and roguish asuras residing and dominating over some regions in Dyauloka, Antarikshaloka and Prithvi.

विद्युन्माली तारकाक्षोऽम्बुजाक्षः सामस्तारस्तारकः षड्भिरेतैः ।
आर्तान्देवान् रक्षितुं देवमुख्या दुर्गांश्चक्रुश्चोपसन्नामकाँस्त्रीन् ।।381।।

पृथ्व्यामग्निः सोम एषोऽन्तरिक्षे विष्णुः स्वर्गे चोपसत्स्वध्यवात्सुः ।
ताँस्त्रीन् देवाश्चासुराः षड्मयांस्तानाश्रित्य प्राग् घोरमामर्दमापुः ।।382।।

The presiding deities then constructed three forts called 'Upasat' to protect the devas harassed by the asuras namely Vidyunmali, Tarakaksha, Ambujaksha, Sama, Tara and Taraka. Agni, Soma, and Vishnu resided in these upasats on the earth, interspace, and heaven respectively. The deities protected by these three gods and the asuras supported by six Maya asuras fought a frightful war against each other.

1.3.1.10.17 त्रयम्बकेण त्रिपुरध्वंसः

1.3.1.10.17 Destruction of Tripur by Shiva

पश्चाच्छम्भुः किञ्चिदुग्रं विचित्रं ब्रह्माण्डाभं स्यन्दनं कारयित्वा ।
तत्रारूढः खेचरे खेचरेऽहन् दैत्यानेतान् पूस्त्रये युध्यमानान् ।।383।।

Shiva then built some big, strong, and mysterious chariots which could be seen from anywhere in the universe. Mounted on it, he fought in Tripur and killed the asuras as he moved around the sky.

घोरं युध्वा नन्दिना दैत्यराजो विद्युन्माली वज्रतो निर्हतोऽभूत् ।
दृष्ट्वा घोरामापदं तां मयोऽसौ वापीमस्यां मायया निर्मिमाय ।।384।।

Nandi and the army of Shiva fought valiantly against the asura king, Vidhyunmali. Seeing the horrible catastrophe inflicted on the asuras, Maya created a stream with the help of magic and illusion.

मृतसंजीवनीं वापीं तारकाक्षसुतो हरिः ।
विनिर्ममेऽमृतमयीं यो मज्जति स जीवति ।।385।।

Hari, the son of Tarakaksha, converted the stream into *mritasanjivani* (an elixir of immortality), which could heal even the most critically wounded.

दैवैर्युद्धे हन्यमानान् विपन्नान् वाप्यां स्नातान् जीवयामास भूयः ।
विद्युन्माली यो गतेऽह्नि प्रमीतः सोप्यन्येद्युर्योधयामास देवान् ।।386।।

Thus, the asuras, critically wounded in the war, cured themselves by diving into the stream. Even the dead asuras would come back to life with the touch of the waters of the magical stream. They would then return to the battleground to fight against the deities the next day.

युद्धेऽमीषां निर्हतानां मृतानां वाप्यां स्नातान्नित्यमुत्थानमित्थम् ।
दृष्ट्वा देवाश्चिन्तया व्यग्रचित्ता विष्णुं वापीध्वंसहेतुं व्यजानन् ।।387।।

This became a source of worry for the deities who saw the dead asuras regaining new life and vigour and fighting against them. They knew only Vishnu could destroy this stream.

विष्णुः कृत्वा वार्षभं रूपमुग्रं मायावापीं तां जगाम त्रिपुर्याम् ।
वापीबालाँश्चासुरान्मर्द्दयित्वा वापीं पीत्वा नर्द्दयन्नाजगाम ।।388।।

Vishnu took an extremely frightening form of Taurus and went to that magical stream, killed the asura guards and returned dancing after drinking up all the water in the stream.

वापीध्वंसाद् ध्वंसितोत्साहवीर्याः सर्वेऽभूवंस्त्रैपुरा दैत्यधीराः ।
मत्वा तत्रोपस्थितामापदं स्वां रक्षार्थं ते युद्धभूमेः परायन् ।।389।।

This put an end to the bravado of the asuras of Tripur. To protect themselves from immediate disaster, they tried hard to run away from the battlefield.

तेऽपक्रान्ता निन्युरेतां पुरीं स्वामूर्ध्वाकाशे द्राग् महीसागरस्य ।
तत्रैवागाच्छाम्भवं पृष्ठलग्नं तूर्णं दिव्यं स्यन्दनं सैन्ययुक्तम् ।।390।।

While running away from the battlefield, the frightened asuras carried their city to the interspace above the Mediterranean Sea. The great and divine chariot of Shiva, along with his army, followed them.

दिव्याश्चर्यं निर्मितं शिल्पिदेवैरारुह्योग्रोऽत्युग्रकर्मा रथाग्र्यम् ।
खस्थं शम्भुः खस्थितायां त्रिपुर्यां तांस्तान् वीरान् युध्यतो निर्जघान ।।391।।

This chariot of Shiva was constructed by brilliant architects among the deities. It was capable of facing most difficult and astonishing tasks. Mounted on it, Shiva destroyed all the asuras.

अत्याश्चर्यं खे चरन्तीः पुरीस्ता बाणेनैकेनाभिनत् पुष्ययोगे ।
पुर्योऽभूवँस्ता महीसागरेन्तर्मग्नाः भग्नाः पातिताः खण्डखण्डैः ।।392।।

Surprisingly, the city, which moved across the sky, was destroyed by an arrow piercing through it at the time of Pushya nakshatra. It broke into tiny particles which fell into the Mediterranean Sea.

पश्चादग्निर्दाहयामास भूयो हर्म्याण्येषामासुराणां पुराणाम् ।
तत्प्राकारा दग्धदग्धैरङ्गारैः सार्धं सिन्धौ प्रस्फुटद्भिर्निपेतुः ।।393।।

Thereafter, Agni burnt down all the palaces of asuras and the burning particles of the city's ramparts fell into the sea.

विद्युन्माली नन्दिना निर्हतोऽभून् निष्प्राणेऽस्मिंस्तेसुरा क्लैव्यमापुः ।
रक्षायास्तेऽन्यानुपायानदृष्ट्वा निस्तारार्थं तारमेवाभिजग्मुः ।।394।।

Vidhyunmali was killed by Nandi and the army of Shiva. After his death, all the asuras became restless and they sought protection from Tara.

तारो वीरः पुत्रपौत्रैः समेतो यावच्छक्यं युध्यमानः च पश्चाद् ।
दृष्टोत्साहभ्रंशमात्मीयसैन्ये भग्नाशः सन् युद्धतोऽस्माविरेमे ।।395।।

The warrior, Tara, with his sons and grandsons, fought bravely. But he was frustrated by the demoralised army and left the battlefield.

1.3.1.10.18 महीसागरोपरिष्टात् त्रिपुरासुरपलायनम्ः

1.3.1.10.18 Escape of Tripurasura from Mahisagar

आदायैकं स्वं गृहं सोऽपसृप्तोपक्रान्तोऽभूत् क्वाप्यविज्ञातदेशे ।
त्यक्त्वा पूर्वोदक् प्रदेशान् स दैवान्नैर्ऋत्येऽन्तेगान्महीसागरस्य ।।396।।

Tripurasura, with his family, secretly ran away to an unknown place. He fled towards the direction of Nerutya in the north-east region.

मिश्रे देशे नीलनद्याः परस्तादन्याप्येका दृश्यते पूस्त्रिपूली ।
मन्येऽनैषीद् भग्नशेषामिहैतां तत्स्मृत्यर्थं निर्ममेऽन्यां त्रिपूलीम् ।।397।।

There is another city called Tripuli on the banks of river Nile in the country named Misra [Egypt]. I believe they might have brought the devastated remains of Tripuli here and another Tripuli might have been constructed in the memory of the original.

भूमध्यसागरस्य प्राक् तटवद्दक्षिणेऽपि तटे ।
एकत्रिंशेऽक्षांशे त्रयोदशे ग्रीनवीचांशे ।।398।।

नष्टा यैषाऽभूत् त्रिपूली पुरीयं तस्याः स्थाने निर्मिताऽन्या त्रिपूली ।
इत्येकस्या अद्भुतायास्त्रिपूल्या ध्वंसात् पश्चाद् द्वे त्रिपूल्यावभूताम् ।।399।।

As happened on the eastern coast of the Mediterranean Sea, the Tripuli, which was destroyed, was replaced by another Tripuli. The demolition of this wonderful Tripuli led to the creation of two Tripulis.

इत्थं शर्वः सर्वमेषां मयानां राष्ट्रं जित्वा संन्यच्छत् सुरेभ्यः ।
यः प्रागासीत् सामदेशः स पश्चाद्देवाक्रान्तः सीरियेति श्रुतोऽभूत् ।।400।।

In this way, Shiva became victorious against the Maya asuras and gave their country to the devas. The country named earlier as Sama, after its defeat, came to be known as Syria.

1.3.1.10.19 तारकासुरसंग्रामः

1.3.1.10.19 The war with Tarakasur

तस्मिन् पश्चात्तारकोऽभ्येत्य भूयो युद्धं चक्रे तत्र बालः कुमारः ।
क्षात्रे वीर्ये पूर्णमात्रेऽभिषिक्तः पूर्णोत्साहोऽयोधयत् तारकं तम् ।।401।।

Tarakasur fought again and again but he was defeated by a confident child named Kartikeya who was made the chief of army.

जम्भक, जम्भ, कुजम्भा, कुञ्जर, महिषौ, च मेघ, शुम्भौ, च ।
निमि, कालनेमि, मथनास्तारकसेनासु नायकास्तु दश ।। 402।।

शृङ्गी, भृङ्गी, नन्दी, नन्दीशः, शङ्कु, कर्ण, रिटी ।

तुण्डी, शाख, विशाखौ, स्कन्दः स्कन्दस्य: नायकाः सैन्ये ।।403।।

Jambhaka, Jambha, Kujambha, Kunjar, Mahisha, Megh, Shumbha, Nibhi, Kalanemi, and Mathana were the chiefs in the army of Tarakasur. Shringi, Bhringi, Nandi, Nandish, Shanku, Karna, Riti, Thundi, Shaka, Vishakha and Skanda headed the army of Skanda.

शिशुरप्येष कुमारः स्कन्दोऽभ्यस्कन्दयन्महाप्रबलम् ।
तारकमेतं पश्चात् सर्वेऽप्यसुरा दिशो जग्मुः ।।404।।

Skanda, despite being a child, overthrew the strong warrior Tarasur and other asuras ran away to the ends of all four corners.

1.3.1.10.20 असुरराजविध्वंसे अपि असुरप्रजाविध्वंसाभाव:

1.3.1.10.20 Asura rulers defeated but not asura people

देवा यद्यपि विजयं प्राप्तास्त्रिपुरासुरान् हत्वा ।
न तथाप्यसुरविशस्ता इलावृतान्निर्हरन्ति स्म ।।405।।

Though the deities were victorious after killing the asuras, the latter remained unvanquished.

असुराक्रमणे देवानासुरधर्मेषु दीक्षयांचक्रुः ।
तेन न संप्रति देवा दृश्यन्तेऽभ्रश्यत स्वर्गः ।।406।।

The invasion of the asuras, however, introduced the asura dharma to the devas which led to the decline of the heaven and the subsequent extinction of the devas themselves.

1.3.1.10.21 प्रकरणोपसंहार:

1.3.1.10.21 In conclusion

इत्थं भूमावन्तरिक्षे दिवि प्राग् देवद्विड्भिः स्थापिता या नगर्यः ।
तासां भूमावायसीं पूरियं भूमध्याब्ध्यन्तं भारतं सुव्यनक्ति ।।407।।

In this way, the city of iron constructed on the earth, among the cities constructed by the enemies of deities on Prithviloka, Antarikshaloka and Dyauloka, prove that Bharatavarsha's frontiers reached as far as the Mediterranean Sea.

भूमिः पृथ्वी मानुषो लोक उक्तो मर्त्यं लोकं भारतं वर्षमाहुः ।
मर्त्ये लोके सा महीसागरप्राक्कूले भूमावायसी पूः प्रसिद्धा ।।408।।

This Bharatavarsha came to be known as Bhumi, Prithvi, Manushyaloka and *Mrityuloka* (mortal world). The iron city was known to be situated on the eastern coast of the Mediterranean Sea on this Mrityuloka.

आद्वात्रिंशाक्षांशतोऽर्वाक् प्रदेशः पृथ्वीलोको मर्त्यलोको निरुक्तः ।
सप्तत्रिंशादुत्तरः स्वर्गलोको द्यावाभूम्योरन्तरे त्वन्तरिक्षम् ।।409।।

The region before 32° latitude is Prithviloka, which is also called Mrityuloka. The Śvargaloka is situated on the 36° north latitude and Antarikshaloka is situated in the middle part of the Dyauloka and Prithviloka.

पृथ्वीलोकं भारतं प्राहुरार्या लोकाध्यक्षत्वेन यत्राग्निरासीत् ।
तत्रैवासीदायसी पूस्ततो भूमध्याब्ध्यन्तं भारतं भावयामः ।।410।।

The Arya called Bharatavarsha as Prithviloka whose *lokadhyaksha* (master) was Agni and this is where the city of iron existed. That is why, the region which stretched to edge of the Mediterranean Sea is known as Bharatavarsha.

1.3.1.11 एकादशं प्रमाणम्-कुमारिकाद्वीपत्वाख्यानम्

1.3.1.11 The Eleventh Evidence—Nine islands of Bharatavarsha

नवानां भारतीयद्वीपानां मध्ये हिन्दुस्तानस्य नवमं कुमारिकाद्वीपत्वाख्यानं भारतवर्षस्य हिन्दुस्तानमात्रपर्यवसायित्वाभावे एकादशं प्रमाणम् ।

It is said that there are nine islands of Bharatavarsha and the ninth is Kumarikadvipa but it is misleading to consider Hindustan as India; this is the eleventh evidence.

अस्य भारतवर्षस्य दक्षिणोत्तरतः सहस्रयोजनत्वं भुवनकोशे निर्दिश्यते यथा मात्स्ये-

योजनानां सहस्रं तु द्वीपोऽयं दक्षिणोत्तरः ।
आयतस्तु कुमारीतो गङ्गायाः प्रवहावधिः ।।
(मत्स्यपुराणम्, 114.9-10)

As per the description given in Bhuvanakosha, Bharatavarsha is spread over one thousand yojana (one yojana = approximately 12 kms or 9 miles) from south to east. It is so written in the Matsya Purana (114): 'This island is spread in one thousand yojana from Kanyakumari in the south to the Ganges in the north.'

मार्कण्डेयेऽपि-

योजनानां सहस्रं वै द्वीपोऽयं दक्षिणोत्तरम् । (मार्कण्डेयपुराणम्, 54.7)

इति। अत्र योजनशब्दः क्रोशपरतया नेयः। तथा हि कुमारीशब्दः सिंहलद्वीपेऽपि वर्तते, स्कान्दे माहेश्वरखण्डीयकुमारिकाऽऽख्यानात्तथावगमात् सिंहलद्वीपश्चत्वारिंशदधिकसप्तमेंऽशे संनिविष्ट इति सोऽवधिर्दक्षिणो भाव्यः। गङ्गाप्रवाहारम्भस्तु षट्त्रिंशेऽक्षांशे। तथा च तयोरन्तरं साधिका अष्टाविशत्यंशाः स्युः। एकैकश्चाक्षांशो मीलतृतीयांशोपेतैरूनसप्ततिमीलैः सम्पद्यते। तेषामष्टाविंशतिगुणत्वे मीलानां द्विसहस्रप्रायतया तावानस्य दक्षिणोत्तरायामो निष्कृष्यते। मीलशब्दश्चार्द्धक्रोशकल्पे पथि निरूढः। तेन सहस्रक्रोशता सिद्धा। एतच्च मानं सिन्धोः पश्चिमतोऽपि लोहितसागरपर्यन्तमुपनीयते। मेशापोटेमियाप्रदेशस्यापि षट्त्रिंशदक्षांशप्रायत्वात्। यत्तु ब्राह्मादिषु

उत्तरेण समुद्रस्य हिमाद्रेश्चैव दक्षिणे ।
वर्षं तद् भारतं नाम भारती यत्र सन्ततिः ॥

(ब्रह्मपुराणम्, 17.1)

It is also described in the Markandeya Purana: This island is spread in 1000 yojana from south to north. Here the word yojana should be taken as *kosa* (two miles). That is why the word 'kumara' is right for the *Sinhaladvipa* (island of Sinhaladvipa) as clarified in the Kumarika-akhyana of Mahesvara-khanda in Skanda Purana. The island of Sinhaladvipa is situated between 7 and 40 kala and its boundary is believed to be in the southern direction. The root of Ganga is situated on 36° and the part between these two is more than 28°. A latitude is made up of 69⅓ miles. In this way, multiplying 69⅓ miles into 28, we get the distance of 2000 miles from north to south. The word 'mile' is conventionalised for the distance of half kosa. It can be the assumed distance between the western parts of Sindhu to the Red Sea because the region called Mesopotamia is situated at 36°.

It is written in the Brahma Purana that 'the great island called Bharatavarsha is situated between the Himalaya mountain in the north to the sea in the south. The people residing here are called Bharatiya (Indian).'

यच्च मात्स्यादिषु-

तिर्यगूर्ध्वं तुविस्तीणः सहस्राणि दशैव तु ।

(मत्स्यपुराणम्, 114.10)

इति निर्दिश्यते तत्र कालदोषाल्लेखप्रमादात् पाठभ्रमः संभाव्यते। दशसहस्रसंख्यायाः सर्वथा प्रत्यक्षविरुद्धत्वात् पूर्वापरस्वोक्तिविरोधाच्च। अथवा वर्गात्मकक्रोशानामयमुल्लेखः संभाव्यते। तथा च पूर्वपश्चिमतो नवत्यंशतया साधिकत्रिसहस्रक्रोशमितं दक्षिणोत्तरतस्तु साधिकाष्टाविंशत्यंशतया

सहस्रक्रोशमितं चेदं भारतवर्षमिति स्थितम्। यदि तु निरक्षदेशाद् व्यवतिष्ठते। तदा षट्त्रिंशदंशतया ततोऽप्यधिकं दक्षिणोत्तरायामः सिध्यतीत्यूह्यम्।

Likewise, it is described in the Matsya Purana: It is spread across 10000 kosa horizontally. There may be a difference of opinion due to *kaladosha* (misgivings) or sloppy writing. The number of 10000 for distance can be challenged. Possibly, this number referred to divisional kosa. In this way, Bharatavarsha, extending in 90° from east to west i.e. more than 3000 kosa, and 28° from south to north, is said to extend upto 1000 kosa. If we were to take a country located at 0° (zero) as a reference point, Bharatavarsha should be understood to spread over a distance of more than 36° south to north.

1.3.1.12 द्वादशं प्रमाणम् - तुरुष्कदेशस्य भारतवर्षीयोत्तरसीमात्वाख्यानम्

1.3.1.12 The Twelfth Evidence—Turushk desha as the northern boundary of Bharatavarsha

तथाहि - वायव्यादिषु भुवनकोशेष्विदं भारतवर्षं चतुःसीमातयाऽऽख्यातम् ।

पूर्वे किराता यस्यान्ते पश्चिमे यवनाः स्थितः ।
आन्ध्रा दक्षिणतो धीरतुरुष्कास्त्वपि चोत्तरे ।।

(वामनपुराणम्, 13.11)

The four boundaries of Bharatavarsha are described in the bhuvanakosha of Vayu Purana: [In Bharatavarsha] the Kirats are populated in the eastern boundary, Yavanas in the western boundary, Andhras in the southern boundary and the warriors called Turushkas in the northern boundary.

तुरुष्कस्थानं चेदानीं म्लेच्छभाषायां "तुर्किस्तान" इति तूरान इति तातार इति तारतार इति टारटरी इति चाख्यायते। तद् राजशासनद्वैविध्यादिदानीं द्विधा विभक्तं भवति। पौरस्त्यं पाश्चात्यं च। तत्र पश्चिमं तुरुष्कं राजशासनाधीनं पौरस्त्यं तु चीनराज्यान्तर्गतमिति भेदः । तयोः पौरस्त्यं पौरस्त्यभारतस्य पाश्चात्यं पाश्चात्यभारतस्योत्तरसीमा भवति। सिन्धुस्थानपारस्थानाभ्यां (हिन्दुस्थान ईरान) द्विधा विभक्तस्य भारतवर्षस्य साम्येनोत्तरतस्तुरुष्कस्थानोपगमात् तस्योत्तरसीमात्वं साधूपपद्यते। तथा च तुर्किस्तानस्य भारतोत्तरसीमात्वाख्यानात् सिन्धुनदपश्चिमानाम् अफगानिस्तान, ईराक, साम इत्यादीनामपि देशानां भारतसीमान्तर्भुक्तत्वमुपपद्यते। तथा चात्र श्लोकाः-

The words like Turushtakstan, Turan, Tatar, Tartar and Tartari in the mleccha language are derived from the word, 'Turashk'. Because of different regimes, Turashk was divided into two parts, east and west. The western part of it is administered by the Turushk state and the eastern by the China state. The eastern part of Turushk is on the northern boundary of eastern Bharatavarsha.

Due to the equal division of Bharatavarsha into Sindhusthana and Parasthana [Hindustan and Iran], western Turkistan is proved to be the northern border of Bharatavarsha. It is proper to believe that countries situated on the western part of river Sindhu, Afghanistan, Iraq and Saam, are within the boundaries of Bharatavarsha.

With reference to this, some hymns are presented here:

स्वर्गोन्तरिक्षं पृथिवीतिभेदाद् द्वीपस्त्रिधासीदिह यो विभक्तः ।
स एष संप्रत्यपि दैवयोगात् म्लेच्छैर्विभक्तोऽस्ति पुनस्त्रिधैव ।।411।।

'This island, as per the trailokya-prasanga [as described in this volume] and other ancient descriptions, was divided into three parts—Svarga, Antariksha and Prithvi. At present, the mlecchas have similarly divided the region into three parts.'

उदक्समुद्रानुगतोऽस्ति रूसः पूर्वापरौ तोयनिधी वगाह्य ।
तद्दक्षिणे भाति तुरुष्कदेशः पूर्वापरौ तोयनिधी वगाह्य ।।412।।

The country named Russia is situated on the coast of North Sea and is bound by sea on its east and west. The country called Turushk, bound by sea on its east and west directions, is situated to the south of Russia.

तद्दक्षिणे दक्षिणसागरेणानु भाषितं भारतवर्षमेतत् ।
पूर्वापरौ तोयनिधी वगाह्य ध्रुवं भवेदन्यविभागसाम्यात् ।।413।।

As described in ancient times, in many ways, Bharatavarsha is situated on the coast of southern sea, to the south of Turushk. It is also bound by the sea on its eastern and western borders.

रूसो द्विधास्ति द्विविधं तुरुष्कस्थानं तथा भारतवर्षमेतत् ।
सिन्धुस्थपारस्थविभागतोऽस्तु द्विधा तथाऽप्यस्ति तदेकवर्षम् ।।414।।

Thus, Russia is divided into two parts and the country called Turushk is also divided into two parts. Though Bharatavarsha is divided into two parts, namely Sindhusthana and Parasthana, it is a united and complete island.

1.3.1.13 त्रयोदशं प्रमाणम्-पश्चिमसमुद्रस्य भारतवर्षीयपश्चिमसीमात्वाख्यानम्

1.3.1.13 The Thirteenth Evidence—Western Sea as the boundary of Bharatavarsha

तथा हि इदं भारतवर्षं मार्कण्डेयादिभुवनकोशेषु दिक्त्रये समुद्रैः संवृतमाख्यायते ।

In the bhuvanakosha of the Puranas like Markandeya Purana, it is described that Bharatavarsha is bound by sea on three directions.

एतत्तु भारतं वर्षं चतुःस्थानसंस्थितम् ।
दक्षिणापरतो ह्यस्य पूर्वेण च महोदधिः ॥
हिमवानुत्तरेणास्य कार्मुकस्य यथागुणः ॥
(मार्कण्डेयपुराणम्, 54.58-59)

Bharatavarsha has four boundaries. On its south-west and east, there is an ocean and on its north there is the Himalayas like the string of a bow.

तत्र नायं नर्मदासंगमनीयः सह्याद्रिपश्चिमस्थः समुद्रो भारतवर्षस्य पश्चिमसीमा भवितुमर्हति। तस्य दक्षिणापथपश्चिमत्वेऽपि आर्यावर्तसाधारणभारतापेक्षया पश्चिमत्वाभावात्। मनुस्मृत्यादिषु त्वार्याणां प्रामाणिकशास्त्रेषु पूर्वतः पश्मितश्चार्यावर्तस्य समुद्रः सीमात्वेनाख्यायते-

आसमुद्रात्तु वै पूर्वादासमुद्राच्च पश्चिमात् ।
तयोरेवान्तरं गिर्योरार्यावर्तं विदुर्बुधाः ॥
(मनुस्मृतिः, 2.22)

To take the sea situated to the west of Sahyadri mountains and the confluence of Narmada river as the western boundary of Bharatavarsha is wrong. Though the sea is situated to the west of southern India, it is not in the west as per the concept of Aryavrat. It is described in genuine treatises like Manusmriti that Aryavrat was bound by the sea on its east and west directions. It is said by the scholars that Aryavrat is situated in the middle part of the two mountains and it is spread from eastern sea to western sea'.

एतेन विन्ध्यपर्वतादुत्तरवर्तिनोऽस्यार्यावर्तस्य पश्चिमतोऽवश्यं समुद्रेण भवितव्यम्। तस्मात् पारस्याखातसमुद्रो लोहितसमुद्रो भूमध्यसमुद्रश्चास्य पश्चिमेऽवधिः साधीयान् संभाव्यते।

As per this statement, there must be a sea to the west of Aryavrat. One should believe that the western boundary of Bharatavarsha is up to the Bay of Parasya (Persia), Red Sea, and Mediterranean Sea.

1.3.1.14 चतुर्दशं प्रमाणम्-भारतवर्षशब्दप्रयोगः

1.3.1.14 The Fourteenth Evidence—use of word Bharatavarsha

ईरान -विलोचिस्तानाफगनस्तानादिशब्दानां शासनक्रान्तिभेदमूलकत्वेनाव्यवस्थित्वात् तेषां गणितव्यव स्थितभारतवर्षशब्दप्रयोगप्रतिरोधकत्वासंभवश्चतुर्दशं प्रमाणम् ।

इह हि भुवनकोशे देशविभागाः द्विविधा निरूप्यन्ते- राज्यशासनव्यवस्थिताः भौगोलिकगणितव्यवस्थिताश्च। तत्र शासनकृतविभागा अनित्या अव्यवस्थिताः काले काले विभिद्यन्ते। ये देशा येन राज्ञा जीयन्ते, ते तदायत्तनामरूपाः पूर्वापेक्षया क्वचिदन्येन नाम्ना निर्दिश्यन्ते। अत एव तु भारतीयानामिमे गान्धारदेशा अफगानिस्तानशब्देन, हिङ्गला देशाः प्रथमं सुगदियानाम्ना, पश्चाद्बिलोचिस्ताननाम्ना व्यवह्रियन्ते स्म। पारस्थानमेव पर्सियाशब्देन, ईरानब्देन कैलडियाश्याब्देन असीरियाशब्देन ईरानशब्देन मेसोपाटेमियाशब्देन च काले कालेऽन्यान्यप्रान्तविभागैर्व्यवह्रियते स्म। वर्मात्र देशः पुरायुगे भारतवर्षीयदेशो मध्ययुगे हिन्दुस्तानात् पृथक् परिगणित आसीत्। स एव पुनरिदानीं युगे हिन्दुस्तानान्तर्गतो व्यवतिष्ठते। एतन्नियमानुरोधेनैवेदं पश्चिमभारतवर्षमिदानीं युगे भिन्नशासनहेतो राजपुरुषीयव्यवहारविशेषानुरोधाद् भारतवर्षनामतो विहीनमभूत्। हिन्दुस्तानमात्रे चेदानीं भारतवर्षशब्दः संकुचितोऽभूत्। किन्तु वस्तुगत्या नैतौ भारतवर्षशब्दहिन्दुस्तानशब्दो पर्यायवाचिनौ वर्तते। भारत वर्षीयप्राचीनभुवनकोशानुसारेण राजशासनव्यवस्थामनपेक्ष्य स्वातन्त्र्येण भौगोलिकगणितव्यवस्थया प्रशान्तसमुद्रमारभ्य लोहितसमुद्रभूमध्यसमुद्रपर्यन्तप्रदेशे भारतवर्षशब्दस्य नियतत्वात्। अथैतस्य सिन्धुस्थानपारस्थानाभ्यां द्वेधा विभक्तस्या सिन्धुस्थानस्य हिन्दुस्तानशब्देन व्यवह्रियमाणतया तस्य भारतवर्षीयप्रान्तविशेषत्वाच्च। नित्यं व्यवस्थितं चेदं संज्ञाकरणं राजशासनानामन्यान्यत्वेऽपि न कदाचिद्विचलितं भवति। अत एव पश्चिमभारतस्य अफगानिस्तान, खुरासान ईरान-इत्यादेर्हिन्दुस्तान त्वाभावेऽपि भारतवर्षत्वं नोपहन्यते। भारतवर्षस्य भूवृत्तपादरूपतया प्राचीनार्यशास्त्रे सिद्धान्तितत्वादिति सर्व सुस्थम्।

The coining of words like 'Iran', 'Afghanistan', and 'Baluchistan' were influenced by the change of regime or administration of these countries or regions. Such names are therefore inappropriate. These names therefore cannot take away the true meaning of the name Bharatavarsha because it is mathematically proper.

It is described in the bhuvanakosha of Bharatavarsha that the country can be divided into two. Firstly, it can be divided by the state for administrative purposes. Secondly as per topographical calculations, the division made by the state is improper, inconsistent, and changes from time to time. The king who wins the country desires to name it differently from its previous name. Thus, Gandhara, a part of Bharatavarsha, is called Afghanistan today while Hingala first became Sugadiya and later came to be known as Biluchistan [Balochistan].

From time to time, Parasthana was also called by the names of its provinces like Persia, Iran, Keladiya [Caledia], Assiriya, Iraq and Mesopotamia. Burma was once a part of Bharatavarsha but during the Middle Ages it ceased to be so. Due to these regime changes and the decisions of successive rulers, the term Bharatavarsha today refers only to a smaller part called Hindustan.

Contrary to popular belief, terms Hindustan and Bharatavarsha are not synonymous. If one were to ignore the political changes and rely only on topographical calculations, Bharatavarsha can be said to extend from the Pacific Ocean to the Red Sea and the Mediterranean Sea.

Keeping in mind the division of Bharatavarsha into Sindhusthana and Parasthana, the use of the word Sindhusthana for Hindustan showed that Hindustan was part of Bharatavarsha. Thus, the name Bharatavarsha is consistent and proper. Though regimes and rulers have changed, this name has remained unchanged. So even if countries on its western part like Afghanistan, Khorasan, and Iran are not part of Hindustan any longer, it does not repudiate the term Bharatavarsha. It can therefore be said that Bharatavarsha, in principle, was in the fourth part of prithvi as stated in the ancient arya shastras.

इत्थं चामीभिश्चतुर्दशभिः प्रमाणैः पूर्वस्यां दिशि चीनसमुद्रमारभ्य पश्चिमतो लोहितसमुद्रपर्यन्तं भारतवर्षस्य सीमा भवतीति सिद्धम्।

In this way, these fourteen criterions clearly prove that Bharatavarsha was bound by sea in the eastern direction of China to the Red Sea in the west.

इति भारतपरिचये सीमाप्रसङ्गः सम्पूर्णः ।

The section on territories in the Introduction to Bharatavarsha is concluded.

1.4. उपद्वीपप्रसङ्गः

1.4 NARRATIVE OF THE SUBCONTINENT

1.4.1 जम्बूद्वीपस्याष्टोपद्वीपभेदाः

1.4.1 Eight sub-islands of Jambudvipa

ननु ब्राह्म-मार्कण्डेय-मात्स्य-स्कान्दादिषु भुवनकोशेष्विन्द्रद्वीपादयो नवोपद्वीपा निरूप्यन्ते।

भागवतादिषु तु केषुचिद् भुवनकोशेषु ततोऽन्ये स्वर्णप्रस्थादयोऽष्टोपद्वीपा उच्यन्ते। तथा च विरोधः प्राप्नोति-इति चेन्न। इन्द्रद्वीपादीनां भारतीयोपद्वीपत्वेन, स्वर्णप्रस्थादीनां तु जम्बूद्वीपोपद्वीपत्वेनाख्यानाद् विरोधाप्रसक्तेः। तथा चोक्तं भागवते - "जम्बूद्वीपस्य च राजन्नुपद्वीपानष्टौ हैक उपदिशन्ति। तद्यथा-स्वर्णप्रस्थश्चन्द्रशुक्ल आवर्तनो नारमणको मन्दरहरिणः पाञ्चजन्यः सिंहलो लङ्केति।" (भागवतपुराणम्, 5.19.29-30)

In the Puranas of Brahma, Markandeya, Matsya and Skanda, nine sub-isles, including Indra island, are described. The mahapuranas like the Bhagavata Purana describe eight sub-islands including Swarnaprastha. The seeming contradiction between the two opinions can be resolved by understanding that Indra island is deemed part of the Indian subcontinent and Swarnaprastha is considered part of Jambudvipa.

The Bhagavata Purana says, 'O king, it is said that Jambudvipa has eight sub-islands. They are Swarnaprastha, Chandrashukla, Avartan, Narmanak, Mandaharina, Panchjanya, Sinhaladvipa and Lanka.'

एषां प्रचलितदेशभाषायां नामानि यथा-

(1) आवर्तनः - वर्तानिया - (इंगलैण्ड-स्काटलैण्ड-आयर्लैण्डादयः)
(अक्षांश उ. 51-58-उज्जयिन्याः पश्चिमदेशान्तरे 75-85)

(2) नारमणक - नारवे । स्वेदन।
(उ. अक्षांशे 59-70, उज्ज. देशा. पश्चि. 45-70)

(3) मन्दर - हरिणो-नोविया-जेम्ल्या ।
(उ.अ.71-78- उ.प.दे. 6/123)

(4) पाञ्चजन्यः - जापान-द्वीपसंघ।
(सांघालियन-जेसो-नीफन-सिकोक-क्यूसू) (उ.अ. 55-30, - उ.पू.दे. 40)
इति पञ्चभिर्जनैस्तस्योपपन्नत्वात् पाञ्चजन्यत्वम् ।

(5) चन्द्रशुक्लः - फीलीपायिन-द्वीपसंघः । चन्द्राय गन्धर्वराजाय पणिभिरुपायनीकृतत्वात् पण्युपायनस्य तस्य चन्दशुक्लत्वम् ।
(उ.अ. 10-18, - उ.पू.दे. 30)

(6) स्वर्णप्रस्थः - वोर्नियो-जावाद्वीपसंघः - सुमात्रा, सिंगापुर, पीनाङ्ग
(द.अ.10. - उ.अ. 16 उ.पू.दे. 10-25)
निकोवर, ऐन्दमन। इत्येतेषां भारतीयोपद्वीपसंघानां स्वर्णप्राचुर्योपलब्ध्या स्वर्णप्रस्थत्वम् ।

(7) सिंहलद्वीप - सीलोन, इति नाम्ना प्रसिद्धः ।
(उ.अ. 6-8- उ.पू.दे. 5)

(8) लङ्काद्वीपः - लक्केदीब, मालदीब - इतिद्वेधा विभक्तो नष्टप्रायः ।
(उ.अ. 1-12, - उ.प.दे. 5)

Their popular names are as follows—

Avartan–Britannia (England–Scotland–Ireland and other islands], [latitude north 51°-58°, longitude–western hemisphere);

Narmanak–Norway and Sweden (latitude north 59° and 70°, longitude north 54° and 70°)

Mandaharina–Nowiya–Jamlya (northern latitude 71°-78°–north-western longitude 6/123)

Panchjanya–Japanese archipelago (Sanghaliya–Jeso–Neefan–Sikok–Kuse), (northern latitude 55°-30°–north eastern longitude 40°). This island was discovered by five persons, hence it was named Panchjanya.

Chandrashukla–The Philippines archipelago. It was so named because the Panis gifted it to the Gandharva king Chandra. (northern latitude 10°–18°, north eastern latitude 30°)

Swarnaprastha–Borneo–Java archipelago including Sumatra, Singapore, Pinar, Andaman and Nicobar. These Indian sub-archipelagos were so called because of the golden ore available in plenty there. (northern latitude 10°–16°, north eastern latitude 10°-25°).

Sinhaldadvipa–popularly known as Ceylon (northern latitude 6°-8°, north eastern longitude 5°)

Lanka island is divided into Lakshadweep and Maldives (northern latitude 1°-12°, north eastern longitude 5°)

इदं तावद् भूगोलं पूर्वीयपश्चिमीयगोलार्द्धाभ्यां द्वेधा विभज्यते। तत्र पूर्वीयगोलार्द्धस्य जम्बूद्वीप इति संज्ञा क्रियते। अस्ति हि पूर्वगोलार्द्धस्य मध्यप्रदेशे हिरण्यपर्वतशृङ्गपर्वतान्निर्गत्य पश्चिमदिशि प्रवहन्ती अरालसमुद्रे प्रविशन्ती काचिन्नदी या वेदे यक्षुरित्याम्नाता।

The earth is divided into northern and southern hemispheres. The northern hemisphere is called Jambudvipa. A river descending from the Hiranya and Shringa mountains, situated in the middle of northern hemisphere, and flowing westward to merge with the Aral Sea, is called 'Yaksha.'

तदपभ्रंशेन च म्लेच्छभाषयाम्। 'अक्सस्'-इति साख्यायते। सैव पश्चात् संस्कृतभाषायां 'जम्बू' - इत्याख्यायत। तदपभ्रंशेन च म्लेच्छभाषायाम्-'अमू'-इत्याख्यायते। तादृशजम्बूनद्युपलक्षितः पामीरप्रदेश एवासीत् पुरात्वे पूर्वीयगोलार्द्धे प्रधानरूपः समृद्धतमः केन्द्रभूतः प्रदेशः। तत्रत्यानां देवयुगीयानामिह गोलार्द्धे एकतन्त्रं स्वाराज्यमासीदिति कृत्वा पूर्वीयगोलार्द्ध जम्बूद्वीपशब्देन प्रसिद्धमासीत्।

This river named Yaksha, because of linguistic corruption, came to be called Aksas in the mleccha language. The same river is known as Jambu in Sanskrit. The word Jambu is known as Amu in the mleccha languages. The region through which this Jambu (Amu) flowed, the Pamir region, was the most prosperous and important region in the northern hemisphere. The men inhabiting this region ruled the entire northern hemisphere in the devayuga. That is why the northern hemisphere was popularly known as Jambudvipa.

वर्तमानयुगप्रसिद्धौ एशिया-यूरोप-देशौ सोपद्वीपौ तस्मिन् पूर्वीय-गोलार्द्धे संनिविशेते। अफरीकाराष्ट्रेलिययोरप्यत्रैव संनिवेशं केचिदिच्छन्ति। तदसत्। सकोत्रा-मदगास्कार-प्रभृतीनामफरीकोपद्वीपानां पापुआप्रभृतीनामाष्ट्रेलियोपद्वीपानां च जम्बूद्वीपोपद्वीपतया भागवतादिष्वपरिगणितत्वात्। तस्मादफरीकाष्ट्रेलिययोर्जम्बूद्वीपाद्बहिष्ट्वमासुरद्वीपत्वं च प्रत्येतव्यम् ।

The present-day [the time when this book was written] Asia and Europe are parts of the northern hemisphere. Some people include Africa and Australia in this group. But this is incorrect because the mahapuranas like Bhagavata Purana do not include Sakotra, Madagascar (parts of Africa) and Australian sub-islands like Papua in the sub-islands of Jambudvipa. Therefore, Africa and Australia should be considered as asura islands and not part of Jambudvipa.

जम्बूद्वीपस्त्वयं दैवतो द्वीपः । तस्यैतस्य महाद्वीपस्यैते आवर्तनादयोऽष्टावुपद्वीपा भवन्तीत्यन्यदेतत्। भारतवर्षस्य तु प्रातिस्विकतया पूर्वोद्रा इन्द्रद्युम्नादयो नवैवोपद्वीपा इष्यन्ते। तेषां भारतसागरान्तर्वर्तित्वात्। अत एवैतद् भारतीयोपद्वीपसंघो वर्तमानयुगेऽपि म्लेच्छभाषायाम् - 'इण्डियनआर्किपैलैगो'-इत्याख्यायते।

Jambudvipa is the island of devas. The eight sub-islands of Jambudvipa like Britannia are different. Bharatavarsha has nine sub-islands including the north-eastern Indradyumna. All these sub-islands are situated in the Indian Ocean. Even in English language they are known as the 'Indian Archipelago'.

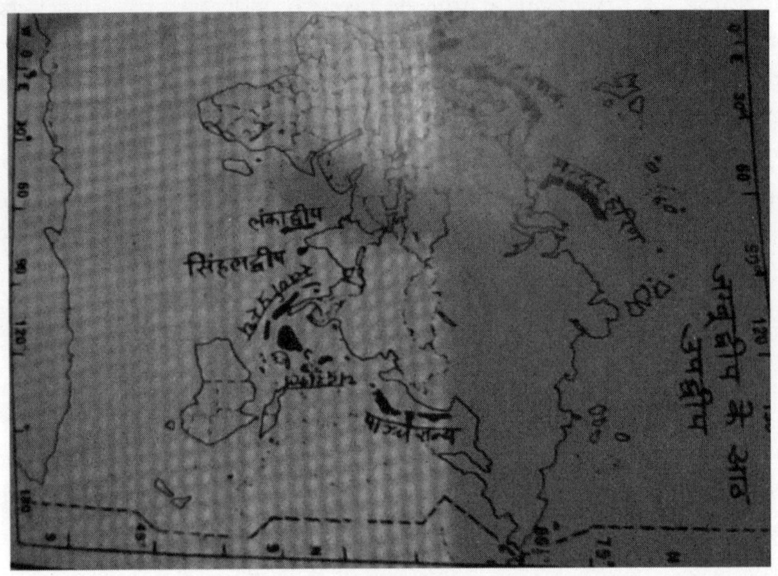

इति भारतपरिचये उपद्वीपप्रसङ्गः सम्पूर्णः ।

The section on subcontinent in the Introduction to Bharatavarsha is concluded.

1.5. लङ्काप्रसङ्गः

1.5 THE LANKA NARRATIVE

1.5.1 सिंहलद्वीपस्य लङ्कात्वभ्रमखण्डने द्वादशविप्रतिपत्तियः-

1.5.1 Twelve objections to disprove that Sinhaladvipa is Lankadvipa

(1) अत्रेदमपरं बोध्यम्। अद्यत्वे केचन विद्वांसः सिंहलमेव द्वीपं लङ्कामाचक्षते, तन्नितान्तं भ्रान्तमिति ब्रूमः । लङ्कादयो हि शब्दा भारतवर्षीयग्रन्थोपलब्धसंज्ञाः सन्तीत्येषां भारतवर्षीयग्रन्थाधारेणैव व्यवस्थावकल्पते न तु स्वकपोलकल्पनया यथेच्छं प्रतिपत्तिः । अन्यथा प्रमादप्रलपितत्वापत्तेः । भारतवर्षीयग्रन्थेषु च सिंहलादन्या लङ्कोपदिश्यते।

अथ दक्षिणेन लङ्का-कालाजिन-सौरिकीर्ण-तालिकटाः ॥
काञ्ची मरुचीपट्टनचेर्यार्यक-सिंहला ऋषभा
-इति बृहत्संहितायां-(बृहत्संहिताया, 14.11,15)

कूर्मविभागे तयोः पृथक्त्वेन निर्देशात्। यदि सिंहलद्वीप एव लङ्काऽभविष्यत्, तदा भागवतादिषु सिंहलस्य सप्तमत्वमाख्याय लङ्काया अष्टमत्वं नोपदिष्टमभविष्यत्। तस्मादन्या लङ्का अन्यश्चायं सिंहलद्वीप इति सिद्धं भवति। इति प्रथमा विप्रतिपत्तिः ।

Some scholars consider Sinhala island and Lanka island to be identical but it is a misconception. Since words like Lanka as noun have originated from the Indian granthas, a resolution of the problem could only be found in these texts. The Koorma section of Brahma Samhita says: In the southern direction are Lanka, Kalajin, Saurikirna, Talikata, Kanchi, Maruchi, Pattanchairya, Aryak, Sinhaladvipa and Rishabha.

One can see that Lanka and Sinhaladvipa have been described as two different entities. If Sinhaladvipa and Lanka were identical islands, Bhagavata Purana would not have described them as different islands. Hence, it is proved that Sinhaladvipa and Lanka are separate islands.

(2) अपिच भारतवर्षीयार्यग्रन्थेषु लङ्केति निरक्षदेशस्य संज्ञा क्रियते। सिंहलद्वीपस्तूत्तरश्चत्वारिंशत्कलोपेते सप्तमेऽक्षांशे संनिविष्ट इति साक्षदेशत्वान्न कदाचिदपि लङ्का भवितुमर्हतीति। इति द्वितीया विप्रतिपत्तिः ।

The Arya texts call Lanka *niraksha* (a place without latitude or 0° latitude) whereas Sinhaladvipa island is situated at 7° 40′ northern latitude. Thus, it cannot be deemed as a country located at 0° latitude.

(3) अपि च यथेदानीं युगे पाश्चात्यैः स्वदेशे ग्रीनवीचनगरे भूमेर्मध्यरेखा प्राकल्प्यत, तथैवेह पुरायुगे भारतवर्षे उज्जयिन्यां नगर्यां सा मध्यरेखा प्रकल्पितासीत् । सा च लङ्कोज्जयिनीमेरुस्पर्शिनी व्याख्यायते।

यल्लङ्कोज्जयिनीपुरोपरि कुरुक्षेत्रादिदेशान् स्पृशत् ।
सूत्रं मेरुगतं बुधैर्निगदिता सा मध्यरेखा भूवः ।।
(सिद्धान्तशिरोमणिः, गोलाध्यायः, मध्यगतिवासना, 24)

इत्यभियुक्तोक्तेः । सेयमुज्जयिनी ग्रीनवीचतः त्रिचत्वारिंशत्कलोपेतपञ्चसप्ततिमिते पूर्वदेशान्तरे प्रारभ्यते, तेन तयोर्मध्यरेखयोः षट्सप्ततिरन्तरांशाः सिध्यन्ति । सीलोननाम्ना प्रसिद्धः सिंहलद्वीपस्तु ग्रीनवीचतः पञ्चाशत्कलोपेताशीत्यंशमिते पूर्वदेशान्तरे संनिविष्ट इत्येकाशीतिरन्तरांशा भवन्ति। तथा च पञ्चभिरंशैरयं सिंहलद्वीपो भवत्युज्जयिन्यपेक्षया पूर्वदिक्स्थ इति सिंहलारब्धरेखाया उज्जयिनीस्पर्शो नितरां कदापि संभाव्यते। लङ्का तूज्जयिन्याः साम्येन दक्षिणतः षट्सप्ततिमिते ग्रीनवीचतः पूर्वदेशान्तरे विवक्ष्यते। तस्मात् सिंहलद्वीपो लङ्का नास्तीति लङ्काशब्देन सिंहलव्यपदेशः केषांञ्चित् साहसमात्रम्। इति तृतीया विप्रतिपत्तिः ।

Just as Greenwich meridian is considered to be the meridian situated at the middle of the globe, the longitude passing through Ujjaini in India was considered the *bhumadhya* (middle of the earth) meridian in ancient times. This meridian used to pass from Ujjaini to Mount Meru.

There is a view among the scholars that 'the meridian which passes through Lanka, Ujjaini and Kurukshetra region to Mount Meru is called the meridian which is located in the middle of the earth.' Ujjaini city is located at 75° 43′ east. Both these central meridians (Indian and western) have a difference of 76 degrees. But Ceylon is situated at 80° 40′ east meridian from Greenwich meridian. This implies that Ceylon is situated 40 degrees east unlike Ujjaini. Therefore, none of the meridians from Ceylon can possibly touch Ujjaini. Therefore Ceylon cannot be considered Lanka.

(4) अपिच-

निरक्षदेशात् क्षितिषोडशांशे भवेदवन्ती गणितेन यस्मात् ।
(सिद्धान्तशिरोमणिः, गोलाध्यायः भुवनकोशः, 15)

इति सिद्धान्तशिरोमणिप्रदर्शितज्योतिर्वित्समयानुसारेणोज्जयिन्या लङ्कापेक्षया सार्द्धद्वाविंशेऽक्षांशे स्थितिरुपपद्यते। सा च विषुवस्पर्शिमालदीवाभिप्रायेण कथंचित्संभवति, सिंहलस्य लङ्कात्वोपगमे तु तस्य निरक्षस्पर्शित्वाभावान्मुख्यनिरक्षस्यवापादानत्वे स्थिते सार्द्धद्वाविंशेऽवन्तीस्थितिर्नोपपद्येत। दशकलाधिकत्रयोविंशेऽशे उज्जयिन्या अवस्थितत्वात्। तस्मात् सिंहलोऽयं लङ्का नास्तीति सिद्धम्। इति चतुर्थी विप्रतिपत्तिः ।

It has also been written that 'according to mathematics, the city of Avanti (Ujjaini) is situated at 16° from niraksha country.' In this way, according to *Sidhanta Shiromani* [an astrological text] time calculation, Ujjaini in comparison to Lanka is located at 22° and half meridian. [Since the circumference of the earth is 360 degrees, its 16th part 360/16 = 22

and ½° north latitude should be the location of Ujjaini]. One can consider Maldives as the niraksha country since it touches the Equator. If one considers Sinhaladvipa as Lanka, we must reckon that the Equator does not pass through it and since its mainland is located far away from niraksha point, we are not able to locate Avanti (Ujjaini) on 22.5°. As Ujjaini is situated at 23° and 101 kala, Sinhaladvipa cannot be confused with Lanka.
(5) अपि च वाल्मीकीये सुन्दरकाण्डे-

योजनानां शतं चापि कपिरेष खमालुप्तः ॥
(रामायणम्, सुन्दरकाण्डम्, 5.1.108)
योजनानां शतस्यान्ते वनराजिं ददर्श सः ॥
(रामायणम्, सुन्दरकाण्डम्, 5.1.192)
शतान्यहं योजनानां क्रमेयं सुबहून्यपि ।
कि पुनः सागरस्यान्तं संख्यातं शतयोजनम् ॥
(रामायणम्, सुन्दरकाण्डम्, 5.2.4)
योजनानां शतं श्रीमाँस्तीर्त्वाऽप्युत्तमविक्रमः ॥
(रामायणम्, सुन्दरकाण्डम्, 5.2.3)
शतयोजनविस्तीर्णं पुप्लुवे लवणार्णवम् ।
(रामायणम्, सुन्दरकाण्डम्, 1.1.72)

इत्येवमभ्यासेन महेन्द्रगिरित्रिकूटगिर्योः शतयोजनात्मकमन्तरमाख्यायते। तेन चतुःशतक्रोशान्तरे लङ्कायाः संनिवेशोऽध्यवसीयते। स चावश्यं विषुवद्रेखायामुपपद्यते। महेन्द्राचलस्य विषुवतो दशाऽक्षांशान्तरितत्वादेकैकांशस्य साधिकोनसप्ततिमीलात्मकतया सार्द्धत्रिशतीक्रोशान्तरितत्वोपपत्तेः। सिंहलस्य त्वस्य शतार्द्धक्रोशमात्रमप्यन्तरं नास्ति तस्मादन्या लङ्का, अन्यश्चायं सिंहलद्वीप इत्यवसितं भवति। इति पञ्चमी विप्रतिपत्तिः ।

In the Sunder-khanda of Valmiki Ramayana, it is said: 'This monkey jumped a distance of hundred yojana in the sky. He saw a grove at the distance of 100 yojana; I can cross hundreds of yojana, how can a distance of mere hundred yojana bother me. Most valiant monkey warriors did not tire after crossing great distances like hundred yojana.' Such sayings clearly imply that there is a distance of 100 yojana between Mount Mahendra and Mount Trikoot. According to this, Lanka is located at a distance of 400 kosa. Lanka lies on the Equator. Since Mount Mahendra is situated at 10° latitude, and each degree is equal to 69.5 miles, the total distance would be 350 kosa (or roughly 700 miles). But Sinhaladvipa is located at a distance of approximately 50 kosa (100 miles). Hence it is proved that Sinhaladvipa and Lanka are two different islands.

(6) अपि च एष खलु सिंहलद्वीपः पञ्चत्रिंशदधिकशत क्रोशदीर्घः सार्द्धद्वाविंशत्यधिकशत क्रोशविस्तीर्ण उपलभ्यते, लङ्काद्वीपस्त्वयं चतुःशतक्रोशदीर्घो विंशत्याधिकशत क्रोशविस्तीर्णो रामायणे स्मर्यते।
त्रिंशद्योजनविस्तीर्णा शतयोजनमायता।
इति। तत्र विस्तारसाम्येऽपि दीर्घत्वे भूयान् भेदोऽस्तीति नायं सिंहलो लङ्का भवितुमर्हति। इति षष्ठी विप्रतिपत्तिः ।

According to the Ramayana, Sinhaladvipa is 135 kosa in length and 122 kosa in width, whereas Lanka is 400 kosa in length and 120 kosa in width. It says, 'Lanka is 30 yojana (120 kosa) in width and 100 yojana (400 kosa) in length.' Although their breadth is almost similar, the difference in length is substantial. So, Sinhaladvipa is not Lanka.

(7) अपि चेहि सिंहले बहवः पर्वता महाबलिनाम्नी गङ्गा च प्रसिद्ध्यन्ति। लङ्कायां तु त्रिकूटसुवेलौ द्वौ पर्वतौ बहुधा स्मर्येते। यदि तत्र महाबलिगङ्गाऽप्यभविष्यत्, तत्तर्हि नूनं तस्या अपि रामायणे चरित्रप्रसङ्गे क्वच्चिदुपयोगोऽभविष्यत्। तस्मात् सिंहलस्य लङ्कात्वाख्यानं प्रमादः । इति सप्तमी विप्रतिपत्तिः ।

In the present day, Sinhaladvipa is known to have many mountains and a river like Ganga known as Mahabali. In the description of Lanka, we find mention of Mount Trikoot and Mount Suvail. The Charitraprasanga of Ramayana would not have omitted an important river like Mahabali. Hence it is wrong to say that Lanka is Sinhaladvipa.

(8) यत्तु–असित खल्वपि सिंहलद्वीपे त्रिकूटाचलो रावणविहारस्थानमशोकवाटिका चेत्येतेषां तत्र सुप्रसिद्ध्यैवास्य सिंहलस्य लङ्कात्वं संभाव्यत इति केचिदालपन्ति तन्न युक्तं प्रतीमः । प्रमाणविरोधे प्रसिद्धिमात्रस्यार्थोपपादकत्वायोगात्। अथवा सन्तु तादृशान्यपि तत्र संस्थानानि। पुष्पकविमानेन लङ्कातो भारतवर्षं प्रत्यासीदतो रावणस्य मध्येमार्गं तत्र सिंहलद्वीपेऽपि विश्रमार्थमवस्थानविहारादेः संभाव्यमानतया तदर्थं रावणाज्ञया तत्र तादृशसंस्थानादेर्निर्माणसंभवात्। किन्तु नैतावता शक्योऽयमपदार्थः कल्पयितुं यदुच्यते सिंहलोऽयं लङ्कास्तीति। तस्मात् सिंहलस्य लङ्कात्वं भ्रान्तिवादः । इति अष्टमी विप्रतिपत्तिः ।

According to some, the present-day Sinhaladvipa has two places called Ravana-vihar and Asoka-vihar on the Trikoot mountain and thus Sinhaladvipa can be considered as Lanka. But these claims are baseless. Besides, there can be a hundred places like Lanka there. To refute such claims, it is best to remember that on his way to Bharatavarsha, Ravana would have stopped over at several places and gardens in Sinhaladvipa. Flying in his *pushpaka vimana* (flying chariot), he would have stopped at places in Sinhaladvipa to rest. This may explain the presence of places named after him. However, it does not prove that Sinhaladvipa is Lanka.

(9) यद्यपि यूनानीयग्रन्थेऽस्य सिंहलद्वीपस्य 'टापरोवेन' इति संज्ञा दृश्यते तस्य च शब्दस्य 'टापू रावण' शब्दापभ्रंशत्वप्रतिपत्त्या सिंहलस्य लङ्कात्ववमध्यवसीयते इति केचिदाहुः । तदपि भ्रान्तम्। टापूशब्दस्य भारतीयग्राम्यशब्दतया यूनानदेशे तत्प्रचारायोगात्। अस्तु वा तस्यापि रावणाधिकृतवाद् रावणटापूत्वं किन्तु नैतावता तस्य लङ्कात्वमुपपद्यते। लङ्कावदेव द्वीपान्तराणामपि महाप्रतापिरावणाधि कृतत्वसंभवात्। वस्तुतस्तु बौद्धग्रन्थे सिंहलस्य ताम्रपर्णसंज्ञोपलभ्यते, तस्यैवापभ्रंशेनायं, 'टापूरोवेन' शब्दः संभाव्यत इति रावणटापूत्वमप्यस्य सिंहलस्य दूरापास्तम्। तस्मादस्य सिंहलस्य लङ्कात्वाख्यानमसङ्गतम्। इति नवमी विप्रतिपत्तिः ।

Since some Greek texts refer to Sinhaladvipa as Taproven, some call it a corrupted form of 'Tapu Ravana'. This is another fallacy because 'tapu' is a Hindi word and not Greek. Ravana was a great warrior and many islands were under his sovereign control. Sinhaladvipa could be one of those islands. Buddhist documents refer to Sinhaladvipa as 'Tamraparna' which could be the source of the distorted word, Taproven.

(10) यदपि च सेतुबन्धरामेश्वरात् सिंहलद्वीपपर्यन्तं मध्येसमुद्रमस्ति किञ्चित्किञ्चिदन्तरेण पर्वतानां सन्निवेशः । तदवश्यं रामचन्द्रकृतसेतोर्भग्नावशेषं लक्षणं संभाव्यते। तदेव चैतस्य सिंहलद्वीपस्य लङ्कात्वे जागरूकं प्रमाणं भवितुमर्हतीति केचिदाक्षिपन्ति। तदुपहासास्पदं तुच्छप्रायम्। नहि सेतुं बध्नता रामेण मध्यसमुद्रं पर्वता अवरोपिताः, येनैतेषां सेतुचिह्नत्वं संभाव्येत। अपि तु समुद्रोपरि तीर्यमाणाभिः शिलाभिरयं सेतुः प्रक्लृप्त आसीत्। ताश्चावश्यं सेतुभङ्गे यतस्ततो विप्लुता विनष्टा एवाभविष्यन्। रामेश्वरसिंहलयोरन्तराले तु पर्वताः पृथ्वीनिर्माणकालादेव प्रकृत्या सिद्धाः संभाव्यन्ते न त्वेते रामेण संस्थापिताः । तस्मादेतान् पर्वतानालोक्य सिंहलस्य लङ्कात्वव्यवस्थापनप्रयासो बालक्रीडामात्रमित्युपेक्ष्यते। इति दशमी विप्रतिपत्तिः ।

Some say that there is a broken-down range of mountains in the sea between Rameshvaram to Sinhaladvipa which could be the remnants of the bridge built by Sri Rama which proves Sinhaladvipa can be part of Lanka. But it is worth remembering that Sri Rama had not established the mountain ranges inside the sea bed. He had built the bridge out of floating rocks. Those rocks would have been lost after the bridge collapsed. These mountain ranges between Rameshvaram and Sinhaladvipa have existed since the creation of planet earth. These could not have been created by Sri Rama and therefore this contention cannot be true.

(11) यच्च भारतवर्षाद्दक्षिणतो निरक्षस्थाने कश्चिदपि स्थलप्रदेशो नोपलभ्यते। तस्मात् सिंहल एवायं लङ्काद्वीपः स्यात्। भारतवर्षीयार्याणां सिंहले निरक्षत्वभ्रमसंभवादिति केचिदुत्प्रेक्षन्ते। तदेतदेषामुक्तमुपहासास्पदं बालचापल्यमात्रमतिधाष्ट्‌र्यं वा। सर्वजगद्गुरूणामार्यमहामहर्षीणां विद्यासंबन्धे भ्रमकल्पनायाः साहसिकत्वात्। को हि नाम सभ्यो विद्वानखिलजगत्कर्तृणां महामहिमभाजामुपदेशे तावदित्थं भ्रमकल्पनां कुर्याद् ऋते संकीर्णहृदयादसभ्यात् पण्डितम्मन्यात्। मेसोपोटेमियादेशे निमरूदप्रतिष्ठापितं बाबिलन्नगरं सम्प्रति नोपलभ्यत इत्येतावता बगदादनगरमेवासीद् बाबिलन्नगरमिति

चेत् कश्चिदभ्युपगच्छेत् को नाम तस्य श्रद्दध्यात्। संभवति हि बहुभिः कालैः कोषांचिन्नगराणां विध्वंसो यथा वेदप्रसिद्धानां यव्यावती वसोर्धाराप्रभृतीनाम्। यथा वा पुराणप्रसिद्धानां वस्वोकसारामहोदयपुष्कलावतीप्रतिष्ठानादीनामद्योपलब्धिर्नास्ति। भवति च बहूनां द्वीपानामपि कालेन समुद्रगर्भे प्रवेशः। उक्तं च तथा स्कान्दे प्रभासखण्डे द्वासप्ततिशततमाध्याये।

भरतो नाम राजाभूदाग्नीध्रः प्रथितः क्षितौ ।
यस्येदं भारतं वर्षं नाम्ना लोकेषु गीयते ।।
(स्कन्दपुराणम्, प्रभासखण्डः, 172.2)

भारतं नवधा कृत्वा पुत्रेभ्यः प्रददौ पृथक् ।
तेषां नामाङ्कितान्येव ततो द्वीपानि जज्ञिरे ।।
(स्कन्दपुराणम्, प्रभासखण्डः, 172.6)

इन्द्रद्वीपः कसेरूश्च ताम्रवर्णो गभस्तिमान् ।
नागद्वीपस्तथा सौम्यो गान्धर्वस्त्वथ चारुणः ।।
(स्कन्दपुराणम्, प्रभासखण्डः, 172.7)

अयं तु नवमो द्वीपः कुमार्यासंज्ञितः प्रिये ।
अष्टौ द्वीपाः समुद्रेण प्लाविताश्च तथापरे ।।

ग्रामादिदेशसंयुक्ताः स्थिताः सागरमध्यगाः ।
एक एव स्थितस्तेषां कुमार्याख्यस्तु साम्प्रतम् ।।
(स्कन्दपुराणम्, प्रभासखण्डः, 172.8, 9)

एतेन पुत्रेभ्यः समानविभागात् तदात्वे, नवानामपि भारतवर्षभागानां विस्तारसाम्यं प्रतीयते। कालेन तु तेष्वष्टद्वीपानां बहुभिर्भागैः समुद्रगर्भे प्रवेशादतितुच्छभागैरद्यावशेषः स्मर्यते। तथा च तद्रीत्या लङ्काद्वीपस्यापि सर्वात्मना संभाव्यते समुद्रगर्भे प्रवेशाद्विलोप इति नैतावता स्थानान्तरस्य स्थानान्तरसंज्ञया व्यपदेशो विद्विद्भिः कर्तुं युज्यते तस्मात्सिंहले लङ्काशब्दप्रयोगो नितान्तमज्ञानाद् इति बोध्यम्। इति एकादशी विप्रतिपत्तिः ।

Some believe that there is no region in the southern part of India which is located on the Equator and hence Sinhaladvipa is mistaken to be located on Equator. If one follows a similar argument, one can claim that Babylon, situated in ancient Mesopotamia, does not exist today and Baghdad can be considered as Babylon. However, we can see how such an argument is absurd and facile. Many ancient cities have been lost over a period of time due to vagaries of nature. Vedic cities like Yavyavati and Vasordhara do not exist any longer. Many islands like Mahodaya and Pushpakalawati, over the ages, have submerged under the ocean. The Prabhas section of Skanda Purana says: 'The great king Bharata ruled Bharatavarsha, a country famous for its prosperity in the three domains.' King Bharata divided this country into nine sections named after his nine sons and they ruled them. These nine islands are thus named—Indra island, Kaseru island, Tamraparna, Naga, Gabhastiman, Saumya, Gandharva and Varun island. The ninth island was known as Kumari. The other eight islands had submerged in the sea along with their towns and villages. Now only an island named Kanyakumari remains.

Dividing Bharatavarsha into nine equal parts for nine sons seems justified. As a great span of time has passed since that time, one can only imagine about the existence of islands which have since submerged. Yet, it is not wise to confuse them with the names of other places. Similarly Sinhaladvipa cannot be confused with Lanka.

(12) अपि वा अस्त्येव खल्वस्या लङ्काया भग्नावशेशचिह्नमद्यापि। तथा हि यस्तावदुपलभ्यतेऽद्यत्वे सिंहलद्वीपात् पश्चिमतो नातिदूरे लक्के दीव इत्युपद्वीपः स एव तु पुरा लङ्काद्वीप आसीदित्यध्यवस्यामः । सन्ति हि तस्य लङ्काद्वीपत्वे षडुपष्टम्भकानि।

Some ruins found in modern times prove that there was an island named Lakkedvipa situated on the western side of Sinhaladvipa. There are six proofs to attest that this 'Lakkedvipa' was in fact Lanka:

(क) तत्र तावन्नामसादृश्यं पश्यामः लक्केदीव इत्यवश्यं लङ्काद्वीपशब्दस्य रक्षोद्वीपशब्दस्य वापभ्रंशो भवितुमर्हतीत्येकम् ।

Lakkedvipa, Lakka, Lanka are similar sounding words and probably can be variations of the same name.

(ख) यच्च लक्केदीवप्रदेशात् दक्षिणतो निरक्षदेशोपह्वरे मालदीवनाम स्थानमुपलभामहे तन्नूनं मालेयद्वीप इति वा मालिद्वीप इति वा संभाव्यते। मालिसंज्ञस्य राक्षसविशेषस्य निवासोपलक्षितं स्थानं मालिद्वीपः । मालिनः पुत्राणां वा अनलानिलहरसंपातीनां मालेयसंज्ञा स्मर्यते। ते चैते विभीषणमातुला विभीषणामात्याश्चासान् ।

अनलश्चानिलश्चैव हरः संपातिरेव च ।
एते विभीषणामात्या मालेयास्ते निशाचराः ।।

(रामायणम्, उत्तरकाण्डम्, 5.43)

इति रामायणोक्तेः । तन्निवासोपलक्षितं स्थानं मालेयद्वीपः । स चायं मालदीवाख्यो मालिद्वीपोऽद्यत्वे लक्कद्वीपात् पृथक्त्वेनोपलभ्यमानोऽपि पुरात्वे नूनमासीदयं लङ्काया एवैको दक्षिणः प्रान्तः। लङ्काधिपतेर्माल्यवतः कनिष्ठभ्रातृत्वेन तत्सेनापतित्वेन च श्रुतस्य मालेर्लङ्कातोऽतिदूरे द्वीपान्तरे स्थातुमनवक्लृप्तत्वात्। तथा च लङ्कावासित्वेन प्रसिद्धस्य मालिनो राक्षसस्य निवासस्थानरूपमालिद्वीपसान्निध्योपपत्या ध्रुवमस्य लक्कदीवस्य लङ्काद्वीपत्वमुपपन्नं भवतीति द्वितीयम् ।

Maldives, located near the south of Lanka, must be the Malay island or Malidvipa. The asura named Mali must have resided there. Mali had four sons named, Anal, Anil, Har, and Sampati. They were known as Malay. They occupied prestigious positions as ministers of Vibhisara. It is said in the Ramayana: Anal, Anil, Har and Sampati were the kin of Vibhisara and were known as Malayrakshasas.

Their habitation was known as Malidvipa. The present day Maldives was once an integral part of southern Lanka. Mali, who was the younger brother and general of Lankan king Malyavan, could not have resided very far from Lanka. He must have resided in Maldives.

(ग) पूर्वं तावदयमेक एवार्थ आसील्लङ्काद्वीपश्च मालिद्वीपश्च अद्यतनोपलब्ध लक्केदीवादारभ्यनिरक्षवृत्तादपि दक्षिणतः कियद्दूरपर्यन्तं लङ्कायाः सन्निविष्टत्वादद्य पृथक्त्वेनोपलब्धयोरपि लक्केदीवमालदीवयोः पुराकाले एकस्या एव लङ्कायाः प्रान्तविशेषत्वेनोपगन्तव्यत्वात्। तथा हि लङ्कायामस्यां सर्वतः पूर्वं साल कटंकटवंश्या राक्षसा वसन्ति स्म। तेषां च तद्वंश्य एव माल्यवन्नाम राजासीत्। माल्यवतोऽवरजः सुमाली प्रधानमन्त्री सर्वकनिष्ठस्तु माली प्रधानसेनापतिरित्येवं त्रयोप्येते भ्रातरः सुकेशपुत्रा विद्युत्केशपौत्राः प्रहेतिप्रपौत्राः अस्या लङ्कायाः प्राधान्येन शासका आसन्। बलदुर्मदान्धैरेतैर्भूयो भूयः प्रपीडितानां प्रजानां रक्षार्थमेते त्रयोपि विष्णुना हृतराज्याधिकारा लङ्कातो निष्कासिता अधस्तात्पातालं गत्वा सपरिवारस्तत्र न्यूषुः । उक्तं चैतत्सर्वमुत्तररामायणे-

ततः काले सुकेशस्तु जनयामास राघव ।
माल्यवन्तं सुमालिं च मालिं च बलिनां वरम् ।।

(रामायणम्, उत्तरकाण्डम्, 5. 5-6)

ऊचुस्ते विश्वकर्माणं शिल्पिनां वरमव्ययम् ।
अस्माकमपि तावत् त्वं गृहं कुरु महामते ।।

(रामायणम्, उत्तरकाण्डम्, 5.18, 20)

विश्वकर्मा ततस्तेषां निवासं निर्द्दिदेश ह ।
दक्षिणस्योदधेस्तीरे त्रिकूटो नाम पर्वतः ।।

सुवेल इति चाप्यन्यो द्वितीयो राक्षेश्वराः ।
शिखरे तस्य शैलस्य मध्यमेऽम्बुदसन्निभे ।।

त्रिंशद्योजनविस्तीर्णा शतयोजनमायता ।
मया लङ्केति नगरी शक्राज्ञप्तेन निर्मिता ।।

(रामायणम्, उत्तरकाण्डम्, 5.21-25)

तस्यां वसत दुर्धर्षा यूयं राक्षसपुङ्गवाः ।
विश्वकर्मवचः श्रुत्वा गत्वा तामवसन् पुरीम् ॥
(रामायणम्, उत्तरकाण्डम्, 5.26, 28)

लङ्कानामपुरी दुर्गा त्रिकूटशिखरे स्थिता ।
तत्र स्थिताः स्म बाधन्ते सर्वान् देवान्निशाचराः ॥
(रामायणम्, उत्तरकाण्डम्, 6.15)

इति माली सुमाली च माल्यवांश्चैव राक्षसाः ।
बाधन्ते समरोद्धर्षा ये च तेषां पुरःसराः ॥
(रामायणम्, उत्तरकाण्डम्, 6.7)

ये त्वया निहतास्ते तु पौलस्त्या नाम राक्षसाः ।
सुमाली माल्यवान् माली ये च तेषां पुरःसरा ।
सर्व एते महाभागा रावणाद् बलवत्तराः ।
(रामायणम्, उत्तरकाण्डम्, 8.24)

अशक्नुवन्तस्ते विष्णुं प्रतियोद्धुं बलार्दिताः ।
त्यक्त्वा लङ्कां गता वस्तुं पातालं सहपत्नयः ॥
(रामायणम्, उत्तरकाण्डम्, 8.22)

सुमालिनं समासाद्य राक्षसं रघुसत्तम ।
स्थिताः प्रख्यातवीर्यास्ते वंशे सालकटङ्कटे ॥
(रामायणम्, उत्तरकाण्डम्, 8.23)

अथ माल्यवत्प्रभृतिषु सालकटङ्कटाख्येषु पातालं गतेषु सत्सु लङ्कमेतां कुबेरः समागत्य शशास। कालेन तु केनचित् माल्यवद्भ्रातुः सुमालिनः कन्यायां कैकस्यां पुलस्त्यान्महर्षे रावणकुम्भकर्णशूर्पणखाविभीषणा उदपद्यन्त। तद्बलदर्पितः सुमाली स्वदौहित्राय रावणाय लङ्कां कुबेराद् ग्रहीतुं प्रेरयामास। स रावणो विनैव युद्धं कुबेराल्लङ्कां गृहीत्वा तत्र राजाऽभवत्। तदवधि पौलस्त्या राक्षसाः प्राधान्येन लङ्कामधिष्ठाय सालकटङ्कटानपि राक्षसान् स्वायत्तान् पालयामासुः । तथा चैतस्या लङ्कानगर्यास्त्रेधा कक्षविभाग आसीत्। तत्र मध्यमे लङ्कार्धे पौलस्त्यानां रावणकुम्भकर्णविभीषणप्रमुखानामधिपतीनां राजप्रासादास्त्रिकूटाचले सन्निविष्टा अभूवन्। उत्तरे तु लङ्कार्धे रावणजातीयाः पौलस्त्या नाम राक्षसा वसन्ति स्म। अथ दक्षिणे लङ्कार्धे सालकटङ्कटा माल्यवत्मालिसुमालिप्रमुखा राक्षसा न्यूषुः । सेयमेकैव लङ्का त्रिधा विभक्तासीत्। तत्र मध्यमो भागो लङ्कायाः समुद्रगर्भे निमग्नः कालेनोच्छिन्नोऽभूदिति नेदानीमुपलभ्यते। उत्तरप्रान्तस्तु भग्नावशिष्टः कश्चिद्भागो रक्षोद्वीपनामा तदपभ्रंशेन लक्केदीव इत्युच्यते। एवमस्या दक्षिणः कश्चन मालेयाध्युषितो भागो भग्नावशेषे मालिद्वीपस्तदपभ्रंशेन मालवदीवनाम्नाभिधीयते । इति तृतीयम् ।

Lanka and Maldives were parts of the same land mass in ancient times. Both were also parts of the same kingdom. In those days, Lanka was ruled by the kings of Salkantkant dynasty. Malyavan was one of their descendants. His younger brother Sumali was the prime minister and the youngest brother Mali was the army chief. These three brothers were corrupt and laid the city to ruins. Vishnu punished them by forcing them into exile. They moved to Pathala [one of the seven subterranean worlds, the nether world] along with their respective families and began living there.

This incident is described in the Uttara Ramayana: Hey Raghunandan (Raghu's son referring to Sri Rama)! Sukesh bore three sons named Malyavan, Mali, and Sumali. Mali was the most powerful of them. They requested the greatest architect Vishvakarma to construct a huge palace for them. After listening to this request, Vishvakarma told them about such a place which was located near the southern seas. It had two famous mountain ranges, Trikoot and Suvale. In the middle range of Trikoot, which was so lush with foliage that it was as blue as a cloud, Indra had asked him to construct a city called Lanka which was 300 yojana wide and 100 yojana long.

He suggested that the asuras should stay in that city. They paid heed to his advice and started living in Lanka.

Living in that inaccessible city on top of the Trikoot mountain, the asuras began harassing the devas who cried for help.

'Mali, Sumali, and Malyavan and their soldiers are bothering us.'

'Hey Rama! The rakshasas from Pulastya dynasty, whom you have slain, were as powerful as Mali, Sumali, and Malyavan. They were more powerful than Ravana.

'But they could not face the wrath of Vishnu and therefore escaped to Pathala with their families.

'Hey Raghushreshta! They took refuge under the great rakshasa king Sumali who hailed from Salkantkant dynasty.'

After the rakshasas from Salkantkant dynasty left for Patala, Kubera ruled Lanka. Ravana, Kumbhakarna, Shurpanakha, and Vibhishna were born from the marriage between Sumali's daughter Kaikashi and sage Pulastya. Impressed by the valour of Ravana, his grand father Sumali coaxed him to snatch the reins of Lanka. Ravana was able to win Lanka without any war and was crowned as the new king. Since then, rakshasas from the clans of Pulastya and Salkantkant lived in Lanka.

Lanka was divided into three parts. On the middle part of Mount Trikoot were the palaces of Ravana, Kumbhakarna, Shurpanakha and Vibhishna. Towards the north, lived the rakshasas from Pulastya clan. Similarly, southern Lanka was populated by the rakshasas of Salkantkant clan. Among them, Mali, Sumali, and Malyavan were the prominent rakshasas. Thus Lanka was divided into three parts, the middle of which had submerged in the ocean after a long passage of time. The northern part was also destroyed and its remnants were called Rakshodvipa which later became Lakkedvipa. Similarly, the remanants of southern Lanka became Maldvipa which got corrupted to become Maldives, a region ruled by King Malaya.

(घ)अपि चास्मिन् लक्कदीवादिमालदीवान्तोपद्वीपे निरक्षगर्भत्वमप्युपपद्यते तथा हि पुरायुगे तावदियं लङ्कानगरी निरक्षोपह्वरस्थे कस्मिंश्चित् सुवेलपर्वतत्रिकूटपर्वताभ्यामुपसंपन्ने द्वीपे त्रिकूटाद्रिमध्यमशिखरोपरि सन्निविष्टाऽऽसीत्। सा च पूर्वापरतो विंशत्यधिकशतक्रोशैर्विस्तीर्णा दक्षिणोत्तरतस्तु चतुश्शतक्रोशदीर्घासीदिति रामायणवचनादवगम्यते।

त्रिंशद्योजनविस्तीर्णा शतयोजनमायतेति तत्रोक्तेः । तेन त्रिकूटैकशिखरस्थाया नगर्याश्चतु:शतक्रोशमितत्वे तदुपलक्षितैतद्द्वीपस्य ततोप्यधिकदीर्घत्वं संभाव्यते। त्रिकूटादुत्तरतः सुवेलशैलाभिव्याप्त्या चतुर्दिक्षु समुद्रकूलेषूपत्यकाप्रदेशाभिव्याप्त्या चैतस्या नगर्या बहिर्द्धा परिसरस्थलानमाधिक्यात्। तथा चावश्यं मालदीवादप्यस्माद्दक्षिणतो निरक्षपर्याप्ता लङ्काद्वीपस्य दक्षिणपरिसरप्रदेशाः पुरात्वे आसन्निति गम्यते । तथा च नगरीविशेषवाचिनो लङ्काशब्दस्य तदुपलक्षित राष्ट्रेऽपि मिथिलादिशब्दवल्लोकव्यवहारसिद्धतया द्वीपाभिप्रायेणापि प्रयुज्यमानत्वाल्लङ्काया निरक्षत्वोपपत्तिः ।

Another noteworthy point in this regard is the fact that only Lakkedvipa and Maldives are the islands situated at 0° latitudinal zones. In ancient times, the city of Lanka was located near an archipelago consisting of regions of Suvale and Trikoot mountains.

According to the Valmiki Ramayana, Lanka was 120 kosa in width and 400 kosa in length. It implied that this city was fairly large because it comprised of valleys of the Suvale mountain and was flanked by great plains on the north. Probably the entire region, including the areas falling under 0° latitude, was known as Lanka. There have been such instances elsewhere also. For instance, the entire township surrounding the city of Mithila was popularly known as Mithila.

(ङ) अथेयमुज्जयिनी नगरी ग्रीनवीचमध्यरेखातः साधिकपञ्चसप्ततिमिते पूर्वदेशान्तरे सन्निविशते। लङ्कापीयं पुरात्वे तावत्येव पूर्वदेशान्तरे संनिविष्टासीदिति लङ्काया उज्जयिन्याश्च दक्षिणोत्तरतः समसूत्रत्वमापतति। समसूत्रत्वाच्च भारतवर्षीयार्यनिदर्शिता भूमध्यरेखा तदुभयस्पर्शिन्युपपद्यते। तेन देशान्तरतोऽपि लक्कदीवमालदीवयोरेव लङ्कात्वं सिध्यतीति पञ्चमम् ।

The city of Ujjaini was located at 75° east of Greenwich meridian. In the ancient era, Lanka was also located at a similar meridian. Hence these meridians of Lanka and Ujjaini were located at a similar longitude, on south and north respectively. Because they were located at similar longitudinal line, the 0° longitude must pass through these two cities. Consequently, it is proved that Lakkedvipa and Maldives were once part of Lanka.

(च) अपि च सिंहलद्वीपे सोमानाम्न्या रजक्या निवासस्थानमासीदिति सोमवत्यमावास्योपाख्यानादवगम्यते। पुराकालादेव तु दक्षिणापथस्थानां द्रविडादीनां सिंहलद्वीपे भूयांसो वाणिज्यव्यापारा: प्रचलन्ति स्म। बहूनां च दाक्षिणात्यानां राज्ञां सिंहलद्वीपे युद्धानि भवन्ति स्मेति प्रचलितकतिपयेतिहासपिटकाद्विज्ञायते। विजयश्रीविक्रमराजादयो बहव: सूर्यवंश्या राजानस्तत्र राज्यं कुर्वन्ति स्म। कुमारदासश्चात्र प्रसिद्धो राजासीत्। तदित्थं मनुष्याणामेवात्र सिंहलद्वीपे पुराकालदारभ्येदानीं यावत् संनिवेशो यातायातं चाख्यायते। न तु राक्षसानामुपनिवेश: पुराकालादिदानीं यावदिह कुत्रापि स्मर्यते। लङ्काद्वीपे तु राक्षासानामेवाऽसीत् पुरात्वे निवासस्थानमिति भेदा:। तस्मान्नायं सिंहलद्वीप: कदापि लङ्कासीदिति निश्चिनुम:। अथैतयोस्तु लक्कदीवमालदीवयोरद्यापि मनुष्यमांसभक्षकत्वं बहुषु दृश्यते इति राक्षसवृत्तिप्राणिनामिहोपनिवेशादनयोर्लङ्कात्वं संभाव्यते। इति षष्ठम् ।

According to the narrative of the origin of Somavati Amavasya, Sinhaladvipa had a washer woman named Soma. Since ancient times, Dravidians used to indulge in commerce with the people of Sinhaladvipa. Some historical documents show that many kings of southern Bharat had fought wars with Sinhaladvipa kings. Suryavanshi kings like Vijaysri Vikram were very famous. Ever since olden times, there is no evidence of rakshasas inhabiting Sinhaladvipa whereas Lanka has always been inhabited by the rakshasas. Though cannibalistic tribes have been found in Lakkedvipa and Maldives, there has never been any evidence of man-eating tribes in Sinhaladvipa.

तथा च सिध्यत्यन्य: सिंहलद्वीपोऽन्यश्च लङ्काद्वीप इति युक्तं भागवतादिषु सिंहललङ्कयो: पार्थक्येनाभिधानम्। अयुक्तं च सिंहलस्य लङ्काभिधानम्। इति द्वादशी विप्रतिपत्ति: ।

To conclude, mahapuranas like Bhagavata Purana also distinguish between Sinhaladvipa and Lanka. Therefore, it is inappropriate to treat the two as a single entity.

इति भारतपरिचये लङ्काप्रसङ्ग: सम्पूर्ण: ।

The section on Lanka narrative in the Introduction to Bharatavarsha is concluded.

1.6 भारतीयभाषाप्रसङ्ग:

1.6 LANGUAGES OF BHARATAVARSHA

1.6.1 भाषाविभाग:

1.6.1 Division of language

छन्दोभाषा संस्कृतभाषाऽथ च नागरी भाषा ।
इत्थं भारतवर्षे कालक्रमतस्त्रिधा भाषा ।।415।।

At various times, three different languages were prevalent in Bharatavarsha. These were: Chhandobhasha [Vedic language], laukika bhasha [Sanskrit] and Devanagari bhasha.

1.6.2 छन्दोभाषा

1.6.2 Chhando bhasha

भारतवर्षे द्विविधा भाषाऽऽसीत् पाणिने: समये ।
छन्दोभाषा दैवी ब्राह्मीनाम्नी तु भारती भाषा ।।416।।

Since the age of Panini [the great and celebrated Indian grammarian who is said to have derived the knowledge of his grammar from Shiva], two languages have been prevalent in Bharatavarsha—the Vedic language [also known as divya or divine language), and the popular language known as Brahmi language.

दैवीभाषा स्वर्ग्या देवेषु प्रचलिताऽभवत् स्वर्गे ।
देवानामुच्छेदादुच्छिन्नाऽप्यस्ति शास्त्रमात्रस्था ।।417।।

Divya language was used by the devas in heaven. With the extinction of the devas, this language fell into disuse and survived only in the shastras.

छन्दोभाषाया: सर्वभाषामूलत्वम् ।

Chhandobhasha is the foundation of all languages.

छन्दोभाषा त्वेषा जननी प्रतिभाति विश्वभाषाणाम् ।
संस्कृतभाषा चासुरभाषा द्वे ज्येष्ठकन्ये स्त: ।।418।।

सम्प्रति भाषा बह्व्यः संस्कृतभाषाविकारतो जाताः ।
यूरोपसर्वभाषा आसुरभाषाप्रसूताः स्युः ॥419॥

Chhandobhasha is the fundamental base of all languages. It is the mother of all the languages in the world. Sanskrit and asura languages are two of its offsprings. All the contemporary languages of Europe have originated from the asura language while several other languages have derived from Sanskrit.

जेन्दावस्ताभाषा त्वासुरभाषा प्रदृश्यते प्रथमा ।
लेटिनभाषा त्वपरा संभाव्यन्ते ततोऽप्यन्याः ॥420॥

Possibly, the language used in the Zendavesta could be the first language to have derived from the asura bhasha; several other languages have sprung from this language.

छन्दोभाषाया एव इण्डोयूरोपियन्भाषात्वम् ।

Chhandobhasha is the Indo-European language.

यत्त्विह वदन्ति लोका इण्डोयूरोपियन्नाम्ना ।
आसीद् काचिद् भाषा सा जननी विश्वभाषाणाम् ॥421।

मन्ये सा हि च्छन्दोभाषैव तु मूलभाषाद्या ।
जेन्दावस्ता छन्दोऽभ्यस्ता सच्छन्द आम्नायः ॥422॥

This Chhandobhasha is considered as the mother of all languages in the world, including that of Indo-European languages. The Zendavesta is a traditional composition of verses in this language.

1.6.3 भारती भाषा

1.6.3 Bharati bhasha

अमरस्य कोशकर्तुः समये सा भारती भाषा ।
ब्राह्मी नाम्ना लोके प्रथिताऽऽसीत् स हि तथैवाह ॥423॥

भारतवर्षमनुष्याः संस्कारैः संस्कृता अभवन् ।
भाषा च भारतीयं पाणिनिना संस्कृताऽक्रियत ॥424॥

According to the author of *Amarakosha* [a compendium on Sanskrit], it was Bharati bhasha which was known as Brahmi bhasha in the world. This

Bharti bhasha was refined by sage Panini.

1.6.4 ब्राह्मी भाषा

1.6.4 Brahmi bhasha

प्राच्योदीच्यभेदाद् ब्राह्मीभाषाद्वैविध्यम् ।

The duality of Brahmi bhasha due to eastern and northern differences.

ब्राह्मी तु भारतीयं भाषाऽऽसीत् प्रचरिता तदा लोके ।
पृथगिव सोदीच्यानां प्राच्यानां चाल्पशो भिन्ना ।।425।।

सा भारती तु भाषा संस्कारभ्रंशतो विकारेण ।
रूपान्तरतामागाद् द्विजातिधर्मा इवेह कालेन ।।426।।

Although it was popular amongst people, there were mild differences in its usage by the eastern and northern people. This language underwent several transformations because of the changes caused by usage over the ages.

दैवी छन्दोभाषा यथाऽभवद् ग्रन्थमात्रस्था ।
तद्वद् ब्राह्मी भाषाऽप्येषाऽभूद् ग्रन्थमात्रस्था ।।427।।

Just as the divine language, Chhandobhasha, is confined to books, Brahmi bhasha too has become limited to books.

1.6.5 नागरी भाषा

1.6.5 Nagari Language

सम्प्रति भारतभाषा प्रर्वतते नागरीनाम्ना ।
वैदेशिकसचिवास्त्विह तामाहुर्हैन्दवीं हिन्दीम् ।।428।।

In the present times, language prevalent in Bharat is popular as Nagari language. Foreigners consider this as Hindi language since it is the language spoken by the Hindus.

इति भारतपरिचये भारतीयभाषाप्रसङ्गः सम्पूर्णः ।

The section on languages of Bharatavarsha in the Introduction to Bharatavarsha is concluded.

1.7 मातृकाप्रसङ्गः

1.7 SECTION ON SET OF ALPHABETS

1.7.1 वर्णमातृका

1.7.1 Alphabets

पथ्यास्वस्तिरिहासीद् देवयुगेऽक्षरसमाम्नायः ।
सप्तनवतिरिह वर्णाश्छन्दोभाषानुगा उक्ताः ॥429॥

During the devayuga, there was an order of alphabets known as Pathyasvasti which contained traditional letters. According to experts on Chhandobhasha, it had 97 alphabets.

यो ब्रह्मराशिरुक्तो वर्णसमाम्नाय उत्तरे तु युगे ।
स चतुःषष्ट्या वर्णैः संस्कृतभाषां प्रवर्तयति ॥430॥

In the post-Vedic era, Sanskrit evolved out of the 64 alphabets present in the collection of alphabets called Brahmi.

त्रिषष्टिर्वा चतुःषष्टिर्वर्णाः संभवतो मताः ।
प्राकृते संस्कृते वापि स्वयं प्रोक्ताः स्वयंभुवा ॥
(पाणिनीय शिक्षा, 3)

इत्थं पाणिनिरवदद् बहुपूर्वं त्वेष भारते जज्ञे ।
पथ्यास्वस्तिरिति प्राग् वेदयुगे वर्णमातृकासंज्ञा ॥431॥

According to sage Panini, Sanskrit or Prakrit contains the 63 or 64 words which were uttered by Brahma himself. Panini had declared that Pathyasvasti alphabets had existed in the Vedic era.

मन्ये ततः स्वयंभूरक्षरमालामिमां ब्राह्मीम् ।
वेदाभिज्ञानार्थं विनिर्ममे सर्वतः पूर्वम् ॥432॥

Brahma had created Brahmi alphabets from Pathyasvasti to disseminate Vedic knowledge. The present 50 alphabets of Devanagari were created by sage Katantra.

या वर्णमातृकेयं पञ्चाशद्वर्णतः कृताऽद्यास्ति ।
कातन्त्रकल्पिता सा वर्तयते नागरीं भाषाम् ।।433।
इति भारतपरिचये वर्णमातृकाप्रसङ्गः सम्पूर्णः ।

The section on set of alphabets in the Introduction to Bharatavarsha is concluded.

1.8 लिपिप्रसङ्गः

1.8 SECTION ON SCRIPT

1.8.1 भारतीयब्राह्मीलिपिः

1.8.1 Brahmi-lipi of Bharata

भारतीयब्राह्मीलिपेः अद्य प्राचरलोपः ।

Loss of the Bharati Brahmi script in the present day.

लिपिरपि खल्वार्याणां ब्राह्मी लिपिरेव सर्वतः पूर्वम् ।
उद्भूद् ब्राह्मी भाषा चेत्युक्तं भारते शान्तौ ।।434।।

इत्येते चतुरो वर्णा येषां ब्राह्मी सरस्वती ।।
विहिता ब्रह्मणा पूर्वं लोभात् त्वज्ञानतां गताः ।।
(महाभारतम्, शान्तिपर्व, 181.15)

ब्राह्मी भाषा संस्कृतभाषेयं ब्राह्मणैरल्पैः ।
विज्ञायते न सर्वैर्ब्राह्मी तु लिपिर्न लिख्यते ह्यधुना ।।435।।

It is written in the Shantiparva of Mahabharata that the first script of the Arya was Brahmi from which the Brahmi language originated. The Brahmi language created by Brahma, and used by all, was lost due to ignorance and greed. This Brahmi language is Sanskrit. Only few brahmins, not all, know this language and its script is not in use any longer.

1.8.2 वेदमन्त्रनिर्माणकाले लिपिविचारः

1.8.2 Script used in creating Vedic mantras

वेदमन्त्रनिर्माणकाले लिपिसामान्याभावमतखण्डनाय श्रुतिशब्दव्यपदेशस्य मौलिकरहस्योपपादनम् ।

Presentation of the fundamental meaning of the word 'shruti' to refute the belief that there was a lack of script during the time when Vedic mantra-s were being created.

ऋग्वेदश्रुतिनिर्मितिकाले काचिल्लिपिर्नासीत् ।
अत एव कण्ठपाठश्रवणाच्छ्रुतयः श्रुता वेदाः ।।436।।

इत्थं ब्रुवते केचित् पाश्चात्याः कल्पनारसिकाः ।
अनभिज्ञास्ते नूनं भारतवैदिकरहस्यविज्ञाने ।।437।।

Some western scholars claim that during the creation of hymns for the Rigveda, there was no lipi and hence they were spoken and heard [and not written] and therefore the Vedas were called *shruti* [spoken verses]. Such scholars rely more on their imagination and are ignorant about the mysteries of Indian Vedic knowledge.

विबुधैस्तु भारतीयैः संकेतित एष यत्रार्थे ।
श्रुतिशब्दः प्राक् कालात् तं संकेतं प्रवक्ष्यामि ।।438।।

Let us look at the origin and meaning of the word 'shruti' and its usage described by the ancient Indian sages.

सत्यानां धर्माणां ज्ञाने हेतुः प्रमाणमित्युक्तः ।
प्रत्यक्षं ह्यनुमानं शास्त्रं चेति त्रिधा तत्स्यात् ।।439।।

The *pramana* (fundamental proofs) of truth are that it must be *pratyaksha* (visible), permit *anumana* (estimable) and should be based on the shastras.

दृष्टिः श्रुतिः स्मृतिर्वा निबन्ध इति हेतवो ज्ञाने ।
दृष्टेः प्रत्यक्षत्वं शास्त्रत्वं तु श्रुतिस्मृत्योः ।।440।।

चक्षुषि सत्यं निहितं चक्षुर्गृह्णात्यदोषमनुपाधि ।
एकं तदेव मुख्यं प्रमाणमन्यत्तु तदपेक्षम् ।।441।।

The three basis of knowledge are—*drishti* (sight), *shruti* (aural) and *smriti* (memory) or *nibandha* (essence of truth). Whatever evidence is seen by the eyes is called pratyaksha; shruti and smriti are its derivatives. Whatever is seen by the eyes is truth because eyes accept only unadulterated, visible facts. Therefore pratyaksha is the only essential basis of truth. The other two basis for knowledge rely on being visible.

वाक्यानपेक्षवाक्यं श्रुतिरिति मीमांसया सिद्धम् ।
दृष्टिः श्रुतिरेकोर्थो वेदाः प्रत्यक्षमित्याहुः ।।442।।

It is established that the words of the eyewitness do not require any evidence to establish their truth. The words of the eyewitness are shruti. The Vedas are pratyaksha shastra or words of the eyewitness.

द्रष्टुर्वाक्यं श्रुतिरिति संकेतो दृष्टिमूला सा ।
दृष्टा दृष्टं ब्रूते शृणुते श्रोता च दृष्टमेवार्थम् ।।443।।

Only the sentences uttered by the seer are shruti or worth listening. Therefore, sight or drishti is the basis of shruti because what the hearer listens to is what the seer witnesses. In other words, this kind of shruti knowledge is also a form of drishti knowledge.

दृष्टिः स्वतःप्रमाणं द्रष्टुर्वाक्यं स्वतःप्रमाणं स्यात् ।
प्राथमिकं तज्ज्ञानं न ज्ञानाज्ज्ञानमवतीर्णम् ।।444।।

Drishti is evidence itself [it witnesses the reality] and therefore the words of a seer do not require any validation. The knowledge acquired by a seer is the primary and fundamental knowledge. It does not rely on any secondary sources of knowledge.

श्रोतुर्वाक्यं स्मृतिरिति संकेतो नात्र वक्ताऽयम् ।
स्वीयां दृष्टिं ब्रूते परानुभूतं गिराऽभिनयेत् ।।445।।

What the listener recounts is smriti. In this kind of knowledge, the speaker does not recite the knowledge that he has witnessed first-hand. Instead, he relies on the secondary information that he has heard from someone else and repeats it.

स्मृतिरिति मतमनुमानं तल्लिङ्गज्ञानतो ज्ञानम् ।
नाप्तः स्वयं स वक्ता श्रुतवानाप्तात् स्मृतः सोऽर्थः ।।446।।

Smriti is conjecture, wherein knowledge is gained through signs or evidence. For instance, the sight of smoke rising from a hilltop suggests the presence of fire. The speaker has not seen the truth himself, he merely understands it by listening to the wise men who have seen the reality.

परपुरुषीयप्रत्ययने योऽस्य प्रत्ययस्तस्मात् ।
परतःप्रमाणमेतद्वाक्यं वाक्यान्तरापेक्षम् ।।447।।

द्रष्टुर्वाक्यं यावन्नोपष्टकम्भकतयाऽयमाश्रयते ।
न च तावत्स्वं वाक्यं शक्नोत्येष प्रमाणयितुम् ।।448।।

The faith we have in the person who has witnessed the reality is known as the *paratah pramana*. But the word of the eyewitness has to be substantiated before it could be accepted.

इत्थं शास्त्रं द्विविधं स्वत:प्रमाणं परप्रमाणं च ।
नात: परं तृतीयं शास्त्रं संभाव्यते किमपि ।।449।।

In this way, shastras can be divided into two types—*svataha pramana* (self validated) and *para pramana* (corroborated externally). There is no other third shastra.

परत:प्रमाणशास्त्रे यत्र द्वैविध्यमापतति ।
विप्रतिपत्तावन्योऽनुमानमत्र प्रवर्तयति ।।450।।

But whenever there occurs a doubt in the parataha pramana shastra, a third *anumana pramana* (estimable evidence) comes into play.

अनुमानाद् यद्युभयोर्विरुद्धवाचो: स तात्पर्यम् ।
पृथगिव नीत्वा सत्यं गृह्णीयात्स हि निबन्ध: स्यात् ।।451।।

If different meanings emerge from two *vani*-s (speeches), the *nibandha* (essence) of the speeches is considered.

अपि च निबन्धं शास्त्रं मन्यन्ते तस्य शास्त्रत्वम् ।
शास्त्रानुबन्धत: स्यादुपचारात् सोऽस्ति तर्कस्तु ।।452।।

If we consider nibandha as a shastra, it can only be known through inference and the knowledge gained from it is the inferred logic.

सर्वमपीदं वाङ्मयमित्थं त्रेधा प्रमाणं स्यात् ।
यत् पुनरेभ्यो भिन्नं तदप्रमाणं प्रलाप: स: ।।453।।

Thus, all the shastras are based on these three kinds of pramana. Any pramana other than these three is fallacious.

न तु केवलमिदमित्थं भारत एव प्रमाणमुपपाद्यम् ।
देशेषु किन्त्वशेषेष्वशेषभाषास्विदं तुल्यम् ।।454।।

These three pramanas are accepted and established in countries other than Bharatavarsha also.

किन्त्विह भारतवर्षे तदिदं मीमांसितं तस्मात् ।
संकेताय नियुक्ता: श्रुतिस्मृतिप्रभृतय: शब्दा: ।।455।।

But Bharatavarsha is the only country where these have been researched, explored, and advanced. The words shruti and smriti are only used as symbols to discuss these grand concepts.

इति पूर्वेषां विदुषां संकेतं ये न जानन्ति ।
भ्रान्तं श्रुतिशब्दार्थं प्रकल्प्य ते भ्रामयन्त्यन्यान् ।।456।।

Those few who do not understand the concepts behind these symbolic words spread confusion about the meaning of shruti.

इह भारतीयविद्यारहस्यशिक्षामनासाद्य ।
भारतशास्त्रपदानां विक्षेपणमित्थमन्याय्यम् ।।457।

It would be grave injustice to make any attempt to give meanings to words contained in the Indian shastras without a proper understanding of its nature and true meaning.

न ह्येष श्रुतिशब्दो मन्त्रार्थे मन्त्रसंहितासूक्तः ।
लिपिकाले त्वविशेषान्मन्त्रे च ब्राह्मणे चोक्तः ।।458।।

The world shruti is not referred to as mantra in any *mantra samhita* (volumes of hymns) but when script came into existence, the word shruti referred to mantra as well as brahmin.

श्रवणाच्छ्रुतिरभविष्यच्छ्रुतिशब्दस्तर्ह्यवश्यमभविष्यत् ।
ऋग्वेदेऽप्युल्लिखितः किन्तु न लिपिशब्दवत्स तत्रास्ति ।।459।।

If the word shruti had originated from *shravana* (listening), then there must have been instances of its usage in the Rigveda. But shruti is not mentioned there unlike the term, lipi.

श्रवणाद्यदि श्रुतिः स्याच्छ्रुतिशब्दस्तर्हि न प्रयुक्तः स्यात् ।
लिपिकालोत्पन्नेषु ग्रन्थेषु ब्राह्मणाख्येषु ।।460।।

If one thinks that shruti originated from the *shravana parampara* (tradition of listening), then surely the brahmana-granthas would have not used the term shruti.

1.8.3 वेदमन्त्रनिर्माणकाले लिपिविषयकानि वैदिकप्रमाणानि

1.8.3 Vedic evidence of script in the era of mantra creation

1.8.3.1 प्रथमं प्रमाणम्

1.8.3.1 First evidence

अपि च ब्रुवते केचिद् लिपिरभविष्यत् वेदसमये चेद् ।
लिपिलेखनीमसीनामप्यभविष्यत् क्वचनोल्लेखः ।।461।।

Some people say that the Vedas would have mentioned ink, writing, and other writing materials if there was a script in the Vedic era.

तत्र ब्रूमो लिप्युल्लेखार्थो न प्रसङ्ग आयातः ।
तेन स तत्र न दृष्टो न तु हेतुर्लिप्यभावे सः ।।462।

The truth is that references to writing materials were not made in the Vedas simply because there was no specific section or discussion dealing with lipi. This should not be taken as the absence of script in those times.

श्रुतिशब्दोऽपि तु मन्त्रे मन्त्रपरत्वेन न क्वचिद्दृष्टः ।
अथ मन्यसे तु मन्त्रे श्रुतिशब्दं तद्वदिह विद्यात् ।।463।।

The word shruti is not mentioned in the hymns of Vedas and if in the hymns the word shruti is accepted as implicit, then this absence too needs to be noted.

अथवा दृश्यत एव तु वेदे लिखनार्थशब्दोऽपि ।
लेखन्याश्च लिपेरपि सत्त्वं शक्यं ततो ज्ञातुम् ।।464।।

In addition, there are references that mean 'writing' in the Vedas. These references should indicate the existence of script.

यजुषश्च संहितायाः पञ्चदशेऽध्याय आम्नातम् ।
छन्दः क्षुरोभ्रज इति क्षुरधातुर्विलिखने दृष्टः ।।465।।

अक्षरपङ्क्तिश्छन्दः, पदपङ्क्तिश्छन्दो विष्टारपङ्क्तिश्छन्दः ।
क्षुरोभ्रजश्छन्दः ।।37।। (यजुर्वेदः, 15.4)

कस्याञ्चिच्छाखायां तु – 'क्षुरश्छन्दः, भ्रजश्छन्दः' – इति
पृथक्त्वेनाम्नायते।

तत्राप्यक्षरपदयोः साहचर्यादिह लोहनिर्मिता पूर्वयुगीया लेखन्येव क्षुरः संभाव्यते। पुरायुगे सूक्ष्मखनित्रेणैव सूच्याकारेणाक्षरलिपेः क्रियायाः संभाव्यमानत्वात्। भ्रज इति पत्रोल्लिखिता प्रकाशमाना वागेव स्यात्।

In the fifteenth chapter of Yajurveda samhita, there is a clear reference to *kshur* as a metre written with a writing tool made of iron. This is a clear proof of the existence of writing implements made of *dhatu* (metal). It is further written in the Yajurveda that 'Veda is the compilation of letters, Veda is the compilation of words, it is the compilation of sentences'. In another section of Yajurveda, it is said: '*kshur* (writing) is Veda, bhraja is verse.' Therefore writing and *patra* (tablet) are mentioned in different places. From the complementary description of *akshara* (letter) and *pada* (verse), it becomes clear that in ancient times, nibs made of iron could have been called kshur. Probably fine and delicate words would have been engraved using nibs which were as sharp as needle tips. The term 'bhraja' means engraved words on patra.

अक्षरपङ्क्तिवर्णैः पदपङ्क्तिः स्यात् पदैर्यथा वाक्यैः ।
विष्टारपङ्क्तिरेवं क्षुरोभ्रजो लिपिकृतं मन्ये ।।466।।

The way alphabets make a row of letters and verses, and a group of sentences makes *vistarpankti* (long sentence), similarly 'kshur illuminated' implies scripted text.

क्षुरसा लेखन्या या लिखनाद् भ्राजेत दृश्येत ।
लिपिरेव सा तु वाक् स्याच्छन्दस्तच्च क्षुरोभ्रजो नाम ।।467।।

The one which is lighted by kshur or pen [made of iron] is called script and that very rhyme, namely bhraja, is *vak* (speech).

छन्दः सर्वं वाङ्मयमक्षरपदवाक्यसाहचर्याच्च ।
अक्षरलिखनादन्यद् विलिखनमिह नोपपद्येत ।।468।।

The entire *vakamaya* is verse. The string of words, verses, and sentences makes vakamaya a verse and akshara means letters.

1.8.3.2 द्वितीयं प्रमाणम्

1.8.3.2 Second evidence

अन्यच्च तत्र काले लिपिसत्त्वेऽस्ति प्रमाणमत्रैव ।
विद्यासूक्ते वक्ति हि बृहस्पतिर्दर्शनं वाचाम् ।।469।।

There is evidence in the Vedas which suggests that script existed in the Vedic era. It is described in the Vidya-sukta where Brihaspati has witnessed the vani.

उत त्वः पश्यन्न ददर्श वाचमुत त्वं शृण्वन्न शृणोत्येनाम् ।
उतो त्वस्मै तन्वं वि सस्रे जायेव पत्य उशती सुवासाः ।।
(ऋग्वेदः, 10.71.4)

It is written in the Rigveda samhita that, 'some do not see the vani due to ignorance and others do not listen to it in spite of hearing it. The vani manifests knowledge like a wife who presents her beautiful self in front of her husband for his pleasure.'

वाचामुच्चरितानां श्रवणं नु यथा तथैव लिखितानाम् ।
वाचां ग्रन्थमयीनां दर्शनमुपपद्यतेऽर्थबोधाय ।।470।।

The vani written in the ancient texts is meant to be understood the same way as the uttered vani is to be heard.

मूर्तिं विना च वाचं दर्शनमुपपद्यते क्वापि ।
तस्माल्लिपिरिह वाचं मूर्तिरवश्यं तदाप्यासीत् ।।471।।

लिपिसंकेताविज्ञः पश्यन्न च तां ददर्श वाक्त्वेन ।
शृण्वन्न शृणोत्येतां वेत्ति न यस्त्वर्थसंकेतम् ।।472।।

The vani cannot be seen without a form and therefore script existed in the shape of vani in ancient times. The person who knows the signs of script cannot perceive it in the form of vani nor can it be heard without understanding its meaning.

1.8.3.3 तृतीयं प्रमाणम्

1.8.3.3 Third evidence

अपि च पुरा देवयुगे सत्त्वे कस्याश्चिदेव देवलिपेः ।
मन्त्रकृतामाचारं वीक्षे नूनं प्रमाणतया ।।473।।

We can know the conduct of the people who created the hymns only with the help of divine script in the devayuga.

कुत्सनृपो गन्धर्वो हृतराज्यो दस्युभिः पुराकाले ।
विकलश्चिन्तामापत् तं प्रति घोरः प्रगाथ इत्याहुः ।।474।।

मा चिदन्यद्वि शंसत सखायो मा रिषण्यत ।
इन्द्रमित्स्तोता वृषणं सचा सुते मुहुरुक्था च शंसत ।।
(ऋग्वेदः, 8.1.1)

In ancient times, Gandharva, the king of Kutsa, became dejected after his kingdom was captured by the asuras. Ghor Pragadha [son of sage Kutsa] thus consoled him: O friends! Do not pray to any other gods. Pray to the Soma-infused might of Indra.

प्रास्मै गायत्रमर्चत वावातुर्यः पुरन्दरः ।
याभिः काण्वस्योप बर्हिरासदं यासद्वज्री भिनत् पुरः ।।
(ऋग्वेदः, 8.1.8)

Let us sing praises in Gayatri mantra for the mighty Indra who destroys the enemy forts with ease. If Indra becomes inspired by these prayers, he might appear next to your seat and destroy your enemies with his vajra.

इत्यादिष्टः कुत्सः शक्रमुपेत्येन्द्रसखकाण्वः ।
गीतान्याह्वानार्थं न्यवेदयद् भद्रसूक्तानि ।।475।।

Kutsa went to Indra and offered him the verses that invoked his help from the sons of Kanva.

आ याहि कृणवाम त इन्द्र ब्रह्माणि वर्द्धना ।
येभिः शविष्ठ चाकनो भद्रमिह श्रवस्यते ।।
भद्रा इन्द्रस्य रातयः ।।
(ऋग्वेदः, 8.51.4)

O great king! We would sing your praises. Prosperity reaches those who have your blessings. Your riches are bountiful.

यच्चिद्धि त्वा जना इमे नाना हवन्त ऊतये ।
अस्माकं ब्रह्मेदमिन्द्र भूतु तेऽहा विश्वा च वर्द्धनम् ।।
(ऋग्वेदः, 8.1.3)

O Indra! You are praised by the people. We call you for our protection and wish that your glory is multiplied.

एन्द्र याहि मत्स्व चित्रेण देव राधसा ।
सरो न प्रास्युदरं सपीतिभिरा सोमेभिरुरु स्फिरम् ।।
(ऋग्वेदः, 8.1.23)

एन्द्र याहि हरिभिरुप कण्वस्य सुष्टुतिम् ।
दिवो अमुष्य शासतो दिवं यय दिवावसो ।।
(ऋग्वेदः, 8.34.1)

O Indra! Please come and give us desired boons. Fill the pond with golden and divine Soma-rasa. Hey Indra! Bring your horses closer to our prayers. O, resident of Dyauloka, ruler of Dyauloka, return to Dyauloka.

कण्वानां तु न चैषां स्वर्गे गमनं श्रुतं तदा काले ।
लिखितं विना नु भारतभूस्थैः शक्यं स आहवः कर्तुम् ।।476।।

In those days, the journey of these Kanvas to heaven was not heard of. These pleas of Kanvas would not have reached heaven unless they were written.

तस्मादवश्यमेते विलिख्य कण्वा इमानि सूक्तानि ।
इन्द्रस्यागमनार्थं कुत्सकरात् प्रेषयामासुः ।।477।।

मन्यामहे ततः प्राग् वैदिकमन्त्रावतारकालेऽपि ।
आसील्लिपिप्रचारो विबुधैरुद्भावितः कुशलैः ।।478।।

Therefore, Kanvas must have given the letter containing their pleas to Indra through the king of Kutsa. It proves that even prior to the creation of Vedic mantras, wise people had used script for writing.

1.8.3.4 चतुर्थं प्रमाणम्

1.8.3.4 Fourth evidence

ऋज्राश्वो नामासीत् पश्चिमभारत ऋषिः कश्चित् ।
जरदस्त्रस्तस्याभूद्दौहित्रो ब्राह्मणद्वेषी ।।479।।

There used to be a sage named Rijrashva in western India. He had a grandson named Zarathustra who hated the brahmins.

ब्राह्मणविद्वेषात् स हि तेषां ब्राह्मीं लिपिं त्यक्त्वा ।
विपरीतां तु खरोष्ठीं लिपिमन्यां कल्पयामास ।।480।।

Because of his intense hatred for the brahmins, he rejected the Brahmi script and developed a script called Kharoshti which could be written from right to left.

ब्राह्मी वामाद्दक्षिणमेति खरोष्ठी तु दक्षिणाद्वामम् ।
शाकद्वीपेऽन्यत्र च लिपिः खरोष्ठी प्रचलिताभूत् ।।481।।

The Brahmi script is written from left to right whereas Kharoshti script is written from right to left. This script was used in countries such as Shaka [Sak] island.

अस्याः पुनः खरोष्ठ्या विकारतोऽनेकलिपयः स्युः ।
विपरीताचरणादथ जरदस्त्रमतानुगा मगाः ख्याताः ।।482।।

Out of this Kharoshti script, many other scripts were born. The hostile behaviour of the followers of Zarathustra reflected the deviating nature of the script. Due to such behaviour, these people came to be known as the Magas.

शाकद्वीपिमगा इह पणिभिः सह भारतेऽभ्येत्य ।
कीकटदेशे न्यूषुस्तं देशं मगधमाचख्युः ।।483।।

The inhabitants of Shakadvipa came to Bharatavarsha and started residing in 'Keekat desha'. That region came to be known as Magadha.

तेषां प्रसङ्गतस्त्विह लिपिः खरोष्ठी समागता मगधे ।
ब्राह्मी लिपिरासीत् प्राक् तेन द्विविधा लिपिः प्रचरिताऽत्र ।।484।।

Due to the influence of people of Maga community, Kharoshti script became popular in Magadha. Before that, Brahmi script was in use there. Thus both the scripts came into existence there.

ब्राह्म्या बह्व्यो विकृतय आसन् खरोष्ठ्याश्च ।
ता अपि वामाद्दक्षिणमथ वामं दक्षिणादयन् ।।485।।

Soon both the scripts, influenced by each other, underwent some structural changes. Some people started using Brahmi from right to left and others started using Kharoshti from left to right.

मगधे पाटलिपुत्रे बूभव सम्राडशोकः प्राक् ।
स लिपी उभयविधे अपि निजराष्ट्रे वर्तयामास ।।486।।

इत्थं द्विविधो लेखो वामावर्ती च दक्षिणावर्ती ।
अद्यावधि प्रचरितो लोके सर्वत्र दृश्यते प्रायः ।।487।।

The great king Ashoka of Magadha's Pataliputra popularised both Brahmi and Kharoshti during his reign. Thus we come across both kinds of scripts in all places.

वामावर्तिन्यास्त्विह जरदस्त्रो जन्मदो लिप्याः ।
ब्राह्मीलिपेर्विरोधादेषा च भिन्नक्रमं लिपौ चक्रे ।।488।।

तेन स्पष्टं सिध्यति जरदस्त्रस्यास्य जन्मतः पूर्वम् ।
ब्राह्मी लिपिः प्रचरिता सर्वत्रासीत् पुराकालात् ।।489।।

Zarathustra was the creator of the script that is written from right to left. He had created it to oppose the Brahmi script. This proves that Brahmi was widely used much before Zarathustra's birth.

1.8.3.5 पञ्चमं प्रमाणम्

1.8.3.5 Fifth evidence

परिपूर्णसभ्यतायां वृत्तायां निर्मिता इमाः श्रुतयः ।
वैज्ञानिकता ह्येषां दृश्यत इह सभ्यतामूलम् ।।490।।

The Vedas came into existence in an evolved and mature civilization. The scientific character of the Vedas revealed the maturity of the times in which they came to be known.

राजप्रजाविभागः सामाजिकता च धर्मनीतिश्च ।
कार्याकार्यविभागो दृश्यत इह सभ्यताचिह्नम् ।।491।।

कालेऽनादौ लक्षाधिकेषु वर्षेष्वतीतेषु ।
वेदा इमेऽवतीर्णा बहुषु च शास्त्रेष्वतीतेषु ।।492।।

The numerous departments and functions of the sovereign and the public, sociology, dharma and law mentioned in the Vedas are symbols of the civilization of that era. The Vedas must have originated millions of years ago after the creation of the shastras.

पूर्वे साध्या देवाः पूर्व्या धर्माश्च पूर्वजा गाथाः ।
पूर्वाण्याख्यानान्यपि बहुधोल्लिख्यन्त इह वेदे ।।493।।

The Vedas are replete with instances of devas belonging to a former age, ancient Vedic dharma, legends of the ancestors, and description of history.

तस्मादेभ्यो वेदग्रन्थेभ्योऽपि च पुरातने काले ।
उन्नत्यवनतिपर्यायधारा लोकेऽवगम्यन्ते ।।494।।

We can thus speculate the progress and development achieved in times prior to the Vedas.

एतद्वेदात् प्रागपि बह्व्यो विद्या अनेकधा भाषाः ।
नाना लिपयो जाताः संभाव्यन्ते विलुप्ताश्च ।।495।।

It is certain that many languages and disciplines must have existed before the Vedas. These languages must have originated from multiple scripts which must have been lost over a great span of time.

प्रकृतिक्रमानभिज्ञाः सहस्रषट्कान्तरार्थमात्रदृशः ।
कालविलुप्तानर्थान्नाभ्युपगच्छन्त्यदर्शनाद्धेतोः ।।496।।

Those who believe in the history of only six thousand years would not understand the concept of the loss of prehistoric knowledge.

अद्यत्वे त्विह वाङ्मयमुपलब्धं यावदेवास्ति ।
सर्वस्मादपि तस्माद्वेदः प्राचीन इति सत्यम् ।।497।।

वेदात्प्रागपि विद्या भाषा लिपयोऽनुवृत्ताश्चेत् ।
ध्रुवमत्र वेदकालेऽप्येता आसन्निति ब्रूमः ।।498।।

The most ancient of the *vakmaya* (collection of words) existing today are the Vedas. Hence we can say that if language, script, and knowledge existed in pre-Vedic times, it certainly must have existed in the Vedic era.

1.8.3.6 षष्ठं प्रमाणम्

1.8.3.6 Sixth evidence

यास्कोऽप्याह निरुक्ते धार्मान् दृष्ट्वर्षयः पुराऽनूचुः ।
श्रुत्वा मन्त्रग्रहणाक्षमा इमं ग्रन्थमामम्नुः ।।499।।

विल्मो विभिन्नखण्डो विल्मग्रहणाय कल्पितो ग्रन्थः ।
लिपिमन्तरेण भिन्नो भिन्नः खण्डो न शक्यमभिनेतुम् ।।500।।

The great sage Yaska has also said: The sages have rendered their discourses after consulting ancient religions. With their grasp over the mantras, the sages must have first heard the mantras and then replicated them in the sacred texts.

It is impossible to understand or grasp these without a script.

1.8.3.7 सप्तं प्रमाणम्

1.8.3.7 Seventh evidence

द्वैपायनश्च कृष्णो हिमवति बदरीवने निवसन् ।
वेदं व्यस्यन् मन्त्रान्संगृह्य तु संहिताश्चक्रे ।।501।।

मन्त्राणां संकलनं तेषां चानेकसंहितारचनम् ।
लिपिमन्तरेण कर्तुं न शक्यमेकेन पुरुषेण ।।502।।

The island-born Veda Vyasa had stayed in the Badri forest of the Himalayas while he compiled the hymns and created samhitas after dividing the Vedas. Without the knowledge of the script, it is impossible for one person to collect all those mantras and create samhitas.

1.8.3.8 अष्टमं प्रमाणम्

1.8.3.8 Eighth evidence

साहसिकः पुनरन्यस्त्वदूरदर्शीत्यदीर्घशीति ।
मागधराजाशोकात् प्राग् लिपिसत्त्वं न भावयति ।।503।।

Ignorant and impertinent people do not believe in the existence of script before the reign of Magadha king Ashoka.

हन्ताशोकस्य द्वाविंशतिशतकल्पवर्षाणि ।
प्रययुः किन्त्विह रामः पञ्चसहस्त्राब्दतोऽभवत्पूर्वम् ।।504।।

It is said that the Magadha king Ashoka lived just 2200 years ago, while lord Rama was born more than five thousand years ago.

रामस्यापि च समये लिपिरासीदिति पुरा हनुमान् ।
नामाङ्किताङ्गुलीयकमदर्शयत्तत्र जानक्यै ।।505।।

In the Valmiki Ramayana, it is said: 'O mother! I am the ambassador of Sri Rama. O goddess! Look at this ring that bears Rama's name.'

वानरोऽहं महाभागे दूतो रामस्य धीमतः ।
रामनामाङ्कितं चेदं पश्च देव्यङ्गुलीयकम् ।।
(रामायणम्, सुन्दरकाण्डम्, 36.2)

There is evidence of the existence of script even during the times of Sri Rama because Hanuman had shown his ring that bore Sri Rama's name to Sita.

चीनपरिव्राडासीदित्यङ्गस्तद्वचः प्रमाणं ये ।
भारतविद्वच्छास्त्रं तु न प्रमाणं वदन्ति ते धन्याः ।।506।।

Un-enlightened scholars do not consider the evidence of the ancient Indian texts as valid, but are quick to reiterate the words of Chinese monks.

इत्थं च वेदकाले लिपिसत्त्वे सन्ति हेतवः कतिचित् ।
सा च लिपिर्ब्राह्मी वा दैवी वा नामतोऽन्या वा ।।507।।

It is clear from all the evidence stated above that script existed in the Vedic era. It may have existed by the names of *daivi* (divine) or Brahmi but its existence is indubitable.

इति भारतपरिचये लिपिप्रसङ्गः सम्पूर्णः ।

The section on scripts in the Introduction to Bharatavarsha is concluded.

1.9 सभ्यताप्रसङ्गः

1.9 SECTION ON CULTURE

1.9.1 देवयुगे भारतवर्षस्य परमोन्नतिः

1.9. 1 Exceptional development of Bharatavarsha during devayuga

अपि पूर्वस्मिन् काले परमोन्नतिशिखरमायाताः ।
एते तु भारतीया विश्वेषां शिक्षका अभवन् ।।508।।

In ancient times, these men of learning from Bharatavarsha had scaled immensely exalted peaks of knowledge and become wise teachers to the entire world.

एष गुरुः सर्वेषां देशानामुत्तमो देशः ।
अत एवास्य मनुः प्रागवर्णयद् गौरवं पूर्णम् ।।509।।

एतद्देशप्रसूतस्य सकाशादग्रजन्मनः ।
स्वं स्वं चरित्रं शिक्षेरन् पृथिव्यां सर्वमानवाः ।।

(मनुस्मृतिः, 2.20)

न तदात्वे यवनानां न रोमकाणां न चीनानाम् ।
ज्ञानं बलं च लक्ष्मीस्तथा यथा भारतीयानाम् ।।510।।

This country was an exceedingly great one and was a teacher to all. Manu has previously described the glory of this country.

It is from the first-born brahmins in this country that all the people on this earth should get knowledge and good conduct [work and business skill]. In that era, these learned men from Bharatavarsha had so much knowledge, strength, and wealth that they could not be rivalled by any amongst the Yavanas, the ancient Greeks, and the inhabitants of Rome and China.

ज्ञानं तेषामधिकं तत इह विद्याश्चतुःषष्टिः ।
भारतवर्षे प्रथमं प्रादुर्भूता असामान्याः ।।511।।

These Indians had superior knowledge, which led to the emergence of the extraordinary sixty-four arts here.

बलमपि तेषामधिकं बहवस्त्विह चक्रवर्तिनोऽभूवन् ।
सप्तसमुद्रां पृथ्वीं मान्धातैकः शशास तच्चोक्तम् ।।512।।

These men from Bharatavarsha were exceedingly powerful: amongst them, many kings became chakravartis; it has been said that a powerful king called Mandhata had, single-handedly, ruled this entire world surrounded by the seven seas.

यावत्सूर्य उदेति स्म यावच्च प्रतिष्ठति ।
सर्वं तद्यौवनाश्वस्य मान्धातुः क्षेत्रमुच्यते ।
(विष्णुपुराणम्, 4.2.65)

अमरीकाख्यो देशो देशो यो वाऽफरीकाख्यः ।
यूरोप एशिया तान् सर्वान् शास्ति स्म मान्धाता ।।513।।

It is written in the Vishnu Purana that Yuvanasva's son Mandhata ruled over so vast a territory that the sun rose and set there. This Mandhata alone ruled over all the countries of America, Africa, Europe, and Asia.

पाताले गन्धर्वैर्वीरा नागाः प्रपीडिताः सन्तः ।
शरणमगुर्मान्धातुः स हि तेषां रक्षणं चक्रे ।।514।।

The valiant people of the Naga race, being persecuted by the Gandharvas of the nether world, had sought the refuge of this Mandhata, who offered them protection.

इक्ष्वाकुश्च ययातिः शशबिन्दुर्हैहयः सगरः ।
एवं क्व च रविवंश्यः क्व च शशिवंश्योऽभवत् सम्राड् ।।515।।

In ancient India, there have been emperors like Ikshvaku, Haihaya, Yayati, Shashbindu and Sagara. Among them, some were Suryavanshis (solar dynasty) and some were Chandravanshis (lunar dynasty).

एषा सुवर्णभूमिगौरेषा दोग्धि भूयसीर्लक्ष्मीः ।
अन्नधनैः स्वान् बिभ्रत्यन्यान् देशान् बिभर्ति साऽद्यापि ।।516।।

This land of Bharata is a land of gold, is like a cow which offers sufficient milk [symbolises wealth] and, even today, maintains itself and other countries with food and wealth.

इति भारतपरिचये सभ्यताप्रसङ्गः सम्पूर्णः ।

The section on culture in the Introduction to Bharatavarsha is concluded.

1.10 धर्मप्रसङ्गः

1.10 SECTION ON DHARMA[2]

1.10.1 भारतीयधर्माणां वैज्ञानिकत्वम्

1.10.1 The scientific nature of bharatiya dharma

अन्नाचारविचाराः वैज्ञानिकनियतिभावनाक्लृप्ताः ।
तेनेह लौकिका अपि धर्मा इह पारलौकिकाः सर्वे: ।।517।।

सर्वेभ्योऽपि च देशान्तरीयधर्मेभ्य उत्कर्षः ।
धर्मेऽत्र भारतीये यदयं लोकद्वयौपयिकः ।।518।।

The rites and practices that exist in the bharatiya dharma are imbued with scientific temperament. What makes it different from other belief systems is that it traverses both the worlds—the world in which we live and the world which is beyond us.

मतभेदा बहवोऽस्मिन्नैको मार्गोऽत्र सुस्थिरः कश्चित् ।
इति दोषं ब्रुवतेऽन्ये भारतवर्षीयधर्मेऽस्मिन् ।।519।।

अनभिज्ञास्ते भारतधर्मरहस्यादसूक्ष्मदृशः ।
नैषा नीतिर्नायं भारतधर्मो यदृच्छया क्लृप्तः ।।520।।

Some people are quick to criticize the bharatiya dharma on the grounds of there being many differences of opinion and the absence of a decided path. These people are uninitiated in the mystery of this dharma. Their vision and capacity for handling mystical knowledge are deficient; this is because the bharatiya dharma is neither a voluntarily adopted faith-system nor merely a code of ethics.

वैज्ञानिकस्तु धर्मः सर्वेषां नैकरूपः स्यात् ।
अपि देशकालपात्रप्रभेदतो भिन्नतौचित्यात् ।।521।।

Dharma based on vijnana do make a distinction between space, time, and personality. Hence, there is no uniformity of behaviour amongst people belonging to different religions.

---

[2]It would be erroneous to understand 'dharma' as religion hence in this text the term has not been translated. Please refer to the glossary for an explanation of dharma.

नरकल्पितस्तु धर्मो नीतित्वात् संभवयत्येकः ।
वैज्ञानिको मनुष्यो न च स्वतन्त्रोऽभिनेतुमेकतया ॥522॥

Religions conceived by humans are mere rules and can be manipulated easily. But a person with a *vaigyanik* (scientific) attitude to dharma will not follow a rule-oriented system.

वैज्ञानिको हि सूक्ष्मोपपत्तिको भारते धर्मः ।
तस्य तदेव महत्त्वं यदनेकत्वं रवीन्दुनियतत्वात् ॥523॥

The bharatiya dharma, influenced by the cosmos, is a more evolved doctrine and is characterised by diversity.

1.10.2 भारतीयधर्मस्वरूपम्

1.10.2 The form of bharatiya dharma

यो धृतः सन् धारयते स धर्मः । स्वरूपसम्पादको गुणो धर्मः । प्रजासंरक्षणे दीक्षितो राजा भवति। दीक्षितोऽधिकारं प्राप्तः । यावता प्रजां स्वदीक्षानुसारेण पालयेत् तावता स राजा स्यात्। दुष्टनिग्रहानुग्रहाभ्यां शान्तिसंरक्षणं पालनम्। स यद्येतन्न कुर्यात् न स तर्हि राजेत्युक्तः स्यात् स स्वरूपाद् विच्यवेत। मनुष्यत्वमस्यावशिष्यते न राजत्वम्। तस्माद्राजस्वरूपसंपादकमिदं कर्म धृतं सद् राजानं धारयति तेनायं राज्ञो धर्मः । अत एवाहुः-

धर्म एव हतो हन्ति धर्मो रक्षति रक्षितः ॥

(मनुस्मृतिः, 8.15)

धर्मो द्विविधः प्राकृतः संस्कृतश्च। यत्र मनुष्याणां हेयत्वोपादेयत्वयोः स्वायत्तत्वं नास्ति स प्रकृत्या सिद्धः सर्वो गुणः प्राकृतो धर्मः । यथा मनुष्यत्वादिः मैथिलत्वसारस्वतत्वादिः । यावांस्तु गुणो मनुष्यैः स्वायत्ततयोपपाद्यते मनुष्येषु मनुष्यैराधीयते स संस्कारजन्यत्वात् संस्कृतो धर्मः । यथा राजत्वं प्राङ्विवाकत्वं गुरुत्वं भृत्यत्वम्। एवमादयो गुणा अधिकारयोगादुत्पद्यन्ते। तस्मात्ते संस्कृता धर्माः ।

The essence of dharma could be explained in these words: The one, when held, becomes the holder. This attribute of subsuming the holder is dharma. Just as a person who becomes a king only when he is initiated into the dharma called 'kingship'—to protect his people. (Here, when the person who accepts the dharma of kingship is also held together and supported by that very dharma he holds onto; in other words, that dharma of kingship makes him the king.)

Achieving the right to rule is initiation in this case. A king remains a king as long as he discharges his responsibilities as ordained by his dharma. The initiation-vows of kingship are: controlling the delinquents, being benevolent to the good, maintaining peace and looking after the subjects. If he fails in these duties, then he does not deserve to be called a king. In such a situation, he would be considered having fallen from the high ideals of kingship. Here, the dharma of being a human would remain but not that of a king. Thus, a king remains a king by following the dharma of being a king. In this way, this initiation into kingship is the religion of kingship. Hence it has been said that, on being destroyed, dharma destroys man. If we safeguard dharma, then dharma protects man.

Dharma is of two kinds: natural and one that is culturally imbued. The natural dharma is the one where humans do not have any control over the actions and attributes, only nature has. The second kind of dharma, on the other hand, is created through cultural practices and interactions practised by humans.

अष्टधा व्याक्रियन्ते हीमे धर्माः

1. दीक्षाव्रतम्।	5. पुष्टिः।
2. संस्कारः।	6. शान्तिः।
3. आचारव्रतम्।	7. स्वस्त्ययनम्।
4. शुद्धिः ।	8. आनृशंस्यम्।

Dharma is of eight kinds: 1. Through initiation, 2. cultural, 3. ritualistic, 4. through purification, 5. by embellishment, 6. meditative, 7. through conciliation, 8. through patronage.

ब्राह्मणक्षत्रियवैश्यानां जन्मना लब्धोऽधिकारो दीक्षा। कुलक्रमागतं कर्म वृत्तिः। अधिकारपूर्तिर्दीक्षाव्रतम्। तत्र ब्राह्मणं व्याख्यास्यामः।

1. स्वयं विज्ञानान्युपार्जयेत्। परेभ्यो विज्ञानान्युपदिशेत। तत् तपः।
2. स्वयं यज्ञैर्यज्ञपुरुषं याजयेत्। परेभ्यो यज्ञैर्यज्ञपुरुषं याजयेत्। स यज्ञः।
3. राजभ्यो धनाढ्येभ्यश्च कररूपेण प्रतिगृह्णीयात्। दीनेभ्यो जीवनं दद्यात्। तद्दानम्।

यथाऽयं क्षत्रियो राजा आधिभौतिकेभ्यो दुःखेभ्यो ब्राह्मणक्षत्रियवैश्यान् प्रजाः संरक्षति। संरक्षणशुल्कतया करं प्रतिगृह्णाति। सत्यामावश्यकतायामधिकमपि समये समये प्रतिगृह्णाति। दीनदरिद्रेभ्यस्तज्जीवनार्थं ददाति च। तथायं ब्राह्मणो ब्रह्मा आधिदैविकेभ्यो दुःखेभ्यो ब्राह्मणक्षत्रियवैश्यान् प्रजाः संरक्षति। संरक्षणशुल्कतया राजभ्योऽपि करं प्रतिगृह्णाति। सत्यामावश्यकतायामधिकमपि समये समये प्रतिगृह्णाति। यथा राज्ञः शासनसभामण्डलाधीनानि धिष्ण्यभवनानि भवन्ति तथामुष्य ब्रह्मणो देवयजनमण्डलाधीनाः पाकादियज्ञशालाः स्थापिता भवन्ति।

भोजमहाभोजौ राजानौ। चक्रवर्तिसार्वभौमो सम्राजौ। इन्द्रमहेन्द्रौ स्वराजौ ब्रह्मविष्णू विराजाविति चतुःकक्षं क्षत्रं भवति। तथा द्विजो विप्रो देवो ब्रह्मेति चतुःकक्षं ब्रह्म भवति। ताविमौ ब्रह्मा मूर्धाभिषिक्तश्च लोकानां दीक्षापालौ भवतः। एतावेव सर्वाः प्रजा अनुशिष्टः। अनयोरपि

क्षत्रमनुशास्ति। तस्माद् ब्राह्मणो राजभ्य: करं प्रतिगृह्णाति। यथा कर्षकाणां सर्वा भूमी राज्ञ:। नगरे सर्वमापणं सर्वा वीथ्यो राजमार्गा राज्ञ एव। राजानुग्रहेण च सर्वा: प्रजा: स्वत्वमनुवर्तयन्ति एवमेवैतेषां राज्ञामपि तत्र तत्राधिकारो ब्राह्मणानुग्रहेण प्रतिपत्तव्य:। सर्वो ब्रह्मस्वं भुङ्क्ते। ब्रह्मा राज्ञोऽधिपति:। राजा वैश्यवर्गस्याधिपति:। यदि प्रजा: सर्वा प्रतिपन्थिन्यो विरुद्धा: स्यु: स्वतन्त्रा: स्यु: राजाज्ञां नानुपालयेयु: स तर्हि राजा क्षत्रवीर्याच्चयुतोऽनधिकारो भवति न स्वधर्मं परिपालयितुं शक्नोति। एवं यदि राजान: सर्वे विप्रतिपन्थिन: स्यु: स्वतन्त्रा: स्यु: ब्राह्मणाज्ञां नानुपालयेयु: स तर्हि ब्रह्मा ब्रह्मवीर्याच्चयुतोऽधिकारो भवति न स्वधर्मं परिपालयितुं शक्नोति। यथा शरीरे आग्नेयम् उदरमण्डलं वायव्यम् उरोमण्डलम् ऐन्द्रं शिरोमण्डलं परस्परानुगृहीतं वीर्यवद् भवति। पृथक्कृतं चैतदेकैकं स्वतन्त्रं सन्निर्वीर्यं मृतं भवति। तथेदं विण्मण्डलं क्षत्रमण्डलं ब्रह्ममण्डलं च पृथक्कृतं सदेकैकं स्वतन्त्रं भूत्वा निर्वीर्यं मृतं भवति। स्वतन्त्रा वैश्या न राजाज्ञामनुपालयन्ति स्वतन्त्राश्च राजानो न ब्राह्मणाज्ञामनुपालयन्ति। तनैते त्रयोऽपि निर्वीर्या मृता इव संप्रति दृश्यन्ते। परस्परानुगृहीतास्त्वेते स्वं स्वं धर्ममसंकीर्णमनुवर्तमाना वीर्यवन्त: स्यु: सर्वैश्चैतै: स्वस्वधर्मानसांकर्येणानुतिष्ठद्भिरेक: समाजात्मा जीवितो भवति तत्रायं ब्राह्मण: समाजात्मन: शिर:स्थानीय:। स एष व्याख्यात:।

एवमुर:स्थानीय: क्षत्रिय:। उदरस्थनीयो वैश्यश्च व्याख्यातव्य:। अस्य हि समाजरूपस्यात्मनोऽयं ब्राह्मणस्तावदाधिदैविकव्यापत्ति- निवर्तकत्वाच्चर्मस्थानीयोन्तरङ्गोऽङ्गरक्षको भवतीति शर्मेत्युच्यते-

चर्मेति मानुषं शर्म देवत्रा। (शतपथब्राह्मणम्, 1.1.4.4)

इति श्रुते:। क्षत्रियस्तु आधिभौतिकव्यापत्तिनिवर्तकत्वाद् वर्मस्थानीयो बहिरङ्गोऽङ्गरक्षको भवतीति वर्मेत्युच्यते। द्वाविमौ गोपयितारौ भवत:। यस्तु ताभ्यामुभाभ्यां संगुप्येते स गुप्तो वैश्य:। तेषामेषां त्रयाणां स्वस्वव्रतोपयोगिशक्तिप्रवर्धककर्मकरणं स्वस्वव्रतोपयोगिशक्तिव्यापादककर्म-परित्यागश्च प्रातिस्विको धर्म: सिद्धो भवतीति विज्ञेयम्।

In the case of brahmins, kshatriyas and vaishyas, their dharma is carrying out their respective inherited socio-cultural duties and responsibilities; this inheritance of familial vocations is dharma for them. Thus, their vocation involves the performance of their time-sanctioned rites and duties.

Now, let us explicate the brahmanical dharma: (1) they should acquire knowledge themselves; hold discourses on vijnana; this is their mission in life; (2) offer respects to the yajna-purusha or the Paramatma, the Supreme-Being, himself; and do the same for others; this is yajna; (3) get wealth from the rulers and the wealthy in the form of taxes; give the gift of life, in the form of knowledge, to both these classes, or the ignorant; this is his gift.

The king protects his brahmin, kshatriya, and vaishya subjects from material tribulations, he accepts taxes in the form of protection-cess, and also, if necessary, accepts excess wealth and gives it in charity to the destitute and poor. Similarly, the brahmin stands for Brahma and protects brahmin, kshatriya, and vaishya subjects from spiritual harm, and, in the form of protection-cess, he accepts formal charity from king, and if necessary, accepts it in excess. Just as a king has his palaces, public halls, and courts, sanctified yajna spaces, essential to worship Brahma, should be established.

Kings are of two types—powerful and very powerful; they are chakravartis and sovereign emperors. Indra and Mahendra are *svaraja* and Brahma and Vishnu are *viraja*.

Similarly, brahmins are also of four kinds: dvija, vipra, deva, and brahma. The brahmins and kshatriyas are both keepers of public conscience and have an inspiring and enforcing role in keeping public order. Hence, brahmins accept taxes from the king. Just as all farm lands in the rural areas, and all shops, lanes and markets belong to the king, and all subjects tend to their duties and enjoy their rights by his permission, so does the kings enjoy all these rights and privileges with the brahmanical sanction.

Everyone enjoys the wealth generated by the brahmins, who are the governors of the state. The king is the overlord of the mercantile community. If all subjects are bent upon rebellion and refuse to accept the bidding of the king, then that king is divorced from his right to his kshatriya-valour and is incapable of attending to his dharma. Similarly, if all kings become tyrannical and do not pay proper respect and obedience to the brahmins, then they are incapable of enjoying the fruits of their *brahmatejas* (power).

In the body, the intestinal regions are controlled by Agni, the chest-regions are controlled by Vayu and the head-area is controlled by Indra. By a process of mutual interaction, they establish a give-and-take mechanism of power. When separated, they lose their integrated synergy and are rendered powerless and nearly dead. Similarly, if the brahmin, kshatriya, and vaishya communities scatter and maintain completely separate and sovereign existence, then they also become powerless and die. The vaishyas, if independent, do not obey the orders of the king, and if the independent king ignores the orders of the brahmins, then all these three sections of society lose their collective power and are rendered almost dead.

If they maintain a mutual equilibrium, then they will, without meanness and pettiness, grow in strength within their own prescribed dharma. All these constitute the soul of a greater society where each individual acts beyond his call of duty and contribute to the holistic growth of the society. Here the soul of the society, taking the form of brahmin, is superior. Thus, the role of the brahmin has been explicated.

In this way, the kshatriya occupies the chest-region of the body of society.

The stomach-area has been given to the vaishyas and thus it should be accepted. The brahmin acts as the skin of the society which preserves a distance between the body of the society in general and the highest functions of the intellect. [Just as, in the body, the skin protects the flesh and bones similarly, it is the brahmin's work and duty to analyse and support the innermost religious-spiritual aspirations and desires in humans.] Hence, because of the brahmin's role as the skin of the society, he is referred to as 'sharm'. According to Shatapatha Brahmana—'what is skin in the popular dialects is called *charmm* in the language of the Vedas'.

The kshatriyas, in their capacity as those who deal with material threats to the society, are categorized as Varma; they act as the protective shield of the society. Thus, these two [the brahmins and kshatriyas] are, by definition, protectors and defenders. The one, who is hidden under the protective layers of these two, is the vaishya, often titled Gupta. The natural dharma of these three is to carry out their responsibilities dutifully and renounce actions and courses detrimental to their dutiful obligations. This is what has been proven, this is what should be followed.

1.10.3 वैज्ञानिकधर्मनिबन्धनं भारतवर्षमहत्त्वम्

1.10.3 Importance of dharma in Bharatavarsha

एतद् भारतवर्षप्रशंसनं यत्पुराणेषु ।
वैज्ञानिकं तदुक्तं धर्मो न यदृच्छयाऽत्र क्लृप्तोऽस्ति ।।524।।

Although the scientific temper of dharma practised in Bharatavarsha has been praised in the Puranas, it is not accepted widely.

अस्मिन्वर्षे वेदविज्ञानधारादीक्षाशिक्षापूर्णपाकोदयेन ।
दिव्या धर्मा यादृशाः सन्ति दृष्टा दृश्यन्ते ते नान्यदेशेषु तद्वत् ।।525।।

The kind of divine dharma that has flowered in Bharatavarsha is a fruition of the stream of Vedic knowledge and is not seen anywhere in the world.

चातुर्वर्ण्यं चातुराश्रम्यमेवं चातुर्वर्ग्यं यज्ञदाने तपश्च ।
इष्टापूर्त्ते दत्तमाराधना वा तीर्थप्रयाणां देवतानां गुरूणाम् ।।1526।।

इत्थं दृष्टा वेदिविद्भिः पुराणैरस्मिन्वर्षे भारते धर्मभेदाः ।
अत्रैवैषामस्ति सम्यग् विधानं देशेऽन्यस्मिन् सन्ति नैषामुदर्काः ।।527।।

Those who are learned in the Puranas and Vedic knowledge have revealed the secrets of dharma in the four varnas, the four ashramas, the *chaturvarga*-s (the four ends of life—dharma, wealth, pleasure, and freedom from birth), yajna, charity, meditation and penance, pilgrimage and worship of devas and gurus.

एतत्सत्यं वर्णयन्ति स्म पूर्वे सूक्ष्मप्रेक्षादक्षपौराणिकाग्र्याः ।
ब्राह्मेऽध्याये पञ्चविंशे पुराणे भूयो भूयोऽन्यत्र चान्यत्र चेति ।।528।।

In the Puranas, especially the twenty-fifth chapter of the Brahma Purana, the wisest of the ancient sages and scholars, enabled by their divine visions, have offered detailed definitions of dharma in many places.

1.10.4 पौराणिकं भारतवर्षमाहात्म्यम्

1.10.4 Greatness of Bharatavarsha in the Puranas

न भारतसमं वर्षं पृथिव्यामस्ति किञ्चन ।
यत्र विप्रादयो वर्णाः प्राप्नुवन्त्यविभवाञ्छितम् ।।
(ब्रह्मपुराणम्, 25.71)

In the Brahma Purana, it is said: In the entire world, there is no country like Bharata where communities like brahmins and others achieve their desired goals through dharma.

धन्यास्ते भारते वर्षे जायन्ते ये नरोत्तमाः ।
धर्मार्थकाममोक्षाणां प्राप्नुवन्ति महाफलम् ।।
(ब्रह्मपुराणम्, 25.72)

Blessed are those epitomes of humanity who are born in Bharatavarsha; they achieve the great fruits of dharma, *artha* (meaning), *karma* (action) and moksha.

प्राप्यते यत्र तपसः फलं परमदुर्लभम् ।
सर्वदानफलं यत्र सर्वयज्ञफलं तथा ।।
(ब्रह्मपुराणम्, 25.73)

Where spiritual practitioners achieve the rarest of rare fruits of spiritual practices, penances and all types of charitable exercises.

तीर्थयज्ञफलं सम्यक् गुरुसेवाफलं तथा ।
देवताराधनफलं गार्हस्थ्ये चैव यत्फलम् ।।
(ब्रह्मपुराणम्, 25.74)

Where the fruits of sacred activities such as yajnas and pilgrimages, and the fruits of serving one's guru, the fruits accrued from the worship of the devas, and those fruits which deserve to be acquired in the course of family life are attained.

यत्र देवाः सदा हृष्टाः जन्म वाञ्छन्ति शोभनम् ।
नाना व्रतफलं यत्र नाना शास्त्रफलं तथा ॥
(ब्रह्मपुराणम्, 25.75)

Where even the gods are only happy to be born anew; where the fruits of multiple vows and fruits of scriptural knowledge are acquired.

अहिंसादिफलं सम्यक् फलं सर्वाभिवाञ्छितम् ।
ब्रह्मचर्यफलं यत्र स्वाध्यायेन च यत्फलम् ॥
(ब्रह्मपुराणम्, 25.76)

Bharatavarsha is where fruits of non-violence can be achieved in full, where it is possible to fulfil all unrequited desires and where fruits of self-learning and celibacy can be achieved.

यत्फलं वनवासेन संन्यासेन च यत्फलम् ।
इष्टापूर्त्तैः फलं चैव तथाऽन्यच्छुभकर्मणाम् ॥
प्राप्यते भारते वर्षे न चान्यत्र क्वचिद्भुवि ।
कः शक्नोति गुणान्वक्तुं भारतस्याखिलानपि ॥
(ब्रह्मपुराणम्, 25.77–78)

The fruits acquired from living in the forest, from the acceptance of *sanyasa* (renunciation vows), from desires and their realisation, and fruits acquired through other kinds of auspicious activities—they are all achievable in this Bharatavarsha, but not anywhere else. Thus, who is capable of articulating all the admirable aspects of this Bharatavarsha?

1.10.5 भारतीयमहर्षीणां वैज्ञानिकतया दूरदर्शित्वम्

1.10.5 The scientific farsightedness of maharshis

अत्रत्या विद्वांसो मान्या ब्रह्मर्षयः पूर्वे ।
विज्ञानं तदपश्यन् येनापश्यन् परत्र कर्मफलम् ॥529॥

The ancient maharshis understood the intricacies of science and deduced the fruits of karma through scientific study.

मरणोत्तरमयमात्मा विलुप्यते सर्वथेति नावेयात् ।
जीवन्निव स तदानीमपि सुखदु:खे तनुं गतो भुङ्क्ते ॥530॥

This soul, after death, is not completely extinguished; but, in that state too, like the living soul, achieves happiness and sorrow.

इह यत्कर्म कृतं स्याच्छुभमशुभं वाफलं ध्रुवं तस्य ।
लभते परत्र जीव: स्वर्गसुखं यातनां यामीम् ॥531॥

This *jeevatama* (individual living soul), depending on its good or bad actions in this loka, realises the comfort of heaven or the trepidations of *Yamaloka* (the abode of the god of death).

यज्ञस्तपश्च दानानीष्टापूर्ते च दत्तं च ।
कर्म स्वर्गप्राप्त्यै दु:खप्राप्त्यै विकर्म चाकर्म ॥532॥

To achieve heavenly pleasures, one should perform the following actions: yajna, *tapa* (spiritual meditation) and *daana* (charity) and carry out their duties; the absence of work, indolence, and harmful work only cause sorrow.

इत्थं यज्ञं कुर्यादित्थं कुर्यात् तपश्च दानं च।
परपीडनं न कुर्याद् वपुषा वचसा च मनसा च ॥533॥

In this manner, as per these precedents and rules, yajna, tapa and daana should be carried out. In thought, word, or deed, no pain should be caused to others.

पारत्रिकमिदमित्थं धर्मश्चार्थश्च कामश्च।
मोक्षश्च भारतीयै: पूर्वैर्विज्ञानतो दृष्टा: ॥534॥

In this scientific manner, ancient sages have developed the dharma by integrating the four meanings of life—dharma, artha, karma, and moksha.

कुर्वन्ति भारतीया एव परलोकसाधनं कर्म ।
उत्तरजन्मन्युत्तमयोनिनिदानं त एव जानन्ति ॥535॥

Only the people of Bharatavarsha perform actions that gives them the otherworldly bliss. Only they know the ways of achieving, after death, births and rebirth in superior manifestations.

इतरजना: श्रद्दधते परलोके नैवमज्ञानात् ।
तेषां सर्वमपीदं कर्मैहिकभोगसाधनं नियतम् ॥536॥

Those who are not from Bharatavarsha, due to ignorance, have no faith in this sort of otherworldly manifestation. All their activities are geared towards achieving pleasure in this world.

अद्येतरवर्षीयप्रोन्नतिकालोऽस्ति किन्तु तत्रापि ।
नैषां तद्विज्ञानं मस्तिष्केऽद्यापि संरूढम् ॥537॥

Today, it is time for other countries to progress, but people there remain unaware of this ethereal knowledge.

धन्यं भारतवर्षं यत्रैतद्बहुपुरातने काले ।
विज्ञानं प्रतिबुद्धं सर्वा पुथ्वी यतोऽनभिज्ञास्ति ॥538॥

Blessed be Bharatavarsha, where in antiquity, this scientific development, which is still unknown to the entire world, took place.

1.10.6 भारतीयानाम् उन्नत्यवनतिविषयको विचारः

1.10.6 On the rise and decline of Bharatavarsha

उन्नत्यवनतिविचारे भारतीयानां प्राचां विदुषां सिद्धान्तः क्षीणभारतोपहासानौचित्यम् ।

The doctrine of progress and decline enunciated by the ancient Indian scholars and the unfairness of ridiculing a weak India.

भारतवर्षस्यास्य प्राचीनं गौरवं श्रुत्वा ।
अद्यत्वेऽवनतं तद् दृष्ट्वोपहसन्ति वैदेश्याः ॥539॥

In view of the decline of Bharatavarsha in later times, foreigners ridicule the ancient glories of this country that they hear.

धाष्ट्र्यं तदेतदेषामनभिज्ञत्वं बालकत्वं च ।
अपमानयन्ति ये तु क्षीणं दैवापराधेन ॥540॥

This is impudence, ignorance, and juvenile impetuousness of those, who by such worthless blasphemies, insult Bharatavarsha's scientific dharma.

अपि युद्धयतोर्द्वयोरिह जयति क्व च दुर्बलो दैवात् ।
दैवापराधतश्च क्वापि पराजीयते प्रबलः ॥541॥

Occasionally, in the course of a battle, due to some misfortune, the weaker side wins and the strong is defeated.

धर्मरक्षोपेक्षाया भारतावनतिहेतुत्वम् ।

The negligence in protecting dharma as the cause of India's decline.

भारतवर्षाधिपतिर्भारतधर्मं न हन्त पालयति ।
संप्रति भारतवर्षे शास्तुरुपेक्षैव हेतुरवनत्याः ॥542॥

It is sad that rulers of Bharatavarsha did not observe their own dharma. It is the negligence of the rulers which is the main reason for the decline of dharma in this country.

भारतवर्षाधिपतिर्यमिदानीमुन्नतेरस्य ।
हेतुं पश्यति च ध्रुवमवनतिहेतुस्ततोऽवनतिः ॥543॥

Nowadays, the progress, which the rulers claim to be beneficial, is the cause of the decline.

चातुर्वर्ण्यव्यवस्थाया अवनतिहेतुत्वाभावः ।

Refutal of claim that chaturvarna caused decline.

अप्यनभिज्ञाः केचिच्चातुर्वर्ण्यव्यवस्थानाम् ।
अवनतिहेतुं प्राहुर्न त्वेते दूरदर्शिनः सन्ति ॥543॥

Some ignorant people, who call the system of chaturvarna to be the cause of this decline, are shortsighted.

भारतवर्षे यावच्चातुर्वर्ण्यव्यवस्थानम् ।
आसीत् सुदृढं तावत् परमोन्नतिरस्य देशस्य ॥545॥

So long as the chaturvarna system was strong in Bharatavarsha, there was all-round development.

यदवधि राज्ञोऽसत्त्वाच्चातुर्वर्ण्यव्यवस्थानम् ।
अभवच्छिथिलं लोके तत आरम्भो निपातस्य ॥546॥

In the absence of kings to defend the chaturvarna system, the world has been on the decline.

चातुर्वर्ण्यव्यवस्थाया अवनतिहेतुत्वाभावः ।

Citing the chaturvarna system as the cause of decline.

यत्तु ब्रूयुः केचिच्चातुर्वर्ण्यव्यवस्थायाः ।
देशान्तरेष्वसत्त्वेऽप्युन्नतिरस्तीत्यहेतुः सा ।।547।।

Some people argue that other countries have progressed without the chaturvarna system and hence this system is not necessary for development.

तत्र ब्रूमः सोन्नतिरेतद्देशोन्नतेस्तुलनाम् ।
नार्हति भारतवर्षोन्नतिरासीदुन्नतिः परमा ।।548।।

On this, it can be argued that development in other countries are not comparable to that of Bharatavarsha. Here, the development has been superior.

भारतवर्षस्योन्नतिरथ चोन्नतिरन्यदेशानाम् ।
भिद्यत इतरेतरतः परमं त्वेवान्तरं हि तयोः ।।549।।

It is fallacious to compare development in other countries with that of Bharatavarsha. There is a big difference between the two.

आत्मोन्नतिरिह परमा भौतिक्युन्नतिरथान्यदेशेषु ।
भौती परसापेक्षा निरपेक्षा त्वात्मनः सिद्धिः ।।550।।

In this country, self-improvement is considered to be of utmost importance, whereas in other countries material improvement is given priority. Material improvement depends on others, whereas self-improvement requires no external effort and is in one's own hands.

विज्ञानतेजसोः संपत्त्यै प्रथमतः शिल्पद्वारा धनापेक्षा ।

Description of how skills can generate money to create wealth in the form of science and light.

आत्मोन्नतिरिह यद्यपि परमोन्नतिरस्ति किन्तु सोदेति ।
न विना धनसंपत्त्या न च राजानुग्रहेण विना ।।551।।

Though self-improvement is the finest kind of improvement, it cannot be achieved without money and royal patronage.

अन्योन्याव्यतिरेकात् सिद्धिरिहान्योन्यसापेक्षा ।
उदरस्य च हृदयस्य च शिरसश्च यथा घनिष्ठसम्बन्धः ।।552।।

Just as there is an intimate relationship between the heart, stomach, and the brain, so also, self-improvement, wealth, property, and royal patronage are inseparable from each other—all these are interrelated.

धनतः प्राणोत्साहो धनतो विज्ञानमुपयाति ।
प्राणोत्साहादपि वा धनमपि विज्ञानमायाति ।।553।।

A meaningful life can only be achieved through wealth and it is from wealth that science could progress. It is the will to live that makes wealth and science attainable.

विज्ञानतो धनं च प्राणोत्साहश्च जायेते ।
सिद्धेनैकेनान्यद् द्वयमपि सिद्धं ध्रुवं भवति ।।554।।

It is from science that wealth and the will to live evolves. If one of these is gained, the other two happen automatically.

यावद् भारतवर्षे नोत्साहो नास्ति विज्ञानम् ।
तावद् धनमधिकाधिकमपेक्ष्यतेऽन्यस्य संसिद्धयै ।।555।।

As long as spirit and science are absent in Bharatavarsha, there will be expectations for more wealth from different quarters.

विज्ञानतेजसोरिह यावदभावोऽस्ति भारते वर्षे ।
शिल्पैरेव तु तावद्धनानि तैः साधनीयानि ।।556।।

Since there is lack of science and spirit in this Bharatavarsha, wealth has to be created through arts.

सिद्धे प्राणोत्साहे विज्ञाने वा पुनर्धनापेक्षा ।
न स्यात् सर्वेऽप्यर्था विज्ञानेनैव साध्येरन् ।।557।।

Once science and spirit are achieved, there will no longer be an expectation of creating wealth through any other means.

विज्ञानं हि महार्थं तद्धनं भवति ।
यद्यद्धनैरसाध्यं तद्विज्ञानेन साध्यते न चिरात् ।।558।।

Science should be the top priority, and acquiring wealth is a general necessity. Those necessities, which cannot be secured through wealth, can be quickly acquired through science.

शिल्पविज्ञानस्य आत्मोन्नतिहेतुविज्ञानत्वाभावः ।

Knowledge of skills cannot lead to self-improvement.

वपुर्बलाभ्युन्नतितो धनोन्नतिः परा ततोऽपि प्रवरा प्रतीयते ।
प्राणोन्नतिः किन्तु ततोऽपि शस्यते ज्ञानोन्नतिर्नास्ति ततः परोन्नतिः ।।559।।

An increase in wealth is better than an increase in bodily strength; better still is life-improvement. However, acquisition of knowledge is superior to life-improvement and is the best, there being nothing greater.

ज्ञानोन्नतिर्यद्यपि शिल्पगाधुनाप्यस्त्येव देशेष्वखिलेषु भूयसा ।
तथापि सा भूतबलव्यपेक्षया पराश्रिताऽस्तीति न सातिशंस्यते ।।560।।

Knowledge has increased in the world but it is still dependent on physical power and hence is not worthy of praise.

यदस्ति शिल्पोन्नतिकारिशिल्पिनां विज्ञानमेतत्तु कथंचिदिष्यते ।
लोकोपकारीह धनाप्तिकारणं तथापि नात्मोन्नतिहेतुरस्ति तत् ।।561।।

Although scientists and artists are working to promote progress and prosperity of the common people, and can be acknowledged and praised, but these do not lead to self-improvement.

आत्मोन्नत्यपेक्षया धानोन्नतेरत्यन्तनिकृष्टत्वम् ।

Creating wealth is relatively inferior to self-improvement.

यथेच्छलब्धिं सुखसाधनानां तत्साधनानामपि साधनानाम् ।
स्वर्णादिकानामुपलब्धिमद्य त्वभ्युन्नतिं प्राहुरिहान्यदेश्याः ।।562।।

People of other countries consider the acquisition of gold and other forms of wealth as the principal goal of all human endeavours.

धनं सुखायास्तु तदेव दुःखस्याप्यस्ति हेतुः क्वचनातिशय्य ।
अमर्षणेर्ष्यादिविरोधमूला उपद्रवा अप्यत उद्भवन्ति ।।563।।

All wealth is acquired for human happiness but is also responsible for suffering; there is no exaggeration in saying this. The jealousies and competitive quarrels caused by wealth lead to unhappiness.

तेनर्षिजाता इह भारतीयाः धनोन्नतिं नोन्नतिमाहुरार्याः ।
आत्मोन्नतिस्तून्नतिरिष्यते तैराध्यात्मिकीमुन्नतिमास्थुरेते ।।564।।

This is why the Arya, sons of sages, had never considered this progress as improvement. They considered self-improvement alone as spiritual development and worthy of pursuit.

तेजोविज्ञानाभ्यामिव धनेन स्वावलम्बनस्वातन्त्र्याभावः ।

Wealth cannot bring self-reliance and independence as science and talent can.

प्राणादपि विज्ञानात् सिध्यत्यात्मावलम्बनं लोके ।
न तथा धनेन शक्यं न धनं सर्वत्र सह भवति ॥565॥

It is possible to become self-sufficient with a spirited life and science but not from wealth alone; the power of wealth in limited.

धनिकानामिह गर्वो यत्र धने तस्य ते स्ववशात् ।
रक्षां कर्तुमशक्ता यदि राजा नानुगृह्णीयात् ॥566॥

The wealthy are proud of their wealth. But it is impossible for the wealthy to safeguard their wealth and its power without the support of the rulers.

धनोन्नतेः निकृष्टत्वे त्रिदोषोत्पादकत्वहेतुः ।

Pursuit of wealth leads to three faults.

धनैरुन्नतिस्तावदेवोन्नतिः स्यान्न यावन्मनःप्राणयोरुन्नतिः स्यात् ।
मनः प्राण आत्मेयमात्मोन्नतिश्चेत् परेषां श्रियोऽप्यस्य सर्वा वशे स्युः ॥567॥

Becoming wealthy can only be considered progress as long as it helps in improving one's self and life. Without such an improvement, wealth has no meaning. If self and life are enhanced, then even the wealth of others comes under one's control.

धनोन्नतिर्भूतपरिग्रहोन्नतिर्नाभ्युन्नतिर्वास्तविकी प्रतीयते ।
दोषाकुलत्वात् सहसा भवन्ति हि त्रयोऽत्र दोषाः सुखबाधनक्षमाः ॥568॥

Acquisition of wealth and material things is not true progress. It creates three *dosha*-s (faults)–impatience, jealousy, and violence—which prohibit happiness.

आराममार्गौ तरवोऽयनस्था राजेच्छया सर्वजनोपभोग्याः ।
तथा धनं सर्वविधं तु बाह्यं राजच्छयैवैकजनो भुनक्ति ॥569॥

Gardens and parks, roads and avenues, trees in royal gardens and other such enjoyable resources are made possible through royal goodwill. Apart from this, all other forms of social wealth are enjoyed by people through royal patronage.

तस्माद्धनं सर्वविधा हि राज्ञो न तु स्वकीयं धनमस्ति किञ्चित् ।
ममेदमस्तीति वृथाभिमानो यथा प्रगृह्यस्य शुकस्य भोग्ये ।।570।।

To boast like a caged parrot that 'all this is mine' is only vanity.

पित्रा भृतः क्लृप्तसमृद्धभावः शिशुः स्वभाग्योपचयात् सुखोऽस्तु ।
भोग्ये न तस्यात्मबलप्रभावस्तस्मान्न सात्मोन्नतिरिष्यतेऽस्य ।।571।।

A well-brought up and well-cared for boy only enjoys his comforts through the goodwill of his father. His own strength has no role to play in this provision of comfort. Hence, this enjoyment cannot be considered self-improvement.

तथा नृपानुग्रहलब्धवित्तः सुखानि भुङ्क्ता किमनेन जातम् ।
राज्ञः कृपा सास्ति, नृपानपेक्षं तद्रक्षणेऽप्यस्ति जनो न शक्तः ।।572।।

Similarly, what is there in enjoying the comforts gained by royal patronage? This is because without royal favours, people cannot protect and secure these comforts.

दुःखं क्षये दुःखत एव लाभो मिथो विरोधाश्च कृते धनानाम् ।
दुःखानुविद्धं धनतः सुखं स्याद्धनं क्वचिज्जीवननाशहेतुः ।।573।।

Wealth is acquired through grief and it causes only grief to see it wasted. Happiness attained through wealth is embedded with grief. Often, wealth can cause the destruction of life.

शास्त्रास्त्रयोगेन तु विक्रमो यस्तद्विक्रमस्योपधिरस्ति शस्त्रम् ।
क्लैव्यं स वैक्लव्यमुपैत्यशस्त्रो न त्वात्मना किञ्चिदलं स कर्तुम् ।।574।।

The power achieved through arms and weapons is primarily because of the weapons. A disarmed person is weak. Without the weapons, he becomes devoid of *purushartha* (strength of character).

धनानि भाराय भवन्त्यशक्तेर्धनानि भाराय भवन्त्यबुद्धेः ।
धनैर्वणिक्त्वं न धनैर्नृपः स्यादुत्साहतः शास्ति नृपो धनाढ्यान् ।।575।।

For a powerless person, wealth is only a burden. The same is true for ignorant people. Wealth may result in achieving mercantile status, but wealth cannot make one a king.

नैसर्गिकोत्साहतेजसोः मध्यमकक्षाकात्मोन्नतित्वम् ।

Considering natural passion and talent as secondary self-improvement.

उत्साह आत्मोन्नतिरस्ति शक्तिस्तेजश्च तत् क्षत्रमनेन सद्यः ।
उपैति भूयांस धनानि लक्ष्मीरुत्साहवन्तं स्वयमावृणोति ।।576।।

Utsaha (passion) alone enhances life and is kshatriya-hood and, with this spirit, the kshatriya swiftly acquires wealth, because Lakshmi [goddess of wealth] herself accepts the company of people with passion.

उत्साह आत्मोन्नतिरस्ति तस्माद् विशालमात्मायतनं विकासि ।
संपद्यते तेन परानन्ल्पानपीक्षतेऽल्पानिव बाधनीयान् ।।577।।

Having utsaha is in itself *atmonnati* (self-evolution) and a passionate person can clear the obstacles in his life without much difficulty.

आत्मा प्राणः प्राण उत्साह एतन्मात्रासाम्याद् वित्तमात्रोपलब्धिः ।
नो दारिद्र्यं वित्ततो यो दरिद्रो यस्योत्साहो नास्ति सोऽयं दरिद्रः ।।578।।

When atma, prana, and utsaha are balanced, wealth gets augmented. Lack of wealth does not create poverty; it is the lack of enthusiasm and positive attitude that make one poor.

वित्तादस्योत्साह उत्साहतो वा वित्तं लोके दृश्यते किन्तु मन्ये ।
यस्तूत्साहो वित्तजन्मा स मन्दो मुख्योत्साहस्त्वात्मनोऽन्यानपेक्षः ।।579।।

The passion that comes from wealth belongs to a lesser category. In reality, inspiration mainly cmanatcs from thc soul.

बाह्यसंपत्त्यपेक्षया प्राणसंपत्तेः अन्तरङ्गत्वात् उत्कृष्टत्वम् ।

Being close to life, living wealth is superior to external wealth.

यावत्यो वा लोके दृश्यन्ते शक्तयः काश्चित् ।
प्राणस्तासां कोशः प्राणविधा एव ताः सर्वाः ।।580।।

All energies present in the world come from prana. These energies are different forms of life.

योऽल्पप्राणः सोसावकिञ्चनोऽत्यल्पशक्तित्वात् ।
यावानधिकः प्राणो यत्र स तावान् विशिष्यते लोके ।।581।।

The faint-hearted person, lacking in true courage, is rendered lonely and incapable of enthusiastic action. Only a powerful person is considered superior in this world.

तस्मादिह बहिरङ्गो न भूतभारस्तथोन्नतेर्मूलम् ।
प्राणोऽयमन्तरङ्गो यथात्मनोऽभ्युन्नतिं कुरुते ॥582॥

Hence, the external manifestations of material development are considered as the basis of progress. But only prana is the closest [to a living being] and leads to atmonnati.

प्राणसंपत्त्यपेक्षया विज्ञानसंपत्तेः आत्यन्तिकोन्नतिहेतुत्वम् ।

Scientific wealth, rather than living wealth, contributes to complete development.

प्राणाभिवृद्धिहेतुर्विज्ञानं साधितं धर्मैः ।
यद्विषये विज्ञानं पूर्णं तत्रैष सिद्धः स्यात् ॥583॥

देशान्तरवदिदानीं भारतवर्षेऽपि जनतायाः ।
वैज्ञानिको न मूर्द्धा प्रदृश्यते हन्त दुर्योगात् ॥584॥

Life can truly be enhanced by science developed through adherence to dharma. When a man acquires such a scientific knowledge, his true development is complete. It is sad that, like in other parts of the world, there is no great scientist in this country.

अपस्वार्थिनां धनहेतुकसुखभोगप्रवणानां मोघजीवत्वम् ।

Selfish lives are lost in fruitless search for money and consumption.

सुखभोगोन्नतिरित्याहुर्भोगलिप्सवो लोकाः ।
ते त्विह पशुसामान्याः पशोर्वोऽपि हि भोगमीप्सन्ते ॥585॥

For people who seek pleasure, self improvement means enjoying material pleasures. Such people are equivalent to animals, because animals also seek only pleasure.

एषा ह्यासुरबुद्धिर्यात्यन्तं स्वार्थपरता स्यात् ।
स सुखप्रवणः पशुवज्जीवत्युदरम्भरिर्मोघम् ॥586॥

मोघाशास्ते मोघकर्माण एते मोघं तेषां जीवितं जन्म मोघम् ।
येषां पाकः कर्म वा जीवितं वा स्वार्थान्धानां सर्वमेवात्महेतोः ॥587॥

Being totally immersed in pleasure is tantamount to *asuri buddhi* (wicked intellect). Such life devoted to pleasures is equivalent to animal-like life. Such people are in deep trouble, as their actions, hopes, life, and birth are all pointless. Their lives are limited to self-indulgence.

किमनेन यत् स जीवति का हानिर्वा न जीवेच्चेत् ।
विज्ञानवीर्याविकलस्य जननि: श्रेयसी धनिन: ।।588।।

What is the point of such a life? The world will be better without such selfish people. Only a person with *vijnana-virya* (scientific temper) can make his progenitor proud.

विज्ञानं वीर्यं वा जीवनसारस्ततो जगत: ।
क्रियतेऽभ्युन्नतिरेतेनेदं जगदुपकृतं भवति ।।589।।

Vijnana-virya is the essence of life. This alone can improve and benefit the world.

विज्ञानं वीर्यं वा भवति मनुष्ये मनुष्यत्वम् ।
विज्ञानवीर्यरहित: सुखभुक् स्याद् राजकृपयैव ।।590।।

Only persons with vijnana-virya are imbued with humanity. Those who are bereft of vijnana-virya depend for their well-being on the patronage of the rulers.

विज्ञानतेजसो: ब्रह्मक्षत्रवीर्ययो: उत्पत्तौ चातुर्वर्ण्यधर्मानुपालनं हेतु: ।

Adherence to the chaturvarna system is the only reason for the generation of talent and science, leading to noetic and martial power.

क्षत्रं वीर्यं ब्रह्म तु विज्ञानं या तदुन्नति: क्रियते ।
सैवोन्नतिरिह वाच्या न धनोन्नतिरुन्नति: कल्प्या ।।591।।

A kshatriya improving his skills and a brahmin increasing his knowledge are in true sense improvements, and not the accumulation of wealth.

आत्मनि मनसि प्राणे यावन्न बलं प्रवर्ततेऽतिशयात् ।
विज्ञानं वीर्यं वा तावत्पुरुषेषु नोदेति ।।592।।

Unless the atma, *mana* (heart) and prana become strong, human beings cannot attain vijnana-virya.

क्वचिदिह मनसि प्राणे तद्बलमुदितं स्वतो भवति ।
अपि वा साधनतस्तत्पुरुषेऽवश्यं समुद्भवति ।।593।।

Sometimes such qualities come naturally to a man, otherwise these qualities can be attained through various practices.

चातुर्वर्ण्यं धर्मं व्यवस्थया यदि तु साधयति ।
पुरुषे बलं तदेदं ब्रह्मक्षत्रं समुद्भवति ।।594।।

If someone follows the chaturvarna system fully, he will be imbued with the power of Brahma, that is vijnana and of kshatriya.

अयथाकृतस्य चातुर्वर्ण्यधर्मस्य वीर्योत्पत्तौ हेतुत्वाभावः ।

Generation of vigour depends on the rule-bound observance of the chaturvarna dharma.

विज्ञानं तु ब्रह्मवीर्यं निरुक्तं यस्तूत्साहः क्षात्रवीर्यं तदाहुः ।
विड्वीर्यं तद् यानि शिल्पानि लोके पूर्वं पूर्वं श्रेष्ठमेषां त्रयाणाम् ।।595।।

The process of creation is considered as the power of Brahma, passion is the characteristic of kshatriya, and the arts and crafts are considered as the power of vaishya. These three powers are named in their order of priority.

बलमबले तु शरीरे व्यायामादिभिरुपायतस्तु यथा ।
जनयति तद्वज्जनयति चातुर्वर्ण्यं व्यवस्थया वीर्यम् ।।596।।

Just as physical exercises strengthen the body, following the chaturvarna system leads to empowerment.

नियतोपायविरुद्धो व्यायामो हानिकृद् वृथा भवति ।
अयथाकृतं तथेदं चातुर्वर्ण्यं वृथा धर्मम् ।।597।।

Just as exercises done incorrectly harm the body, no benefit is accrued by not following the chaturvarna system properly.

तदिदं चातुर्वर्ण्यं वैदिकज्ञानतः सम्यग् ।
ज्ञातं सम्यक् चरितं ब्रह्मक्षत्रादिवीर्यजनकं स्यात् ।।598।।

That is why it has been explained in the Vedic vijnana that pursuing the chaturvarna system enhances science and valour.

तस्मात् प्रथमं वैदिकविज्ञानं साधु जानीयात् ।
तेनाधिदैविकार्था अध्यात्मं साधु नीताः स्युः ।।599।।

It is therefore important to understand the Vedic vijnana first and from it one can attain spiritual power.

चातुर्वर्ण्यस्येदं शैथिल्यं तु व्यवस्थायाः ।
अवनतिहेतुर्भारतवर्षस्याद्यत्व आभाति ॥600॥

The laxity in following the chaturvarna system is the cause of the present degradation of Bharatavarsha.

धर्मप्राणं भारतवर्षं शिल्पे श्लथं पुरैवाभूत् ।
धर्मेप्यधुना शिथिलं भूत्वोभयतोऽभवद् भ्रष्टम् ॥601॥

Dharma was the source of strength for this country and not technological expertise; with the dharma on decline, there is all-round deterioration in this country.

भारतस्य पुनः अभ्युत्थाने चातुर्वर्ण्यधर्मानुपालनस्य एव हेतुत्वम् ।

The indispensability of the chaturvarna system for India's greatness.

चातुर्वर्ण्ये धर्मे यदि भूयोऽभ्युन्नतिं कुर्यात् ।
नूनं प्राग्वदिदानीमप्यात्मोन्नतिमलं यायात् ॥602॥

If the chaturvarna system was to be improved today, all-round development would be possible.

चातुर्वर्ण्ये धर्मेऽभिज्ञानार्थं प्रवृत्त्यर्थम् ।
वैदिकविज्ञानानां बाहुल्येन प्रचार उपपाद्यः ॥603॥

There is, therefore, a need to promote the teaching of Vedic vijnana to understand the true meaning and importance of the chaturvarna system.

भारतधर्मरहस्यं वैदिकविज्ञानतः प्रतीयेत् ।
ज्ञानादुदियाच्छ्रद्धा ततः प्रवृत्तिः स्वतः प्रभवेत् ॥604॥

वैदिकधर्माचरणात् प्रवर्द्धते वीर्यमुन्नतिश्च ततः ।
आत्मोन्नत्या प्राणोन्नत्या वित्तानि सहजानि ॥605॥
इत्युन्नत्यवनतिविचारः ।

The essence of the dharma can only be gained through Vedic vijnana. Knowledge leads to humility and humility leads to dharma. The pursuit of the Vedic dharma leads to atmonnati and *pranonnati* (enhancement of life).

इति भारतपरिचये धर्मप्रसङ्गः सम्पूर्णः ।

The section on dharma in the Introduction to Bharatavarsha is concluded.

1.11 विद्याप्रसङ्गः

1.11 SECTION ON KNOWLEDGE SYSTEMS

1.11.1. भारतवर्षीयविद्याः

1.11.1 Knowledge systems of Bharatavarsha

भारतवर्षीय-ब्रह्मवीर्याख्यानम् भारतवर्षमहत्त्वहेतवः चतुःषष्टिविद्याः ।

Examination of India's brahmanical vigour: The sixty-four kinds of knowledge crucial to the greatness of India.

भारतवर्षगुरुत्वं पुरायुगे विश्वविख्यातम् ।
आसीत् तत्र च हेतुर्विद्यैवासीद् विशेषेण ॥606॥

In ancient times, India's greatness was known to everyone. The reason for this greatness was mainly due to the knowledge it possessed.

प्राकृतविद्या, लौकिकविज्ञानं पार्थिवार्थविषयं यत् ।
दिव्या विद्या, वैदिकज्ञानं सूर्यरसविषयम्॥607॥

This knowledge was of several kinds—knowledge of nature, popular science, knowledge regarding physical worldly substances, knowledge regarding divine world, the Vedic knowledge, and the vital knowledge regarding the sun.

तत्र प्राकृतविद्या निगमागमभेदतो द्विविधा ।
इत्थं त्रिविधा विद्या भारतवर्षस्य गौरवे हेतुः ॥608॥

This knowledge can be divided into two categories—one that is natural and another which is gained through *nigama* (inference) and *agama* (cognitive awareness). These forms of knowledge are the reasons for the glory of Bharatavarsha.

लौकिकसिद्धेरक्षतिमार्गः क्लृप्तस्तु नीतिः स्यात् ।
वैदिकसिद्धेरक्षतिमार्गो दृष्टस्तु धर्मः स्यात् ॥609॥

The right path to worldly attainment is ethics and the road that leads to Vedic siddhi is dharma.

1.11.1.1 निगमविद्या

1.11.1.1 Nigama-vidya

आसु च दिव्या विद्या भवति चतुःषष्टिभेदतो भिन्ना ।
नैगमविद्यास्तत्र च मुख्यतयाऽष्टादश प्रथिताः ॥610॥

आगमविद्या विंशशतमित्थं सर्वविद्यानाम् ।
द्विशती द्व्यधिका संख्याऽवान्तरभेदास्तु बहवः स्युः ॥611॥

Of these forms of knowledge, *divya-vidya* (divine knowledge) is divided into sixty-four sub-categories, the nigama-vidya is of eighteen types and the agama-vidya is of 120 types. Thus, the total number of all knowledge forms is 202.

वेदा सहोपवेदा अष्टावथ षट् तदङ्गानि ।
इतिहासः सुपुराणो योगो न्यायश्च मीमांसा ॥612॥

वेदा अथोपवेदा वेदाङ्गानि च तथोत्तराङ्गानि ।
चत्वारश्चत्वारः षाट्चत्वारीति नैगमश्रेणी ॥613॥

The four Vedas, along with four Upavedas, make eight Vedopavedas; there are six Vedangas, the Puranas with Itihasa (history), and texts of Yoga, Nyaya and Mimamsa. Thus, altogether, there are four Vedas, four Upavedas, six Vedangas and four subsequent texts (the Puranas including the Itihasa, Yoga, Nyaya and Mimamsa), which make it eighteen in all.

ज्योतिःशास्त्रं त्रिविधं गणितं फलितं च संहिताशतकम् ।
ताराज्ञानं कण्डक्षत्रमिति वृष्टिविज्ञानम् ॥614॥

The study of *jyotish-shastra* (astrology) has three divisions: mathematical astrology, applied astrology and *samhita shataka* [the one based on collected texts]. This is also known as the knowledge of heavenly bodies, *kundakshetra* (the site of yajna) and knowledge about rains.

विद्यागणिते प्रबला ऋतुपर्णनलौ यया तु वृक्षाणाम् ।
पर्णानि दूरतः प्रागगणयतां नानृतं तत्र ॥615॥

Rituparna and King Nala were the greatest exponents of mathematical science, who had, in ancient times, counted the leaves of a tree from a distance, and they made no errors.

1.11.1.2 आगमविद्या

1.11.1.2 *Agama-vidya*

आगमविद्या षोढा-सिद्धान्तः संहिताकल्पः ।
यामलडामरातन्त्राण्येषां भेदाश्च बहवः स्युः ॥616॥

The agama-vidya comprises sixteen categories—siddhanta, samhita, kalpa, yamala, damara and tantra are some of them and all of these had different classifications.

षट्कल्पाः सिद्धान्ताश्चतुर्दशाष्टादशेह सांहितिकाः ।
तन्त्राणि चतुःषष्टिर्यामलदशकं च डामरा अष्टौ ॥617॥

मणिमन्त्रौषधिभेदात् त्रिविधा विद्याः सहस्रशस्तन्त्रे।
ताभिः किं न हि सिध्येत् कः स्पर्द्धेतेह तद्विद्भ्यः ॥618॥

There are six kalpas, 14 siddhantas, 18 samhitas, 64 tantras, 10 yamalas and eight damaras. Then, there is the knowledge of therapeutic mantras and gems and all these forms of knowledge have hundreds of offshoots. It is impossible to acquire all this knowledge. Who can compete against this knowledge?

CLASSIFICATIONS OF NIGAMA AND AGAMA VIDYA

निगमविद्याविभागाः ॥18॥	आगमविद्याविभागाः ॥120॥
4 वेदाः ऋग्यजुःसामाथर्वाणः श्रुतयः । 4 उपवेदाः आयुर्वेदधनुर्वेदगन्धर्ववेदार्थवेदाः । 6 वेदाङ्गानि शिक्षाछन्दोव्याकरणनिरुक्तज्योतिः कल्पाः । 4 उत्तराङ्गानि इतिहासपुराणन्यायमीमांसायोगाः ।	18 संहिताः इतिहासादयो नानाप्रकीर्णविषयाः । 14 सिद्धान्ताः रसायनादयो वैज्ञानिकविद्याः । 6 कल्पाः आम्नायाः ऊ.पू.द.प.उ.अ. 10. यामलानि वृष्टिविज्ञानादिनैमित्तिकविज्ञानानि। 8 डामराः । अभिचाराः सनिवर्तनाः । 64 तन्त्राणि-मणिमन्त्रौषधयः ।
18	129

EIGHTEEN KINDS OF NIGAMAS	ONE HUNDRED AND TWENTY AGAMAS
Four Vedas—Rigveda, Yajurveda, Samaveda, Atharvaveda	Eighteen samhitas—itihasas and other mixed subjects
Four upavedas—ayurveda, dhanurveda, gandharvaveda and arthaveda	Fourteen Siddhantas—rasayana and other scientific knowledge
Six vedangas—shiksha, chhanda, kalpa, nirukta, vyakarana and jyotisha	Six kalpas—urdhava, purva, dakshina, paschima, vama and adhara
Four uttarangas—itihasa, Purana, nyaya, mimamsa and yoga	Ten yamalas- including vrshtivijnana
	Eight damaras—abhichara including nivarana
	Sixty four tantras—therapeutic mantras and gems

सनिवर्तनाभिचारा डामरविद्याथ यामलेत्याख्या ।
नैमित्तिकी हि विद्या वृष्ट्यादिर्ज्ञायते यत्र ।।619।।

Damara and yamala constitute the knowledge of malicious incantations and magic-spells that can debilitate or cause death, and their antidote, Naimittika is the knowledge of predicting rain.

कल्या औपासनिकास्तेषु षडाम्नायभेदाः स्युः ।
ऊर्ध्वः पूर्वो दक्षिणपश्चिमवामाधरा इति हि ।।620।।

There are six kalpas dealing with worship-related practices: urdhava, purva, dakshina, paschima, vama and adhara.

ऊर्ध्वाम्नायो योगः पूर्वो वेदोदितो यज्ञः ।
स्मार्तो दक्षिणमार्गः पश्चिमको यावनो म्लेच्छः ।।621।।

Urdhava is about yoga, purva is about sacrificial rites as described in the Vedas, Dakshina is *smartha-vidya*, Paschima is the knowledge of the yavanas and mlechhas, the people who had intruded from the west.

वामः पञ्चमकारोऽघोरो मार्गोऽधराम्नायः ।
विज्ञानाद्भूतविद्या रसायनाद्या तु सिद्धान्तः ।।622।।

Vamana describes the panchamakara as *madya* (wine), *matsya* (fish), *mamsa* (meat), *mudra* (parched grain) and *maithuna* (sexual intercourse). The way of the aghora is called aghora-marga. Chemistry and physics forms the siddhanta aspect of agama-vidya.

क्रीडाकौतुकविद्या रत्नपरीक्षा च पुंपरीक्षा च ।
सामुद्रिकी च शकुनं पशुतन्त्रं मुकुटभूषादि ।।623।।
विद्या दगार्गलाख्या नीतिः सर्वा पुराणमितिहासः ।
एवंविधाः प्रकीर्णा बहुविषयाः संहितासूक्ताः ।।624।।

Different kinds of recreational activities are given in the samhitas. These are the art of entertainment through physical actions, the science of examining gemstones; examining men, the discernment of auspicious and inauspicious aspects from bodily signs, knowledge about animals and birds, knowledge of auspicious and inauspicious aspects of crowns and other jewellery, and a craft called Dagaagrala; detailed descriptions of all these in the form of Itihasa and Puranas have been given in the anthology of samhitas.

यद्यप्यासां काश्चित्संप्रति देशान्तरेऽपि दृश्यन्ते ।
किन्त्वद्यापि च कृत्स्ना सर्वा साऽत्रैव देशेऽस्ति ।।625।।

Though some of these skills and knowledge exist in foreign countries, today all these arts, in an integrated form, exist only in this country.

यज्ञाः सवेदविद्या आगमभेदाः पुराणयोगाश्च ।
धर्मत्रयं निरुक्तं न्यायो मीमांसनं फलितम् ।।626।।

अद्याप्येता विद्या दृश्यन्त इहैव भारते वर्षे ।
देशान्तरस्थजनता नासां जानाति महात्म्यम् ।।627।।

The yajna with Veda-vidya, the agama-vidyas and all its varieties, the Puranas, Yoga, Nirukta, Nyaya and Mimamsa are acknowledged as part of dharma. These arts, even today, are seen in Bharatavarsha. Foreigners do not know the significance of these skills.

अद्य तु यद्यपि विद्या भारतवर्षे श्लथा सर्वा ।
किन्त्वार्याणां तत्र च परवशता विद्यते हेतुः ।।628।।

However, at present, all this knowledge has lost its importance in Bharatavarsha, mainly due to the bondage of the Arya.

1.11.1.3 दिव्यविद्या

1.11.1.3 Divya-vidya

एताः प्राकृतविद्या अद्भुतविद्यास्तु सन्ति तद्भिन्नाः ।
आत्मबलादुत्पन्नास्ताभ्यो भारतशिरोऽत्युच्चम् ।।629।।

These knowledge forms are esoteric in nature and are distinct from *adhbhuta-vidya* (mystical knowledge). This knowledge is gained by *atma-bala* (power of self). It is this knowledge which has given Bharatavarsha a pride of place in the world.

दिव्यं ज्ञानं योगजसिद्ध्याऽऽत्मबलं यदुद्भवति ।
तस्य कला आलम्बनसंदीपनभेतश्चतस्रः स्युः ।।630।।

Divine knowledge can only be gained through atma-bala attained through yoga. This knowledge has four forms divided into two categories, *alambana* and *sandipana* (cause and effect).

मानसकलाऽधिदैवतकला तथेन्द्रियकलाऽध्यात्मम् ।
शिल्पकलेति विभेदादात्मबलं तच्चतुष्कलं भवति ।।631।।

The art of manasa, adhidhaivata and indra are all spiritual arts. Likewise, atma-bala too is imbued with four forms of art.

विज्ञानमेक आत्मा, तत्र चतुर्भ्यो निधीयते हि बलम् ।
प्रज्ञामनसो, धीन्द्रियकर्मेन्द्रियभूतयोगेभ्यः ।।632।।

Vijnana is like the soul which is nourished in four ways—use of knowledge, application of conscious mind, use of senses and integration of knowledge and physical reality.

आलम्बनं मनो यदि मन एवोद्दीपनं यदा भवति ।
आत्मबलं तन्मानसमेतद्भेदा अनेकधा दृष्टाः ।।633।।

शिरसो बलं यदर्जितमुद्दीपयतीह दैवतैर्यदि तत् ।
आत्मबलं तद् दैविकमस्य च बहवः स्मृता भेदाः ।।634।।

Alambana is mind and when it gets enlightened, it becomes *manasa atma-bala* (power of the mind) and these are of different types. When this mind power is embellished by additional power, it becomes *daivika atma-bala* (divine power of self).

यज्ञजबलं यदात्मनि तद् यदि यज्ञात् प्रदीपितं भवति ।
आत्मबलं तद् याज्ञिकमेतद् भेदाश्च बहवः स्युः ।।635।।

The atma gains strength through yajna and this too has different categories.

शिल्पकलाविज्ञानं शिक्षाप्राप्तं यदुद्यमातिशयात् ।
व्यवसायाध्यवसायैर्दीपयते भौतिकं तत् स्यात् ।।636।।

Arts and crafts are mechanical in nature and can be acquired through diligent practice. Material and physical knowledge are acquired through vocation and perseverance.

मानस-दैविक-याज्ञिक-भौतिक-भेदाच्चतुर्विधा विद्या ।
प्रत्येकं षोडशधा तत इह विद्याश्चतुःषष्टिः ।।637।।

Knowledge is thus divided into four types—manasa, daivika, yajnika and bhautika. Given that all the four above have 16 subtypes each, the knowledge that demonstrates self-empowerment is of 64 types.

भारतवर्षीयार्यैरेता विद्याश्चतुःषष्टिः ।
प्रथमं दृष्टास्तस्माज्जगतो गुरवस्त एवासन् ।।638।।

The first to visualize these 64 arts were the Arya of Bharatavarsha. This is why Bharatavarsha has been considered as guru to the whole world.

आत्मबलप्रदर्शिनी तालिका

1.	मानसबलानि षोडश (16)	2	धीन्द्रियबलानि षोडश (16)
	मनःसंयमाद् योगबलसिद्धयोऽष्टौ		हृदयसंयमात् तपोबलसिद्धयोऽष्टौ
1	अणिमा	1	देवसाक्षात्कारच्छायापुरुषसिद्धिः
2	महिमा	2	वलगा (कृत्याभिधाना)
3	गरिमा	3	आत्मोत्क्रमसाक्षात्कारः
4	लघिमा	4	मृतपुरुषसाक्षात्कारः
5	प्राप्तिः	5	विश्वरूपदर्शनम् (विराट्रूपदर्शनम्)
6	प्राकाम्यम्	6	मायाव्यामोहनम्
7	ईशित्वम्	7	उपश्रुतविद्या
8	वशित्वम्	8	संस्कारोपधानी

1	इन्द्रियसंयमाद् दिव्यदृष्टिसिद्धयोऽष्टौ	2	प्राणसंयमाद्-देवबलसिद्धयोऽष्टौ
9 10 11 12 13 14 15 16	अतीतानागतज्ञानजन्मान्तरज्ञानम् दूरपरोक्षज्ञानम् सर्वभूतरुतज्ञानम् मनोविज्ञानम् भूगर्भविज्ञानम् भुवनज्ञानम् ओषधिप्रभावज्ञानम् ताराज्योतिःप्रभावज्ञानम्	9 10 11 12 13 14 15 16	कायव्यूहः परकायप्रवेशः प्राणहारिणी मृतसंजीवनी दैवी शक्तिः स्थाणुसंजीवनी छायानिग्रहणी आकृतिपरिवर्तिनी लिंङ्परिवर्तिनी
3	याज्ञिकानि कर्मेन्द्रियबलानि षोडश (16)	4	भूतबलानि षोडश (16)
	नैगमीयमन्त्रबलसिद्धयोऽष्टौ		**महौषधिबलसिद्धयोऽष्टौ**
1 2 3 4 5 6 7 8	सर्पाकर्षिणी अग्निजलस्तम्भिनी अक्षयकरणी निग्रहानुग्रहणी पुत्रसंजननी पुत्रेष्टिः प्रावृषेण्या जलवर्षिणी आपोनप्त्रीयम् मधुविद्या	1 2 3 4 5 6 7 8	मृतसंजीवनीगुटिका संजीवनीकरणी विशल्यकरणी सावर्ण्यकरणी सन्धानकरणी अरिष्टभैषज्या डिम्भप्रसविनी बलातिबले
3	आगमीयमन्त्रबलसिद्धयोऽष्टौ	4	यन्त्रबलसिद्धयोऽष्टौ
1 2 3 4 5 6 7 8	मारणम् मोहनम् उच्चाटनम् वशीकरणम् विद्वेषणम् स्तम्भनम् आकर्षणम् संरक्षणम्	1 2 3 4 5 6 7 8	दिव्यविमानं त्रिचक्रं रथाकारम् पुष्पकविमानं हंसरयो वर्द्धिष्णुः सोमविमानं नगराकारम् सूतविमानं नौकाकारम् हर्य्यश्वविमानं हययुग्माकारम् प्लवविमानं पक्ष्याकारम् अमृतगवी विश्वरूपा शिलासंतरणी संतरणशिला

LIST DEMONSTRATING ATMA-BALA

I	SIXTEEN TYPES OF SELF-EMPOWERMENT	II	SIXTEEN SENSUAL POWERS
	The eight attainments of Yogic power through mind control		**The eight attainments of ascetic power by controlling the heart**
1	Ahimsa	1	Encountering the Divine and attainment of the power to acquire shadow-personality
2	Mahima		Balaga, an attainment called kritya
3	Garima		Ability to see soul leaving body
4	Laghima		Ability to see dead people
5	Prapti		Seeing the cosmic emanation: visvarupa or viratarupa
6	Prakamya		Maya-vyamoh (an art of confusing the enemy)
7	Ishitva		The science of upasruti, oracular intervention or soothsaying
8	Vashitva		The science that analyses different customs and traditions and rationalizes them
II	**The attainment of eight realizations through sensual control**	**III**	**The attainment of eight realizations by controlling prana**
9	The knowledge of past, future, and birth	9	To become shapeless and formless
10	The knowledge of what is far and indirect	10	Ability to enter a foreign body
11	The knowledge of all languages of all beings	11	The science of taking life
12	Psychology	12	Mritsanjivini—the divine power of resurrecting the dead
13	The knowledge of what is going on under the Earth's surface	13	Sanjivni vidya—resuscitating the injured
14	Cosmography	14	Chaya nigrahara—becoming a shadow
15	The knowledge of remedies and their effects and powers	15	The knowledge of shapeshifting
16	The knowledge of stars and astronomy and their effects	16	The knowledge of sex-change

III	**16 sacrificial powers of the karmendriya (sense-organs of action)**	IV	**16 material powers**
	Eight nigama power attainments		Eight attainments of powerful medicines
1	The power to attract snakes	1	The capsule for resurrecting the dead
2	The power to control over fire and water	2	That which resuscitates the wounded
3	Powers of indestructibility	3	The one which heals arrow-wounds
4	Suppressing and favouring powers	4	That which establishes caste/class equality
5	The power to facilitate the birth of a son	5	That which seeks out
6	The power to control monsoon	6	Extractive and curative powers
7	Aponputriya	7	That which helps in delivery
8	The knowledge of honey	8	Powers, potions and charms
	Attainments of eight agama powers		**Attainment of eight mechanical powers**
9	Killing power	9	Celestial vimana shaped like a chariot
10	Enchantment power	10	Three-wheeled-pushpaka-vimana in the form of a swan
11	Powers of ruining adversaries	11	City-shaped lunar vehicle
12	Imperious curse	12	A chauffer-driven vehicle in the shape of a boat
13	Magical art performed to excite hatred	13	Haryashva-vimana, a vehicle in the shape of two horses
14	Petrifying attainment	14	Floating vehicle in the shape of a bird
15	Attracting attainment	15	Cows with amrita, the nectar of immortality
16	Protective-defensive attainment	13	The knowledge of making stones float on water

1.11.1.4 विद्यानां प्रयोगोदाहरणानि

1.11.1.4 Applications of divine knowledge

1.11.1.4.1 मनःसंयामाद् अष्टौ योगबलसिद्धयः

1.11.1.4.1 Eight yogic siddhis through mind control

(1) अणिमा अणुता ह्रस्वकायता। विशालकायस्य संकल्पमात्रेण तत्क्षणादेवावयवापचयेन मशकादिवत् क्षुद्रशरीरोपपादनम्। यथा हनुमान् समुद्रलङ्घनकाले विशालकायेन ग्रसन्त्याः सुरसाया मुखे मशकवत् क्षुद्रो भूत्वा प्रविश्य निर्गतः । रावणगृहे सीताशोधनाय प्रवृत्तो वृषदंशकवत् क्षुद्रशरीरो भूत्वा प्रच्छन्नो गृहान् परिशोधयामास । लङ्कायामशोकवाटिकायां सीतारावणसंवादं श्रोतुमतिक्षुद्रशरीरो भूत्वा वृक्षान्तरे प्रच्छन्नस्तस्थौ ।

Anima: Acquiring a subtle form by shrinking the body. This is the power with which one can reduce the size of the body through power of thought, or shed parts of the body or acquire difficult-to-see forms. Just as Hanuman had, while leaping across the sea, escaped the mouth of Surasa by transforming himself into a mosquito. On another occasion, while searching for Sita in the palace of Ravana, Hanuman turned into a cat. In order to eavesdrop on the conversation between Sita and Ravana in the Ashoka *vatika* (garden) in Lanka, he reduced his size immensely and took shelter under a tree.

(2) महिमा महत्ता कायवैपुल्यम्। क्षुद्रशरीरस्य सतो महाविशालशरीरसंपादनम्। यथा हनुमान् समुद्रलङ्घनकाले सुरसामुखे प्रवेशाभावाय कायं महाविशालं चक्रे । यथा वा चाक्षुषमन्वन्तरे मत्स्यस्य मनुहस्तपतितस्यातिक्षुद्रशरीरस्यापि क्षणेन महाविशालशरीरोपपत्तिः ।

Mahima: Mahima is the art of acquiring gigantic forms; it is the ability to acquire a huge body, despite being in subtle form. Just as Hanuman had made himself immensely big after entering Surasa's mouth. Similarly, in the epoch of the sixth Manu, the fish which fell into Manu's hands, despite its small size, in no time turned into a fish of enormous size.

(3) गरिमा गुरुत्वं शरीरभारवर्द्धनम्। यथा निषधपर्वते संचरतो भीमस्य बलाभिमानं नाशयितुं मध्येमार्गं पतितेन हनुमता शरीरगुरुत्वं प्रवर्द्धितमिति स जराग्रस्तः क्षुद्रकायोऽपि कपिरनेन भीमेनोत्थापयितुमशक्योऽभूत् । अङ्गदो लङ्कायां रावणसभायां पादमवरोप्य बलिष्ठैरपि सर्वैं राक्षसैरनुत्थाप्यपादो विजिग्ये । बालकेन श्रीकृष्णेन महाकायमहाबलिष्ठचाणूरमल्लपरिमर्द्दनमक्रियत।

Garima: It is the power to increase the weight of the body and make it heavier.

Once, in order to break the pride of Bhima, Hanuman increased the weight of his body. He had pretended to be an old ape but increased the weight of his seemingly shrivelled body so that Bhima could not lift him. In the same way, Angada, in the court of Ravana in Lanka, challenged the asuras to lift his leg which he made big and heavier. The asuras could not lift his leg and thus Angada attained victory. Likewise, infant Sri Krishna had killed the two extremely powerful and large-bodied asuras, Chanura and Malla.

(4) लघिमा गुरुतरशरीरस्यापीषीकातूलवत् शरीरलघूकरणाद् विमानादिसाधनं विनापि आकाशे संचार: । यथोक्तं योगसूत्रे -

कायाकाशयो: संबन्धसंयमाल्लघुतूलसमापत्तेश्चाकाशगमनम् । (योगसूत्रम्, 3.42)

इति। यथा हनुमान् शरीरलघूकरणादाकाशमार्गेण पवनाधारेण समुद्रमुल्ललङ्घे। नारदश्चानेकवारमाकाशमार्गेण सञ्चरन् द्वारकायां श्रीकृष्णान्तिकमन्यत्रान्यत्र चाजगाम। विभीषणाश्चाकाशमार्गेणागत्य रामसेनायामाजगाम ।

उत्तरं तीरमासाद्य खस्थ एव व्यतिष्ठत ।
स उवाच महाप्राज्ञ: खस्थ एवं विभीषण: ।।
(रामायणम्, युद्धकाण्डम्, 17.10,11)

खात् पपातावनिं हृष्टो भक्तैरनुचरै: सह ।
(रामायणम्, युद्धकाण्डम्, 19.2)

Laghima: This is the power of assuming infinitesimally small dimension, like a wisp of cotton, and travel in the sky freely. Likewise, it is written in the Yogasutras: 'If the relationship between the body and the dyau is made equivalent, then the heaviest of bodies can float in the sky like the lightest pieces of cotton.' Just as Hanuman, utilising the *akasha marga* (ethereal way), could leap over the sea by making his body extremely light.

Narada, on several occasions, had also used the akasha marga to come to visit Sri Krishna in Dvaraka as well as other people at different places. Vibhishana too had used the akasha marga to join the army of Sri Rama. Two statements written in the Yuddha-khanda of Ramayana bear this out: 'While standing above the northern shore of the sea, in the sky, Vibhishana said.' and then: 'Vibhishana, being pleased, with his devotees and servitors, descended down on the earth.'

(5) प्राप्ति: एकत्र स्थितवता बहुविप्रकृष्टार्थस्यानायासेनेन्द्रियैर्ग्रहणम्। यथा भूमिस्थ एवाङ्गुल्यग्रेण चन्द्रमसं स्पृशति। पर्वताग्रस्थितादुद्यानात् फलमवचिनोति ।

Prapti: This is the ability to perceive distant objects without moving. Such as, touching the moon with one's finger while standing on the ground, or selecting flowers in the garden located on a mountain peak.

(6) प्राकाम्यम् पृथिव्यादितत्तद्धर्मानभिघातान् मनोवृत्त्यप्रतिबन्धः भूमावपि मज्जति यथोदके मज्जति। शिलामप्यनुविशति। नापः स्निग्धाः क्लेदयन्ति। नाग्निरुष्णो दहति। न वायुः परिणामी वहति। अनावरणेऽप्याकाशेऽयमावृतकाय इव भूत्वा सिद्धानामप्यदृश्यो भवति। आतपस्थोऽप्यातपावरणाच्छायायामिव भवति। अप्रतिरुद्धगतित्वाद् बन्दीगृहतोऽपि बहिर्भावः । यथा द्वारकान्तिके रैवतकपर्वते जरासन्धसैनिकैः सर्वतः प्रतिरोधितस्यापि श्रीकृष्णस्य द्वारकायां प्रवेशः । मथुरायां जरासन्धसैनिकैः कालयवनसैनिकैश्चावरोधितस्यापि तस्यैकेनाह्ना द्वारकायां नवनिर्मितायाम खिलबालवृद्धस्त्रीनिकायसंप्रापणं युद्धाय पुनरागमनं च । अद्भुतकर्मणोऽप्यत्रैव संनिवेशः । यथोक्तं भारते दमयन्तीं प्रति केशिन्या नलचरिते-

Prakamya: This is a knowledge which transcends reality and empowers the person to feel water without touching it, pass through rock, fire, and water effortlessly. A person with this knowledge, can disappear even in uncovered empty spaces, as it happens with *siddha-purusha*-s, those who have acquired special powers. Such persons can easily escape from prisons. For instance, the entry of Sri Krishna into Dvaraka despite being surrounded on all sides by the soldiers of Jarasandha on the Raivatak mountain near Dvaraka.

Despite being besieged by the soldiers of Jarasandha and Kala Yavana in Mathura, Sri Krishna could return to Mathura within a day for the battle, after escorting all the minors, female, and elderly citizens to the newly-built Dvaraka. Adbhuta-karma or the mystical actions, should also be understood in this way. Just as, in the story of Nala in Mahabharata, Kesini tells Damayanti:

स्वमासाद्य संचारं नासौ विनमते क्वचित् ।
तं तु दृष्ट्वा यथा सङ्गमुत्सर्पति यथा सुखम् ।।
(महाभारतम्, आरण्यकपर्व, 73.9)

संकटेऽन्यस्य तु महान् विवरो जायतेऽधिकः ।
तस्य प्रक्षालनार्थाय कुम्भास्तत्रोपकल्पिताः ।।
ते तेनावेक्षिताः कुम्भाः पूर्णा एवाभवंस्ततः ।
तृणमुष्टिं समादाय सवितुस्तं समादधत् ।।
अथ प्रज्वलितस्तत्र सहसा हव्यवाहनः ।
तदद्भुतममं दृष्ट्वा विस्मिताहमिहागता ।।
(महाभारतम्, आरण्यकपर्व, 73.9-13)

'That King Nala does not bend when he sees low door-frames. Upon seeing such doors he comfortably passes through them…Even in narrow places, gateways become immensely large for him. For his bath, empty *kumbha*-s (vessels) used to be kept for him; upon being looked at by the king they would automatically fill up. Upon his pointing a bundle of straws and twigs to the sun, they would get ignited. I have come here upon being amazed by these extraordinary acts.

अन्यच्च तस्मिन् सुमहदाश्चर्यं लक्षितं मया ।
यदग्निमपि संस्पृश्य नैवासौ दह्यते शुभे ।।
(महाभारतम्, आरण्यकपर्व, 73.14)

'I have seen other intriguing things of this King Nala. Oh, auspicious one, he does not get burnt even while touching fire.

छन्देन चोदकं तस्य वहत्यावर्जितं द्रुतम् ।
अतीव चान्यत् सुमहादाश्चर्यं दृष्टवत्यहम् ।।
यत् स पुष्पाण्युपादाय हस्ताभ्यां ममृदे शनैः ।
मृद्यमानानि पाणिभ्यां तेन पुष्पाणि नान्यथा ।।
भूय एव सुगन्धीनि हृषितानि भवन्ति हि ।
एतान्युद्भुतलिङ्गानि दृष्ट्वाहं द्रुतमागता ।।
(महाभारतम्, आरण्यकपर्व, 73.15–17)

'Advancing water stops immediately upon his wish. Many other such miracles have been seen in this king. When he kneaded flowers in his palm they did not change shape; furthermore, those flowers get even more fragrant and they blossom even better. By seeing these awe-inspiring signs I have come here.'

(7) ईशित्वम् अलौकिककर्मकरणे सामर्थ्यलाभः । अणिमादीनां षण्णां योगविभूतीनां स्वस्मिन्निवापरस्मिन्नपि संपादनम्। यथा हनुमान् द्रोणाचलमुत्थापपितुं श्रीकृष्णो वा गोवर्धनमुत्थापयितुं तस्य तस्याचलस्य विग्रहे लघिमानं जनयामास। तेनैव हनुमान् हस्तेन द्रोणाचलमुद्धृत्य लङ्कामानयत्। विश्वामित्रस्त्रिशङ्कुराजानं जीवन्तमेव दिवि प्रतिष्ठापयामास । वसिष्ठश्च नन्दिनीखुरतः परःसहस्राणि सैनिकानि जनयामास । श्रीकृष्णो द्वारकास्थ एव हस्तिनापुरे द्रौपद्याश्चीरं परिवर्द्धयामास । अगस्त्येन समुद्रः परिशोषितः । मनुमत्स्यो जलप्रलयनौकां शुङ्गेन दधार । अन्तर्द्धानमप्यत्रैव संनिविशते। तच्चोक्तं योगसूत्रे–

कायरूपसंयमात् तद्ग्राह्यशक्तिस्तम्भे चक्षुःप्रकाशासंप्रयोगेऽन्तर्द्धानम् ।
(योगसूत्रम्, 3.20)। इति।

Ishitva: The capability of performing otherworldly or extraordinary actions and implanting the eight yoga-siddhis in self as well as others. For instance, Hanuman, while lifting the Dronachala mountain and Sri Krishna, while lifting the Govardhana mountain, had made the mountains light. It is through this power that Hanuman had brought the Dronachala mountain in his hand to Lanka. [1] Vishvamitra had established King Trishanku, who was still alive, in the sky. [2] Vasishta had produced thousands of soldiers from the hooves of the cow Nandini. [3] Sri Krishna, despite being in Dvaraka, had augmented Draupadi's clothes in Hastinapura. [4] Sage Agastya had dried the ocean. [5] The matsya-avatara had, at the time of the Great Flood, secured the ark of Manu on his horn. [6] The antarddhana-vidya, the science of making one to vanish, is subsumed in this. It has been said in the Yoga shastras: 'Through physical discipline, making oneself vanish is called antarddhana-vidya.'

(8) वशित्वम् प्रबलस्य वशीकारः । यथा श्रीकृष्णो नागं वशीचक्रे । ऋषीणामाश्रमेषु सिंहादयो हिंस्रजीवा वशीकृता अद्रोहिणस्तस्थुः । भूतवशीकारोऽप्यत्रैव संनिविशते। इतोऽन्या अप्यनेकधा योगसिद्धयो योगपातञ्जले विभूतिपादे प्रदर्शिताः । इत्यष्टौ संयमसिद्धयः ।

Vashitva: This power is used to tame and control the powerful. Just as Sri Krishna had established control over the Nagas. [1] In the hermitages of the sages, predators like lions and other violent animals used to live without rancour, after coming under the spiritual control of the sages. [2] The science of taming ghosts also comes under the purview of this power.

In the vibhutipada of Patanjali's Yogasutra, many siddhis, other than these, are mentioned.

1.11.1.4.2 इन्द्रियसंयमाद् अष्टौ दिव्यदृष्टिसिद्धयः

1.11.1.4.2 Eight divine insight siddhis gained by controlling the senses

(1) अतीतानागतज्ञानं भूतभविष्यद्ज्ञानम्। तत्रातीतज्ञानं तावत् चिरकालातीतविषयाणां प्रत्यक्षविद्यमानवद् ग्रहणम्। यथा वसिष्ठो दिलीपराजाय दत्तं कामगवीशापं ददर्श। वाल्मीकिमुनिश्च परोक्षं रामचरितं सर्वं यथावद्ददर्श। पातञ्जले योगसूत्रे तु–

धर्मलक्षणावस्थापरिणामत्रसंयमादतीतानागतज्ञानम्। (3.16) इत्युक्तम् ।
संस्कारसाक्षात्कारणात् पूर्वजातिज्ञानम्। (योगसूत्रम्, 3.18) इति योगसूत्रोक्तं

जन्मान्तरज्ञानमप्यतीतज्ञानमेव। यथा जैगीषव्यस्य दशसु महासर्गेषु जन्मपरिणामक्रममनुपश्यतो विवेकजं ज्ञानं प्रादुरभूत्। श्रीकृष्णश्चाह

बहूनि मे व्यतीतानि जन्मानि तव चार्जुन ।
तान्यहं वेद सर्वाणि न त्वं वेत्थ परन्तप ।।
(श्रीमद्भगवद्गीता, 4.5)

Knowledge of *atitanagath* (the past and the future): The knowledge of the past and the future is known as atitanagath-jnana. Here, atitajnana is a means to have direct knowledge of the things and events of the past in the present. As the curse given by Kamadhenu to King Dilip was envisioned by sage Vasishta. It is mentioned in the Yogasutra of Patanjali that 'by *sayama* (control) over the three-fold changes of dharma, *lakshana* (secondary quality) and *avastha* (condition) comes the knowledge of the past and the future'; and 'by bringing residual potencies into consciousness, comes the knowledge of previous birth.' Thus in the Yogasutra, the knowledge of previous births is also known as atitajnana. Jaigishvyaya obtained discretionary knowledge after having seen the direct succession of births during ten great creations. Sri Krishna says: 'O Arjuna! Both you and I have taken so many births. But O subduer of the enemy! I know all about these births, you do not.'

यथा महाभारतयुद्धे प्रवृत्तानाम्। कर्णदुर्योधनादीनां जन्मान्तरस्थासुरयोनित्वं वेदव्यासो दृष्ट्वा आदिपर्वणि वर्णयामास। शुकदेवस्य च पूर्वजन्मनि शुकपक्षित्वं शिवगौरीसंवादश्रोतृत्वं चाख्यातमार्यैः। अथ भविष्यज्ञानम् अनागतज्ञानम्। तद् यथा संभलग्रामे कल्की भविष्यतीति भारतीयाः पश्यन्ति । पुराणे भविष्यन्तो राजवंशाः प्रदर्शिताः । शुद्राश्च ब्राह्मणाचारा ब्राह्मणाः शूद्रवृत्तय इत्येवमादयः कलिधर्मो भविष्यन्तः पुराणे प्रदर्शिताः । सूर्यचन्द्रोपरागा भविष्यन्तः कथ्यन्ते । कालज्ञानमप्यत्रैव संनिविशते। अनया विद्ययात्मनः परस्य च मृत्युकालो विज्ञातो भवति। कालज्ञानोपायभेदे छायापुरुषसिद्धिरप्यस्ति।

In the Adi-parva of Mahabharata, Veda Vyasa described Karna and Duryodhan witnessing their previous births in *asura-yoni* (asura form). Similarly Shukadeva was a Shuka bird in his previous birth, according to scholars.

As far as *anagathjnana* (knowledge of the future) is concerned, it is the knowledge of future things and events. The knowledge of the birth of Kalki-incarnate in Sambhal village is an example of this knowledge. There are also descriptions of future kings in the Puranas. In the Bhavishya Purana, it has been mentioned that in Kaliyuga the shudras would have the conduct of the brahmins and the brahmins that of the shudras. By this knowledge, the lunar and solar eclipses are also predicted. The knowledge of time is also included in it. By this knowledge one can predict one's own death and that of others. Through knowledge of time, *chayapurusha* (a shadow person) can be created.

(2) दूरातिक्रान्तदर्शनश्रवणम्। तत्रादौ दूरपरोक्षदर्शनम्। यथा सञ्जयो हस्तिनापुरे स्थितो वेदव्यासदत्तदिव्यदृष्टिप्रभावेण दूरदेशे कुरुक्षेत्रे जायमानं युद्धं यथावत् पश्यन् धृतराष्ट्राय कथयति स्म। श्रीकृष्णो द्वारकास्थितो हस्तिनापुरस्थाया द्रौपद्याश्चीरहरणं दुःशासनकृतमपश्यत् तदुक्तम् –

प्रवृत्त्या लोकन्यासात् सूक्ष्मव्यवहितविप्रकृष्टज्ञानम् । (योगसूत्रम् 3.25)

इति । अथ विदुरश्रुतिः । सञ्जयो वेदव्यासप्रदत्तविद्याप्रभावेण दूरे कुरुक्षेत्रे भवन्तं कृष्णार्जुनगीतासंवादं स्वदेशस्थो यथायथं शुश्राव ।

श्रोत्राकाशयोः संबन्धसंयमाद् दिव्यं श्रोत्रम् । (योगसूत्रम्, 3.44)।

Knowledge of seeing and hearing remote or unseen objects: Sanjay was able to see and describe the battlefield of Kurukshetra and its events to Dhrithrashtra, even though he was in Hastinapur, with the help of *divya drishti* (the extraordinary vision) given by Veda Vyasa. Similarly, Sri Krishna, even while he was at Dvaraka, saw the seizing of Draupadi's clothes forcefully by Dushasan. It is mentioned in the following Yogasutra: 'By directing the higher sense-activity one gets knowledge of the subtle, the veiled and the remote objects.'

By this very knowledge given by Veda Vyasa, Sanjay was able to hear the exact dialogue between Sri Krishna and Arjuna in Kurukshetra, sitting at a remote place. The following Yogasutra says: 'By establishing a connection between the hearing and sky, an extraordinary power of hearing can be obtained.'

(3) सर्वभूतरुतज्ञानम्। तदुक्तं योगसूत्रे –

शब्दार्थप्रत्ययानामितरेतराध्यासात् संकरस्तत् प्रविभागसंयमात्सर्वभूतरुतज्ञानम् । (योगसूत्रम्, 3.17)

इति । युधिष्ठिरविदुरादयः पक्षिरुतं जानन्ति स्म । ब्रह्मदत्तश्च काम्पिल्यो राजा पिपीलिकारुतं जानाति स्म।

Knowledge of the *shabda* (sound) of all living beings: One of the Yogasutras hold that this knowledge is gained when the distinction between the word, object and idea is eliminated. By this knowledge, Yudhishtira and Vidura were able to understand the meaning of the sounds made by the birds. The Kampilya king, Brahmdatta, could understand and make sense of the sound of an ant by this very knowledge.

(4) मनोविज्ञानम् । मनसः संकल्पनकाले शारीरः प्राणवायुः क्षोभितो विकृतिमापद्यते। विकुर्वाणेन च तेन रोमकूपेभ्यो बहिर्भवता विक्षिप्तः परिक्षुब्धोऽयं शरीरमभितो बाह्यवायुः पुरुषमनसोऽभिज्ञानाय प्रभवति । यथोक्तं वेदमन्त्रे–

मनसा संकल्पयति, तद्वातमभिगच्छति ।
वातो देवेभ्य आचष्टे तथा पुरुष ते मनः ।। इति
(शतपथब्राह्मणम्, 3.4.2.7)

ब्राह्मणेऽपि श्रूयते –

मनो देवा मनुष्यस्यऽऽजानन्तीति ।
मनसा संकल्पयति, तत् प्राणमपि पद्यते ।
प्राणो वातम्, वातो देवेभ्य आचष्टे तथा पुरुषस्य मनः इति ।।
(शतपथब्राह्मणम्, 3.4.2.6)

Science of the mind: When the mind is engaged, *pranavayu* (the vital air) of the body gets contracted and becomes impure. This air then comes out through the pores and spreads around the body. This impure air enables the study of a man's mind. One of the Vedic hymns explains it in the following manner: 'Vayu is life. Whatever man thinks, it spreads in vayu. O man! As your mind is, the Vayu informs the gods likewise.'

The brahmins also hold: 'The gods know the mind of man. As the man thinks, it becomes the pranavayu.' 'The vital power is a kind of air which informs about the mind of man to the gods' (*Shatapatha Brahmana*). In the Yogasutra it is said: 'By controlling the notions, the mind of others can be known.'

(5) भूगर्भज्ञानम्। महौषधसंस्कृतचक्षुषा अधोमुखजातेन भूतलाधस्ताद्दशहस्तपर्यन्तं स्थितानां भावानां साक्षात्कारः शक्यते कर्तुम्। तत्र दिव्याञ्जनप्राधान्येऽपि तेन दैवीदृष्टिरेवानुगृहीता भवतीत्यत्र समावेशः।

Knowledge of the subterranean world: This is the knowledge which enables one to see, with the help of a magic potion applied to the eyes, the objects buried ten feet under the ground. This knowledge also includes the knowledge of *divya netrajnana* (magical collyrium), *adrishyajnana* or *daividrishti* (extraordinary vision).

(6) भुवनज्ञानम्। अस्ति हि सप्तलोकसंग्रहश्लोकः।

ब्राह्मस्त्रिभूमिको लोकः प्राजापत्यस्ततो महान् ।
माहेन्द्रश्च स्वरित्युक्तो दिवि तात भुवि प्रजाः ।। (योगसूत्रम्, 3.26)

इति। आवीचेः प्रभृति मेरुपृष्ठं यावद् भूलोकः। मेरुपृष्ठादारभ्याध्रुवाद् ग्रहनक्षत्रतारा विचित्रेऽन्तरिक्षलोकः। तत्परः पञ्चविधो माहेन्द्रः स्वर्गलोकः । प्राजापत्यो महर्लोक। जनलोकस्तपोलोकः सत्यलोक इति त्रयो ब्रह्मलोकाः। एषां साक्षादिव दर्शनं भुवनज्ञानम्। भुवनज्ञानं सूर्ये संयमादिति योगसूत्रम्।

Knowledge of *bhuvana* (the domains): A hymn of *Saptalokasamgraha* unfolds thus: 'Brahmaloka is a three-fold Brahma domain and bigger than this is the *Prajapatialoka* (domain of the Supreme Being). The Dyauloka includes the stars and the heavens. The five-fold *Mahendraloka* (domain of the sky) is known as the heaven. From south up to the back of Meru is Bhuloka. Beginning from the back of Meru up to the Pole Star, adorned with planets, asterisms and stars, is the Antarikshaloka.

Thereafter is the five-fold domain of Mahendraloka. Then comes the *Mahaloka* (domain of the lords of Creation). After this, there is the three-fold Brahma domain. These are *Jnanaloka* (domain of knowledge), *Tapoloka* (domain of asceticism) and *Satyaloka* (domain of truth). The knowledge of these domains is known as Bhuvanajnana. To obtain this knowledge, it has been said in the following Yogasutra: 'By sayama over the sun, comes Bhuvanajnana.'

(7) ओषधिप्रभावज्ञानम्। यथा सोमहरीतकीविभीतकजङ्गिडापामार्गादीनामोषधीनामतुलिता: प्रभावा आथर्वणसंहितायां मन्त्रैराम्नाता: तेषां प्रभावाणां यथावत्परिज्ञानमार्षं भवति नत्वनृषिश्चक्षुरयोग्यं प्रभावं ज्ञातुं शक्नोति। उक्तं चाभियुक्तै:–

आविर्भूतप्रकाशानामनुपप्लुतचेतसाम् ।
अतीतानागतज्ञानं प्रत्यक्षान्न विशिष्यते ।।
अतीन्द्रियानसंवेद्यान् पश्यन्त्यार्षेण चक्षुषा ।
ये भावान् वचनं तेषां नानुमानेन बाध्यते ।।

(वाक्यपदीयम्, ब्रह्मकाण्डम्, 37, 38)

Knowledge of *aushadhiprabhav* (the effect of the medicinal herbs): The effects of herbs like Soma, haritaki, vibhitaki, jangida and apamarga have been described explicitly in the hymns of the Atharvaveda samhita. A person devoid of extraordinary vision can never understand the effects of these herbs. The sages hold that only those beings are capable of knowing the effect of the herbs who possess the light of extraordinary knowledge, whose mind is not obstructed by worldly engagements, who possess the knowledge of the past and the future as clear as that of the present, who are capable of seeing the objects beyond the senses by their extraordinary vision and whose words are not affected by presumptions.

(8) ताराज्योति: प्रभावज्ञानम्। यावत्य इमा रोचन्ते रोचना दिवि तासामेकैकस्या ज्योतिष: प्रभावग्रहण ामृषीणामेव शक्यम्। असंख्यातास्वपि तासु–एकता द्विता त्रिता–इत्येवं त्रेधा विभक्तासु त्रितानां प्रायेण ााप्त्यानां प्रभावा वेदे श्रूयन्ते। यथा–

जज्ञान: सप्तमातृभिर्मेधामाशासत श्रिये ।
अयं ध्रुवो रयीणां चिकेतदा ।।

इत्यादिभिर्मन्त्रैर्ध्रुवादितारकाणां प्रभावा आम्नाताः ।
चन्द्रे ताराव्यूहज्ञानम् ॥
(योगसूत्रम्, 3. 27) इति ।

Knowledge of the stars or astronomy: It is only the rishis who are capable of knowing the effect of all the planets and stars shining in Dyauloka. Dividing the stars into three kinds of constellation, the Vedas describe their effect based on their mutual relationship. For example, 'The constellation of seven stars known as Saptarshi, being the cause of creation of the world, occupies the place of a mother. Along with this mother-like constellation of seven stars, Dhruva (the Pole Star) is born with the Creation. The Pole Star, which is the *yajamanat* (host) is endowed with wealth.' In the above hymns, the effect of the Pole Star and that of such other stars has been described in the Yogasutra: 'By sayama over the moon, comes the knowledge of star systems.'

1.11.1.4.3 हृदयसंयमात् अष्टौ तपोबलसिद्धयः

1.11.1.4.3 Eight tapobala siddhis gained by control over heart

(1) देवप्रत्यक्षीकरणम् कतिचिद् भावमालम्ब्य तत्र धारणाध्यानसमाधिसंयमे हृदयस्थमनस एवोपादानात् तत्तद्देवतारूपाविर्भावः एतच्च पुरायुगे तपश्चरतामृषीणां मनुष्याणां वा भूयः श्रुतिमितिहासपुराणेषु। भरद्वाजपुत्रो यवक्रीतो ब्राह्मणानामनधीता एव वेदाः प्रतिभान्त्विति कामनया घोरं तपस्तप्त्वेन्द्रं प्रत्यक्षीचकार। तमिन्द्र उवाच।

अमार्ग एष विप्रर्षे येन त्वं यातुमिच्छसि ।
किं विघातेन ते विप्र गच्छाधीहि गुरोर्मुखात् ॥
(महाभारतम्, आरण्यकपर्व, 135.22)
इति। छायापुरुषसिद्धिरप्यत्रैव संनिविशते ।

Knowledge of *devapratyakshikarana* (invoking a deity in person): In the Puranas and Itihasa, there are stories of sages and others engaged in *tapasya* (austerities) invoking gods in person by controlling the mind nestled in the heart through *dharana* (concentration), *dhyana* (meditation) and *samadhi* (communion).

The appearance of Indra before Yavakrita is an example of this knowledge. The story goes like this: Yavakrita, the son of sage Bharadvaja, wanted to acquire the knowledge of the Vedas without any teacher. So, with this desire of acquiring the knowledge of the Vedas, he practised hard penance and made Indra to appear before him in person. Indra spoke, 'O Brahmin! Is there any sense in harming yourself? Return home and acquire knowledge from a teacher' (Mahabharata, Vana-parva). The knowledge of devapratyakshikarana also includes the power of invoking a chayapurusha.

(2) बलगा कृत्या अभिचारविद्या। परविद्रोहाय पुरा क्रूराः कृत्यापुरुषाः स्त्रियो वा तपःप्रभावादुत्पाद्यन्ते स्म । राक्षसपुरुषाः स्त्रियो वा राक्षस्यस्तत्कालं जनिता निर्दिष्टपुरुषस्य प्राणानपहरन्ति विभीषयन्ति वा। यथा भारद्वाजरैभ्यौ सखायावास्ताम्। भरद्वाजपुत्रो यवक्रीतो रैभ्याश्रमं गत्वा रैभ्यपुत्रस्यार्वावसोः पत्नीं बलादाक्रम्य मैथुनायोपचक्रमे। रुदन्त्यास्तस्या वृत्तमभिज्ञाय स रैभ्यो मन्युनाविष्टो जटामेकामवलुञ्च्ययाग्नौ जुहाव। ततो जटाकारा नारी समुत्तस्थौ। पुनरन्यां जटामालुञ्च्याग्नौ जुहाव। ततो घोराक्षं भीमदर्शनं रक्षोऽभवत्। यवक्रीतो वध्यतामिति तौ रैभ्योऽब्रवीत्। भुञ्जानस्य यवक्रीतस्यादौ कृत्या कमण्डलुं जहार। ततः शूलहस्तेन रक्षसा काल्यमानोऽयमुच्छिष्टमुखोऽन्यत्र शरणमपश्यन्नग्निहोत्रशालां गन्तमैच्छत्। तत्रान्धेन गृहरक्षिणा निगृहीतः पपात। शूलेन रक्षसाऽऽहतः प्राणाँस्तत्याज। (महाभारतम्, आरण्यकपर्व, 136)

Knowledge of *balaga* (spells for malevolent purpose): In the ancient period, a phantom like image of a man or a woman was created by observing certain austerities in order to harm others. Such evocation of spirits of man or woman through rigorous austerities, killed or terrified the intended persons. The end of Yavakrita is an example of this knowledge. The story goes like this: Once there lived two brahmins, Bharadvaja and Raibhya, who were close friends. One day Yavakrita, the son of sage Bharadvaja came to the hermitage of Raibhya and tried to rape his daughter-in-law by drugging her. When Raibhya came to know about the incident from his weeping daughter-in-law, he plucked a hair from his knotted lock and offered it as an oblation in the fire. At once there emerged a woman-like image of the size of the hair from the knotted lock. Then the sage again plucked a hair from another knotted lock and offered it as an oblation in the fire. Now an asura of huge size with terrible eyes rose from the fire. Then Raibhya instructed both of them to kill Yavakrita. The woman snatched the bowl of water from Yavakrita while he was taking his food and then the terrible asura rushed towards him with a spear. Knowing that his mantras would be of no avail, until he cleansed himself with water, Yavakrita rushed towards water but in vain. Then, he fled to the sacrificial hall where the blind guard of the sacrificial hall caught hold of him and he fell down. And thus he was killed by the asura created by Raibhya.

(3) आत्मप्रयाणदर्शनं मुमूर्षोः शिरःप्रदेशादूर्ध्वमाकाशे सद्य उत्क्रममाणमात्मानं प्रत्यक्षमनुपश्यति। यथा वेदव्यासो द्रोणास्यात्मानमूर्ध्वं गच्छन्तं ददर्श ।

Knowledge of direct perception of a departing soul: A seer is capable of seeing the soul going upward from the forehead of the dying person. For example: Veda Vyasa saw the soul of Dronacharya going upward.

(4) मृतपुरुषदर्शनम्। मृतानां पुरुषाणां प्रतिकृतयश्छायापुरुषाः प्रत्यक्षं दर्श्यन्ते। यथा वेदव्यासो भारतयुद्धे मृतानां पुरुषाणां छायापुरुषान् परिदर्शयामास।

एष राजा दशरथो विमानस्थः पिता तव ।
लक्ष्मणेन सह भ्रात्रा त्वमेनमभिवादय ।।

लक्ष्मणेन सह भ्राता ददर्श पितरं विभुः ।
विमानशिरस्थस्य प्रणाममकरोत् पितुः ।।

(रामायणम्, युद्धकाण्डम्, 119.7–10)

इति रामायणे युद्धकाण्डे रावणवधान्ते रामेण दशरथो दृष्टोऽनुभाषितश्च ।

एतस्तिन्नेव काले तु जरत्कारुर्महातपः ।
वायुभक्षो निराहारः शुष्यन्नहरहर्मुनिः ।।

स ददर्श पितृन् गर्ते लम्बमानानधोमुखान् ।
निराहारान् कृशान् दीनान् गर्तेऽऽर्तांस्त्राणमिच्छतः ।।

(महाभारतम्, आदिपर्व, 41.1,3,5)

इति भारतादिपर्वणि पितृदर्शनमुक्तम् ।

Knowledge of direct perception of a dead person: The figures of dead people appear like chayapurusha. In the battle of Mahabharata, Veda Vyasa showed the figures of dead persons in the form of chayapurusha.

There is a reference to this knowledge in the Ramayana of Valmiki: 'It is your father, King Dasharatha only, sitting in the celestial car. Pay your salutations to him, along with your brother, Lakshmana. Then Rama paid his salutation to his father, King Dasharatha, sitting on the top of the celestial car. In the 121st sarga of the Yuddha-khanda of Ramayana, it is written that after killing Ravana, Rama saw his father Dasharatha and conversed with him. There is also a reference to the direct perception of dead father in the Mahabharata: 'In that age the great ascetic Jaratkaru, who was observing hard austerities without eating anything except air and thus becoming weaker by day, saw his father with his face hung down towards a pit. He was weak and was stooping. And being in a very miserable condition, he desired liberation' (Mahabharata).

(5) विराट्पुरुषदर्शनम्- यथा श्रीकृष्णेन भारतमहायुद्धोपक्रमेऽर्जुनाय भविष्यत्क्षणसंभावितस्य विश्वरूपस्य प्रागेव साक्षात्कारः कारितः । यथा वा श्रीकृष्णेन दुर्योधनसभायां धृतराष्ट्राय दिव्यचक्षुः

प्रदाय सर्वेभ्यः सभासद्भ्यो विश्वरूपं प्रदर्शितम्। यथा वा यशोदायै स्वमुखान्तरतो नानावैचित्र्यं परिदर्शितम् ।

Knowledge of *viratapurushadarshan* (vision of the transcendental personality): There are many instances of such a vision. In the beginning of the battle of Mahabharata, Sri Krishna had shown Arjuna the future and his 'cosmic personality'. Similarly in the assembly of Duryodhana, Sri Krishna showed his 'cosmic personality' to Dhrithrashtra and all other members of the assembly, by providing divine sight to the former. Likewise, Sri Krishna had displayed his cosmic personality by opening his mouth before Yashoda.

(6) मायाव्यामोहनी-यथा नारदाभिमानखण्डनार्थं कनखलप्रदेशे मायापुरी निर्माणं तत्र सुन्दरीस्वयंवरविधानं च। यमुनायां स्नानार्थमभिप्लुतस्य नारदस्याभिप्लवनोत्प्लवनयोरन्तरतः क्षणमात्रेऽवकाशे चत्वारिंशद्वर्षाणि माययातिवाहितानि । तत्र च नारदस्य स्त्रीभावं गमितस्य राज्ञा विवाहः पुत्रपौत्रादिसृष्टयः तेषां निःशेषाणां मृत्युः । ततो दुःखकातराया राजमहिष्यास्तस्याः शुद्धिस्नानार्थे यमुनायामागतायाः स्नात्वा जलादुत्प्लवन्त्याः पुनर्नारदस्वरूपेणाविर्भावः पुराणेतिहासेषु स्मर्यते। मार्त्तिकावतनगराधीशः शाल्वः कृष्णेन सह युध्यन् द्वारकाधीशाहुकपरिचारकरूपेण स्वमायापुरुषेण वसुदेवमृत्युसंवादं कृष्णाय श्रावयामास। क्षणेन पुनः शाल्वविमानाद्वसुदेवशिरश्छिद्यमानमध स्तात्कृष्णान्तिके निपातयामास। तद् दृष्ट्वा कृष्णः पूर्वं चिन्ताग्रस्तोऽभूत्। पश्चात्पुनः शाल्वकृतां मायां विज्ञाय निर्विषादः शाल्वं निपातयामास।

तमेवमुक्त्वा रुदतीं सीतां मायामयीं च ताम् ।
शितधारेण खड्गेन निजघानेन्द्रिजत् स्वयम् ।।

(रामायणम्, युद्धकाण्डम्, 81.29)

रामायणे मेघनादेन मायासीतावध उक्तः ।

Knowledge of creating illusion or hypnotism: There are many instances of creating illusion in the scriptures. It is mentioned in the Itihasa and the Puranas that Narada's gender was changed by the power of illusion, to destroy his arrogance. It is said that for this a place called Kankhal was created. It was an illusion. So when Narada came here for a bath in river Yamuna, and took the first dip, a long period of forty years passed in that brief moment before he could come out of the river. During the course of this bath, Narada became a woman. She got married to a king; sons and grandsons were born; and all of them died. Then plunged in sorrow, the queen [actually Narada] came to river Yamuna for a bath to cleanse herself. And as soon as she came out of the river after taking bath, she became Narada again. Shalva, the king of Martikavana, also used the power of illusion in the battle of Mahabharata. Engaged in fighting with

Sri Krishna, he created a *mayapurusha* (an illusionary person) as Ahuka, the servant of Sri Krishna in Dvaraka, who gave him the message of the death of Vasudeva. Then within a moment, Shalva, by his power of illusion, hurled the chopped head of Vasudeva, from his extraordinary flying chariot near Sri Krishna. Seeing the head, Sri Krishna first got worried, but knew instantly that it was an illusion created by Shalva; he composed himself and killed Shalva. There is also a reference to this kind of illusion in the Ramayana: 'Saying so, Indrajit himself chopped off the head of the Sita created by illusion'. (Ramayana, Yuddha Khanda, 81).

(7) उपश्रुतिविद्या खलु रात्रिनाम्नी सा विद्या यया गुप्तं विलीनमह्नुतमज्ञातप्रदेशस्थमर्थं प्राणिनं वा परिमार्गमाणास्तमनायासेनोपलभन्ते। आकाशवाण्या वा शिशुवाचा वा कर्मान्तरव्यापृतमनुष्यवाचा प्रकारान्तरेण वा तत्स्थानमुपश्रुतं भवति यत्रैष परिमार्जितव्योऽर्थः स्थितो भवति। यथा देवराजे ब्रह्महत्यादोषेण क्वचित् प्रच्छन्ने नहुषे चैन्द्रं पदमध्यारूढे शची तयोपश्रुतिविद्यया तं देवराजं क्वचित्सरसि प्रच्छन्नं व्यजानात् । तदुक्तं भारते-

Knowledge of *upasruti* (revealing hidden things): This knowledge is known as *ratridevi* (the goddess of night), through which one can find hidden treasures and persons. The place where the treasure is hidden is known by broadcast, by speech of a child, by the speech of the person engaged in the work or by other such means. Once Indra went into hiding as he had committed the sin of killing a brahmin and Nahusa had occupied his place. Then Sachi, Indra's wife, with the help of this siddhi, found Indra hidden in a pond.

In the Mahabharata, Sachi, in order to know about the hiding place of Indra, says:

पुण्यां चेमामहं दिव्यां प्रवृत्तामुत्तरायणे ।
देवीं रात्रिं नमस्यामि सिध्यतां मे मनोरथः ।।

(महाभारतम्, उद्योगपर्व, 13.23)

I invoke the presiding deity of the forthcoming divine night of *Uttarayana* (period of the sun turning to north). O Goddess, fulfil my desire.

यत्रास्ते देवराजोऽसौ तं देशं दर्शयस्व मे ।
इत्याहोपश्रुतिं देवीं सत्यं सत्येन दृश्यताम् ।।

(महाभारतम्, उद्योगपर्व, 13.25)

Show me the place where Indra, the king of gods, is hidden. Saying so, she worshipped the goddess, Upasruti, to reveal the fact.

प्रयतां च निशां देवीमुपातिष्ठत तत्र सा ।
पतिव्रतात्वात् सत्येन सोपश्रुतिमथाकरोत् ।।
(महाभारतम्, उद्योगपर्व, 13.24)

Thus Sachi worshipped ratridevi keeping mind and senses in control. Being a devoted, truthful, and a virtuous wife, she invoked the goddess, Upasruti.

सरसस्तस्य मध्ये तु पद्मिनी महती शुभा ।
बिसतन्तुप्रविष्टं च तत्रापश्यच्छतक्रतुम् ।।
(महाभारतम्, उद्योगपर्व, 14.19)

There was a very big *padmani* (lotus) in the middle of the pond, by entering its *bistantu* (flower's core), the Satkritu Indra was found.

(8) संस्कारोपधानी-सा विद्या यया योगिराजः कस्यचिच्छिशोर्मूद्धनि हस्तं निधाय तस्मिन् सर्वविद्याप्रबोधान् संस्कारविशेषान् मन्त्रप्रभावेणाधत्ते। तदुक्तं मन्त्रमहोदधौ पञ्चमतरङ्गे-

विद्वत्कुलसमुद्भूतमष्टवर्षं शिशुद्वयम् ।
उपवेश्य तयोर्मूर्ध्नि करौ दत्वा जपेन्मनुम् ।।

वेदान्तन्यायसंयुक्त्या विवदेते उभावपि ।
यः कौतुकी स आश्चर्यं विद्यायाः पश्यतु ध्रुवम् ।।
(मन्त्रमहोदधिः, 5.89-90)

Knowledge of *samskaropadhani-sa* (attributing knowledge to a child): A person equipped with this knowledge blesses a child to acquire all kinds of knowledge by chanting a particular hymn and putting his hands on the head of the child. In the fifth taranga of the Mantramahodadhi, it is written: After getting two children of a virtuous family, if the recitation of hymns is made by putting hands on their heads, both of them acquire the knowledge of Vedanta and nyaya, and start participating in scholarly discussions.

दूर्वोत्थया तु लेखन्या रोचनारसयुक्तया ।
बालस्याच्छिन्ननालस्य जिह्वायां विलिखेन्मनुम् ।।
संप्राप्ते चाष्टमे वर्षे सर्वशास्त्रज्ञतामियात् ।
मन्त्रेणायुतसंजप्तां वचां बालस्य कण्ठतः ।।
बध्नीयात् पूवसंप्रोक्तं बलिं दत्वा विधानतः ।
द्वादशे वत्सरे प्राप्ते भक्षिता सा कवित्वकृत् ।।
(मन्त्रमहोदधिः, 5.83-85)

Write down the mantra on the tongue of the baby before cutting the umblical cord with the pen made of *durva* (grass) steeped in the juice of *gorochan* (a yellow pigment obtained from the bile of a cow or elephant). At the age of eight, the child would imbibe the knowledge of all religious texts. After infusing a herb named Vacha with 10,000 mantras, it is tied around the throat of the child and at the age of 12 it is untied and given to the child to eat. This would give the child tremendous poetic power.

1.11.1.4.4 प्राणसंयामात् अष्टौ दैवसिद्धय:

1.11.1.4.4 Eight divine powers gained by controlling prana

(1) कायव्यूह:- युगपदनेकशरीरधारणमनेकदेशे भिन्नशरीरेणावस्थानं च। यथा श्रीकृष्णो रासलीलायां प्रतिगोपीशरीरसहकारेणान्यान्यशरीरोपपन्नस्तस्थौ। यशोदासदेशं तिष्ठन् गोपीनां गृहेष्वपि तत्कालं तस्थौ।

Knowledge of acquiring multiple bodies, *kayavyuha rachna*: This knowledge helps in acquiring many bodies or being present simultaneously at many places. Sri Krishna, during the course of *rasalila* [dance], accompanied each *gopi* [his female companions] in different physical forms even as he was present with Yashoda.

(2) परकायप्रवेश:-स्वशरीरं पृथक् संस्थाप्य शुद्धेनात्मना शरीरान्तरे प्रवेश: तदुक्तं योगसूत्रे (3.38) बन्धकारणशैथिल्यात् प्रचारसंवेदनाच्च चित्तस्य परशरीरावेश: इति ।
यथा शङ्कराचार्यो राज्ञ: शरीरे विवेश। यथा वा किन्दिमो नाम मुनिर्मृगशरीरे प्रविश्य मृग्या सह रेमे । (महाभारतम्, आदिपर्व, 123)

Knowledge of *parakaya-pravesha* (entering other's body): This siddhi enables one to leave one's physical form and enter the body of a pious soul. It is written in the Yogasutra : 'The mind may enter another body by undoing the cause of bondage, and with the knowledge of the passage of time.' Shankaracharya entered the body of a king by this power. According to the Mahabharata (Adi-parva), with this knowledge, Kindhim, a sage, entered the body of a deer and had sexual experience with a she-deer.

(3) प्राणसंहारिणी-यथा वेनस्य राज्ञ उन्मार्गं गच्छत: प्राणान् कुशाघातेन महर्षयोऽपजह्नु: ।

Knowledge of *pranasamhara* (destroying the vital force): Once the maharshis destroyed the vital force of King Vena, when he was on an evil path, by merely striking him with a blade of *kusha* (grass).

(4) मृतसंजीवनी दैवीशक्ति:-उत्क्रान्तप्राणे शरीरे पुन: प्राणसंधानम्। यथातिवेगेन धावमानानां रथाश्वानां प्रत्याघातान्मृतं ब्राह्मणशिशुं जान: पुरोहित: पुनरुज्जीवयामासेति बृहद्देवतायामुक्तम्।

सान्दीपनिना गुरुदक्षिणात्वेन मृतं मे पुत्रमानयेत्युक्तः कृष्णस्तत्पुत्रं स्वयमुज्जीव्य गुरवेऽर्पयामास। अथ रैभ्यभरद्वाजौ सखायावास्ताम्। रैभ्यः कृत्यामुत्पाद्य भरद्वाजसुतं यवक्रीतं मारयामास। पुत्रशोकपरितप्तो भरद्वाजः स्वयं प्राणांस्तत्याज। अथ रैभ्यपुत्रो ज्येष्ठः परावसुर्मृगभ्रमात् स्वपितरं घातयामास। रैभ्यस्य कनिष्ठपुत्रोऽर्वावसुः ज्येष्ठभ्रातुर्ब्रह्मवध्याप्रायश्चित्तमचरत्। सोऽर्वावसुरुग्रं तपः कृत्वा सूर्यस्य रहस्यवेदं चक्रे। तेन कर्मणावार्वसोरग्न्यादयो देवाः प्रीता अभवन्। अर्वावसुप्रार्थनया प्रसन्ना देवा रैभ्यं भरद्वाजं यवक्रीतं चेत्येतान्मृतान् पुनरुज्जीवयामासुः । सूर्यवेदस्य च प्रतिष्ठां चक्रुः ।

अर्वावसुप्रार्थनया देवाः सेन्द्रपुरोगमाः ।
संजीवयित्वा तान् सर्वान् पुनर्जग्मुस्त्रिविष्टपम् ।।

(महाभारतम्, आरण्यकपर्व, 139.23)

अथ हैहयकुमारोऽरिष्टनेमिस्ताक्ष्र्यस्य पुत्रं मृगभ्रमाज्जघान। स ब्रह्मवध्यानिर्विण्णस्तन्निष्कृत्यै ताक्ष्र्याश्रमं गत्वा निष्कृतिमर्थयामास। ताक्ष्र्यस्तूचे। यस्त्वया ब्राह्मणो हतः सोऽयं ममैव पुत्र आसीत्। स मयोज्जीवितोऽयं तवाग्रे तिष्ठति। कथमयं जीवितोऽभूदिति विस्मयेन पृष्टस्ताक्ष्र्य उवाच-

Knowledge of *mritsanjivani* (restoring life): The herb known as mritsanjivani is impregnated with the extraordinary power of restoring life to the dead. There is a reference to this in the Brihaddevata: 'The priest made the boy of a brahmin alive, who had died due to injury caused by galloping horses of a chariot. Sage Sandipani, asking for his guru-dakshina, said to Sri Krishna: 'Bring my son back to life.' On hearing this, Sri Krishna restored the son of his teacher to life and gave him back. An example of this power can be cited from the Mahabharata also. Raibhya and Bharadvaja were two friends. Raibhya, killed Yavakrita, by creating an asura. Plunged into grief by the death of his son, Bharadvaja ended his own life. Thereafter, Paravasu, the elder son of Raibhya, killed his father, thinking him to be a deer. Arvavasu, the younger son of Raibhya, repented for his elder brother's sin of slaughtering a brahmin. Having observed austerities, Arvavasu obtained the mysterious knowledge of the sun. By this act, Agni and other gods were pleased with Arvavasu. In response to the prayer of Arvavasu, the gods made the dead Raibhya, Bharadvaja and Yavakrita alive again. In the Mahabharata, it is clearly mentioned, 'Accepting the prayer of Arvavasu, Indra and other gods became happy, made them all alive again and went to heaven.'

Arishtanemi, the son of Haihaya, had killed the son of Taksharya, thinking him to be a deer. Then he, grieving at the sin of killing a brahmin, prayed to Taksharya for a solution. Taksharya spoke thus: 'The brahmin, killed by you, is my son. Now he has been made alive by me and is sitting before you.' Then Arishtanemi asked how he had restored life to his son. Taksharya replied:

सत्यमेवाभिजानीमो नानृते कुर्महे मनः ।
स्वधर्ममनुतिष्ठामस्तस्मान्मृत्युभयं न नः ॥
(महाभारतम्, आरण्यकपर्व, 182.17)

We know only truth, and never engage our mind in untruth. We engage in righteous acts of truth only and hence, we are not afraid of death.

यद् ब्राह्मणानां कुशलं तदेषां कथयामहे ।
नैषां दुश्चरितं ब्रूमस्तस्मान्मृत्युभयं न नः ॥
(महाभारतम्, आरण्यकपर्व, 182.18)

We examine only the righteous act of brahmins; we never look at their evil conduct. Hence we are not afraid of death.

अतिथीनन्नपानेन भृत्यानत्यशनेन च ।
संभोज्य शेषमश्नीमस्तस्मान्मृत्युभयं न नः ॥
(महाभारतम्, आरण्यकपर्व, 182.19)

We eat only the food that is left after serving food to guests and servants. Hence we are not afraid of death.

शान्ता दान्ता क्षमाशीलास्तीर्थदानपरायणाः ।
पुण्यदेशनिवासाश्च तस्मान्मृत्युभयं न नः ।
(महाभारतम्, आरण्यकपर्व, 184.21)

We are calm by nature; we suppress our senses; we forgive others for their vices; we give alms and live at pious places, hence we are not afraid of death. (Mahabharata, Vana-parva)

अकालमृत्युप्रतिघातः प्रदर्शितः। स्वायुःप्रदानमप्यैत्र संनिविशते। यथा सर्पदंशनेन मृतायाः प्रमद्वराया रुरुणा स्वार्धायुःप्रदानेन पुनरुज्जीवनम्। यथा वा रामचन्द्राय दशरथेन स्वजीवनशेषायुः प्रदानम्। विषहरविद्याप्यत्रैव संनिविशते। यथा ब्रह्मणा कश्यपाय विषहरविद्यादानम्। यथा वा हरिद्वारे नागेन भीमाय विषहरविद्यादानम्।

This knowledge also includes the power of negating the blow of untimely death and that of giving one's age to others. Ruru made Pramadvara, who was killed by snake bite, alive again. King Dasharatha blessed Rama by giving his remaining age. The knowledge of sucking venom also belongs to this knowledge. Brahma blessed Kashyapa by providing him with the knowledge of sucking venom. Like the Nagas at Haridwar had blessed Bhima by providing him with this knowledge.

(5) स्थाणूज्जीवनी-शुष्कतरोः पुनरार्द्रीभावात् पर्णोद्गमनम्। गायत्रीमन्त्रप्रभावेणाभिमन्त्रिताभिरद्भिः परिषिक्तः शुष्कतरुस्तं रसमात्मानं गृहीत्वा पुनरुज्जीवितो भवति। अतस्तत्र सद्यः पर्णान्याविर्भवन्ति। यथोक्तं यजुर्ब्राह्मणे-'तं हैतमुद्दालक आरुणिर्वाजसनेयाय याज्ञवल्क्यायान्तेवासिने उक्त्वोवाच-य एतं शुष्के स्थाणौ निषिञ्चेत् जायेरन् शाखा प्ररोहेयुः पलाशानीति।' (शतपथब्राह्मणम्, 14.9.3.15)

Knowledge of *sthanujivani* (reviving a dead tree): By this knowledge, a dead tree is revived and leaves start growing on it. A dead tree, having been irrigated with the water charged by the recitation of Gayatri mantra, regains its juice and becomes green again. In the Brahmana of Yajurvaveda, it is written: Uddalaka Aruni said to his disciple Vajasaneya Yagyavalkya, 'If a dead tree is irrigated with the water charged by the recitation of Gayatri mantra, green leaves grow on its branches'.

(6) छायाग्रहणी-प्राणिनः शरीरच्छायां तच्छरीरगन्धपर्याप्तामाक्रम्य तद्द्वारा तत्प्राणिशरीरानुकर्षणम्। यथाऽऽकाशमार्गेण समुद्रल्लङ्घयतो हनुमतश्छायां ग्रसित्वा सिंहिकया समुद्रस्थया हनुमानाकाश-स्थोऽधस्तान्निपातितः ।

Knowledge of *chayagrahan* (becoming a shadow of another person): The power which affects a person physically by working on the shadow and smell of his body, is called *chayagrahana-vidya* (the power of assuming another person's shadow). It was with the help of this power that Singhika [rakshasi] swallowed the shadow of Hanuman flying over the ocean and made him to fall from the sky.

(7) आकृतिपरिवर्तिनी-शरीराकृतेरन्याजातीयाया अन्यजातीयतासम्पादनम्। यथा-मृग्यामैथुनं चरतो मृगरूपस्य किन्दिमस्य मुनेः पाण्डुना मृगयां चरता हननम्। यथा वा मनुष्याकारो विष्णुर्वराहो मोहिनी वा समपद्यत। धर्मः शुनो रूपं दध्रे। शिविपरीक्षायामग्निः कपोतोऽभूदिन्द्रः श्येनः ।

इन्द्रः श्येनः कपोतोऽग्निर्भूत्वा यज्ञेऽभिजग्मतुः ।
ऊरुं राज्ञः समासाद्य कपोतः श्येनजाद्भयात् ॥
शरणार्थी तदा राजन्निलिल्ये भयपीडितः ।

(महाभारतम्, आरण्यकपर्व, 130.19-20)

Knowledge of *akratiparivartan* (changing the form of one's body): The power to change the form by acquiring a new form of body is known as akratiparivartana-vidya. By this knowledge, sage Kindhim acquired the form of a deer in order to have sexual experience with a she-deer; and the human bodied god Vishnu acquired the form of a pig and that of a charming damsel. Likewise Yama acquired the form of a dog. Agni acquired the form of a pigeon in order to test King Sivi and Indra acquired the shape of a falcon. It is written in the Mahabharata: 'Agni acquired the form of a pigeon and Indra the form of a falcon and then the pigeon, scared of the falcon, took refuge in the lap of the king.'

स तदा राक्षसेन्द्रेण संदिष्टो रजनीरः ।
शुको विहङ्गमो भूत्वा तूर्णमाप्लुप्त्य चाम्बरम् ।।
स गत्वा दूरमध्वानमुपर्युपरि सागरम् ।
संस्थितो ह्यम्बरे वाक्यं सुग्रीवमिदमब्रवीत् ।।
(रामायणम्, युद्धकाण्डम्, 20. 13-14)

इति रामायणे राक्षसः शुकरूपधारणमुक्तम् । रूपान्तरीकरणमिदं पुरायुगे देवकुले भूयसाभ्यस्तमासीत् अद्भुतरूपकरणमप्यत्रैव संनिविशते। यथा नृसिंहो यथा वा शरभः ।

There is a reference to this power in the Ramayana also where an asura has been described as acquiring the form of a Shuka bird: 'Then the asura, who had brought the message of Ravana, the king of asuras, acquiring the form of Shuka bird and flying in the sky over the sea, began saying this to Sugriva.'

In the ancient period, there were many persons in the family of deities, equipped with this power of changing form. The power of acquiring strange forms is also included here. The forms of *Narasimha* (half-human and half-lion) and the lion-killer *Sharaba* (part-lion and part-bird) also exemplify this power.

(8) लिङ्गपरिवर्तिनी लिङ्गयोनिव्यत्यासः । अनया विद्यया पुंसां स्त्रीत्वं स्त्रीणां पुंस्त्वं च शक्यते कर्तुम्। यथा शिवः कदाचिदुमावने प्रविशतः सुद्युम्नस्य राज्ञः स्त्रीत्वमिलायाश्च पुंस्त्वं चक्रे। इति भारताख्याने पुराणेषु च सर्वेष्विलोपाख्याने सुप्रसिद्धम् ।

Knowledge of *lingaparivartan* (changing gender): With this knowledge it is possible to change from a male into a female and vice versa. There is a famous story in the Puranas. Once Shiva changed the genders of King Sudyumna and Ila, the former from male into female and the latter from female into male, while they were entering the forest of Parvati.

1.11.1.4.5 अष्टौ नैगमीयमन्त्रबलसिद्धयः

1.11.1.4.5 Eight siddhis gained through mantras

(1) सर्पाकर्षिणी-सर्पाकर्षिण्या विद्यया मन्त्रबलेन सर्पाः दूरस्था अपि अभीष्टदेशे आकृष्यन्ते निगृह्यन्ते निर्विषीक्रियन्ते यथा जनमेजयकृते सर्पसत्रे याजकाः समिद्धेऽग्नौ मन्त्रैः सर्पानाजुहुवुः ।

Knowledge of *sarpakarshan* (attracting snakes): By reciting some specific mantras, serpents from distant places can be attracted, caught and their venom taken out. In *nagayajna* (the sacrifice of serpents), priests offered serpents as oblation in the burning fire by this very knowledge. In the Mahabharata, there is a description of this yajna in which serpents are attracted:

क्रोशयोजनमात्रा हि गोकर्णस्य प्रमाणतः ।
पतन्त्यजस्रं वेगेन प्रदीप्ते हव्यवाहने ॥
(महाभारतम्, आदिपर्व, 52.7)

Some of the serpents were as long as one kosa and a yojana and some of them were of the shape of the cow-ear. Such snakes began to fall rapidly into the burning sacrificial fire.

उच्चावचाश्च बहवो नानावर्णा विषोल्बणाः ।
घोराश्च परिघप्रख्या दन्दशूका महाबलाः ॥
(महाभारतम्, आदिपर्व, 52.10)

Some of them were very long and some were very short and they were of different colours and full of venom; some of them were like iron rods and others small and strong like a drawbar and all began to fall in the fire of naga-yajna.

(2) अग्निस्तम्भनी विद्या सा यया मन्त्रेणाग्निः शीतलीक्रियते। तेनाग्नौ प्रविष्टोऽपि पुरुषो न दह्यते। सोऽग्निस्तम्भस्त्रेधा सम्पद्यते। सत्येन मन्त्रेण मणिना च। सत्येन यथा धर्माधिकारिभिरपराधी पुरुषो दिव्यपरीक्षया हस्तनिहितेनाग्निना परीक्ष्यते। यथा वा सीता लङ्कायां सत्येनाग्नौ प्रवेशिता परीक्षिताऽऽसीत् । मन्त्रेण यथा नीलो महाराजोऽग्निं स्तम्भयति स्म ।

तदुक्तं भारते -

अन्यच्च तस्मिन् सुमहदाश्चर्यं लक्षितं मया ।
यदग्निमपि संस्पृश्य नैवासौ दह्यते शुभे ॥
(महाभारतम्, आरण्यकपर्व, 73.14)

Knowledge of *agnistambhan* (restraining the burning intensity of fire): With the knowledge of specific mantras, the burning quality of fire can be tempered down. This fire, restrained by hymns, does not burn a person even when he or she enters into it. This power is of three kinds—the fire restrained by the power of truth, the fire restrained by the power of hymns and the fire restrained by the power of gems.

A *dharamadhikari* (judicial functionary) takes an extraordinary test of a criminal by making him touch the flame. Sita was tested by this power of truth by making her enter into fire. King Nala also restrained the burning quality of fire. It is written in the Mahabharata: 'Auspicious! I have seen many strange things in King Nala. It is strange that he does not get burnt even with the touch of fire.'

अथ ग्रामदाहे तृणगृहान् प्रदहन्नग्निर्मन्त्रेण स्तम्भितो गृहान्तरं न दाहयति इति मन्त्रशास्त्रे निरूप्यते। अथ मणिश्चन्द्रकान्तमणिः । स द्विविधः औषधिः प्रस्तरश्च। तत्रैते श्लोका द्रष्टव्याः-

In the Mantrashastra, it is said that 'if a fire, which begins damaging the houses made of straw in a village, is restrained, it will not burn other houses'.

अमरलता वितता स्याद् यस्य तरोरुपरि तस्य चाधस्तात् ।
भूमावन्तर्निहितं तस्या मूलं तु कन्दमन्वेष्यम् ॥639॥

वृक्षाधस्तात् परितस्तृणान्युपस्तीर्य दाहयेच्छिखिना ।
यत्र तु न दह्यते तत् तत्रैवाधः स्थितं कन्दम् ॥640॥

अतिशीतं तत्कन्दं स उच्यते चन्द्रकान्तमणिः ।
तत्सानिध्यादग्निः शीतलतामेति नैष दाहयति ॥641॥

तद्रसलिप्ते हस्ते धारयितुं शक्यते वह्निः ।
तद्रसलिप्तशरीरः शक्नोत्यग्नौ प्रवेष्टुमक्लेशात् ॥642॥

एवं प्रस्तरोऽप्ययश्चन्द्रकान्तमणिः । सोऽतिशीतलः प्रस्तरः संनिधानमात्रेणाग्निं शीतलयति। तत्संनिहितोऽग्निः स्पृष्टोऽपि न दाहयति। चन्द्रकान्तसंनिहितोऽप्यग्निः सूर्यकान्तमणिसंनिधनात्पुनर्दाहयति। चन्द्रकान्तोपजनितशीतलतायाः सूर्यकान्तेन निरस्तत्वात् ।

Fire can be restrained by *chandrakanta-mani* (moon-herb or diamond). This herb is of two types—*agnibela* (the creeper of fire) and *mani* (diamond). Regarding the former, the following hymn is worth mentioning: One should find out the main root of agnibela hidden in the ground under the tree it spreads about. After collecting the leaves scattered around the tree, set fire to them. The place, where the leaves do not burn, should be considered as the place where the roots of the creeper are located. This creeper is extremely cold and so is known as chandrakantamani. Mere presence of this root restrains fire and a person does not get singed by this fire. After applying the juice of this root, one can hold fire in one's hands. After applying the juice of this root, a person can enter fire without experiencing any pain.

As it has already been stated, the second type of moon-herb is also a kind of diamond. It too has such a cold effect that its presence alone restrains fire. If a person were to keep this diamond with him, he will not be harmed by fire. But if the *suryakantamani* (sun-diamond) is kept there beside this moon-herb, fire would burn again. The heat of suryakantamani negates the cooling effect of chandrakantamani.

(3) अक्षय्ययकरणी–सा विद्या यया गृहभाण्डस्थमन्नं परः सहस्रैर्भुज्यमानमपि न क्षीयते। पूर्वं तावत् सूर्यमाराध्यमानेन युधिष्ठिरेण सूर्यादेकं पिठरमुपलब्धं तत्प्रभावादन्नमक्षय्यमासीदित्युक्तं भारते–

Knowledge of *akshayyakaran* (producing endless supply of food): By this knowledge, food vessels in the house never get empty, even after serving food to thousands of persons. In the ancient period, Yudhishtira, as a result of his austerities, obtained a vessel which held a never-ending supply of food. It is written in the Mahabharata:

गृह्णीष्व पिठरं ताम्रं मया दत्तं नराधिप ।
यावद् वर्त्स्यति पाञ्चाली पात्रेणानेन सुव्रत ।।
(महाभारतम्, आरण्यकपर्व, 3.72)

O King! I give you this copper vessel. Accept it. O man of good conduct! As long as Draupadi continues serving food, without herself eating, she will be able to cook four kinds of vegetables and other food articles in this vessel and there will be never-failing supply.

फलमूलामिषं शाकं संस्कृतं यन्महानसे ।
चतुर्विधं तदन्नाद्यमक्षय्यं ते भविष्यति ।।
(महाभारतम्, आरण्यकपर्व, 3.73)

The amount of food, prepared from a meagre amount of four kinds of food articles, continues increasing. Its supply remains never-failing. And using this vessel, the Pandavas began serving the brahmins.

संस्कृतं प्रसवं याति स्वल्पमन्नं चतुर्विधम् ।
अक्षय्यं वर्धते चान्नं तेन भोजयते द्विजान् ।।
(महाभारतम्, आरण्यकपर्व, 3.82)

Four kinds of food in a small quantity, when cooked in this *patra* (pot), kept on increasing in amount. The Pandavas started giving this food to the brahmins.

भुक्तवत्सु च विप्रेषु भोजयित्वाऽनुजानपि ।
शेषं विघससंज्ञं तु पश्चाद् भुङ्क्तेयुधिष्ठिरः ।।
(महाभारतम्, आरण्यकपर्व, 3.83)

Yudhishtira used to eat only after food was served to the brahmins and his younger brothers.

युधिष्ठिरं भोजयित्वा शेषमश्नाति पार्वती ।
द्रौपद्यां भुज्यमानायां तदन्नं क्षयमेति च ।।

(महाभारतम्, आरण्यकपर्व, 3.84)

Panchali herself used to eat food that was left after serving it to Yudhishtira. The food got over in the vessel after Draupadi had taken her share.

अथ यत्किञ्चिन्मात्रेणैकस्मिन्नव्ययात्मनि तर्पिते ततोऽन्येषामात्मनां तर्पणमप्यत्रैव संनिविशते।

The knowledge of satisfying the hunger of others by eating merely a tiny bit of food is also included here. It is written in the Mahabharata:

ततः कदाचिद्दुर्वासाः सुखासीनाँस्तु पाण्डवान् ।
भुक्त्वा चावस्थितां कृष्णां ज्ञात्वा तस्मिन् वने मुनिः ।।

(महाभारतम्, आरण्यकपर्व, 263.1)

अभ्यागच्छत् परिवृतः शिष्यैरयुतसंमितैः ।
दृष्ट्वायान्तं तमतिथिं स च राजा युधिष्ठिरः ।।

(महाभारतम्, आरण्यकपर्व, 263.2)

विधिवत् पूजयित्वा तमातिथ्येन न्यमन्त्रयत् ।
जगाम च मुनिः सोऽपि स्नातुं शिष्यैः सहानघः ।।

(महाभारतम्, आरण्यकपर्व, 263.4,5)

O King! In the meanwhile, one day maharshi Durvasa, knowing that the Pandavas were resting after their meals, and Draupadi had also taken her meal and resting, came there along with his ten thousand disciples. Then Yudhishtira, seeing the guest approaching, honoured and invited him. Then the pious sage with his disciples went to the river to bathe.

एतस्मिन्नन्तरे राजन् द्रौपदी योषितां वरा ।
चिन्तामवाप परमामन्नहेतोः पतिव्रता ।।

(महाभारतम्, आरण्यकपर्व, 263.6)

O King! Faithful Draupadi, the best among all the women, was greatly troubled.

सा चिन्तयन्ती च तदा नान्नहेतुमविन्दत ।
मनसा चिन्तयामास कृष्णं कंसनिषूदनम् ।।

(महाभारतम्, आरण्यकपर्व, 263.7)

When she did not find any way of finding food, she thought of Sri Krishna.

द्रौपद्याः संकटं ज्ञात्वा द्वारकास्थः स माधवः ।
पार्श्वस्थां शयने त्यक्त्वा रुक्मिणीं केशवः प्रभुः ॥
(महाभारतम्, आरण्यकपर्व, 263.17-18)

Knowing this despairing predicament of Draupadi, Sri Krishna, leaving Rukmani, who lay beside him on the bed, at once appeared there and said:

तत्राजगाम त्वरितो ह्यचिन्त्यगतिरीश्वरः ।
ततस्तामब्रवीत् कृष्णः क्षुधितोऽस्मि भृशातुरः ॥
(महाभारतम्, आरण्यकपर्व, 263.18-19)

शीघ्रं भोजय मां कृष्णे लज्जिता वाक्यमब्रवीत् ॥
(महाभारतम्, आरण्यकपर्व, 263.20)

स्थाल्यां भास्करदत्तायामन्नं मद्भोजनावधि ।
भुक्तवत्यस्म्यहं देव तस्मादन्नं न विद्यते ॥
(महाभारतम्, आरण्यकपर्व, 263.21)

'Draupadi, I am very hungry, I am suffering from hunger. Bring food without any delay and do other jobs afterwards.' Hearing the words of Sri Krishna, Draupadi was filled with shame; she spoke: 'O Master! The vessel given by the Sun-god supplies food only until I eat. O Deity! Today even I have taken my food. So there is no food left in the vessel'.

कृष्णे न नर्मकालोऽयं क्षुच्छ्रमेणातुरे मयि ।
शीघ्रं गच्छ मम स्थालीमानयित्वा प्रदर्शय ॥
(महाभारतम्, आरण्यकपर्व, 263.23)

Then Sri Krishna said, 'O Draupadi! I am terribly hungry and tired. It is not the time for excuses. Go immediately and show me the vessel.'

स्थाल्याः कण्ठेऽथ संलग्नं शाकान्नं वीक्ष्य केशवः ।
उपयुज्याब्रवीदेनामनेन हरिरीश्वरः ॥
(महाभारतम्, आरण्यकपर्व, 263.24)

विश्वात्मा प्रीयतां देवस्तुष्टश्चास्त्विति यज्ञभुक् ।
आकारय मुनीन् शीघ्रं भोजनायेति चाब्रवीत् ॥
(महाभारतम्, आरण्यकपर्व, 263.25,26)

Sri Krishna saw a tiny cooked vegetable stuck to the neck of the vessel and ate it. He said: 'May Sri Hari [the soul of the Universe] be satisfied with it.' Saying this Sri Krishna asked, 'Go immediately and invite all the sages to eat.'

ते चावतीर्णाः सलिले कृतवन्तोऽघमर्षणम् ।
दृष्ट्वोद्गारान् सान्नरसान् तृप्त्या परमया युताः ।।
(महाभारतम्, आरण्यकपर्व, 263.28,29)

At that time, the sages were reciting the Aghamarsana mantra in the water. Suddenly they felt well-fed and belched.

(4) निग्रहणी-ययायमगस्त्य ऋषिर्विंध्यपर्वतं निजग्राह। यया श्रीकृष्णो जयद्रथवधे सांयकाले सूर्यं निजग्राह। यया कपिलमहर्षिः सगरपुत्रान् षष्टिसहस्रमितान् सागरकूले निगृह्य भस्मसाच्चक्रे। यया नहुषो देवेन्द्रपदं प्राप्तोऽपि गौतमादिभिर्निगृहीतः सर्पोऽभूत्। नृगश्च राजा महर्षिशप्तः कृकलासोऽभूत्। राजा परीक्षिच्च शमीकपुत्रेण शृङ्गिणा शप्तस्तक्षकसर्पदंशात् प्राणाँस्तत्याज। च्यवनक्रोधाद्राज्ञः शर्यातेर्नगरे सर्वेषां मलमूत्रनिरोधोऽभूत्। विश्वामित्रक्रोधाद्हरिश्चन्द्रो राजा पीडितोऽभूत् ।

Knowledge of *nigrahan* (giving curse): By using this knowledge, sage Agastya intercepted the movement of the Vindhyachal mountain. Sri Krishna intercepted the movement of the sun in the evening at the time Jayadratha was killed. Sage Kapil, by cursing the 60,000 sons of King Sagara, burnt them on the bank of the ocean. Nahusa, even after obtaining the place of Indra, was turned into a python by the curse of Gautam and other sages; The Naga king was turned into a chameleon by the curse of a great sage. King Parikshita, son of Shamika, died after being bitten by a serpent Takshaka, as cursed by sage Shringi. Cursed by sage Chyavana, citizens in the kingdom of King Sharyati could neither urinate nor defecate. Similarly King Harishchandra was made to suffer by the curse of Vishvamitra.

अनुग्रहणी-यया गौतमशापात् प्रस्तरभूताया अहल्यायाः शापोद्धारानुग्रहं स्वचरणस्पर्शेन चकार भगवान् रामचन्द्रः । यमलार्जुनवृक्षः कृष्णस्पर्शादनुगृहीतः । समुद्रे निमज्जतो भुज्युराजस्याश्विभ्यामुद्धरणमुक्तं वेदे ।

Knowledge of *anugrahan* (showing grace): Sri Rama, by the grace of the touch of his feet, redeemed Ahilya who had turned into a stone by the curse of sage Gautam. Two oxen by the name of Yamalrjuna, received grace by the touch of Sri Krishna. Similarly, as has been said in the Vedas, the kingdom of Bhujjyu, sinking in the ocean, was rescued by the horse-riders.

(5) पुत्रजननीयम्-या एता लोके बन्ध्याः स्त्रियः तासां पुत्रजननप्रतिबन्धका दोषाः शुक्रशोणितपितृनागग्रहादिभेदादष्टौ वैद्यैः स्मर्यन्ते। तेषामष्टानामपि दोषाणामेकेन यज्ञेनैव शक्यते निवृत्तिः कर्तुम्। यथा विभाण्डकसुत ऋष्यशृङ्गोऽयोध्यायां पुत्रेष्टियज्ञं संपाद्य चरुप्राशनेन दशरथपत्नीषु रामलक्ष्मणादींश्चतुरः पुत्रान् संभावयामास। ऋचीकमहर्षिकृतचरुभक्षणात् परशुरामविश्वामित्रयोरुत्पत्तिः। द्रुपदस्य राज्ञो यज्ञाद् द्रौपदी जज्ञे धृष्टद्युम्नश्च। श्रद्धादेवस्य मनोर्यज्ञादिलाकन्या जज्ञे।

Knowledge of *putrajanan* (giving birth to a son): There are eight causes, enumerated by the vaidyas, like shukra, shonita, pitra and naga in a woman who is unable to give birth to a son. These eight causes of deficiency can be resolved by performing a single *putreshtiyajna* (sacrifice to beget a son). For example, sage Shringa, son of Vibhandaka, performed the putreshtiyajna in Ayodhya and enabled Dasharatha's wives to give birth to sons—Rama, Lakshmana, and others—by serving them *charurupa prasad* [a kind of oblation]. Vishvamitra and Parashurama were born by eating the charu prepared by maharshi Richika. Draupadi and Drishtadyumna were born after a similar yajna was performed by King Draupada. Similarly, Ila was born after a sacrifice performed by Manu.

(6) प्रावृषेण्या-वृष्टिकरणीयं विद्या। अवग्रहकाले कारीरीष्ट्यादिभिर्वृष्टिः शक्यते कर्तुम्। यथा विभाण्डकपुत्र ऋष्यशृङ्गः समागत्यायोध्यायां जलं वर्षयामास।

Knowledge of *pravrshenay* (bringing rain): This is the knowledge of causing rain. It is possible to bring rain during drought by performing kariri yajna. By this very knowledge, sage Shringa visiting Ayodhya, made it rain there.

(7) आपोनप्त्रीयम् अपां नानारूपाणि यत्र तत्र भिद्यन्ते अम्भो मरीचिर्मरः श्रद्धारस इत्यादीनि। सूर्यादूर्ध्वप्रदेशे प्रत्युत्पन्नं सर्वजगदव्यापकमुदकमदृश्यरूपमम्भः । सूर्यरश्मौ मरीचिः । मृत्तिकात्वे मरः । चन्द्ररश्मौ श्रद्धा। एवं वायौ रसः । तत्र या इमा रसात्मिका आपो वायौ नित्यं तारतम्येनाहिता भवन्ति। त इमे रसा अहरहः पृथिव्यां प्रत्यर्थमुपसीदन्ति। तेषां संग्रहणविज्ञानाद् यथेच्छं यत्र तत्र निर्जलेऽपि देशे वायुतः प्रतिमूर्च्छनया जलान्युपार्जयितुं शक्यन्ते। तत्प्रकारश्च वेदे आपोनप्त्रीयसूक्ते सुविशदं प्रदर्शितः । पुरात्वे खलु कवष एलूषः प्राचीसरस्वतीकूले सत्रमातिष्ठमानैर्ब्राह्मणैर्निराकृतो मरुधन्वप्रदेशं प्रापितः सन्नेतया विद्यया वायोर्भूयांसि जलान्याविष्कुर्वन् परिसारकनदीं जनयामास।

Knowledge of *aponaptriya* (obtaining water from air): Water has been classified variously from time to time, like ambha, marichi, mara, shraddha and rasa. The water present in the upper part of the sun is called ambha; water present in the rays of the sun is called marichi; water present in *mrittika* (soil) is called mara; water present in the rays of the moon is called shraddha; and water present in the air is called rasa. A slightest amount of this form of water known as rasa is present continuously in the air. This water is obtained in the form of *rasa*-s (juices) every moment by all persons and things on the earth. After accumulating these juices by the science of accumulation or samgrahana vijnana, rain can be created at will by intercepting the air. There are many procedures of this power delineated in detail in aponaptriya-vidya hymn of the Vedas.

In the ancient period, on being boycotted by a congregation of brahmins in a sacrifice on the eastern bank of the Sarasvati, Kavasha-Elusha created the Parisaraka river in the Marudhanva area by accumulating adequate amount of water from the air with the help of *pratimurchana-vidya* (knowledge of intercepting air).

(8) मधुविद्या–मधुमक्षिकायाः मधुकोशमिवैतत् सूर्यमण्डलं भावयित्वा तद्रश्मिसूत्रैरधः परिस्रुतानां मधुबिन्दूनां परिग्रहणं मधुविद्या। मधुशब्दोऽयमुपलक्षणं दधिघृतामृतानाम्। येन पृथिव्याः शरीरं संगठितं कठिनं वाऽन्यत् किञ्चिद् भवति। स सूर्यरसो दधि कथ्यते, येनान्तरिक्षस्वरूपं संपद्यते तद् घृतम्। येन दिव्यस्तन्मधु। येन दिव ऊर्ध्वं तदमृतम्। चत्वारोऽप्येते भावा अहरहः सूर्यात् पृथिव्यामस्यां परिवर्षन्ति तेषां परिवर्षणक्रमविज्ञानाद्बहवोऽर्था यथेच्छं साधयितुं शक्यन्ते। दधन्युपादाने घृतमधुनोः संश्लेषणयोर्योगादनेकभावोत्पत्तिसंभवात्। तामिमां मधुविद्यां दध्यङ्ङाथर्वणो जानाति स्म। ततोऽश्विनौ च।

Knowledge of obtaining *madhu* [honey, ghee, nectar and curd]: The act of accumulating drops of honey from the rays of the sun, perceived as a bee-hive in the solar system, is called *madhu-vidya* (the power of obtaining ghee, nectar and curd). Here *madhu* (honey) is merely a symbol which refers to ghee, nectar and curd. The element which has made the outer crust of the earth hard is known as *dadhi*. The element which has made antariksha is *dhrit*. The element by which the Dyauloka is created is madhu; and the element by which the upper part of Dyauloka is created is known as *amrita* (nectar). These four blessings or *bhava*-s rain down on this earth daily from the solar system. On knowing the sequence of this rain of elements clearly, several elements can be obtained at one's own will. There is a possibility of obtaining many blessings by combining honey and ghee. Sage Dadhyantharvana knew this power and the ashvin kumars had learnt it from him.

1.11.1.4.6 अष्टौ आगमीयमन्त्रबलसिद्धयः

1.11.1.4.6 Eight agamic siddhis through mantras

अथ मारणमोहनोच्चाटनवशीकरणविद्वेषणस्तम्भनाकर्षणादयो मन्त्रशास्त्रोक्ताः सिद्धयः पुरश्चरणानुष्ठान

पूर्वकप्रयोगसाधिताः शारदातिलकमन्त्रमहोदधितन्त्रसारादिग्रन्थेभ्यो विज्ञेयाः ।

The vidyas like marana, mohana, ucchatana,vashikarna, vidveshana, stambhana and akarshana are narrated in the Mantrashastra. These accomplishments are written in granthas like Tantra-shastra, Sharadatilaka and Mantramahodadhi.

1.11.1.4.7 अष्टौ महौषधिबलसिद्धयः

1.11.1.4.7 Eight siddhis through extraordinary herbs

(1) मृतसंजीवनी-इयं महौषधिरभिमन्त्रिता सती स्वप्रभावेण मृतानामपि प्राणिनां शरीरं पुनः प्राणेन संयोज्य पुनरुज्जीवितं तदुत्थापयति। यथा शुक्रः पुरात्वे देवासुरसंग्रामेऽहरहर्मृतानामप्यसुराणां मृतसञ्जीवन्योषधिप्रभावेणाहरहर्जीवयति स्म। यथा वा बृहस्पतिपुत्रः कचः शुक्रशिष्यैरसुरैर्भूयो भूयो व्यापादितोऽपि संजीवन्या विद्यया शुक्रेण पुनरुज्जीवितोऽभूत् । वेनाङ्गुष्ठमथनेन पृथुः पुत्रो जनित इति सेयं विद्यापि मृतसंजीवन्यां विद्यायां संनिविशते।

Knowledge of *mritsanjivani*, a herb for restoring life: It is a herb which, after being charged by the recitation of hymns, restores life to the dead. In the ancient days, Shukracharya, the guru of asuras, used mritsanjivani to revive the asuras killed in the battle with the deities. Shukracharya also restored life to Kacha, killed many times by the asuras, with mritsanjivani. The birth of Prathu by rolling the toe of King Vena is also an example of this power of mritsanjivani.

(2) सञ्जीवकरणी-इयमोषधिर्मूर्च्छया नष्टसंज्ञानां तत्क्षणात् पुनश्चैतन्योत्पादनायोपयुज्यते।

Knowledge of *sanjivani*, a herb for restoring consciousness: This herb restores consciousness to the persons rendered unconscious by some fatal stroke. It is mentioned in the Valmiki Ramayana:

श्रुत्वैतद्वानरेन्द्रस्य सुषेणो वाक्यमब्रवीत् ।
देवासुरमहायुद्धमनुभूतं पुरातनम् ॥
तदा स्म दानवा देवान् शरैर्जघ्नुर्मुहुर्मुहुः ।
तानार्तान्नष्टसंज्ञांश्च गतासूंश्च बृहस्पतिः ॥
विद्याभिर्मन्त्रयुक्ताभिरोषधीभिश्चिकित्सति ।
तान्यौषधान्यानयितुं क्षीरोदं यान्तु सागरम् ॥

(रामायणम्, युद्धकाण्डम्, 50.26-29)

Listening to Sugriva, the king of *vanara*-s (monkeys), Sushena said, 'We saw the battle between the devas and asuras which took place in the past. There the asuras wounded all the devas with their arrows. Then Brihaspati, the guru of the devas, was asked to go at once to the banks of the Kshirsagara to bring this herb for the treatment of the devas. He treated the devas wounded, rendered unconscious, and lifeless in the battle with the power of hymns and extraordinary herbs.

हरयस्तु विजानन्ति पार्वती ते महौषधी ।
संजीवकरणीं दिव्यां विशल्यां देवनिर्मिताम् ।।

(रामायणम्, युद्धकाण्डम्, 50.30)

The whole vanara class knows where the two divine extraordinary herbs are found on the mountains. These two herbs are sanjivani and *vishalyakarani* [herb for healing wounds].

चन्द्रश्च नाम द्रोणश्च क्षीरोदे सागरोत्तमे ।
अमृतं यत्र मथितं तत्र ते परमौषधी ।।

(रामायणम्, युद्धकाण्डम्, 50.31)

On the banks of the Kshirsagara, amidst all the oceans, there are two mountains, Chandra and Drona where *amritmanthan* [churning of the ocean by the gods to extract amrit] took place. On these mountains, these extraordinary herbs could be found.

समीपस्थमुवाचेदं हनुमन्तं महाकपिम् ।
सौम्य शीघ्रमितो गत्वा पर्वतं हि महोदयम् ।।
दक्षिणे शिखरे जातां महौषधिमिहानय ।
विशल्यकरणीं नाम्ना सावर्ण्यकरणीं तथा ।।
संजीवकरणीं वीरसंधानीं च महौषधिम् ।
संजीवनार्थं वीरस्य लक्ष्मणस्य स्वमानय ।।

(रामायणम्, युद्धकाण्डम्, 101.29–32)

Sushena said to Hanumana standing beside him, 'O modest being! Go immediately and bring here vishalyakarani or savarnyakarani, *sanjivakarani* [herbs for restoring consciousness] and *sandhani* [herbs for joining fractures]. O, brave! It is only by these herbs the life of brave Lakshmana will be saved'.

ततः संक्षोदयित्वा तामोषधीं वानरोत्तमः ।
लक्ष्मणाय ददौ नस्तः सुषेणः परमौषधिम् ।।

(रामायणम्, युद्धकाण्डम्, 101.43)

Sushena, the best among the apes, after preparing the herb, gave it to Lakshmana through his nose.

स तस्य गन्धमाघ्राय सशल्यो लक्ष्मणस्तदा ।
विशल्यो विरुजः शीघ्रमुदतिष्ठन्महीतलात् ।।
(रामायणम्, युद्धकाण्डम्, 101.44)

The whole body of Lakshmana was pierced by the arrows. As soon as Lakshmana inhaled the herb, all arrows came out of his body and being free from sickness, he stood up on the ground.

(3.4) विशल्यकरणी-इयं महोषधिः सावर्ण्यकरणी च नियुद्धे शस्त्रास्त्रविहतानां तत्क्षणादेकरात्रेण नैरुज्योत्पादनेन पुनर्युद्धयोग्यतासंपादनार्थमुपयुज्यते। भीष्म-परशुरामयुद्धे त्रिसप्ताहकालिकेऽह रहर्विक्षतयोर्मूर्च्छामागतयोरपि तयोः पुनर्द्वितीयेऽहनि पूर्ववद् बलोत्साहौ सज्जता च स्मर्यन्ते।

छिन्नाङ्गोद्भावनमप्यत्रैव संनिविशते। तच्च विच्छिन्नानामसतामङ्गानां सूर्यरश्मिप्रभावेण पुनरुत्पादनम्। यथा सुद्युम्नेन राज्ञा स्तेयदण्डरूपेण लिखितस्य ऋषेर्हस्ते छिन्ने पुनः शंख ऋषिः सैतवाहिन्यां नद्यां संस्नाप्य पूर्ववत् तद्बाहुमुत्पादयामास।

Knowledge of *vishalyakarani* and *savanyakarani* herbs that heal wounds: These herbs are useful in healing wounds of warriors caused by weapons and making them capable of fighting in the war instantly or overnight. It is said that Bheema and Parashurama daily used to restore themselves to their original strength and zeal even after being wounded and rendered unconscious in a battle that lasted for three weeks.

These herbs also helped in the growth of new organs of the body in place of the broken ones. In conjunction with the rays of the sun, these herbs help grow new organs in place of the old ones. When a hermit named Likhit had his arms broken as a punishment meted out by King Sudyumna for stealing, his arms were restored by another hermit, Sankha who took him for a bath in the Sautavahini river.

(5) सन्धानकरणी-विच्छिन्नाङ्गसन्धानायोपयुज्यते। यथा ग्रीवातिरिक्तानामङ्गानां शस्त्रच्छिन्नानां संश्लेषणद्रव्यसंयोगं विनैव देवराज इन्द्रः संधत्ते स्मेति ऋग्वेदसंहितायामाख्यातम् ।

य ऋते चिदभिश्रिषः पुरा जत्रुभ्य आतृदः ।
सन्धाता सन्धिं मघवा पुरुवसुरिष्कर्ता विह्रुतं पुनः ।।
(ऋग्वेदः, 8.1.12)

Knowledge of *sandhanakarani*, the herb to heal fractures: This herb is used to join the fractured parts of the body. It is mentioned in the Rigveda: 'Indra joined the parts of the neck cut by the weapons, without using any gluing substance.' It is also mentioned in the Rigveda, 'The very prosperous Indra, who joined the neck without any bandage even before the blood could flow, heals the wound again'.

मधु विद्यां ब्रुवत: शिरश्छेत्स्यामीति देवराजेनोक्ते तां शिक्षितुमादावेवाश्विनौ दधीचस्य शिरश्छेदं कृत्वा शिर: संयोज्य हयशिरसो दधीचीन्मधुविद्यामुपलेभाते। अथ देवेन्द्रणाश्वशिरसि विच्छेदिते पुनराश्विभ्यां तदीयं पौर्विकं शिरो यथावत् संयोजितमिति प्रसिद्धमितिहासेषु।

According to the Puranas, Indra had threatened to cut off the head of anyone divulging the secrets of obtaining the power of madhu. The ashvin kumars, therefore, first cut the head of sage Dadhichi and implanted it on the body of a horse. When they gained the madhu vidya from the horse's mouth, the implanted head was cut by Indra. The ashvin kumars then joined the head of Dadhichi to his body.

(6) अरिष्टभैषज्या नाम योगविद्यानुगृहीता महौषधि: । यया सौभरिणा राजकन्यानां शतमितानां कुब्जानां स्वहस्तास्फालनेन कुब्जत्वं निरस्तम्। लङ्कायां मेघनादेन युद्धे शरबन्धविक्षतयो रामलक्ष्मणयोर्गरुडोऽकस्मादाकाशादुपेत्य स्वाङ्गस्पर्शेन सर्वाङ्गव्रणशोधनं कृत्वा निर्व्रणत्वं नैरुज्यं च संपादयामास।

There is an extraordinary herb called arishtabhaishajya which is charged by yogic knowledge. Sage Saubhari cured the hunchback of a hundred princesses by the touch of his hand. In the battle, when Rama and Lakshmana were seriously wounded by the arrows of Meghanatha, Garuda appeared out of nowhere and by his gentle touch cured all their wounds and made them healthy.

It is written in the Ramayana:

ततः सुपर्णः काकुस्थौ स्पृष्ट्वा प्रत्यभिनन्द्य च ।
विममर्श च पाणिभ्यां मुखे चन्द्रसमप्रभे ।।

(रामायणम्, युद्धकाण्डम्, 50.38)

Thereafter Garuda, touching both the Raghuvanshis, welcomed them and cleansed their moon-like faces.

वैनतेयेन संस्पृष्टास्तयोः संरुरुहुर्व्रणाः ।
सुवर्णे च तनू स्निग्धे तयोराशु बभूवतुः ।।

(रामायणम्, युद्धकाण्डम्, 50.39)

By the touch of Garuda, all the wounds of Rama and Lakshmana were healed and their bodies became attractive and radiant instantaneously.

तेजोवीर्यं बलं चौज उत्साहश्च महागुणाः ।
प्रदर्शनं च बुद्धिश्च स्मृतिश्च द्विगुणा तयोः ।।
(रामायणम्, युद्धकाण्डम्, 50.40)

All the extraordinary qualities of radiance, bravery, strength, elegance, and enthusiasm, intellect, and memory became doubled.

(7) डिम्भप्रसविनी-यथा सगरमहाराजस्य षष्टिसहस्राणि पुत्राणां, धृतराष्ट्रस्य च शतं पुत्राणामौषधिप्रभावादुदपद्यन्त। डिम्भमेकं खण्डशः कृत्वा तान् खण्डान् घृतकलशे महौषधिघृताढ्ये निक्षप्य कैश्चिन्मासैः परिपक्वांस्तान् गर्भांस्ततः प्रादुर्भावयामासुर्महर्षयः ।

Knowledge of *dimbhaprasavani*, herbs used for giving birth to a son: This is a herb which is used for preparing an artificial embryo to give birth to children. The seventy thousand sons of King Sagara and hundred sons of King Dhritarashtra were born by the power of this herb. For giving birth to children, the great seers, divided an artificial embryo into many pieces, kept them in a pitcher filled with ghee and dimbhaprasavani herb and then after a due course of time created matured embryos out of these pieces. It is written in the Brahma Purana:

कनिष्ठा सुषुवे तुम्बीं बीजपूर्णामिति श्रुतिः ।
तत्र षष्टिसहस्राणि गर्भास्ते तिलसंमिताः ।।
घृतपूर्णेषु कुम्भेषु तान् गर्भान्निदधे ततः ।
ततो दशसु मासेषु समुत्तस्थुर्यथाक्रमम् ।।
कुमारास्ते यथाकालं सगरप्रीतिवर्द्धनाः ।
सम्बभूवुर्यथाकालं ववृधुश्च यथासुखम् ।।
(ब्रह्मपुराणम्, 6.68–71)

The youngest queen gave birth to a gourd with a seed in which there were sixty thousand embryos shaped like thin straws. These were then kept in *ghrit* (ghee) *kalasha*-s (vessels). In due course of time, these embryos were born as the illustrious sons of King Sagara who began to grow up happily.

(8) बलातिबले-मन्त्रयुक्ते महौषधी एते। यथोक्तं रामायणे वाल्मीकीये-

Knowledge of *balatibal-aushadhi*, herbs that give extraordinary strength: These herbs known as bala and atibala are charged by hymns. There is a reference to these herbs in the Valmiki Ramayana:

गृहाण वत्स सलिलं माभूत् कालस्य पर्ययः ।
मन्त्रग्रामं गृहाण त्वं बलामतिबलां तथा ॥
(रामायणम्, बालकाण्डम्, 22.12-13)

Sage Vishvamitra tells Rama: O, dear child! Sip water from the palm of hand. Do not waste your time. Now obtain the herbs of bala and atibala and the hymns to charge them.

बला चातिबला चैव सर्वज्ञानस्य मातरौ ।
एतद्विद्याद्वये लब्धे न भवेत् सदृशस्तव ॥
(रामायणम्, बालकाण्डम्, 22.17)

These bala and atibala are the mothers of all powers. After obtaining them, there will be no one as valorous as you are.

न श्रमो न ज्वरो वा ते न रूपस्य विपर्ययः ।
न च सुप्तं प्रमत्तं वा धर्मयिष्यन्ति नैर्ऋताः ॥
(रामायणम्, बालकाण्डम्, 22.13-14)

You will not suffer from fatigue and fever. Nor will there be any change in your body. Nor will the asuras be able to suppress you even while you are in a state of sleep or intoxication.

न बाह्वोः सदृशो वीर्ये पृथिव्यामस्ति कश्चन ।
त्रिषु लोकेषु वा राम न भवेत् सदृशस्तव ॥
(रामायणम्, बालकाण्डम्, 22.14-15)

There will be nobody like you in regard to the strength of your arms. And O Rama! There will be nobody like you in all the three worlds.

न सौभाग्ये न दाक्षिण्ये न ज्ञाने बुद्धिनिश्चये ।
नोत्तरे प्रतिवक्तव्ये समो लोके तवानघ ॥
(रामायणम्, बालकाण्डम्, 22.16)

O, Sacred one! There will be nobody equal to you in regard to fortune, intelligence, knowledge, intellect, determination, and wit.

बलामतिबलां चैव पठतस्तात राघव ।
क्षुत्पिपासे न ते राम भविष्येते नरोत्तम ॥
(रामायणम्, बालकाण्डम्, 22.18)

O son, Raghava! O! the greatest one among all men! You will not suffer from hunger and thirst.

विद्याद्वयमधीयाने यशश्चाथ भवेद् भुवि ।
पितामहसुते ह्येते विद्ये तेजःसमन्विते ।।
(रामायणम्, बालकाण्डम्, 22.19)

The use of these two powers shall enhance your fame. These two powers which are the daughters of Brahma, are impregnated with radiance.

ततो रामो जलं स्पृष्ट्वा प्रहृष्टवदनः शुचिः ।
प्रतिजग्राह ते विद्ये महर्षेर्भावितात्मनः ।।
(रामायणम्, बालकाण्डम्, 22.21-22)

Then Rama, after purifying himself by touching water, and with cheerful disposition, obtained both the powers from maharshi Vishvamitra.

1.11.1.4.8 अष्टौ यन्त्रबलसिद्धयः

1.11.1.4.8 Eight siddhis gained with mechanical power

(1) दिव्यविमानम्-ऋभुनिर्मितमुक्तमृग्वेदे चतुर्थमण्डले षट्त्रिंशसूक्ते भगवता वामदेवेन-

अनश्वो जातो अनभीषुरुक्थ्यो रथस्त्रिचक्रः परिवर्तते रजः ।
महत् तद्वो देवस्य प्रवाचनं द्यामृभवः पृथिवी यच्च पुष्यथ ।।
(ऋग्वेदः, 4.36.1)

Knowledge of *divya vimana* [divine flying chariot]: In the thirty-sixth sukta of the fourth mandala of Rigveda, Bhagwan Vamadeva said: 'O extraordinary being! Your chariot, devoid of horses and reins, having three wheels, is praiseworthy. It moves all around in space. Your act of strengthening the Dyauloka and Prithviloka is great and is an expression of your godly nature.'

(2) पुष्पकविमानं रामायणे निरूपितम् -

Knowledge of *pushpaka vimana* [a flying chariot]: There is a description of pushpaka vimana in the Ramayana:

एतत्पश्य तथा क्षिप्रं प्रतिगच्छाम तां पुरीम् ।
अयोध्यां गच्छतो ह्येष पन्थाः परमदुर्गमः ।।
(रामायणम्, युद्धकाण्डम्, 121.7)

Bhagvan Rama said, 'Let us now think how we can reach Ayodhya as soon as possible because the path leading to Ayodhya is very difficult.'

एवमुक्तस्तु काकुत्स्थं प्रत्युवाच विभीषणः ।
अह्ना त्वां प्रापयिष्यामि तां पुरीं पार्थिवात्मज ।।
(रामायणम्, युद्धकाण्डम्, 121.8)

Responding to him, Vibhishana spoke: 'O Princes! Do not worry about this. I shall help you reach Ayodhya just in a day.'

पुष्पकं नाम भद्रं ते विमानं सूर्यसन्निभम् ।
मम भ्रातुः कुबेरस्य रावणेन बलीयसा ।।

हृतं निर्जित्य संग्रामे कामगं दिव्यमुत्तमम् ।
त्वदर्थं पालितं चेदं तिष्ठत्यतुलविक्रमम् ।।
(रामायणम्, युद्धकाण्डम्, 121.9-10)

'May God bless you! There is a sun-like pushpaka vimana of my elder brother, Kubera, which the great warrior Ravana had confiscated after defeating him. O incomparable, valorous Rama! this chariot which flies, according to one's desire, is reserved for you.'

तदिदं मेघसंकाशं विमानमिह तिष्ठति ।
येन यास्यसि यानेन त्वमयोध्यां गतज्वरः ।।
(रामायणम्, युद्धकाण्डम्, 121.11)

'This extraordinary chariot which looks like a cloud and by which you will be able to reach Ayodhya, is before you here.'

ततः काञ्चनचित्राङ्गं वैदूर्यमणिवेदिकम् ।
कूटागारैः परिक्षिप्तं सर्वतो रजतप्रभम् ।।
(रामायणम्, युद्धकाण्डम्, 121.24)

'One of the parts of this chariot is made with gold and inside there are balconies studded with blue diamonds. It has several secret rooms; and it shines like silver on all sides. Such is the beauty of this chariot.'

पाण्डुराभिः पताकाभिर्ध्वजैश्च समकलङ्कृतम् ।
काञ्चनं काञ्चनैर्हर्म्यैर्हैमपद्मविभूषितैः ।।
(रामायणम्, युद्धकाण्डम्, 121.25)

'This chariot is embellished with white and golden banners, and flags. There are golden mansions of many storeys, decorated with golden lotus which made the chariot resplendent.'

प्रकीर्णं किङ्किणीजालैर्मुक्तामणिगवाक्षकम् ।
घण्टाजालैः परिक्षिप्तं सर्वतो मधुरस्वनम् ।।
(रामायणम्, युद्धकाण्डम्, 121.26)

'The entire chariot is embedded with small bells and hangings. It has windows of pearls and gems; It has bells tied all around it, which produce musical sounds.'

तं मेरुशिखराकारं निर्मितं विश्वकर्मणा ।
बृहद्भिर्भूषितं हर्म्यैर्मुक्तारजतशोभितैः ।।
(रामायणम्, युद्धकाण्डम्, 121.27)

'This chariot, designed by Vishvakarma, stands tall like the Sumeru mountain and is equipped with big rooms embellished with pearls and silver'.

तलैः स्फटिकचित्राङ्गैर्वैदूर्यैश्च वरासनैः ।
महार्हास्तरणोपेतैरुपपन्नं महाधनैः ।।
(रामायणम्, युद्धकाण्डम्, 121.28)

'Its floor is embedded with unique crystals and gems. There are royal seats of blue diamond where precious sheets are spread out on them'.

तद्विमानं कामगमं पुष्पकं पुष्पभूषितम् ।
निवेदयित्वा रामाय तस्थौ तत्र विभूषणः ।।
(रामायणम्, युद्धकाण्डम्, 121.29)

'This chariot moves according to one's own will, and is beautified by flowers.' Informing Sri Rama about such a chariot, Vibhishana stood there.

ततः स पुष्पकं दिव्यं सुग्रीवः सह वानरैः ।
आरुरोह मुदा युक्तः सामात्यश्च विभीषणः ।।
(रामायणम्, युद्धकाण्डम्, 122.24)

Then Vibhishana along with vanaras, Sugriva and the counsellors ascended joyously into that divya pushpaka vimana.

तेष्वारूढेषु सर्वेषु कौबेरं परमासनम् ।
राघवेणाभ्यनुज्ञातमुत्पपात विहायसा ।।

खगतेन विमानेन हंसयुक्तेन भास्वता ।
प्रहृष्टश्च प्रतीतश्च बभौ रामः कुबेरवत् ॥
(रामायणम्, युद्धकाण्डम्, 122.25-26)

After all of them ascended, the pushpaka vimana began to fly in the sky under the command of Sri Rama, who looked splendid like Kubera himself.

ते सर्वे वानरर्क्षाश्च राक्षसाश्च महाबलाः ।
यथासुखमसम्बाधं दिव्ये तस्मिन्नुपाविशन् ॥
(रामायणम्, युद्धकाण्डम्, 122.25-27)

All apes, bears, and other great warrior asuras delightfully and comfortably were sitting in the chariot. Nobody was creating any obstacle.

(3) सौभविमानं-मार्तिकावतराजस्य शाल्वस्यासीत्। युद्धविमानमेतद्बहुविस्तृतमासीत्। उक्तं च भारते वनपर्वणि कृष्णेन ।

Knowledge of saubha vimana: This vimana [flying chariot] was in the possession of King Shalva of Martikavata. This vimana, meant for war, was big in size. In the Vanaparva of Mahabharata, Sri Krishna says:

खे विषक्तं हि तत् सौभं क्रोशमात्र इवाभवत् ।
शाल्वराजो युध्यमानो वियदभ्यगमत् पुनः ॥
(महाभारतम्, आरण्यकपर्व, 21.25)

That saubha vimana entered the sky with such speed as if it had travelled a kosa; King Shalva, while fighting, thus flew into the sky.

ततो नादृश्यत तदा सौभं कुरुकुलोद्वह ।
अन्तर्हित मायया ऽभूत् ततो ऽहं विस्मितो ऽभवम् ॥
(महाभारतम्, आरण्यकपर्व, 23.3)

O Kurukula shiromani! that time the saubha vimana was made to vanish by the power of illusion. It could not be seen by any means. I was astounded by this.

ततः प्राग्ज्यौतिषं गत्वा पुनरेव व्यदृश्यत ।
सौभं कामगमं वीरो मोहयन्मम चक्षुषी ॥
(महाभारतम्, आरण्यकपर्व, 23.9)

When the saubha vimana, which moves according to one's own will, reached near Pragajyotishapur, it began to reappear before my astonished eyes.

आग्नेयमस्त्रमादाय युद्धे मतिमधारयम् ।
वधाय शाल्वराजस्य सौभस्य च निपातने ।।
(महाभारतम्, आरण्यकपर्व, 23.26-27)

Armed with a weapon of extraordinary power, Agneya, I decided to kill King Shalva and to knock down the saubha vimana.

रूपं सुदर्शनस्यासीदाकाशे पततस्तदा ।
द्वितीयस्येव सूर्यस्य युगान्ते प्रतपिष्यतः ।।
(महाभारतम्, आरण्यकपर्व, 23.32)

Once in the sky, the *sudarshana-chakra* [an extraordinary weapon] shone like the sun rising during *pralayakala* [great flood].

तत् समासाद्य नगरं सौभं व्यपगतत्विषम् ।
मध्येन पाटयामास क्रकचो दार्विवोच्छ्रितम् ।।
(महाभारतम्, आरण्यकपर्व, 23.33)

That extraordinary weapon, reaching Shaubhanagar, cut the chariot as a saw chops a wood.

द्विधाकृतं ततः सौभं सुदर्शनबलाद्धतम् ।
तस्मिन्निपतिते सौभे चक्रमागात्करं मम ।।
(महाभारतम्, आरण्यकपर्व, 23.34-35)

Then with the power of sudarshana-chakra, the saubha vimana was cut into two pieces. On felling the saubha vimana, the sudarshana-chakra came back into my hands.

तन्मेरुशिखराकारं विध्वस्ताट्टालगोपुरम् ।
दह्यमानमभिप्रेक्ष्य स्त्रियस्ताः संप्रदुद्रुवुः ।।
(महाभारतम्, आरण्यकपर्व, 23.39)

All the multi-storeyed buildings in Shaubhanagar, built like the Meru mountain, were destroyed. Seeing it burning, all women of the city ran helter skelter.

(4) अथ सूतविमानं तु त्रिकक्षं पारदाभ्रकैः ।
आस्थानयन्त्रभागाभ्यां द्विविभक्तं मनोजवम् ।।643।।

Knowledge of suta vimana: Made of mercury and mica, this vimana with three sections could move with the speed of mind. It had two parts—one was a seating place while another was a place for the engine.

यन्त्रभागे निम्नकोष्ठे सुदीप्तेनाग्निनाचितम् ।
तदूर्ध्वपादेनाढ्यं तदूर्ध्वं चाभ्रकाचितम् ।।644।।

In the lower part of the machine, a bright fire was lit, the upper part was covered with mercury and the uppermost part with mica.

तिर्यगूर्ध्वाधरान् देशान्नमितं तद्यथेच्छया ।
आयसीभिर्भूयसीभिर्नलिकाभिः समाचितम् ।।645।।

In order to move it sideways, downwards or upwards, there were many iron levers in this suta vimana.

गन्धकैरपि तद्युक्तं निपुणैर्निर्मितं पुरा ।
गौरीशंकरवीर्याभ्यां विमानं कृतमद्भुतम् ।।646।।

In the ancient period, this vimana, made of sulphur, was designed by skilled and expert craftsmen. In this way this unique vimana was prepared by the power of sulphur and mercury.

(5) हर्यश्वविमानम्-इन्द्राय दारुविनिर्मितं संयुक्तं हयद्वयात्मकम्। यथोक्तं वेदे-

Knowledge of *haryashva vimana* (an extraordinary horse-chariot): This chariot of Indra, driven by two horses, was made of wood. It is written in the Rigveda:

शच्याकर्त पितरा युवाना शच्याकर्त चमसं देवपानम् ।
शच्या हरी धनुतरावतष्टेन्द्रवाहावृभवो वाजरत्नाः ।।

(ऋग्वेदः, 4.35.5)

With your skill, you maintained the youth of your parents. Again with your skill you made *chamasa* (drinking vessel) worthy of the devas. O! famed *ribhus* (part divine, part human beings)! By your expertise you trained horses to carry Indra, with a speed faster than that of the arrows.

ये हरी मेधयोक्था मदन्त इन्द्राय चक्रुः सुयुजा ये अश्वाः ।
ते रायस्पोषं द्रविणान्यस्मे धत्त ऋभवः क्षेमयन्तो न मित्रम् ।।

(ऋग्वेदः, 4.34.10)

O ! Ribhus, who, being delighted by hymns, trained the horses with their expertise; who trained the horses for Indra to be yoked easily to the chariot, grant us wealth and prosperity.

(6) प्लवविमानं-समुद्रसंतरणसाधनदारुनिर्मितं पक्षिरूपमश्विकृते सुधन्वराजपुत्रैर्ऋभुभिर्विनिर्मितम्। नैतत्समुद्रे निमज्जति स्म। एतदारूढा अनायासेन समुद्रमत्यूर्मिमालाकुलमपि संतरन्ति स्म।

Knowledge of *plava vimana* [a bird-shaped ship]: This ship, made of wood, meant for sailing and crossing oceans, was prepared for the ashvin kumars by ribhus, sons of King Sudhyanva. This ship did not sink in the ocean. A man sailing in this ship could cross very easily even a turbulent ocean.

(7) अमृतगवी-

रथं ये चक्रुः सुवृतं नरेष्ठां ये धेनुं विश्वजुवं विश्वरूपाम् ।
त आतक्षन्त्वृभवो रयिं नः स्ववसः स्ववसः सुहस्ताः ॥

(ऋग्वेदः, 4.33.8)

ऋभुभिर्गौरति भव्या कामगवी निर्मिता चित्रा ।
एषा यदेव किञ्चित् प्राश्नोत्यमृतं ततो दुग्धे ।।647।।

Knowledge of *amritgavi* (nectar-producing cow): It is written in the Vedas: Ribhus, you are the one who, while performing the worldly duties, prepared chariots for men and created a cow with many qualities. The ones whose work is of highest standards, who possesses excellent means of protection and are endowed with excellent hands, grant us prosperity.

An extraordinary cow called Kamagavi was created by the ribhus; that cow produced amrita-like milk from whatever she ate.

(8) शिलासंतरणी-

नलेन कपिवीरेण वायुवेशाल्लघूकृतैः ।
शिलाखण्डैः संतरिद्भः सेतुरब्धौ प्रवर्तितः ।।648।।
अद्यत्वे गङ्गायां पञ्चभिरब्दैर्भवेन्न वा सेतुः ।
पञ्चभिरहोभिरब्धौ रामः सेतुं शिलामयं व्यदधात् ।।649।।
पूर्वयुगे यद्वीर्यं यच्चाद्भुतकर्म चक्रिरे वीराः ।
अनुकर्तुं तदशक्ता अनृतं मन्यन्त आत्मनस्तुष्ट्यै ।।650।।
अद्यातिहीनवीर्या अल्पारम्भा स्वमानरक्षार्थम् ।
पूर्वेषामिह कीर्तिं न सहन्ते कूपमण्डूकाः ।।651।।

Knowledge of building with floating stones or *shilasantarani*: Brave vanara Nala built a bridge over the sea by floating light-weight boulders. Today it is not sure whether such a bridge can be built over Ganga in five years but Rama built a bridge of boulders over the sea in just five days. In the ancient period, those brave persons performed this heroic deed. Those who are incapable of doing such heroic deeds, to please themselves, consider these events as imaginary and fiction. It is a matter of lamentation that such weak persons of limited knowledge, capable only of doing ordinary jobs, do not accept the heroic fame of their ancestors merely out of ego.

1.11.1.4.9 स्वयंवहादयः यन्त्रविशेषा

1.11.1.4.9 Special automatic machines

आभ्यः सर्वाभ्यो विद्याभ्योऽप्यधिकचमत्कारवती नितान्तमुपयोगिनी स्वयंवहयन्त्रविद्या भवति। तया दैनिकं षष्टिघटिकापलविपलादिज्ञानमतिसूक्ष्ममसंशयितं यथार्थरूपमुपसंपद्यते। तन्निर्माणप्रयोगादिप्रकाराः सूर्यसिद्धान्ते सिद्धान्तशिरोमणौ च विशिष्योल्लिखिता द्रष्टव्याः ।

Of all such sciences, the most miraculous and extremely useful is the science of the special automatic machines, svayamvah. With the help of this science, one can derive exact, subtle, and flawless knowledge of the sixty *ghari*-s (minutes or moments) of the day and its sub-units *pala*-s and *vipala*-s (Indian astrology divides the total period of a full natural day and night into sixty gharis which are further divided into sixty pala-s and the palas are further divided into sixty vipalas). Its manufacturing and application techniques are especially illustrated in *Surya Sidhanta* and *Shiromani Sidhanta.*

1.11.1.5 सर्वासां विद्यानां प्रादुर्भावः

1.11.1.5 Beginning of all knowledge

एवं केचिद् विद्या विभजन्ते भारतीयास्ताः ।
एता एव स्वपरे ब्रुवते पुनरन्यथा दृष्ट्वा ॥652॥

People call these knowledge systems by different names. These branches of knowledge are understood differently and are explained in several ways.

ब्राह्मणवीर्याण्यष्टौ दैवाद् योगेन यज्ञतस्तपसा ।
मणिमन्त्रौषधियन्त्रैरेषां भेदाश्च बहवः स्यु ॥653॥

These branches of knowledge were born out of eight energies of the brahmins, and are categorized into eight types. These are: those born of divine grace, through the energy of yoga, through the fruits of yajna, through ascetic heat, through the powers of diamond, through chanting, through herbs, and through the power of yantras.

एकैकविद्ययापि च लभतेऽपूर्वं जनस्तु सामर्थ्यम् ।
नातः परं तु किञ्चिद्बलमधिकं संभवत्यत्र ।।654।।

Man accomplishes unprecedented powers by achieving even one of these vidyas. There is no other conceivable power than the one attained by the knowledge of these vidyas.

दैवबली योगबली यज्ञबली वा तपोबली निगमात् ।
मणिमन्त्रतन्त्रयन्त्रैरागमतः स्याद्बली विप्रः ।।655।।

A brahmin, with the help of divine knowledge, can become sufficiently powerful by acquiring classical knowledge by the power of yoga, meditation, mani, yantra, shastras and tantra.

नास्ति पृथिव्यां सोऽर्थो वीर्यात् पूर्णान्न यः सिध्येत् ।
दैवाद् योगाद् यज्ञात् तपसो मन्त्रान् महौषधितः ।।656।।

There is no material goal on the earth which cannot be achieved with the knowledge of divine powers, yoga, meditation, sacrifice, incantations, and knowledge of medicinal herbs. That means all that is attainable can be achieved.

सर्वविद्यानां सर्वार्थसिद्धौ हेतुत्वं तुल्यम् ।

Ways to attain vidya and siddhi are similar.

इत्थं विद्याः कारणकार्यविभागेन दर्शिता एताः ।
किन्त्वविशेषात् सर्वाः सिद्धय एभ्योऽष्टवीर्येभ्यः ।।657।।

On the cause and effect analysis, all these vidyas are defined differently. Especially the supreme siddhis or accomplishments are gained with the help of eight energies of the brahmins.

दैवाद् योगाद् यज्ञात् तपसो मणिमन्त्रतन्त्रयन्त्रेभ्यः ।
तुल्यवदेव समग्राः कामा निश्चित्य सिध्यन्ति ।।658।।

The eight *brahmvirya*-s (energies of brahmins) are divine grace, yoga, yajna, mani, tapa, mantra, tantra, and yantra.

1.11.1.6 नवनिधयः

1.11.1.6 Nine treasures

एता हि सिद्धयोऽष्टौ बहुभिर्यत्नैः प्रसाधनात् सिद्धेः ।
अथ नवनिधयस्त्वन्ये गृहे निधानं ह्यपेक्षते तेषाम् ।।659।।

The aforesaid eight siddhis are achieved through persistent efforts and sustained meditation. But possession of different powers called *nidhi*-s (treasures) make these siddhis automatically attainable.

महापद्मश्च पद्मश्च शङ्खो मकरकच्छपौ ।
मुकुन्दकुन्दनीलाश्च खर्वश्च निधयो नव ।।
(अमरकोशः, स्वर्गवर्गः, 165, 166)

The nine treasures are *mahapadma* (the great lotus), *padma* (lotus), *shankha* (conch shell), *makara* (a half terrestrial, half aquatic sea creature), *kachhapa* (tortoise), *mukunda* (precious stone or mercury), *kunda* (chameli flower or pearl), *neel mani* (blue diamond), and *kharva* (vessels baked in fire).

एषामेकोऽपि गृहे निहितः परमां श्रियं तनुते ।
सपरिच्छदान्नवस्त्रप्राचुर्यं भोगसौभाग्यम् ।।660।।

Even one of the treasures stored in one's home could fetch endless prosperity and fortune. It will bring jewellery, grains, sufficient clothes, and every kind of good fortune.

नापेक्ष्यतेऽत्र मन्त्रो न यन्त्रतन्त्रे न यज्ञयोगौ वा ।
केवलनिधानमङ्गे गृहेऽपि लक्ष्मीं विवर्द्धयति ।।661।।

For acquiring these treasures no means like mantra, tantra, yajna or yoga power are needed. Keeping these nidhis on your person or in your house alone increases prosperity and fortune.

निधिविशेषा अष्टौ मणयः ।

Some medicines too are nidhis.

औषधयोऽपि च निधयो निधिप्रभावाः प्रसिद्ध्यन्ति ।
कतिचित् तासामष्टौ मणिसंज्ञा अत्र कथ्यन्ते ।।662।।

अष्टमणय:	1.	2.	3.	4.	5.	6.	7.	8.
	इन्द्रमणि:	जङ्गिड-मणि:	प्रतिसर-मणि:	वरुण-मणि:	दर्भ-मणि:	औदुम्बर-मणि:	शतवार-मणि:	अस्तृत-मणि:

Their powers are proved when they assimilate the magical influence of nidhi. These treasures in the form of medicines derive their names from mani.

The list of these diamonds or manis is given below:

Eight manis	**1**	**2**	**3**	**4**	**5**	**6**	**7**	**8**
	indra-mani	jangid-mani	pratisara-mani	varuna-mani	darbha-mani	audhumbara-mani	shatvara-mani	astrata-mani

शक्तिर्गुणश्च वीर्यं रसो विपाकः प्रभावश्च ।
प्रत्योषधि भिद्यन्ते मणित्वमेषां प्रभाववैशेष्यात् ।।663।।

The effect of *shakti* (strength or energy), *guna* (quality), *virya* (virility), *rasa* (essence), *vipaak* (flavour) and *prabhava* (influence or effect) respectively causes different levels of efficacy in each medicine. Owing to the impact of the diamonds, these medicines are also considered as forms of diamonds.

सन्त्योषधयः सर्वाः प्रभाववत्योऽथ तास्वष्टौ ।
मणयः स्युरिन्द्रजङ्गिडप्रतिसरवरणादयः ख्याताः ।।664।।

All medicines are effective but eight of them are forms of precious stones. Among these are indra, jangid, pratisara, and varuna.

हस्ते धृतेन्द्रमणिरिह महौषधिः स्वप्रभावेण ।
दिव्यां दृष्टिं दत्ते यथोक्तमाथर्वणे वेदे ।।665।

It is said in the Atharvaveda that wearing of indra-mani on the arm imparts divine vision:

आपश्यति प्रतिपश्यति परापश्यति पश्यति ।
दिवमन्तरिक्षमाद् भूमिं सर्वं तद्देवि पश्यति ।।

(अथर्ववेदः, 4.20.1)

Hey goddess, should a man were to wear jangid-mani, he would be able to see everything. He could see every matter, see into distance and beyond, see Dyauloka, Antarikshaloka and *bhumi*.

तिस्रो दिवस्तिस्रः पृथिवीः षट् चेमाः प्रदिशः पृथक् ।
त्वयाऽहं सर्वा भूतानि पश्यानि देव्योषधे ॥

(अथर्ववेदः, 4.20.2)

O divine remedies, may I see all the three divine spheres, three spheres of earth and six sub-directions (east, west, north, south, up and down) distinctly and see all the living beings in the world with your help and powers that you possess.

ता मे सहस्राक्षो देवो दक्षिणे हस्त आदधत् ।
तयाऽहं सर्वं पश्यामि यश्च शूद्र उतार्य्यः ॥

(अथर्ववेदः, 4.20.4)

The thousand-eyed sun has tied to my arm the divine medicine. Now with the magical powers of the medicine I can look into the hearts of both the shudras and the Arya.

दर्शय मा यातुधानान् दर्शय यातुधान्यः ।
पिशाचान् सर्वान्दर्शयेति त्वारम्भ ओषधे ॥

(अथर्ववेदः, 4.20.6)

O, *aushadhi* (medicine)! Show me all the rakshasa-s, rakshasi-s and the spirits surrounding you, for that I seek your help.

यो अन्तरिक्षेण पतति दिवं यश्चातिसर्पति ।
भूमिं यो मन्यते नाथं तं पिशाचं प्रदर्शय ॥

(अथर्ववेदः, 4.20.9)

O, aushadhi! Wearing you on my person, show me all the rakshasa-s, rakshasi-s and all the ghosts and spirits, for this I invoke your help.

अथ जङ्गिडमणरन्यो धृतः शरीरे प्रवर्द्धयत्यायुः ।
कृत्यादोषं हरति च यथोक्तमाथर्वणे वेदे ॥666॥

One who wears jangid-mani the medicine, increases his or her life span. It is said in the Atharvaveda that a person wearing jangid-mani medicine cannot be harmed by the evil impact of black magic.

दीर्घायुत्वाय बृहते रणायारिष्यन्तो दक्षमाणाः सदैव ।
मणिं विष्कन्ध दूषणं जङ्गिडं बिभृमो वयम् ।

(अथर्ववेदः, 2.4.1)

For attaining longevity and for the bliss of great joy we all wear jangid-mani which prevents decay of our energy and increases our strength.

जङ्गिडो जम्भाद् विशराद् विष्कन्धादभिशोचनात् ।
मणिः सहस्रवीर्यः परिणः पातु विश्वतः ।

(अथर्ववेदः, 2.4.2)

May the jangid-mani endowed with thousand efficacies protect us from the disease responsible for yawning and the diseases which drain strength.

अयं विष्कन्धं सहतेऽयं बाधाते अत्रिणः ।
अयं नो विष्वभेषजो जङ्गिडः पात्वंहसः ।।

(अथर्ववेदः, 2.4.3)

This jangid-mani protects us from excessive consumption. The diamond saves us from the influence of mani-eating ashes [excessive eating and general weakness] disease. This jangid-mani is in fact an essence of all the medicines. May this diamond protects us from sin!

देवैर्दत्तेन मणिना जङ्गिडेन मयोभुवा ।
विष्कन्धं सर्वा रक्षांसि व्यायामे सहामहे ।।

(अथर्ववेदः, 2.4.4)

May we forever bury all excess consumptions, and all the viruses, which are the root cause of diseases, with the help of this comfort giving jangid-mani given to us by the divine men.

शरणश्च मा जङ्गिडश्च विष्कन्धादभिरक्षताम् ।
अरण्यादन्य आभृतः कृष्या अन्यो रसेभ्यः ।।

(अथर्ववेदः, 2.4.5)

May sharan and jangid-mani protect me from excessive consumption! One of the medicines is culled from forest while the other is cultivated in the fields, and both are extracts of medicines.

कृत्यादूषिरयं मणिरथो अरातिदूषिः ।
अथो सहस्वान् जङ्गिडः प्रण आयूंषि तारिषत् ।।

(अथर्ववेदः, 2.4.6)

The diamond saves us from violence and cures us from hostile diseases. May this powerful jangid-mani increase our life span.

एकोनविंशकाण्डस्यायं सूक्ते चतुस्त्रिंशे ।
पञ्चत्रिंशे तद्वन्मणिरुक्तो जङ्गिडो भूयः ।।667।।

This 'jangid-mani' is mentioned in detail in the thirty-fifth mantra of thirty-fourth sukta in nineteenth khanda of Atharvaveda.

एवं प्रतिसरमणिरयमष्टमकाण्डस्य पञ्चमे सूक्ते ।
वरणो मणिरधिदशमं तृतीयसूक्ते विशिष्योक्तः ।।668।।

In the same way, there is a reference to pratisara-mani in the fifth sukta of the eighth mandala of Atharvaveda and reference to varuna-mani is found in the third sukta of the tenth mandala of the same Veda.

एकोनविंशकाण्डस्याष्टाविंशादिषट्सूक्तैः ।
दर्भो मणिरौदुम्बरमणिविशेषादिहाख्यातौ ।।669।।

Darbha-mani and audhumbara-mani find reference especially in the twenty-eighth to thirty-third sukta, i.e. total six hymns, of the nineteenth mandala.

एतत्काण्डे सूक्ते षट्त्रिंशे त्वस्ति शतवारः ।
अस्तृतमणिरिह गदितः षट्चत्वारिंशके सूक्ते ।।670।।

In the thirty-sixth and forty-sixth sukta of the same mandala, we find descriptions respectively of shatvara-mani and astrita-mani.

इत्थमनेका ओषधिविद्या आर्यैः पुरातनैर्दृष्टाः ।
आथर्वणे तु वेदे प्रदर्शितास्तास्ततो ज्ञेयाः ।।671।।

In this way, the ancient Arya discovered several branches of knowledge of medicines which find mention in the Atharvaveda.

विद्याप्रकारणोपसंहारः ।

Conclusion of the chapter on knowledge.

देवानामिह समये देवैः प्रोत्साहनात् सुयुक्त्वाच्च।
भारतवर्षीयार्यैरेता उद्भाविता विद्याः ।।672।।

The Arya of Bharatavarsha explored these branches of knowledge with the encouragement and cooperation of gods in the devayuga.

एतासां विद्यानां कारव आसन् पृथक् पृथक् कतिचित् ।
तत्प्रतिपत्तिग्रन्थाः कालविलुप्ता न लभ्यन्ते ।।673।।

Different seer-scientists had conceptualized these sciences or branches of knowledge. The original and authentic volumes of these sciences have disappeared long time ago and are not available today.

इतिहासेषु प्राय: प्रसङ्गतश्चर्चिता एता: ।
तेनास्तित्वं ह्यासां पूर्वयुगे भारते विद्म: ।।674।।

Discussions on these branches of knowledge emerge in the respective contexts in history books. On the basis of these discussions, we come to know that these knowledge systems did exist in Bharatavarsha.

1.11.1.7 भारतवर्षे युद्धोपयोगिचतु:षष्टिदिव्यास्त्राणि

1.11.1.7 Sixty-four divine weapons for warfare in Bharatavarsha

ब्रह्मशिरो ब्रह्मास्त्रं पाशुपतं वैष्णवं च वरुणास्त्रम् ।
नाराणास्त्रमैन्द्रं प्राजापत्यास्त्रमाग्नेयम् ।।675।।

वायव्यं कौबेरं पार्जन्य-त्वाष्ट्रकालयाम्यानि ।
दानवमथ च स्कान्दं प्रमथं वैनायकं च कूष्माण्डम् ।।676।।

गणगान्धर्वे राक्षसपैशाचे भौतवैताले ।
शारभताक्ष्यशावरफैरवमातङ्गनागमकरास्त्रम् ।।677।।

सौपर्णं भारुण्डं चौलूकं गालणं चेति ।
पाषाणकालकूटे चाक्रैषीके बलातिबले ।।678।।

औदुम्बरं च राजसहैमनगुह्यानि शौरमुन्माद: ।
स्तम्भनकम्पनजृम्भणजम्भकमूर्च्छानिमीलनोत्पाता: ।।679।।

प्रस्वापनं च मोहनमचेतनं भ्रामकं ज्वरास्त्रं च ।
वैद्युततैमिरतामसभेदादासंश्चतु:षष्टि: ।।680।।

दिव्यास्त्रतालिका

सं.	दैवास्त्राणि	सं.	यौनास्त्राणि	सं.	भौतास्त्राणि	सं.	कर्मास्त्राणि
1.	ब्रह्मशिरोऽस्त्रम्	17.	स्कान्दास्त्राणि	33.	मकरास्त्रम्	49.	उन्मादास्त्रम्
2.	ब्रह्मास्त्रम्	18.	प्रथमास्त्रम्	34.	सपर्णास्त्रम्	50.	स्तम्भनास्त्रम्
3.	पाशुपतास्त्रम्	19.	वैनायकास्त्रम्	35.	भारुण्डास्त्रम्	51.	कम्पनास्त्रम्
4.	वैष्णवास्त्रम्	20.	कूष्माण्डास्त्रम्	36.	उलूकास्त्रम्	52.	जृम्भकास्त्रम्
5.	वारुणास्त्रम्	21.	गणास्त्रम्	37.	गालणास्त्रम्	53.	जम्भकास्त्रम्

6.	नारायणास्त्रम्	22.	गान्धर्वास्त्रम्	38.	पाषाणास्त्रम्	54.	मूर्च्छास्त्रम्
7.	ऐन्द्रास्त्रम्	23.	राक्षसास्त्रम्	39.	कालकूटास्त्रम्	55.	निमीलनास्त्रम्
8.	प्राजापत्यास्त्रम्	24.	पैशाचास्त्रम्	40.	चाक्रास्त्रम्	56.	उत्पातास्त्रम्
9.	आग्नेयास्त्रम्	25.	भौतास्त्रम्	41.	ऐषीकास्त्रम्	57.	प्रस्वापनास्त्रम्
10.	वायव्यास्त्रम्	26.	वेतालास्त्रम्	42.	वलास्त्रम्	58.	ज्वरास्त्रम्
11.	कौरवेयास्त्रम्	27.	शरभास्त्रम्	43.	अतिवलास्त्रम्	59.	भ्रामकास्त्रम्
12.	पार्जन्यास्त्रम्	28.	तार्क्ष्यास्त्रम्	44.	औदुम्बरास्त्रम्	60.	अचेतनास्त्रम्
13.	त्वाष्टास्त्रम्	29.	शावरास्त्रम्	45.	राजसास्त्रम्	61.	मोहनास्त्रम्
14.	कालास्त्रम्	30.	फैरवास्त्रम्	46.	हेमनास्त्रम्	62.	वैद्युतास्त्रम्
15.	याम्यास्त्रम्	31.	मातङ्गास्त्रम्	47.	गुह्यास्त्रम्	63.	तिमिरास्त्रम्
16.	दानवास्त्रम्	32.	नागास्त्रम्	48.	शौरस्त्रम्	64.	तामसास्त्रम्

TABLE OF DIVINE WEAPONS

S. N.	Devastrani	S. N.	Yonastrani	S. N.	Bhautastrani	S. N.	Karmastrani
1.	Brahmoshirostram	17.	Skandastrani	33.	Makarastram	49.	Unmadastram
2.	Brahmastram	18.	Pramatastram	34.	Sapranastram	50.	Sthambanastram
3.	Pashupathasvam	19.	Vainaykastram	35.	Bharundastram	51.	Kampanastram
4.	Vaishnvastram	20.	Krishnandastram	36.	Ulukastram	52.	Jhumbanastram
5.	Varunastram	21.	Ganastram	37.	Galanastram	53.	Jhambakastram
6.	Narayanastram	22.	Gandharvastram	38.	Pashanastram	54.	Murchanastram
7.	Aindrastram	23.	Rakshasatram	39.	Kalakutastram	55.	Nimilnastram
8.	Prajapatyastram	24.	Paishachastram	40.	Chakrastram	56.	Utpathastram
9.	Agneyastram	25.	Bhautastram	41.	Aishikastram	57.	Prasvapnastram
10.	Vayvyastram	26.	Vetalastram	42.	Valastram	58.	Jvarastram
11.	Kauverastram	27.	Sharabastram	43.	Ativalastram	59.	Bramakastram
12.	Parjanyastram	28.	Taksharyastram	44.	Audhumbarastram	60.	Achetanastram
13.	Tvashtastram	29.	Shavarastram	45.	Rajsastram	61.	Mohanastram
14.	Kalastram	30.	Fairavastram	46.	Hemanastram	62.	Vaidyutastram
15.	Yamyastram	31.	Matangastram	47.	Guhyastram	63.	Timirastram
16.	Danavastram	32.	Nagastram	48.	Shaurastram	64.	Tamasastram

दिव्यास्त्राणि पुरात्वे देवयुगे भारते वर्षे ।
मन्त्रैर्यन्त्रैस्तन्त्रैरद्भुतकर्माणि तान्यासन् ।।681।।

In the divine era of Bharatavarsha, there were divine weapons made by mantra, yantra, and tantra.

शरनाराचकृपाणप्रभृतीन्यष्टादशास्त्राणि ।
लौहानि सर्वदेशे दिव्यास्त्रविधास्तु भारतेऽत्रैव ॥682॥

Here in Bharatavarsha, the science of weapons was prevalent all over the country which involved the use of eighteen varieties of iron weapons like arrow, handsaw, and sword.

1.11.1.8 रामायणोक्तानि दिव्यास्त्राणि

1.11.1.8 Fifty divine weapons mentioned in the Ramayana

रामायणे तु विश्वामित्रो रामाय पञ्चाशत् ।
दिव्यास्त्राणि निरूप्य प्रददौ तान्यप्यतो विद्यात् ॥683॥

The Valmiki Ramayana refers to fifty divine weapons which were moulded by Vishvamitra and given to Sri Rama. These weapons should also be included in the list of aforementioned weapons.

चक्राणि पञ्च पाशत्रयमशनी द्वे गदे च द्वे ।
शक्ती द्वे च महास्त्रं षोढा षौढैव तीव्रास्त्रम् ॥684॥

साधारणास्त्रभेदाः सन्ति चतुर्विंशतिस्तत्र ।
मन्त्राहितानि सर्वाण्यमोघवीर्याणि सिध्यन्ति ॥685॥

Five discs, three ropes, two *ashani*-s (a weapon thrown into distance), two maces, two *bhakti*-s, six *maha-astra*, six *teevra-astra* and twenty-four kinds of ordinary weapons, all of which were empowered by the mantras. Enjoined with the mantras these weapons became *amoghaveerya* (assuredly destructive).

अथ चैषामस्त्राणां संहारा रामभद्राय ।
पञ्चाशदेव कथिता विश्वामित्रेण तान् ब्रूमः ॥686॥

Vishvamitra has talked about fifty sub-varieties of divine weapons. We enlist them now.

पञ्चाशद्दिव्यास्त्र तालिका

1.	1. दण्डचक्रम् 2. धर्मचक्रम् 3. कालचक्रम् 4. विष्णुचक्रम् 5. ऐन्द्रचक्रम्	5.	1. कङ्कालमुसलशक्तिः 2. कायालकिङ्कणीशक्तिः
2.	1. धर्मपाशः 2. कालपाशः 3. वारुणपाशः	6.	1. वज्रास्त्रम् 2. शैवास्त्रम् 3. शूलवतास्त्रम् 4. ब्रह्मशिरोस्त्रम् 5. ऐषीकास्त्रम् 6. ब्राह्मस्त्रम्
3.	1. शुष्का अशनिः 2. आर्द्रा अशनिः	7.	1. पिनाकास्त्रम् 2. नारायणास्त्रम् 3. आग्नेयास्त्रम्-शिखरमग्निदयितम् 4. वायव्यास्त्रम् 5. हयग्रीवास्त्रम् 6. क्रौञ्चास्त्रम्
4.	1.मोदकी गदा 2.शिखरी गदा	8.	1. विद्याधरास्त्रम् नन्दमसिरत्नम् 2. गान्धर्वास्त्रम् मोहनम् 3. प्रस्तावनम् 4. प्रशमनम् 5. सौम्यम् 6. वर्षणम् 7. शोषणम् 8. संतापनम् 9. विलापनम् 10. मादनम् 11. कन्दर्पास्त्रम् कन्दर्पदयितम् 12. गन्धर्वास्त्रम् गन्धर्वदयितम् मानवम् 13. पिशाचास्त्रम् पिशाचदयितम् मोहनम् 14. तामसम् 15. सौमनम् 16. संवर्तम् 17. मौसलम् 18. सत्यास्त्रम् 19. मायास्त्रम् 20. सौरास्त्रं, तेरःप्रभं, परतेजोपकर्षणम् 21. सौपास्त्रम् शिशिरम् 22. त्वाष्ट्रास्त्रम् दारुणम् मगास्त्रम्, दारुणम् शीतेषु-मानदम्

FIFTY DIVINE WEAPONS

1	2	3	4	5	6	7	8
dhandachakram	dharmapash	shushka ashni	modhaki gadha	kandalmusalshakti	vajrastram	pinakastram	vidyadharastram nandamasiratnam
dharmachakram	kalapash	adhra ashni	shikhari gadha	kayalakidanishakti	shaivastram	narayanastram	gandharvastram mohanam
kalachakram	varunapash				shulavatastram	agneyastram-shikaramagnidayitam	prasthavanam
vishnuchakram	dharmapash				brahmashirostram	vayavyastram	prashamanam
aindrachakram					aishikastram	haygrivastram	sumyam
dhandachakram					brahmastram	kaunjchastram	varshanam
dharmachakram							shoshanam
							santhapanam
							vilapanam
							madhanam
							kandrapastram kandhapradhyitam
							gandharvastram gandharvadayitham manavam
							pishachastram pishachadayitam mohanam
							tamasam
							saumanam
							samvartam

							mausalam
							satyastram
							mayastram
							saurastram, therprabham, paratejhopakarshanam
							saupastram shishiram
							tvashtrastram darunam, magastram, darunam, sheeteshu-manadam

पञ्चाशद् दिव्यास्त्रसंहाराः।

1.	सत्यवान्	18.	स्वनाभः	35.	पित्र्यः
2.	सत्यकीर्तिः	19.	ज्यौतिषम्	36.	सौमनसः
3.	धृष्टः	20.	शकुनम्	37.	विधूतः
4.	रमसः प्रतीहारः तरः	21.	नैरास्यः	38.	मकरः
5.	अपराङ्मुखम्	22.	विमलः	39.	परवीरः
6.	अवाङ्मुखम्	23.	योगधरः	40.	रतिः
7.	लक्ष्यः	24.	विनिद्रः	41.	धनम्
8.	अलक्ष्यः	25.	दैत्यः	42.	धान्यम्
9.	दृढनाभः	26.	प्रथमतः	43.	कामरूपः
10.	सुनाभः	27.	शुचिबाहुः	44.	काकरूपः
11.	दशाक्षः	28.	महाबाहुः	45.	मोहः
12.	शतवक्त्रः	29.	निष्कलिः	46.	आवरणम्
13.	दशशीर्षः	30.	विरुचिः	47.	जृम्भकः
14.	शतोदरः	31.	सार्चिमाली	48.	सर्पनाथः
15.	पद्मनाभः	32.	धृतिमाली	49.	पन्थानः
16.	महानाभः	33.	वृत्तिमान्	50.	वरुणः
17.	दुन्दुनाभः	34.	रुचिरः		

FIFTY DIVINE OFFENSIVE WEAPONS MENTIONED IN RAMAYANA

1.	Satyavan	18.	Svanaba	35.	Pitraya
2.	Satyakirti	19.	Jyotisham	36.	Somnasa
3.	Dhrusht	20.	Shakunam	37.	Vidyuta
4.	Ramasa Pratihar Taraha	21.	Nairasya	38.	Makara
5.	Apranamukham	22.	Vimala	39.	Paravira
6.	Avanamukham	23.	Yogadyara	40.	Rati
7.	Lakshya	24.	Vinidra	41.	Dhanam
8.	Alakshya	25.	Daitya	42.	Dhyanyam
9.	Dhridnabaha	26.	Pratamata	43.	Kamarupa
10.	Sunabha	27.	Shuchibahu	44.	Kakarupa

11.	Dashaksha	28.	Mahbahu	45.	Moha
12.	Shatvakatraha	29.	Nischkali	46.	Avaranam
13.	Dashshirsha	30.	Viruchi	47.	Jhumbaka
14.	Shatodara	31.	Sachirmaali	48.	Sarpnatha
15.	Padyanabha	32.	Drtimaali	49.	Panthana
16.	Mahanabha	33.	Vrittiman	50.	Varuna
17.	Dhundhnabha	34.	Ruchira		

1.11.1.9 अष्टादश साधारणानि शस्त्राणि

1.11.1.9 Eighteen ordinary weapons

सहचर्मखभेदाः सधनुर्बाणाश्च परिघश्च ।
पट्टिश-तोमर-कुन्ताः खेट-गदा-परशु-चक्र-शूलानि ।।687।।

शक्ति-मुद्गरपाशौ हलमुसलभिन्दिपालमसिपुत्री ।
सशतघ्ना च भुशुण्डीत्येते शस्त्रास्त्रभेदाः स्युः ।।688।।

There are eighteen varities of daggers, arrows without bow, sticks, fish hook, wooden rod, javelin, dagger, mace, axe, discus, cudgel, halter/trap, plough head, catapult, kitchen knife, mortar, and guns.

एषामेकैकस्य च बहवो भेदाः पुरातनैः क्लृप्ताः ।।
प्राधान्यतस्त्वमन्त्राण्येतान्यष्टादशास्त्राणि ।।689।।

Each of them has several sub-categories defined by ancient practitioners of weapons. These eighteen weapons were chiefly used without mantras; mantras were not required for their use.

अष्टादशास्त्रभाषानामतालिका

सं.	संस्कृतम्	पर्यायाः	विशेषः
1.	खड्गः सचर्मा	कृपाणः, ऋषिः, असिः, करवालः	
2.	धनुः सशरम्	चापः, धन्वः	
3.	परिधः कालदण्डः	परिघातिनः	लोहबद्धो हस्तप्रमाणो लगुडः

4.	पट्टिशम्	0000	
5.	तोमर:	सर्वला	
6.	कुन्त:	प्रास:	
7.	खेट:	ईलो करवाली 1	
8.	गदा	0000	
9.	परशु:	परश्वध:, स्वधिति:, कुठार:	
10.	चक्रम्	0000	
11.	शूलम्	0000	
12.	शक्ति:	कास:	
13.	मुद्गर:, कूटमुद्गर:	धन:, द्रुघण:	
14.	पाश:	0000	
15.	हलमुसलम्	0000	
16.	भिन्दिपाल:	सृग:	
17.	छुरिका	शस्त्री, असिपुत्री	
18.	शतघ्नी, भुशुण्डी	0000	

THE LIST OF EIGHTEEN WEAPONS

S. N.	In Sanskrit	Sanskrit Synonym	In English
1.	Khadag sacharma	kripan, rishi, assi, karaval	sword
2.	dhanu-sasharam	chap, dhanv	bow and arrow
3.	paridh, kaldhand	paridhathin	cane
4.	pattisham	...	spear
5.	tomar	sarvala	iron javelin
6.	kunth	pras	javelin
7.	khet	ilo karvali 1	dagger
8.	gadha	...	mace
9.	parashu	parshvadh, svadhithi, kutar	axe
10.	chakram	...	disc
11.	shulam	...	spear
12.	shakti	kasah	lance
13.	mudgar, kutumudgar	dhan, dhrughan	hammer

14.	pash	...	lasso
15.	halamusalam	...	mortar
16.	bhindipal	srig	sling
17.	churika	shastri, asiputri	knife
18.	shathagni, bhushundi	...	gun

1.11.1.10 भारतीयविड्वीर्याख्यानम्

1.11.1.10 A Treatise on the Mercantile Powers of Bharata

भारतीयानां भग्नावशिष्टानामपि शिल्पानामतुलनीयत्वम् ।
वाणिज्यं च पुरासीदत्युत्कृष्टं हि भारतीयानाम् ।
इतरे सर्वे देशा आयान्ति स्मात्र भूयसा क्रेतुम् ॥690॥

Even if in the shape of ruins the sculptures of India are incomparable, the commercial knowledge of ancient India was excellent. As a result, several businessmen would come to purchase goods from Indian markets.

यद्यपि भारतवर्षे शिल्पिकला: शिथिलतां क्रमादगमन् ।
किन्तु न तत्रार्याणामलसत्वं मूढतापि वा हेतु: ॥691॥

Although the Indian mercantile power gradually declined, it was definitely not because of lethargy or ignorance.

राजास्त्यभारतीयो न स धर्माणामिहत्यशिल्पानाम् ।
वृद्धिं रक्षां वैषां कुरुते तस्मादियं दसाऽवनता ॥692॥

आद्याप्यवनतिकाले हीनदशानामपि क्वाचार्याणाम् ।
शिल्पं भारतवर्षे प्रदृश्यतेऽन्यैरतुलनीयम् ॥693॥

Here, at the moment, the ruler is not Indian. The king does not care for the promotion and growth of our religion and handicrafts. This is the reason for the decline of the handicraft industry. Even in this state of decline and inferiority, the handicraft of the Indian Arya appears to be superior and incomparable.

कश्मीरे शालपटश्चोर्णावस्त्रं च दिव्यमप्रतिमम् ।
मलमलवस्त्रं ढाकानगरे सूक्ष्मातिसूक्ष्मतरम् ॥694॥

The shawls and woollen clothes of Kashmir and the transparent velvet of Dhaka city are divine and unique even today.

रूप्यकसहस्रसप्तकमूल्याः शाला विनिर्मिता हस्तैः ।
सौष्ठवमौष्ण्यं मृदुतां हृद्यत्वं यादृशं धत्ते ।।695।।

The hand-woven shawls, which cost seven thousand during the British period, were unparalleled for their beauty, warmth, softness and attractiveness.

ढाकामलमलवस्त्रं सूक्ष्मतमत्वेऽपि यादृशं धत्ते ।
मसृणत्वं च दृढत्वं सौक्ष्म्यं चौष्ण्यं मनोहरताम् ।।696।।

The silk work of Dhaka, not withstanding its transparent quality, was so extraordinarily soft, durable and fine—the qualities which cannot be found anywhere in the world.

न च तत्तुलनां कर्तुं शक्ता अद्यापि यत्नवन्तोऽपि ।
सन्त्युत्तमयन्त्रकलायुक्ता अपि भिन्नदेशीयाः ।।697।।

Even today such shawls and silk-works cannot be matched by foreign machine-made garments.

अंशुकपट्टविशेषा दारुमृदश्मादिरम्यपात्राणि ।
अद्याप्यवनतिसमये भारतवर्षे प्रशंसनीयानि ।।698।।

Today even in the age of decline, highly artistic silk work, wood work, pottery made of clay and stone in India remain exceptional.

अद्याप्यत्र बहूनि श्लाघ्यानि भवन्ति दीनहतकानाम् ।
कारूणामिह शिल्पान्येभिर्भारतशिरोऽत्युच्चम् ।।699।।

The handicraft magic of the poor craftsmen in India is highly appreciated all over the world.

इति भारतपरिचये विद्याप्रसङ्गः सम्पूर्णः ।

The section on knowledge in the Introduction to Bharatavarsha is concluded.

इति मधुसूदनविद्यावाचस्पतिप्रणीतस्य ब्रह्मविज्ञानशास्त्रसम्बन्धिनो
भारतवर्षीयार्योपाख्याने भारतपरिचयः प्रथमः प्रक्रमः सम्पूर्णः ।

Thus the translation of the first chapter namely the 'Introduction to Bharatavarsha' in the Bharatavarshiyaryopakhyan section related to Brahmavijnanashastra of Madhusudan Ojha is concluded.

प्रक्रमः द्वितीयः

आर्यदासीयः

CHAPTER SECOND

THE ARYA-DASA CONFLICT

2.1 भारतीयार्याणां मौलिकभारतीयत्वसिद्धान्तात् वैदेशिकत्वमतखण्डनम्

2.1 REFUTING THAT ARYA WERE FOREIGNERS

ओंकार एष येषामविशेषान्मन्त्र आराध्यः ।
येषां भिन्नमतानामप्यत्रास्त्येकबन्धुत्वम् ।।1।।

The Arya, whose main prayer was 'omkara', lived in great harmony with the people pursuing different faiths.

येषां शास्त्रं वेदश्चातुर्वर्ण्ये विभाजितो धर्मः ।
धेनुर्गङ्गाऽऽराध्या तेषां देशोऽस्ति भारतं वर्षम् ।।2।।

आर्यास्तेऽमी उदिताश्चातुर्वर्ण्ये विभाजिता लोकाः ।
तेषां स्वोऽयं देशो न तु परदेशादिहागता एते ।।3।।

Their scripture was the Vedas, their religion was divided into four varnas or castes and their objects of faith were the cow and River Ganga. Their country was Bharatavarsha.

पूर्वसमुद्रारब्धो देशो यः पश्चिमाब्धिपर्यन्तः ।
पूर्वोऽस्यार्यावर्तः पश्चिम आर्य्यायणं भागः ।।4।।

The stretch of land between the Eastern Sea [China Sea] and the Western Sea [Red Sea] was Bharatavarsha. Its eastern part was known as Aryavarta and the western as Aryayana.

2.2 आर्यवीराणां भारतवर्षीयमूलनिवास्यनार्यजातिपरिभावकाः पञ्चहेतवः

2.2 FIVE THEORIES ABOUT ARYA MIGRATION

एशियामध्यदेशात् आगतानाम् आर्यवीराणां भारतवर्षीयमूलनिवास्यनार्यजातिपरिभावकत्वं पञ्चभिर्हेतुभिः एके मन्यन्ते ।

Five viewpoints presented in favour of the theory of migration of brave Arya coming to Bharatavarsha through Central Asia and defeating the non-Arya communities of India.

प्राहुः केचिद् भारते पूर्वमासन् वन्या जाल्मास्तैरनार्यैर्नियुध्य ।
जित्वा चैतान्भारतेऽस्मिन् न्यवात्सुः पामीराद्रेरागता आर्यवीराः ॥5॥

Some people [historians] say that in ancient times, barbarians and dacoits inhabited the land of Bharatavarsha. The Arya came from Pamira desha or the land of Pamir and started living here after defeating the barbarians.

योऽद्रिर्विलूरतागो मुस्तागो वा तयोश्च पश्चिमतः ।
जम्बूनदीसदेशेऽत्युच्चे न्यूषुर्य आर्याः प्राक् ॥6॥

They lived on the extreme heights of the western slopes of Vilurtag and Mustang mountains situated near the Jambu river.

ते खलु भारतवर्षेऽभ्याक्रम्यैतत् प्रदेशसंभूतान् ।
वासान्निहत्य जयिनो भारतवर्षनिवासिनोऽभूवन् ॥7॥

They invaded Bharatavarsha, vanquished the non-Arya living there and began to live there.

यद्वत् पूर्व्यान् स्काटलेण्डप्रसूतान् हत्वा तत्र न्यूषुरन्ये प्रवीराः ।
एवं मन्ये भारते भारतीयान् वन्यान् जित्वा सभ्यवर्णा इहाऽस्थुः ॥8॥

The way warriors of a certain race decimated the Scottish community and settled over there in the olden times, in the same way the barbarian communities were vanquished by the more civilized people who began to live here.

ये हीदानीं भारते भारतीयाः सभ्या एते सन्ति वैदेशिकास्ते ।
पञ्चैतस्मिन् हेतवः सन्ति वादे तात्पर्यस्य ग्राहकास्तान् वदामः ॥9॥

All the civilized people living in Bharatavarsha at the moment are foreign migrants. There are five evidences to prove this point. We present the thesis of the scholars supporting this theory.

आर्याः सर्वे रोमका यावना वा पूर्वं पूर्वोदक्प्रदेशादुपेताः ।
देशे देशे तत्र तत्र न्यावात्सुः सेत्थं ख्यातिः श्रूयते पूर्वकालात् ।।10।।

Right from ancient times, it is a commonly accepted belief that all the Arya, whether Romans or Greeks, travelled through the eastern watersheds and settled at different places.

आदिस्थां पारसीकोपदेष्ट्राऽवेस्ताग्रन्थे ह्यैर्यनम्बीज उक्तम् ।
मन्ये स स्यादेष पामीरदेशस्तत्रैवार्याः पूर्वमासन् वसन्तः ।।11।।

In the Zendavesta, the scripture of the Parsi community, their original dwelling place has been mentioned as 'Aerianbeez'. This, I believe, referred to the Pamir country where the Arya had been living.

अनुप्रत्नस्यौकसो हुवे तुवि प्रतिनरम् ।
यं ते पूर्वं पिताहुवे ।।

(अथर्ववेदः, 1.30.9)

It is written in the Atharvaveda, 'O Indra, you who goes to your previous land to meet your devotees, I invite you; my father had also invited you earlier.'

अत्र प्रत्नस्यौकसो वर्णनेन प्राप्ता एते भारतीया विदेशात् ।
प्रत्नं ह्येषां धाम पामीरमासीन्मन्ये नूत्नं भारतं वर्षमेतत् ।।12।।

Descriptions of the old settlements brings to light the fact that the people of this country came here from other lands. I believe their old dwelling place was the Pamir region and Bharatavarsha was their [Arya] new habitation.

ओघोत्थाने पूर्वकाले कदाचिद् यस्मान्नावोदग् गिरेः पारमायन् ।
तस्मान्मन्येऽत्रागता उत्तरात् ते वेदग्रन्थे तच्छ्रुतं पारयानम् ।।13।।

Long ago, when the entire earth was submerged under water at the time of the epic flood, the Uttaragiri mountain from where Manu rowed his boat across was the place in the north from where the Arya came here. This migration is described in the Vedas.

मनवे हवै प्रातरवनेग्यमुदकमाजह्रुः ।
तस्य मत्स्यः पाणिं आपेदे ।। स औघ

उत्थिते नावमापेदे। तं स मत्स्य उपन्या पुप्लुवे ।
तस्य शृङ्गे नावः पाशं प्रति मुमोच।
तेनैतमुत्तरं गिरिमतिदुद्राव तदप्येतदुत्तरस्य
गिरेर्मनोरवसर्पणम् । ओघो हताः सर्वाः प्रजा
निरुवाह। अथेह मनुरेवैकः परिशिशिषे। (शतपथब्राह्मणम्, 1.8.1.1-6)
वेदग्रन्थे वर्णितं यन्नियुद्धं तच्चात्रत्यैः प्रागसभ्यैः सहैषाम् ।
सभ्यानां स्यादागतानां विदेशात् जित्वा चैतान् भारते ते न्यवात्सुः ॥14॥

एतन्मतप्रत्याक्षेपः । तदुपोद्बलकहेतूनामप्रामाण्यात्।

Early in the morning, Manu went to fetch water for his *sandhya* [morning and evening chanting of Gayatrimantra] yajna. A fish came into his hands. At the time of the great deluge, when Manu boarded an ark, the same fish came to him. Manu tied his ark to the horn of the fish and the fish pulled the ark across the Uttaragiri mountain. Since that day, Uttaragiri mountain is called Manu's Descent. The deluge submerged the entire population of Manu's state and he was the only survivor ('Manupakhyan' of Shatapatha Brahmana).

The civilized groups, coming from the foreign land, fought with the civilized groups of this land and, after subduing the latter, began to live here. This war is described as a duel in the Vedas.

I outrightly reject this thesis because the logic of this theory is flawed.

इत्थं केचिद् भारते भारतीयानेतान् सभ्यान् हन्त पामीरदेशात् ।
प्राप्तानाहुः किन्तु मन्ये तदेषां मिथ्याक्लृप्तं भ्रान्तमस्त्यप्रमाणम् ॥15॥

It is regretful that some scholars consider civilized communities living in Bharatavarsha to have come from outside. I believe this to be a false hypothesis; it is an unauthentic and confusing concept.

ख्यातिस्तावन्न प्रमाणं स्वतन्त्रा यावत्तस्मिन्नान्यदस्ति प्रमाणम् ।
ये त्वत्रान्ये हेतवः केचिदुक्ता हेत्वाभासास्तेऽखिला न प्रमाणम् ॥16॥

There is a reason to reject such a hypothesis—the thesis treats as evidence a common hearsay which cannot be treated as evidence in the scholarly traditions. A prevalent opinion is always independent of facts. All other evidences, presented in support of this thesis, only appear to be so and are not concrete evidences.

पारस्यानामैर्य्यनम्बीज उक्तो योऽयं देश: सोन्य आर्याणक: स्यात् ।
तत्राप्यासन् प्राक् तुषारप्रपाता येभ्यो लोका भूयसासन् विपन्ना: ।।17।।

Aerianbeez, reported to be the land of the Parsis, should be part of some other country of the same community called Aryanaka. There, a snowfall killed many men and women.

तुषारवर्षैर्बहुलैस्तमकाण्डनिपातिभि: ।
आर्याणाकाभिधे देशे विपन्नं केचिदूचिरे ।।18।।

Some people [scholars] say that this untimely and repeated snowfall destroyed the country, Aryanaka.

प्रत्नं त्वोक: स्वं शुन:शेप एतत् प्रीतिप्राप्त्यै स्मारयत्यागताय ।
इन्द्रायेन्द्र: प्रागजीगर्तयज्ञे हूत: प्रीतोऽनेकधाऽवाप हव्यम् ।।19।।

In ancient times, when Indra was invited to the yajna organized by Ajigarta, he was pleased when Shunashape reminded him of his old dwelling place. And thus pleased, Indra received havya several times.

ओक: प्रत्नं स्वर्गरूपं यदत्र व्याचष्टेऽसौ सायणास्तावतापि ।
इन्द्रस्याजीगर्तयज्ञे गतस्य प्रत्नौकस्तद् भाव्यते न त्वमीषाम् ।।20।।

The dwelling place described here has been termed as a form of heaven by Sayana. Nevertheless, this dwelling place was that of Indra and not of the Arya

शौन:शेपो मन्त्र एष ह्यमीषां सर्वार्याणां प्रत्नमोकोऽविशेषाद् ।
पामीरं तल्लक्षयत्येवमुक्ति: पाश्चात्यानां साहसाद् भ्रान्तिमूलात् ।।21।।

The mantra associated with Shunashape gives a general description of the ancient dwelling of all the Arya. The western scholars are wrong in declaring the Pamir region as the ancient home of the Arya.

पुराणमोक: सख्यं शिवं वां युवोर्नराद्रविणां जाह्नाव्याम् ।
पुन: कृण्वाना: सख्या शिवानि मध्वा मदेन सहनू समाना: ।।
(ऋग्वेद:, 3.58.6)

It is mentioned in the Rigveda, 'O you men, your original dwelling and your ancient friendship is auspicious. Your wealth is treasured near Sindhu river. Therefore, you should once again engage in fruitful friendship and, with this friendly sentiment, enjoy sweet juices and feel the bliss.'

विश्वामित्रो जाह्नवीप्रान्तक्लृप्तां राजस्थाने स्वे कृतां यज्ञशालाम् ।
त्यक्त्वाऽरण्ये स्वाश्रमं कल्पयित्वा यज्ञं धत्ते पूर्वसाम्येन क्लृप्तम् ।।22।।

Sage Vishvamitra moved away from his place of yajna constructed on the banks of Janhvi in Rajasthan and created a new shelter in the forest and continued to perform yajna as he was doing earlier.

त्यक्त्वा पूर्वं स्थानमन्यत् प्रगृह्णन् कश्चित् विद्वान् प्रत्नमोकः स्मरेत् स्वम् ।
सर्वेऽप्यार्यास्तावता प्रत्नमोकस्त्यक्त्वाऽत्रैता इत्यसाधुः प्रवादः ।।23।।

So, if a sage leaves his original dwelling place to move to a new place and there he gives description of his old home, it is wrong to conclude that all sages have left their original dwelling place.

यद्वै नावोदग्गिरेः पारयानान्मन्यन्ते ते पारयानं हिमाद्रेः ।
तच्च भ्रान्तं सा हि नावाभिपत्तिः पामीरादत्युत्तरे पश्चिमेऽभूत् ।।24।।

And it is equally wrong for scholars to believe that sailing across Uttaragiri in an ark was like sailing across the Himalayas. This ark incident took place in the north-west part of Pamir.

आर्मीन्याख्ये म्लेच्छदेशे गिरिर्योऽरारातो भात्यार्कनौस्तस्य पादे ।
दुद्रावाद्रौ तत्र नावा मनुः प्राग् म्लेच्छे देशेऽस्ति प्रसिद्धिस्तथैव।।25।।

In the mleccha desha called Armenia, there is a mountain named Ararat. In its lap is nestled a place called Arkanau. In ancient times, the ark of Manu sailed across the same mountain, which is well-known in those lands.

नायं शैलो नापि देशोऽयमासीत् प्राचामेषां प्राक्तनी वासभूमिः ।
तस्मादेषौधश्रुतिः प्राक्तनानां पूर्वावासद्योतिका नोपपन्ना ।।26।।

But neither this mountain nor this province is the ancient abode of these ancient Arya. Therefore, the old hearsay indicating this place to be the ancient abode of Arya is not justified.

वेदग्रन्थे वर्णितं यत् समीकं तच्चानार्यैर्भारते पूर्वजातैः ।
वीरार्याणां भारतेऽभ्यागतानामासीत् पूर्वं पाञ्चनद्यप्रदेशे ।।27।।

इत्थं प्राहुः पण्डिता केऽपि तेषामुक्तं मन्ये भ्रान्तमेतन्नितान्तम् ।
नार्या वीरा भारतस्थाननार्यान् निर्वास्य प्राग् भारतेऽस्मिन् न्यवात्सुः ।।28।।

Some scholars say that the war mentioned in the Vedas, known as Sameek, which was fought with the Bharata-born Arya, took place in the panchanadha [Punjab] province. This was a war fought by the heroic Arya already settled in Bharatavarsha. But this hypothesis is misleading because the Arya fighters did not settle in Bharata by displacing the non-Arya living in this place.

सर्वाण्येवैतानि युद्धानि वेदाख्यातान्यासन् यैर्यथा यत्र येषाम् ।
स्वर्गख्यातावस्ति तेषां विशेषादुक्तिः किञ्चित् त्वत्र चोदाहरामः ।।29।।

All the wars described in the Vedas, the names of warring groups, the nature of war, the arena of war and the stakeholders—everything is given special treatment in the book *Svarga Khyati*[1]. Here only a few of them have been quoted as examples.

[1]Another work by Pandit Madhusudan Ojha

2.3 भारतीयानां विदेशादागतत्वे देवासुरसंग्रामस्य हेतुत्वप्रत्याख्यानम्

2.3 WRONG TO CITE DEVA-ASURA CONFLICT AS EVIDENCE

भारतीयानां विदेशात् आगतत्वे हेतुत्वेन परोपन्यस्तस्य वेदोक्तसंग्रामस्य हेत्वाभासत्वम् ।

The citation of the *devasurasangram* (war between devas and asuras) described in the Vedas as the evidence of the migration of Bharatiyas from a foreign land is not convincing; it merely has the appearance of a reason.

तत्रादौपुरायुगीयानां नराणां संक्षेपतः त्रैविध्यम् ।

Three-fold short narration of the ancient communities.

अखिला नराः पुरात्वे त्रेधा भिन्नाः प्रधानतो ह्यभवन् ।
देवा अथ च मनुष्या देवविरोधात् त्वदेवाश्च ।।30।।

The human beings in the beginning were classified under three divisions—devas, manushya and *adaiva*-s (demons) who opposed the devas.

अत्युन्नतविज्ञानाः प्रभाववन्तोऽभवन् देवाः ।
विज्ञानदुर्बला अपि बहुलप्रज्ञा महाबला असुराः ।।31।।

The devas were endowed with the knowledge of highly developed vijnana and were very influential; whereas the asuras were highly intelligent, extremely powerful, but very ignorant of vijnana.

साधारणी तु जनता मनुष्यनाम्ना प्रतीताऽऽसीत् ।
तत्रादेवा आसन् दानवा दैत्याश्च दस्यवः पणयः ।।32।।

Ordinary humans were identified as manushya. The asuras were divided into four categories: *danava* (ruthless enemies of devas), *daitya* (sons of asura Diti), *dasyu* (dacoits) and *pani* (misers).

अफरीकाद्या देशा दैत्यानां दानवानां च ।
फीनीशिया पणीनां दस्यूनां हेमकूटाद्याः ।।33।।

Prominent among the places where the asuras lived was Africa; the daityas lived around the same place; Phoenicia belonged to the panis, and the dasyus lived in Hemkut and other countries.

अथ देवानां यावान् देशः सा द्यौः स हि स्वर्गः ।
यस्त्विह मनुष्यदेशः सा पृथ्वीभारतं वर्षम् ।।34।।

यद्यप्यासन् स्वर्गे स्वर्णरसंज्ञा अदेवदेवा अन्ये ।
किन्तु न तेषां देशो भारतवर्षं मनोः प्रजा नैताः ॥35॥

The place where the devas lived was called the Dyau which was the heaven. The place which belonged to the humans was Prithviloka and Bharatavarsha was located there. [This matter has been clarified in the trailokya-prasanga.] A select group of humans lived in the heaven and were called adaiva-daivas. But they did not belong to Bharatavarsha and were not the progenies of Manu.

2.4 वेदोक्तसंग्रामाणाम् आरम्भकनिमित्तभेदात् पाञ्चविध्यम्

2.4 FIVE CATEGORIES OF WAR DIFFERENTIATED BY THEIR CAUSE MENTIONED IN THE VEDAS

वेदग्रन्थे कथिताः समराः सर्वेऽपि पञ्चभेदाः स्युः ।
देवानां तैः पणिभिर्दानवदैत्यैश्च दस्युभिश्चार्यैः ।।36।।

All the wars narrated in the Vedas have been classified into five categories. These wars were fought by the devas with panis, daityas, danavas, dasyus and the Arya.

सूर्यश्चन्द्रः पृथिवी गावश्चेति हि चतुष्टयं तेषाम् ।
देवानमसुरैः सह निमित्तमन्योन्यसंमर्द्दे ।।37।।

These wars were terrible and was fought for the possession of sun, moon, earth, and cows.

देवाः सूर्ये दासैः, पणिभिर्गोष्वद्रिसोमके: दैत्यैः ।
क्षित्यर्थे दानवकैरार्यैर्युयुधुः प्रकीर्णविषयेषु ।।38।।

With the dasyus, the devas fought for the possession of the sun, with the panis for the cows, with the daityas for the possession of the Soma mountain, with the danavas for land and with the Arya for different causes.

आर्याणां सममार्यैसंघर्षो नातिबहुलोऽभूत् ।
पण्यादिभिस्त्वनार्यैश्चिरहानिकरा हि संगरा घोराः ।।39।।

The war between the Arya and non-Arya was not serious but the wars which the Arya fought with the panis and non-Arya were terrible and caused long-lasting damages.

तेष्वपि विशेषतो द्वे युद्धे आस्तां महारम्भे ।
भूम्यर्थे संग्रामाः सूर्यार्थे दस्युयुद्धानि ।।40।।

Of these serious wars, two were the most formidable. These great wars were fought with the dasyus for the possession of land and for the dominance over the sun.

इत्थं पञ्चविधा ये संग्रामा यत्र तत्रासन् ।
सर्वेषु तेषु देवा एकत आसन्नथान्यतोऽदेवाः ।।41।।

Thus, in all, five kinds of wars took place from time to time and always the warring parties were—daivas versus adaivas.

2.4.1 देवानाम् आर्यैः संग्रामः

2.4.1 Wars between devas and Arya

आर्याणां क्वचिदार्यैः संग्रामाः केचिदासन् प्राक् ।
सोमहृता गुरुपत्नी यथेन्द्रवरुणाभिमर्दहेतुरभूत् ।।42।।

In earlier times, there were conflicts between two groups of Arya; one reason was the abduction of Brihaspati's wife by Chandrama and another a result of the mutual conflict between Indra and Varuna.

गुर्वङ्गिरो द्वेषवशाद् भृगुस्तदा सोमस्य पक्षं जगृहे वृतोऽसुरैः ।
भृगोः पितासौ वरुणो भृगुं गतो याज्यो गुरोरिन्द्र इमं गुरुं गतः ।।43।।

Out of jealousy towards his guru [Brihaspati], Bhrigu sided with the asuras in favour of Chandrama. Bhrigu's father Varuna supported Bhrigu while Brihaspati's patron, Indra sided with his guru Brihaspati.

देवेश इन्द्रो वरुणोऽसुरेशस्ततश्च देवासुरयोः प्रमर्दः ।
गन्धर्वराज्याश्रितमन्त्रिसभ्याः समेत्य तन्निर्णयमत्र चक्रुः ।।44।।

Thus, a formidable war took place between Indra and Varuna. All those who could chant mantras in Gandhara came together and took some decisions regarding the war.

तेऽवदन् प्रथमा ब्रह्मकिल्विषेऽकूपारः सलिलो मातरिश्वा ।
वीळूहरास्तप उग्रो मयोभूरापो देवीः प्रथमजा ऋते ।।
(ऋग्वेदः, 10.109.1)

It has been said in the Rigveda: 'These prominent gods speak about the sins of Brihaspati. Standing far off, the Surya and Varuna devas are endowed with the energy of wind.' The fierce sun, soothing Soma [moon], and *apa-tatva* have first originated from Satya.

सोमो राजा प्रथमो ब्रह्मजायां पुनः प्रायच्छदहृणीयमानः ।
अन्वर्तिता वरुणो मित्र आसीदग्निर्होता हस्तगृह्या निनाय ।।
(ऋग्वेदः, 10.109.2)

King Soma granted Brihaspati a devout wife; Varuna and Mitra supported the decision. Then, Agni held her hand and took her away.

सोमान्तःपुरतोऽग्निर्मनुष्यपो ब्रह्मजायां ताम् ।
तारां करे गृहीत्वा गुरवे प्रत्यर्पयामास ।।45।।

The protector of humans, Agni held the hand of Tara, wife of his guru, and led her from King Soma's dwellings and handed her to the guru.

हस्तेनैव ग्राह्य आधिरस्या ब्रह्मजायेयमिति चेदवोचत ।
न दूताय प्रह्ये तस्थ एषा तथा राष्ट्रं गुपितं क्षत्रियस्य ।।46।।

It is written in 'taraharan-akhyan', which forms the fifth mandala of Atharvaveda, that: 'This is the command that this hand should be held only with the proper yajna procedure of *panigrahana* (wedding). If this is the wife of a brahmin, she is not allowed to be escorted by a messenger. By following this procedure alone can a king keep his kingdom secure.'

देवा एतस्यामवदन्त पूर्वे सप्त ऋषयस्यपसे ये निषेदुः ।
भीमा जाया ब्राह्मणस्योपनीता दुर्धा दधाति परमे व्योमन् ।।47।।

In the former age, the devas have also said the same, and the ones who sit on meditation, those saptrishis, have also said the same. A brahmin's wife if abducted becomes dangerous and continues to torment even in the heaven.

ब्रह्मचारी चरति वेविषद् विषः स देवानां भवत्येकमङ्गम् ।
तेन जायामन्वविन्दद् बृहस्पतिः सोमेन नीतां जुह्वं न देवाः ।।48।।

The *brahamchari*-s (celebates) wander around the world, serving the mankind. With the powers of the same brahmacharya, Brihaspati succeeded in getting a wife, in the same way the devas receive offerings brought to them by Soma.

पुनर्वै देवा अददुः पुनर्मनुष्या उत ।
राजानः सत्यं कृण्वाना ब्रह्मजायां पुनर्ददुः ।।49।।

Following this principle, the devas blessed the brahmin again with a woman, the men did the same and the virtuous king also did the same.

पुनर्दाय ब्रह्मजात्यां कृत्वा देवैर्निकिल्विषम् ।
ऊर्जं पृथिव्या भक्त्वा योरुगायमुपासते ।।50।।

This brahim woman is pure and is the energy of Prithvi; she pays obeisance to the devas.

आथर्वणे च पञ्चमकाण्डे सूक्ते तु सप्तदशे ।
ताराहरणाख्याने मन्त्रा एकादशान्ततोऽधीता: ।।51।।

In the seventeenth sukta of the fifth mandala of Atharvaveda, eleven mantras have been dedicated to taraharan-akhyan.

तत्राकूपाराद्यैस्तदा व्यवस्थापकै: सभ्यै: ।
ब्रह्मस्त्रीसंबन्धे ध्रुवा व्यवस्थापिता नीति: ।।52।।

Then prominent devas, important people, and administrators crafted a definite policy about brahmin women.

ब्राह्मणजायापहता राष्ट्रे जनयतितरां बहून् दोषान् ।
ब्राह्मणजाया तस्मादत ऊर्ध्वं नापहरणीया ।।53।।

As per their law, if the wife of a brahmin is abducted, the aberration causes several kinds of miseries in a nation [is prone to calamities]. Therefore, hereafter, wife of a brahmin should not be abducted.

यामाहुस्तारकैषा विकेशीति दुच्छुनां ग्राममवपद्यमानाम् ।
सा ब्रह्मजाया विदुनोति राष्ट्रं यत्र प्रापादिशश उल्कुषीमान् ।।54।।

That which brings calamities to the village is called the Taraka, free from all bonds. An aggrieved wife of a brahmin jolts a nation in the same way in which a nation is shaken by the shooting star [falling stars are considered to be inauspicious sign for a nation].

ये गर्भा अवपद्यन्ते जगद् यच्चापलुप्यते ।
वीरा ये तृह्यन्ते मिथो ब्रह्मजाया हिनस्ति तान् ।।55।।

All miscarriages, death of moving creatures, and infights among warriors are caused by the humiliation of a brahmin's wife.

उत यत् पतयो दश स्त्रिया: पूर्वे अब्राह्मणा: ।
ब्रह्मा चेद्धस्तमग्रहीत् स एव पतिरेकधा ।।56।।

The non-brahmin women [of other varnas] can have ten [several] husbands. But a brahmin himself holds the hand of his wife, he becomes her husband once and for all.

ब्राह्मण एव पतिर्न राजन्यो न वैश्यः ।
तत् सूर्यः प्रब्रुवन्नोति पञ्चभ्यो मानवेभ्यः ।।57।।

Moving on its axis, the sun keeps saying, 'Brahmin alone is husband once, not vaishya and kshatriya' [such is the eternal law for five categories of men].

नास्य जाया शतवाही कल्याणी तल्पमाशये ।
यस्मिन् राष्ट्रे निरुध्यते ब्रह्मजाया चित्या ।।58।।

In a country where the wife of a brahmin is restricted by ignorance, even a virtuous woman capable of producing hundred issues should not sleep on the bed.

न विकर्णः पृथुशिरास्तस्मिन् वेश्मनि जायते ।
नास्य क्षता निष्कग्रीवः सूनानामेत्यग्रतः ।।59।।

In a country where the wife of a brahmin is restricted by ignorance, sons with beautiful ears and broad forehead are not born. In that country, boys do not go decorated with gold ornaments to court girls.

नास्य श्वेतः कृष्णकणा धुरियुक्तो महीयते ।
नास्य क्षेत्रे पुष्करिणी नाण्डीकं जायते विसम् ।।60।।

In that country, horses with white ears and black ears are not yoked. In such a country, lotus flowers do not blossom and stalks do not grow in the lotus flowers.

नास्मै पृश्निं विदुहन्ति येऽस्या दोहमुपासते ।
यस्मिन् राष्ट्रे निरुध्यते ब्रह्मजाया चित्या ।।61।।

In such a country those who want to milk cows are not obliged by the cows [do not milch].

नास्य धेनुः कल्याणी नानड्वान् सहते धुरम् ।
विजानिर्यत्र ब्राह्मणो रात्रिं वसति पापया ।।62।।

In a country where a brahmin, bereft of a woman, is full of sinful thoughts, in that country neither the auspicious cow exist nor can the ox bear the load of the harness.

2.4.2 गवार्थे देवानां पणिभिः संग्रामः

2.4.2 Conflict between devas and panis for cow

गावो बृहस्पतेः प्राग् बलेन पश्चादिमाश्च देवानाम् ।
पणिभिर्मुषितास्ताः पुनरादातुं घोरविग्रहः समभूत् ।।63।।

The panis first abducted the cows of Brihaspati and then those of the gods. This caused a terrible war.

यदा पर्णीं रराघसो निवाधस्व महाँ असि ।
नहि त्वा कश्चन प्रति ।।

(ऋग्वेदः, 8.53.2)

The Rigveda says: O Indra, you are great. Crush under your feet the unfaithful unwilling to give money for performing yajna. You have no rivals at all.

अयं ते मानुषे जने सोमः पुरुषु सूयते ।
तस्ये हि प्रद्रवा पिव ।।

(ऋग्वेदः, 8.53.10)

O Indra, this Soma is squeezed for your sake in the presence of humans and noble citizens. Come quickly and drink of it.

अयं ते शर्य्यणावति सुषो मातामधिप्रियः ।
आर्जीकीये मदिन्त मः ।।

(ऋग्वेदः, 8.53.11)

This Soma grows along the river Sushoma in the province of Sharanyavat. Stored in a pot, this stimulating drink is dear to you.

इत्थं पणिनिग्रहणे विपाड् विनिर्गमगिरौ कृतं सवनम् ।
पणिसरमासंवादो दशमेऽष्टशते प्रदर्शितः सूक्ते ।।

(ऋग्वेदः, 10.108.11)

In this way, by containing the panis, the Soma creeper was crushed at the Vinigram mountain and then consumed. In the hundred and a eighth sukta of the tenth mandala of Rigveda, the *sarmapani samvad* (dialogue between sarama and panis) is discussed.

2.4.3 भूम्यर्थे देवानां दैत्यदानवैः संग्रामः

2.4.3 Conflict between devas and daityas for land

तत्र प्राक् प्रक्रान्तयज्ञोपयुक्तभूमेर्देवदायत्वम् ।

In ancient times, the devas controlled a large piece of land suitable for yajna.

देवा असुराः सर्वे प्राक् सयुजः सह वसन्त एवासन् ।
देवाः शान्ता विबुधा असुरास्त्वासन् महोद्धता बलिनः ।।64।।

Earlier the devas and asuras used to live together in harmony. The devas were calm but intelligent and the asuras were arrogant and violent.

सर्वां पृथ्वीं प्रबला आक्राम्यन्तासुरा यर्हि ।
देवास्तत्र विरोधं चक्रुस्तद्भागलाभाय ।।65।।

When the powerful asuras threatened to occupy the land meant for yajna, and posed a threat to the entire earth, then the devas protested, claiming their share.

असुरा ऊचुर्यावद् भूमिर्यज्ञाय विष्णुविधृतास्ति ।
देवेभ्यो दास्यामो वेदिमितां तावदेव भूमिमिमाम् ।।66।।

The asuras said they would give to them only that much of space which Vishnu had accorded for yajna, and not the entire area.

नाकविभागे कश्चिद् यज्ञविधानाय विष्णुना विधृतः ।
खर्वः प्रदेश आसीत्तावत् प्रतिजज्ञिरेऽसुरास्तेभ्यः ।।67।।

In the heaven, Vishnu had earmarked a smaller area for yajna. The asuras promised to give the same measure of land to the devas.

देवास्तदौषधीनां मूल्यान्युच्छिद्य पूर्वपश्चिमतः ।
महतीं वेदीं कृत्वाऽऽहवनीयं पूर्वतो न्युदधुः ।।68।।

Then the devas uprooted the medicinal plants and cleared the eastern and western part of the province and created a huge altar along with a sacrificial pit.

यज्ञोपकरणभागैराच्छन्द्यैतां महावेदीम् ।
देवयजनमयभूमिं लब्ध्वा लोकैस्त्रिभिर्व्यभजन् ।।69।।

Covering this grand altar with tools and materials used in the yajna, the devas divided the land earmarked for the yajna into three lokas.

एतद्वाजसनेयब्राह्मणके श्रूयते चरितम् ।
काण्डस्य प्रथमस्य प्रपाठके तु द्वितीये हि ।।70।।

This characterization is heard in the second *prapathaka* (lecture) of the first khanda of Vajsneya Brahmana.

2.5 देवत्रैलोक्यादसुराणां बहिष्कारः

2.5 EXPULSION OF ASURAS FROM DAIVA TRAILOKYA

अररुरदेवो मानुषभूमौ न्युषितो निराकृतः सततः ।
ऐच्छद्दिवमुपगन्तुं किन्त्वग्निस्तं न्यषेधयत् तस्मात् ॥71॥

In the land of humans lived an adaiva named Ararur. Expelled from there, he expressed his desire to go to the Dyauloka but this was protested by Agni.

तदपाररुमिति मन्त्रव्याख्याने शतपथे कथितम् ।
काण्डस्य प्रथमस्य प्रपाठके तु द्वितीये च ॥72॥

This narration is made in Aparumantra Vyakhyan in the second prapathak of the first khanda of Shatapatha Brahmana.

2.6 देवयजनभूमेः त्रैलोक्यविभक्ताया ऐश्या संज्ञा

2.6 DIVINE YAJNA LAND DESIGNATED IN TRAILOKYA IS ASIA

भारतवर्षं पृथिवी हैमवतं वर्षमन्तरिक्षं स्यात् ।
उत्तरमब्धिं यावत् कुरुवर्षान्तं त्रिविष्टपं तु द्यौः ॥73॥

This Bharatavarsha is the earth, Haimatvarsha is the sky, and the tract stretching from the northern seas to Kuruvarsha is *trivishtapa* (triple summit), and this itself is dyau.

ब्रह्मण एकं विष्टपमपरं विष्णोस्तृतीयमिन्द्रस्य ।
एभिस्त्रिभिरधिपतिभिः स्वर्गो लोकस्त्रिविष्टपं भवति ॥74॥

The first is the *vishtapa* (summit) of Brahma, the second that of Vishnu and the third that of Indra. Owing to the ownership of these three vishtapas by three principal gods, the heaven is also known as trivishtapa.

अपि मैत्रिसंहितायां विष्णुमुखानामयं स्वर्गः ।
असुरान् प्रणुद्य लब्धः प्रथमचतुर्थे निरुक्तोऽस्ति ॥75॥

In the fourth chapter of the first khanda of Maitrani Samhita, it is written: This heaven has been gained by the *Vishnumukhadevas* [deities in Vishnu's lineage] by expelling the asuras from here.

देवेभ्यस्त्रैलोक्यं यावद् व्यभजत् स्वयंभूः सः ।
तदभूत् प्रसिद्धमासुरभाषायामैशिया नाम ॥76॥

The part of trailokya allotted to the devas by Svayambhu came to be called Asia by the asuras.

ईशो मनुः स्वयंभूस्त्रैलोक्येऽस्मिन् स्वयं न्यवसत् ।
तस्मादियं त्रिलोकी प्रथिताभूदैशिया नाम्ना ॥77॥

In this divya trailokya lived Svayambhudish Manu and hence this area came to known as Asia.

2.7 दहरैशिया स्वायम्भुवी

2.7 SVAYAMBHU NAMED ASIA MINOR

त्रैलोक्यमैशियाख्यं देवेभ्यो वसतयेऽभवन्नियतम् ।
तस्यान्तरतः क्षुद्रैशियाख्यदेशः स्वयंभुवोस्य मनोः ।।78।।

This trailokya known as Asia was earmarked for the dwelling of the devas. The area beyond it, known as Kshudra Asia [Asia Minor], was the dwelling place of Svayambhu Manu.

सोऽयं प्रथमो देशस्तत्र प्रथमे नरा अभवन् ।
अत्र जलप्लावननौ स्तब्धाऽद्रौ चाक्षुषेऽन्तरे हि मनोः ।।79।।

At this place, on a mountain, the ark of Chakshush Manu had come to rest after the great deluge.

तारसशैलात् प्राच्यां योऽयं शैलोस्त्यरारातः ।
मत्स्यस्तत्र हि चाक्षुषमनुनौकां शृङ्गतो दध्रे ।।80।।

The place where the fish held the ark of Chakshush Manu on its horns was the Ararat mountain, located east of the Taras mountain.

निषधकुलाद्रेः शाखाशैलः पश्चादरारातः ।
तत्पश्चादिह तारसशैलोऽस्ति च रोमके देशे ।।81।।

This Ararat mountain was the western ridge of the Nishadh mountain and on its western side lay the country called Rome where the Taras mountain was located.

सप्तत्रिंशेऽक्षांशेऽथोज्जयनात् तारसः स पश्चिमतः ।
एकत्रिंशादंशात् षट्चत्वारिंशदंशान्तः ।।82।।

This Taras mountain falls at 37° latitude towards the west of Ujjaini and the mountain is situated at 31°-46° longitude.

पश्चिमसमुद्रकूलप्रान्ते स हि तारसः शैलः ।
निषधाकुलाद्रेः पश्चिमसीमा सेयं त्रिलोक्याश्च ।।83।।

This Taras mountain is situated at the western sea shore which is also the western boundary of the Nishadh mountain. And this too is the western boundary of the [mythical] trailokya state.

आसीत् तारकनामा पुराऽसुरस्त्रिपुरनिर्माता ।
तारकनिवासहेतोस्तारसशैलोयमाख्यात: ।।84।।

In the mythical times lived Tarakasura, the creator of Tripur. Since it was the dwelling of Tarakasura, this mountain came to be known as Taras.

वज्राङ्गापरनामा तारो नामाऽसुर: पूर्वम् ।
आसीत् तस्य च तारकनाम्ना पुत्रोऽभवत् प्रबल: ।।85।।

Once upon a time, there lived an asura called Tar, who was also known as Vajrang. He had an extremely powerful son named Taraka.

ब्रह्मकृपावशत: स हि शार्विकतीर्थे महीसमुद्रतटे ।
स्वमुपनिवेशं चक्रे तारस्याख्ये महीधरप्रवरे ।।86।।

With the blessings of Brahma, he set up his colony on a mountain known as Taras in the pilgrim centre of Sharvik along the coast of Mahisamundra [Mediterranean Sea].

तारस्तस्य पितासीत् तस्मात् स्वावासपर्वतस्यास्य ।
तारस्येत्यभिधानं चक्रेऽसौ तारको मन्ये ।।87।।

Tar was the father of Taraka, and hence, according to me, the mountain was named Tarasya.

तारस्य पर्वतोऽयं यस्मिन् प्रान्तेऽस्ति तं पुरा प्राहु: ।
शार्विकतीर्थनाम्ना स्कान्दकुमारे स्मृतं खराध्याये ।।88।।

In the olden days, the province where this Tarasya mountain stood was called Sharvik—such is the description found in the twenty-second chapter of Skanda Purana.

तं च प्रान्तं व्यदधान्मेरुसमं मेरुसमसूत्रम् ।
दैवं स्वर्गमिवासुरमेतं स्वर्ग स नामतश्चक्रे ।।89।।

This province which is similar to Meru, was created on the axis line of Meru and was given a name '*asur svarga*' [heaven of the asuras] as a parody of '*deva svarga*' [heaven of the gods].

पृथ्व्यन्तरिक्षकं द्यौरित्थं देवस्त्रिलोकमातेनु: ।
तत् प्रतिकृत्या त्वसुरास्त्रिपुरं व्यदधुर्महीसमुद्रतटे ।।90।।

In the same way as the gods conceived the idea of trailokya consisting of the earth, sky, and heaven, the asuras conceived the plan of Tripur on the coast of Mahisagara.

त्रिंशे तूरगिरौ भुवि लौही, त्रिपुरी तु राजती वियति ।
पञ्चत्रिंशे सप्तत्रिंशे दिवि तारसे गिरौ हैमी ।।91।।

On the earth, at 30° latitude existed the *lauh nagari* (the city of iron) at the Turgiri mountain. In the antariksha, at 35° latitude, was the *rajati nagari* (the city of silver) and in the Dyauloka, at 37° latitude, on top of the Taras mountain was the *svarna nigari* (the city of gold) which was also the Tripur of the asuras.

देवस्वर्गं त्वैश्याशब्देनोचुः पुराऽसुरा यद्वत् ।
ऐश्याशब्देनैव प्रोचुः स्वर्गं तमासुरं तद्वत् ।।92।।

As the asuras had named the heaven of the deities as Asia, the asura-svarga was also called Asia.

2.8 आसुरदेशाः त्रैलोक्यविभक्ताः

2.8 DIVISION OF ASURA COUNTRY INTO THREE LOKAS

दायविभागे ब्रह्मा देवेभ्यस्त्रीन् ददौ यथा लोकान् ।
तद्वत् त्रीनसुरेभ्योऽप्यन्यान् देशान् ददौ बृहतः ॥93॥

As Brahma granted three lokas to devas, he also granted three other large countries to asuras.

विपुलास्त्रयः प्रदेशा असुरेभ्यो येऽर्पितास्ते तु ।
अमरौकोऽप्यपरौको यवरूपाश्चोदिता असुरैः ॥94॥

The three provinces granted to the asuras were given the names of Amrauk [America], Aparauk [Africa], and Yawarup [Europe] by the asuras.

2.9 देवत्रिलोक्याम् असुराक्रमणम्

2.9 INVASION OF DIVYA TRAILOKYA BY ASURAS

असुरास्तत्र बलिष्ठाः स्वान् लोकान् सम्यगासाद्य ।
दैव्यामपि त्रिलोक्यामाचक्रमिरे हठादनीतिस्था ।।95।।

These powerful asuras after controlling their domains, invaded the divya trailokya, arbitrarily and forcefully.

स्वायंभुवं तु देशं प्रकल्प्य तीर्थं मनुप्रणाममिषात् ।
असुरास्ते मनुसविधे यातायातं प्रचक्रिरे प्रायः ।।96।।

On the excuse of paying tribute to Manu, the asuras succeeded in getting Svayambhu province declared as a shrine, and then began to have their parleys at Manu's place.

क्रमशो विरोधमाप्ता अफरीकातोऽप्युपागता असुराः ।
स्वायंभुवमनुदेशानैश्यामायिनरसंज्ञकानजयन् ।।97।।

Gradually, in spite of resistance, the asuras coming from Africa captured the country of Svayambhu Manu, then known as the Asia Minor.

तस्मिन् देशे योऽभूद्देवासुरविग्रहस्तत्र ।
असुरा व्यजयन्तामी तेन ततः प्रान्त आसुरः सोऽभूत् ।।98।।

The battle that took place in the country of Svayambhu Manu led to the victory of asuras. As a result, the province became an asura state.

पूर्वं काले केचिदासन्नदेवा देवेभ्यो यैस्ते जिताः सर्वदेशाः ।
तेषां वंशे रोमकाद्या अभूवंस्तेऽर्वाक्काले‌ऽन्यान्यरूपैर्विभेजुः ।।99।।

In ancient times, adaivas (asuras) conquered the entire province from the devas. In their clan were born men [rulers] like Romak and others, who in the succeeding period, were known by different names.

असुरो रोमक आसीत् तन्नाम्ना रोमकोऽभवद्देशः ।
तद्वंश्यैरिह पश्चात् प्रान्तविभागोऽसुरैः क्लृप्तः ।।100।।

Romak was an asura whose name was given to a country called Romak. Later, the region was divided by the descendants of Romak.

आर्मीनिया च कुर्दिस्थानं वा शामदेशश्च ।
अर्वः फीलिस्थानं मेशोपोटेमिया चेति ।।101।

The region was divided into following countries: Armenia, Kurdistan, Shamdesh (Syria), Arab, Philisthan [Palestine] and Mesopotamia.

आर्मीनियाप्रदेशे योऽयं शैलोऽस्त्यरारातः ।
जूदीपर्वत उक्तो म्लेच्छैः पूर्वं स युद्धहेतुत्वात् ।।102।।

The Ararat mountain, which lies in the Armenia province, was renamed by the mlecchas as the Judi [Judaen] mountain because of the war.

जूदीशैलप्रभृतिर्देशो भूमध्यसागरान्तो यः ।
देवासुरसंग्रामास्तत्रैवासन् सुविस्तृते प्रान्ते ।।103।।

The Judi mountain and other provinces, stretching up to the shores of the Mediterranean Sea, became a battleground for the devas and asuras.

देवासुरसंग्रामः कुर्दिस्थाने बभूवुरधिकाः प्राक् ।
कतिधा देवाः कतिधा त्वसुरा देशानिमान् जिग्युः ।।104।।

The maximum number of wars between the devas and asuras took place in the Kurdistan province in which both the groups had their share of victory and defeat.

असुराणां बलमधिकं मेशोपोटेमियादेशे ।
तस्मादसीरियेति प्रख्यातोऽभूदयं देशः ।।105।।

The strength of the asura army was greater in Mesopotamia. Hence, this country came to be known as Assyria.

ये कालकञ्जकालकदौर्हृदमौर्याश्च कालकेयास्ते ।
कालदियाख्ये देशे (केलडिया) न्यूषुर्यमिराक इत्याहुः ।।106।।

Those who are known as Kalkanj, Kalak, Dorhrids or Mauryas were in fact from the stock of Kalakeya race. They lived in Kaladiya [Caledia], a country which today is known as Iraq.

असुरागमनद्वारं यत आसीच्छामदेशोऽयम् ।
तेनारुध्यत स सुरैस्तस्मादुक्तः स सीरियानाम्ना ।।107।।

The country which became the route for the asuras was known as Samadesha and the country where the asuras were stopped by the devas came to be known as Syria.

2.10 इन्द्रविष्णुभ्यां वराहासुरप्रतीकारः

2.10 RETALIATION OF INDRA AND VISHNU AGAINST VARAHA

सर्वत्र देवानसुराः पुरस्तान्यपीडयन् तत्प्रतिकारहेतोः ।
देवा अपीमानसुरान्निजघ्नुः स एष देवासुरसंप्रहारः ।।108।।

In the ancient days, the asuras troubled the devas all the time and everywhere. Thus, in retaliation, the devas too killed the asuras and this came to be known as the great battle between the devas and asuras.

स्वर्गे सुराणामधिपः स इन्द्रः सर्वाः प्रजाः प्रत्यहभोजनेन ।
तद्रक्षणेनापि सभाजयंस्ता न्ययोजयत् कर्मसु नित्यमासाम् ।।109।।

In svarga, Indra, the king of devas, bestowed food to all his *praja* (subjects) and took care of them and engaged them in works of daily life.

संवत्सरान्त्येऽह्नि सबालवृद्धाः प्रजा अगण्यन्त तदर्थमन्नम् ।
संवत्सरोपक्रमदेयमासीत् तद्वाममारक्षति वामदेवः ।।110।।

On the last day of *sanvatsara* (year), all the people, including children and older citizens, counted the grains for Indra. The grain, which was offered to Indra at the start of sanvatsara, was guarded by Vamadeva.

धनं गृहं मार्गसरो वनादि वा सर्वं पृथक् रुद्रगणैररक्ष्यत ।
रुद्रा अनन्ता अभवन् प्रभुस्त्वभूदीशान एको दिवि देवसंसदि ।।111।।

All the money, wealth, house, land, ponds, and forests were taken care of by different rudraganas. These rudraganas were many, but their master was the one from Dyauloka, Ishana.

वामान्नरक्षाऽधिकृतो बभूव यः स वामदेवः खलु नामतोऽभवत् ।
वामं तदन्नं परिरक्षितं वसोर्धारानगर्यां ध्रियते स्म सञ्चितम् ।।112।।

The one who was appointed to take care of *vama* and *anna* (women and foodgrains) was called Vamadeva. Both were protected in a city called Vasodhara.

ज्येष्ठः सुतो ब्रह्मण औरसो वसोर्धारानगर्यां विनुयुक्त आबभौ ।
ओंकारनामैष तदाज्ञया प्रजास्वन्नं वितीर्णं भवति स्म तन्मुहुः ।।113।।

This Vamadeva was the elder son of Brahma and he was given charge of the city called Vasodhara. He was also called by the name Omkara, on whose orders grains were distributed among people.

तदन्नमाहर्तुमनेकधा व्यधादुपद्रवं दानवसङ्घ आकुलम् ।
ओंकार एषः प्रतिचक्र आक्रमं स वामदेवः प्रहरंस्तमासुरम् ॥114॥

When a group of asuras began harassing the people for seizing this grain, Vamadeva named Omkara repulsed their attempts with his might.

एमूषसंज्ञस्त्वसुरो वराहोपाख्यस्तदासीद् गिरिसप्तकस्य ।
स्थितः परस्तात् स हि वाममन्नं क्रमात्तदाक्रम्य जहार सर्वम् ॥115॥

On the other side of the Saptaka mountain lived an asura named Emusha who was given the title of Varaha, and it was he who had taken in his possession the entire vamanna by force.

यासीद् वराहस्य पुरी तथा वसोर्धारापुरी या पथि चान्तरे तयोः ।
पुर्योऽश्ममय्यो बभुरेकविंशतिर्वामं स तासां परतो मुमोष ह ॥116॥

There were twenty-one cities made of stones located between the city of Varaha and Vasodhara. He snatched the grains and stored it in those cities.

यो लोकपालोन्नकुलस्य विष्णुस्तस्थौ सुधर्म्मा सदसि प्रशास्ता ।
श्रुत्वाऽसुराक्रान्तिमयं जगामाऽविज्ञात एमूषवराहदेशान् ॥117॥

After hearing the news of these attacks by the asuras, Vishnu, the guardian deity and administrator of the gods, reached the place of Emusha clandestinely.

अन्वेषयन्विष्णुमियाय चेन्द्रस्तत्रैव कालेन वराहदेशे ।
इन्द्रश्च विष्णुश्च विधाय मन्त्रं स्वं स्वं पृथक् कर्म तदाध्यवास्थत् ॥118॥

Searching for Vishnu, Indra too reached there and two of them decided on a plan to counter attack the asuras.

उरुक्रमो विष्णुरयं पुरस्तादाचक्रमे चानुमते मघोनः ।
वराहमातुः सवनत्रयार्थं प्रक्लृप्तमन्नं स जहार सद्यः ॥119॥

On the instructions of Indra, the valiant Vishnu attacked first and seized the grains kept by the mother of Varaha to perform three sacrifices.

महानसे यत् पचतं गृहे वा चार्वन्नवर्गो निहितोऽस्य मात्रा ।
तत्सर्वमेषोऽपजहार विष्णुः क्षीरौदनं वा महिषान् शतं च ।।120।।

Vishnu soon captured all the grains stored in the house and kitchen of Varaha, the grains kept by the mother of Varaha, together with hundreds of buffaloes.

ये यथा मां प्रपद्यन्ते तांस्तथैव भजाम्यहम् । (श्रीमद्भगवद्गीता, 4.11)
इति विष्णोः क्रियानीतिः सोन्नमन्नमुषोऽहरत् ।।121।।

Following his rule, 'as you surrender unto me, I reward you accordingly', Vishnu seized all the grains from the grain-thief.

इन्द्रः पुरीस्ता व्यधमद् गिरींस्तान्दुर्गान् परास्थन्निजघान योद्धृन् ।
अविध्यदेमूषवराहवक्षःस्थलं गतप्राणममुं स चक्रे ।।122।।

Indra then destroyed the city of Varaha, demolished the mountains and castles of that city and slaughtered the warriors. He ripped apart the chest of Emusha Varaha and killed him.

स वाममोषे निहते वराहे पुरीषु तस्याश्ममयीषु गुप्तम् ।
वामं यदन्नं मुषितं तदासीत् तत् सर्वमप्याहरदेष विष्णुः ।।123।।

Vishnu took in his possession all the grains stored secretly in the cities of stone after the death of Varaha.

ऋक्संहितायां प्रथमे तु मण्डले तदेकषष्टिप्रमितेऽस्ति सूक्तके ।
सूक्तेऽष्टमस्यास्ति च सप्तसप्ततिप्राये तदाख्यानमिदं प्रदर्शितम् ।।124।।

This episode has been narrated in the sixty-first sukta of the first mandala and seventy-seventh sukta of the eighth mandala of Rigveda samhita.

अस्येदु मातुः सवनेषु सद्यो महः पितुं पपिवाञ्चार्वन्ना ।
मुषा यद् विष्णुः पचतं स हीमान् विध्यद्वाराहं तिरो अद्रिमस्ता ।125।।

It is written in the Rigveda: That great Indra, the creator of the world, drank havya and Soma kept for the sacrifices and that all-pervading Vishnu took possession of the ripe grains of the enemies. The vajra-wielding Indra also slaughtered Megha.

विश्वेत् ता विष्णुराभरदुरुक्रमस्त्वेषितः ।
शतं महीषान्क्षीरपाकमोदनं वराहमिन्द्र एमुषम् ।।
(ऋग्वेदः, 8.66.10)

In the Rigveda it is said, O Indra! Inspired by you, the valiant Vishnu brought with him hundred powerful oxen, rice cooked in milk and cloud full of water.

व्याख्यातमेतद्धयपि तैत्तिरीयके षष्ठद्वितीयस्य तुरीयभागके ।
निदर्शनं तावदिदं प्रदर्शितं तथाऽन्ययुद्धान्यपि कानिचिद् विदुः ।।126।।

In Taittiriya Upanishad, all these battles have been narrated as examples. It is said that other battles had also taken place.

विष्णुर्यज्ञो देवेभ्य आत्मानमन्तरधात् तमन्यदेवता नाविदन् । इन्द्रस्त्ववेत् । विष्णुरिन्द्रमब्रवीत्-को भवानिति । इन्द्रोऽब्रवीत्-दुर्गाणामसुराणां हन्ताऽहम् । भवान् कः । विष्णुरब्रवीत् । अहं दुर्गादाहर्ताऽस्मि। त्वं तु दुर्गहन्ताऽसीत्यतो वराहमसुरं जहि । स हि वराहो वाममुष एकविंशत्या पुरां पारेऽश्ममयीनां वसति । तस्मिन्नसुराणां वसुवाममस्ति । तत इन्द्रस्ताः पुरो भित्वा वराहस्य हृदयमविध्यत् । ततस्तत्र यदासीत्- तद्विष्णुराहरत् ।

Vishnu made himself invisible to the gods so that they would not recognize him. But Indra identified him. Indra asked Vishnu, 'Who are you? I'm the possessor of enemy forts.' Vishnu replied, 'I capture things from the forts. You are the destroyer of the forts, therefore kill asura Varaha. That Varaha, who has stolen grains from Vama's area, lives beyond those twenty-one cities made of stone. Those cities have the vamanna and riches of the asuras.' Then Indra destroyed those forts and ripped apart the heart of Varaha. Then Vishnu took in his possession all the belongings of the forts.

यज्ञोन्नमन्नस्य पतिः स विष्णुदेवाननुक्त्वैव वराहमागात् ।
किं कर्तुकामोऽत्र भवानुपागादित्याह यत् प्राह भवान् क एवम् ।।127।।

That Vishnu, the lord of the sacrificial grains, went over to Varaha's place without informing the gods. When asked about the motive of his visit, Vishnu said, 'Who are you to question me?'

भूयोऽप्येवं देवतानां त्रिलोक्यामाक्रम्यन्तात्युग्रचेष्टा अदेवाः ।
इन्द्रो विष्णुस्तत्प्रतीकारहेतोरास्तां नित्यप्रोद्यतौ धर्मधीरौ ।।128।।

Whenever the aggressive and troublesome asuras attacked the three domains of the gods, Vishnu and Indra were always ready to come to their rescue.

इन्द्रस्य कर्तव्यं कर्माख्यातं स्कान्दे कौमारखण्डे एकोनत्रिंशाध्याये

Duties and acts of Indra given in the Skanda Purana.

इन्द्रो दिशति भूतानां बलं तेजः प्रजाः सुखम् ।
प्रज्ञां प्रयच्छति तथा सर्वान् दायान् सुरेश्वरः ॥

(स्कन्दपुराणम्, 1.2.183)

Indra provides brilliance, strength, progeny, happiness, and wisdom to all his subjects. The king of gods, Indra also provides every other thing that is needed by his subjects.

दुर्वृत्तानां स हरित वृत्तस्थानां प्रयच्छति ।
अनुशास्ति च भूतानि कार्येषु बलवत्तरः ॥

(स्कन्दपुराणम्, 1.2.184)

This Indra takes away everything from the sinners and hands it over to the noble ones. He is very powerful and he assigns duty to the living beings.

असूर्ये च भवेत् सूर्यस्तथाऽचन्द्रे च चन्द्रमाः ।
भवत्यग्निश्च वायुश्च पृथिव्या जीवकारणम् ॥

(स्कन्दपुराणम्, 1.2.185)

This Indra assumes the role of surya where surya is not present and chandrama (the moon) where chandrama is absent. On the earth, he is also Vayu and Agni.

एतदिन्द्रेण कर्तव्यमिन्द्रो हि विपुलं बलम् ॥

(स्कन्दपुराणम्, 1.2.186)

These are the duties and acts of Indra, who is very powerful.

2.11 देवासुराणां द्वादश महासंग्रामाः

2.11 TWELVE GREAT DEVA-ASURA WARS

प्रत्यक् कृष्णादम्बुधेः काश्यपीयादार्मीन्याख्ये सीरियाऽसीरियादौ ।
स्वर्गे भूम्यां चात्र देवासुराणां संग्रामाः प्राग्द्वादशासन् महोग्राः ॥129॥

In ancient times, twelve fierce battles took place between the devas and asuras near the shores of Caspian Sea and Black Sea in the provinces of Syria and Assyria situated in a region called Armenia.

आडीबक, कोलाहल, हालाहल, जलधिमन्थनान्येवम् ।
त्रैपुर, मान्धक, तारक, वार्त्र, ध्वजयुद्ध, बलिबन्धाः ॥130॥

हैरण्याक्ष नृसिंहावेते द्वादश पुरायुगे जाताः ।
देवासुरसंग्रामा इतरेऽप्यभवन्नितः क्षुधा ॥131॥

These twelve battles were: Adibak, Kolahal, Halahal, Samudramanthan, Traipur, Mandhak, Tarak, Vatra, Dhvajayudha, Balibandha, Hiranyaksha and the one with Narasimha. There were also several other minor battles.

यद्यपि वेदग्रन्थे स्पष्टं त इमे न दृश्यन्ते ।
किन्त्वनुमिनुमो लुप्तान् सन्ति पुराणेतिहासयोर्हि धृताः ॥132॥

There is no clear description of these minor battles in the Vedas. The books which mention these wars have disappeared now. But the wars do find mention in the Itihasa and Purana texts.

आग्नेयस्याध्याये षट्सप्ततियुक्शतद्वयप्रमिते ।
मात्स्यस्य सप्तचत्वारिंशाध्याये च संग्रामाः ॥133॥

The description of these wars is recorded in the two-hundred and seventy-sixth chapter of Agni Purana and in the forty-seventh chapter of Matsya Purana.

निजघानान्धकमसुरं भगवान् रुद्रः सुरैरुक्तः ।
त्रैपुरयुद्धेऽप्येष न्यवधीत् त्रिपुरासुरत्रिपुरम् ॥134॥

On the request of the devas, Bhagvan Rudra [Shiva] slew Andhak asura and in the Traipur war, the same Rudra killed Tripurasura who was then haunting all the three lokas.

उत्तरशामप्रान्ते तिरपूली नाम या नगरी ।
तन्मन्ये त्रिपुरं स्यात् तत्र त्रिपुरासुरो निहतः ।।135।।

In the northern region of Samadesha, there is a city named Tirpuli. In my opinion, it was Tripurnagar and Tripurasura was killed there.

इन्द्रेण हतो वृत्रस्त्वष्टृसुतो वृत्रवधसमरे ।
निहतश्च विप्रचित्तिमायाछत्रः सहानुजो ध्वजके ।।136।।

Vrittasur, son of Tvashta, was killed by Indra in a battle. In dhvaja yudha (battle of flags), Maya Chatra-Viprachiti was also killed along with his younger brother.

हालाहले तु घोरा निहता इन्द्रेण दानवा दैत्याः ।
रजिना नहुषभ्रात्रा कोलाहलपर्वते हता दैत्याः ।।137।।

In the Halahal battle, Indra killed extremely powerful demons. Nahusha's brother Raji killed a number of demons in the Kolahal war.

इन्द्रार्थे तु वराहो जघान विष्णुर्हिरण्याक्षम् ।
नरसिंहोऽपि च विष्णुर्हिरण्यकशिपुं जघान दैत्येशम् ।।138।।

On behalf of Indra, Vishnu, disguised as Varaha, killed Hiranyaksha and in the manifestation of Narasimha, Vishnu killed Hiranyakashipu, the lord of asuras.

द्वासप्ततिलक्षैरयमशीतिसाहस्रसंयुक्तैः ।
सैन्यैर्हिरण्यकशिपुर्भारतवर्षे पुराक्रामीत् ।।139।।

इन्द्रस्य सैनिकानां संख्यानं न स्मरन्त्यत्र ।
सैनिकयुद्धे देवा दैत्यादस्मात् पराजिता अभवन् ।।140।।

Hiranyakashipu with his army of 72,80,000 soldiers attacked Bharatavarsha. There is no mention of the latter's army and its numbers. In this battle, the devas were defeated by Hiranyakashipu.

भारतवर्षे दैत्यो हिरण्यकशिपुर्बलात्प्रविष्टोऽभूत् ।
मूलस्थानं नगरं निर्माय्यैषोऽकरोद् राज्यम् ।।141।।

This asura, Hiranyakashipu, invaded Bharatavarsha and founded a city called Mulsthana [Multan], and began to rule there.

आसुरभाषाशब्दो मूरः सूर्यार्थकस्ततो मूराः ।
सूर्यापासकदैत्यास्तत् स्थानं सूर्याधामाद्यम् ।।142।।

In the asura language the word 'mur' stands for surya. That is why the worshippers of sun were called Muras.

मूलस्थानं नगरं हिरण्यकशिपोस्तदद्य मुलतानम् ।
ब्रूते तत्र हि चतुरः पुरुषान् व्याप्यास्थितं राज्यम् ।।143।।

This place was inhabited by the sun worshippers and was also known as *suryadham* (shrine of sun). This place is today known as Multan. It is said that the kingdom of Hiranyakashipu lasted for four dynastics.

आदौ हिरण्यकशिपुः प्रह्लादोऽन्यो विरोचनोऽथ बलिः ।
चक्रे राज्यं तदिदं बलिसमये ध्वंसितं तु सुरैः ।।144।।

First, Hiranyakashipu, then Prahlada, and then Virochan and in the end Bali ruled here and finally during the regime of Bali, this city was destroyed by the devas.

प्रह्लादस्तु तदानीमनीतिमालक्ष्य तत्र दैत्यानाम् ।
पितृद्वेषी विष्णोः पक्षं जग्राह शान्तिकामाय ।।145।।

Realizing the evil policy of the asuras, Prahlada rebelled against his father and wanted to make peace with the devas; he joined the group of Vishnu.

शान्त्यै युद्धनिवृत्त्यै प्रह्लादाऽनुमतिमाप्य विष्णुरयम् ।
अन्तः प्रविश्य योगात् सिंहाकृतिरिह जघान दैत्येशम् ।।146।।

To end the war, Vishnu, with the consent of Prahlada, took the form of a lion through his power of yoga, entered the city and killed the asura king Hiranyakashipu.

षण्णवतिस्तु कलानामसुरैर्यद्वत् प्रकाशिता पूर्वम् ।
तद्वद्देवैराविष्कृतास्तु विद्याश्चतुःषष्टिः ।।147।।

The ninety-six forms of art practised by the asuras in the ancient times were equalled by the devas by inventing sixty-four forms of vidya of their own.

तत्रैका विद्यासीदाकृतिपरिवर्तिनी देहे ।
विष्णुर्यया वराहोऽभवद्विचित्रश्च नरसिंहः ।।148।।

One such vidya was the power to transform one's body. With the help of this vidya, Vishnu transformed himself into a boar and that of Narsimha.

अदधाद् रूपं विष्णुर्मोहिन्याश्चारुकामिन्याः ।
सेयमपूर्वा विद्या देवयुगे योगमायोक्ता ।।149।।

It was with the same vidya that Vishnu assumed the form of a beautiful woman called Mohini. It was the same art which was known by the name of yogmaya during the early period of devayuga.

अत्यद्भुतं स्वरूपं स नारसिंहं विधाय यद्विष्णुः ।
स्कम्भादाविरभूत् तद्विज्ञेयं योगमायातः ।।150।।

This may be known that with the help of yogmaya, Vishnu emerged from a pillar assuming the form of a grotesque Narasimha.

नारदसुपाञ्चरात्रे पञ्चविधं ज्ञानमाख्यातम् ।
निर्विषयं यज्ज्ञानं परतत्त्वं ब्रह्म तच्छुद्धम् ।151।।

Five kinds of jnana are described in the *Narada Pancharatra* [a text of knowledge authored by Narada]. The jnana, which is *nirvishaya* (free of any objective), is associated with pure parabrahma. That very jnana is the pure jnana.

कर्मजमगुणब्रह्मज्ञानं परमुक्तिदं तद्वत् ।
सगुणब्रह्मोपास्तिजमवरविमुक्तिप्रदं ज्ञानम् ।।152।।

Similarly, nirguna *brahmajnana* (attributeless truth), issuing forth from karma, secures *paramukti* (salvation) for us. The knowledge gained from the worship of Saguna Brahman grants us *apara* (after death) salvation.

दिव्यं ज्ञानं योगजसिद्धिरूपं तच्च षोडशधा ।
अणिमा महिमा गरिमा लघिमेशित्वं वशित्वं च ।।153।।

व्याप्तिश्च प्राकाम्यं भूतभविष्यत्परोक्षदूरेक्षा ।
दूरश्रवणं कायव्यूहः परकायवेशश्च ।।154।।

परजीवहरणजीवप्रदानके सर्गकर्तृताशिल्पम् ।
संहारकरणमिति तत् षोडशधा योगजं ज्ञानम् ।।155।।

Originating from yoga, this divine knowledge is *yogasiddhi jnana* (knowledge gained by yogic accomplishments) and is composed of sixteen kinds of accomplishments. These are: anima, mahima, garima, laghima, ishitva, vashitva, prapti, prakamya, knowledge of past and (present, cognition from a distance and indirect knowledge, hearing a distant voice, kayavyuha, parjivharan, parkayapravesh, granting life to others, art of creating the cosmos and destroying it. Thus, this knowledge originates from sixteen kinds of Yoga.

अथ पञ्चमं तु विषयज्ञानं न्यूनाधिकं लोके ।
इन्द्रियसेवाविषयानुराग आत्मोन्नतिश्चेति ॥156॥

The fifth kind of knowledge is about the enjoyment of worldly pleasures, and this knowledge is known to every human being. This knowledge is concerned with serving the senses and self growth by fulfilling our desires for material things.

ज्ञाने पञ्चविधेऽस्मिन् विषयज्ञानं तु चेतने सहजम् ।
दिव्यज्ञानमृषीणां देवानां योगिनां चासीत् ॥157॥

Out of the five varieties of knowledge, the knowledge pertaining to sensory organs is present instinctively in all animate beings. The divine knowledge, however, remains the absolute privilege of the one who meditates, sages, and yogis [they alone can achieve that knowledge].

नानाविधार्थनिर्मितिरिव निजरूपान्यता शिल्पम् ।
स्यात् सर्गकर्तृतायां तेनाभून्नारसिंहवपुः ॥158॥

Like the process of creating various new objects [knowledge of creating the universe], is the knowledge of transforming one's own shape into other forms. With this vidya, Vishnu assumed the form of Narasimha.

वाग्बद्ध एष विष्णुः सौहार्द्येनानुगृह्य तं तु तदा ।
प्रह्लादं तद् राज्यासने प्रतिष्ठापयामास ॥159॥

The same Vishnu, bound by his commitment to his devotees, blessed Prahlada and consecrated him on the royal throne.

इन्द्रेण प्रह्लादो विजितोऽमृतमन्थने पश्चात् ।
इन्द्रेण प्रह्लादिर्विरोचनस्तारकामये निहतः ॥160॥

Thereafter at the time of churning of amrita [in Samudramanthan], Indra once again conquered Prahlada and his son Virochana was killed by Indra during the battle provoked by Tarakasura.

वैरोचनिर्बलिश्च प्रतरां निगृहीत इन्द्रविष्णुभ्याम् ।
एते बहुभिर्वर्षैः पञ्चैकस्मिन् कुलेऽभवन् समराः ॥161॥

Virochana's son Bali was contained many times by Indra and Vishnu. In this way, this family faced five great wars for many years.

षष्टिसहस्रोपेते द्वे लक्षे प्रस्तुते आस्ताम् ।
बलिदैत्यसैनिकानां रणाङ्गणे तत्र बलिबन्धे ॥162॥

In that war called Balibandh, 2,60,000 soldiers of Bali fought in the battlefield.

यावच्छण्डामर्कौ द्वावसुराणां पुरोधसावास्ताम् ।
असुरास्तावद्विजिता अभवन् जयमाप्नुवन् क्वापि ॥163॥

Till the two priests of the asuras, Shanda and Armaka, lived, they had mixed success in the battlefield.

यदवधि भृगुर्बृहस्पतिसदृशप्रतिभः पुरोहितस्तेषाम् ।
अभवत् तत आरभ्य व्यजयन्तेहासुराः प्रायः ॥164॥

And when Brihaspati acted as their priest, the asuras won almost every time.

2.12 देवानां पराजयः

2.12 THE DEFEAT OF DEVAS

मध्यतो बहुधा विजयलाभेऽप्यन्ततो देवानां पराजयः।

In spite of several victories in the interregnum, the deities met with defeat in the end.

स्वार्थैकसिद्धिपरता धर्मान्तरबाधने स्वधर्मत्वम् ।
एतद्द्वयमसुराणां विद्रोहोत्थापने हेतुः ॥165॥

The asuras had an upper hand in the wars as they were focussed only on their victory and their only dharma was to obstruct the duty of others.

शान्तिप्रियताऽत्यर्थं धर्मे प्रवणत्वमानृशंस्याख्ये ।
एतद्द्वयमार्याणां प्रत्यभिमर्दे पराभवे हेतुः ॥166॥

The devas, on the other hand, were known for their peaceful attitude and firm adherence to *anrshansya dharma* [compassion]. These virtues in fact became the cause of their defeat.

बुद्धिश्चाक्रमणं च द्वे अप्येते बले भवतः ।
उभयोर्मिथोभियोगे विजयः कुत्रेति दुरभिगमम् ॥167॥

Strength is of two types—*buddhibala* (strength of intellect) and *akramanabala* (strength of attack or offensive). It is difficult to say which one will lead to victory.

यच्चिरकारि विवेकापेक्षं तज्जीयते बुद्ध्या ।
आक्रमणं सा बुद्धिर्जयति सदा सावधाना या ॥168॥

The outcome of a prolonged war depends on acute judgement and victory is gained through intellect and this intellect is the offensive power.

यत् क्षिप्रकारि पूर्णोत्साहं तज्जयति नूनमाक्रमणम् ।
समयापेक्षा बुद्धिस्तत्राक्रमणेन जीयते प्रायः ॥169॥

The offensive attack, which is expeditious and leads to complete obliteration, undoubtedly brings victory whereas pausing to think over the attack leads to defeat.

कर्त्तुं योग्मयोग्यं वेति धिया यावदेव विविनक्ति ।
धृष्टस्तावत् सहसैवाक्रम्यार्थं निजं प्रसाधयति ॥170॥

A sober person reflects through intellect on the appropriateness and inappropriateness of action, whereas a bold person completes his work by attacking suddenly.

सूर्यो लुप्तश्चन्द्रो लुप्तः संप्रति न दृश्यते प्रायः ।
दैवतसंस्थालोपोत्तरमसुरैस्तद् द्वयोच्छेदात् ॥171॥

In this way, the sun disappeared and somalata [the moon] was destroyed. Because of the cutting off of the two by the asuras, the assembly of devas was destroyed after which these were rarely seen.

यज्ञजसिद्ध्या येषामात्मा दैवोऽपरो मनुष्याणाम् ।
कृत्रिम उत्पनः स्यात् तेषु मनुष्येष्वभूत्तु देवत्वम् ॥172॥

Those human beings who gained divine power through yajna, they were extraordinary beings and were imbued with divinity.

यज्ञक्रियाविलोपादप्रत्युत्पन्नदैवतात्मानः ।
केवलमनुष्यभावा न पुनर्देवा अकथ्यन्त ॥173॥

But with the loss of yajna rituals and in the absence of daivata atma, these human beings remained simply humans and cannot be addressed as devas.

स्वर्गः कृत्स्नो मानुषलोकः समभूदशेषदेवाश्च ।
अभवन् मानुषरूपा आसुरधर्मे प्रविष्टाश्च ॥174॥

That svarga has totally become the world of humans, and all devas have been reduced to human forms who follow the asura ideology.

आसुरधर्मे गमनाद्देवैरपि भूरभूदियं हीना ।
लोकत्रयव्यवस्थालोपाद् भूर्नाद्य दैवताधीना ॥175॥

With the conversion of devas into the asura ideology, there are no devas left in svarga any longer. With the disappearance of the trailokya lokas, Prithviloka has ceased to be under the authority of devas.

देवासुरसंग्रामा यत्र यथा यैरभूवन् प्राक् ।
विशदं तद्द्रष्टव्यं मत्कृतदेवासुरख्यातौ ॥176॥

In the olden times, how was the battle of gods and asuras fought, when and between whom, one should get a clear view of this in *Devasurkhyati*[2].

[2]Another work by Pandit Madhusudan Ojha

2.13 सोमार्थे देवानां दैत्यैः संग्रामः गंधर्वविनियोगश्च

2.13 THE DEVA-DAITYA WAR OVER SOMA

चन्द्रस्तु सोमवल्लीरूपो यो हेमकूटाद्रौ ।
यज्ञैकसाधनं तद्देवानामुदखनन्नसुराः ।।177।।

On the Hemakut mountain, the moon in the form of a Soma plant, which was the only means of offering yajna for the devas, was uprooted by the asuras.

यज्ञात् सिद्धीर्देवतानामनेका दृष्ट्वा यज्ञं कर्तुमैच्छन्नदेवाः ।
किन्त्वस्मिंस्ते यज्ञविज्ञानशिक्षाशून्याः सिद्धिं नाप्नुवन् विध्यबोधात् ।।178।।

Seeing that the devas were attaining various types of powers through yajna, the asuras also expressed their wish to perform such a yajna. But due to their ignorance of *yajnajnana* (science of yajna), and the lack of knowledge of the proper method, the asuras remained unsuccessful.

यज्ञज्ञानायोग्यतां स्वस्य दृष्ट्वा जातामर्षा विद्विषन्तश्च देवान् ।
तेषां सिद्धौ हेतुभूतस्य यज्ञस्यैच्छन् कर्तुं हन्त निर्मूलनाशम् ।।179।।

Once they realized their inability to perform yajna, the asuras became angry with the devas and vowed to destroy the yajna, the source of their power.

सूर्यं श्रुत्वा यज्ञविज्ञानहेतुं चन्द्रं श्रुत्वा तद्विधाने च हेतुम् ।
आक्रम्यैते सूर्यचक्रे विहन्तुं दासानादौ प्रेरयामासुरुग्रान् ।।180।।

Learning that the sun and moon helped the devas in their yajna, the asuras unleashed their agents of destruction to annihilate suryachakra.

एवं कर्तुं हन्त निर्मूलनाशं दैत्यव्रातः सोमवल्ल्याख्यचन्द्रम् ।
भूयो भूयो हेमकूटाद्रिदेशानेत्योच्चखनुस्ते यथाशक्ति सोमम् ।।181।।

Simultaneously, a group of asuras were despatched to the Hemkut mountain to destroy Soma which gave power to the devas.

इन्द्रः श्रुत्वा सोमवल्लीविनाशं तद्रक्षार्थं दैत्यमार्गश्च रोद्धुम् ।
गन्धर्वाख्यान् वासयामास वीरान् सिन्धोः पाश्चाद् व्याप्य गान्धारदेशे ।।182।।

When Indra heard about the imminent destruction of somalata by the asuras, he established a settlement of brave warriors named Gandharvas in the Gandhara region on the western bank of Sindhu river.

गन्धर्वास्ते पूर्वमासन् हिमाद्रेर्द्रोण्यावासा नृत्यगीतानुरक्ता: ।
तेषां वृत्तिं तां निवर्त्याथ योद्धुं वृत्तिं तेषां कल्पयामास देव: ।।183।।

These Gandharvas lived in caves on the Himalayas, and spent their time in songs and dances. After putting an end to this practice, Indra engaged them in the practice of warfare.

गन्धर्वास्ते तत्र काले द्विधाऽसन् दिव्या अन्ये केचिदन्ये तु मर्त्या: ।
दिव्यास्त्रेधोत्कृष्टकर्माण आप्ता मर्त्यास्त्वेके क्षुद्रकर्माण आसन् ।।184।।

In that era, Gandharvas were of two types: some were divya-gandharvas, and others were matsya-gandharvas. The divya-gandharvas would perform three types of noblest deeds—yajna, daana, and *tapa* (meditation)—and were trustworthy. The matsya-gandharvas performed ordinary deeds.

2.14 सोमसंरक्षणाय नियुक्ता गन्धर्वाः

2.14 GANDHARVAS RECRUITED TO PROTECT SOMA

हाहाहूहूहंसगोमायुनन्दितुम्बुर्वख्याश्चित्रविश्वावसू च ।
एते मर्त्या अष्टगन्धर्वभेदा हैमाद्रिस्था नृत्यगीतानुषक्ताः ।।
(अग्निपुराणम्, 360.1)

There were eight types of Gandharvas—Haha, Huhu, Humsa, Gomayu, Nandi, Tumburva, Chitra and Vishvavasu.

दिव्या वर्गाः स्वर्ग एकादशासन् बम्भारिश्चाऽङ्घारिहस्तौ सुहस्तः ।
मूर्धन्वान् वा सूर्यवर्चाः कृशानुः कृध्वभ्राजौ स्वानविश्वावसू च ।।
(ऋग्वेदे, 10/139)

Divya-gandharvas were of eleven types—Bambhari, Adhari, Hasta, Suhasta, Murdhanvan, Suryavarcha, Krishanu, Kridhu, Abhraja, Svana and Vishvavasu. They lived in svarga.

क्रमः	क्षुद्रगन्धर्वाः	प्राधेयगन्धर्वाः 30000000	मौनेयगन्धर्वाः 60000000	दिव्यगन्धर्वाः
1	हाहाः	सिद्धः	भीमः	अङ्गारिः
2	हूहूः	पूर्णः	भीमसेनः	अम्भारिः
3	हंसः	बर्ही	उग्रसेनः	मूर्धन्वान्
4	गेमायुः	पूर्णायुः	कलिः	कृधुः
5	नन्दी	ब्रह्मचारी	पर्जन्यः	सुर्यवर्चाः
6	तम्बुरुः	रतिगुणाः	गोपतिः	कृशानुः
7	चित्रसेनः	सुपर्णः	प्रयुतः	हस्तः
8	विश्वासुः	भानुः	धृतराष्ट्रः	सुहस्तः
9		चन्द्रः	सुर्यवर्चाः	स्वाञ्ची
10		विश्वावसुः	वरुणः	विश्वावसुः
11			सुपर्णः	
12			अर्कपर्णः	
13			वशी	
14			शालिशिराः	
15			नारदः	
16			चित्ररथः	

Serial number	kshudragandharva	pradhyeygandharva: 30000000	mauneyagandharva: 60000000	Divyagandharva
1	haha	sidha	bhima	adhari
2	huhu	purna	bhimasena	bambhari
3	hansa	barhi	ugrasena	murdhavan
4	gomayu	purnayu	kali	kridhu
5	nandi	brahmachari	pajranjya	suryavarcha
6	tumburva	ratiguna	gopati	krishanu
7	chitrasena	suparna	prayutha	hastha
8	vishvasu	bhanu	dhritrastra	suhasta
9		chandra	suryavarcha	svana
10		vishvavasu	varuna	vishvavasu
11			suparna	
12			Akraparna	
13			Vasi	
14			shalishira	
15			Narada	
16			chitraratha	

स्वर्ग क्रीत्वा सोमसंरक्षणं वै वृत्तिर्ह्येषामाहरन्ति स्म तेभ्य: ।
सोमं देवा: दिव्यगन्धर्वभेदानेतानूचे तित्तिरि: षष्ठकाण्डे ।।185।।

It was their duty to protect Soma in svarga for a price. The gods used to accept Soma from them. The names of different types of divya-gandharvas are described in the eighth mandala of Taittiriya Brahmana.

एभ्यो भिन्ना वीरगन्धर्ववर्गा आसन् द्वेधा तत्र मौनेयसंज्ञा: ।
पातालस्था: कोटिषट्कप्रमाणा नागैर्द्वेषाद् युद्धमासीत्तु तेषाम् ।।186।।

Other than these, there were two other classes of Gandharvas, who were equally brave. The one called Mauneya lived in *pathala*. They were six crores in number. Due to malice, they were involved in a battle with the Nagas.

कलिभीमसेनभीमोग्रसेनपर्जन्यगोपतिप्रयुता: ।
धृतराष्ट्रसूर्यवर्चो वरुणसुपर्णार्कपर्णचित्ररथा: ।।187।।

शालिशिरा अथ नारदवशिनावति षोडशैतानि ।
गन्धर्वाणामासन् मौनेयानां कुलानीह ।।188।।

These Mauneya-gandharvas had sixteen clans: Kali, Bhimsena, Bhima, Ugrasena, Pajranya, Gopati, Prayuta, Dhrtrastra, Suryavarcha, Varuna, Suparna, Arkaparna, Chitraratha, Shalishira, Narada, and Vasi.

प्राधेयाः पुनरन्ये गान्धर्वाः कोटयः पुरा तिस्रः ।
सिन्धोः पश्चाद्देशे गान्धाराख्ये वसन्ति स्म ।।189।।

सिद्धः पूर्णो बर्ही पूर्णायुर्ब्रह्मचारी च ।
रतिगुणसुपर्णविश्वावसवो भानुश्च चन्द्रश्च ।।190।।
एते दश कुलभेदाः प्राधेयानां प्रसिध्यन्ति ।
एषा च राजधानीपुरमासीद् वर्द्धमानपुरम् ।।191।।

Pradheyas were the other class of Gandharvas. They were three crores in number. Their races included Siddha, Purna, Barhi, Purnayu, Brahmachari, Ratiguna, Suparna, Vishvavasu, Bhanu, and Chandra. In the olden times, Vardhamanpur was their capital.

वाल्मीकिये सन्ति रामायणे ते प्रोक्ता, भ्राता रामचन्द्रस्य येभ्यः ।
युद्धवा जित्वा स्वस्य पुत्रद्वये तद् राज्यं सर्वं संविभक्तं व्यधत्त ।।192।।

It is mentioned in the Valmiki Ramayana that Sri Rama's brother Bharata defeated the Gandharvas in a battle, won the town, and divided it between his two sons.

ते चैते प्राधेया मूजवदाद्यद्रिजातसोमानाम् ।
सिन्धु सुवास्तु वितस्ता सरस्वती प्रभृति सरिदप्सु ।।193।।

वहमानानां विचितिं रक्षां कर्तुं न्ययुज्यन्त ।
इत्थं वदन्ति कौषीतकिनः स्वब्राह्मणे मुनयः ।।194।।

These pradheya-gandharvas were recruited to protect Soma that grew on Munjavana and other mountains and flowed in rivers like Sindhu, Suvastu, Sarasvati and Vitasta. It is said so by the sages of Kaushitki lineage in their Brahmanas.

गन्धर्वा ह वा इन्द्रस्य सोममप्सु प्रत्यायिता गोपयन्ति ।
त उह स्त्रीकामाः ते हा-सुमनांसि कुर्वते ।।
(कौषीतकीब्रह्मणम्, 12.4.3)

These Gandharva [rays of the moon] hid the Soma which flowed under the waters of Indra. They are such who harbour desire for the apsaras, and certainly have a beautiful heart.

2.15 विश्वावसुप्रधानानां गन्धर्वाणाम् आधिपत्ये चन्द्राभिषेकः

2.15 SUPREMACY OF GANDHARVAS AND ANOINTMENT OF CHANDRA

एषां राजाऽभूच्च विश्वावसुः प्राग् दैतेयानां मार्गरोधं स चक्रे ।
भूयो भूयो मार्गरोधे कृतेऽपि प्राग्र्या दैत्या नो निवृत्ता बभूवुः ॥195॥

Vishvavasu was the king of these Gandharvas. He checked and obstructed the ways of the asuras. The daityas, however, remained unrestrained.

दैत्यक्रान्तेः सोमरक्षां विधातुं धात्रेऽभ्येत्याभ्यर्थमास शक्रः ।
गन्धर्वाणां शासकं कश्चिदन्यं त्वैच्छत् सोमं योऽभिरक्षेद् विशिष्य ॥196॥

In order to protect Soma from the asuras, Indra went to Brahma or *Vidhata* (Supreme God) and prayed to appoint someone else as the ruler of the Gandharvas, who was capable of protecting Soma from the asuras.

ब्रह्मा दृष्ट्वा कश्चिदत्रेस्तु पुत्रं योग्यं युक्तं ब्राह्मवीर्येण तावत् ।
क्षात्रं वीर्यं धातुमत्राभिषिच्य प्रागास्येनाभ्रामयत् कृत्स्नपृथ्व्याम् ॥197॥।

Brahma selects one of Atri's sons as suitable and competent as he was imbued with brahmavirya. Brahma anoints him and takes him along on a trip around the earth from the western direction, in order to engender in him the attributes of an army commander.

गन्धर्वाणामौषधीनां च सोमादीनां चक्रे तत्र राजानमेतम् ।
गन्धर्वेऽस्मिंस्तं प्रतिष्ठाप्य देशे सोमस्थानं रक्षितुं तं न्ययुङ्क्त ॥198॥

This son of Atri is made the king of Gandharvas, herbs, and Soma. He was established in the Gandharva region, and appointed to protect Soma.

चन्द्रांशुभ्यो जातमूलं तु सोमं ज्योतिष्मन्तं रक्षितुं यन्नियुक्तः ।
तस्मात् स्वर्गे लोकपालः स भूत्वा चन्द्रः सोमो नामतः ख्यातिमागात् ॥199॥

He was appointed to secure the *jyotishmana* (the light) that was born out of the rays of the moon. Therefore, he became lokapala in the heaven, and became famous as Chandrasoma.

पुत्रस्तस्यासीद् बुधो राजपुत्रो नाम्ना ख्यातो हस्तिविद्याप्रवीणः ।
यस्तत्पुत्रोऽभूदिलागर्भजन्मा तस्मादासीच्चन्द्रवंशप्रवृत्तिः ॥200॥

Bhudha, who became famous by the name Rajaputra, was born to him. He was an expert in palmistry or *hastavidya*. From Chandrasoma's son that was born to Ila began the *Chandravamshaja* (the lunar dynasty).

चन्द्रस्येत्थं चान्तरिक्षावकाशे गन्धर्वाणामाधिपत्ये नियोगम् ।
पूर्णोद्योगं दैवतानां च दृष्ट्वा कञ्चित्कालंस्तम्भितास्ते बभूवुः ॥201॥

In this manner, Chandrama is appointed as the king of Gandharvas in the antariksha. The asuras were astonished by the effort and the robust preparedness of the devas.

2.16 दैत्यैः कृतः सोमवल्लीविध्वंसः

2.16 DESTRUCTION OF SOMA CREEPER BY DAITYAS

एवं सोमध्वंसने चान्तरायं दृष्ट्वा दूरादागमे चान्तरायम् ।
योद्धुं दैत्या यत्नमातस्थिरे ते प्रान्तेऽत्रैव स्वयं निवासं विधाय ।।202।।

The daityas decided to settle in the region as it was becoming difficult to carry out the destruction of Soma after travelling long distances.

सैन्यग्रामं ते महान्तं सम्भारञ्च प्राप्य सोत्साहयत्नम् ।
आक्रम्यास्मिन् भारते सिन्धुदेशान् मूलस्थाने स्थापयन्ति स्म राज्यम् ।।203।।

With a large army and abundant weaponry, the asuras excitedly attacked the neighbouring regions, and established Mulasthana as their kingdom.

प्रह्लादोऽस्मिंस्तत्पिता तस्य पुत्रस्तत्पौत्रे वा दैत्यराजः प्रसह्य ।
दैतेयान् स्वान् सैन्यचारादिभृत्यान् सोमस्थाने चारणायादिदेश ।।204।।

This region that is Multan had great kings like Prahlada, his father, his son, and grandson, who forcibly ordered the asura soldiers like Charana and other spies to roam in Somasthana.

तस्मिन्काले दैवयोगेन रुष्टां याज्यं मत्वा चन्द्रसद्माभ्युपेताम् ।
तारां देवाचार्यपत्नीं स चन्द्रो हृत्वा देवैर्भर्त्सितश्चिन्तितोऽभूत् ।।205।।

It was one of those days when fate so ordained that Tara, wife of an acharya of gods, being offended for some reason, went to the abode of Chandra, taking him to be a *yajamana*. The devas thought Chandra had abducted Tara, and tortured him. Chandra was upset by this.

गन्धर्वाणामेष राजा तदासीत् तेषां नीतौ स्त्रीषु वैवाहिकोऽयम् ।
नासीद्बन्ध प्रीतिदायेन पुंसां स्वीया स्त्री स्यादेष जह्ने ततस्ताम् ।।206।।

Chandra was the king of the Gandharvas and there were no restrictions among Gandharvas about marriage. Men and women entered a wedlock merely by expressing love for each other. So it was believed that Chandra had abducted Tara.

आक्रुष्टोऽभूद्दैवतैस्तत्र चन्द्रस्तस्मिन्काले लब्धवेला अदेवाः ।
चन्द्रस्यार्थं साधयन्तः स्वसैन्यैः स्वीये पक्षे चन्द्रमेतं व्यनैषुः ।।207।।

After the devas offended chandra, the asuras, sensing an opportunity, got him on their side by catering to his needs using their military strength.

पक्षग्राहक्रीत एष श्लथोऽभूत् स्वे कर्तव्ये सोमसंरक्षणेऽर्थे ।
इत्थं दैत्याः सोमवल्लीवितानध्वंसे जाताश्चन्द्रदोषात् समर्थाः ।।208।।

Chandra, who came under the temptations of the asuras, became lax about protecting Soma and this helped the asuras to destroy the Soma-valli.

काले काले सोमवल्लीविनाशे कुर्वद्भिस्तैर्यत्नमन्यत्र युद्धात् ।
दुष्टैर्नीचैर्ब्राह्मवीर्याः प्रशस्ता सौम्या वल्लयो नाशितः कृत्स्नशस्ताः ।।209।।

Gradually, the asuras, short of waging a war, systematically destroyed Soma that gave strength to the devas.

अद्यत्वे यच्चक्षते सिन्धुपारे बोलन्घाटी पर्वतप्रान्तभागे ।
माजन्दारान् नामतः ख्यातशैले सोऽयं सोमो लभ्यतेऽद्यापि भूयान् ।।210।।

It is believed that Soma is available in plenty on a mountain famous as Majandaran, located on the outskirts of Bolanghati side of the mountain beyond Sindh.

किन्तु ब्रूमो नैव सोमोऽस्ति मुख्यो यो ब्रह्मण्यः सोम आसीत् स नष्टः ।
यद्वद् ब्राह्मीं नाम मण्डूकपर्णीमाहुः केचित् तद्वदन्यः स सोमः ।।211।।

But people say that the Soma found there is not the real one. The real Soma was Brahmana (Brahmi) Soma, which was destroyed. Today as Mandukaparni is called Brahmi, this Soma is also some other Soma and not the real one.

2.17 सोमप्रतिनिध्येन सुरोत्पादनम्

2.17 SURA CREATED TO REPLACE SOMA

अप्राप्य सोममसुराः सोमविधं मादकं विधापयितुम् ।
असुराधीशं वरुणं राजानं प्रार्थयामासुः ।।212।।

In the event of their inability to possess Soma, the asuras prayed to their chief, King Varuna, to create an intoxicating substance that was like Soma.

वरुणस्ततः प्रयत्नाद् विनिर्ममे वारुणीं मदिराम् ।
पास्यामस्त्वसुरानिति सुरामिमां नातश्चक्रुः ।।213।।

Varuna then made varuni madira. The asuras named it sura by declaring that 'we would drink these suras.' [Suras also mean devas.]

एकादशप्रकाराः सुरास्ततस्त्वासवाः पृथग् बहवः ।
भिन्नास्ततश्च शीधव इत्यवरे मादकाः सोमात् ।।214।।

This sura is of eleven types, and, apart from it, there are different types of liquor. Besides, drinks like Shidhav are considered inferior to Soma.

सोमो धृतिविज्ञाने वर्द्धयते संस्करोति मस्तिष्कम् ।
माल्यं, सुरा तु हरते तद् विज्ञानं, शिरोऽपि दूषयति ।।215।।

Soma enhances concentration or *dharana-shakti* (concentration power) and intelligence. It cultivates the brain. Sura is impure and it weakens intelligence and pollutes the brain.

2.18 सोमरसगुणप्रकाशका वेदमन्त्राः

2.18 MANTRAS THAT ENHANCE SOMA

बुद्धिः शौर्यसमृद्धी बलमारोग्यं महत्त्वमभयत्वम् ।
रिपुदमनक्षमता सुखदीर्घायुष्ट्वे जयश्च सोमेन ।।216।।

Soma makes it possible to attain intellect, courage, prosperity, valour, strength, fearlessness, happiness, long life, and victory.

अद्रौ हैमे त्वोषधीनामधीशो योऽयं सोमः कश्चिदासीत् पुरात्वे ।
यो यस्तस्यासीद् गुणस्तं प्रगाथः काण्वः सम्यग् वर्णयामास विद्वान् ।।217।।

This lord of herbs, Soma, existed on the Himalayas in ancient times. Its merits have been adequately described by learned Kanva Pragatha.

स्वादोरभक्षि वयसः सुमेधाः स्वाध्यो वरिवोवित्तस्य ।
विश्वे यं देवा उत मर्त्यासो मधु बुवन्तो अभिसञ्चरन्ति ।।
(ऋग्वेदः, 8.48.1)

'I, Kanva, with excellent intellect, and who has examined different forms of soma-rasa, have eaten Soma which both the devas and humans say is delicious and worthy of worship.'

अन्तश्च प्रागा अदितिर्भवास्यवयाता हरसो दैवस्य ।
इन्दविन्द्रस्य सख्यं जुषाणः श्रौष्टीव धुरमनुराय ऋध्याः ।।
(ऋग्वेदः, 8.48.2)

'Soma, O, destroyer! The moment you enter the human body, you remove anger. O Soma, you are inclined towards giving wealth in the similar manner as the steeds, after accepting Indra's friendship, are inclined towards getting attached to the axle of the chariot.

अपाम सोमममृता अभूमागन्म ज्योतिरविदाम देवान् ।
किं नूनमस्मान्कृणवदरातिः किमु धूर्तिरमृतमर्त्यस्य ।।
(ऋग्वेदः, 8.48.3)

'We have now drunk Soma, and we have become immortals. We have now attained light, and are known as the gods. O, Soma that is amrita, now enemy or mischievous men cannot harm us.

शं नो भव हृद आपीत इन्दो पितेव सोम सूनवे सुशेवः ।
सखेव सख्य उरुशंस धीरः प्रण आयुर्जीवसे सोम तारीः ॥
(ऋग्वेदः, 8.48.4)

'O Chandrasoma! When we drink you, may you benefit us. May you be benevolent to us in the same manner as a father is to his son or a friend is to his friend. O praiseworthy Soma! You are steady, hence bestow us long life, and make our life longer.

इमे मा पीता यशस उरुष्यवो रथं न गावः समनाह पर्वसु।
ते मा रक्षन्तु विस्रसश्चरित्रादुत मा स्रामाद्यवयन्त्विन्दवः ॥
(ऋग्वेदः, 8.48.5)

'This Soma that is glorious, and protects us, when imbibed it makes the joints of my body as strong as a bull's that pulls a chariot. O Soma, make my weak legs strong and free from disease.

अग्निं न मा मथितं संदिदीपः प्रचक्षय कृणु हि वस्यसो नः ।
अथा हिते मद आसोममन्ये रेवां इव प्रचरा पुष्टिमच्छ ॥
(ऋग्वेदः, 8.48.6)

'O, Soma! make me resplendent as the shining Agni, make me luminous and wealthy. O Soma! In bliss, I invoke you to come strolling like a wealthy person and nourish us.

इषिरेण ते मनसा सुतस्य भक्षीमहि पित्र्यस्येव रायः ।
सोमराजन्प्रण आयूँषि तारीरहानीव सूर्यो वासराणि ॥
(ऋग्वेदः, 8.48.7)

'O Soma, extracted with a willing mind! May we enjoy you in the similar way as a son enjoys his father's wealth. O splendid Soma! As the sun expands the life-affirming days, may you extend our life.

सोमराजन्मृडयानः स्वस्ति तव स्मसि व्रत्या स्तस्य विद्धि ।
अलर्ति दक्ष उत मन्युरिन्दो मानो अर्यो अनुकामं परा दाः ॥
(ऋग्वेदः, 8.48.8)

'O splendid Soma! Make us happy for our welfare. We are going to observe fast, consider as your own. O Chandrasoma! Bestow on us competence and *sattvika krodha* (righteous anger). Do not subordinate us to the enemies [in other words, make us stronger than the enemies].

त्वं हि नस्तन्व: सोमगोपा गात्रे गात्रे निषसत्था नृचक्षा: ।
यत्ते वयं प्रमिनाम व्रतानि सनो मृड सुषखा देववस्य: ।।
(ऋग्वेद:, 8.48.9)

'O Soma! You are the guardian of our bodies. The one who inspects human beings, you enter each limb of our bodies in order to provide power. Though we violate your laws, may you, like a good friend, make us happy.

ऋदूदरेण सख्या सचेय यो मा नरिष्येद्धर्यस्व पीत: ।
अयं य: सोमो न्यधाय्यस्मे तस्मा इन्द्रं प्रतिरमेम्यायु: ।।
(ऋग्वेद:, 8.48.10)

'O Indra, the one with the best horses! May I obtain the friendship of Soma that can be digested easily, and would not cause sorrow on being drunk. I pray to Indra that through Soma that has entered our bodies, he provides us with long life.

अपत्या अस्थुरनिरा अमी वा निरत्रसन्तमिषीचीरमैषु: ।
आ सोम अस्माँ अरुह द्विहाया अगन्म यत्र प्रतिरन्त आयु: ।।
(ऋग्वेद:, 8.48.11)

'We have obtained this great Soma, so make our debilitating diseases go away. May those diseases that have given us pain and suffering go away and we go only there where Soma enhances life.

यो न इन्दु: पितरो हृत्सुपीतोऽमर्त्या मर्त्या आविवेश ।
तस्मै सोमाय हविषा विधेम मृलीके अस्य सुमतौ स्याम ।।
(ऋग्वेद:, 8.48.12)

'O ancestors! That immortal Soma which on being drunk has entered our mortal bodies, we worship that same Soma through oblations. May we attain the best intellect in its worship.

त्वं सोम पितृभि: संविदानोऽनुद्यावा पृथिवी आ ततन्थ ।
तस्मै त इन्द्रो हविषा विधेम वयं स्याम पतयो रयीणाम् ।।
(ऋग्वेद:, 8.48.13)

'O, Soma! You, accompanied by the sages, expand the Dyauloka and Prithviloka. O Chandrasoma! We offer oblations while worshiping you. May we become masters of wealth.

त्रातारो देवा अधि वोचता नो मा नो निद्रा ईशत मोतजल्पिः ।
वयं सोमस्य विश्वह प्रियासः सुवीरासो विदथमा वदेम ।।
(ऋग्वेदः, 8.48.14)

'O guardian gods! Bestow on us advice so that we do not waste our time in laziness and useless babble. May we, with our exceptional sons and grandsons, become dear to Soma, and everyday sing invocations to it.

त्वं नः सोम विश्वतो वयोधास्त्वं स्वर्विदा विशा नृचक्षाः ।
त्वं नः इन्द ऊतिभिः सजोषाः पाहि पश्चात्तादुत वा पुरस्तात् ।।
(ऋग्वेदः, 8.48.15)

'O Chandrasoma! You are the one who provides us with food from everywhere. You are the one to know happiness and inspect human beings. May you enter inside us, and happily protect us with your guardianship.'

एवं कृत्नुर्भार्गवः सोममस्तौदूनाशीत्या वाष्टषष्ट्यामिते वा ।
सूक्ते सम्यङ् मण्डलस्याष्टमस्य प्रायः प्रोचुर्मण्डले वोत्तरेऽन्ये ।।218।।

In a similar manner, Kritnu Bhargava has also invoked Soma in the eighty-ninth and sixty-eighth mantras of eighth mandala in Rigveda. Likewise, Soma has been invoked in other sections also.

2.19 इन्द्रभवने प्रत्यहं त्रिंशतः सोमसरसाम् उपयोगः

2.19 THIRTY TYPES OF SOMA RASA IN INDRA'S PALACE

सोमलतारसपूर्णान्यासन् प्रातिस्विकानि शक्रस्य ।
गन्धर्वरक्षितानि त्रिंशत् स्वर्गे सरांसि क्लृप्तानि ॥219॥

In the heaven, there are thirty traditionally built pools guarded by the Gandharvas; these are Indra's personal pools which are filled with Soma.

ऐन्द्रे भुक्तिप्रमहे सहभुग् जनता बहुत्वतस्त्रिंशत् ।
सोमसरांसि निपीतान्येकोपक्रमतया भवन्ति स्म ॥220॥

At Indra's dinner, there would generally be thirty persons to dine with him and one by one, they would drink from these thirty Soma-filled pools.

एकया प्रतिधाऽपिबत् साकं सरांसि त्रिंशतम् ।
इन्द्रः सोमस्य काणुका ॥ (ऋग्वेदः, 8.66.4)

It is written in the Rigveda: 'This Indra drank Soma from thirty beautiful vessels at one go in one breath.'

सोमवल्लीस्वरूपम्

Descriptions of Soma creeper.

सुश्रुतचिकित्सितेऽपि च स चतुर्विंशतिविधो विनिर्दिष्टः ।
(सुश्रुतसंहिता, चिकित्सास्थानम्, 29.5.7)
वल्ली-प्रतानरूपा क्षुपरूपा वा भवेच्च सोमविधा ॥221॥

Even in the Suhsruta Samhita, there are twenty-four instructions given about Soma.

The Soma is of three kinds—*valli rupa* (one which appears like a creeper), one which appears like a *pratana rupa* (tendril) and one which appears like a small thorny bush.

पाङ्क्तत्रैष्टुभजागतगायत्राः सांकराश्च काश्मीरे ।
क्षुद्रकसरसि प्राप्या गिरिषु वितस्तोत्तरेषु चन्द्राख्यः ॥222॥

In the Kashmir region, various species of Soma like Pandakth, Trayshtubha, Jagat, Gayatra, and other mixed class of species are found. On the mountain north to Vitasta river, in small ponds named Kshudraka and others, Soma-valli called Chandra is found.

अपि मुञ्जवान् स शैले मुञ्जवतीहांशुमानयं गिरिषु ।
अपि शर्यणावदादिषु गरुडः श्वेताक्ष इत्याद्याः ॥223॥

On the mountain named Munjavana, in the river named Munjavati, grows Anshumana Soma. On Sharyyanavada and other mountains, Soma named Garuda and Shvetaksha are found.

अलवर्ज नामतो यं पर्वतमाचक्षते म्लेच्छाः ।
सोमस्तत्र च लभ्यत इत्येवं प्रायशः ख्यातिः ॥224॥

It is well-known that on the mountain that the mlecchas call Alavarj, Soma is found in plenty.

सोमे श्वेतं क्षीरं प्रवर्तते मूलगः कन्दः ।
रस एतस्यास्वादुः श्वेतः पीतोऽथ चित्रपृश्निश्च ॥225॥

The milky juice of soma-lata is white, and the plant has a bulb in its root which is of different colours, often white and yellow, but it is not good to taste.

सोमलताया दण्डे पञ्चदशैवच्छदा भवन्ति स्म ।
पञ्चदशाहं स्थित्वा ध्रुवं व्यशीर्यन्त षोडशेऽहनि ते ॥226॥

On its stalk, the soma-lata has only fifteen leaves. These leaves stay on the branches for fifteen days and fall on the sixteenth day, without fail.

दर्शे पर्णाभावः प्रतिपदि पूर्णोद्गमोऽन्वधः पर्व ।
प्रतितिथि पर्णोद्गमनात् पूर्णायां पञ्चदश तानि ॥227॥

On the first day of the amavasya, the stalk of the creeper would look completely bare as it would bore no leaves. On the first day of the lunar fortnight, *pratipada*, leaves would begin to appear; on every lunar day, a new leaf would be born so that by *purnima* [the full moon day], there would be fifteen leaves on the stalk.

प्रतिपद्यधरे पर्वणि पर्णनिपातः क्रमादुपर्येवम् ।
दर्शे पर्णाभावो ज्योतिष्मन्त्यस्य पर्णानि ॥228॥

Starting from the first day of the lunar fortnight, which falls after the full moon, the leaves are lost in a sequence, and on the first day of the new moon, the plant is bereft of leaves. The leaves of this Soma creeper are bright and shining.

सोमरसोऽयं पीतो दिव्यां दृष्टिं मनोगता कुरुते ।
भूतं भव्यं चार्थं दूरपरोक्षं च दर्शयति ।।229।।

On drinking, this Soma juice bestows *divya drishti* (extraordinary sight) as desired by the one who drinks it. It enables one to view past and future, and observe meaning of remote objects.

सर्वे नूनं मादका: शीर्ष्णि दोषानुत्पाद्यालं घ्नन्ति बुद्धे: प्रभावम् ।
सोमस्त्वेको मादक: पीयमान: शीर्ष्ण: सर्वान्नाशयत्याशु दोषान् ।।230।।

All other intoxicating substances destroy the intellect by producing faults in the brain, but Soma is the only substance that immediately destroys such imperfections when imbibed.

मस्तिष्काङ्गं पोषयन्नेष सोमो ब्राह्मं वीर्यं क्षात्रवीर्योपपन्नम् ।
सृष्ट्वा सूते शिल्पविज्ञानविद्या: सोमस्तस्मादोषधीनामधीश: ।।231।।

This Soma, while nourishing parts of the brain, creates great vigour and enhances creativity.

2.19.1 ब्रह्मवीर्यम्

2.19.1 Brahmavirya

ब्राह्मे वीर्ये योगजा: सिद्धय: स्यु: सूक्ष्मेऽप्यर्थे भाति विज्ञानमग्र्यम् ।
धृत्युत्कर्ष: स्यात् स्थितप्रज्ञता वा शान्तिर्देवी संपदत्राऽनृशंस्यम् ।।232।।

In brahmavirya, one attains several siddhis and becomes aware of even the most subtle elements of *sreshtajnana* (superior knowledge). The self attains concentration, righteousness and patience. Extraordinary peace is gained from Soma; in other words, extraordinary qualities are produced, and compassion rises forth in the self by drinking Soma.

सोमध्वंसाद् ब्रह्मवीर्यापध्वंस: ।

The destruction of brahmavirya with the destruction of Soma.

ब्राह्मं वीर्यं भाति विज्ञानहेतो: सूर्योपास्ते: सोमपेयाच्च यज्ञात् ।
ब्राह्माद् वीर्यात् त्वेषु सक्ति: प्रवृत्ति: ब्राह्मं वीर्यं सर्वसिद्धेरुपाय: ।।233।।

The brahmavirya is attained through vijnana, worship of surya, drinking of Soma, and by performing yajna. On the other hand, it is due to brahmavirya that these come forth and gain strength. Therefore, brahmavirya is the propitiator of all powers.

यद्वद्दासैर्नाशितं सूर्यचक्रं तद्वद्दैत्यैर्नाशिता सोमवल्ली ।
भूमिः कृत्स्ना दानवैस्तैर्जितेयं हन्तेदानीं ब्रह्मवीर्यं निरस्तम् ।।234।।

In the same way as the suryachakra was destroyed by a group of asuras, another group of asuras destroyed the Soma plant. The entire land was won over by the asuras. It is said that in this period brahmavirya too was destroyed.

विड्वीर्यात्तु क्षात्रवीर्यं वरेण्यं क्षात्राद्वीर्याद् ब्राह्मवीर्यं वरेण्यम् ।
ब्राह्मं शास्तृ क्षात्रविड्वीर्ययोः स्याद् विड्वीर्यस्य क्षात्रवीर्यं प्रशास्तृ ।।235।।

Kshatravirya (virility of a warrior) is superior to *vidvirya* (vaishyavira), brahmavirya is superior to kshatravirya and vidvirya; kshatravirya rules over vidvirya.

विड्वीर्यात्तु तु प्रायशोऽस्त्यत्र लभ्यं भूयांसो वै सन्ति लोके विशस्ताः ।
तासां शास्तृ क्षत्रमत्यल्पमाप्यं राजा ह्येको भूयसीनां प्रशास्ता ।।236।।

Vidvirya is, usually, found in great abundance on earth but their superior, kshatravirya is scarce as one king rules over a large number of citizens.

यावत्क्षत्रं किञ्चिदस्तीह लोके तस्मादेतद् ब्राह्मवीर्यं कनीयः ।
नाना क्षत्रं शास्ति हि ब्राह्मणोऽसावेकः कश्चिद् यो गुरुः क्षत्रियाणाम् ।।237।।

Whatever the number of kshatravirya be in this world, brahmavirya is even less, because one brahmavirya alone rules over many kshatravirya-s and is the guru of kshatriyas.

किन्तु ब्रूमो भूयसाल्पं विनष्टं कर्त्तुं शक्यं वस्तुधर्मस्तथास्ति ।
साध्यं श्रेयो दूरमस्तीति मन्दं सिद्धात् पापाद्धन्यते वा सदेशात् ।।238।।

But we say that the one with the strength of large numbers destroys the one with fewer numbers. It is because that is reality. Noble actions are possible but difficult. The fruits of virtue are slow in coming but that of sin is fast and tangible.

क्षुद्रश्चन्द्रः सूर्यमेतं महान्तं खग्रासे हि च्छादयन् संतनोति ।
ध्वान्तं सूर्यज्योतिषः स्यान्निरोधास्तद्वद् ब्राह्मं क्षात्रतोऽभूद्विनष्टम् ।।239।।

This moon is small, and the sun is great and glorious. The moon, the smaller form of the sun, gets concealed during the solar eclipse, and spreads darkness. With the concealment of the sun, its light is also lost. In this way, brahmavirya is destroyed by higher kshatravirya.

अग्नेर्जातो वर्द्धितो रक्षितोऽस्माद् अग्नी रक्षत्येषु वंशप्रकाण्डः ।
तत्रैवान्यो घर्षजन्माऽग्निरुग्रं शान्तं चाग्निं वंशमप्याशु हन्ति ।।240।।

Like the bamboo wood, brahmavirya is born out of agni; it matures due to agni, which also guards it. But agni, born out of friction, which is more aggressive, immediately destroys the cool bamboo wood despite being *agnisvarupa* (a form similar to fire).

2.20 सूर्यार्थे देवानां दस्युभिः संग्रामः

2.20 DEVA-DASYU CONFLICT FOR SURYA

तत्र विज्ञानौपयिके सूर्येऽसुरप्रेरितानां दासानाम् आक्रमणम् ।

Provoked by the asuras, the dasas attack the surya suited for vijnana.

देवानामिह सूर्यादुदगाद् वैज्ञानिकः प्रभावः सः ।
सौमिकयज्ञवशात् ते प्रापुर्लोकातिगां भूतिम् ।।241।।

The devas gained scientific knowledge through the sun and with the Soma yajna, they gained fame in the world.

बलिनोऽसुरास्त एते महाविभूतिं महाप्रभावं च ।
देवानामिह दृष्ट्वा यज्ञं कर्तुं यतन्ते स्म ।।242।।

Witnessing the great powers and influence of the devas, these strong asuras also decided to perform yajna.

विज्ञानदुर्बलत्वादप्रारयन्तस्तु ते यज्ञे ।
विज्ञानोदयनार्थं सूर्येऽस्मिन्नाक्रमन्ते स्म ।।243।।

But, because of their ignorance about the science and process of this ritual, the asuras met with failure and in protest they attacked the sun which, according to the asuras, was the source of strength of the devas.

सूर्यः पृथ्व्यां चक्रद्वयरूपः कश्चिदासीत् प्राक् ।
देवैर्विनिर्मितस्तं हर्तुं दासान् न्ययोजयन्नसुराः ।।244।।

In the olden times, there was a surya with two wheels on prithvi created by the devas; the asuras employed dasas to abduct this surya.

यद्देवदासीयनियोधनं तद् यैर्यत्र येषामभवद् यदर्थम् ।
तज्ज्ञायते वेदवचोऽवधानात् तत्किंचिदत्रापि निदर्शयामः ।।245।।

This triggered a battle between the devas and dasas, the details of which are in the vedic hymns and some of which is mentioned here.

प्राक् स्वर्णरं सप्तगुमभ्यवोचद् वैकुण्ठ इन्द्रः प्रमहेऽमराणाम् ।
स्वं कात्स्न्र्यतो जीवनकर्म तस्मिन् अवर्णयद्दासकुलैः स्वयुद्धम् ।।246।।

In olden times, in the festival of devas in heaven, Vaikunta [Indra] narrated to Manavasaptagu the deeds of his life, and his battle with dasas in that life.

2.20.1 दासानां त्रैविध्यम्

2.20.1 Three types of dasas

स एष दासस्तु न देव आसीन्न दानवो नापि मनुष्य आसीत् ।
आर्यैर्द्विषन् कश्चिदनार्यः पृथग्वदेवैष विभाग आसीत् ।।247।।

This dasa Dasakula was neither a deva nor an asura. He was not even a human being. He was of a different class and had only malice for the Arya.

बर्बरभिन्नाः सभ्या आर्या दासा इति द्विविधाः ।
आर्या बहुधा भिन्ना देवपितृप्रभृतयः कथिताः ।।248।।

The Arya were markedly distinct from this savage and cruel class. The people who were civilized and sober than dasas were divided into two groups. The Aya were of innumerable types, who were known as deva and pitra.

सभ्येष्वेकेऽनार्या जात्या दासा हि दस्यवो वृत्त्या ।
चौर्याद्भयाच्च दैन्यात् पलाय्य दासा उपक्षयिणः ।।249।।

अमनुष्याश्च मनुष्य इत्थं दासा अमी द्विविधाः ।
भारतवर्षाभिजना वन्यनिषादा मनुष्यदासाः स्युः ।।250।।

Among the civilized, some were from the non-Arya class, who were called the dasas and they were dasyus by nature. Reduced to a miserable state by stealing, fear and poverty, these dasas divided themselves into two groups, humans and non-humans. In other words, they became dasas of two types. Among these were forest-dwelling people in Bharatavarsha like Nishada-s.

तेषामार्यैः साकं क्वापि कदापि श्रुतं न युद्धमिदम् ।
नैते जिता न चैते भारतवर्षान्निराकृता न हताः ।।251।।

Any war between the Arya and these human dasas have not been heard of. They were either won over, or were pushed out of Bharatavarsha.

दस्युनियुद्धादस्मात् प्रागेवैषां बहोः कालात् ।
सहवासोऽनार्याणमार्याणां भारतीयानाम् ।।252।।

From a long time, prior to the dasyu-war, the Arya and non-Arya had lived together.

मनुना स्मृतौ त एते स्मर्यन्तेऽद्यापि दृश्यन्ते ।
भारतवर्षबहिःस्थास्त्वमनुष्या गिरिचरा दासाः ।।253।।

In the Manusmriti, Acharya Manu has recounted the presence of the forest-dwelling human dasas. Even today, people who look identical to the human dasas dwell on the mountains in the outer regions of Bharatavarsha.

तेषां प्रभवं प्रकृतिं भेदान् वसतीश्च युद्धसंस्थानम् ।
तदभिज्ञानविशेषानत ऊर्ध्वं दर्शयिष्यामः ।।254।।

The birth, nature, type, abode, and warfare, identification marks of these dasas is mentioned here.

2.20.1.1 अमनुष्यदासानां प्रभवः

2.20.1.1 Non-human dasas

ते दशधा भिन्ना अमीषु भूतगणाः ।
आसन्नेके तेऽपि द्विविधाः सभ्या असभ्याश्च ।।255।।

The *devayoni*-s (extraordinary beings) are divided in such a way that some of them are *bhuta*-s who, in turn, are of two types—*sabhya* (civilized) and *asabhya* (uncivilized). Ten devayonis are described in the Puranas: vidyadhara, apsara, yaksha, rakshasa, gandharva, kinnar, pishacha, guhyaka, siddha and bhuta.

सभ्यनिकाये भुक्ता आर्यनिदेशानुकारिणः सभ्याः ।
ये विपरीता एभ्योऽसभ्यास्ते दस्यवोऽपगणाः ।।256।।

Those who lived in a society, and followed the directions of the Arya were civilized. Those who disobeyed them were uncivilized, and belonged to the inferior dasyu class.

प्रमथप्रमुखा बहवो गणाः सुराणां तु सैनिका आसन् ।
उत्सवसङ्केताद्याः केऽपि गणाः भारते कथिताः ।।257।।
(महाभारतम्, सभापर्व, 27)

There were many *ganas* (groups or tribes) whose chief was Pramatha. They were soldiers of the devas. A few ganas like Utsava and Sanketa find mention in the Mahabharata. They have been described in the twenty-sixth chapter of the Sabha-parva of the epic.

एभ्यो ये विपरीता लुठच्चरास्तेऽपरीतयः प्रोक्ताः ।
मन्ये त एव साम्प्रतमफरीदीत्याख्ययाख्याताः ।।258।।

Those who rebelled against the norms, and became bandits, came to be called *apariti* (rebels). I believe today they are known by the name Afridi.

हीरोदोतस एवान्-अपरीतईत्येवमाचष्ट
तस्मात् पूर्वयुगेऽमी अपरीयत एवं चाख्याताः ।।259।।

A writer named Hirodotus has called these people aparitayi. In times, prior to this, they were called apariti.

युद्धस्थलान्न येषां परिच्युतिस्तेऽपरीतयः सुदृढ़ाः ।
परिगलितं यन्न स्यादपरीतत्वं श्रुतं तस्य ।।260।।

Why were they given the name 'apariti'? In this context, it is said—those who did not face defeat or expulsion and remained strong were called apariti. That which does not melt or flow, that which does not drip is called and heard as aparitatva.

विश्वमना वैयश्वोऽप्रतिरुद्धं वक्तुमिन्द्रबलम् ।
अपि गौतमः क्रतून् प्रतिरुद्धान् वक्तुमाह शब्दं तम् ।।261।।

Vaiyashva's son Vishvamana has used the word apariti for describing the unbound and superior strength of Indra and even Gautama has termed uninterrupted yajna as apariti.

इन्द्र यथा ह्यस्तितेऽपरीतं नृतो शवः ।
अमृताराति: पुरुहूत दाशुषे ।।

(ऋग्वेदः, 8.24.9)

It is written in the Rigveda: Great Indra! In the same way as your strength is limitless for the enemies; O Indra, who is invoked by many! Your gifts that you give to the donors are also indestructible.

आ नो भद्राः क्रतवो यन्तु विश्वतोऽदब्धासो अपरीतास उद्भिदः ।
देवानो यथा सदमिद् वृधे ।
असन्न प्रायुवो रक्षितारो दिवे दिवे ।।

(ऋग्वेदः, 1.89.1), (शुक्लयजुर्वेदः, 25.14)

May it be instilled in us, from all directions, actions that would give us prosperity and higher status, and not those that lead to ruin. May such devas who do not stop progress but rather give protection everyday enhance our growth.

अथवा ये प्रतिरुद्धाः परिच्युता आपरीतयस्ते स्युः ।
एषां वेश्म समन्तात् प्रतिरुद्धं चापरीतिनस्ते वा ।।262।।

The aparitis are those who are stopped or imprisoned, *pratirudha*; those who have absconded, and whose houses have been surrounded from all directions are aparitis.

दैवतरीत्यपकर्षादेषामरीतिता गणानां स्यात् ।
अपकृष्टत्वादेषामपगणशब्देन विश्रुतिश्चासीत् ।।263।।

Due to the degeneration of *daivata riti* (divine characteristics) there has been a complete loss of culture or *parititva* among these ganas, and because of their downfall, they became infamous as apagana.

त इमेऽफगाननाम्ना अफगन् नाम्ना च साम्प्रतं प्रथिताः ।
एषामेव तु वैदिकसमये दासत्वमुपपन्नम् ।।264।।

They are the same people who are presently known by the name Afghan and Afganna. It is reasonable to assume that they could have been the dasas during the Vedic period.

अमनुष्यदासप्रकृतिः ।

The nature of non-human dasas.

उग्रप्रकृतय आसन् एते हत्यापरायणाः क्रूराः ।
घोरा द्रुहश्च योद्धुं सन्नद्धाः स्वैरचर्याश्च ।।265।।

These non-human dasas are aggressive in nature, are expert killers, cruel, terrible, conspiring, always engaged in war, and obstinate.

अमनुष्यदासप्रभेदाः ।

Types of non-human dasas.

एषां बहवो भेदा अद्यत्वे चाभवन्नये ।
आसन् पुरापि बहवः साङ्कर्येण गण-नाग-दैत्यानाम् ।।266।।

The non-human dasas have been of various types, many of them were known to be present till now; their known types in the past were gana, naga, and the ones born from mixed daitya parentage.

अमनुष्यदासानां प्रमुखाः कतिपये वेदे नामतो निर्दिश्यन्ते ।

The description of major names of non-human dasas in the Vedas.

बहवः श्रेणय एषामेकैकश्रेणिनायको भिन्नः ।
प्रमुखा अराजकानां दासानां मन्त्रविश्रुताः केचित् ।।267।।

These non-human dasas had various ranks, each rank or class had a different leader. One usually hears a few mantras about these stateless dasas.

शंबरः कुयव-शुषण-पिप्रवाः पङ्गृभिः स्मदिभ-रोहिणाऽहयः ।
व्यंस-वेश-मृगया-इलीलिविशः-शूश्रुवांश्चमुरि-तुग्रकौ धुनिः ।।268।।

पर्वतनिवासिशंबर एवाममर्मोच्यते तुजिर्वर्ची ।
दस्यव एते दासा असुरा वृत्राश्च सर्व उच्यन्ते ।।269।।

The major names of these stateless dasas were: shambar, kuyava, sushana, piprava, pargrabhi, smadibha rohina, ahaya, vyansa, vesha, mrigya, ililivisha, sushruvana chamuri, tugraka and dhuni. Those who lived on the mountains were called shambar. These dasyu-dasas and people of vritta class were called the asuras.

अमनुष्ययदासानां हिमवत्प्रदेशे सिन्धुनदप्रान्ते निवासः ।

The habitation of non-human dasas in the Himalayan region and on the banks of Sindhu river.

हिमवति च हेमकूटे यावन्तः पादपर्वतास्तेषु ।
सिन्धुनदोत्तरभागे द्रोण्यां निवसन्ति दासगणाः ।।270।।

The dasas used to live on all the small hills in the Himalaya and Hemakut regions, and in the northern caves on the bank of Sindhu river.

गान्धारोत्तरसीम्नि च निषधात् प्राच्या य उज्जिहानदेशोऽस्ति ।
अद्यत्वे तं देशं म्लेच्छा आहुस्तु काफिरस्थानम् ।।271।।

The region by the name Ujjihana, which is on the northern border of Gandhara region and the eastern border of Nishadh mountain, is presently called 'Kafirsthana' by the mlecchas.

जाह्नवहाटकदेशौ सम्प्रति चित्राललद्दाखौ ।
कथितौ तत्र प्रान्ते दस्यव एते वसन्ति स्म ।।272।।

These dasas used to reside in Jahanvand Hataka regions, which are at present known as Chitral and Ladakh.

दुर्गमगिरिगहनेऽस्मिन् श्वेतागिरेः प्रागुपत्यकाप्रान्ते ।
विषमेऽङ्गणे निगूढे निवसन्ति स्मापरीतिनोऽपगणाः ।।273।।

The aparitis lived in Upatyaka (the western edge of Shvetagiri mountain) in the difficult and inaccessible Himalayas.

गान्धराद्या देशा आर्याणामथ च हेमकूटाद्याः ।
दासानामुभये ते विभिन्नसप्तनदवास्तव्याः ।।274।।

Place like Gandhara were home to the Arya and Hemakut to the dasas, and so these two classes used to live in different Saptanada regions.

2.20.1.1.1 सिन्धुनदप्रान्ते सप्तनदत्रयम्

2.20.1.1.1 Saptanada region near Sindhu

सिन्धौ तावत् सप्त स्रवन्त्यः संगच्छन्ते वामतो दक्षतश्च।
सिन्धौ प्राच्यामन्यदन्यत् प्रतीच्यां तस्योदीच्यां सङ्गमस्थानमन्यत् ।।275।।

Seven rivers that flow from the left and right directions got merged in the Sindhu river. There was a confluence of seven more rivers to the east of Sindhu, and another of seven more to its west.

प्रसप्त सप्त त्रेधा हि चक्रमुः प्रसृत्वरीणामतिसिन्धुरोजसा ।
त्रिः सप्त सस्रा नद्यः ।।
(ऋग्वेदः, 10.75.1)

With his vigour, Indra made seven different divisions of Sindhu, most superior of all rivers. In this way, twenty rivers flowed together.

त्रिः सप्त सस्रा नद्यो महीरपो वनस्पतीन् पर्वताँ अग्निमूतये ।
कृशानुमस्तॄन् तिष्यं सधस्थ आ रुद्रं रुद्रेषु रुद्रियं हवामहे ।।
(ऋग्वेदः, 10.64.8)

The Rigveda contains description of these seven rivers: Sarasvati, Sarayu, Sindhu, and other flowing rivers, great *jala* (water), vegetation and mountains and Gandharvas named Krishanu who protected Soma, Gandharvas who were archers and attendants, Pushya-nakshtra (constellation), *havibhargayogya* (capable of accepting havya) rudras, we call all these for the invocation of the best among the rudras.

अभि त्वा सिन्धो शिशुमिन्न मातरो वाश्रा अर्षन्ति पयसेव धेनवः ।
राजेव युध्वा नमसि त्वमित् सिचौ यदासामग्रं प्रवतामिनक्षसि ।।
(ऋग्वेदः, 10.75.4)

O Sindhu! Just as mothers come to their sons with love and cows go to their calves, similarly the rivers, making sound, flow in your direction. Like a warring king, you lead the rivers for irrigation and you flow ahead of these rivers.

2.20.1.1.1.1 पूर्वसप्तनदः

2.20.1.1.1.1 Eastern Saptanada region

इमं मे गङ्गे यमुने सरस्वति शुतुद्रि स्तोमं सचता परुष्ण्या ।
असिक्न्या मरुद्वृधे वितस्तयाऽऽर्जीकीये शृणुह्या सुषोमया ।।
(ऋग्वेदः, 10.75.5)

About the eastern parts of the Saptanada region, it is written in the Rigveda: O Gange, Yamune! Sarasvati! Shutudri! Parushini, Asikina Marudhvridhe! Vitasta Sushoma and Ajrikiye! Listen to us by accepting this hymn of ours!

इत्थं शतद्रुश्च इरावती च या चन्द्रभागा च विपाड् वितस्ता ।
ताभिः कृतः पञ्चनदप्रदेशः प्राच्यां स्थितः सप्तनदः स एव।।276।।

In this way, because of these five rivers—Shatadruscha, Iravati, Chandrabhaga, Vipad and Vithasta—this region to the east of Sindhu river is called Saptanada [east Saptanada].

2.20.1.1..1.2 पश्चिमसप्तनदः

2.20.1.1.1.2 Western Saptanada region

यद्वत्सिन्धोः प्राच्यां सप्तनदान्तर्गतोस्ति पञ्चनदः ।
तद्वत् ततः प्रतीच्यां सप्तनदे पञ्चगौरदेशोस्ति ।।277।।

Just as to the east of Sindhu, there is Punjab [a territory with five rivers] that lies within the Saptanada region, similarly the region has panchagaura territory to the west of the river.

तृष्टा मया प्रथमं यातवे सजूः सु सर्त्वा रसया श्वेत्या त्या ।
त्वं सिन्धो कुभया गोमती क्रुमुं मेहत्न्वा सरथं याभिरीयसे ।।
(ऋग्वेदः, 10.75.6)

It is written in the Rigveda: O Sindhu! You first coursed with Trishta river to assimilate the flowing Gomti river. Thereafter you unite with Susatru, Rasa Shveti, Kubha, and Mehantu rivers. And thereupon you move along, mounted on a horse accompanied by all these on a single chariot. (The confluence of these seven rivers takes place to the west of Sindhu, and, thereafter, they flow assimilated into one river.)

कुरम क्रमुर्गोमल गोमतीसिदुम् श्वेती कुभा काबुल उच्यतेऽधुना ।
रसा वुरिंडू च सुवात् सुसर्त्तुस्तृष्टां मिकोर्ध्वं गिलघिट सरिन्मता ।।278।।

Kuram, Kramu, Gomala, Gomti, Sindum, Shveti, and Kubha rivers are today said to be in Kabul. Apart from these, Rasa, Vurindu, Suvata, Susatru, Trishta, Mikodhrava, and Gilgit have been considered rivers.

मेहत्नूः स्याद् वर्णुनद्यो वमन्येयत्सम्बन्धाद् वर्णुदेशः प्रसिद्धः ।
वर्णुर्देशो दक्षिणे स्यात् कुभायास्तस्यास्तूदक् पञ्चगौरप्रदेशः ।।279।।

It is possible that Mehatnu river is Varnu river. I believe that it is the reason there is a well-known territory by the name Varnu. To the south of Kubha river is Varnudesha, and to its north is the panchagaura territory.

संगच्छते सुवास्तुर्यस्यां सा वास्तुरेकधा भूत्वा ।
संगच्छते कुभायां कुभा तु सिन्धौ समन्वेति ।।280।।

The Vastu river, joined by Suvastu river, unites with another river before it assimilates itself into Kubha river, and, finally, Kubha river joins and becomes part of Sindhu.

वास्तोः पश्चात् कुभया चित्राख्याऽन्वेति सा गौरी ।
जाह्नवी सा गङ्गा चित्रालो जाह्नवो देशः ।।281।।

To the west of Vastu, Chitra river meets Kubha, and it becomes Gauri. The Jahanvi river is Ganga, and the region called Chitrala is Jahanv region.

गाओरीति म्लेच्छा गौरी तामाहुरितरत्र ।
देशं च पञ्चगौरं वदन्ति ते पञ्चकोरेति ।।282।।

The mlecchas call this same Jahanvi river as Gaora river. And some other people call it Gauri river. Likewise, they call the panchagaura region as Panchakora.

सिन्धोरस्ति स पश्चात् हिर्मण्डाख्यां (हेलमण्ड) हिरण्वतीं यावत् ।
या अस्य पञ्चनद्यस्ता उक्ताभारते भैष्मे ।।283।।

The five rivers that flow till Hiranvati river [also known as Himmaranda or Helamanda], which is to the west of Sindhu river, are mentioned in the Bhishma-parva section of Mahabharata.

वास्तुं सुवास्तुं गौरीं च कम्पनां च हिरण्यवतीम् ।
वरां वीरकरां चापि पञ्चमीं च महानदीम् ।। (महाभारतम्, भीष्मपर्व, 1 0.14)

Vastu, Suvastu, Gauri, Kalpana, Hiranyavati, Vara, Virkara, and Mahanadi are rivers; the last [Mahanadi] is either the fifth, or part of another which is the fifth river, that is, Hiranyavati.

सश्वा सिन्धुः सुरथा सुवासा हिरण्यमयी सुकृता वाजिनीवती ।
ऊर्णवती युवतिः सीलनावत्यु ताधिवस्ते सुभगामधु वृधम् ।। (ऋग्वेदः, 10.76.8)

The river fields [irrigated land] are rich in horses, rich in chariots, rich in clothes, and rich in good ornaments. They are rich in food, rich in wool, rich in fiber grass, ever fresh. They are full of medicinal plants. This auspicious river irrigates honey-growing flowers.

2.20.1.1.1.3 उत्तरसप्तनदः

2.20.1.1.1.3 Northern Saptanada region

तत्पञ्चगौरदेशादुत्तरतोऽन्योऽस्ति सप्त नददेशः ।
कुलिशी च वीरपत्नी शिफाञ्जसीत्यादिभिः क्लृप्तः ।।284।।

Towards the west from the panchagaura territory, there is another Saptanada region, which has been described by Kulishi, Virapatni, and Shiphanjasi.

2.21 आर्यदासानां सप्तनदवासित्वम्

2.21 RESIDENCE OF ARYA-DASA IN SAPTANADA

परस्परतो युध्यमानानाम् आर्यदासानां पश्चिमोत्तरविभिन्नसप्तनदवासित्वम् ।

The abode of the warring class of arya and dasas in different north-eastern regions.

इत्थं सप्तनदेषु त्रिषु सिन्धोरुत्तरं तु सप्तनदम् ।
तद्दासानां स्थानं भारतवर्षाद्बहिश्चैतत् ।।285।।

In this way, of the three Saptanada regions, the one that lies to the west of Sindhu is the dwelling place of the dasas, and is outside Bharatavarsha.

सप्तनदे पुनरन्ये सिन्धोः पौरस्त्यपाश्चात्ये ।
ते द्वे भारतवर्षान्तर्भुक्ते वसतिरार्याणाम् ।।285।।

The two other Saptanada regions, to the north and west of Sindhu, are inside Bharatavarsha, and they are the dwelling place of the Arya.

पूर्वसप्तनदे दासकुलाभिजनासत्त्वात् तत्र युद्धाभावः ।

Absence of war in the east Saptanada region due to the absence of the dasas.

तेषु च सप्तनदेषु त्रिषु पूर्वस्मिन्नभूदिदं युद्धम् ।
इति पाश्चात्या आहुः प्रत्यगुदक्प्रान्तयोस्तु तद्ब्रूमः ।।286।।

The western scholars say that a war took place in each of the Saptanada regions in the olden times. But we believe that this war happened in the outer regions towards the west.

चित्रालदेशतो यः पूर्वोत्तरदेशगोऽस्ति सप्तनदः ।
तत्रत्यदस्युभिः सह पश्चिमसप्तनदवासिनां युद्धम् ।।287।।

The residents of Saptanada had a war with the dasyus of that Saptanada region which belongs to the territory west of Chitral.

द्विविधं युद्धमिहासीत् प्रथमं युद्धं तु दासकृतम् ।
उत्तरमिन्द्रकृतं तत् तदुभयमन्यान्यदेशेऽभूत् ।।288।।

Here, two types of war took place. The first war was fought by the dasas, and the second was at the behest of Indra. Both these wars were fought in some other territories, outside Bharata.

यत् प्राथमिकं युद्धं तदभूद्गान्धारदेशेऽस्मिन् ।
स्वस्थानस्थानार्यान् दस्यव एत्याभ्यमदर्दयंस्तत्र ॥289॥

The first war took place in the Gandhara territory. In this war, the dasyus came forth and crushed the resident Arya and inflicted extreme pain upon them.

यत्तु श्वेतगिरेः प्राग् मूजवतः पर्वतादपि प्रत्यक् ।
अभवद् द्वितीययुद्धं तत्राक्रम्यावधीद्धरिर्दस्यून् ॥290॥

The second attack and war took place to the west of Munjavana mountain, which lies to the east of Shvetagiri mountain. In this war, Indra, in an offensive mode, slaughtered the dasyus.

पश्चिमसप्तनदस्था आर्यास्ते स्थायिनो युद्धे ।
उत्तरसप्तनदस्था दस्यव इह यायिनः प्रथमे ॥291॥

The Arya, who lived in the east Saptanada region, remained stationed at their place during the war, while the dasyus of the north Saptanada region were the ones who kept travelling during that period.

पश्चात्तु दस्यवस्ते प्राप्तजयाः स्थायिनोऽभूवन् ।
इन्द्रो दीनसहायो यायी जयमाप्य कुत्समातस्थे ॥292॥

The dasyus, despite their defeat, stayed put and consolidated their position while Indra, after the victory, went away to protect Kutsa.

पूर्वस्मिंस्तु न कश्चित् सभ्योऽनार्योऽपि वात्र सप्तनदे ।
स्थायी यायी वाऽसीत् तस्माद् युद्धं न तत्राभूत् ॥293॥

In the east Saptanada region, neither the civilized Arya nor the non-Arya were stationary or on the move. That is why no war took place there.

उत्तरसप्तनदवासिनां दासानां भारतवर्षीयत्वाभावः ।

The fact that dasa residents of north Saptanada region are not the residents of Bharata.

उत्तरसप्तनदं यद्दासानां स्थानमेतच्च ।
भारतवर्षाद्बहिरिति दासा न हि भारतीयाः स्युः ।।294।।

The dwelling-places of the dasas,which was in the north Saptanada region, was outside Bharatavarsha. Therefore, the dasas were definitely not bharatiya.

2.22 भारतवर्षसीमाचतुष्टयी

2.22 BHARATAVARSHA'S FOUR BORDERS

एतद्भारतवर्षं रक्तसमुद्रान्तमस्ति पश्चिमतः ।
पीतसमुद्राश्लिष्टप्रशान्तसागरपरं प्राच्याम् ।।295।।

This Bharatavarsha reached till the end of Red Sea in the west, and, in the east, it stretched till Pacific Ocean, which adjoined Pita or *Pila Sagara* (the Yellow Sea) or the South China Sea.

याम्ये समुद्रमध्ये विषुवान्तं तत् यथोदीच्याम् ।
हिमवत्पर्वतपरमं प्रवदीन्तीत्थं चतुःसीमम् ।।296।।

In the south, it extended till the Equatorial Line that existed in the middle of the Indian Ocean, and in the north, it stretched till the Himalayas. In this way, this Bharatavarsha had four borders.

त्रैलोक्यस्य विभागे त्वेतद्वर्षं हि मानुषो लोकः ।
स इरावतीविनिर्गमदेशादर्वाग् निरूपितः पूर्वैः ।।297।।

The ancient scholars, in their *trailokyavibhajana* (three-fold division of the world), have described this Bharatavarsha as falling in the manushyaloka. It was said to be situated at the outlet of Iravati river.

पश्चादष्टमतोंऽशात् पूर्व्यं यावत्तु सप्तदशमंशम् ।
भारतवर्षं ब्रुवते सा सीमा राजशासनस्याद्य।।298।।

Later, scholars described Bharatavarsha to be located 17° east and 8° to the west. This location is identical to that of the present-day territorial border.

पूर्वे किराता यवनाश्च पश्चिमे याम्ये समुद्रो हिमशैल उत्तरे ।
पौराणिका इत्थमनेकधाऽब्रुवन् तद्भारतं सीमचतुष्टयं कृतम् ।।299।।

In the Puranas and Pauranikas, while describing the four borders of Bharatavarsha, it has been said many a time: 'This is Bharatavarsha, to the east of which lies Kirata, to its west is Yavana, ocean (southern ocean) is to its south, and to its north lies the Himalayas.'

पूर्वसमुद्रारब्धो रक्तसमुद्रान्तविस्तृतो देशः ।
भारतवर्षं ज्ञेयं पूर्वापरतो नवत्यंशैः ।।300।।

Starting from the ocean in the east and stretching till the Red Sea is the country of Bharatavarsha.

प्राग् मेरुकर्णिकस्य हि भूपद्मस्यास्य सन्ति पत्राणि ।
चत्वारि दिक्षु चतसृषु क्लृप्तानि समं नवत्यंशैः ।।301।।

This country that exists to the east of Pragmerukarnika has four plates or *patra*-s, which have been mapped in all four directions. [According to the ancient borders of this desha, in the four directions of Bharatavarsha, from 90° to 90°, Bhadrashvavarsha, Kuruvarsha, Ketumalavarsha, and Lankapuri have been described in the given order. The elaborate description is given in the earlier chapter on Simaprasanga.]

नववर्षाणि यदानीं कल्प्यन्ते भूतलस्यास्य ।
तर्ह्यपि भारतवर्षं दक्षिणतः स्यान्नवत्यंशम् ।।302।।

Bharatavarsha was mapped upto 90° in the south when the earth had nine continents.

क्लृप्ता तु मध्यरेखा मेरुस्पृग् भारते वर्षे ।
तस्याः प्रागपि पश्चाच्चत्वारिंशच्च पञ्च चांशाः स्युः ।।303।

The intermediary line that touches Meru-parvata [Meru mountain] has been located in Bharatavarsha, and to the 45° east and west of this line lies this country.

2.23 भारतवर्षस्य ऐन्द्रवारुणाभ्यां पूर्वपश्चिमाभ्यां विभागः

2.23 DIVISION OF BHARATAVARSHA INTO EAST AS AINDRA AND WEST AS VARUNA

तत्सिन्धुना विभक्त ।। तत्रैन्द्रं भारतं पूर्वम् ।
तत्पश्चिमं तु भारतमस्तीदं वारुणं विद्यात् ।।304।।

That Bharatavarsha which was to the east of Sindhu river, that Aindra (follower of Indra) was Bharata. That part of Bharatavarsha, which was west to Sindhu, was Varuna (related to Varuna), and should be considered Bharata.

भूमध्यसागरात् प्राक् सिन्धोः प्रत्यक् समुद्रतस्तूदक् ।
आरालकाश्यपीयनजलधिभ्यां दक्षिणो यावान् ।।305।।

एतं देशं ब्रुवते म्लेच्छजना ओरियंसशब्देन ।
तदिदं भारतवर्षं वारुणमासीत् पुरायुगे मन्ये ।।306।।

The area that lies to the east of the Mediterranean Sea, to the west of Sindhu, to the north of ocean [southern ocean], and to the south of Arala and Kashyipana (Caspian) seas, is called Oriyansa by the mlecchas but I believe that in the ancient time, this was Varuna Bharatavarsha.

वारुणभारतभागे न्यवसन् प्राधेयगन्धर्वाः ।
गन्धर्वदेश एव प्रथते गान्धारनाम्ना सः ।।307।।

The Gandharvas dominated in this Varuna Bharatavarsha. It was this Gandharvadesha which came to be called Gandhara.

वर्णुश्च पञ्चगौरो जाह्नव एवोज्जिहानश्च ।
हाटक एवं बहवो गान्धारे पूर्वतो देशाः ।।308।।

To the east of Gandhara lay several countries like Varnu, Panchagaura, Jahanav, Ujjihana and Hataka.

मद्रा उत्तरमद्रा गान्धारेभ्यः स्युरुत्तरे पश्चात् ।
उत्तरमद्रा देशा मिदिया मादेति वोदिता म्लेच्छैः ।।309।।

To the north of Gandhara were countries like Madra and Uttara-Madra. At some point of time, these Uttara-Madra countries were called Midia and Madha by the mlecchas.

अप्येत आरियाना दक्षिणमद्रास्तु पारसेत्युक्ताः ।
उभयविधा अपि मद्रा भारतवर्षस्य पश्चिमा देशाः ।।310।।

In the same way, the South Madra region was called Ariyana and Paras. Thus both Madra countries were situated on the west of Bharatavarsha.

गान्धार-मद्रदेशे सिन्धुनदात् पश्चिमे भागे ।
यवन-म्लेच्छाक्रमणादार्यास्तत्राल्पशोऽद्य निवसन्ति ।।311।।

Due to frequent attacks carried out by the Yavanas and mlecchas, there were fewer Arya in the Gandhara-Madra region, located on the western margin of Sindhu river.

2.24 पश्चिभारते गान्धारदेशे दासकृतं प्रथमं युद्धम्

2.24 FIRST WAR BY DASAS IN GANDHARA, WEST OF BHARATAVARSHA

दस्युनियुद्धात् प्राक् त्विह सिन्धोः प्राच्यां प्रतीच्यां च ।
भारतवर्षीयार्या न्यूषुर्युद्धप्रतीच्येषु ।।312।।

Before the war imposed by the dasyus, the Arya used to reside in this region, which was to the east and west of Sindhu river. During that time, the war took place in the western parts.

गान्धारे तु वसन्तोऽनार्या वार्याः पुरा वृचीवन्तः ।
आर्यस्य चायमानस्यासन् विद्वेषिणस्तत्र ।।313।।

In the early times, the Arya and non-Arya used to live in Gandhara. These non-Arya were the descendants of *Vrichivana* (literally, those who walked on a crooked path). They hated the Arya, who were descendants of *Chayamana* (the superior one who performed the best deeds).

हरियूपीया नद्याः कूले यव्यावती नगरी ।
तस्यां वरशिख आसीद् वृचीवतः कस्यचित् कुलजः ।।
(ऋग्वेदः, 6.27.5-6)

There was a town called Hariyupiya, which was on the bank of Yavyavati river. In this town, Varshikha, who was the descendant of one Vrichivana, used to live.

त्रिंशं शतं त आसन् वीराः प्रथिता वृचीवन्तः ।
अभ्यावर्त्यभिधस्याभिघातिनश्चायमानस्य ।।314।।

It has been said that Vrichivana, who had 3,000 valorous soldiers, was a mortal enemy of a Chayamana named Abhyavarti, who was the son of Chayamana.

अन्ये तु हेमकूटद्रोण्यावासा लुठच्चरा दासाः ।
गन्धारमद्रदेशे न्यपीडयन्निवसतो हि गन्धर्वान् ।।315।।

There was another kind of dasas, who were robbers and lived in the caves of the Hemakut mountain. They lived in the Gandhara-Madra region and tormented the Gandharvas.

भारतवर्षबहि:स्था दासा आक्रम्य पीडयन्ति स्म ।
चिरकालादिह भारतवर्षे वसतो नृपानार्यान् ।।316।।

In the olden times, the dasas living outside Bharatavarsha kept on tormenting the Arya kings who lived through numerous attacks.

गान्धारेऽस्मिन्देशे सिन्धुप्रान्तस्थकुत्सनृपराष्ट्रे ।
अपगणदस्युभिरासीदार्याणां मन्त्रविश्रुतं युद्धम् ।।317।।

In the Gandhara region, in the outer areas close to Sindhu river, in the country ruled by King Kutsa, the Arya had a war with the inferior dasyus, which is described in the hymns.

सिन्धोः पश्चिमदेशे पुरायुगादद्यपर्यन्तम् ।
या गान्धारपुरीयं तदुपह्वरतोऽर्जुनी तु नदी ।।318।।

In the region close to the Gandhara town, which lies to the west of Sindhu river and has existed since ancient times, there flows a river called Arjuni.

अर्जुन्याः सरितोऽस्या अर्गन्दारेति नाम च ब्रुवते ।
अद्यत्वे म्लेच्छाद्याः, सैव स्यादर्जुनीधारा ।।319।।

The mlecchas of the present-age address this very Arjuni river by the name 'Argandara'.

कूलेऽर्जुन्या नद्या या नगरी वेतसूस्तया क्लृप्तः ।
कश्चिज्जनपद आसीत् तत्र नृपोऽभूत् कथं रुरुर्नाम ।।320।।

On the bank of this Arjuni river was a town called 'Vetasu'; there lived a community whose king was someone named 'Kanthamruru.'

पुत्रोऽस्य कुत्स आसीद् गन्धर्वः शिक्षितः स विद्यायाम् ।
सिन्धुप्रान्तनिवासिभिरभूद् वसिष्ठश्रुतर्याद्यैः ।।321।।

The son of this Kanthamruru was a Gandharva named Kutsa. He was educated in various disciplines by teachers like Vasishta and Shrutyarya who lived in the outer regions along Sindhu.

दभीतितुर्वीतिमुखाः परेऽपि स्युस्तस्य सामन्तनृपा अधीनाः ।
यतोऽर्जुनीसंनिहितोऽस्य वासस्ततः स कुत्सो मत आर्जुनेयः ।।322।।

There were other major kings who were subservient to this Kutsa. Since he used to reside near Arjuni river, he came to be known as Kutsa Arjuneya.

याभिः कुत्समार्जुनेयं शतक्रतू प्र तुर्वीतिं प्र च दभीतिमावतम् ।
याभिर्ध्वसन्तिं पुरुषन्तिमावतं ताभिरूषु ऊतिभिरश्विनागतम् ॥
(ऋग्वेदः, 1.112.23)

It is also written in the Rigveda, 'O Shatkrato [the doer of hundreds of deeds], Ashvidevo! With the power you protect the sons of Arjuni—Kutsa, Turviti, Dabhiti, Dhvansati, and Purushanti—come to us here accompanied with the same protective powers.'

यत्त्वार्जुनेयस्य पदस्य सायणो ब्रूतेऽर्थमिन्द्रस्य हि पुत्रमित्यपि ।
न साधु मन्ये तदमुष्य सख्यता त्विन्द्रेण कुत्सस्य न पुत्रता श्रुता ॥323॥

Sayana has described the meaning of the word 'Arjuneya' as 'Indra's son,' but we do not accept this, because Indra was a friend of Kutsa, and he was not his son.

'मरुत्वन्तं सख्याय हवामहे' इत्येवन्तं कुत्स ऊचे सखायम् ।
सखायं कृत्वा कुत्समिन्द्रः प्रतस्थे हन्तुं कुत्सद्वेषिणो दस्युसङ्घान् ॥324॥

'We call Marutvana [Indra] for friendship'—with such statement, the friendship of Kutsa and Indra has been indicated. By calling Kutsa as his friend, Indra proceeded to slaughter Kutsa's enemies.

यद्वाऽर्जुन्या स्याज्जनन्याऽऽर्जुनेयो यद्वाऽर्जुन्या स्याद्वसत्यार्जुनेयः ।
अश्विस्तुत्यामिन्द्रसम्बन्धिताया आख्यानं स्यादिन्द्रदस्रावमत्यै ॥325॥

He came to be called 'Arjuneya,' as he was the son of Arjuni, or he was so called because his residence was near the Arjuni river. Perhaps, in the Asivastuti of Rigveda, Indra's relationship has been narrated in order to insult him and the ashvin kumars.

ध्वंसन्ति तुर्वीतिदभीति भूपतीन् कुत्सानुगान् प्राक् पुरुषन्तिनाऽन्वितान् ।
न्यपीडयन्दस्युगणाः पुरायुगे ररक्षतुः शक्रनियोगतोऽश्विनौ ॥326॥

In ancient times, the asuras tormented the followers of Kutsa like Turviti and Dabhiti kings as well as some other kings including Purushanita; on the orders of Indra, the Ashvidevas gave them protection from the asuras.

परमतनिरासेन सिद्धान्तस्थापनम् ।

The establishment of siddhanta by refuting others' views.

अद्याप्येते दस्यवः सिन्धुपारे चित्रप्रान्ते गूहितान्तर्निकेताः ।
दृश्यन्ते ये पश्चिमोदक्प्रदेशे सभ्यान् लोकान् पीडयन्ति प्रसह्य ।।327।।

Across the river Sindhu, in Chitra, people of the asura class live in hiding even today; these people forcefully torment the civilized people of north-western region.

एतानेव प्रोद्धतान् वृत्तिमाप्तान् भीष्मान् दस्यून् दण्डयामास धृष्टान् ।
एत्य स्वर्गात् सोऽमरावत्यधीशः प्रत्यावृत्तः स्वर्गमेवाभ्यगात् सः ।।328।।

These haughty, impudent, and dreadful asuras, who had flourished, were in turn tormented and punished by the master of Amaravati, who came forth for this purpose. Thereafter, Indra returned to the heaven.

कुत्सादीनां सिन्धुपारे स्थितानां रक्षार्थं तद्दस्युभिर्लुण्ठितानाम् ।
इन्द्रः कुत्साभ्यर्थितस्तद्धिमाद्रिद्रोण्यावासान्नाशयामास दस्यून् ।।329।।

After listening to the prayers of Kutsa for the protection of people including him, who lived across the Sindhu river, Indra destroyed those asuras, who lived in the valleys of the Himalayas.

बध्यान् दासान् भारतस्यादिवासान् भ्रान्त्या कश्चित्साहसं कल्पते तत् ।
बध्या दासा भारताद् बाह्यसीमाप्रान्तेष्वासन् भारतं नाध्यवात्सुः ।।330।।

These primitive dasas, who deserve to be punished, are daringly called bharatiya by some, but, in reality, these dasas lived in the outer regions and not in Bharatavarsha.

तस्माद् ब्रूमो भारतवर्षे वसतो नृपानार्यान् ।
भारतबहिः प्रदेशादेत्याक्रामन्निमे दासाः ।।331।।

Therefore, we say that these dasas used to come from outside in order to attack the Arya kings living in Bharatavarsha.

भारतवर्षे वसतो दासानाद्यानिहाक्रम्य ।
देशान्तरादुपेता आर्या युयुधिर इति भ्रान्तम् ।।332।।

The view that by attacking the primitive dasas living in Bharatavarsha, the Arya, who had come from a foreign country, waged a war is completely false.

मेरुभ्रष्टा आर्या विदेशिनः पौर्विकान् दासान् ।
हत्वा भारतवर्षे न्यवसन्निति हन्त निःसारम् ।।333।।

It is also completely baseless to say that the depraved and wanton foreign Arya from the regions of Meru mountains invaded and forcibly occupied Bharatavarsha after killing the dasas living in the north.

2.25 ऋभुपरिचयः

2.25 INTRODUCTION TO RIBHUS

दस्युयुद्धाद् बहुपूर्वम् आर्याणां भारतवर्षनिवासित्वे पूर्वमनुष्याणाम् ऋभूणां भारतीयत्वं हेतुः ।

Long before the war with the dasyus, the presence of the *manushya* (human) ribhus in the north, is the primary evidence of the fact that Arya were natives of Bharatavarsha.

अप्यस्ति हेतुरन्यो यत एषोऽर्थोऽवधार्यते नितराम् ।
दस्युपराजयमूलो नार्याणां भारते वासः ।।334।।

There are other evidence in this context which makes it certain that the Arya had not settled in Bharatavarsha after killing the dasyus.

पूर्वं हि दस्युयुद्धादार्याणां भारतीयत्वम् ।
विज्ञायते यतः प्राक् पूर्वमनुष्या इहभवो न्यूषुः ।।335।।

The bharatiyata of the Arya is proved even before the war, because the ribhus from the north used to live here [in Bharata] prior to this war.

दस्युनियुद्धादस्माद् बहुपूर्वं भारते वर्षे ।
आसीन्नृपः सुधन्वा पुत्रास्तस्य त्रयस्त्वासन् ।।336।।

ऋभुरथ विभ्वावाजस्त्वाष्टुः शिष्यास्त्रयोऽप्यभूवंस्ते ।
त्वष्टात्वाष्ट्रे कर्मणि तान् सम्यक् शिक्षयामास ।।337।।

Even before this war, there was a king named Sudhanva in Bharatavarsha; he had three sons. These three sons studied under Ribhu, Vibhva and sage Tvashta.

त इमे कलाविभागे निजनैपुण्याभिमानतो जातु ।
देवचमसनिर्माणात् प्रथितं त्वष्टुर्यशः पराक्षिप्यन् ।।338।।

Because of their pride, which rested on their skillfulness in the field of arts, they insulted and abused the glory and fame of Tvashta, questioning the validity of his role in the making of *devachamasa* [divine wooden vessel for drinking Soma].

त्वष्टृविनिर्मितचमसे निर्मातुः कौशलं न पश्यामः ।
यत्रोत्पन्नश्चमसो माहात्म्यं तस्य दारुणो भवति ।।339।।

In the Rigveda, 'chamasa' also means food. They denied the skill of the maker of the vessel, Tvashta, and claimed that it was the wood which should be given the credit.

त्वष्टृविनिर्मितचमसाद् देवानां सोमपानार्थात् ।
अत्युत्कृष्टं चमसं निर्मातुं नः प्रतिज्ञास्ति ।।340।।

The disciples said, 'We pledge to make a vessel superior to the one made by Tvashta for drinking Soma by the gods.

एकं चमसं सद्यश्चतुर्विधं शक्नुमः कर्तुम् ।
इत्थमृभूणां वचनं त्वष्ट्रेऽचकथत् दिवं गतस्त्वग्निः ।।341।।

'We can immediately develop one vessel in four types; in other words, we have the ability to immediately make four types of vessels from one.' Agni went to svarga, and reported the words of the ribhus to Tvashta.

निन्दिष्यन्ति तु चमसं देवानां सोमपानं ये ।
तान् ध्रुवमत्र हनिष्याम्येवं क्रुध्यन्नवोचत त्वष्टा ।।342।।

An angry Tvashta declared, 'I will kill those who insult chamasa, the vessel for the devas to drink Soma.'

प्रत्यावृत्य स्वर्गाच्छ्रावयितुं त्वष्टृरोषवचः ।
एष ऋभूणां सदनं मनुष्यलोकेश आजगामाग्निः ।।343।।

In order to report Tvashta's words of anger and warning, Agni, the master of the human world, returned from svarga, and came to the residence of the ribhus.

आगच्छन्तं दृष्ट्वा तमग्निमृभवो व्यतर्कयन् स्वगतम् ।
किमयमकस्मादग्निर्देवो नः सदनमभ्येति ।।344।।

When the ribhus saw Agni coming towards them, they wondered why was he coming to their home.

किमयं श्रेष्ठोस्त्यस्माननुग्रहीतुं समायाति ।
अस्ति यविष्ठो वायं किञ्चिन्नोर्थयितुमभ्येति ।।345।।

अथवा त्वष्टुर्विषये पूर्वं यत् कुत्सितं न्यवोचाम ।
तत्रैति दूत्यमेतत् किञ्चिद् धृतं निवेदयिष्यति नः ।।346।।

'Is this the superior Agni, who is coming to oblige us? Or is he only an ordinary being, a *yavisht* (fire produced from wood), who is coming to entreat us for something?' [In the Vedas, Agni has been called a guest or an attendant on Soma, with respect to whom Grihasthi reflects that 'this guest is superior to us and is worthy of worship', or he is yavisht, whom we should gratify by giving gifts.] 'Or has he come as an emissary, to talk about the defamatory words that we had said about Tvashta.'

इत्थं वितर्क्य पक्षे त्रयस्तृतीयो प्रतीतिमास्थाय ।
दैवी गर्हाऽनुचिता मर्त्यैरिति दोषमक्षिपन् स्वीयम् ।।347।।

After deliberating upon the issue, and with confidence in the third party [who had come as Tvashta's emissary], they accepted this fault on their part of insulting the gods and agreed that it should not be done.

ऋभवः प्राहुर्न वयं निन्दामस्त्वष्टृनिर्मितं चमसम् ।
ब्रूमस्तु दारुणस्तं प्रभावमत्रास्ति यश्चमत्कारः ।।348।।

The ribhus said, 'We have not insulted the vessel made by Tvashta. We just called it the *chamatkara* (miracle) of the wood.'

ऋभुभ्यः स्वकौशलं दर्शयितुं देवानाम् आदेशः ।

The ribhus are commanded by the devas to show their skills.

ऊचे भगवानग्निर्निभृतं प्रोत्साहयन्नृभूनेतान ।
आदिदिशुर्वो देवाश्चमसं चैकं चतुर्विधं कर्तुम् ।।349।।

Then Agni, after talking to them individually, said that the devas had commanded them to make one four-layered chamasa. [If the chamasa is taken to mean as *anna* (food-grains) then making chamasa four-layered would amount to dividing the food grains into four parts, of which the first part will be for the svarga family, the second for the guests, the third for his relatives and the fourth for the animals.]

खेचरमश्वमनश्वं रथमथ गां चर्मणोनिर्ऋताम् ।
वृद्धस्य च तारुण्यं वक्तुमिमामागतोस्मि देवाज्ञाम् ।।350।।

Agni said that he had come to convey the commands of the devas. He said, Devas have commanded that a horse capable of traversing the sky should be created, a chariot capable of moving without the aid of the horse should be created, make the skinny cow fat and healthy and make the old people youthful.

देवादिष्टानर्थान् प्रणीय गच्छत दिव्यं स्वयं यूयम् ।
यद्येव प्रकरिष्यथ तर्हि भविष्यथ नु यज्ञिया देवाः ॥351॥

'After creating all these things commanded by the devas, you should proceed to svarga. If you follow these commands, then you will also become as praise-worthy as the devas and will be established as such.

चमसचतुष्टयमेतद् दृष्ट्वा त्वष्टाभविष्यति ह्नीणः ।
इत्याकर्ण्य वचोऽग्नेर्ऋभवः पुनरब्रुवन् प्रतिज्ञाय ॥352॥

'Seeing this four-layered food-grains [making of the food grains four-layered] Tvashta will feel humbled.'

अग्निकथितमादेशं देवानां दृढमिमं प्रतिश्रुत्य ।
निर्माय वाहनानि च देवेभ्यः स्वर्गमागमिष्यामः ॥353॥

After hearing this firm command of the devas as stated by Agni, the ribhus said, 'We will proceed to heaven after creating these vehicles for the devas.'

अग्निर्ऋभून् पुनरूचे स्वर्गे चामन्त्र्य मां तु युष्माभिः ।
देयानि मत्समक्षं देवेभ्यः शिल्पजातानि ॥354॥

Agni told the ribhus again that he himself will be present in the heaven and all these skillful creations will be offered to the devas in his presence.

एवं कृते वयं वः सख्यं देवेषु भावयिष्यामः ॥
देवेन्द्रेण च सग्धिं सवने क्वापि प्रवर्तयिष्यामः ॥355॥

Agni said, 'By so doing we will establish your friendship with the devas and give you an opportunity to partake food with Indra [in other words, being of equal status with Indra].'

प्रातरपां यदि पानं मध्यदिने मुञ्जने जनं वा चेत् ।
अनुरुचितं वो न स्यात् सायं सग्धिस्तदा ध्रुवं वः स्यात् ॥356॥

Agni said, 'If you do not like to take intoxicating drinks in the morning or Soma brought from the Munjavana mountain in the afternoon, then surely you will find a place in the company of Indra for dinner.'

इत्यादिष्टा ऋभवश्चमसविधाने त्रयोऽपि सहयुक्ताः ।
अभवन् विप्रवदन्तः स्वस्वाकूत्याऽनुसंवदन्तश्च ।।357।।

Having received these commands, the three ribhus together started the work of creating vessels for drinking Soma and also engaged themselves in dialogue and discussion.

आपो भूयिष्ठास्तत् प्रातरपां सग्धिरुत्कृष्टा ।
भूयिष्ठोऽग्निरतोह्नो मध्ये सग्धिः प्रकर्षाय ।।358।।

सायं बहवः साकं बहुविधिभोज्यानि चात्र भुञ्जन्ति ।
तस्मात् सायं सग्धिः श्रेष्ठेति च ते मिथे मता न्यूचुः ।।359।।

The ribhus expressed their views—one said water was best, it was the purest of all, therefore the morning-time meeting with Indra was the best. The other expressed his view that fire was best therefore noon-time meeting was ideal. The third said that the evening-time meeting was the best, because various kinds of foods were consumed in the evening. [The devas take various kinds of food in the evening.] In this manner the three expressed their views.

शक्नोमि चमसमेकं कर्तुं द्वेधेत्यवोचत ज्येष्ठः ।
त्रेधेति मध्यमोऽसौ किन्तु चतुर्धा व्यधुः कनिष्ठगिरा ।।360।।

[In order to indicate the mutual superiority of the elements from each other, at some places the superiority has been ascribed to water, at other places to fire and at other places to earth. It is true that life cannot exist without water, therefore water is superior, the body cannot sustain itself without fire and if there is no earth, all the elements will be destroyed in the absence of a sustaining ground. Therefore, earth is superior to them all.] In connection with the action of making the four-layered vessel, the eldest of the ribhus said, 'I can make one double-layered vessel'; the middle one said, 'I can make one triple-layered vessel', but they finally made the four-layered vessel as the youngest of them wished.

पञ्चदशात् इष्टान्यनादिष्टानि च बहूनि शिल्पानि प्रदर्शयितुम् ऋभूणां स्वर्गे गमनम्।

The journey of ribhus to heaven in order to exhibit fifteen commanded and many uncommanded skills.

अथ कुशला ऋभवस्ते त्रेधा शिल्पानि कल्पयामासुः ।
पञ्च परोक्षार्थेऽपि च दश सख्यार्थे बहूनि कीर्त्यर्थे ।।361।।

Then, these proficient ribhus thought of three different types of skills which would be needed for their task—of these, five skills were connected to education, ten to friendship and other skills were for achieving fame.

आदिष्टकौशलानि तु पञ्चादिष्टोपयोजनानि दश ।
उपबृंहणानि चानादिष्टानि तु विदधिरे कतिचित् ।।362।।

Out of these, there were commanded skills [those that the devas had commanded] and ten were commanded subordinate skills. These were gathered with great effort. Some other non-commanded skills were also created which could be progressively increased. [As two from one, three from two and four from three, so on and so forth.]

एकं चमसं चतुरश्चमसान् शिलष्टान् विबर्हयेति ।
पुनरेकं च चतुर्णां संपादयतीति कौशले परमम् ।।363।।

A vessel which contained four vessels within and on opening, spread out into four vessels! What a wonderful skill it is!

आश्वादश्वमतक्षद् द्वौ चाश्वावेक एवाश्वः ।
अपि बहवोऽश्वाः सहिता दिवि ते प्रचरन्ति भूमौ च ।।364।।

From one horse another horse was made and the one horse was like two horses [containing the power of two horses]. Many horses roamed together on the earth and sky. Here the intended meaning can be of transforming one horse into many.

उक्थ्यो रथऽप्यनश्वोऽभीषुरेतीर्वानामतो विपुलः ।
परिवर्तते च चक्रैस्त्रिभिः समं दिवि भुवि प्रचरन् ।।365।।

There is a description of a huge chariot created by the ribhus, which has three wheels but no horse or harness attached to it, which roams over the earth and sky with equal ease. [The chariot without horse and harness is the chariot of the sun; the morning, noon, and evening are its three wheels with the help of which the sun traverses the whole of earth and sky.]

अनश्वो जातो अनभीषुरुक्थ्यो रथस्त्रिचक्रः परिवर्तते रजः ।
महत्तद्वो देवस्य प्रवाचनं द्यामृभवः पृथिवीं यच्च पुष्यथ ।।

(ऋग्वेदः, 4.36.1)

It is written in the Rigveda, 'O Ribhus, your chariot is without horse and harness, consisting of three wheels and is praiseworthy. The chariot moves around in the four corners of the cosmos. You strengthen the heavens and earth. This great action of yours is indicative of your godliness.'

द्विविधा तु निर्मिता गौरग्नेर्वचनाद् बृहस्पतेर्वचनात् ।
आदिष्टकौशलेऽन्या आदिष्टे तूपयोजने साऽन्या ।।366।।

The ribhus created two types of cows in accordance with the advice of Agni and Brihaspati. One cow was created according to the commanded skill and the other for serving a secondary purpose.

गौः श्वेतरी तु पूर्वा बृहस्पतेर्विश्वरूपाख्या ।
गौः श्वैतरीयमेकाऽनेकतनुः स्यान्निकृत्तचर्मवशात् ।।
(ऋग्वेदः, 1.161.7)

Brihaspati began to use various types of speech. The white cow of Agni means the sun offering its shining rays to Agni. [Here the intended meaning of cow can also be taken as signifying speech.]

अन्या गौरतिभव्या कामगवी निर्मिता चित्रा ।
एषा यदेव किञ्चित् प्राश्नात्यमृतं ततो दुग्धे ।।367।।

The other cow was very haughty and strange; it was Kamagavi, the one who has the ability to fulfil desires; whatever she ate, she produced milk like amrita.

मातापितरौ यौ यौ जरसा भूमौ शयानौ स्तः ।
यन्त्रप्रभावतस्तौ पुनर्युवानौ प्रचक्रिरे सद्यः ।।368।।

The old and aged parents, who were sleeping on the earth, immediately became youthful with this magic potion.

इत्थं चमसानश्वं रथमथ धेनुं युवानौ च ।
निर्माय सुष्ठु पश्चाद् व्यधुरादिष्टो योजनानि दश ।।369।।

In this manner, after creating the vessels, the chariots, the cows, and making the old people youthful, the ribhus created ten commanded auxiliaries.

इन्द्रस्य हरी हरितः सूर्यस्याग्नेस्तु रोहितो नाम ।
श्यावाः सवितुः पूष्णस्तस्त्वजाश्च मरुतां पृषन्नाम ।।370।।

The horse of Indra was called Hari, the horse of surya was called Harit [yellowish green], the horse of Agni was called Rohit [red colour], the horse of Savita was called Shyava [black colour], the horse of Pusha was called Aja and that of the marutas was called Prishat.

नियुतो वायोरुषसोऽरुण्यो गावोऽथ विश्वरूपा गौः ।
विहिता बृहस्पतेरथ रासभयुग्मं तथाश्विनोः क्लृप्तम् ।।371।।

Then was created a horse for Vayu called Niyukta, Aruni cow for Usha, *Rasabhayugam* [many-splendoured vani] for Brihaspati and a pair of donkeys for the ashvin kumars.

दश चैतान्यादिष्टोपयोजना प्रसिद्ध्यन्ति ।
एतान्यारुह्यैते यान्ति स्माकाशमार्गेण ।।372।।

These ten commanded auxiliaries are famous. Riding them the ribhus travelled through the sky.

इन्द्राय चक्रुर्हरिसंज्ञकौ हयौ श्लिष्टौपृथिव्यां दिवि च प्रचारिणौ ।
यथेच्छमाभ्यां भुवि खे च संचरन् हर्यश्व उक्तो हरिवाहनोऽपि सः ।।373।।

The ribhus created a pair of horses named as Hari for Indra which were able to traverse the heaven and earth. Therefore Indra, roaming the heaven and earth, on these horses according to his will, was called Indra Haryashva and Harivahana.

हरिप्रभावाद्धरिवान् पराक्रमं स मानुषः सन्नतिमानुषं व्यधात् ।
ताभ्यां स सानोः परसानुमारुहन्नस्पृष्टकर्त्वं बहुदस्युहत्यके ।।374।।

With the help of these horses, Indra performed supernatural feats. Riding these horses, climbing one mountain after other without even touching them, he was able to kill many demons.

प्राथमिकषष्ठतुर्ये तित्तिरयः संहितायां तु।
सूर्यस्यैतशमाहुः सोऽपि स्याद्धरित एवाश्वः ।।375।।

In the fourth hymn of the beginning of the sixth chapter of Taittiriya Samhita, the name of the surya's horse is given as Etasha [full of power]. It was a horse of yellowish-green colour.

त्वं सूरो हरितो रामयो नृन् भरचक्रमेतशो नायमिन्द्रः ।
(ऋग्वेदः, 1.121.13)

अस्मिन्मन्त्रे ह्येतशो नानियुक्तो नृणां हरितां स्थान इन्द्रेण पूर्वम् ।।376।।

It is written in the Rigveda, 'O Indra, you project these yellowish-green rays [that sap the energy of rasas] for the benefit of human beings, and like the energetic rays of the sun, the wheel of your chariot always moves on.'

अर्थाहरणे कर्मणि ये नियता व्यापृता नरा भृतकाः ।
हरितो नरास्त उक्ताः शिरसा रश्मिभिरिमे हरन्ति रथम् ।।377।।

The servants, appointed for carrying the goods meant for trade, are called Harita because they pull the chariot by the *lagam* (harness) tied to their head.

हरितो हरन्ति शिरसा पृष्ठेन च किमपि संभारम् ।
हरितां तु नायको यो वहनेऽधिकृतः स वह्निराख्यातः ।।378।।

These Haritas also pull some of the baggage with the help of their head and back. The hero of these Haritas, who is the administrator of the transport, is called *vahana* [vahana also means the officer of transport]. Since Agni passes on the offerings of human beings to the devas, he is, therefore, an administrator of transport.

अपि यो मनुष्यलोकेश्वरोऽग्निरस्थात्तु भारते वर्षे ।
वह्निः स उक्त एष हि देवैर्देयं दिवे वहति ।।379।।

Agni, the master of human world, who lives in Bharata, is called Vanhi. He carries this Vanhi to the world of the devas.

इत्यधिभूतं विद्यादधिदैवं तूदिता दिशो हरितः ।
ता इह विद्याच्छन्दांस्येवाहोरात्रवृत्तानि ।।380।।

This fact must be admitted by the the humans as well as the devas [Adhibhutas]. The directions have been indicated with the help of the word Harita. Here those directions should be recognized with the help of '*ahoratra vritra chhand*'.

नरदेवानामेषां यानि यु यानाभिधानानि ।
प्रायेण तानि क्लृप्तान्यधिदैवतयानसामान्यात् ।।381।।

Whatever the vehicles of these human-gods were called, these were usually called by names similar to that of the devas.

ऋक्सामे हरिसंज्ञे अधिदैवतमिन्द्रयाने स्तः ।
यजुरिन्द्रं हरतस्ते अधिभूताश्वो हरिस्तदिन्द्रस्य ।।382।।

In devaloka, Rik [the sun] and Sama [sun rays] are Indra's vehicles and Yaju is the name of his horse. [Rik is the name of every cosmic body and its aura is Sama. The element of motion between the two is Yaju.]

इत्थं पञ्चदशार्थानादिष्टानग्नये निवेद्यैतान् ।
दर्शयितुं स्वं कौशलमृभवः स्वर्गे विमानतो जग्मुः ॥383॥

After creating these fifteen commanded objects and presenting them to Agni, the ribhus proceeded on a vehicle to the heaven to demonstrate their skills.

ऋभुकौशलविमुग्धैः देवैः ऋभुभ्यः देवत्वेन्द्रसग्धित्वादिपारितोषिकप्रदानम् ।

Impressed by their skills, the devas rewarded the ribhus with a form of *devatva* and the right of Indra's association.

अग्निसमक्षं भगवानिन्द्रः शिल्पानि तानि चालोच्य ।
देवसभायां प्रमहे देवेभ्यो वाहनानि ददौ ॥384॥

After examining those skills, Indra presented these vehicles to the devas, at the time of festivities in the presence of Agni.

अस्थिभिरस्य दधीचोऽतो वज्रं प्रागजीजनत् ।
सोमग्रहणं चमसं योऽपूर्वं दारुणोऽकुरुत ॥385॥

तस्मादप्याचार्यात् त्वष्टुर्देवान्मनुष्याणाम् ।
ऋभ्वादीनामेषामप्रथत यशोऽधिकं स्वर्गे ॥386॥

The fame of these human ribhus that spread to the heaven was greater than that of the vajra, a weapon of bones created earlier by sage Dadhichi for Indra and the unmatched wooden vessel for drinking Soma made by Tvashta.

यशांसि भूयांसि सुपर्वणां कुले प्रगीयमानानि निशम्य वासवः ।
तुतोष मेने मनुजेषु सत्क्रियामग्नेर्मनुष्याधिपतेर्विचारतः ॥387॥

After hearing the singing of elaborate praise in honour of the ribhus in the clan of the devas, Indra was greatly pleased and Agni was honoured and acknowledged as the leader of humans.

स्वाराट् स दृष्ट्वा हरिसप्तिनिर्मितौ लोकातिगं कौशलमस्य शिल्पिनः ।
सम्मानहेतोः सह पारितोषिकैः सग्धिं तृतीये सवनेऽन्वकल्पयत् ॥388॥

Witnessing the unparalleled skill of these artisans involved in creating the seven horses, Indra granted them the right of evening companionship, as a reward.

महती हि सा प्रतिष्ठा स्वर्गे लोके यदिन्द्रतः सग्धिः ।
तेनोत्साहितचित्ताः शिल्पान्यन्यानि भूरिशश्चक्रुः ।।389।।

The companionship of Indra in heaven is a great honour. Inspired by this gesture, they also created many other artefacts.

परिनिष्ठितकर्माणो विश्वैर्देवैस्त आहूताः ।
यानानि ते च तेषां व्यदधुर्विविधानि शस्त्रणि ।।390।।

The performers of these faithful actions, the ribhus [who have full faith in their action] have been invoked by all the devas. They created many vehicles and armaments for them.

अत्यद्भुतं स पक्षिणमेकं व्यधात् प्लवं नाम ।
इन्द्राज्ञया जगृहतुस्तमश्विनौ देवकर्मार्थम् ।।391।।

These ribhus created a wonderful bird named Plava which was received by the ashvin kumars with the permission of Indra for divine actions.

यावन्मितमिह वेगं निवेश्य नोदेन गमयेत् तम् ।
तावन्मिते प्रदेशे गत्वा परिवर्त्य चायाति ।।392।।

About this bird, it is said that it is filled with so much energy and motivation that it returns after covering long distances.

पृष्ठारूढं स वहन्नारूढं वा विनैव नोदनया ।
विचरन् विहायसाऽयं याति मनोनीतमास्पदं तरसा ।।393।

With or without carrying someone on its back, moved by inspiration, it traverses the sky and soon reaches the intended place of mind's desire.

एष समुद्रे प्लवते बलाज्जलाधो निधीयमानोऽपि ।
तत्पृष्ठस्था बहवो मनुजाः प्रतरन्ति सागरेऽप्यभयम् ।।394।।

This bird could swim in the sea and easily carry humans on its back across the waters without any fear.

अथ यांस्ते देवेभ्यो रथाननश्वान् विहङ्गमान् व्यदधुः ।
तानि विमानान्याहुस्तानि च नानाविधान्यासन् ।।395।।

After this, the horses and birds, which were created by the ribhus for the devas, were named *vimana*-s (flying machines) and these crafts were of many kinds.

प्रथमं बृहस्पतिकृते प्रणयन्ति स्म त्रिबन्धुर सुरथम् ।
अश्विभ्यामपि रासभरथं प्रचक्रुस्त्रिबन्धुरं सुदृढम् ।।396।।

First of all a beautiful chariot was created for Brihaspati which had three parts. Then a strong chariot driven by donkeys was created for the ashvin kumars, this was also divided into three parts.

क्रमतोऽत्र सिद्धहस्ता ऋभव इमे शिल्पिमूर्द्धन्याः ।
आविश्चक्रुर्नानाविधानि तेभ्यो विमानानि ।।397।।

These master craftsmen, ribhus, soon achieved perfection and they invented many types of flying machines for the devas.

एतद्विमानकौशलदर्शनतो हृष्ट एष देवेन्द्रः ।
बहुभिः सुपुरस्कारैः सत्कृत्य ऋभून् सभाजयामास ।।398।।

Happy with their skills in building flying machines, Indra gave the ribhus choicest awards.

इन्द्रस्तैर्ऋभुभिः सममारुह्यैतं विमानरथम् ।
व्यचरद्दिवि देवानिव तान् यज्ञे सोमपायिनो व्यदधात् ।।399।।

Indra traversed the sky with the ribhus sitting alongside and then gave them the right to take Soma at the yajna like the devas.

एषां च मनुषाणां सम्मानायाददात् स देवत्वम् ।
महती कीर्तिरमीषामभूत् ततो यज्ञभागभुजाम् ।।400।।

To honour these humans, Indra conferred the title of Devatva on them and thus the fame of the ribhus, the partakers of a part of yajna, spread far and wide.

इन्द्रस्यासन् बहवो मनोनपात् संज्ञयाऽमात्याः ।
एषामपि स ऋभूणां मनोनपात्वं ददाविन्द्रः ।।401।।

Indra had many or *manonpata*-s (counsellers). Indra offered the ribhus a place in the council of his advisors.

अग्निर्भूम्या, वातोऽन्तरिक्षतो, दिव इमे मरुतः ।
शवसोनपात इच्छन्त्यृभून् समुद्रस्य वरुणश्च ॥
(ऋग्वेदः, 1.161.14)

To seek the ribhus, Agni came from earth, Vayu from antariksha and from Dyau came Maruta and the presiding deities of ocean.

अपि वामदेव ऊचे रत्नानां दुर्लभाद्भुतानां ते ।
शवसोनपात ऋषभोऽभवंश्च देवेन्द्रसाम्राज्ये ॥402॥

Vamadeva thus spoke, 'In the empire of Indra, those ribhus, precious, and wonderful jewels, became the presiding gods.'

2.25.1 विद्वद्भिः निर्मितं कीर्तिसूक्तम्

2.25.1 Paens to ribhus

2.25.1.1 दीर्घतमसा कृतं सूक्तम्

2.25.1.1 Paens by Dirghatma

ऋभूणां यशःस्थैर्याय देवेन्द्रनिदेशात् देवसभाविद्विद्भिः कीर्तिसूक्तनिर्माणम् ।

Composition of kritisukta by the wise men of the court of devas on the command of Devendra for steady fame of ribhus.

दीर्घतमा औचथ्यो ममतापुत्रोन्यदर्शयत्प्रायः ।
चरितमृभूणामेषामप्रथत यथा तु शिल्पिनां सुयशः ॥403॥

Dirghatma, the son of Mamta, has praised the character of the ribhus which was instrumental in spreading the fame of these craftsmen.

किमु श्रेष्ठः किं यविष्ठो न आजगान्किमीयते दूत्यङ् कद्यदूचिम ।
न निन्दिम चमसं यो महाकुलोऽग्ने भ्रातर्द्रुण इद्भूतिमूदिम ॥
(ऋग्वेदः, 1.161.1)

In the 161st sukta of first mandala of Rigveda, Dirghatma says: What is that which is most excellent? Or that which is small? That has come to us. As whose envoy has it come? Of whose description should we offer? O Agni, the great provider! Those born into a great clan do not defame the vessel of the devas; instead supremacy of food should be extolled.

एकं चमसं चतुस्कृणोतन तद्वो देवा अब्रुवन्तद्व आगमम् ।
सौधन्वना यद्येवा करिष्यथ साकं देवैर्यज्ञियासो भविष्यथ ।।
(ऋग्वेद:, 1.161.2)

O sons of Sundhva! Make four parts of one chamasa [food], as the devas have told you to. I have come here to convey this to you. If you do this, you will also become worthy of worship along with the devas.

अग्निं दूतं प्रति यदब्रवीत नाश्व: कर्त्वो रथ उतेह कर्त्व: ।
धेनु: कर्त्वा युवशा कर्त्वा द्वा तानि भ्रातरनु व: कृत्व्येमसि ।।
(ऋग्वेद:, 1.161.3)

O Ribhus! You have told Agni, the messenger of the devas, that you have to make horses strong and healthy, and have to make a chariot and make old people young. After doing all these things, O Agni! We are with you.

चकृवांस ऋभवस्तदपृच्छतक्वेदभूद्य: स्य दूतो न आजगन् ।
यदावाख्यच्चमसाञ्चतुर: कृतानादित्त्वाष्टामग्नास्वन्तर्न्यानजे ।।
(ऋग्वेद:, 1.161.4)

The wise men asked the ribhus, 'Where was that one born, who has come to us as a messenger? When Tvashta made the vessel radiant and four-layered, only then was he able to become a messenger, and roam around the lands.'

हनामैनां इति त्वष्टा यदब्रवीच्चमसं ये देवपानमनिन्दिषु: ।
अन्या नामानि कृण्वते सुते सचां अन्यैरेनान्कन्या नामभि: स्परत् ।।
(ऋग्वेद:, 1.161.5)

Tvashta said, 'Let us kill those people who revile the food worthy of the devas. Soma is known by several names after it is prepared; virgins refer to it [Soma] by its many names. [In other words we should not revile the food worthy of consumption by the devas.]

इन्द्रो हरी युयुजे अश्विना रथं बृहस्पतिर्विश्वरूपामुपाजत ।
ऋभुर्विभ्वा वाजो देवाँ अगच्छत स्वपसो यज्ञियं भागमैतन ।।

निश्चर्मणो गामरिणीता धीतिभिर्या जरन्ता युवशा ताकृणोतन ।
सौधन्वना अश्वादश्वमतक्ष युक्त्वा रथमुप देवाँ अयातन ।।
(ऋग्वेद:, 1.161.6–7)

'Indra has harnessed the horse, the ashvin kumars have readied the chariot, and Brihaspati has started speaking in his beautiful vani. Therefore O Ribhus! You please go to the devas and receive part of the yajna after performing good deeds. O sons of Sundhava! You have made strong even the weak and skinny cows by your efforts. You have created horses from a horse and then, harnessing them to your chariot you have gone to the devas.

इदमुदकं पिबतेत्यब्रवीत नेदं वा घा पिबता मुञ्जनेजनम् ।
सौधन्वना यदि तन्नेव हर्यथ तृतीये घा सवने मादयाध्वै ॥
(ऋग्वेद:, 1.161.8)

'O sons of Sundhva! Please drink this water, the Soma brought from the Munjavana mountain. If you have no desire to drink this just now, as you had said, then do enjoy this in the evening.

आपो भूयिष्ठा इत्येको अब्रवीदग्निर्भूयिष्ठ इत्यन्यो अब्रवीत् ।
वर्धयन्ती बहुभ्य: प्रैको अब्रवीदृता वदन्तश्चमसाँ अपिंशत ॥
(ऋग्वेद:, 1.161.9)

'The water is the best of all, someone has said so, it is the fire, the other one has said so, and someone else has told that the earth is the best. Speaking truth in this manner, all of them have divided the best things of the world.

श्रोणामेक उदकं गामवाजति मांसमेक: पिंशति सूनयाभृतम् ।
आ निम्नुच: शकृदेको अपाभरत्किंस्वित्पुत्रेभ्य: पितरा उपावतु: ॥
(ऋग्वेद:, 1.161.10)

'One of the sons takes the cows to water, the other feeds the cows well and makes them strong and healthy. One of the sons clears the cow dung in the evening, what more can the parents of such sons expect of them.

उद्वत्स्वमा अकृणोतना तृणं निवत्स्वप: स्वपस्यया नर: ।
अगोह्यस्य यदसस्तना गृहे तद्येदमृभवो नानुगच्छथ ॥
(ऋग्वेद:, 1.161.11)

'O persons of imposing personality! Procure grass for these cows and preserve the sources of water in the lands of high altitude by your good actions. As long as you live in a house devoid of cows, you cannot hope to enjoy luxury.

सम्मील्य यद्भुवना पर्यसर्पत क्व स्वित्तात्या पितरा व आसुतः ।
अशपत यः करस्नं व आददे यः प्राब्रवीत्प्रो तस्मा अब्रवीतन ॥
(ऋग्वेदः, 1.161.12)

'O Ribhus! Where would your father and mother go when you roam the four directions after covering the world with clouds? Curse the person who tries to obstruct you. And bless the person who praises you.

सुषुप्वांस ऋभवस्तदपृच्छतागोह्य क इदं नो अबूबुधत् ।
श्वानं वस्तो बोधयितारमब्रवीत्संवत्सर इदमद्या व्यख्यत ॥
(ऋग्वेदः, 1.161.13)

'O rays of sun [ribhus]! You asked the sun while in sleep—O ever awake sun! Who has awakened us? Then the sun, who provides reason to everyone, has told you that it was the air that has awakened you. You have enlightened this world today after one year.

दिवा यान्ति मरुतो भूम्याग्निरयं वातो अन्तरिक्षेण याति ।
अद्भिर्याति वरुणः समुद्रैर्युष्माँ इच्छन्तः शवसोनपातः ॥
(ऋग्वेदः, 1.161.14)

'O the sustainers of power, ribhus! Desiring you, marutas come from Dyau, Agni goes from the earth, Vayu goes from the sky and Varuna goes from the turbulent ocean.'

2.25.1.2 वामदेवेन कृतं सूक्तम्

2.25.1.2 Paens by Vamadeva

अपि वामदेव ऊचे विस्तरतस्तन्महर्षिराङ्गिरसः ।
चरितमृभूणामेषामप्रथत यथा तु शिल्पिनां सुयशः ॥404॥

The great sage, Angirasa Vamadeva, has described the character of these ribhus in detail, on account of which the fame of these craftsmen has spread far and wide.

प्र ऋभुभ्यो दूतमिव वाचमिष्य उपस्तिरे श्वैतरीं धेनुमीळे ।
ये वातजूतास्तरणिभिरेवैः परि द्यां सद्यो अपसो बभूवुः ॥
(ऋग्वेदः, 4.33.1)

It is written in the thirty-third sukta of fourth mandala of Rigveda: Like a messenger, I bring praises for the ribhus, and ask for milk-yielding cows to prepare the best of Soma. The ribhus, who are fast like air and are full of creativity and who, with the help of their fast horses, are able to reach Dyau very fast.

यदारमक्रन्नृभव: पितृभ्यां परिविष्टी वेषणा दंसनाभि: ।
आदिद्देवानामुप सख्यमायन्धीरास: पुष्टिवहन्मनायै ॥

(ऋग्वेद:, 4.33.2)

The ribhus were able to procure the friendship of devas only when they made themselves efficient by serving their parents and by their good deeds. And then those wise ribhus made their mind powerful.

पुनर्ये चक्रु: पितरा युवाना सना यूपेव जरणा शयाना ।
ते वाजो विभ्वाँ ऋभुरिन्द्रवन्तो मधुप्सरसो नोऽवन्तु यज्ञम् ॥

(ऋग्वेद:, 4.33.3)

Then ribhus made their old and extremely weak parents strong and young once again. May those ribhus [Vaja and Vibhva], after receiving the blessings of Indra and taking the sweet Soma protect our yajna.

यत् संवत्समृभवो गामरक्षन् यत् संवत्समृभवो मा अपिंशन् ।
यत्संवत्समभरन्भासो अस्यास्ताभि: शमीभिरमृतत्वमाशु: ॥

(ऋग्वेद:, 4.33.4)

When the ribhus protected the cow for a year and made it strong by making it fat. When the cow was filled with strength for one year, only then due to their good deeds the ribhus achieved immortality.

ज्येष्ठ आह चमसा द्वा करेति कनीयान् त्रीन्कृणवामेत्याह ।
कनिष्ठ आह चतुरस्करेति त्वष्ट ऋभवस्तत्पनयद्वचो व: ॥

(ऋग्वेद:, 4.33.5)

The eldest of the ribhus said, 'Let us make two parts of the vessel', then the younger one said, 'Let us make three parts of it.' And then the youngest one said, 'Let us make four parts of it.' Tvashta has praised the ribhus for these actions.

सत्यमूचुर्नर एवा हि चक्रुरनु स्वधामृभवो जग्मुरेताम् ।
विभ्रजमानाँश्चमसाँ अहेवाऽवेनत् त्वष्टा चतुरो ददृशवान् ॥

(ऋग्वेद:, 4.33.6)

The human-like ribhus spoke the truth, as they did whatever they promised. After this the ribhus received this offering. Tvashta looked at the four vessels, shining like day and praised them.

द्वादश द्यून्यदगोह्यस्यातिथ्ये रणन्नृभवः ससन्तः ।
सुक्षेत्राकृण्वन्ननयन्त सिन्धून्धन्वातिष्ठन्नोषधीर्निम्नमापः ॥
(ऋग्वेदः, 4.33.7)

When those ribhus enjoyed the hospitality of aditya [sun], then these ribhus in the form of rays made the agricultural fields fertile, they guided the rivers, produced medicinal plants in the dry regions and made the water flow downstream.

रथं ये चक्रुः सुवृतं नरेष्ठां ये धेनुं विश्वजुवं विश्वरूपाम् ।
त आतक्षन्त्वृभवो रयिं नः स्ववसः स्वपसः सुहस्ताः ॥
(ऋग्वेदः, 4.33.8)

Those ribhus who created well-crafted chariots fit for human beings, who created well-endowed cows, those ribhus are performers of good deeds and have such worthy arms that are capable of best defence. May such ribhus provide us with all the luxuries of life!

अपो ह्येषामजुसन्त देवा अभि क्रत्वा मनसा दीध्यानाः ।
वाजो देवानामभवत्सुकर्मेन्द्रस्य ऋभुक्षा वरुणस्य विभ्वा ॥
(ऋग्वेदः, 4.33.9)

The devas, illustrious and heroic in mind and action, have accepted the actions of these ribhus. On account of his good actions, a ribhu named Vaja became dear to the devas, Ribhuksha became dear to Indra and Vibhva became dear to Varuna.

ये हरी मेधयोक्था मदन्त इन्द्राय चक्रुः सुयुजा ये अश्वा ।
ते रायस्पोषं द्रविणान्यस्मे धत्त ऋभवः क्षेमयन्तो न मित्रम् ॥
(ऋग्वेदः, 4.33.10)

Those ribhus, after being delighted by the praises, created two excellent horses with the help of their intellect, they also created a horse for Indra that was easy to harness. O such Ribhus! Like a friend desirous of doing good, provide abundant wealth, power and affluence.

इदाह्नः पीतिमुत वो मदं धुर्न ऋते श्रान्तस्य सख्याय देवाः ।
ते नूनमस्मे ऋभवो वसूनि तृतीये अस्मिन्सवने दधात ॥
(ऋग्वेदः, 4.33.11)

O Ribhus! At this time of the day, the devas have provided Soma and pleasure for you. Even the devas do not become friends without enduring difficulties. Therefore O Ribhus! Provide wealth to us in this third part of the day.

ऋभुर्विभ्वा वाज इन्द्रो नो अच्छेमं यज्ञं रत्नधेयोप यात ।
इदा हि वो धिषणा देव्यह्नामधात्पीतिं सं मदा अग्मता वः ॥
(ऋग्वेदः, 4.34.1)

In the Rigveda, sage Gautama has also showered praises on the ribhus: May Ribhu Vibhva, Vaja, and Indra come straight to us towards yajna to give us gems. Today Vagdevi has given you Soma to drink. You may receive this enjoyable Soma.

विदानासो जन्मनो वाजरत्ना उत ऋभुभिर्ऋभवो मादयध्वम् ।
सं वो सदा अग्मत सं पुरन्धिः सुवीरामस्मे रयिमेरयध्वम् ॥
(ऋग्वेदः, 4.34.2)

O Ribhus, possessing the best quality of anna! Being knowledgeable of the births of all beings, receive pleasure in all the seasons. May you receive this enjoyable Soma forever! May you continue to receive the best of intellect! You may provide us with wealth and brave sons.

अयं वो यज्ञ ऋभवोऽकारि यमा मनुष्यवत्प्रदिवो दधिध्वे ।
प्र वोऽच्छा जुजुषाणासो अस्थुरभूत विश्वे अग्रियोत वाजाः ॥
(ऋग्वेदः, 4.34.3)

O Ribhus! This yajna has been arranged for you. Accept this yajna as a bright human being! These enjoyable Soma comes straight to you. Due to this, O powerful Ribhus! You are supreme.

अभूदुवो वो विधते रत्नधेयमिदा नरो दाशुषे मर्त्याय ।
पिबत वाजा ऋभवो ददे वो महि तृतीयं सवनं मदाय ॥
(ऋग्वेदः, 4.34.4)

O leader Ribhus! May the performers of yajna for you receive jewel-like bounties from you. I offer you lots of Soma to drink, for your enjoyment.

आ वाजा यातोप न ऋभुक्षा महो नरो द्रविणसो गृणानाः ।
आ वः पीयतोऽभिपित्वे अह्नामिमा अस्तं नवस्व इव ग्मन् ॥
(ऋग्वेदः, 4.34.5)

O powerful leader ribhus! May you come to us attaining fame as the most powerful being! At the end of the day, the Soma flows towards you like the cows, who have recently delivered, rush expectantly towards home.

आ नपातः शवसो यातनोपेमं यज्ञं नमसा हूयमानाः ।
सजोषसः सूरयो यस्य च स्थ मध्वः पात रत्नधा इन्द्रवन्तः ॥
(ऋग्वेदः, 4.34.6)

O shining Ribhus! Come to this yajna with love, being invited to it in an intelligent and respectful manner. Drink Soma possessing enjoyable qualities in the company of Indra, to whom you belong.

सजोषा इन्द्र वरुणेन सोमं सजोषाः पाहि गिर्वणो मरुद्भिः ।
अग्रेपाभिर्ऋतुपाभिः सजोषा ग्नास्पत्नीभी रत्नधाभिः सजोषाः ॥
(ऋग्वेदः, 4.34.7)

O Indra! Enjoy Soma, in the loving company of Varuna. O praiseworthy Indra! Enjoy Soma lovingly in the company of marutas. Enjoy Soma lovingly in the company of the devas who are the first drinkers and drink according to the seasons. And enjoy Soma in the company of ladies who have attained affluent status.

सजोषस आदित्यैर्मादयध्वं सजोषस ऋभवः पर्वतेभिः ।
सजोषसो दैव्येना सवित्रा सजोषसः सिन्धुभी रत्नधेभिः ॥
(ऋग्वेदः, 4.34.8)

O Ribhus! Enjoy happily in the company of the adityas, enjoy happily in the company of the mountains, enjoy happily in the company of deva Savita, who is well disposed towards the devas and enjoy in the company of the ocean-possessing gems.

ये अश्विना ये पितरा य ऊती धेनुं ततक्षुर्ऋभवो ये अश्वा ।
ये अंसत्रा य ऋधग्रोदसी ये विभ्वो नरः स्वपत्यानि चक्रुः ॥
(ऋग्वेदः, 4.34.9)

Those ribhus, who have made the ashvin kumars capable by giving them tools to protect, who made the elders capable, made cows to yield milk in plenty and made the horses strong, who have created the shields, who have separated the earth and the realms of light, who, as powerful leaders, have performed wonderful deeds.

ये गोमन्तं वाजवन्तं सुवीरं रयिं धत्थ वसुमन्तं पुरुक्षम् ।
ते अग्रेपा ऋभवो मन्दसाना अस्मे धत्त ये च रातिं गृणन्ति ।।
(ऋग्वेद:, 4.34.10)

O Ribhus! You are the ones that possess most abundant material resources in the shape of cows, horses, and brave off-springs, whose offering is praised everywhere. You, who are the first ones to drink Soma, please fill us with affluence after you are filled with enjoyment.

नापाभूत न वोऽतीतृषामानि: शस्ता ऋभवो यज्ञे अस्मिन् ।
समिन्द्रेण मदथ सं मरुद्भि: सं राजभी रत्नधेयाय देवा: ।।
(ऋग्वेद:, 4.34.11)

O Ribhus! Do not go away from us. Let us not leave you thirsty but keep providing you Soma. O Ribhus! Endowed with divine quality and free from hate, be happy to participate in this yajna along with Indra. O Ribhus! To provide precious jewels, enjoy with the glorious marutas.'

इहोप यात शवसो नपात: सौधन्वना ऋभवो माप भूत ।
अस्मिन्हि व: सवने रत्नधेयं गमन्त्विन्द्रमनु वो मदास: ।।
(ऋग्वेद:, 4.35.1)

Offering praises to the ribhus, Vamadeva Gautama has said, O Ribhus, protectors of strength and armed with excellent bows! Come to us, do not go away from us and you may also receive the enjoyable Soma worthy to be received by Indra who provides precious gems in this yajna.

आगन्नृभूणामिह रत्नधेयमभूत्सोमस्य सुषुतस्य पीति: ।
सुकृत्यया यत्स्वपस्यया चँ एकं विचक्र चमसं चतुर्धा।।
(ऋग्वेद:, 4.35.2)

Let the gifts of precious gems for the ribhus come here, and let the drinking of well-prepared Soma continue. O ribhus! You have made the vessel four-layered with your power, duty and skill.

व्यकृणोत चमसं चतुर्धा सखे वि शिक्षेत्यब्रवीत ।
अथैत वाजा अमृतस्य पन्थां गणं देवानामृभव: सुहस्ता: ।।
(ऋग्वेद:, 4.35.3)

O Ribhus! You have divided the chamasa into four parts. O friend, you wanted to offer charity, after this you travelled on the path of immortality. O possessors of best hands! You have joined the assembly of the devas.

किं मय: स्विच्चमस एष आस यं काव्येन चतुरो विचक्र ।
अथा सुनुध्वं सवनं मदाय पात ऋभवो मधुन: सोम्यस्य ।।
(ऋग्वेद:, 4.35.4)

O Ribhus! Of what material was the drinking vessel made of that you could divide it into four parts! O Ritvijas! Grind and press the Soma and taste this sweet Soma for pleasure.

शच्याकर्त पितरा युवाना शच्याकर्त चमसं देवपानम् ।
शच्या हरी धानुतरावतष्टेन्द्रवाहावृभवो वाजरत्ना: ।।
(ऋग्वेद:, 4.35.5)

O Ribhus! With your able deeds you have made your parents youthful, with your skill you have made a vessel fit for the devas to drink. O affluent Ribhus! With your skill you have made the horses of Indra run even faster than an arrow.

यो व: सुनोत्यभिपित्त्वे अह्नां तीव्रं वाजास: सवनं मदाय ।
तस्मै रयिमृभव: सर्ववीरमा तक्षत वृषणो मन्दसाना: ।।
(ऋग्वेद:, 4.35.6)

O powerful Ribhus! After being delighted in every way, give wealth along with valiant progeny to a person who presses and prepares flavoured Soma for your enjoyment at the end of the day.

प्रात: सुतमपिबो हर्यश्व माध्यन्दिनं सवनं केवलं ते ।
समृभुभि: पिबस्व रत्नधेभि: सखीं याँ इन्द्र चकृषे सुकृत्या ।।
(ऋग्वेद:, 4.35.7)

O Indra, possessor of best horses! Please drink the Soma pressed in the morning. The midday Soma is also only for you. O Indra! Please drink Soma in the company of those gem-bearing ribhus, whom you have befriended today on account of their excellent deeds.

ये देवासो अभवता सुकृत्या श्येना इवेदधि दिवि निषेद ।
ते रत्नं धात शवसोनपातः सौधन्वना अभवतामृतासः ।।
(ऋग्वेदः, 4.35.8)

O Ribhus! With the help of those very excellent deeds you become the devas, you have been established as *Suparna* [sun-bird] in the realms of light. O Ribhus, sustainers of power! Provide us gems. O Sudhanvana, bearers of best bowls! You have become immortal.

यत्तृतीयं सवनं रत्नधेयमकृष्णुध्वं स्वपस्या सुहस्ताः ।
तदृभवः परिषिक्तं व एतत्संमदेभिरिन्द्रियेभिः पिबध्वम् ।।
(ऋग्वेदः, 4.35.9)

O *Suhasta* [having the best and capable hands]! With you excellent deeds, you have made the third *savana* [a term used to denote a specific time for yajna] as the provider of gems. Therefore, O Ribhus! Please drink Soma which has been pressed and prepared for you with all care.'

अनश्वो जातो अनभीशरुक्थ्यो रथस्त्रिचक्रः परिवर्तते रजः ।
महत्तद्वो देव्यस्य प्रवाचनं द्यामृभवः पृथिवीं यच्च पुष्यथ ।।
(ऋग्वेदः, 4.36.1)

Vamadeva has praised the ribhus in the Rigveda: O Ribhus! Your chariot, having three wheels, devoid of horses and devoid of harness, is praiseworthy. That chariot roams in all directions in the sky. Your journey through Dyauloka and Prithviloka is an admirable deed and is indicative of your *devatva*.

रथं ये चक्रुः सुवृतं सुचेतसोऽविह्वरन्तं मनसस्परि ध्यया ।
ताँ ऊ न्वस्य सवनस्य पीतय आ वो वाजा ऋभवो वेदयामसि।।
(ऋग्वेदः, 4.36.2)

O Ribhus, the possessors of excellent mind who have made the well-turning and never bending chariot. O powerful Ribhus! You invite those people to drink this Soma.

तद्वो वाजा ऋभवः सुप्रवाचनं देवेषु विभ्वो अभगन्महित्वनम् ।
जिव्री यत्सन्ता पितरा सनाजुरा पुनर्युवाना च रथाय तक्षथ ।।
(ऋग्वेदः, 4.36.3)

O powerful and shining Ribhus! This most important deed of yours, with which you have made your extremely old and weak parents youthful again, has been intensely praised by all the devas.

एकं विचक्र चमसं चतुर्वयं निश्चर्मणो गामरिणीत धीतिभिः ।
अथा देवेष्वमृतत्वमानश श्रुष्टी वाजा ऋभवस्तद्व उक्थ्यम् ।।
(ऋग्वेदः, 4.36.4)

O powerful Ribhus! You have made one vessel which is four-layered and with your deeds, you have made an extremely old and skinny cow very strong and healthy again. Such a deed of yours soon became praiseworthy and you have won the praises of the devas.

ऋभुतो रयिः प्रथमश्रवस्तमो वाजश्रुतासो यमजीजनन्नरः ।
विभ्वतष्टो विदथेषु प्रवाच्यो यं देवासोऽवथा स विचर्षणिः ।।
(ऋग्वेदः, 4.36.5)

May we receive that wealth, which is the best of all and provider of fame, which was created by the ribhus, who are the leaders and are known for their power. The excellent chariot created by the ribhus is praiseworthy in the wars. O devas! That one, whom you defend, becomes famous in the world.

स वाज्यर्वा स ऋषिर्वचस्यया स शूरो अस्ता पृतनासु दुष्टरः ।
स रायत्पोषं स सुवीर्यं दधे यं वाजो विभ्वाँ ऋभवो यमाविषुः ।।
(ऋग्वेदः, 4.36.6)

That person whom vaja, vibhva, and ribhu defend is powerful and progressive, he is the seer of hymns and is praiseworthy; he is valiant. Therefore he is victorious in the wars; he is the receiver of wealth, food, and of remarkable deeds.

श्रेष्ठं वः पेशो अधिधायि दर्शतं स्तोमो वाजा ऋभवस्तं जुजुष्टन ।
धीरासो हि ष्ठा कवयो विषश्चितस्तान् व एना ब्रह्मणा वेदयामसि।।
(ऋग्वेदः, 4.36.7)

O powerful Ribhus! Your charming beautiful form is the best of all. You are patient, farsighted and intelligent. Please perform your deeds in accordance with the above praises we have showered on you. We call you through the medium of mantras.

यूयमस्मभ्यं धिषणाभ्यस्परि विद्वांसो विश्वा नर्याणि भोजना ।
द्युमन्तं वाजं वृषशुष्ममुत्तममा नो रयिमृभवस्तक्षता वयः ॥
(ऋग्वेदः, 4.36.8)

O Ribhus! You are wise. Provide us resources beyond even our own imagination that is capable of serving the interests of all beings, the privileges of wealth, the best of food, strength and affluence.

इह प्रजामिह रयिं रराणा इह श्रवो वीरवत्तक्षता नः ।
येन वयं चितयेमात्यन्यान्तं वाजं चित्रमृभवो ददा नः ॥
(ऋग्वेदः, 4.36.9)

O Ribhus! Being pleased, please provide us most excellent progeny in the world, the best of food combined with valour and affluence. Provide us such excellent power with the help of which we may surpass other people.

उप नो वाजा अध्वरमृभुक्षा देवा यात पथिभिर्देवयानैः ।
यथा यज्ञं मनुषो विक्ष्वासु दधिध्वे रण्वाः सुदिनेष्वह्नाम् ॥
(ऋग्वेदः, 4.37.1)

In the thirty-seventh sukta of fourth mandala of Rigveda, sage Vamadeva Gautam says in praise: O powerful Ribhus! Come to us at our yajna through the ways of devas. O presentable Ribhus! Receive the offerings of yajna made in the best of the day by humans.

ते वो हृदे मनसे सन्तु यज्ञा जुष्टासो अद्य धृतनिर्णिजो गुः ।
प्र वः सुतासो हरयन्त पूर्णाः क्रत्वे दक्षाय हर्षयन्त पीताः ॥
(ऋग्वेदः, 4.37.2)

O powerful Ribhus! These yajna may please your mind and heart. You may receive Soma as enriched as ghee, and worthy of drinking. The fully pressed Soma may be brought to you. The Soma taken by you may please you so that you could express your skills and valiant deeds.

त्र्युदायं देवहितं तथा वः स्तोमो वाजा ऋभुक्षणो ददे वः ।
जुह्वे मनुष्वदुपरासु विक्षु युष्मे सचा बृहद्दिवेषु सोमम् ॥
(ऋग्वेदः, 4.37.3)

O powerful Ribhus! In the same manner as the hymns are offered to you, I offer you Soma, prepared thrice a day and fit for the devas. Best among praiseworthy humans, I offer you Soma.

पीवो अश्वाः शुचद्रथा हि भूताय: शिप्रा वाजिनः सुनिष्काः ।
इन्द्रस्य सूनो शवसो नपातोऽनु वश्चेत्यग्नियं मदाय ।।
(ऋग्वेदः, 4.37.4)

O powerful Ribhus! You are the bearers of strong horses, glowing chariots, and bearers of the protected shields of horses, be you the givers of excellent wealth. O Ribhus! Born of power, sons of Indra, this excellent Soma is offered to you for your enjoyment.

ऋभुमृभुक्षणो रयिं वाजे वाजिन्तमं युजम् ।
इन्द्रस्वन्तं हवामहे सदासातममश्विनम् ।।
(ऋग्वेदः, 4.37.5)

O Ribhus! We call your group which is brilliant, affluent, powerful and dear to Indra, and lives in unity, we call forth such a group.

सेदृभवो यमवथ यूयमिन्द्रश्च मर्त्यम् ।
स धीभिरस्तु सनिता मेधसाता सो अर्वता ।।
(ऋग्वेदः, 4.37.6)

O Ribhus! That person, whom you and Indra protect, only he is considered the best and only he is equipped to enjoy desirable objects due to his good deeds. Only he is with the horse at the time of yajna.

वि नो वाजा ऋभुक्षणः पथश्चितन यष्टवे ।
अस्मभ्यं सूरयः स्तुता विश्वा आशास्तरीषणि ।।
(ऋग्वेदः, 4.37.7)

O powerful Ribhus! Show us the best way to perform good deeds. O wise Ribhus! When we offer praises to you, show us the most successful way to cross all directions.

तं नो वाजा ऋभुक्षण इन्द्र नासत्या रयिम् ।
समश्वं चर्षणिभ्य आ पुरु शस्त मघत्तये ।।
(ऋग्वेदः, 4.37.8)

O powerful Ribhus! O Indra and Ashvani devas! Please bless us humans so that we may receive abundant wealth and horses.

एषां कतिपयमन्त्रा अधिदैवतपक्ष उपनेयाः ।
शेषाः सर्वे मन्त्रा अधिभूतं तूपनीयन्ते ।।405।।

Out of this, some of the hymns should be taken in a metaphysical sense and the rest of the hymns are to be taken in a physical sense [related with specific individuals].

2.25.2 ऋभूणां माध्यमेन आर्याणां भारतीयत्वसिद्धान्तः

2.25.2 Ribhus prove that Arya were bharatiya

युद्धात् प्राक्तनानाम् ऋभूणां भारतीयमनुष्यतया दस्युयुद्धात् प्रागेवार्याणां भारतीयत्वसिद्धान्तः ।

The theory of Arya as the original inhabitants of Bharat is proved by the fact that ribhus, before their war with dasyus, were residents of Bharat.

इत्थमृभूणामेषां शिल्पं शृणुमः पुरा मनुष्याणाम् ।
भारतवर्षाभिजना ध्रुवमासंस्ते मनुष्यत्वात् ।।406।।

In this manner, we hear about the craft of the ancient human-like ribhus. As a matter of fact, being humans they were inhabitants of Bharatavarsha.

एभिश्च निर्मितौ तावश्वौ हरिसंज्ञकौ समारुह्य ।
इन्द्रो दस्यूनवधीत् तस्मादृभवः पुरैवासन् ।।407।।

'Mounting on the twin horses, created by them, named Hari, Indra killed the asuras.' It is evident from this that the ribhus were already living here.

एष सुधन्वा राजा जनक ऋभूणां च मानुषे लोके ।
आसीद् भारतवर्षे तस्मादार्याः पुराप्यासन् ।।408।।

In the world of humans, the king named Sudhanva was the father of ribhus, which proves that Arya were already living in Bharatavarsha.

2.25.3 दस्युयुद्धात् बहुपूर्व सभ्यानाम् आर्याणां भारतीयत्वसिद्धान्तः

2.25.3 Before the war with dasyus, Arya lived in Bharat

यस्मिन्नकाले स्वर्ग इन्द्रोऽयमासीत् पामीरे वा ब्राह्मणो वास आसीत् ।
पामीरोऽयं देवपूर्णो यदासीत् तर्ह्येवासन् भारतेऽप्यार्यसभ्याः ।।409।।

When Indra lived in the heaven and Pamir was the abode of Brahma, and Pamir was full of devas, at that time civilized Arya lived in Bharatavarsha.

नैषां वासः स्वर्गलोके कदाचित् पामीराद्वा नागता भारतेऽस्मिन् ।
नो वाऽनार्याधिष्ठितं देशमेतं जित्वा तत्र स्वान्निवासानकार्षुः ।।410।।

These Arya never lived in Svargaloka and they had neither come to Bharatavarsha from the Pamir region nor had they made this country their abode after defeating the non-Arya who lived here.

युद्धेऽप्यायुः श्रूयतेऽस्मिन् सहायः सोऽयं राजैलेयपुत्रः श्रुतोऽस्ति ।
ऐलेयश्चेक्ष्वाकुणा तुल्यकालोऽयोध्यायां चेक्ष्वाकुरार्येश आसीत् ।।411।।

In the context of this war, the name of Ayu is mentioned as a helper, who, according to an oral tradition, was the son of king Aileya. This Aileya was the contemporary of Ikshavaku; Ikshavaku was the king of Arya in Ayodhya.

तस्मान्मन्ये भारतीयार्यसंघा दस्योर्युद्धात्पूर्वमेवात्र देशे ।
अस्थुस्तेषामेष देशः स्वकीयो न त्वेवास्मिन् सन्ति वैदेशिकास्ते ।।412।।

So, I believe that the Arya lived in this country long before the war [between the asuras and devas]. Therefore this country was of their own, they were not outsiders in this country. [In other words they were natives, it was their own country.]

इति मधुसूदनविद्यावाचस्पतिप्रणीतस्य ब्रह्मविज्ञानशास्त्रसम्बन्धिनो
भारतवर्षीयार्योपाख्याने आर्यदासीयः द्वितीयः प्रक्रमः सम्पूर्णः ।

Thus, the second chapter namely the arya-dasa conflict in the Bharatavarshiyaryopakhyan related to Brahmavijnanashastra of Madhusudan Ojha is concluded.

प्रक्रमः तृतीयः

विज्ञानभवनम्

CHAPTER THIRD

SCIENTIFIC INSTITUTION

3.1 विज्ञानशालानिर्माणम्

3.1 CONSTRUCTION OF SCIENCE LABORATORY

पुरायुगे दिव्यप्राणपरीक्षणार्थं विज्ञानशालानिर्माणम् आर्यानार्यविद्रोहनिमित्तभूतं सिन्धुसरस्वतीसंभेदे सूर्याधिष्ठानम् ।

In the ancient period, the construction of the science block for the examination of *divyaprana*, the establishment of surya-bhavan in the context of Sindhu and Sarasvati, as a result of the conflict between the Arya and non-Arya.

आर्याणां दस्यूनां सूर्योऽभ्यामदर्दने निमित्तमभूत् ।
तद्दर्शयामि तावद् यत्र स सूर्यो यथा चासीत् ।।1।।

The surya [sun] was the cause of the conflict between the Arya and dasyus. Now I describe about surya, as to what he was and where he was.

वेत्तुं वसिष्ठमुख्याः सूर्यस्य गवां तथोषसो विद्याम् ।
चक्रे सूर्यं नामाधिष्ठानं प्राक् सरस्वतीकूले ।।2।।

On the shores of ancient Sarasvati, a building named after surya was constructed under the leadership of sage Vasishta to study the rays of the sun and the knowledge of *usha* (dawn).

अस्ति वितस्तासिन्धोरन्तरतः सा सरस्वती धारा ।
सरयूसहिता काचित् सान्या प्राचीसरस्वत्याः ।।3।।

The river that flowed between Vitasta and Sindhu was none other than river Sarasvati.

सरस्वती सरयू: सिन्धरूर्मिभिर्महो महीरवसा यन्तु वक्षणी: ।
देवीरापो मातर: सूदयित्न्वो घृतवत्पयो मधुमन्नो अर्चता ।।
(ऋग्वेद:, 10.64.9)

It is described in the Rigveda samhita–Sarasvati, Sarayu, and Sindhu, the great and most excellent rivers full of waves, may come to protect us. These inspiring and mother-like rivers may provide us butter and honey-like water.

इयं शुष्मेभिर्बिसखा इवारुजत् सानु गिरीणां तविषेभिरूर्मिभि: ।
पारावतघ्नीमवसे सुवृक्तिभि: सरस्वतीमा विवासेम धीतिभि: ।।
(ऋग्वेद:, 6.61.2)

Like the breaking of the lotus stalks, this Sarasvati breaks the higher edges of the mountains with the forceful strikes of its powerful and gushing currents. We serve this Sarasvati with devotion for our protection.

सा पारसीकवेदे हरखूवतीत्याख्यया पठिता ।
सर्पसरोवरतोऽस्या निर्गमनं दर्शितं मात्स्ये ।।4।।

In the Zendavesta, Sarasvati river has been mentioned as Harkuati (Harkuvati). In the Matsya Purana, its source has been shown in the *sarpa sarovara* [lake of serpents].

हेमकूटस्य पृष्ठे तु सर्पाणां तत्सर: स्मृतम् ।
सरस्वती प्रभवति तस्माज्ज्योतिष्मती तु या ।।
(मत्स्यपुराणम्, 161.64–65)

This sarpa sarovara has been mentioned as being located behind the Hemakut mountain. Sarasvati has its source in that sarpa sarovara and therefore that river has been mentioned as jyotishmati.

मन्ये सर्पसरस्तत् पञ्चाशत् क्रोशदीर्घ यत् ।
सार्द्धक्रोशप्रततं भाषायामद्य 'पानकाङ्गा' यम् ।।5।।

I believe that this sarpa sarovara is fifty-kosa long and one-and-a-half-kosa wide, which has been mentioned in the common language as 'pankanga'.

काश्मीरेष्वेव नगरस्य भवनं तक्षकस्य च ।
वितस्ताख्यामिति ख्यातं सर्वपापप्रमोचनम् ।।
(पद्मपुराणम् स्वर्गखण्ड:, 25.2)

In Kashmir, there is a building named after Takshaka naga [serpent], which is famous as Vitasta and is the destroyer of all sins.

इत्थं पाद्मे स्वर्गखण्डे वितस्ता नामाख्याता तक्षकाणां पुरी या ।
आसन्नेऽस्यास्तत्सरस्तक्षकाणां तीर्थं तस्मात्सा सरस्वत्युपेता ।।6।।

In this manner, as mentioned in the Svarga-khanda of Padma Purana, in the city of Takshaka, named Vitasta, there is a lake known as Tiratha, that is why that river became famous as Sarasvati.

काश्मीरादुत्तरतो बिन्दुसरस्तत्सरीकुलेत्युक्तम् ।
'सरपस' नाम च तस्मात्सरस्वतीत्याहुरन्ये तु ।।7।।

Towards the north of Kashmir, there is a lake named Bindusara, also known as 'Sarpasa', which some people call Sarasvati.

सिन्धोः सङ्गमदेशे तस्या वामे च दक्षिणे च तटे ।
यासीत्सरस्वती पूस्तस्यां सूर्यप्रतिष्ठाऽऽसीत् ।।8।।

Near the east and west coast of the confluence of Sindhu, where there is a city named Sarasvati, the surya was established there.

ऊचे वसिष्ठ एतां सरस्वतीं पुरि सरस्वत्याम् ।
प्रवहन्ती रथ्यामिव तत्र वसिष्ठः स वसति स्म ।।9।।

Sage Vasishta tells that this Sarasvati river flowed like chariot lanes through the city of Sarasvati; it is where sage Vasishta lived.

स्थानं यदुन्नतं स्यान्निसर्गजं कृत्रिमेण वा विधिना ।
तत्रास्ति धरुणशब्दः सरस्वती पूरियं धरुणम् ।।10।।

The place which became higher either due to natural causes or through artificial means, it became known as *dharuna* (sustainer of all) and hence it was called the city of Sarasvati.

प्रक्षोदसा धायसा सस्र एषा सरस्वती धरुणमायसी पूः ।
प्र वा बधाना रथ्येव याति विश्वा आपो महिना सिन्धुरन्याः ।।
(ऋग्वेद:, 7.95.1)

In the ninety-fifth sukta of seventh mandala of Rigveda, it is written: This Sarasvati river is full of water and flows rapidly. It protects everyone like a city made of iron. This river flows majestically like a charioteer, obstructing all other waters.

एकाऽचेतत् सरस्वती नदीनां शुचिर्यती गिरिभ्य आ समुद्रात् ।
रायश्चेतन्ती भुवनस्य भूरेर्घृतं पयो दुदुहे नाहुषाया ।।
(ऋग्वेद:, 7.95.20)

Of all the rivers, Sarasvati, filled with consciousness, is the only river that runs its course all the way from the mountains to the ocean. This river projects the infinite wealth of the earth and provides butter and milk to the people living near its banks.

इमा जुह्वाना युष्मदा नमोमिः प्रतिस्तोमं सरस्वति जुषस्व ।
तव शर्मन् प्रियतमे दधाना उपस्थेयाम शरणं न वृक्षम् ।।
(ऋग्वेद:, 7.95.5)

O Sarasvati! We, the performers of yajna, receive these cereal-offerings from you with gratitude. Hear our praises. We are your most dear ones. Like the shelter of a tree, may we remain with you.

अयमुते सरस्वती वसिष्ठो द्वारावृतस्य सुभगे व्यावः ।
वर्धशुभ्रे स्तुवतेरासि वाजान् यूयं पात स्वस्तिभिः सदा नः ।।
(ऋग्वेद:, 7.95.6)

O Epitome of good fortune Sarasvati! This Vasishta sage opens both the doors of yajna for you. O Bright one! Come forward and provide food to the persons praising you. Please protect us with all good means.

3.2 भरद्वाजकृता सरस्वतीस्तुतिः

3.2 PRAISE OF SARASVATI BY BHARADVAJA

पुत्रो बृहस्पतेः प्रागत्रैवासीत् पुरा भरद्वाजः ।
सहकारी स वसिष्ठस्यासीत् स च तां सरस्वतीं स्तौति ॥11॥

In ancient times, Bharadvaja, son of Brihaspati, lived here. He was a collaborator of Vasishta. He praises that Sarasvati.

इयमददाद्रभसमृणच्युतं दिवोदासं बध्न्यश्वाय दाशुषे ।
या शश्वन्तमाचखादावसं पणिं ता ते दात्राणि तविषा सरस्वति ॥
(ऋग्वेदः, 6.61.1)

In the Rigveda, sage Bharadvaja offers praises to the river thus: This Sarasvati granted a son, Devodasa to Baddhnyashva, who was known as *danadata* (giver of grains). This son was tolerant and free of any debt. While being wealthy, he destroyed the miserly. O Sarasvati! Majestic are such blessings of yours.

इयं शुष्मेभिर्विसखा इवारुजत् सानु गिरीणां तविषेभिरूर्म्मिभिः ।
पारावतघ्नीमवसे सुवृक्तिभिः सरस्वतीमाविवासेम धीतिभिः ॥
(ऋग्वेदः, 6.61.2)

This river breaks the high corners of the mountains with its gushing currents, like breaking the lotus stalks. For our protection, we serve the forceful Sarasvati with devotion.

सरस्वति देवनदो निबर्हय प्रजां विश्वस्य वृसयस्य मायिनः ।
उत क्षितिभ्योऽवनीरविन्दो विषमेभ्यो अस्रवो वाजिनीवति ॥
(ऋग्वेदः, 6.61.3)

O Sarasvati! Please destroy the persons condemning the god. Destroy all the false and vicious persons. Please provide land for the protection of earth. O *Vajinivati* [one who feeds]! You have made the water flow for this world.

प्रणो देवी सरस्वती वाजेभिर्वाजिनीवती ।
धीनामवित्र्यवतु ॥
(ऋग्वेदः, 6.61.4)

Provided with food, Sarasvati is the bearer of food. Protector of intellect, she may guard us.

यस्त्वा देवि सरस्वत्युपब्रूते धने हिते ।
इन्द्रं न वृत्रतूर्ये ॥

(ऋग्वेद:, 6.61.5)

O Sarasvati! Guard that person who, before the beginning of war, offers you prayers like Indra, the slayer of Vritra.

त्वं देवि सरस्वत्यवा वाजेषु वाजिनी ।
रदा पूषेव न: सनिम् ॥

(ऋग्वेद:, 6.61.6)

O Sarasvati, the bearer of anna! Please protect us in war. Provide us wealth like *pusha* (a deity).

उत स्या न: सरस्वती घोरा हिरण्यवर्तनि: ।
वृत्रघ्नी वष्टि सुष्टुतिम् ॥

(ऋग्वेद:, 6.61.7)

This powerful Sarasvati, mover of the golden chariot-wheel, destroys Vritra. That Sarasvati desires to hear the best of our praises.

यस्या अनन्तो अह्रुतस्त्वेषश्चरिष्णुरर्णव: ।
अमश्चरित रोरुवत् ॥

(ऋग्वेद:, 6.61.8)

The flow of that Sarasvati river transcends limits, is extremely fast, continuously in motion and never remains static at any one place. Such a flow goes on continuously making noise.

सा नो विश्वा अतिद्विष: स्वसृरन्या ऋतावरी ।
अतन्नहेव सूर्य: ॥

(ऋग्वेद:, 6.61.9)

This Sarasvati river expels all our enemies.This Sarasvati is a follower of truth; it takes us afar from all of its sisters [rivers]. This river spreads light like the sun during the day.

उत नः प्रिया प्रियासु सप्तस्वसा सुजुष्टा ।
सरस्वती स्तोम्याभूत् ।।

(ऋग्वेदः, 6.61.10)

This river is dear to us than all the dearest objects. This Sarasvati is worthy of our best service, therefore it is the best of the seven sisters [rivers].

आपप्रुषी पार्थिवान्यूरु रजो अन्तरिक्षम् ।
सरस्वती निदस्पातु ।।

(ऋग्वेदः, 6.61.11)

May this Sarasvati river, provider of worldly wealth and capable of covering the vast space with its light, protect us from our detractors.

त्रिषधस्था सप्तधातुः पञ्चजाता वर्धयन्ती ।
वाजे वाजे हव्याभूत् ।।

(ऋग्वेदः, 6.61.12)

This Sarasvati is capable of pervading in all the three spaces [*bhu* (universe), *bhuva* (interspace), *sva* (heaven)], is the magnifier of five objects combined with seven metals [four varnas and nishada], therefore in every war, it is always worthy of prayers.

प्रया महिम्ना महिनासु चेकिते द्युम्नेभिरन्या अपसामपस्तमा ।
रथ इव बृहती विभ्वने कृतोपस्तुत्या चिकितुषा सरस्वती ।।

(ऋग्वेदः, 6.61.13)

This Saravati appears best among all rivers because of its unique importance and brilliance. The flow of this river is faster than the flow of other rivers. This river is like a chariot. Created by god, this Sarasvati is worthy of every praise.

सरस्वत्यभि नो नेषि वस्यो माप स्फरीः पयसा मा न आधक् ।
जुषस्व नः सख्या वेश्या च मा त्वत्क्षेत्राण्यरणानि गन्म ।।

(ऋग्वेदः, 6.61.14)

O Sarasvati! Provide us our desirable wealth. Don't harm us with your flow of water. Don't keep us away from you. Accept our friendship and service. Let us not go away from you to other fields.

3.3 सूर्यसंस्थापनस्वरूपम्

3.3 NATURE OF SURYA'S INSTALLATION

अस्याः सिन्धुप्रान्ते प्रवहन्त्या अनुतटं सरस्वत्याः ।
नगरी सरस्वती या तस्यां सौरं बृहत् सदनम् ॥12॥

There is a city named as Sarasvati situated on the banks of Sarasvati river, flowing in the region of Sindhu river. Here, the huge surya-*sadhana* (solar observatory) was situated.

तत्र वसिष्ठप्रमुखा द्विचक्रयन्त्रेण सूर्यसंज्ञेन ।
उषसं सूर्यज्योतिश्चन्द्राद्यंशून् परीक्षयामासुः ॥13॥

There, Vasishta and other sages used to examine usha, and the rays of sun and moon.

वैज्ञानिकैर्महर्षिभिरासीद् रचितं पुरा परीक्षार्थम् ।
यत्सूर्यमन्दिरं तत् स्तूपाकारं शिलामयं वृत्तम् ॥14॥

This surya-sadhana, constructed by the wise sages for the purpose of research in ancient times, was a circular, conical-building, shaped like a stupa.

स्तूपादस्माद् बाह्यभागे समन्तान्नानाशालाश्रेणिसंभक्तमूर्तिः ।
प्रासादोऽभूदम्बरोल्लेखिशृङ्गो नानाकक्षोऽग्र्यः शतस्तम्भरम्यः ॥15॥

Around the outer section of this stupa was a complex containing rows of rooms and high-rising towers. Consisting of hundred columns, that building was most beautiful and excellent.

प्रासादेऽस्मिन् मुख्यवेश्माध्यवात्सीत् सूर्यः पश्चादेतशश्चोषश्च ।
बार्हस्पत्योऽन्ये वसिष्ठादयो वा सर्वेऽप्यासन् मन्दिरेऽस्मिन्नियुक्ताः ॥16॥

In the main building of this complex stood the sun and in other buildings *aitasha* [brilliance] and usha were established. Bharadvaja, son of Brihaspati, Vasishta, and others were appointed as administrators of this complex.

प्रासादानां मध्यभूमौ तदासीत् स्तूपकारं सद्म वैवस्वतं तत् ।
द्विप्राकारं छन्नसोपानगम्यातिध्वान्तान्तर्वेश्मनिम्नावकाशम् ॥17॥

At the centre of the building, there was a surya-bhavana in the shape of a stupa, which had two sub-sections and covered staircases. In the inner part of the building, there was a pitch-dark inner section, in which there were many minute holes for the light to enter.

सूर्यस्थानं निस्तलं वर्तुलं तद् ब्रह्माण्डाभं श्लक्ष्णबाह्यान्तरङ्गम् ।
अन्तर्भूम्या अर्द्धमूर्ध्वं बहिर्धा तत्रागारं निम्नभूमीतलेऽन्तः ।।18।।

This building was circular in shape and had different levels. It was filled with the radiance of the cosmos and was beautiful and smooth from inside as well as outside. Inside, it had a sunken floor as half of its base was underground and the other half was overground.

रन्ध्रैरच्छाश्मावरुद्धैः कृतोर्ध्वं भाभैः सूक्ष्मैर्नीलदेशोपपन्नैः ।
तत्सोपानं द्वारयोः क्लृप्तमन्तर्द्वारं द्वारधः स्थितं भिन्नभित्तौ ।।19।।

There were two staircases adjacent to the two doors of the building, covered with clean slates that had beautiful, blue radiant glow coming through the holes. Its inner door was built in the opposite wall.

द्वारेकस्मिन् बाह्यभित्तौ ततोऽन्तः प्रादक्षिण्यात् सम्मुखी द्वारधस्तात् ।
अन्तर्भित्तौ या तयाऽन्तःप्रविष्टः सूर्यं साक्षाच्चक्रगं पश्यति स्म ।।20।।

There was a door on the outer wall and there was another wall built on the opposite side. On entering the door, which was on the inner wall, the sun could be seen directly fixed in a circle.

सूर्यगृहस्यैतस्यच्छदिपटलेऽकृत सा रन्ध्राणि ।
दुर्लक्ष्याणि यथैभ्यो रश्मिश्चक्रे समं न्यपपत् ।।21।।

On the roof of this building, there were many minute holes made in such a manner that the rays of the sun fell on the sun-circle in equal proportion.

अष्टाचत्वारिंशद्रेखाः पूर्वापराः पटले ।
प्रतिरेखं रन्ध्राणामभवदशीतिशतं न्यस्तम् ।।22।।

On the eastern and western part of the roof of this building, there were forty-eight lines and on every line there were 180 small holes.

संवत्सरेण सूर्यो व्योम्नि चरन् यत्र यत्र देशे स्यात् ।
तत्तत्सम्मुखरन्ध्रादंशुनिपातोऽत्र चक्रे स्यात् ।।23।।

Irrespective of the sun's position in the sky during the year, the rays of the sun, through these holes, fell on the sun-circle carved inside the laboratory.

यर्ह्येवायं प्रागुदेति स्म सूर्यस्तर्ह्येवास्मिन्नश्मके बिम्बितः स्यात् ।
खे संचारेऽप्यत्र चक्रे स्थिरोऽर्कोऽथास्तंभावे नक्तमत्राप्यदृश्यः ।।24।।

When the sun rose in the eastern direction, then the rays of the sun were reflected on this sun-circle and the rays were reflected on the circle even when the sun was moving across the sky. And these rays fell on the circle even before the setting of the sun. This circle was not visible at night.

तत्राश्चर्यं संवृतेऽस्मिन्नागारे ध्वान्ते गाढे सूर्य एकत्र तस्थौ ।
नाभौ चक्रस्याश्मके बिम्बितोऽभात् प्रातःकालात् सायमन्तं स सूर्यः ।।25।।

It was a very strange sight, the sun's rays reflecting in the sun-circle in a pitch-dark room through out the day.

3.4 सूर्यचक्रस्वरूपम्

3.4 SHAPE OF SUN-DISC

तत्रागारेन्त:स्थले चक्रयुग्मं हैमं सांशुश्लिष्टमासीत् स सूर्य: ।
नाभिस्थोऽयं नास्य तत्रावलम्बोऽत्रात्याश्चर्य खे निराधार एव ।।26।।

Inside the mansion, there were two [bright] golden discs. That was the sun, embraced by its rays. That sun was positioned on the navel [centre] of the disc. Surprisingly, that disc was suspended in space without any perpendicular support.

सूर्ये द्विचक्ररूपे एकं चक्रं बृहत् तदन्तरत: ।
क्षुद्रं चक्रं निहितं तत्र प्रतिबिम्ब एति बृहतोऽस्य ।।27।।

बृहदपि चक्रं द्विकृतं परिवर्तते क्रमेण ते चक्रे ।
संवत्सरेण सौरेणैते परिवृत्तिमायात: ।।28।।

One of the discs, shining like the sun, was bigger and inside it was another smaller disc in which the image of the bigger disc could be seen. The bigger disc was in two parts. Both the discs revolved respectively in *uttarayana* [northern circumambulation] and *dakshinayana* [southern circumambulation] in the order of sanvatsara.

चक्रद्वितये चैकं भवति निगूढं सदैवकद् ददृशे ।
षण्मासै: पर्यायाद् दृष्टमदृष्टं बभूव तच्चित्रम् ।।29।।

Since one of the two discs remained hidden, they appeared always as one disc. Surprisingly, it could be seen for six months and for remaining six months, it became invisible.

द्वे ते चक्रे सूर्ये ब्रह्माण ऋतुथा विदु: ।
अथैकं चक्रं यद् गुहा दतद्धातय इद् विदु: ।।
(ऋग्वेद:, 10.85.16)

The two discs of your chariot—sun and moon—are known to the brahmins and the third, sanvatsaratmaka disc, which was hidden from sight, is only known to the learned.

एतच्चक्राधस्ताद् भूमौ चक्रं समाहितं धरुणे ।
ऊर्ध्वस्थसूर्यरश्मिग्राहि परीक्षास्ति तत्रैव ।।30।।

On the ground, below this disc, there was another disc which received the rays and there the sun was observed carefully.

3.5 सूर्यविज्ञानात् आधिदैविकसिद्धिः

3.5 CELESTIAL SIDDHIS FROM SURYAVIJNANA (SOLAR SCIENCE)

गौर्ज्योतिरायुरेते सूर्ये सन्ति त्रयो भावाः ।
भूतग्रामो देवग्रामात्मग्रामकौ च तेभ्यः स्युः ॥31॥

The sun is considered to possess three different functional forms—*gau* (a ray of light; also the earth), *jyoti* (light) and *ayu* (living beings taken collectively). Out of these three, *bhutasamuha* (group of material objects) originate from gau, *devasamuha* (group of devas) originate from jyoti, and *atmasamuha* (groups of atma) originate from ayu.

सर्वं व्योम व्याप्नुवन् सोम एतत् सूर्यप्राणे द्वादशात्मन्यपीतः ।
ज्योतिर्भावं भावयत्यत्र देवाः सेन्द्रा इन्द्रः शुक्लकृष्णादिरूपम् ॥32॥

The moonlight spread across the sky is the reflection of this sun; all the gods including Indra, manifest this light. Indra reflects both white and dark parts of this light.

3.6 सूर्यविज्ञानात् आधिभौतिकसिद्धिः

3.6 MATERIAL SIDDHIS FROM SURYAVIJNANA

तस्मिंश्चक्रे शङ्कवोऽन्ते सहस्रं तीव्रज्योतिर्भासते चक्रमध्ये ।
ज्योतिष्यस्मिन् ये सहस्रं विभागास्तेषामेकः सत्यकृत् कामधुक् च ।।33।।

To that disc, thousands of spikes were attached and an intense light emitted from the middle of the disc. Out of the thousand sections in this light, one was of the form of truth and fulfilled desires.

शेषा गावस्तास्त्रिधा स्युर्विभक्ता आदित्यानां रुद्रकाणां वसूनाम् ।
चक्रेऽन्यस्मिन् द्वादशैकादशाष्टौ द्वौ चेति स्युस्त्रिंशदंशास्त्रयश्च ।।34।।

Remaining rays were divided into three parts—adityas, rudras and vasus, In the other disc, there were twelve adityas, eleven rudras, and eight vasus. And along with the ashvin kumars (both morning and evening twilight), there were, in all, thirty-three types of rays.

शङ्कुग्रामे शक्तिवैचित्र्यहेतोर्गोभ्यो वर्णाः सप्त पार्थक्यतः स्युः ।
अन्योन्यस्मिन् घातविक्षेपकर्मद्वारा नानाशक्तयः प्रादुरासन् ।।35।।

In that conical group, seven colours used to get segregated from these rays. This separation of colours was caused by varied energies. Several powers used to originate due to various combinations of these seggregated coloured rays.

इति चक्रद्वययोगात् प्रतिफलिता अंशवो विभक्ताः स्युः ।
विशकलितास्ता गावो भवन्ति ते सप्तसप्तका मरुतः ।।36।।

Thus as a result of the combination of the two discs, the rays themselves got divided and in their advanced stage, they transformed into forty-nine marutas.

गन्धादींस्तु विशेषान् जनयन्तीमानिमे मरुतः ।
तत एव भूतभेदा भवन्ति नानाविधा लोके ।।37।।

These forty-nine marutas give shape to form, taste, odour, and other qualities and these create differences among various types of animals in the world.

मरुतां पुनर्विभागादेकादशजातयो हि ते रुद्राः ।
रुद्राणां च विभागादादित्या द्वादशाविःस्युः ॥38॥

Eleven rudras originate on further division of marutas and from the division of rudras originate twelve adityas.

इन्द्रस्तेषामेकोऽस्त्योकःसारीश्वरो महावीर्यः ।
आदित्यरुद्रमरुतोऽवलम्बिताः सन्ति तत्रेन्द्रे ॥39॥

Indra [surya] is the only abode for all these. He is the only controller and is very powerful. The adityas, rudras and marutas, all reside in this Indra.

यथाग्निगर्भा पृथिवी तथा द्यौरिन्द्रेण गर्भिणी । (शतपथब्राह्मणम, 14.9.4.21)
इत्थं वदन्त ऋषयः सूर्येऽपश्यन् विशिष्यैतम् ॥40॥

It is written in the Shatapatha Brahmana, 'As the earth is in the middle of fire, the heaven is in the middle Indra'. Thus speak sages after looking at this sun.

आयुः स एष इन्द्रः स हि सर्वेषां भवत्यात्मा ।
प्रत्यर्थमेष तिष्ठन् देवान् भूतानि वा जनयेत् ॥41॥

It is the atma of Indra. This Indra pervades the atma of all beings. Integral to all the elements, it gives birth to devas and other beings.

देहे देहे बृहतीसहस्रभेदास्त्रिधा प्रवर्तन्ते ।
प्राणगनोवाग्भेदादायुरतत् तत्र राग्यगैक्षन्त ॥42॥

In every body, there are three forms of *brihati sahasra*—prana, mana and vak: ayu envelops them completely and uniformly.

आयुस्त्वमृतः प्राणस्तत आदित्या भवन्ति तैरात्मा ।
प्रत्यात्मतस्तु गावः सहस्रमभितः प्रवर्तन्ते ॥43॥

That ayu element is the basic life-breath out of which are born the adityas. Out of these adityas originate atma: Gau originates from every atma and that usha gets transformed into thousand forms all around.

योगाद् गवां तु रुद्रा एकादशजातिका विजायन्ते ।
रुद्रे तु रुद्रयोगान्मरुतः स्युः सप्तसप्तकास्तत्र ॥44॥

When the gau come together, eleven rudras are born. By the coming together [either by striking or by mixing] of rudras, forty-nine marutas are created.

एषामेव तु मरुतां योगविभेदाद् भवन्ति वसवोष्टौ ।
गन्धो रसश्च रूपं स्पर्शो वाग् धृतिमती ध्रुवत्वं च ।।45।।

In varied ways of coming together of these marutas, eight vasus are created and also odour, taste, form, touch, speech, *dhriti* (self-command), *mati* (intellect) and *dhruvatva* (firmness).

मात्राभिराभिरेव प्रज्ञानप्राणभूतानि ।
प्रभवन्त्येषां ग्रामा धातूद्भिच्चेतनैस्त्रिविधा: ।।46।।

From these mantras are born *prahnan* (intellect), prana, and physical elements. From these are born *dhatu* (primary or elementary substance), *utbhijja* (plants) and *chetna* (consciousness).

यत्किञ्चिदत्र वीक्षे तत् खनिजोद्भिज्जचेतनत: ।
त्रेधा विभक्तमेतत् सर्वं सवितु: प्रसूतमंशुभ्य: ।।47।।

All that is seen in the world is divided into these three types—[dhatu, utbhijja and chetana]. All these originate from the rays of sun.

नूनं जना: सूर्येण प्रसूता अयन्नर्थानि कृण्वन्नपांसि । (ऋग्वेद:, 7.63.4)
इत्थं वसिष्ठ ऊचे सर्वेषां सूर्यजनितत्वम् ।।48।।

All that can be created have originated from the sun's rays and this creates order among 'all that is desired'. Thus has sage Vasishta theorized about the origin of all beings from the sun.

जगति हि सृष्टिविधाने यद्वैचित्र्यं प्रदृश्यते क्वापि ।
तस्यैष एव सूर्य: कारणमस्तीति सिद्धान्त: ।।49।।

सूर्ये द्युस्थे के के सन्ति पदार्था: कथं च तैर्विश्वम् ।
उत्पद्यते कुतो वा नानाभेदा इहोत्पन्ना: ।।50।।

कथमिह वायु: पवते निर्वातं वा कुतो भवति ।
कथमिह मेघा वृष्ट्यै कदाचिदुद्भूय शाम्यन्ति ।।51।।

What are the substances in the sun situated in the Dyauloka? And how did this world originate from them? And from where did such variety of beings originate in this world? How does the wind blow and where does it go? From where do these clouds originate and become quiety after shedding rain?

एतत् सर्वं ज्ञातुं भूमौ सूर्यं प्रतिष्ठाप्य ।
चक्रद्वयप्रभावान् सर्वानर्थान् परीक्षयामासुः ।।52।।

To know all these mysteries, lets us establish a sun [sun-house] on the ground and examine the elements by the influence of the dual discs [two sun-discs].

चक्रद्वयेऽत्र सौरान् रश्मीन् संश्लेष्य विश्लेष्य ।
नाना भावा जनिताः सर्वं विज्ञानमुपलब्धम् ।।53।।

Various beings [*bhava*-s] originate by synthesis and analysis of the sun rays in the two discs; and thus all vijnana can be availed.

3.7 सूर्यविज्ञानात् आध्यात्मिकसिद्धिः

3.7 METAPHYSICAL SIDDHIS FROM SURYAVIJNANA

संकलितैर्व्यवकलितैरंशुभिरर्था बहिः क्रियन्ते स्म ।
देवानामिदमेव तु विज्ञानं यज्ञयोनिरभूत् ।।54।।

All desirables [elements] have manifested clearly by the integration and disintegration of the rays. This is the knowledge of the devas and this knowledge is why the yajna is performed.

संकलितैर्व्यवकलितैरंशुभिरात्मनि बलं हितं यज्ञात् ।
आत्मा परोक्षदर्शी परोक्षकारी च यज्ञतो भवति ।।55।।

Strength is imported to atma by these integrated and disintegrated rays [as a result of the action of mutual exchange]. Through the yajna are gained the unobserved [secret] knowledge and even the unobserved knowledge gained by mutual exchange originate from yajna.

अपि मृतमुज्जीवयते यज्ञात् सिद्ध्यन्ति भुक्तयः सर्वाः ।
या चाष्टयोगसिद्धिः सा यज्ञादात्मनि प्रभवेत् ।।56।।

By yajna, even dead objects can be brought to life and all enjoyable substances can be accomplished. And the *ashtayogasiddhi* (eight yoga accomplishments) can be acquired through these yajna.

अणिमा महिमा चैव गरिमा लघिमा तथा ।
प्राप्तिः प्राकाम्यमीशित्वं वशित्वं चाष्ट सिद्धयः ।।
(अमरकोशः, 1.1.17 प्रक्षिप्त)

एतद्यज्ञविधाने यजमाननियुक्त ऋत्विगाख्यातः ।
ऋत्विज ऋषयो ह्यृषिता वैज्ञानिकता हि सूर्यविज्ञानात् ।।57।।

There are eight siddhis known as—anima, mahima, garima, laghima, prapti, ishitva and vashitva. In such a yajna, the priest appointed by the host alone is important. The priest is sage and the sage-hood, that is, acceptance of his *vaijnanikata* (knowledge status) is attested and accomplished by suryavijnana.

3.8 विज्ञानशालास्थिता सूर्यप्रतिमायाः प्रतिमाराधनबीजत्वम्

3.8 IDOL OF THE SUN IN SCIENTIFIC LABORATORY, PRECURSOR OF IDOL WORSHIP IN BHARAT

अत एव सूर्यसदनाद् देवप्रतिमाप्रकल्पनारम्भः ।
वेदऽन्योऽपि च देवप्रतिमार्चायाः प्रचार आम्नातः ।।58।।

The conceptualization of the god's idol was initiated from the sun-house. The popularity of god's idols have been described at many other places in the Vedas.

ऋग्वेदसंहितायां चतुर्थमण्डलचतुर्विंशे ।
सूक्ते दशमर्च्यैन्द्र्या मूर्तेः क्रयमाह वामदेव ऋषिः ।।59।।

In the tenth verse of the twenty-fourth hymn of the fourth mandala of Rigveda samhita, sage Vamadeva has talked about the purchase of Indra's idol.

उत्कृष्टं बहुमूल्यं विक्रीणन् द्रव्यमल्पमूल्येन ।
पूजाफलोपलब्धौ समयं प्रत्यर्पणाय चक्रे सः ।।60।।

'While buying an excellent and highly priced object at a cheap price, the buyer promised to return it after having attained the merits of worship.

भूयसां वस्नमचरत् कनीयोऽविक्रीतो अकानिषं पुनर्यन् ।
स भूयसा कनीयो नारिरेचीद् दीना दक्षा विदुहन्ति प्रवाणम् ।।
(ऋग्वेदः, 4.24.9)

'Someone gave a lot of money and then got an object. When that object could not be sold anywhere, then he went to get his money back. But the seller did not agree to give back a large amount of money for that object.

क इमं दशभिर्ममेन्द्रं क्रीणाति धेनुभिः ।
यदा वृत्राणि जङ्घनद् अथैनं मे पुनर्ददत् ।।
(ऋग्वेदः, 4.24.10)

'Who can give ten cows for this idol of Indra? O buyers, after this Indra has killed your enemies, you may return this Indra to me'.

इन्द्रप्रतिमापूजाप्रकारमप्ययमुपादिक्षत् ।
देहोपचारभोगाहवनमनःप्रेमभावनास्तुतिभिः ।।61।।

The ways of worshipping the idol of Indra—by obeisance, offerings, invocations, heart filled with *manaprema* (love), emotion, and incantations—are also preached.

आदिद्ध नेम इन्द्रियं यजन्ते आदित् पक्तिः पुरोडाशं रिरिच्यात् ।
आदित्सोमो विपपृच्यादसुष्वीनादिज्जुजोष वृषभं यजध्यै ।।
(ऋग्वेदः, 4.24.5)

'After this the warriors adore the power of Indra. Then the cook prepares *purodasa* (offerings). After this, the ones who perform the Soma yajna remove those *nastika*-s (non-believers) who do not perform yajna. Then, for the yajna, the warriors attend to Indra.

कृणोत्यस्मै वरिवो य इत्था इन्द्राय सोममुशते सुनोति ।
सध्रीचीनेन मनसाऽविवेनं तमित् सखायं कृणुते समत्सु ।
(ऋग्वेदः, 4.24.6)

'This way Indra gives wealth for him who extracts Soma for him. Those wishing Indra good with the best of intentions makes that performer of Somayajna their friend.

य इन्द्राय सुनवत् सोममद्य पचात् पक्तीरुत भृज्जाति धानाः ।
प्रति मनायोरुचथानि हर्य्यन् तस्मिन्दधद्वृषणं शुष्ममिन्द्रः ।।
(ऋग्वेदः, 4.24.7)

'Today Indra, while listening to *stotra*-s (incantations), will endow those with strength who extracts Soma, prepares purodasa and roasts *dhana* (paddy) for him.'

सर्वप्रथमे मन्ये देवयुगे वामदेव एवायम् ।
देवप्रतिमापूजां मानुषलोके प्रचारयामास ।।62।।

It is believed that during the devayuga, it was sage Vamadeva who had first introduced the practice of worshipping god's idol on earth.

यद्यपि ततोऽपि पूर्वं सारस्वतसूर्यसदनेऽभूत् ।
अपि सूर्यचक्रमूर्तेरुपासनारम्भ इत्युक्तम् ।।63।।

It has been said that worship of an idol in the form of sun-disc was prevalent in the sun-house of knowledge.

किन्त्वासीदिह सेयं विज्ञानार्थैव सूर्यचक्रस्य ।
अंशुपरीक्षोपासा दैवप्रतिमार्चना नैवम् ।।64।।

But what took place in the sun-house was not an idol worship; it was a scientific investigation of the sun's rays captured in the sun-disc for gaining specific knowledge.

योगस्त्रिधा क्रियाया भक्तेर्ज्ञानस्य भेदेन ।
भक्तेस्ते चत्वारो हठलयवन्मन्त्रराजयोगाख्याः ।।65।।

There are three kinds of yoga: bhaktiyoga, jnanayoga and karmayoga. There are four kinds of bhaktiyoga: hatha, laya, mantra and raja.

देवप्रतिमायामियमुपासनामन्त्रयोगोऽस्ति ।
योगान्नियमाचरिताद् दैवीं रक्षामपेक्षितां लभते ।।66।।

The worship of god in adoration is mantrayoga. The desired protection is obtained by mantrayoga and a restrained conduct.

को देवानामवो अद्यावृणीते क आदित्यां अदितिं ज्योतिरीट्टे ।
कस्याश्विनाविन्द्रो अग्निः सुतस्यांशोः पिबन्ति मनसाऽविवेनम् ।
देवानामिदवो महत् तदा वृणीमहे वयम् ।
वृष्णामस्मभ्यमूतये ।।

(ऋग्वेदः, 4.25.3)

In the twenty-fifth sukta of fourth mandala of Rigveda, it is said: Nowadays who adores the gods? Who desires for the light of sun? By whom is that Soma filtered which is relishingly accepted by the ashvin kumars, Agni and Indra? We pray to the adorable and powerful devas for our protection.

इत्थं महर्षयः प्राग् दैवीं रक्षां परामुपादिक्षन् ।
मन्त्राराधितदेवः प्रत्यासन्नो भवन्नवति ।।67।।

This way ancient sages prayed first for the protection of the devis; then offered mantras or hymns to ensure the protection of the devas.

यत्र न विज्ञानार्थो न मन्त्रयोगाय वा मनोयोगः ।
सविकल्पकः समाधिर्न यत्र सार्चा वृथा क्रियते ।।68।।

If the desired aim of worship is to gain neither scientific knowledge (vijnana), nor mantrayoga, nor manoyoga, nor *savikalpaka* (discriminate perception) samadhi, it is then useless to worship by the repetition of invocations.

3.9 विज्ञानशालायां नियुक्तानां सूर्यैतशोषसाम् इतिवृत्तम्

3.9 APPOINTMENT OF STAFF IN THE SOLAR LAB

3.9.1 सूर्योषसोः सूर्यायतनप्रन्धकर्तृत्वम्

3.9.1 Surya and usha appointed to surya-sadana

सौरं धामैतद्ध्यधीष्टे दिविष्ठो वागध्यक्षो देवतानां पुरोधाः ।
भूमिष्ठोऽयं तद्वसिष्ठोऽध्यतिष्ठद् बार्हस्पत्यस्तस्य चासीत् सहायः ।।69।।

The master of speech and priest of the devas, Brihaspati, was the chief of *dhama* (abode) in the heavens. Vasishta was the chief of *sauradhama* (solar-abode) on the earth and Brihaspati's son Bharadvaja was his assistant.

भरद्वाजश्च शंयुश्च बार्हस्पत्यौ प्रसिद्ध्यतः ।
उभावपि तु पर्यायादत्रास्तां सूर्यमन्दिरे ।।70।।

Brihaspati's son Bharadvaja and Shanyu managed this sun temple.

यद्यप्यत्रासन् बृहस्पत्यधीना द्रष्टारोऽन्येऽन्ये वसिष्ठादयश्च ।
किन्तु स्थाने नित्यरक्षास्वभूवन् सूर्याधीना बह्व्य एवोषसः प्राक् ।।71।।

Though there were many sages like Vasishta and such others under Brihaspati in this surya-sadhana, many ushas functioned with sun as their guardian.

स्वश्वो नाम बभूव क्षितिपतिरेतस्य पुत्रस्तु ।
सूर्य इति स्वं विरुदं सूर्योपासकतया जगृहे ।।72।।

There was a king called Svashva who had a son named Surya. He had adopted this name as he was a sun worshipper.

स च सौवश्वः सूर्यो गन्धर्वः ख्यायते जात्या ।
घोरः प्रगाथ ऊचेऽष्टमादिमैकादशे हि तथा ।।73।।

This son of Svashva was a Gandharva of surya lineage—a sage known as Ghora Pragatha has said so in the eleventh sutra of eighth mandala of Rigveda.

सूर्यायतनाध्यक्षः स हि सूर्योऽभूत् सहोषसा पूर्वम् ।
सूर्यं च दिवस्पुत्रं विदुरुषसं तां दिवस्पुत्रीम् ।।74।।

First that surya along with usha became the administrators of the surya-sadana. For this, that surya was known as the son and usha as the daughter of Dyauloka.

वरुणस्य कापि जामिर्भगस्वसाऽसीदुषा इति प्रथिता ।
सूर्यायतने सासीदुषसां प्रवरा तु बह्वीनाम् ।।75।।

Varuna had a daughter named Bhargasvasa, who was famous as usha. That usha was the most eminent among all.

रक्षति सूर्यं सूर्यः सोषा आप्तान् जनान् सभाजयति ।
सूर्यः सूर्यपरीक्षामुषःपरीक्षामुषा जनयेत् ।।76।।

A person named Surya (son of Svashva) protected the surya-sadana and usha provided hospitality to the learned people. This Gandharva Surya investigated the sun and usha investigated the usha *tatva*-s (elements) of dawn.

3.9.2 एतशोषसोः सूर्यायतनप्रबन्धकर्तृत्वम्

3.9.2 Aitasha-Usha appointed as administrators of surya-sadana

इन्द्रक्रोधात् सूर्ये निराकृते पश्चात् एतशोषसोः सूर्यायतनप्रबन्धकर्तृत्वम्।

After an angry Indra sacked Surya, Aitasha and usha were appointed as administrators of surya-sadana.

सूर्येण सख्यमभवद्दस्योः कृष्णस्य लम्पटस्येति ।
सूर्यायेन्द्राऽक्रुद्ध्यत्कृष्णासुरसौहृदाद्धेतोः ।।77।।

Surya [head of the sun-house] made friends with a rogue asura named Krishna. Indra got angry with Surya for his friendship with Krishnasura.

अत एवैतशनामा तैर्यग्योनोऽश्वजातिः सुष्विः ।
आचक्रमे ग्रहीतुं सूर्यं सूर्याय दुद्रोह ।।78।।

So, an arrogant brave born in triyagayoni called Sushvi of the ashva clan revolted against Surya and attacked him to imprison him.

तत्र च सूर्यैतशयोस्तयोः प्रवृत्तेऽत्यभीमदर्दे ।
आस्कन्दयत् स सूर्यस्तमेतशं कृष्णसहयोगात् ।।79।।

Aitasha also revolted against Aurya; the latter then sought the help of his friend, Krishnasura to defeat Aitasha.

तत्र स इन्द्रोऽश्वाभ्यां वातजवाभ्यां समानयत्कुत्सम् ।
अप्रच्छन्नं सूर्यं गन्धर्वं छद्मनाऽऽक्राम्यत् ।।80।।

Indra came on galloping horses, along with Kutsa, and deceitfully attacked the Gandharva surya and defeated him.

एतशमेतमरक्षत् समरे सूर्यं पराभाव्य ।
इन्द्रोऽनुगृह्य तस्मिन् सूर्यायतने न्ययुङ्कतापि।।81।।

Indra then appointed Aitasha as the new head of the sun-house.

अस्मा इदुत्यदनुदाप्येषामेको यद् वव्रे भूरेरीशानः ।
प्रैतशं सूर्ये पस्पृधानं सौवश्व्ये सुष्विमावदिन्द्रः ।।
(ऋग्वेदः, 1.6.15)

'This Indra alone is the master of all divine qualities. Singers eulogize him with the song he desires. Indra, waging war with Svashva's son Surya, saved Aitasha who performed Somayajna.

यत् तुदत् सूर एतशं बङ्कू वातस्य पर्णिना ।
बहत्कुत्समार्जुनेयं शतक्रतुस्त्सरद् गन्धर्वमस्तृतम् ।।
(ऋग्वेदः, 8.1.11)

'When surya shook the horse [cloud] named Aitasha with the force of a fierce wind, then Shatakratu Indra, that is, thunderbolt took away the [sun's] scintillating light and reached the cloud [Aitasha], not hurt or killed by anyone.'

इन्द्रकृतैतशरक्षा चक्रापहृतिश्च सूर्यस्य ।
तुर्ये सप्तदशस्य त्वृच्याम्नाते चतुर्दश्याम् ।।82।।

Aitasha's protection by Indra and stealing of the sun-disc are described in the fourteenth mantra in the seventeenth sukta of the fourth mandala of Rigveda.

अयं चक्रमिषणात् सूर्यास्य नेतशं रीरमत् ससृमाणम् ।
आकृष्ण ईं जुहुराणो जिघर्ति त्वचो बुध्ने रजसो अस्य योनौ ।।
(ऋग्वेदः, 4:17.14)

'Indra inspired the sun-disc and made Aitasha, who was coming to fight, return. Clouds moving obliquely in the sky bear this Indra. [When sun-rays enter black clouds, these cause mutual friction and create Indra or light.]

नोधा गौतम इव तत् प्रोवाचावस्युरात्रेयः ।
पञ्चम एकत्रिंशस्यैकादश्यामृचि द्वितयम् ।।83।।

Like Nodha Gautam, Atreya Avasyu has also said in the eleventh mantra in the thirty-first sukta of fifth mandala of Rigveda.

सूरश्चिद्रथं परितक्यायां पूर्वं करदुपरं जूजुवांसम् ।
भरच्चक्रमेतशः संरिणाति पुरो दधत् सनिष्यति क्रतुं नः ।।
(ऋग्वेदः, 5.31.11)

'In the past, Indra had stopped chariots moving even faster than the sun. He snatched the disc of Aitasha and destroyed the enemy. Such an Indra may accept the services of our yajna.'

पञ्चम ऊनत्रिंशे शाक्त्यो यद् गौरवीतिरिन्द्रमिमम् ।
महयति यस्मिन्नेतशसंरक्षणमुपदिशत्येषः ।।84।।

In the thirty-ninth sukta of fifth mandala of Rigveda, Shaktya Gorviti has eulogized Indra, and has mentioned the act of saving Aitasha.

अधकृत्वा मघवन्तुभ्यं देवा अनुविश्वे अददुः सोमपेयम् ।
यत्सूर्यस्य हरितः पतन्ती पुरः सतीरुपरा एतशे कः ।।
(ऋग्वेदः, 5.29.5)

'O Indra! When you stopped the sun's rays for protecting Aitasha, then O Maghavan! All the devas were pleased with you, offered you Soma for drinking.'

3.9.3 एतशस्य आधिदैविकवद्वृत्तिः

3.9.3 Divine qualities of Aitasha

संवत्सरे तु कतिधा रथमारूढं स एतशः सूर्यम् ।
स्वयमुपबृहन्नुदग् दिशि सीमाप्रान्ते दिवो नयति ।।85।।

Though a man, Aitasha conducted himself as a presiding god. Several times in a year, he took surya on his chariot to the Dyauloka.

उदुत्यद्दर्शतं वपुर्दिव एति प्रतिह्वरे ।
यदी माशुर्वहति देव एतशो विश्वस्मै चक्षसे अरम् ॥
(ऋग्वेदः, 7.66.14)

This discernible *mandala* [aureole] of the sun rises from the edge of the heavens. This sun can be seen to the whole world; this sun gets movement by its rays.

अर्थाहरणे कर्मणि ये नियता व्यापृता नरा भृतकाः ।
हरितो नरास्त उक्ताः शिरसा रश्मिभिरमे हरन्त्यर्थान् ॥86॥

Those appointed for collecting wealth were called Harit and they captured material elements from ray-like heads. [The rays of the sun are the Harit named horses of sun and these sun-rays capture all elements of the world and also capture Time or Kaal-chakra.]

इन्द्रश्चक्रं स यदा दिवमनयत् यत्र हरितो नॄन् ।
व्यरमयतेन्द्रो ना त्वयमेतश एकोऽहरच्चक्रम् ॥87॥

When Indra took that sun-disc to the heaven, then Indra stopped all men known as Harit and Aitasha alone went ahead with that chakra.

त्वं सूरो हरितो रामयो नॄन् भरच्चक्रमेतशो नायमिन्द्र ।
प्रास्यपारं नवतिं नाव्यानामपि कर्तमवर्तयोऽयज्यून् ॥
(ऋग्वेदः, 1.121.13)

'O Indra! Like sun, you manifest these rays which help men in accomplishing their well-being. The discs of Indra's chariot are always in motion. You have done a great favour by throwing those who do not perform the yajna across ninety rivers [which can be crossed on boat].'

3.9.4 एतशाश्वकृतपरीक्षा

3.9.4 Research conducted by Aitasha

सूर्यसंस्थाननियुक्तः स एतशः सूर्यमन्वीक्ष्य ।
आयुर्ददर्श सम्यक् सूर्यादध्यात्ममुपसृप्तम् ॥88॥

Appointed to the suryasansthan, Aitasha investigated the sun and its affect on all elements of ayu. He saw prana emanating from the sun to the body.

वरुणस्य राजधान्यां बाह्लीके भृगुमहर्षिरभूत् ।
भृगुवंश्य एतशोऽयं कौषीतकिनोदितस्त्रिंशे ।।89।।

In the capital Bahlika of Varuna, there was a great sage known as Bhrigu. This Aitasha was the descendent of Bhrigu—this has been said in the thirtieth khanda by Kaushitakis.

अपि चैतरेय ऊचे त्रिंशाध्याये त्रयस्त्रिंशे ।
एतश आयुरपश्यच्छन्दांस्यप्येतशप्रलाप इति ।।90।।
(ऐतरेयब्राह्मणम्, 3.33)

In the thirty-third chapter of the thirtieth khanda of Aitreya Brahmana, it has been stated that Aitasha has properly seen the elements of age and he has described also the verse form of circle of days and night.

3.10 एतशस्य सूर्याश्वत्वम्

3.10 CYCLE OF DAY AND NIGHT

अहोरात्रवृत्तानां छन्द:संज्ञानाम् ऐतशनाम्ना विवक्षितानां सूर्याश्वत्वम् ।

Designation of Aitasha as the mount of surya.

तत्परीक्षकत्वात् सुष्विराजस्य मनुष्यस्याप्येतशत्वम्

प्रजापते: सूर्यसतोऽक्षि पृथ्व्यां यदश्वयत् सोऽश्व इति प्रसिद्ध: ।
स सप्तसंस्थो विषुवाध ऊर्ध्वप्रदेशभेदादिह सूर्यदृष्टे: ।।91।।

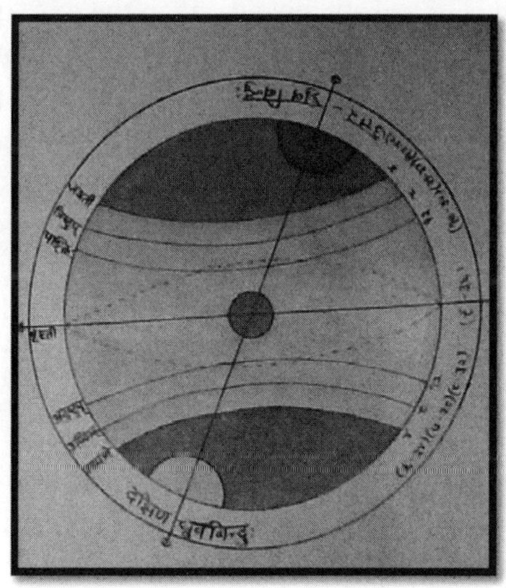

The sage, who propagated the existence of sun-like Prajapati on the earth, is also known by the name of Ashva. This critical circle *samkramnnavritta,* depending upon the position of sun, is divided into seven parts above and below the Equinox line.

विषुवन्मण्डलतोऽर्वाक् त्रीणि त्रीण्येव तूदक् च ।
सन्ति समानान्तरवत् कृतान्यहोरात्रवृत्तानि ।।92।।

To the south of Equinox, there are three *chhanda*s (metre or measure)—gayatri, ushnika, anushtupa and to its north are three chhandas—pankti, trishtupa, jagati which create the cycle of day and night. These chhandas are of 6, 7, 8, and 10, 11, 12, alphabets or *akshara*-s in that order, and in the middle is the Brihati *chhanda*.

सप्तानामपि तेषां गायत्र्युष्णिक् तथाऽनुष्टुप् ।
बृहती पंक्तिस्त्रिष्टुप् जगतीति च सन्ति नामानि ।।93।।

These seven chhandas are called—gayatri, ushnika, anushtupa, brihati, pankti, trishtupa, and jagati.

गायत्र्यामुदगयनं दक्षिणमयनं जगत्यां स्यात् ।
रात्र्यहनी तु समाने भवतः सूर्ये बृहत्यां चेत् ।।94।।

Uttarayana is in gayatri chhanda and dakshinayana is in jagati chhanda. And when the sun is in brihati chhanda, then the day and night are equal. The gayatri chhanda is at the end of southern trajectory of *surya sankrmana vritta* (sun's circular movement). Where the sun starts returning towards the northern direction after having finished its southern journey on 22 December—this is called dakshinayana. In this journey, the sun moves towards north on 23 December and is at the middle point on 21 March on its way towards south. When the sun is at the middle point, the night and day are equal. This middle point is called brihati chhanda.

यावान् सप्तच्छन्दोभिरवच्छिन्नो दिवः प्रदेशोऽयम् ।
सूर्यरथं तं ब्रूमः सप्ताश्वं चैकचक्रं च ।।95।।

That area of this heaven, demarcated by gayatri and other seven chhandas, is called the chariot of surya which is drawn by seven horses and has one disc. Those seven chhandas of *krantivritta* (celestial circle) on which the sun moves, are seven horses and this entire circle in which the sun moves is the chariot of the sun.

यद् भास्वद्गतिवर्म प्रसिद्ध्यति क्रान्तिवृत्ताख्यम् ।
रथचक्रं तद् ब्रूमस्तत्सयुजः सन्ति सप्ताश्वाः ।।96।।

The path of movement named krantivritta is called *ratha-chakra* (chariot-disc) in which the seven chhandas are seven horses.

एषा वै परिभाषा पशवश्छन्दांसि देवानाम् ।
शतपथचतुर्थकाण्डे तार्तीयकपञ्चमेऽधीता ।।

(शतपथब्राह्मणम्, 4.3.5.11)

These seven chhandas are seven *pashu*-s (animals) of the devas—this has been said in the fifth chapter of the third discourse of Shatapatha Brahmana.

सप्तच्छन्दांस्यश्वाः सप्तमुखो वा स एक एवाश्वः ।
एतशमेतं ब्रुवते एतश एतं ददर्श सम्यगृषिः ।।97।।

These seven chhandas are seven horses of the sun. Sage Aitasha has properly observed these horses which are in the form of *sampurna krantivirtta* (a full celestial circle).

तिर्यग्योनावश्वयोनिर्य आसीत् कश्चिद्वर्गस्तस्य राजैव सुष्विः ।
सूर्यस्याश्वं यद्ददर्शैताख्यं तस्मादेषोऽप्येतशोऽभूत् प्रसिद्धः ।।98।।

This Aitasha was a king named Sushvi of some order of the horses in the animal world. Since he saw the sun called Aitasha, he became famous as Aitasha.

3.11 सूर्यायतनस्थाया उषसः प्रभेदाः

3.11 CLASSIFICATION OF USHAS IN SURYASTHANA

आसन्नुषसी बह्व्यः पर्यायेणात्र कर्मकारिण्यः ।
तासामेका सूर्यायतनस्था सूनरी नाम ॥99॥

There were many ushas who worked by turn at suryasthana. One of them was usha named sunari.

प्रागुदयादिह चक्रे केतौ चित्र प्रभोदेति ।
तां सूनरी ह्युपास्ते नाखिलभास्ते तु साऽभास्ति ॥100॥

Before it comes up (rising of sun), a spiral of light originates in the upper part of that disc. The usha named sunari lives near this spiral illumination. But when the sun becomes fully bright, this illumination vanishes.

योषा सूर्यसदेशे नक्तं शेते विभावरी सोक्ता ।
सैव पुनः स्यादहना प्रातर्यात्रां प्रकुर्वाणा ॥101॥

That usha which sleeps at night in the sun's abode is known as vibhavari. That vibhavari while travelling during the morning time is called ahana.

अहना चरित गवाश्वोपेतं वाजं प्रयच्छन्ती ।
दिवि तु भुवनस्य पत्नी याति मनुष्येषु मानुषीनाम्ना ॥102॥

This usha named ahana provides grains along with cows and horses and is known as the wife of *bhuvan* [world of earth] in the Dyauloka and men know it as *manushi* (woman).

पञ्चक्षितिषु सरन्ती यतस्ततः पुंश्चली भवत्वेषा ।
तेन भुवनस्य पत्नीत्यहना सा या दिवि क्रमते ॥103॥

This usha is known as punshchali when she moves aound the moon, earth, sun, Parameshti and Svayambhu Prajapati. This way the usha called ahana moves around in the heavens and so is known as the wife of bhuvana.

अपि सा सर्वाध्यक्षा तेन च भुवनस्य पत्नी सा ।
यो विश्वकर्मजनको भुवनः सा तस्य पत्नी वा ॥104॥

This ahana is the leader of all ushas and so also is known as the wife of bhuvana. (Ahana is wife of that bhuvana which is the origin of all actions or karmas.)

सूर्यस्यैका योषा तामाहुर्वाजिनीवतीं नाम्ना ।
स हि गन्धर्वः सूर्यः सूर्यायतनेऽधिकारवानासीत् ।।105।।

Surya (a Gandharva named Surya) has a wife named Vajinivati. That Surya is a Gandharva who was an authority in the sun-house.

स्वर्ग्यधनाढ्यैर्वसुभिः काले काले प्रदीयमानस्य ।
क्रोशं धनस्य रक्षति या सा चित्रा मघा नाम ।।106।।

The ushas named Vichitra and Magha protect the wealth donated by affluent people of heaven.

ते वह्न्यो वहन्ति तु ये संभारान् कुतश्चिदन्यत्र ।
वह्नी नामाध्यक्षा काचिदुषा सा मघोन्याख्या ।।107।।

That dominant usha, who takes things from one place to other, is known as maghoni.

ऋषयस्तु सूर्यरश्मीन् परीक्षितुं येऽत्र समवयन्त्यसकृत् ।
तेषां परिचर्यायां जरयन्ती नाम काचिदुषा ।।108।।

An usha named jarayanti used to provide hospitality to the sages who would come together for examining the rays of the sun.

विश्वपिशेति तृतीया कृतं पदं सायणः प्राह ।
अथवा विश्वपिशा सा या बहुरूपा रथेनैति ।।109।।

Sayana has said that the word vishvapisha means 'third' but it also means that usha which travels in the chariot with multiple forms.

मधुधा च रोचनान्या ऋतावरी रेवती चान्या ।
इत्थं बहवो भेदा आसन्नुषसो दिवस्पुत्र्याः ।।110।।

Daughter of Dyauloka, usha is of different types—madhudha, rochana, ritavari and revati.

एताः कर्मनियुक्ता उषसः कर्माख्यया ख्याताः ।
इतरा विश्राम्यन्तः सर्वा भद्राभिधानाः स्युः ।।111।।

These ushas were named after the work they did. And the ushas, who were on rest, were called bhadra.

उषसः सर्वा आसन् प्रसन्नहृदयाः सदा हसद्वदनाः ।
मधुभाषिण्यः प्रेम्णा कर्षन्त्यश्चारुसर्वाङ्ग्यः ।।112।।

All these ushas were always happy and smiling. These ushas spoke sweetly and attracted everyone with their beautiful limbs and loving nature.

3.12 उषस मानुष्याः आधिदैविकवद्वृत्तिः

3.12 USHAS ACTED LIKE DEITIES

सूर्योदयादेव रथं हिरण्मयं सारुह्य दूरानभियाति मानुषान् ।
अध्यासितं तत्सहचारि दैवतैः शतं रथानामनुयापि पृष्ठतः ॥113॥

After sunrise, this usha, riding on the chariot, goes close to the humans. Hundred devas follow her on chariots.

वाजैश्च पूर्ण वसुभिश्च भूरिभिर्नयन्त्यनोऽश्वानपि गाश्च भूयसीः ।
सूर्यप्रसादोपहृतान् विभाजयत्यर्थानिमान् प्राणिजने दिने दिने ॥114॥

This usha takes horse-carts full of wealth and lots of cows along with her. This way she distributes among living beings the wealth brought by the grace of sun.

गृहे गृहे संप्रचरन्त्यनातुरा समीक्ष्य सा दीनजनान् नवान्नवान् ।
तेभ्यः प्रयच्छत्यहना यथोचितं धनानि वाजानपि गाश्च वाजिनः ॥115॥

या द्वेषिणोऽन्योन्यविरोधिनो जनान् प्रवृज्य धत्ते सुभगाऽतिसौभगम् ।
तां भासमानामभिलाषपूरणीं विश्वं जगद् द्रष्टुमिमां नमाम ह ॥116॥

The usha named ahana goes from house to house and provides grains, horses, cows, and wealth to the needy people, except to those who are jealous and who quarrel. An usha named subhaga brings affluence to all. And I bow to such a subhaga who is so radiant and who fulfils all our desires.

चित्रं तु वाजं प्रविभज्य मानुषे जनेन्तरिक्षं च कदाप्युपेत्य सा ।
विश्वांश्च देवानिह सोमपीतये संतर्पणायाह्वयति स्म दक्षिणा ॥117॥

This dakshina usha, after having distributed various grains, reaches antariksha and calls out the devas for drinking Soma to their satisfaction.

संयाति सूर्यायतनादितस्ततस्त्रिंशत्समन्तादिह योजनानि सा ।
पुंसां समक्षं चरतीयमत्र सा निवर्तते नित्यमुपह्वराद् दिवः ॥118॥

This usha moves around at a distance of thirty yojanas, among the people, and returns to the Dyauloka every day.

या चाद्य विश्राणयते धनान्नं रथेन गत्वोषसि मानुषेभ्यः ।
निवृत्य विश्राम्यति सा परेद्युः पराऽहना याति रथेन दातुम् ॥119॥

After distributing wealth and grains among men, usha returns by her chariot and takes rest. Next day, the same usha, bearing the name ahana, goes by a chariot to distribute wealth.

उषसो या मे दानं विशेषपुण्यातिशयकृत् स्यात् ।
इत्येव घोषयन्ती ददात्युषा उषसि कण्व इत्याह ।।120।।

Sage Kanva has said about usha, 'That usha gives me donations in an act of special piety.'

3.13 विश्वामित्रकृता उषःस्तुतिः

3.13 INVOCATION OF USHA BY VISHVAMITRA

पञ्चनदाख्ये देशे विश्वामित्रो महर्षिरासीत् प्राक् ।
एष सुदासो राज्ञः पुरोहितः स्तौति तामुषसम् ।।121।।

In ancient times, there was a great sage Vishvamitra in Panchanada, who was the priest of king Sudasa. He invokes usha in the sixty-first sukta of third mandala of Rigveda.

उषो वाजेन वाजिनि प्रचेताः स्तोमं जुषस्व गृणतो मघोनि ।
पुराणी देवि युवतिः पुरन्धिरनुव्रतं चरसि विश्ववारे ।।

(ऋग्वेदः, 3.61.1)

O Usha, who has all grains and wealth! May you listen attentively to this invocation! O Usha, who qualifies to be adored by the world! Despite being ancient, you are new, wise, and self-restrained.

उषो देवमर्त्या विभा हि चन्द्ररथा सूनृता ईरयन्ती ।
आ त्वा वहन्तु सुयमासो अश्वा हिरण्यवर्णां पृथपाजसो ये ।।

(ऋग्वेदः, 3.61.2)

O Usha, one who sits in a chariot as beautiful as the moon, the one who inspires sweet speech, the one who beholds the eternal self-form! May you be more brilliant. You are golden, so powerful. May independent horses bring you here.

उषः प्रतीची भुवनानि विश्वोर्ध्वा तिष्ठस्य मृतस्य केतुः ।
समानमर्थं चरणीयमाना चक्रमिव नव्यस्या ववृत्स्व ।।

(ऋग्वेदः, 3.61.3)

O Usha! You are the flag bearer of amrita in all worlds; you sit on a high pedestal. O Usha! You are new and youthful. To achieve one goal, you move around like a disc. May you again move around.

अवस्यूमेव चिन्वती मघोन्युषा याति स्वसरस्य पत्नी ।
स्वर्जनन्ती सुभगा सुदंसा आन्तादि्दवः पप्रथ आ पृथिव्याः ।।

(ऋग्वेदः, 3.61.4)

This usha drives away darkness like light rays; she is affluent, wife of sun and moves around. This usha radiates light. She is fortunate and beautiful; she spreads light to the end of Dyauloka and Prithviloka.

अच्छा वो देवीमुषसं विभातीं प्र वो भरध्वं नमसा सुवृक्तिम् ।
ऊर्ध्वं मधुधा दिवियाजो अश्रेत्प्रोचना रुरुचे रण्वसंदृक् ।।

(ऋग्वेद:, 3.61.5)

This usha provides light to all those who invoke her. You should all invoke her. She bears sweetness and establishes her brilliance in higher parts of Dyauloka. The light of usha is everywhere; she is radiant and beautiful.

ऋतावरी दिवो अर्कैरबोध्या रेवती रोदसी चित्रमस्थात् ।
आयातीमग्न उषसं विभातीं वाममेषि द्रविणं भिक्षमाण: ।।

(ऋग्वेद:, 3.61.6)

This usha has been recognized as the one who follows the truth and the one who spread its rays in the Dyauloka. This affluent usha establishes varied splendours in Dyauloka as well as Prtihviloka.

ऋतस्य बुध्न उषसामिषण्यन्वृषा मही रोदसी आविवेश ।
मही मित्रस्य वरुणस्य माया चन्द्रेव भानुं वि दधे पुरुत्रा ।।

(ऋग्वेद:, 3.61.7)

The powerful sun, inspiring the ushas at dawn, enters this vast sky and earth. The golden radiance of dawn, with the power of Mitra and Varuna, spreads around the sun in all directions.

3.14 वसिष्ठकृता उषःस्तुतिः

3.14 INVOCATION OF USHA BY VASISHTA

अस्तु वसिष्ठो राज्ञो वरुणस्यासीत् पुरोहितः पूर्वम् ।
पश्चात्सूर्यायतने नियुक्त आसीत् स चोषसं स्तौति ।।122।।

That Vasishta, who was earlier the priest of King Varuna and was later appointed to the sun-house, invokes usha.

व्युषा आवो दिविजा ऋतेनाविष्कृण्वाना महिमानमागात् ।
अपद्रुहस्तम आवरजुष्टमङ्गिरस्तमापथ्या अजीगः ।।
(ऋग्वेदः, 7.75.1)

Sage Vasishta invokes usha in the Rigveda: This usha enters the sky and begins radiating in her unique manner. She comes manifesting her majesty by her brilliance. This usha drives away enemies and unpleasant darkness and enlightens the walking path.

महेनो अद्य सुविताय वोध्युषो महे सौभगाय प्रयन्धि ।
चित्रं रयिं यशसं धेह्यस्मे देवि मर्तेषु मानुषि श्रावस्युम् ।।
(ऋग्वेदः, 7.75.2)

O Usha! For our happiness, please wake up and give us affluence. O human goddess! Give the beings of mortal world famous and rich sons.

एते त्ये भानवो दर्शतायाश्चित्रा उषसो अमृतास आगुः ।
जनयन्तो दैव्यानि व्रतान्यापृणन्तो अन्तरिक्षा व्यस्थुः ।।
(ऋग्वेदः, 7.75.3)

Eternal and magnificent rays of usha are spreading all around. They are creating divine laws and are according a fullness to the sky where these rays reside.

एषा स्या युजाना पराकात्पञ्च क्षितीः परि सद्यो जिगाति ।
अभिपश्यन्ती वयूना जनानां दिवो दुहिता भुवनस्य पत्नी ।।
(ऋग्वेदः, 7.75.4)

Despite staying far, this usha inspires all humans. Observing the people working, this usha, the daughter of Dyauloka, nourishes all the worlds.

वाजिनीवती सूर्यस्य योषा चित्रा मघा राय ईशे वसूनाम् ।
ऋषिष्टुता जरयन्ती मघोन्युषा उच्छति वह्निभिर्गृणाना ।।

(ऋग्वेद:, 7.75.5)

She is endowed with strength-giving grains and special affluence. She is the wife of sun, mistress of affluence and wealth. Sages invokes her. That affluent usha destroys everyone's ayu. She is radiant by the eulogies of Agni and Kala-chakra.

प्रति द्युतानामरुषासो अश्वाश्चित्रा अदृश्रन्नुषसं वहन्त: ।
याति शुभ्रा विश्वपिशा रथेन दधाति रत्नं विधते जनाय ।।

(ऋग्वेद:, 7.75.6)

The horses carrying radiant usha are seen over there. This radiant usha goes by the best chariot. She provides gems and wealth to people who work hard.

सत्या सत्येभिर्महती महद्भिर्देवी देवेभिर्यजता यजत्रै: ।
रुजदृह्लानि ददुस्त्रियाणां प्रतिगाव उषसं वावशन्त ।।

(ऋग्वेद:, 7.75.7)

This usha is the one who obeys truth and is worthy of being worshipped. Living along with the devas, who follow Truth, she destroys dense darkness. For cows, usha gives light and so cows call out for usha.

नूनो गोमद्वीर वद्धे हि रत्नमुषो अश्वावत्पुरु भोजो अस्मे ।
मानो बर्हि: पुरुषता निदेकर्यूयं पात स्वस्तिभि: सदा न: ।।

(ऋग्वेद:, 7.75.8)

O Usha! Give us cows, horses, wealth, brave sons and plenty of food! May our yajnas not be despised in society! May you always protect us with all means for our well-being!

उदु ज्योतिरमृतं विश्वजन्यं विश्वानर: सविता देवो अश्रेत् ।
क्रत्वा देवानामजनिष्ट चक्षराविरकर्भुवनं विश्वमुषा: ।।

(ऋग्वेद:, 7.76.1)

Radiance is protected by deity savita, who is eternal, is good to all and leads the world. He has risen for the devas, and the entire world is lit up by usha.

प्रमे पन्था देवयाना अदृश्रन्नमर्धन्तो वसुभिरिष्कृतासः ।
अभूदु केतुरुषसः पुरस्तात्प्रतीच्यागादधिहर्म्येभ्यः ।।
(ऋग्वेदः, 7.76.2)

I have seen many paths of the devas who are radiant and peaceful. In the east, usha is spreading her light like a flag and is lighting up high altars there.

तानीदहानि बहुलान्यसन् या प्राचीनमुदिता सूर्यस्य ।
यतः परिजार इवा चरन्त्युषो ददृक्षे न पुनर्यतीव ।।
(ऋग्वेदः, 7.76.3)

O Usha! Long before the sunrise, you start radiating as you attend to your husband sun. And you are not restrained.

त इद्देवानां सधमाद आसन्नृतावानः कवयः पूर्व्यासः ।
गूह्ळं ज्योतिः पितरो अन्वविन्दन्त्सत्यमन्त्रा अजनयन्नुषासम् ।।
(ऋग्वेदः, 7.76.4)

Those who are learned and follow truth, and have been blessed by the mantras, and nourished everyone like a father, sat with the devas for drinking Soma, they have attained the light of sun who has manifested usha.

समान ऊर्वे अधिसङ्गतासः सं जानते न यतन्ते मिथस्ते ।
ते देवानां न मिनन्ति व्रतान्यमर्धन्तो वसुभिर्यादमानाः ।।
(ऋग्वेदः, 7.76.5)

They come together for a great work and express their thoughts. They don't quarrel. They do not flout the rules of the devas and do not attain affluence by violent means.

प्रति त्वा स्यौमैरीडते वसिष्ठा उषबुर्धः सुभगे तुष्टुवांसः ।
गवां नेत्री वाजपत्नी न उच्छोषः सुजाते प्रथमा जरस्व ।।
(ऋग्वेदः, 7.76.6)

O Auspicious one! In the morning, sages like Vasishta invoke you. You nourish the cows. Remain lighted for us. O high born usha, you are best among the devas.

एषा नेत्री राधसः सुनृतानामुषा उच्छन्तीरिभ्यते वसिष्ठैः ।
दीर्घश्रुतं रयिमस्मे दधाना यूयं पात स्वस्तिभिः सदा नः ।।
(ऋग्वेदः, 7.76.7)

This usha inspires divine words, she drives away darkness and is eulogized by those who invoke her and provides us affluence. O such usha! May you always protect us.

उषो रुरुचे युवतिर्न योषा विश्वं जीवं प्रसुवन्ती च रायै ।
अभूदग्निः समिधे मानुषाणामकर्ज्योतिर्बाधमाना तमांसि ॥
(ऋग्वेदः, 7.77.1)

This usha radiates like a youthful woman; she inspires all beings. She enlightens humans and lights the flame which dispels darkness.

विश्वं प्रतीची स प्रथा उदस्थाद्रुसद्वासो विभ्रती शुक्रमश्वैत् ।
हिरण्यवर्णा सुदृशी कसन् दृग्गवां माता नेत्र्यह्नामरोचि ॥
(ऋग्वेदः, 7.77.2)

This usha has manifested before the whole world and she moves ahead wearing bright clean dress. This is radiant like gold and is worth watching. That usha, who manages the day, radiates like a pleasure giving cow.

देवानां चक्षुः सुभगा वहन्ती श्वेतं नयन्ती सुदृशीकमश्वम् ।
उषा अदर्शि रश्मिभिर्व्यक्ता चित्रामघा विश्वमनुप्रभूता ॥
(ऋग्वेदः, 7.77.3)

Usha, glowing with the radiance of the devas, driving the horses of the sun made of beautiful white rays, is clearly visible in the form of rays. This usha is full of glory and is growing in stature before the whole world.

अन्ति वामा दूरे अमित्रमुच्छोर्वी गव्यूतिमभयं कृधी नः ।
यावयद् द्वेष आभरा वसूनि चोदय राधो गृणते मघोनि ॥
(ऋग्वेदः, 7.77.4)

O Usha, who brings wealth to us! Illuminate all but our enemies. Make the land meant for us more fertile, keep our enemies at bay and bless us with wealth. O glorious one! Offer wealth to those who adore you.

अस्मे श्रेष्ठेभिर्भानुभिर्वि भाह्युषो देवि प्रतिरन्ती न आयुः ।
इषं च नो दधती विश्ववारे गोमदश्वावद्रथवच्च राधः ॥

यां त्वा दिवो दुहितर्वर्धयन्त्युषः सुजाते मतिभिर्वसिष्ठाः ।
सास्मासुधा रयिमृष्वं बृहन्तं यूयं पात स्वस्तिभिः सदा नः ॥
(ऋग्वेदः, 7.77.5-6)

O Usha! Illuminate us with the finest rays of the sun. The propagator of our life, adored by all usha! Bless us with the wealth of grains, cows, and horses with chariots. O Daughter of Dyauloka, born in high family! The learned ones pray to you with their wisdom. Provide us with unlimited wealth and protect us with possible means.

प्रति केतवः प्रथमा अदृश्रन्नूर्ध्वा अस्या अञ्जयो विश्रयन्ते ।
उषो अर्वाचा बृहता रथेन ज्योतिष्मता वाममस्मभ्यं वक्षि ॥
(ऋग्वेदः, 7.78.1)

The first rays of this usha appear like a flagstaff. Its moving rays take shelter in higher sphere. This usha, seated in her shining chariot, comes closer to the human beings.

प्रति षीमग्निर्जरते समिद्धः प्रति विप्रासो मतिभिर्गृणन्तः ।
उषा याति ज्योतिषा बाधमाना विश्वा तमांसि दुरिताप देवी ॥
(ऋग्वेदः, 7.78.2)

The learned ones are engaged in their acts of worship by reciting hymns in her praise. This usha moves across, removing darkness with her bright rays.

एता उत्याः प्रत्यदृश्रन्पुरस्ताज्ज्योतिर्यच्छन्तीरुषसो विभातीः ।
अजीजन्त्सूर्यं यज्ञमग्निमपाचीनं तमो अगादजुष्टम् ॥
(ऋग्वेदः, 7.78.3)

These ushas appear before us shining forth. These ushas have produced the sun, fire, and sacrifice and removed the painful darkness.

अचेति दिवो दुहिता मघोनी विश्वे पश्यन्त्युषसं विभातीम् ।
आस्थाद्रथं स्वधया युज्यमानमायमश्वासः सुयुजो वहन्ति ॥
(ऋग्वेदः, 7.78.4)

When usha, the glorious daughter of Dyauloka, appears, the whole world looks up to her. This usha rides a chariot full of grains and the horses take her to her destination.

प्रतित्वाद्य सुमनसो बुधान्तास्माकासो मघवानो वयं च ।
तिल्विलायध्वमुषसो विभातीर्यूयं पात स्वस्तिभिः सदा नः ॥
(ऋग्वेदः, 7.78.5)

O Usha! This day our glorious and wise men pray to you. Illuminate the world with your kind light and protect us with your blissful means.

व्युषा आ वः पथ्याजनानां पञ्चक्षितीर्मानुषीर्बोधयन्ती ।
सुसन्दृग्भिरुक्षभिर्भानुमश्रेद्वि सूर्यो रोदसी चक्षसावः ।।
(ऋग्वेदः, 7.79.1)

That usha is the benefactor of human beings and has appeared for a special reason. She wakes up all the people and shines with the glory of superior cows. The sun, too, strengthens the heaven and earth with its light.

व्यञ्जते दिवो अन्तेष्वक्तून्विशो न युक्ता उषसो यतन्ते ।
सं ते गावस्तम आवर्तयन्ति ज्योतिर्यच्छन्ति सवितेव बाहू ।।
(ऋग्वेदः, 7.79.2)

These ushas send forth their light to the farthest parts of the heaven. They strive to remove all darkness. O Usha! Your rays end darkness. They spread their light in the same way as the sun does.

अभूदुषा इन्द्रतमा मघोन्यजीजनत्सुविताय श्रवांसि ।
वि दिवा देवी दुहिता दधात्यङ्गिरस्तमा सुकृते वसूनि ।।
(ऋग्वेदः, 7.79.3)

Exceptional and affluent usha has appeared. This usha has created grains for the prosperity of all. This usha, the daughter of Dyauloka, radiates like Agni and provides wealth to those who do good deeds.

तावदुषो राधो अस्मभ्यं रास्व यावत्स्तोतृभ्यो अरदो गृणाना ।
यां त्वा जज्ञुर्वृषभस्यारवेण विदृह्लस्य दुरो अद्रेरौर्णोः ।।
(ऋग्वेदः, 7.79.4)

O Usha! Give us the same amount of wealth as you have given to those who invoke you. Everyone knows you by the name of ox and you have brought out all the cows after opening the door of a strong mountain.

देवं देवं राधसे चोदयन्त्यस्मद्र्यक्सूनृता ईरयन्ती ।
व्युच्छन्ती नः सनये धियो धा यूयं पात स्वस्तिभिः सदा नः ।।
(ऋग्वेदः, 7.79.5)

O Usha! You inspire all the devas to gain wealth, you inspire speaking of truth, you dispel darkness and may you get the thought of giving us wealth.

May you protect us with all means.

प्रति स्तोमेभिरुषसं वसिष्ठा गीर्भिर्विप्रासः प्रथमा अबुध्रन् ।
विवर्तयन्ती रजसी समन्ते आविष्कृण्वतीं भुवनानि विश्वा ।।

(ऋग्वेदः, 7.80.1)

Learned sages wake up usha with their first incantations and speech. This usha revolves around the sky and earth equally and enlightens all the world.

एषास्या नव्यमायुर्दधाना गूढ्वी तमो ज्योतिषोषा अबोधि ।
अग्र एति युवतिरह्रयाणा प्राचिकितत्सूर्यं यज्ञमग्निम् ।।

(ऋग्वेदः, 7.80.2)

This usha rises after dispelling darkness and creates a new day. She walks in front like a young woman and manifests herself before surya, Agni, and yajna.

अश्वावतीर्गोमतीर्न उषासो वीरवतीः सद्मुच्छरन्तु भद्राः ।
घृतं दुहाना विश्वतः प्रपीता यूयं पात स्वस्तिभिः सदा नः ।।

(ऋग्वेदः, 7.80.3)

This usha is propitious and accompanies horses, cows, and brave men. May she always bring them to us! This usha extracts ghee and is well nourished. O Usha! May you protect us with propitious means!

प्रत्यु अदर्श्यायत्युच्छन्ती दुहिता दिवः ।
अपोमहि व्ययति चक्षसे तमो ज्योतिष्कृणोति सूनरी ।।

(ऋग्वेदः, 7.81.1)

That usha, who dispels darkness, is seen coming from the heaven. This dispels dense darkness and brings light for everyone's eyes.

उदुस्रियाः सृजते सूर्यः सचाँ उद्यन्नक्षत्रमर्चिवत् ।
तवेदुषो व्युषि सूर्यस्य च सम्भक्तेन गमेमहि ।।

(ऋग्वेदः, 7.81.2)

The sun spreads light with rays and before the sunrise makes stars radiant, O Usha! May we get grains from you and the sun shining bright.

प्रति त्वा दुहितर्दिव उषो जीरा अभुत्स्महि ।
या वहसि पुरुस्यार्हं वनन्वति रत्नं न दाशुषे मयः ।।

(ऋग्वेदः, 7.81.3)

O Usha, the daughter of sky! Those who do their duty truthfully will tell you so; O affluent one! You bear adorable wealth and bring happiness and wealth for those who donate.

उच्छन्ती या कृणोषि मंहना महि प्रख्यै देवि स्वर्दृशे ।
तस्यास्ते रत्नभाज ईमहे वयं स्याम मातुर्न सूनवः ।।

(ऋग्वेदः, 7.81.4)

O Usha! You are great, you dispel darkness and spread light and brilliance all around. We invoke you, the one with jewels. May we be dear to you as children are dear to their mother.

तच्चित्रं राध आभरोषो यद्दीर्घश्रुत्तमम् ।
यत्ते दिवो दुहितर्मर्तभोजनं तद्रास्व भुनजामहै ।।

(ऋग्वेदः, 7.81.5)

O Usha! May you give us that affluence, which is varied and glorious. O Usha, the daughter of sky! May you give us food so that we may fill our hunger.

श्रवः सूरिभ्यो अमृतं वसुत्वनं वाजाँ अस्मभ्यं गोमतः ।
चोदयित्रि मघोनः सूनृतावत्युषा उच्छदपस्रिधः ।।

(ऋग्वेदः, 7.81.6)

O Usha! May you give nectar like wealth and glory to braves like us! May you give us grains with cows! O Affluent one! O Usha! Endowed with truthful speech, you are the destroyer of enemies.

3.15 प्रस्कण्वकृता उषःस्तुतिः

3.15 PRASKANVA PRAISES USHA

प्रस्कण्वोपि च काण्वो महर्षिरुषसं परिष्टौति ।
काण्वाः सूर्यायतने परोक्षयन्ति स्म सूर्यविज्ञानम् ।।123।।

Kanva's son Praskanva, too, prays to usha and examines the science related to the sun in the sun-house.

सह वामेनन उषो व्युच्छा दुहितर्दिवः ।
सह द्युम्नेन बृहता विभावरिरायादेवि दास्वती ।।

(ऋग्वेदः, 1.48.1)

In the Rigveda, sage Praskanva eulogizes usha: O Usha, the daughter of sky! May you be radiant for us with vamanna. O golden vibhavari! May you be radiant with majesty as you give boons with grace.

अश्वावतीर्गोमतीर्विश्व सुविदो भूरि च्यवन्त वस्तवे ।
उदीरय प्रतिमा सुनृता उषश्चोदराधो मघोनाम् ।।

(ऋग्वेदः, 1.48.2)

May usha, who has all the wealth, horses and cows, and through her rays takes care of my progeny, let her shower blessings on me. O Usha! May you give us the wealth worthy of affluent people!

उवासोषा उच्छाच्च नु देवी जीरा रथानाम् ।
ये अस्या आचरणेषु दध्रिरे समुद्रे न श्रवस्यवः ।।

(ऋग्वेदः, 1.48.3)

That usha, who lives in this world, drives a chariot. May that usha be more radiant! This usha drives chariots in the same way as those who desire wealth in the sea ride their boats.

उषो ये ते प्रयामेषु युञ्जते मनो दानाय सूरयः ।
अत्राह तत्कण्व एषां कण्वतमो नाम गृणाति नृणाम् ।।

(ऋग्वेदः, 1.48.4)

O Usha! Among those learned people, who offer everything for the time of your arrival, the most learned sage Kanva eulogizes you.

आ घा योषेव सूनर्युषा याति प्रभुञ्जती ।
जरयन्ती वृजनं पद्वदीयत उत्पातयति पक्षिणः ।।
(ऋग्वेदः, 1.48.5)

Usha arrives like a *grahini* (a housekeeper). That usha makes every one strong; she moves on her own feet and makes birds fly.

वि या सृजति समनं व्यर्थिनः पदं न वेत्योदती ।
वयो नकिष्टे पप्तिवांस आसते व्युष्टौ वाजिनीवति ।।
(ऋग्वेदः, 1.48.6)

That usha inspires intelligent people, inspires those who desire for wealth and she does not stay at one place.

एषा युक्तः परावतः सूर्यस्योदयनादधि ।
शतं रथेभिः सुभगोषा इयं वियात्यभिमानुषान् ।।
(ऋग्वेदः, 1.48.7)

She prepares her chariots before sunrise. This affluent usha rides on hundred chariots to the humans.

विश्वमस्या नानाम चक्षसे जगज्ज्योतिष्कृणोति सूनरी ।
अपद्वेषो मघोनी दुहिता दिव उषा उच्छदपस्रिधः ।।
(ऋग्वेदः, 1.48.8)

The whole world greets this usha with their eyes. This usha is a majestic woman; she spreads light. This usha is the daughter of Dyauloka, is affluent and drives away violent enemies.

उष आ भाहि भानुना चन्द्रेण दुहितर्दिवः ।
आवहन्ती भूर्यस्मभ्यं सौभगं व्युच्छन्ती दिविष्टिषु ।।
(ऋग्वेदः, 1.48.9)

O Usha, the daughter of Dyauloka! May you be radiant with pleasing rays! You dispel darkness for completing the chores of the day.

विश्वस्य हि प्राणनं जीवनं त्वे वि यदुच्छसि सूनरी ।
सा नो रथेन बृहता विभावरि श्रुधि चित्रामघे हवम् ।।
(ऋग्वेदः, 1.48.10)

O Usha, the one who leads in the best manner! You dispel darkness; the life of the whole world resides in you. O Usha! With varied affluence and wealth, may you hear our incantations from your great chariot.

उषो वाजं हि वंस्व यश्चित्रो मानुषे जने ।
तेना वह सुकृतो अध्वराँ उप ये त्वा गृणन्ति वह्नयः ॥
(ऋग्वेदः, 1.48.11)

O Usha! May you accept the wealth that the humans possess. May you take good men to the yajnas after being satisfied with the incantations of those who invoke you.

विश्वान्देवाँ आवह सोमपीतयेऽन्तरिक्षादुषस्त्वम् ।
सास्मासु धा गोमदश्वा वदुक्थ्य मुषो वाजं सुवीर्यम् ॥
(ऋग्वेदः, 1.48.12)

O Usha! May you bring all the devas from the sky for drinking Soma! O Usha! May you endow us with food, cows, and horses.

यस्या रुशन्तो अर्चयः प्रति भद्रा अदृक्षत ।
सो नो रयिं विश्ववारं सुपेशसमुषा ददातु सुग्म्यम् ॥
(ऋग्वेदः, 1.48.13)

Such an usha whose beautiful propitious rays are seen, may give us wealth that can please us.

ये चिद्धि त्वामृषयः पूर्व ऊतये जुहूरेऽवसे महि ।
सा नः स्तोमाँ अभिगृणीहि राधसोषः शुक्रेण शोचिषा ॥
(ऋग्वेदः, 1.48.14)

O radiant great Usha! Ancient sages prayed to you for protection and grains. May you, who is endowed with success, valour, and radiance, accept our incantations.

उषो यदद्य भानुना विद्वारा वृणवो दिवः ।
प्र नो यच्छ तादवृकं पृथुछर्दिः प्रदेवि गोमती रिषः ॥
(ऋग्वेदः, 1.48.15)

O Usha! As you have opened the entrances of heaven with your light, may you give us big houses for living. O Usha! May you give us wealth with cows.

सं नो राया बृहती विश्वपेश सामिमिक्ष्वा समिलाभिरा ।
संद्युम्नेन विश्वतुरोषो महि संवाजैर्वाजिनीवती ॥
(ऋग्वेदः, 1.48.16)

O Usha! May you make us affluent with your great and praiseworthy wealth! May you endow us with cows. O Usha endowed with grains! May you endow us with grains and wealth which can help us destroy our enemies.

उषो भद्रेभिरागहि दिवश्चिद्रोचनादधि ।
वहन्त्वरुणप्सव उप त्वा सोमिनो गृहम् ॥

(ऋग्वेद:, 1.49.1)

O Usha! May you come from bright places of the sky, through propitious paths! May the red horses bring you to the place of somayajna.

सुपेशसं सुखं रथं यमध्यस्था उषस्त्वम् ।
तेना सुश्रवसं जनं प्रावाद्य दुहितर्दिव: ॥

(ऋग्वेद:, 1.49.2)

O Usha! May you protect humans with good grains from that majestic chariot on which you sit with happiness.

वयश्चित्ते पतत्रिणो द्विपच्चतुष्पदर्जुनि ।
उष: प्रारन्नृतूँ रनुदिवो अन्तेभ्यस्परि ॥

(ऋग्वेद:, 1.49.3)

O white Usha! As you start moving, all humans with two legs and all animals with four legs, and all flying birds fly to Dyauloka for welcoming you.

व्युच्छन्ती हि रश्मिभिर्विश्वमाभासि रोचनम् ।
तां त्वामुषर्वसूयवो गीर्भि: कण्वा: अहूषत ॥

(ऋग्वेद:, 1.49.4)

O Usha! You dispel darkness and brings light to the whole world. Sage Kanva invokes you.

3.16 दैर्घतमःकृता उषःस्तुतिः

3.16 DIRGHATMA PRAISES USHA

दीर्घतमा औतथ्यो बृहस्पतेर्भातृपुत्रो यः ।
सूर्यायतने पश्यति कर्म भरद्वाजवत् सोऽपि ।।124।।

Son of Brihaspati's brother, Autathya Dirghatma, who looks after the yajnas (karma) related to the sun in the sun-house like Bharadvaja, invokes usha.

पृथूरथो दक्षिणाया अयोज्यैनं देवासो अमृतासो अस्थुः ।
कृष्णा दुदस्था दर्या विहायाश्चिकित्सन्ती मानुषाय क्षयाय ।
(ऋग्वेदः, 1.123.1)

The vast chariot of dawn is yoked. The immortals are seated in it. Usha, great and venerable, has emerged from deep darkness, yearning to illuminate the hearts of men.

पूर्वा विश्वस्माद्भुवनादबोधि जयन्ती वाजं बृहती सनुत्री ।
उच्चाव्यख्यद्युवतिः पुनर्भूरोषा अगन्प्रथमा पूर्वहूतौ ।।
(ऋग्वेदः, 1.123.2)

This usha remains awake for all beings. She is on her way to give away great boons. She is going to create great wealth. This usha is youthful who is going to manifest again and again. This usha comes first to the first havan and watches it from a higher plane.

यदद्य भागं विभजासि नृभ्य उषोदेवि मर्त्यत्रा सुजाते ।
देवो नो अत्र सविता दमूना अनागसो वोचति सूर्याय ।।
(ऋग्वेदः, 1.123.3)

O brilliant Usha, of a noble family! O nourisher of humans! As you are bestowing good fortune on all mortals, may the divine sun, the household friend of us all, through you, recommended us to the god as being sinless.

गृहङ् गृहमहना यात्यच्छा दिवे दिवे अधि नामा दधाना ।
सिषासन्ती द्योतना शश्वदागादग्रमग्रमिद्भजते वसूनाम् ।।
(ऋग्वेदः, 1.123.4)

This usha goes everyday from house to house and assumes new names. This usha has no hesitation in accepting the offerings made in the morning and accepts the first offering of all wealth.

भगस्य स्वसा वरुणस्य जामिरुषः सुनृते प्रथमा जरस्व ।
पश्वा सदध्यायो अघस्य धाता जयेम तं दक्षिणया रथेन ।।

(ऋग्वेदः, 123.5)

O Usha with beautiful speech! You are the sister of Bhaga and Varuna. May you be adorable! After your eulogies, may the sinners be imprisoned and may we conquer the enemy with your wisdom.

उदीरतां सूनृता उत्पुरन्धीरुदग्नयः शुशुचानासो अस्थुः ।
स्पार्हा वसुनि तमसाप गूह्लाविष्कृण्वन्त्युषसो विभातीः ।।

(ऋग्वेदः, 1.123.6)

May beautiful speech be uttered! May great minds be active! May fires be lighted and enflamed! May radiant usha throw light on wealth covered by darkness.

अपान्यदेत्यभ्यन्यदेति विषुरुपे अहनी सञ्चरेते ।
परीक्षितो स्तमो अन्या गुहाकर द्यौ दुषाः शोशुचता रथेन ।।

(ऋग्वेदः, 1.123.7)

When dark night and bright usha moves across towns, then the darkness of night emerges from one side. The night soon covers everything in darkness and usha brings light from a bright chariot.

सदृशीरद्य सदृशीरिदु श्वो दीर्घं सचन्ते वरुणस्य धाम ।
अनवद्यास्त्रिंशतं योजनान्येकैका क्रतुं परियान्त सद्यः ।।

(ऋग्वेदः, 1.123.8)

On all days, these pure ushas serve the vast space inhabited by Varuna. Each of these ushas always move thirty yojanas ahead of the sun.

जानत्यह्नः प्रथमस्य नाम शुक्रा कृष्णा दजनिष्टश्वितीची ।
ऋतस्य योषा न मिनाती धामाहरहर्निष्कृतमाचरन्ती ।।

(ऋग्वेदः, 1.123.9)

Knowing how important the first part of the morning is, this usha rises from dense darkness. This usha is youthful and is never detracted from its avowed duty and moves everyday on her journey.

कन्येव तन्वा शाशदानाँ एषि देवि देवमियक्षमाणम् ।
संस्मयमाना युवतिः पुरस्तादार्विवक्षांसि कृणुषे विभाती।।
(ऋग्वेदः, 1.123.10)

O Usha! You are like the woman who is happy to be with her husband, seeking his approval and pleasure.

सुसङ्काशा मातृमृष्टेव योषा विस्तन्वं कृणुषे दृशेकम् ।
भद्रा त्वमुषो वितरं व्युच्छनतत्ते अन्या उषसो नशन्त ।।
(ऋग्वेदः, 1.123.11)

Like a beautiful woman, you make everyone look up to you. O Usha! You are generous; may you distribute light. Other ushas cannot be radiant like you.

अश्वावतीर्गोमती विश्ववारा यतमाना रश्मिभिः सूर्यस्य ।
परा च यन्ति पुनराच यन्ति भद्रा नाम वहमाना उषासः ।।
(ऋग्वेदः, 1.123.12)

Such ushas, who come with the gifts of horses and cows, and is adored by everyone, and who spreads light with sun's rays, travel long distances and return.

एषा दिवो दुहिता प्रत्यदर्शि ज्योतिर्वसाना समना पुरस्तात् ।
ऋतस्य पन्था मन्वेति साधु प्रजानतीव न दिशो मिनाति ।।
(ऋग्वेदः, 1.124.3)

This usha is the daughter of Dyauloka, she wears bright white dress. She is seen in the east and carries enormous wealth. This usha is capable of moving on the path of rita. This usha moves like a learned woman and does not cause any disruptions.

एवेदेषा पुरुतमा दृशे कं ना जामिं न परिवृणक्ति जामिम् ।
अरेपसा तन्वा शाशदाना नार्भादीषते न महो विभाती ।।
(ऋग्वेदः, 1.124.6)

Generous usha does not abandon those belonging to others nor those who belong to her while distributing light. Manifesting a sinless body, usha does not abandon neither the small nor the big ones and enlighten both.

अभ्रातेव पुंस एति प्रतीची गर्तारुगिव सनये धनानाम् ।
जायेव पत्य उशती सुवासा उषा हस्रेव निरिणीते अप्सः ॥
(ऋग्वेदः, 1.124.7)

This usha spreads her light like the joy a woman experiences on returning to her parent's home or when she goes to her husband dressed in beautiful clothes.

स्वसा स्वस्रे ज्यायस्यै योनिमारैगपैत्यस्याः प्रतिचक्ष्येव ।
व्युच्छन्ती रश्मिभिः सूर्यस्या ञ्ज्यङ्क्तेसमनगा इव व्राः ॥
(ऋग्वेदः, 1.124.8)

Ratri goes away as soon as she looks at usha in the same way as a younger sister vacates the place for an elder sister, dispelling darkness with rays of the sun, this usha brings the rays of light together.

आसां पूर्वासामहसु स्वसृणामपरापूर्वामभ्येति पश्चात् ।
ताः प्रत्नवन्नव्यसीर्नूनमस्मे रेवदुच्छन्तु सुदिना उषासः ॥
(ऋग्वेदः, 1.124.9)

Of these two sisters, the younger one travels during the day and the elder goes later. These ushas are ancient as well as new—they brighten the day with affluence.

3.17 अष्टादंष्ट्रकृता उषःस्तुतिः

3.17 EULOGY OF USHA BY ASHTADAMSHTRA

सचन्त यदुषसः सूर्येण चित्रामस्य केतवो रामविन्दन् ।
आ यन्नक्षत्रं ददृशे दिवो न पुनर्यतो न किरद्धा नु वेद ॥
(ऋग्वेदः, 10.111.7)

'When ushas are associated with the sun, his rays acquire wonderful beauty but when (during the day hours) the constellations of heaven are not seen, no one really knows his rays as he moves (across space).'

एषां कतिपयमन्त्र आधिदैवतापक्ष उपनेयाः ।
सर्वे त्वपरे मन्त्रा अधिभूतं समनुगच्छन्ति ॥125॥

Some of these mantras should be considered in the context of tutelary devas and others in context of desired tutelary material.

3.18 आप्त्यकृता उषःस्तुतिः

3.18 APTYA'S EULOGY OF USHA

केचिन्मत्रा उषसस्त्वधिदैवतमेव पर्याप्ताः ।
आप्त्यस्त्रितो यथोचे संधे सूक्तेऽन्तताऽष्टमगे ।।126।।

In the fourty-seventh sukta of eight mandala of Rigveda, sage Trita Aptya has said that some mantras of the Vedas are entirely related to the celestial goddess, usha.

यच्च गोषु दुः ष्वप्न्यं यच्चास्मे दुहितर्दिवः ।
त्रिताय तद्विभावर्यात्याय परावहानेहसो व उतयः सुऊतयो व ऊतयः ।।
(ऋग्वेदः, 8.47.14)

O daughter of Dyauloka! Vibhavari! May you keep bad dreams away from Trita Aptya. May your protection be without condition and superior.

निष्कं वा घा कृण्वते स्रजं वा दुहितर्दिवः ।
त्रिते दुःष्वप्नयं सर्वमाप्त्ये परिद्मस्यनेहसो व ऊतयः सुऊतयो व ऊतयः ।।
(ऋग्वेदः, 8.47.15)

O daughter of Dyauloka! May you keep bad dreams of a goldsmith and a gardener away from Trita Aptya.

तदन्नाय तदपसे तं भागमुपसेदुषे ।
त्रिताय च द्विताय चोषो दुःष्वप्न्यं वहानेहसो व ऊतयः सुऊतयो व ऊतयः ।।
(ऋग्वेदः, 8.47.16)

May you take the bad dreams away from that Trita and Dvit who acccpt grains and who work hard. Your protection is flawless; your protection is the best protection (one who accepts grains achieved through sinful acts is also a sinner; may his sins be destroyed).

यथा कलां यथाशफं यथा ऋणं सन्न यामसि ।
एवादुःष्वप्न्यं सर्वमाप्त्ये सं नयामयस्य नेहसो व ऊतयः सुऊतयो व ऊतयः ।।
(ऋग्वेदः, 8.47.17)

Like we pay back our loans along with interest, you take all bad dreams away from me. Your protection is generous and strong.

अजैष्माद्यासनाम चाभूमानागसो वयम् ।
उषो यस्माद्दु:ष्वप्न्यादभैष्मापतदुच्छत्वनेहसो व ऊतय सुऊतयो व ऊतय: ।।
(ऋग्वेद:, 8.47.18)

We have gained victory as well as revenue today. We have been expiated from sins today. O Usha! May the hideous dream that frightens us disappear. Your protection is devoid of sin, the safety you provide is supreme.

3.19 देवेन्द्रेण सूर्यचक्रपरीहरणं सूर्याधिष्ठाने दस्यूनामाक्रमणं च

3.19 DASYUS ATTACK SUN-HOUSE TO STEAL SUN

विज्ञानशालास्थितात् सूर्यचक्रद्वयात् एकस्य देवेन्द्रेण परीहरणम् ।

Devendra taking away one of the two sun-discs located in the science block.

उषःकारणात् सूर्याधिष्ठाने दस्युनाम् आक्रमणम् इन्द्रकुत्साभ्यां तन्निबर्हणं च ।

Attack of dasyus on the sun-house due to usha and the counter offensive of Indra and Kutsa.

उषा विलज्जा चरतीति शुष्णो बबन्ध तां प्रेम्णि कदाप्यभीक्ष्य ।
तत्प्रेमपाशानुविकर्षितः सन्नुषः समीपं स उपैत्यभीक्ष्णम् ।।127।।

The usha moves uninhibited across the sky. Once an asura named Shushna got enamoured by her and he came again and again to meet her.

सूर्यनिवृत्त्या कृष्णो विरतोऽभूत् किन्तु तत्पश्चात् ।
सूर्यायतने शुष्णो यातायातं व्यधादुषोहेतोः ।।128।।

An asura namd Krishna had earlier attacked the sun-house and now it was another asura named Shushna, infatuated by usha, who attacked the sun-disc several times.

शुष्णो दस्युः सूर्यं बहुधागत्य व्यमर्दयद् धृष्टः ।
अकुतोभयः स सूर्यद्वारं पिदधे निजह्नुवे सूर्यम् ।।129।।

That insolent asura crushed the sun-disc many times. He shut the door of the sun-house without any fear to hide the sun.

इन्द्रः शुष्णाक्रमणं सूर्यापह्नुतिमुपद्रवातिशयम् ।
बार्हस्पत्यस्य गिरा श्रुत्वा सद्यः समाययौ सूर्यम् ।।130।।

Indra came to hear about Shushna's attack from Brihaspati's son and how the sun was hidden.

दासाक्रमणनिरोधोपायानृषि सदसि चिन्तयंस्तत्र ।
सूर्यसदनरक्षार्थं कमपि नृपं मार्गयामास ।।131।।

The sages at the sun-house discussed ways to stop such attacks. A king was appointed for the protection of the sun-house.

तत्रावोचदगस्त्यः सौराच्चक्रद्वयादेकम् ।
दिवि नीत्वा परचक्रं स्थापयितुं कुत्सरक्षणे युक्तम् ॥132॥

Then sage Agastya took one of the sun-discs to the heaven and entrusted another disc with Kutsa for protection.

वह कुत्समिन्द्र यस्मिञ्चाकन्त्स्यू मन्यू ऋज्रा वातस्याश्वा ।
प्रसूरश्चक्रं बृहतादभीकेऽभिस्पृधो यासिषद् वज्रबाहुः ॥
(ऋग्वेदः, 1.174.5)

In the first mandala of Rigveda it is said: O Indra! Take the fast running, pleasure loving and straight moving horse to Kutsa in the same yajna in which you want to go. May the sun move its chakra near that place and let Indra with thunder-like arms go to attack the enemies.

रपत्कविरिद्रार्क सातौक्षां दासायोपवर्हणीं कः ।
करत् तिस्रो मघवा दानुचित्रानिदुर्योणे कुयवाचं मृधिश्रेत् ॥
(ऋग्वेदः, 1.174.7)

O Indra! Sages glorify you to obtain blessings. You throw the evil forces obstructing the path of their progress and crush the evils one for all. O bounteous lord, you set open the doors of three-fold progress—physical, mental, and spiritual, and annihilate evil forces which put obstacles in our progress.

मुषाय सूर्यं कवे चक्रमीशान ओजसा ।
वह शुष्णाय वधं कुत्सं वातस्याश्वैः ॥
(ऋग्वेदः, 1.175.4)

O poet of wisdom! By your strength, you have carried away the sun-disc. You are master of all. May you proceed with the swiftness of the wind to reach Kutsa and kill Shushna.

शुष्मिन्तमो हि ते मदो द्युम्निन्तम उत कतुः ।
वृत्रघ्ना वरिवोविदा मंसीष्ठा अश्चसातमः ॥
(ऋग्वेदः, 1.175.5)

O Indra! Your *mada* (pride) gives strength to all and your karma yield plenty of grains. You are famed for donating horses. So, may you give us the weapons which would kill Vritra and give us wealth.

इत्यगस्त्यपरामर्शं युयुत्सुरनुमोदयन् ।
हत्वैकं चक्रमन्यस्य रक्षायै कुत्समाह्वयत् ॥133॥

This way Agastya's advice for war was accepted, according to which Kutsa was called for the protection of the disc which was then removed.

गत्वोशनसा साकं कुत्सगृहं तं न्ययोजयत् त्रातुम् ।
वातजवाश्वैः सूर्यस्थानेऽत्रानाय्य चादिशत् कुत्सम् ॥134॥

Sage Ushna went to Kutsa's house and appointed him to protect the sun-disc. A fast horse brought the sun to the sun-house and the sage commanded Kutsa to protect it.

गान्धारमद्रभूपान् न्युङ्क्त कांश्चिच्च कुत्ससहकर्तॄन् ।
वार्षागिरान् दभीति ध्वसन्ति पुरुषन्ति पूर्वांश्च ॥135॥

Along with Kutsa, Vrishagiri's sons, Dabhiti, Dhvasanti and Purushanti, who had worked with Kutsa and kings of Gandharva and Madra, were appointed.

इन्द्रस्तत्र तदानीं दासाक्रान्तिं निरोधयितुम् ।
सहदेवैः कुत्सेन च सूर्यस्थानादताडयच्छुष्णम् ॥136॥

For countering the asura attack on the suryasthana, Indra along with the devas and Kutsa launched a combined attack on Shushna.

स यथाऽयमिन्द्र एतं सह कुत्सेन न्यवर्हनच्छुष्णम् ।
शाक्त्यो हि गौरवीतिः स्मारयतीन्द्राय तत् स्तोतुम् ॥137॥

Sage Shaktya Gauraviti has described how Indra and Kutsa attacked Shushna.

उशना यत् सहस्यैरयातं गृहमिन्द्रजूजुवानेभिरश्वैः ।
वन्वानो अत्र सरथं ययाथ कुत्सेन देवैरवनोर्हशुष्णम् ॥
(ऋग्वेदः, 5.29.9)

'O Indra! On a chariot driven by galloping horses, you first went with Ushna to the [sun] house and then you and Kutsa rode the same chariot and killed Shushna'.

षष्टिः षष्टिश्चेत्थं मरुतां सेनासु कल्पिता व्यूहाः ।
त्रि:षष्टिर्मरुतोऽत्राभिक्रमणे प्रस्तुता आसन् ॥138॥

Sixty-member squadrons were created in the army of the marutas and they were kept in the state of readiness for a war.

3.20 सूर्यसंस्थासंरक्षणार्थो देवेन्द्रकृतः स्थानिकः प्रबन्धकः

3.20 APPOINTMENT OF LOCAL ADMINISTRATOR BY DEVENDRA TO SAFEGUARD SURYASANSTHANA

ये द्वेचक्रे सूर्यस्तत्रैकं दिवि समाधातुम् ।
दस्योः शङ्कित इन्द्रो हत्वाऽन्यत् कुत्सरक्षणे न्यदधात् ॥139॥

Of the two surya-chakras, the one meant to be placed in the Dyauloka was carried away by Indra and kept at another place under the protection of Kutsa.

प्रथमस्य मथकसूक्ते चतुर्थमन्त्रे तदेतदाम्नातम् ।
पञ्चममण्डलधारासूक्तस्य च दशममन्त्रेऽपि ॥140॥

It has also been narrated in the fourth mantra of mathak sukta in the first mandala as well as in the tenth *richa* (mantra) of dhara sukta in the fifth mandala of Rigveda.

सूर्यस्यास्य विधाने नियुक्त आसीत् तदैतशः सुष्विः ।
सूनर्युषोऽभिधाना पुत्री दिव उषस उपचारे ॥141॥

A king named Sushvi was appointed as the protector of the sun. An usha named sunari was appointed for its ministration.

चक्रं हत्वापीन्द्रः कृपयाऽरक्षत् तमेतशं मर्त्यम् ।
उषसं त्ववधीदुषसः शकटं भङ्क्त्वा विपाशि निक्षिप्य ॥142॥

Before carrying off the disc, to defend the besieged defender, Aitasha, Indra, had killed usha; he broke her chariot and threw it into Vipasha.

उषसो दिवः सुतायाः प्रेमवशादेव गतागतं चक्रे ।
शुष्णः सूर्यस्थाने दासाक्रमणे निमित्तमेषोषाः ॥143॥

This usha was the cause of the attacks on the surya sansthana; enamoured by this usha, an asura named Shushna had attacked the sun-house.

अत एवेन्द्रः क्रुद्धस्तदुषोऽधिकृतं तदेकरविचक्रम् ।
स्वर्गे निनाय शकटं वाजावहमिक्षपद् विपाशायाम् ॥144॥

An enraged Indra carried off that one surya-chakra entrusted with usha to the heaven and threw the chariot driven by her horses into Vipasha.

उषसः सम्बन्धादिह सर्वविधानं व्यवर्जयत् किन्तु ।
एतशहयानुवाहितचक्रमरक्षत् तदैतशाधिकृतम् ।।145।।

To protect the surya-chakra, all the activities related to usha were banned.

एतच्च वामदेवस्त्रिंशे सूक्ते चतुर्थमण्डलगे ।
उषसो निवर्हणं तद् व्याचष्टे शकटभङ्गं च ।।146।।

Sage Vamadeva describes the end of usha and the destruction of her chariot in the Rigveda.

यत्रोत बाधितेभ्यश्चक्रं कुत्साय युध्यते ।
मुषाय इन्द्रसूर्यम् ।।

(ऋग्वेदः, 4.30.4)

O Indra! You protected Kutsa, who was fighting the enemies, and carried away the surya-chakra.

यत्रोत मर्त्याय कमरिणा इन्द्र सूर्यम् ।
प्राव: शचीभिरेतशम् ।।

(ऋग्वेदः, 4.30.6)

O Indra! You speedily send forth the power of the sun for the sake of mortals and protect the the diligent and wise man with your radiance.

एतद्धे दुतवीर्यमिन्द्र चकर्थ पौंस्यम् ।
स्त्रियं यद्दुर्हणा युवं बधीर्दुहितरं दिवः ।।

(ऋग्वेदः, 4.30.8)

O Indra! You performed this work valiantly, full of manliness; in the same way you killed usha, daughter of Dyauloka, who harboured desires to annihilate you.

दिवश्चिद् घा दुहितरं महान्महीयमानाम् ।
उषासमिन्द्र संपिणक ।।

(ऋग्वेदः, 4.30.9)

O Indra! You are great. It is true that you destroyed the chariot of usha who was endowed with the glory of Dyauloka.

अपोषा अनसः सरत्सन्पिष्टादह विभ्युषी ।
नियत्सीं शिष्लथद्व्रषा ।।

(ऋग्वेदः, 4.30.10)

As the mighty Indra destroyed her chariot, a frightened usha stood clear of her broken vehicle.

एतदस्या अनः शये सुसम्पिष्टं विपाश्या ।
ससारसीं परावतः ॥

(ऋग्वेदः, 4.30.11)

This broken chariot of usha is lying on the banks of river Vipasha and usha had moved away from there.

सूर्यस्य दस्युगणतो रक्षार्थं ये न्ययुज्यन्त ।
ते खलु कुत्साधीना राजानः सूर्यमासेदुः ॥147॥

The kings appointed to defend the sun against the asuras were under the command of Kutsa and they went near the sun.

अधितिष्ठति तं सूर्यम् कुत्सदभीति ध्वसन्ति तुर्वीति ।
सह राजचक्रमेव वार्षागिर पञ्चराज कुलम् ॥148॥

A group of five kings, including the sons of Kutsa, Dabhiti, Dhvasanti, Turviti and Vrishagiri, had been appointed to protect that sun.

इत्थं सूर्यस्थाने विधाय शान्तिं कृतेऽखिले सुस्थे ।
सबृहस्पतिरियमिन्द्रः समरुत्सेनोऽभ्यगात्स्वर्गम् ॥149॥

Thus, having established peace and order in the sun-house, Indra, accompanied by Brihaspati and the army of devas, left for svarga.

3.21 सूर्यस्य दिव्यारोपणस्थानम्

3.21 INSTALLATION OF SUN IN SVARGA

पृथिव्यां प्रतिष्ठापितसूर्यद्वयात् एकस्य सूर्यस्य दिव्यारोपणम् ।

Of the two surya-s enshrined in prithvi, installation of one surya in svarga.

एकं चक्रं कुत्साभिरक्षणे तत्र संस्थाप्य ।
अपरं चक्रं हृत्वा तं दिवमारोहयत् सूर्यम् ॥150॥

After putting one sun in the protection of Kutsa, the second surya-chakra was carried away and installed in the Dyauloka.

प्रान्यच्चक्रमबृहः सूर्यस्य कुत्सायान्यद् वरिवो यातवेऽकः ।
अनासो दस्यूं रमृणो वधेन निदुर्योण आवृणङ् मृध्रवाचः ॥
(ऋग्वेदः, 5.29.10)

'O Indra! You segregated one disc of surya and constructed another disc to provide wealth to Kutsa. O Indra! You killed the nose-less [flat-nosed people living in the mountains] asuras with your weapons. You annihilated those speaking foul words in the war.'

3.22 अग्निपुरस्कृतानां देवानां स्वर्गे सहगमनम्

3.22 DEVAS LED BY AGNI GOING TO HEAVEN

तत्सूर्यचक्रं तु मनुष्यलोकाद्दिवि प्रणेतुं विहिते विमर्शे ।
अग्नादयस्तत्र सहोपगन्तुं चक्रुः समारम्भमनेकदेवाः ॥151॥

Agni and many other gods decided to go forth to the heaven to propose the installation of a surya-chakra in the manushyaloka.

अग्निरिन्द्रो वरुणो मित्रो अर्यमावायुः पूषा सरस्वती सजोषसः ।
आदित्या विष्णुर्मरुतः स्वर्बृहत् सोमो रुद्रो अदितिर्ब्रह्मणस्पतिः ॥
(ऋग्वेदः, 10.65.1)

Agni, Indra, Varuna, Mitra, Aryama, Vayu, Pusha, Sarasvati, Sajoshasa, Aditya, Vishnu, Marut, Swar Brihat, Soma, Rudra, Aditi, and Brahmanaspati, all these go forth to the cosmic space together.

इन्द्राग्नी वृत्रहत्येषु सत्पती मिथो हिन्वानातन्वा समोकसा ।
अन्तरिक्षं मह्यापप्रुरोजसा सोमोघृतश्रीमहिमानमीरयन् ॥
(ऋग्वेदः, 10.65.2)

Staying together and invigorating each other, Indra, Agni, and Soma, protectors of the virtuous, have filled the antariksha with their splendour.

दिवस्पतिर्यः पृथिवीपतिर्यः प्रधानतो दासवधोद्यतौ तौ ।
सोमोऽन्तरिक्षस्य पतिघृतश्रीस्त्रयोन्तरिक्षं विपुलं तदाक्षुः ॥152॥

The lord of the heaven, Indra, along with the lord of the earth, Agni, the killers of dasas, and the lord of antariksha, Soma, all three encompass the vast space.

ब्रह्म गामश्वं जनयन्त ओषधीर्वनस्पतीन् पृथिवीं पर्वताँ अपः ।
सूर्यं दिवि रोहयन्तः सुदानवः आर्याव्रता विसृजन्तो अधिक्षमि ॥
(ऋग्वेदः, 10.65.11)

स्वर्णमन्तरिक्षाणि रोचना द्यावाभूमीं पृथिवीं स्कम्भुरोजसा ।
पृक्षा इव महयन्तः सुरातयो देवाः स्तवन्ते मनुषाय सूरयः ॥
(ऋग्वेदः, 10.65.4)

Producing knowledge, holy cows, herbs, earth, water, and mountains, installing the sun in the sky, enlightening the human beings of Dyauloka and Antariskhaloka, the devas thus infused the heaven and earth with their radiance.

दिव्यन्तरिक्षे भुवि च प्रचक्रुर्ज्योतींषि भूमिं च सुसज्जितां ते ।
ये स्वर्णरास्तान् व्यदधुः सुदीप्तान् कृतोत्सवान् राजनिदेशयोगात् ।।153।।

These human deities propagated festivities celebrated with royal permission across the heaven, earth, and interspace.

विश्वेपि देवा दिवि सप्रयातुं प्रतिष्ठमानाहि मनुष्यलोकात् ।
नृभ्यो वसूनि व्यतरन् प्रहर्षात् तेभ्यः स्तवन्ते स्म च मानुषेभ्यः ।।154।।

On the occasion of their departure from the manushyaloka to svarga, all the devas together distributed wealth among the humans and prayed for them.

देवोऽधिकारो मरुतां यथासीद् यथान्तरिक्षेऽधिकृतश्च वातः ।
यथाप्सु चाब्धौ वरुणस्तथाग्निर्भूम्याः पतिर्दीर्घतमा जगाद ।।155।।

Sage Dirghatamas has said that Agni is the lord of Prithviloka in the same way as maruta reign over Dyauloka, Vayu pervades antariksha and Varuna holds sway over the water of oceans.

यद्यप्यमरावत्यां देवसभायां सुधर्मायाम् ।
धिष्ण्यानधितिष्ठन्ति हि दिक्पाला लोकपालाश्च ।।156।।

सन्ति तथापि ततोऽन्ये चत्वारो लोकपतयोऽमी ।
स्वे स्वे लोके प्रत्यासन्नाः शवसोनपात् संज्ञाः ।।157।।

Though Dikpala and Lokpala sit at their respective seats in the assembly of devas called Sudharma in Amaravati, the lords of four lokas (Agni, Vayu, Varuna, and Maruta) are different from them and assume the title of *shavasonapat* (presiding authority) of their respective lokas.

शवसोनपात् स शास्ता यः स्थानीयः प्रबन्धकर्ता स्यात् ।
राजप्रतिनिधिभूतः प्रान्ताध्यक्षः पुराकाले ।।158।।

Shavasonapat is an administrator who takes care of the territory under his command. In ancient times, a shavasonapat ruled over the territory as a representative of the king.

योऽग्निः स देवोऽधिकृतः पृथिव्यां मनुष्यलोकेऽधिपतिर्नियुक्तः ।
वह्निः स देवेभ्य इतः प्रदानं प्रगृह्य दिव्यर्पयति प्रणीय ॥159॥

Agni, who was appointed as the lord of manushyaloka on earth, was authorized by the devas as the one who carried the oblations from earth to the heaven for them.

त्वमग्ने यज्ञानां होता विश्वेषां हितः ।
देवेभिर्मानुषे जने ॥

(ऋग्वेदः, 6.16.1)

O Agni! You are the performer of all the sacrifices among human beings. You have been placed here by the devas.

यो अग्निः सप्त मानुषः श्रितो विश्वेषु सिन्धुषु ।
तमागन्मत्रिपस्त्यं मन्धातुर्दस्युहन्तारमग्निं यज्ञेषु पूर्व्यम् ।
नभन्ता मन्यके समे ॥

(ऋग्वेदः, 8.39.8)

That Agni who pervades in all human beings and all rivers, protects the learned ones living in the three domains [bhumi, antariksha, and Dyauloka]. Let's reach out to that Agni, the most important one in the yajna, the annihilator of asuras. Our remaining enemies will automatically be destroyed.

इत्थं ब्रूते काण्वो नाभाकस्त्रिषु समुद्रकूलेषु ।
भवनानि त्रीण्यग्नेर्मन्त्रकृतः सप्तमानुषान् सभ्यान् ॥160॥

After constructing three houses, with mantras, for Agni on the banks of three oceans, sage Kanva addressed the seven noblemen thus.

मनुष्यलोकाधिपतित्वहेतोरग्निः प्रधानः स इतः पृथिव्याः ।
चक्रप्रणीतौ दिवि तेन केतुः सूर्यप्रणेतृत्वममुष्य वक्ति ॥161॥

Being the *adhipati* (sovereign) of human world, this Agni is the lord of prithvi. He [Kanva] has said this about the installation of surya-chakra in Dyauloka.

अग्ने नक्षत्रमजरमासूर्यं रोहयो दिवि ।
दधज्ज्योतिजनेभ्यः ॥

(ऋग्वेदः, 10.156.4)

O Agni, that sun which bears light for people, you have honoured that immortal star in the heaven.

तान् प्रस्थितान् दिव्यमरान्मनुष्यास्ते स्वस्तिवाकैर्बहुधाऽभ्यनन्दन् ।
यूयं समं धीभिरितः प्रयान्तः स्वः प्राप्य तत् स्वस्तिगिरो जुषध्वम् ।।162।।

The humans repeatedly greeted the devas going towards the heaven with various invocations and said, may you all rejoice in the eulogies showered on you.

विश्वदेवाः सह धीभिः पुरन्ध्वा मनोर्यजत्रा अमृता ऋतज्ञाः ।
रातिषाचो अभिषाचः स्वर्विदः स्वर्गिरो ब्रह्मसूक्त ।। जुषरेत ।।
(ऋग्वेदः, 10.65.14)

स्वं स्वं दिविस्थानमभिप्रयातान् ववन्दिरे भक्तिवशान्मनुष्याः ।
वसिष्ठपूर्वा भुवि सूर्यसंस्था-प्रतिष्ठिताः स्वं च यशोऽर्थयन्तः ।।163।।

'May all the gods, including Indra, full of wisdom and responsibility, who know the importance, essence and customs of the yajna, receivers of oblations, staying together in the yajna, and who are familiar with svarga, accept our grain imbued with prayers and sacred chanting.' The human beings thus eulogized the devas going to their respective seats in the heaven. After seeking the blessings of the devas, they returned to their positions in the surya sansthana, under the leadership of Vasishta.

देवान् वसिष्ठो अमृतान् ववन्दे ये विश्वा भुवनाऽभिप्रतस्थुः ।
तेनो रासन्तामुरुगायमद्य यूयं पात स्वस्तिभिः सदा नः ।।
(ऋग्वेदः, 10.65.15)

The descendants of sage Vasishta eulogized the immortal devas, famous in all realms of the world for their radiance. O deities, provide us with radiant grains. O all deities! Protect us always.

3.23 एतशेन सूर्यरथवहनम्

3.23 AITASHA RIDING THE CHARIOT OF SUN

अर्थाहरणे कर्मणि ये नियता व्यापृता नरा भृतकाः ।
हरितो नरास्त उक्ताः शिरसा रश्मिभिरिमे हरन्त्यर्थान् ॥164॥

The attendants, appointed for *arthasamgraha* (collection of money) were also called Harita. Those human beings called Harita absorb all the riches from the world through streaks of light radiating from the forehead [like the rays of sun].

इन्द्रश्चक्रं स यदा दिवमनयत् तत्र हरितो नॄन् ।
व्यरमयतेन्द्रो ना त्वयमेतश एकोहरच्चक्रम् ॥165॥

When Indra took that sun-disc to the heaven, he stopped the humans called Harita and let Aitasha alone carry the disc.

त्वं सूरो हरितो रामयो नॄन् भरच्चक्रमेतशो नायमिन्द्र ।
प्रास्य पारं नवतिं नाव्यानामपि कर्तमवर्तयोऽयज्यून ॥
(ऋग्वेदः, 1.121.13)

'O Indra! You generate the rays that accomplish the duties of humans like the radiant sun. The wheel of Indra's chariot remains always in motion. You have done a great favour by throwing those who do not perform yajna across ninety rivers, navigable by boats only.'

यद्यपि नद्यो बह्व्यस्तथापि या नौकया तार्याः ।
मध्ये मार्गं नवतिस्तत्पारे चक्रमेतशो निन्ये ॥166॥

Though rivers are numerous, yet the rivers which can be navigated only by boat are ninety in number, and Aitasha carried the disc to the middle of these rivers and dropped it there.

3.24 दिवि सूर्यारोपणस्थानम्

3.24 PLACE OF SURYA (SUN) IN DYAULOKA

स्वर्गस्त्रिविष्टपाख्यो विष्टपमेतस्य मण्डलं खण्डम् ।
ऐशान्यामपराजितदिशि चैन्द्रं विष्टपं त्वासीत् ।।167।।

Svarga is known as trivishtapa and its one section or sphere is called vishtapa.

प्राग्मेरुलक्षितं तु ब्राह्मं विष्टपमवाग् दिशि प्रथितम् ।
तत उत्तरदिक्प्रथितं नाकारब्धं तु विष्टपं विष्णोः ।।168।।

South of Pragmeru is the vishtapa of Brahma, from here towards the north is the vishtapa of Vishnu.

ब्रह्माविष्णुरथेन्द्रस्त्रयोऽक्षरा मुख्यतोऽधिदैवमिमे ।
अग्निः सोम इतीमावनुगौ पञ्चाक्षरं विश्वम् ।।169।।

Brahma, Vishnu, and Indra, these three are *akshar devas* (all-powerful, immortal gods). They have the power of celestial deities. Agni and Soma follow these presiding deities. In this way, this whole world is *panchakshar* (made up of five elements). On these five elements this world is based, these are the *panch pundir*-s which uphold the seat of universe by revolving in each other's orbits.

लोकत्रयमधिभूतं तद्वदिदं पञ्चमण्डलं क्लृपाम् ।
एकं मनुष्यलोकोऽन्तरिक्षमेकं त्रिविष्टपं तु द्यौः ।।170।।

In the same way as one manushyaloka prithvi, one Antarikshaloka and one trivishtapa Dyauloka pervade the three domains, this universe is made up of five spheres. This five-sphere universe comprises the spheres of moon, earth, sun, parameshti, and Prajapati; and this is the *panch pundir vidya*.

ब्राह्मस्य वैष्णवस्यान्तरे स्थितं विष्टपस्यास्य ।
ब्रध्नस्य विष्टपं तत् प्रकल्पितं यज्ञसूर्याभ्याम् ।।171।।

The vishtapa of the sun lies between the vishtapa of Brahma and Vishnu, illuminated by the sun and yajnas.

आसीद्दिवस्तु मध्ये लोको ब्रध्नस्य विष्टपस्तत्र ।
संप्रत्युत्तरतः प्राग्मेरोरंशे तु सप्तदशे ।।172।।

In the present-day Pragmeru region, at 17° latitude, the site of surya vishtapa, was Dyauloka in ancient times.

मध्ये चतुष्पथं यः स्कम्भोधरुणाख्य उन्नतः क्लृप्तः ।
तदुपरि चाश्मा पृश्निर्नामहितं सूर्यचक्रं तत् ।।173।।

Here, there is a *chatushpath* (cross-road) known as Skambhodharu which has been constructed at some height, and on it the surya-chakra called Ashma Prashni has been installed.

इन्द्रो दीर्घाय चक्षस आसूर्यं रोहयद्दिवि ।
विगोभिरद्रिमैरयत् ।।

(ऋग्वेदः, 1.7.3)

Surya was installed in the heaven for the light engulfing Indra. That sun created the cloud with its rays.

इन्द्रो दिवः प्रतिमानं पृथिव्या विश्वा वेद सवना हन्ति शुष्णम् ।
महीं चिद्द्यामातनोत् सूर्येण चास्कम्भ चित्कम्भनेन स्कभीयान् ।।

(ऋग्वेदः, 10.111.5)

Indra is the epitome of heaven and earth, therefore he knows about all the yajnas. That Indra annihilates Shushna. He illuminates the vast space and earth with the sun. He supports the heaven with his rays.

अद्रिः सोऽश्मा पृश्निः समन्ततो गोभिराकीर्णः ।
अहनि च दिवा च दीर्घत्विषेऽत्रसूर्ये तमाधत्त ।।174।।

That sun namely Ashma Prashni was surrounded by rays from all sides. Everyday during daytime, the rays fall profusely on this sun and eliminate darkness.

स्कम्भस्यास्य चतुर्षु च पाश्वेष्वासीच्चतुर्भद्रम् ।
वृषभो ह्रदश्च चन्द्राश्वः पक्षी ते शिलाकायाः ।।175।।

There was a *chaturbhuj* (quadrangle) in the flank of this fulcrum located on chatushpath. This quadrangle had four forms or names: vrishabh, sarovar, chandra, and ashva, these were built of stones.

दिवो यः स्कम्भो धरुणः स्वातत आपूर्णो अंशु पर्येति विश्वतः ।
सेमे मही रोदसी यक्षदावृतासमीचीने दाधार समषिः कविः ।।

(ऋग्वेदः, 9.74.2)

This central pillar of Dyauloka, which supports everything, pervades everywhere, and fills all the places with its presence. May this omnipresent Soma bestow his actions on this great expansive earth. This knowledge enhancing Soma supports both earth and heaven, and also bears the grains.

स्कम्भो दाधार द्यावापृथिवी उभे इमे स्कम्भो दाधारोर्वन्तरिक्षम् ।
स्कम्भो दाधार प्रदिशः षडुर्वीः स्कम्भ इदं विश्वं भुवनमाविवेश ॥
(अथर्ववेदः, 10.5.35)

This fulcrum [Indra] supports the heaven and earth; it also upholds antariksha as well as the six directions; this fulcrum pervades the whole universe.

उक्षा समुद्रो अरुषः सुपर्णः पूर्वस्य योनिं पितुराविवेश ।
मध्ये दिवो निहितः पृश्निरश्मा विचक्रमे रजसस्पात्यन्तौ ॥
(ऋग्वेदः, 5.47.3)

The sun with its radiant rays fills the ocean with water. The sun has come to the eastern part of its parent, *akasha* (sky). This sun, like a multicoloured meteor, has been installed in the sky and it revolves there. It protects the farthest parts of Dyauloka.

स्कम्भोऽधिदैवतमयं व्याख्यातोऽथर्वसंहितायां यः ।
दशमे काण्डे सप्तमसूक्ते सोपीन्द्रतः क्लृप्तः ॥176॥

This fulcrum as a presiding deity has been described in the seventh mantra of the tenth khanda of Atharvaveda, according to which this fulcrum, too, is pervaded by Indra.

स्कम्भे लोकाः स्कम्भे तपः स्कम्भेऽध्यृतमाहितम् ।
स्कम्भ त्वा वेद प्रत्यक्षमिन्द्रे सर्वं समाहितम् ॥
(अथर्ववेदः, 10.5.29)

This fulcrum is the all-supporting Paramatma, that fulcrum constitutes tapa, and on its base resides rita. I know that in you [Indra] alone resides everything.

इन्द्रे लोका इन्द्रे तप इन्द्रेऽध्यृतमाहितम् ।
इन्द्रं त्वां वेद प्रत्यक्षं स्कम्भे सर्वं प्रतिष्ठितम् ॥
(अथर्ववेदः, 10.5.30)

All the domains, worship, and seasons reside within Indra. O Indra! I know it for sure that you are the fulcrum around which everything revolves.

यत्परममवमं यच्च मध्यमं प्रजापतिः ससृजे विश्वरूपम् ।
कियता स्कम्भः प्रविवेश तत्र यन्न प्राविशत्कियत् तद् बभूव ॥
(अथर्ववेदः, 10.5.8)

Indra has pervaded everywhere in the world created by Prajapati. There is hardly any place left where he has not been.

यस्मिन् भूमिरन्तरिक्षं द्यौर्यस्मिन्नध्याहिता ।
यत्राग्निश्चन्द्रमाः सूर्यो वातस्तिष्ठन्त्यार्पिताः ॥
(अथर्ववेदः, 10.5.12)

Tell me who is the one who supports prithvi, antariksha, and Dyauloka where Agni, surya, chandra, and Vayu have taken shelter?

यस्य त्रयस्त्रिंशद्देवाः अङ्गे सर्वे समाहिताः ।
स्कम्भं तं ब्रूहि कतमः स्विदेवसः ॥

यत्र ऋषयः प्रथमजा ऋचस्साम यजुर्मही ।
एकर्षियस्मिन्नार्पितः स्कम्भं तं ब्रूहि कतमः स्विदेवसः ॥
(अथर्ववेदः, 10.5.13-14)

Tell me about the one who bears all, in which the most ancient sages and Rigveda, Samaveda, Yajurveda, and the great Atharvaveda have resided.

अस्त्यधिदैवं स्कम्भो नाकाद्वितयान्तरा ततो विपुलः ।
सूर्येण क्लृप्तगर्भस्तत्प्रतिमो भौमदिवि स कृतः ॥177॥

Between the two heavens is a huge fulcrum whose front portion is covered with sun and a similar fulcrum has been constructed on the earth and heaven.

अस्ति सुषुम्णा वृषभो वरुणः समुद्रः खगश्चन्द्रः ।
स्कम्भं परितस्तस्माद् भौमस्कम्भानुगा अपि ते ॥178॥

This mighty quadrangle is, in fact, the prime ray of the sun and it is Varuna who is the ocean and the bird is chandrama. All these pervade around the fulcrum. That is why the replica of the divine pillar or *deva-skambha* has been constructed on the earth.

अस्ति च वेदो वृषभोऽस्त्यपां समुद्रः क्षितिश्चन्द्रः ।
स्कम्भं परितस्माद् भौमे स्कम्भे परितस्ते ॥179॥

And in the same way, the Veda is vast and supreme. The ocean full of water, prithvi and chandrama, all these surround the the divine pillar, therefore they pervade the earthly pillar as well.

3.25 अश्मा पृश्निः

3.25 ASHMA PRASHNI

देवयुगे प्रागभवद् विश्वविदितमद्भुतत्रितयम् ।
एकं मानुषलोके सूर्यायतनं सरस्वत्याम् ।।180।।

In ancient times, there were three famous wonders in the devayuga, of which one was situated in the suryasthana in the city of Sarasvati in the manushyaloka.

अन्यत् स्वर्गे प्रेङ्खं वरुणाधीनं हिरण्मयं विपुलम् ।
तत्रैवान्यद्धरुणं यत्राश्मा पृश्निराहितो रेजे ।।181।।

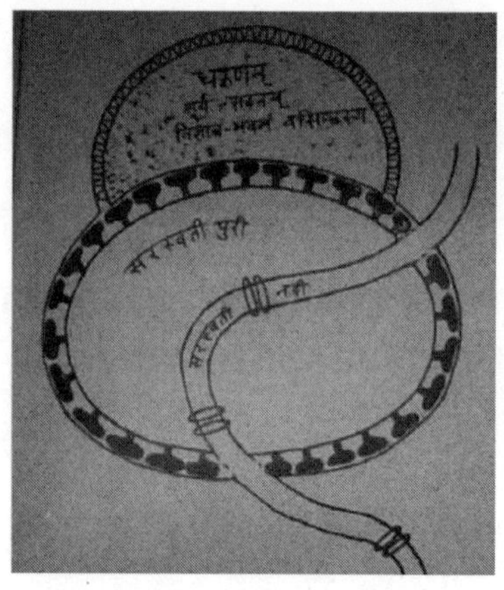

The second one was the great golden cradle in svarga under the authority of Varuna and the third one was Dharuna itself, adorned by Ashma Prashni in the form of surya.

विशदं स्वरूपमेषामन्यत्र स्वर्गवर्णने कथितम् ।
स्वर्गे सोऽश्मा पृश्निः सुप्रथितोऽत्यद्भुतश्चासीत् ।।182।।

Their form has been discussed in great detail elsewhere in *Svargakhyati* [another work by Pandit Madhusudan Ojha], in which it is mentioned that in the heaven that extraordinary Ashma Prashni was famous.

तत उत्तरतः पन्था विष्णोश्चेन्द्रस्य ब्रह्मलोकस्य ।
पितृलोकस्य प्राच्यां दक्षिणतो ब्रह्मलोकस्य ।।183।।

Suryasadana [svarga dharuna parilekh]

To the north of this domain of Brahma is the way to Nakaloka of Vishnu, to the west is the domain of Chandraloka and to the north is the domain of Pitra.

तत्र चतुष्पथमध्ये स्कम्भस्योपरि विहायसि क्रान्तः ।
सप्तशिरा हैमाश्वोऽश्मनि पृश्नौ चक्रमदधात् तत् ।।184।।

In the middle of this chatushpath and above the *skambha* (pillar) is that Ashma Prashni bearing the seven-headed sun-disc comprising golden horses. [The rooms around the sun-house located in Sarasvatipur are so constructed that Ashma Prashni lies on the middle pillar bearing radiant rays, that is the sun, to the west of which lies the chandra, in the north is the abode of Vishnu and towards the south are the *shalas* (working place) of Pitraloka.]

नक्त ।। दिवा च तुल्यं सूर्यमयूखप्रसारतो ज्योतिः ।
सर्वासु दिक्षु पथिषु प्रयतामयनान्यदर्शयत्साधु ।।185।।

Examining the rays of the sun, dispersed equally in all directions, in the surya sansthana, the learned have witnessed the motion of the wheel of Time and Universe. [This was the observatory where knowledge regarding the whole universe could be acquired.]

इत्थं भगवानिन्द्रः स्वर्गेप्येकं स सूर्यमारोप्य ।
कीर्तिं स्वामप्रथयत् भूमौ शान्तिं च संस्थाप्य ।।186।।

Thus, that majestic Indra enhanced his glory by installing the sun in Dyauloka and establishing peace in the world.

इति मधुसूदनविद्यावाचस्पतिप्रणीतस्य ब्रह्मविज्ञानशास्त्रसम्बन्धिनो ।
भारतवर्षीयार्योपाख्याने विज्ञानभवनाख्यस्तृतीयः प्रसङ्गः सम्पूर्णः ।।

Thus, the translation of the third chapter namely scientific institution in the Bharatavarshiyaryopakhyan related to Brahmavijnanashastra of Madhusudan Ojha is concluded.

प्रक्रमः चतुर्थः

दस्युनिग्रह

CHAPTER FOURTH

SUBJUGATION OF DASYUS

4.1 भारते वैदेशिकानार्यदासानामाक्रमणम्

4.1 ATTACK OF DASYUS ON BHARATAVARSHA

दस्यूनाम् उपद्रावकाणां पुनराक्रमणम् ।

Re-invasion by the riotous dasyus.

गतवति कतिपयकाले पुनरपि शान्तिर्व्युलुप्यत प्रायः ।
अत्युद्धतस्वभावैराक्रम्यन्तार्यराष्ट्राणि ॥1॥

After the passage of some time, peace virtually disappeared again because the extremely turbulent asuras reinvaded the Arya nation.

एतेऽपगणप्रमुखा आर्यान् गन्धर्वदेशवास्तव्यान् ।
शश्वत् प्रपीडयन्तो व्याकुलयाञ्चक्रुरत्युग्राः ॥2॥

These extremely aggressive apagana [Afghan] chiefs, who have been continuously tormenting the Arya living in the Gandhara country, made them restless.

आर्यो दशद्युरन्यः श्वैत्रेयोन्यो मुहुर्नियुध्यापि ।
बलवद्दस्युभिरेतैर्हृतश्रियौ जग्मतुः परां विपदम् ॥3॥

One Arya, Dashadyu, and another Shvaitreya, both after being repeatedly tormented by the powerful asuras lost their power and fell into deep trouble.

सव्यं षड्गृभि-शुष्णौ वेशस्त्वायुं पुरूरवःपुत्रम् ।
वैदथिनमृजिश्वानं पिप्रुर्मृगयश्च शूशुवान् व्यरुजन् ।।4।।

Among these asuras, Shadgribhi and Shushna oppressed Arya Savya, Vesha tormented Ayuraj, son of Pururav, while Pipru and the powerful Mrigaya tormented Vaidathin Mrajishvan.

वयं चतूर्वयाणं सुश्रवसं चातिथिग्वमार्य नृपम् ।
बङ्गृद-करञ्ज-पर्णयमुख्या बहुधा निपीडयामासुः ।।5।।

The Aryas, Vaya, Chaturvayana, Susravans and the Arya king Atithigva were repeatedly troubled by Badgradh-Karanj, Parnaya and other asura chiefs.

चुमुरिर्धुनिर्दभीति-ध्वसन्ति-पुरुषन्ति-तुर्वीतीन् ।
वार्षागिरांश्च पञ्चभ्रातृन् भूपान् प्रपीडयतः। ।6।।

The asuras, Chumuri and Dhuni, tormented five brother kings, Dabhiti, Dhvasanti, Purushanti, Turviti and Varshagir.

राज्ञो यदा पिठीनस आसीद् रज्यां विवाह आदिष्टः ।
चुमुरिर्धुनिर्बलादिव तां रजिमपजह्रतुस्तर्हि ।।7।।

When the marriage of King Pithinas was fixed with Raji, then Chumuri and Dhuni forcefully abducted Raji.

राजादभीतिरेतौ परिभावयितुं यदा प्रवृत्तोऽभूत् ।
प्रबलौ तदा दभीतिं चुमुरिर्धुनी तौ तमर्दयतः ।।8।।

When King Dabhiti decided to confront Chumuri and Dhuni, then those powerful asuras tormented Dabhiti too.

देवेन्द्रः श्रुतवृत्तः समादिशन्ति ग्रहीतुं तौ ।
इन्द्रकृपातो राजा पिठीनसा सा रजिर्लब्धा ।।9।।

After after these incidents, Indra issued orders to arrest these two [Chumuri and Dhuni] and by the grace of Indra, Raji was restored to King Pithinas.

षष्टिसहस्राण्यस्मिन्नभिमर्दे निहताः सुभटाः ।
दासानामित्यूचे बार्हस्पत्यो भरद्वाजः ।।10।।

Bharadvaja, son of Brihaspati, has said that 60,000 brave warriors were killed in this battle.

कुवयकृतः कुत्सपराभवः ।

Defeat of Kutsa by Kuyava.

कुयवः शुष्णः पिप्रुस्तुग्रः स्मदिभश्च दस्यवोऽत्युग्राः ।
आक्रम्य सूर्यसंस्थामशान्तिमातेनिरे भूयः ॥11॥

Powerful asuras like Kuyava, Shushna, Pipru, Tugra and Smadibha reinvaded the Suryasansthana and caused turbulence again.

वेतसुनगराधीशे कुत्से तत्सूर्यसंस्थायाः ।
त्रणार्थमागते सति बभूव दासैरमुष्य संमर्द्दः ॥12॥

King Kutsa of Vetasu came forward to defend the surya sansthana and he was engaged in a fierce battle with the asuras.

प्रबलः कुयवस्तमिमं कुत्सं छलतः पराभाव्य ।
वेतसुजनपदसीम्नः सहसा निष्कासयामास ॥13॥

The powerful Kuyava deceitfully defeated King Kutsa and banished him immediately from the territory of Vetasu-*janapada* [republic].

अपहृत्यैतत् क्षेत्रं तुग्रस्मदिभौ तु शासकत्वेन ।
कुयवस्तत्र तदानीं वेतसुराष्ट्रे नियोजयामास ॥14॥

After acquiring that territory, Kuyava appointed Tugra and Smadibh as rulers of the Vetasu state.

सिन्ध्वादिस्रोतोभ्योऽपां ग्रहणं वर्जितं चक्रे ।
जलनिग्रहाय शुष्णं पिप्रुं चापि प्रयोजयामास ॥15॥

He prohibited the release of water from rivers like Sindhu [Indus], and employed Shushna and Pipru to block the release of this water.

प्रस्तरखण्डप्रचयाज्जलप्रवाहो न्यरोधि सिन्धूनाम् ।
हिमवद्द्रोण्यामजिरे कृतोऽर्णवः कृत्रिमोऽवरुद्धाद्भिः ॥16॥

The flow of rivers like Sindhu was blocked by putting huge stones in their channels. An artificial lake was formed in the basin region of the Himalayas due to the blockage of this water.

कृष्णस्तदधिष्ठाता मध्येऽर्णवमुन्नते गिरौ न्युषितः ।
अहिशम्बरौ च नौभ्यो यातायातं गृहेषु चुक्रुरिमे ॥17॥

The ruler of that ocean was an asura named Krishna, who lived on the lofty mountain peak in the middle of the ocean. Both Ahi and Shambar used to commute to their abodes on boats.

4.1.1. कुत्सादीनाम् आर्यनृपाणां परित्राणोपायचिन्तासमितिः

4.1.1. Committee to protect Kutsa

दस्युनिग्रहणार्थं भारतीयार्याणां देवेन्द्रसाहाय्यलाभाय प्रयत्नः ।

Efforts by the Arya to procure help from Indra to drive out dasyus.

कुत्सादयोऽतिखिन्नाः किं करवामेति चिन्तयामासुः ।
घौरः प्रगाथ एतानूचे समयोचितं तत्र ॥18॥

Kutsa and other kings became very anxious and did not know what to do. When they were reflecting seriously over this, Ghor Pragatha gave them a timely suggestion.

मा चिदन्यद् विशंसत सखायो मा रिषण्यत ।
इन्द्रमित् स्तोता वृषणं स चासुते मुहुरुक्था च शंसत ॥
(ऋग्वेदः, 8.1.1)

There are some suktas in the Rigveda in this context, for example, the first sukta of the eighth mandala says: O friends! Don't pray to any other god. Don't be sad. Let all of you pray together in Somayajna and repeat the prayers to Indra many times.

अवक्रक्षिणं वृषभं यथाजुरं गां न चर्षणी सहम् ।
विद्वेषणं संवननो भयङ्करं मंहिष्ठमुभयाविनम् ॥
(ऋग्वेदः, 8.1.2)

Pray to Indra, formidable like the ox, slayer of enemies, nourisher of human beings like the immortal Kamadhenu, revered by all, punishing as well as condescending, extraordinarily glorious and protector of living world.

य ऋते चिदभिश्रिषः पुरा जत्रुभ्य आतृदः ।
सन्धाता सन्धिं मघवा पुरुवसुरिष्कर्ता विहुतं पुनः ॥
(ऋग्वेदः, 8.1.12)

That Indra who had fixed the wounds without putting any bandage, even before blood could spill out of the neck, only that munificent and brilliant

Indra heals the wound again.

प्रो अस्मा उपस्तुतिं भरता यज्जुजोषति ।
उक्थैरिन्द्रस्य माहिनं वयो वर्धन्ति सोमिनो भद्रा इन्द्रस्य रातयः ।।
(ऋग्वेदः, 8.51.1)

It is said in the sixty-second sukta of eighth mandala of Rigveda: O Ritvijas! If this Indra wants to remain silent, pray to him. Sing hymns praising Soma for this Soma-lover Indra. This Indra is generous in giving alms.

अयुजो असमो नृभिरेकः कृष्टीरयास्यः ।
पूर्वीरति प्रवावृधे विश्वा जातान्योजसा भद्रा इन्द्रस्य रातयः ।।
(ऋग्वेदः, 8.51.2)

This immortal Indra is the only one of his kind. He bestows strength to old as well as the newly born human beings to enhance his glory. The riches of Indra are auspicious.

सुपूर्व्यो महानां वेनः क्रतुभिरानजे ।
यस्य द्वारा मनुष्पिता देवेषु धिय आनजे ।।
(ऋग्वेदः, 8.52.1)

Pragatha Kanva prays in the sixty-third sukta of the eighth mandala of Rigveda: The means to reach Indra, which only Manu could acquire among the gods, that enlightened and ancient Indra has been reached only through actions.

दिवो मानं नोत्सदन्त्सोम पृष्ठासो अद्रयः ।
उक्थ्या ब्रह्म च शंस्या ।।
(ऋग्वेदः, 8.52.2)

The stones that grind Soma, praise worthy hymns and knowledge do not leave Indra, the lord of Dyauloka.

स विद्वाँ अङ्गिरोभ्य इन्द्रो गा अवृणोदप ।
स्तुषे तदस्य पौंस्यम् ।।
(ऋग्वेदः, 8.52.3)

That learned Indra rescued cows for the Angira sages, therefore, I admire his strength.

स प्रत्नथा कविवृध इन्द्रो वाकस्य वक्षणिः ।
शिवो अर्कस्य होमन्यस्मत्रागन्त्ववसे ॥

(ऋग्वेदः, 8.52.4)

May the promoter of learning, receiver of prayers, auspicious Indra come to our Somayajna to protect us.

आदूनुते अनुक्रतुं स्वाहा वरस्य यज्यवः ।
श्वात्रमर्का अनूषतेन्द्रगोत्रस्य दावने ॥

(ऋग्वेदः, 8.52.5)

O Indra! After this only the performers of the yajna in Agni and those offering prayers narrate your deeds for donating wealth.

इन्द्रे विश्वानि वीर्या कृतानि कर्त्वानि च ।
यमर्का अध्वरं विदुः ॥

(ऋग्वेदः, 8.52.6)

Indra, whom devotees consider non-violent, has the strength to do everything already done or to be done.

यत्पाञ्चजन्यया विशेन्द्रे घोषा असृक्षत ।
अस्तृणद्बर्हणा विपोर्यो मानस्य सक्षयः ॥

(ऋग्वेदः, 8.52.7)

When Indra is eulogized by his subjects, then he slays the enemies with his might. May this *sarveshvar* (greatest of all gods) Indra be honoured by me!

अस्य वृष्णो व्योदन उरुक्रमिष्ट जीवसे ।
यवं न पश्व आददे ॥

(ऋग्पेदः, 8.52.9)

From this mighty warrior Indra, all of us human beings procure grains like barley, and we are able to perform the great deeds of life only after getting the grains.

तद्दधाना अवस्यवो युष्माभिर्दक्षपितरः ।
स्याम मरुत्वतो वृधे ॥

(ऋग्वेदः, 8.52.10)

To enhance the glory of that *maruta-sakha* (the friend of marutas), Indra, may we, needing protection and glory ourselves, own that grain!

प्रास्मै गायत्रमर्चत वावातुर्यः पुरन्दरः ।
याभिः काण्वस्योपबर्हिरासदं या सद्वज्री भिनत्पुरः ।।
(ऋग्वेदः, 8.1.18)

Sing Gayatri hymns in praise of that Indra, destroyer of fortresses, who bestows grace upon the devotees. Those hymns will inspire him to go to the seat of the yajna of Khajava's son. May that vajra-wielding Indra destroy the enemy cities!

अन्यन् मा प्रयतध्वं मा क्लिश्यध्वं तमेकमेवेन्द्रम् ।
शरणं यात स एवाऽखिलकृच्छ्रात् तारयिष्यति नः ।।19।।

O human beings! Don't make any other effort, don't harbour any feeling of tribulation. Take recourse only to that Indra, because he only will redeem us of our miseries.

ग्रीवाछेदात्पूर्वं संधानद्रव्यमन्तरेणैव ।
स च्छिन्नमङ्गमखिलं सद्यः संधाय संस्कुरुते ।।20।।

That Indra fixes all the broken organs together in no time, without any means, even before the neck could be slit.

दासानां प्रबलानामिन्द्रोऽस्त्येको निबर्हणे शक्तः ।
तस्मादिन्द्रं यातेत्यादिश्योचे स कुत्सादीन्।। 21।।

Only Indra is capable of crushing the dasyus, therefore, go to Indra. He thus commanded Kutsa and others.

कुत्सं त्वामिह सूर्यायतनेऽस्मिन् स न्ययुङ्क्तेन्द्रः ।
प्राक् स यदा गन्धर्वं सूर्यं हत्वैतशं तत्र ।।22।।

Indra, having initially slain Aitasha, had appointed a Gandharva named Surya to take care of the surya-sadana, there in this surya-sadhana, Indra has appointed you, Kutsa.

तस्मादत्र विपन्नः शरणं याहीन्द्रमेव तं तूर्णम् ।
अहमपि तमाह्वयामि तु कामगवीमिव समस्तकामदुहम् ।।23।।

Therefore, in this state of calamity, go immediately to seek refuge of that Indra. Even I shall invoke Indra like Kamadhenu is invoked to fulfil our desires.

गायत्रमिन्द्रसविधे नयतेत्युक्त्वा प्रगाथ एतददात् ।
वाग् ब्रह्म भद्रसूक्तं गायत्रं नाम कुत्साय ।।24।।

Go to Indra with this Gayatri hymn. Having said this to Kutsa. Pragatha Kanva gave the hymn or Gayatri—'Vag-Brahma-Bhadra'.

देवानामाह्वानं त्वाहव इत्युच्यते तत्र ।
आश्रावणं तदुक्तं यच्चाश्रावयति देवेभ्य: ।।25।।

अभ्यर्थनां तु देवा अभ्युपगच्छन्ति तच्छ्रौषट् ।
अभ्यर्थनामयं यद्विनयवचस्तद्धि गायत्रम् ।।26।।

The invocation of the devas has been called 'ahava' here. The narrative recited to the gods is called 'ashravana'. The prayer that draws the devas near is called 'Sraushada'. The humble requests made in the prayer are called Gayatra.

काण्वो हीन्द्रप्रणयी काण्वकृताभ्यर्थनास्तोत्रम्।
नीत्वा यातेत्यददात् कुत्सकरे विनयपत्रं स: ।।27।।

Kanva was dear to Indra, therefore that Pragatha Kanva handed over that letter of request to Kutsa for him to go to Indra carrying that hymn of prayer composed by Kanva.

तत्र प्रथमं काण्व: प्रगाथ एवार्थनांचक्रे ।
दस्युवधार्थं कुत्सत्राणार्थं त्वरितमायातुम् ।।28।।

There, Pragatha Kanva was the first one to entreat Indra to come immediately to the protection of Kutsa and for the annihilation of asuras.

मेधातिथि-मेध्यातिथि-नीपातिथयस्तदेन्द्राय ।
काण्वा एत्य त्रातुं चक्रुरिहाभ्यर्थनासूक्तम् ।।29।।

After this, Kanvas namely Medhatithi, Medhyatithi, and Nipatithi came forward to compose prayers for Indra for their protection.

4.2 देवेन्द्राभ्यर्थनासूक्तम्

4.2 PRAYERS FOR DEVENDRA

4.2.1 प्रगाथकृतम् अभ्यर्थनासूक्तम्

4.2.1 Prayer by Pragatha

आयाहि कृणवाम त इन्द्र ब्रह्माणि वर्धना ।
येभिः शविष्ठ चाकनो भद्रमिहश्रयस्यते भद्रा इन्द्रस्य रातयः ॥
(ऋग्वेदः, 8.51.4)

The prayer hymn composed by Kanva Pragatha is found in the sixty-second sukta of eighth mandala in Rigveda, which narrates: O Indra! We will sing hymns in your praise, do come here! O powerful Indra! You wish to bring about well-being of the host of the yajna aspiring for glory. The riches of Indra are auspicious.

धृषतश्चिद्धृषन्मनः कृणोषीन्द्र यत्त्वम् ।
तीव्रैः सोमैः सपर्यतो नमोभिः प्रतिभूषतो भद्रा इन्द्रस्य रातयः ॥
(ऋग्वेदः, 8.51.5)

O Indra! When you strengthen the mind of the host who honors you with robust Soma-rasa, adores you with greetings and slays the enemies, then your gifts become auspicious.

अवचष्ट ऋचीषमोऽवताँ इव मानुषः ।
जुष्ट्वी दक्षस्य सोमिनः सखायं कृणुते युजं भद्रा इन्द्रस्य रातयः ॥
(ऋग्वेदः, 8.51.6)

This Indra, fond of incantations, watches all in the same way as human beings look into the wells. Thus pleased, Indra makes the performer of Somayajna his friend. Therefore, the riches of Indra are auspicious.

विश्वे त इन्द्र वीर्यं देवा अनुक्रतुं ददुः ।
भुवो विश्वस्य गोपतिः पुरुष्टुत भद्रा इन्द्रस्य रातयः ॥
(ऋग्वेदः, 8.51.7)

O Indra! By following you, all the devas have attained strength and wisdom. O Indra, worthy of prayer! You are the lord of all the domains and cows.

Therefore, the riches of Indra are auspicious.

गृणे तदिन्द्र ते शव उपमं देवतातये ।
यद्धंसि वृत्रमोजसा शचीपते भद्रा इन्द्रस्य रातयः ॥
(ऋग्वेदः, 8.51.8)

O Shachipathe! For this reason you killed Vritra with force. Therefore, O Indra! I describe that extraordinary power of yours in the yajna. I want to benefit from the auspicious wealth of Indra.

समनेव वपुष्यतः कृणवन्मानुषा युगा ।
विदे तदिन्द्रश्चेतनमधश्रुतो भद्रा इन्द्रस्य रातयः ॥
(ऋग्वेदः, 8.51.9)

The way a woman of calm disposition attracts a powerful man, similarly Indra takes in his control all the living beings and *Kala* (Time). Indra is honored everywhere for performing knowledgeable acts. Therefore, the riches of Indra are auspicious.

उज्जातमिन्द्र ते शव उत्त्वामुत्तवक्रतुम् ।
भूरिगो भूरि वा वृधुर्मघवन्तवशर्मणि भद्रा इन्द्रस्य रातयः ॥
(ऋग्वेदः, 8.51.10)

O brilliant Indra, owner of many cows! The yajamana, who attains the strength produced by you, promote your actions and rejoice in pleasing you. The riches of Indra are auspicious.

अहं च त्वं च वृत्रहन्त्संयुज्याव सनिभ्य आ ।
अराती वा चिदद्रिवोऽनु नौशूर मंसते भद्रा इन्द्रस्य रातयः ॥
(ऋग्वेदः, 8.51.11)

O Indra, slayer of Vritra! Let you and me join together to acquire wealth. O valiant Indra! In this way even the poor human beings will support us. The riches of Indra are auspicious.

सत्यमिद्वा उतं वयमिन्द्रं स्तवाम नानृतम् ।
महां असुन्वतो वदो भूरि ज्योतींषि सुन्वतो भद्रा इन्द्रस्य रातयः ॥
(ऋग्वेदः, 8.51.12)

We pray to that true Indra, not any false Indra. Those who do not perform Somayajna face dreadful destruction. However, may the riches of Indra be auspicious to those preparing Soma.

यदिन्द्र प्रागपागुदङ्न्यग्वा हूयसे नृभिः ।
आयाहि तू यमाशुभिः ॥

(ऋग्वेदः, 8.54.1)

There is a prayer of Kanva Pragatha in the sixty-fifth sukta of eighth mandala in Rigveda: O Indra! Since you are called forth by human beings from all sides, come soon on your fast horses.

यद्वा प्रस्रवणे दिवो मादयासे स्वर्णरे ।
यद्वा समुद्रे अन्धसः ॥

(ऋग्वेदः, 8.54.2)

O Indra! You are pleased to be in the place of origin of water of Dyauloka or in the yajna that leads to the heaven, or under the influence of Soma-rasa.

आत्वागीर्भिर्महामुरुं हुवे गामिव भोजसे ।
इन्द्रसोमस्य पीतये ॥

(ऋग्वेदः, 8.54.3)

O Indra! I invite you, the mighty Indra, by my invocation to drink Soma-rasa in the same way as the cow is called for feeding.

आतइन्द्र महिमानं हरयो देव ते महः ।
रथं वहन्तु बिभ्रतः ॥

(ऋग्वेदः, 8.54.4)

O divine Indra! May these glorious horses of yours, bring you here in your chariot!

इन्द्रगृणीष उ स्तुषे महाँ उग्रईशानकृत ।
एहि नः सुतं पिब ॥

(ऋग्वेदः, 8.54.5)

O brave, great, and lord of all, Indra! I narrate your attributes and pray to you, so come and drink the Soma prepared by us.

सुतावन्तस्त्वा वयं प्रयस्वन्तो हवामहे ।
इदं नो बर्हिरासदे ॥

(ऋग्वेदः, 8.54.6)

O Indra! We possess grain and perform Somayajna, we invite you to come and sit on our seat.

यच्चिद्धि शश्वतामसीन्द्रसाधारणस्त्वम् ।
तं त्वा वयं हवामहे ॥

(ऋग्वेद:, 8.54.7)

O Indra! We invoke you because you are revered by many.

इदं ते सोम्यं मध्वधुक्षन्नद्रिभिर्नरः ।
जुषाण इन्द्र तत्पिब ॥

(ऋग्वेद:, 8.54.8)

O Indra! The performers of the yajna grind with stones sweet Soma for you, therefore, drink it and be pleased.

विश्वाँ अर्यो विपश्चितोऽतिख्यस्तूयमागहि ।
अस्मे धेहि श्रवो बृहत् ॥

(ऋग्वेद:, 8.54.9)

O Indra! Come soon to see and examine the learned men and provide us with abundant grains.

दाता मे पृषतीनां राजाहिरण्यवीनाम् ।
मा देवा मघवा रिषत् ॥

(ऋग्वेद:, 8.54.10)

O Gods! Indra, the lord of cows of Hiranyavarna, bestow wealth upon me and eschew violence.

सहस्रे पृषतीनामधिश्चेन्द्रं बृहस्पृथु ।
शुक्रं हिरण्यमाददे ॥

(ऋग्वेद:, 8.54.11)

By the grace of Indra, I acquire the pleasant, great, and brilliant gold containing virtues of a thousand cows.

न पातो दुर्गहस्य में सहस्रेण सुराधसः ।
श्रवो देवेष्वक्रत ॥

(ऋग्वेद:, 8.54.12)

May my helpless and aggrieved people get thousand types of supreme wealth and achieve glory among the gods!

इयमुते अनुष्टुतिश्चकृषे तानि पौंस्या ।
प्रावश्चक्रस्य वर्तनिम् ।

(ऋग्वेदः, 8.52.8)

O Indra! You have performed those brave acts, therefore this prayer is most suitable for you. Protect the path of our chariot-wheels.

ववृत्वियाय धाम्न ऋक्वभिः शूर नो नुमः ।
जेषामेन्द्र त्वया गुजा ॥

(ऋग्वेदः, 8.53.11)

O mighty warrior Indra! We eulogize you with hymns for the brilliant one and protector of yajna. May we be victorious by your grace.

अस्मे रुद्रा मेहना पर्वतासो वृत्रहत्ये भरहूतौ सजोषाः ।
यः शंसते स्तुवते धायिपज्र इन्द्रज्येष्ठा अस्मां अवन्तु देवाः ॥

(ऋग्वेदः, 8.53.12)

That Indra, who is very powerful, goes in person to those who eulogize and praise him. May Indra, rudra, the rain-bearing clouds, among which Indra reigns supreme, and all the gods join hands to protect us in our battle with Vritra!

4.2.2 मेधातिथिकृतम् अभ्यर्थनासूक्तम्

4.2.2 Medhatithi's eulogies

यच्चिद्धि त्वा जना इमे नाना हवन्त ऊतये ।
अस्माकं ब्रह्मेदमिन्द्र भूतु तेऽहा विश्वा च वर्द्धनम् ॥

(ऋग्वेदः, 8.1.3)

Medhatithi eulogizes Indra in the first sukta of eighth mandala of Rigveda: O Indra! Though all these subjects pray to you daily for their protection, let these prayers enhance your glory every day.

विततर्य्यन्ते मघवन्, विपश्चितोऽर्योविपोजनानाम् ।
उपक्रमस्व पुरुरूपमाभर वाजं नेदिष्ठमूतये ॥

(ऋग्वेदः, 8.1.4)

O Maghavan (the munificent one)! The knowledgeable and remarkable person, the provider of people, your worshippers steer clear of difficulties. Therefore, come to us, and provide us with that power which has many forms and always protects us.

महेचन त्वामद्रिवः परा सुल्काय देयाम् ।
न सहस्राय नायुताय वज्रिवो न शताय शतामघ ॥
(ऋग्वेदः, 8.1.5)

O Indra, the wielder of divine thunderbolt and replete with hundreds of merits! I won't let you go for any amount of money. O Indra! I won't give you to those paying thousands, not even for ten thousand, nor for several hundreds. [A devotee can never sell his lord for any price.]

वस्याँ इन्द्रासि मे पितुरुत भ्रातुरभुञ्जतः ।
माता चमे छदयथः समावसो वसुत्वनाय राधसे ॥
(ऋग्वेदः, 8.1.6)

O Indra! You are richer than my father, or my miser brother who does not spend his money. But you are like my mother. O Vaso! Make me and both of them capable of gaining wealth and abode.

क्वेयथ क्वेदसि पुरुत्रा चिद्धि ते मनः ।
अलर्षि युध्म खजकृत् पुरन्दर प्रगायत्रा अगासिषुः ॥
(ऋग्वेदः, 8.1.7)

O Indra! It is impossible to find out places where you go or where you live, because your mind knows all the places. O Destroyer of fortresses, expert in warfare! Come to us. We, devotees, pray to you.

ये ते सन्ति दशग्विनः शतिनो ये सहस्रिणः ।
अश्वासो ये ते वृषणो रघुद्रुवस्तेभिर्नस्तूयमागहि ॥
(ऋग्वेदः, 8.1.9)

O Indra! These horses of yours can run for ten yojana, hundreds of yojana and thousands of yojana. Ride on your powerful and sprinting horses to come fast to us.

आ त्वाद्य सवर्दुघां हुवे गायत्र वेपसम् ।
इन्द्रं धेनुं सुदुघामन्यामिषमुरुधारामरं कृतम् ॥
(ऋग्वेदः, 8.1.10)

O Indra! This day, to fete you, I invoke the decorated *dhenu* or *vani* (holy cow) that fulfils all wishes, has a voice similar in tune to Gayatri hymn, procures all the fruits easily, has many streams and provides grain.

यत्तुदत्सूर एतशं वङ्कूवात्स्य पर्णिना ।
वहत्कुत्समार्जुनेयं शतक्रतुस्तत्सरद् गन्धर्वमस्तृतम् ।।
(ऋग्वेद:, 8.1.11)

When the sun tormented Aitasha with *vanku pani* (strong currents) of Vayu, then the son of Arjuna, Kutsa took away the shining light to Gandharva Megha. [Here the meaning can be inferred that when the sun moved the cloud with strong currents of air, the friction produced by the moving clouds produced lightning and the clouds hung low, just before the rains.]

मा भूमनिष्ट्या इवेन्द्र त्वदरणा इव ।
वनानि न प्रजहितान्यद्रिवो दुरोषासो अमन्महि ।।
(ऋग्वेद:, 8.1.13)

O Indra, the wielder of thunderbolt! May we not be like incapable human beings! Let us not be bereft of joys when we are with you, not even like dry forests. Living in a quiet house, may we pray to you!

अधज्मो अधवादिवो वृहतो रोचनादधि ।
अया वर्धस्व तन्वागिरा ममा ज ता सुक्रतो पृण ।।
(ऋग्वेद:, 8.1.18)

O Indra! At this moment whether you are on prithvi or antariksha or even above this Dyauloka, even then may this small prayer enhance your greatness! O *Sukriti* (performer of virtuous acts)! You fulfil the desires of my sons and all, too.

मात्वा सोमस्य गल्दया सदा याचन्नहं गिरा ।
भूर्णि मृगं न सवनेषु चुक्रुधं क ईशानं न याचिषत् ।।
(ऋग्वेद:, 8.1.20)

O Indra! May I always please you by filtering Soma in the yajna and my speech! By always praying humbly to you, may I never enrage you, who are angry like a lion! Who does not beg from his lord? In other words, the lord is always the one who gives.

इहि तिस्रः परावत इहि पञ्चजनां अति ।
धेना इन्द्रावचाकशत् ।

(ऋग्वेदः, 8.32.22)

O Indra! Listen to our prayers and come to us on all three periods of the day. Come to us ignoring others.

4.2.3 मेध्यातिथिकृतम् अभ्यर्थनासूक्तम्

4.2.3 Medhyatithi's eulogies

एन्द्र याहि मत्स्व चित्रेण देव राधसा ।
सरो न प्रास्युदरं सपीतिभिरासोमेभिरुरु स्फिरम् ।।

(ऋग्वेदः, 8.1.23)

While composing the hymn to eulogize Indra in the eighth mandala of Rigveda, Medhyatithi says: O Indra! You are the brilliant one. Make us rejoice by providing desired wealth. Fill your vast abdomen with golden Soma-rasa like a water-filled pond.

आत्वा सहस्रमाशतं युक्ता रथे हिरण्यये ।
ब्रह्म युजो हरय इन्द्र केशिनो वन्तु सोमपीतये ।।

(ऋग्वेदः, 8.1.24)

O Indra! Come with a hundred horses. May thousands of horses empowered with supreme power or brahmashakti bring you in your golden chariot for the Soma-rasa!

अत्वा रथे हिरण्यये हरी मयूरशेव्या ।
शितिपृष्ठा वहताँ गध्वो आधरोबिनक्षणरग गीतगे ।।

(ऋग्वेदः, 8.1.25)

O Indra! This is the pleasure giving Soma-rasa, which you desire. May your horses of peacock colours and white bring you in the golden chariot to drink this!

पिबात्वस्य गिर्वणः सुतस्य पूर्वया इव ।
परिष्कृतस्य रसिन इयमासुतिश्चारुमदाय पत्यते ।।

(ऋग्वेदः, 8.1.26)

O Indra! Drink today also the extraordinary nectar that has been squeezed and filtered like before. This well-extracted Soma-rasa will give you pleasure.

य एको अस्ति दसना महाँ उग्रो अमिव्रतैः ।
गमत् स शिप्री न स योषदागमद्धवं न परिवर्जति ।।

(ऋग्वेदः, 8.1.27)

That Indra is mighty powerful, for he has performed extraordinary deeds alone and has never broken the rules. May this most beautiful Indra come to us, never go away, come to our yajnas and never abandon our yajna!

त्व पुरं चरिष्णवँ बधैः शुष्णस्य सं पिणक् ।
त्वं भा अनुचरो अधद्विता यदिन्द्रहव्यो भुवः ।।

(ऋग्वेदः, 8.1.28)

O Indra! You destroyed the city of asura named Shushna with your deadly weapons. You follow the divine path. Therefore you are worthy of eulogy.

ममत्वा सूर उदिते मम मध्यन्दिने दिवः ।
मम प्रतित्वे अपि शर्वरे वसवा स्तोमासो अवृत्सत ।

(ऋग्वेदः, 8.1.29)

O Indra! May my prayers reach you on sunrise. May my prayers reach you at the time of midday and sunset, too.

वयँ घत्वा सुतावन्त आपो न वृक्त बर्हिषः ।
पवित्रस्य प्रस्रवणेषु वृत्रहन् परिस्तोतार आसते ।।

(ऋग्वेदः, 8.33.1)

O Indra, the annihilator of Vritrasura! We, the devotees, sit around the Soma-rasa trickling down from the filter.

स्वरन्ति वा सुतेनरो वसो निरेक उक्थिनः ।
कदा सुतं तृषाण ओक आगम इन्द्रस्वब्दीव वंसगः ।।

(ऋग्वेदः, 8.33.2)

O Indra, who provides shelter to all! Your devotees eulogize only you while filtering Soma. When will you, thirsty for Soma, come to our place like a thundering ox?

सत्यमित्था वृषेदसि वृषजूतिर्नोऽवृतः ।
वृषा ह्युग्र शृण्विषे परावति वृषो अर्वावति श्रुतः ॥
(ऋग्वेदः, 8.33.10)

O powerful Indra! It is true that you are that much powerful. You reach the powerful ones immediately, you are famed for your strength, and no one ever can besiege you. You are known as the powerful one in lands far and near.

वृषणस्ते अभीशवो वृषा कशा हिरण्ययी ।
वृषा रथो मघवन् वृषणाहरी वृषा त्वं शतक्रतो ॥
(ऋग्वेदः, 8.33.11)

O Indra! Your chariot is strong, both your horses are vigorous, even your golden whip is powerful and so are your reins. In the same way as *shatkrato* (performer of hundred deeds); you yourself are powerful.

एन्द्र याहि पीतये मधुशविष्ठ सोम्यम् ।
नायमच्छा मघवा शृणवद् गिरो ब्रह्मोक्था च सुक्रतुः ॥
(ऋग्वेदः, 8.33.13)

O powerful Indra! Come to us to drink this honey like Soma. O powerful one, the performer of splendid acts! Listen patiently to our voice, knowledge, and prayers.

वहन्तु त्वा रथेष्ठामा हरयो रथयुजः ।
तिरश्चिदर्य्यं सवनानि वृत्रहन्नन्येषां या शतक्रतो ॥
(ऋग्वेदः, 8.33.14)

O Shatkrato, the annihilator of Vritra! May the horses pulling the chariot in which the supreme Indra is seated, bring him to our yajna, overlooking the yajna of others.

नहिषस्तव नो मम शास्त्रे अन्यस्य रण्यति ।
यो अस्मान् वीर आनयत् ॥
(ऋग्वेदः, 8.33.16)

The brave Indra is our hero. He neither likes to be governed by you, nor by me, or anyone else.

अधः पश्यश्व मोपरि संतरां पादकौ हर ।
माते कशप्लकौ दृशन् स्त्री हि ब्रह्मा वभूविथ ।।

(ऋग्वेदः, 8.33.19)

O woman! Always look downwards, never upwards, walk keeping your feet close together. May the two portions of your body (upper and lower one) not be revealed, because you are the wife of Brahma.

4.2.4 नीपातिथिकृतम् अभ्यर्थनासूक्तम्

4.2.4 Prayer by Nipatithi

एन्द्र याहि हरिभिरुप कण्वस्य सुष्टुतिम् ।
दिवो अमुष्य शासतो दिवं यय दिवावसो ।।

(ऋग्वेदः, 8.34.1)

Hymns of prayers composed by Nipatithi as narrated in the thirty-fourth sukta of eighth mandala of Rigveda: O Indra! Riding your horses, go to the place where Kanva is praying. O Indra, resident of Dyauloka! You, the ruler of this Dyauloka, return to your home in Dyauloka.

आ त्वा ग्रावा वदन्निह सोमी घोषेण यच्छतु ।
दिवो अमुष्य शासतो दिवं यय दिवावसो ।।

(ऋग्वेदः, 8.34.2)

O Indra! May the stone used in the yajna to extract Soma-rasa reach you. O Divavaso! Return to Dyauloka.

अत्रा वि नेमिरेषामुरां न धूनुते वृकः ।
दिवो अमुष्य शासतो दिवं यय दिवावसो ।।

(ऋग्वेदः, 8.34.3)

O Indra, dweller of Dyauloka! In this Somayajna, the vine of Soma makes the stones tremble the in the same way as the wolf makes the sheep shiver. O Indra! Return to Dyauloka.

आ त्वा कण्वा इहावसे हवन्ते वाजसातये ।
दिवो अमुष्य शासतो दिवं यय दिवावसो ।।

(ऋग्वेदः, 8.34.4)

O Indra! The sons of Kanva invoke you to come in this yajna for protection and grains. O Indra, dweller of Dyauloka! Return to Dyauloka.

दधामि ते सुतानां वृष्णे न पूर्वपाय्यम् ।
दिवो अमुष्य शासतो दिवं यय दिवावसो ॥

(ऋग्वेदः, 8.34.5)

O Indra! First of all, I offer you the nectar of Soma like Vayu. O Indra, dweller of heaven! Return to Dyauloka.

स्मत्पुरन्धिर्न आ गहि विश्वतो धीर्नं ऊतये ।
दिवो अमुष्य शासतो दिवं यय दिवावसो ॥

(ऋग्वेदः, 8.34.6)

O Indra! You are wise, you spread wisdom in all directions, so come for our protection. O Indra, dweller of Dyauloka! Return to Dyauloka.

आ नो याहि महेमते सहस्रोते शतामघ ।
दिवो अमुष्य शासतो दिवं यय दिवावसो ॥

(ऋग्वेदः, 8.34.7)

O great wise one, who forgives in a thousand ways and provides hundreds of types of wealth, Indra! Come to us. O Indra, dweller of heavens! Return to Dyauloka.

आ त्वा होता मनुर्हितो देवत्रावक्षदीड्यः ।
दिवो अमुष्य शासतो दिवं यय दिवावसो ॥

(ऋग्वेदः, 8.34.8)

O Indra! May this Agni, well-wisher of mankind and worthy of prayer by the gods, bring you to us! O Indra, dweller of heavens! Return to Dyauloka.

आ त्वा मदच्युता हरी श्येनं पक्षेव वक्षतः ।
दिवो अमुष्य शासतो दिवं यय दिवावसो ॥

(ऋग्वेदः, 8.34.9)

O Indra! The way the eagle moves forward on its wings, similarly may the salivating horses bring you to us! O Indra, dweller of Dyauloka! Return to Dyauloka.

आ याह्यर्य आ परि स्वाहा सोमस्य पीतये ।
दिवो अमुष्य शासतो दिवं यय दिवावसो ॥

(ऋग्वेदः, 8.34.10)

O pious Indra! Come to us to have this excellently dedicated Soma. O Indra, dweller of Dyauloka! Return to Dyauloka.

आ नो याह्युपश्रुत्युक्थेषु रणया इह ।
दिवो अमुष्य शासतो दिवं यय दिवावसो ।।

(ऋग्वेद:, 8.34.11)

O Indra! After listening to the prayers, come to our yajnas and make us happy. O Indra, dweller of heavens! Return to Dyauloka.

सरूपैरा सु नो गहि संभृतैः सम्भृताश्वः ।
दिवो अमुष्य शासतो दिवं यय दिवावसो ।।

(ऋग्वेद:, 8.34.12)

O Indra, owner of excellent horses! Come to us on your beautiful and strong horses. O Indra, dweller of Dyauloka! Return to Dyauloka.

आ याहि पर्वतेभ्यः समुद्रस्याधि विष्टपः ।
दिवो अमुष्य शासतो दिवं यय दिवावसो ।।

(ऋग्वेद:, 8.34.13)

O Indra! Come to us from the regions of mountains and oceans. O Indra, dweller of Dyauloka! Return to Dyauloka.

आ नो गव्या न्यश्व्या सहस्रा शूर दर्द्दहि ।
दिवो अमुष्य शासतो दिवं यय दिवावसो ।।

(ऋग्वेद:, 8.34.14)

O valiant Indra! Give us thousands of cows and horses. O Indra, dweller of Dyauloka! Return to Dyauloka.

आ नः सहस्रशो भरायुतानि शतानि च ।
दिवो अमुष्य शासतो दिवं यय दिवावसो ।।

(ऋग्वेद:, 8.34.15)

O Indra! Make us affluent by giving us hundred and thousand types of riches. O Indra, dweller of Dyauloka! Return to Dyauloka.

4.2.5 भर्गप्रगाथकृतम् अभ्यर्थनासूक्तम्

4.2.5 Euologies of Bharga Pragatha

उभयं शृणवच्च न इन्द्रो अर्वागिदं वचः ।
सत्राच्या मघवा सोमपीतये धिया शविष्ठ आगमत् ।।
(ऋग्वेदः, 8.50.1)

According to the sixty-first sukta of eighth mandala of Rigveda, the hymns of prayer composed by sage Bharga Pragatha are: May that Indra listen to our direct and indirect prayers closely and the brilliant and valiant Indra come to us to drink Soma-rasa after listening to prayers sung in unison by us.

तं हि स्वराजं वृषभं तमोजसे धिषणे निष्टतक्षतुः ।
उतोपमानां प्रथमो निषीदसि सोमकामं हि ते मनः ।।
(ऋग्वेदः, 8.50.2)

This Prithviloka and Dyauloka make that big and powerful Indra more powerful and excellent. O Indra! You are supreme among the gods, because your mind craves for Soma-rasa.

आवृषस्व पुरूवसो सुतस्येन्द्रान्धसः ।
विद्मा हित्वा हरि वः पृत्सु सासहिमधृष्टं चिद्दधृष्वणिम् ।।
(ऋग्वेदः, 8.50.3)

O supreme Indra! May you shower grains in the form of Soma! O vanquisher of enemies in battlefield, owner of horses, invincible, lover of others, we know you.

अप्रामि सत्य मघवन्तथे दसदिन्द्र क्रत्वा यथावशः ।
सनेमवाजं तव शिप्रिन्नवसा मक्षूचिद्यन्तो अद्रिवः ।।
(ऋग्वेदः, 8.50.4)

O supreme one, follower of truth, Indra! Whatever you desire from your acts, happens. O mighty Indra! May we acquire grain won under your protection!

शग्ध्यूषु शचीपत इन्द्र विश्वाभिरूतिभिः ।
भगं नहि त्वा यशसं वसुविदमनुशूर चरामसि ।।
(ऋग्वेदः, 8.50.5)

O Shachipath Indra! Make us capable of self-defense of every kind. O valiant

Indra! May we follow you by obtaining glorious riches replete with fortune!

पौरो अश्वस्य पुरुकृद्गवा मस्युत्सो देव हिरण्ययः ।
न किर्हि दानं परिमर्धिषत्वे यद्यद्यामि तदाभर ।।

(ऋग्वेदः, 8.50.6)

O Indra! You are the lord of subjects, making cows and horses abundant and you are the origin of gold, no one can destroy alms gifted by you, therefore, give me all that I entreat you for.

त्वं ह्येहि चेरवे विद्राभगं वसुत्तये ।
उद्वावृषस्व मघवन् गविष्टय उदिन्द्राश्वमिष्टये ।।

(ऋग्वेदः, 8.50.7)

O royal Indra! We are at your service, give us a fortune so that we can give alms. Come and give us cows and horses as desired by us.

त्वं पुरू सहस्राणि शतानि च यूथादानाय मंहसे ।
आ पुरन्दरं चकृम विप्रवचस इन्द्रं गायन्तोऽवसे ।।

(ऋग्वेदः, 8.50.8)

O Indra! You give hundreds and thousands of horses and cows for being gifted away. We sing prayers imbibed with knowledge. We pray with the wish of being protected by Indra, the destroyer of fortresses.

अविप्रो वा यदविधद्विप्रो वेन्द्रते वचः ।
स प्रममन्दत्वाया शतक्रतो प्राचामन्यो अहंसन ।।

(ऋग्वेदः, 8.50.9)

O Shatkrato Indra! You perform hundreds of deeds, you have unbridled passion and self-respect. Whoever, learned or otherwise, prays to you, is rewarded by you.

उग्रबाहुर्म्रक्ष कृत्वा पुरन्दरो यदि मे शृणवद्धवम् ।
वसूयवो वसुपतिं शतक्रतुं स्तोमैरिन्द्रं हवामहे ।।

(ऋग्वेदः, 8.50.10)

That Indra, having long hands, is slayer of enemies and destroyer of the enemy cities. If he listens to my prayers, then we, owners of fortune, will invoke Indra, performer of hundred acts, with prayers to seek more fortune.

न पापासो मनामहे नारायसो न जल्हवः ।
यदिन्विन्द्र वृषणं स चा सुते सखायं कृणवामहै ।।
(ऋग्वेदः, 8.50.11)

Because we all invoke this powerful Indra for friendship in Somayajna, he is not considered a sinner or an atheist.

उग्रं युयुज्म पृतनासु सासहि मृणकाति मदाभ्यम् ।
वेदा भृमं चित्सनितारथी तमो वाजिनं यमिदूनशत् ।।
(ऋग्वेदः, 8.50.12)

We take on our side that Indra who destroys enemies, keeps debt away and is aggressive and valiant. That excellent charioteer owns the quickest horses. Whoever gets him becomes happy.

यत इन्द्र भयामहे ततो नो अभयं कृधि ।
मघवञ्छग्धि तव तन्न ऊतिभिर्विद्विषो वृमृधो जहि ।।
(ऋग्वेदः, 8.50.13)

O Indra! Make us fearless from all quarters which cause fear in us. O royal Indra! Make us capable with those weapons of yours and defeat those who hate us and indulge in violence.

त्वं हि राधस्पते राधसो महः क्षयस्यासि विधतः ।
तं त्वा वयं मघवन्निन्द्रगिर्वणः सुतावन्तो हवामहे ।।
(ऋग्वेदः, 8.50.14)

O Indra, lord of wealth! You are the enhancer of fortune and riches of the yajamana. O worthy of prayers, royal Indra! We, the performers of Somayajna, invoke you.

इन्द्र स्पलुत वृत्रहा परस्यानो वरेण्यः ।
सनो रक्षिषच्चरमं समध्यमं सपश्चात्पातु नः पुरः ।।
(ऋग्वेदः, 8.50.15)

That Indra is knower of all, slayer of Vritra, provider of noble men, and is acceptable to us. May that Indra protect the mighty ones as well as the average ones amongst us! May that Indra protect us on all sides!

त्वं नः पश्चादधरादुत्तरात्पुर इन्द्र निपाहि विश्वतः ।
आरे अस्मत्कृणु हि देव्यं भयमारे हेतीरदेवीः ॥
(ऋग्वेदः, 8.50.16)

O Indra! Protect us in all directions. Protect us from divine fear and misfortunes and save us from the weapons of the asuras.

अद्याद्याश्वः श्व इन्द्र त्रास्व परे च नः ।
विश्वाचनो जरितृन्त्सत्पते अहादिवानक्तं च रक्षिषः ॥
(ऋग्वेदः, 8.50.17)

O Indra! Protect us today, tomorrow, and every day. O Protector of gentlemen, Indra! Protect us, because we pray to you all day and night.

प्रभङ्गी शूरो मघवा तुवीमघः सम्मिश्लो वीर्यायकम् ।
उभाते बाहू वृषणा शतक्रतो निया वज्रं मिमिक्षतुः ॥
(ऋग्वेदः, 8.50.18)

That Indra is valiant, affluent, giver of wealth, destroyer of enemies and he mixes Soma in water for courage. O Indra, the performer of hundred deeds! Your arms, which wield the vajra are very powerful.

4.3 दस्युपरिपीडितानाम् आर्याणामिन्द्रशरणे गमनम्

4.3 ARYAS SEEKING INDRA'S PROTECTION FROM DASYUS

इत्थं कृतमतिराप्तप्रणयवचोयुक् स विह्वलः कुत्सः ।
अन्यच्छरणमपश्यन्निन्द्रायैवामरावतीं प्रययौ ।।30।।

Thus, a worried and perturbed Kutsa, finding no other means of protection, left for Amaravati to pray to Indra.

वैकुण्ठस्तु ददानीमासीदिन्द्रोऽमरावत्याम् ।
स्वर्गेऽपराजितायां दिशि तस्यासीदियं नगरी ।।31।।

During those days, Indra ruled from Amaravati to Vaikuntha. This city of that Vaikuntha Indra was located in the north and was decorated with gold.

तत्र स गत्वा कुत्सो महेन्द्रभवनं पुरः समासाद्य ।
काण्वनिवेदितसूक्तान्यस्मै प्रणयादुपाजह्ने ।।32।।

After reaching the palace of Indra, Kutsa confidently uttered those hymns composed by Kanva before Indra.

इन्द्रेण पृष्टवृत्तः स्वं तत् कष्टं निवेदयामास ।
येन स विधिना कुत्सो हृतराज्यो दीनतामापत् ।।33।।

When Indra asked about his problem, Kutsa narrated how he was deprived of his kingdom and brought to that wretched condition.

4.4 देवेन्द्रस्य दस्युनिग्रहार्थं भारतवर्षे सपरिकरम् आगमनम्

4.4 DEVENDRA COMING WITH HIS ARMY TO BHARATAVARSHA TO DEFEAT DASYUS

इन्द्राय कुत्सप्रमुखानां स्वदुःखाश्रावणम् ।

Kutsa and his companions narrating their miseries to Indra.

कौत्से राष्ट्रे दस्युभिः सिन्धुपश्चात्प्रान्ते नानोपद्रवा अक्रियन्त ।
क्षेत्राणां चाप्स्रोतसां चावरोधास्तार्णान्नादिस्तूपदुर्निग्रहाश्च ।।34।।

The asuras unleashed violence in the kingdom of Kutsa, located in the western province of Sindhu river. Farms and sources of water were blocked. The granaries and animal husbandry storages were subdued.

सिन्धुश्लिष्टा या सरस्वत्यमुष्याः कूलस्थाया पूः सरस्वत्यपूर्वा ।
तस्यां यासीद् सूर्यसंस्था वशिष्ठाधीना तां च प्रोद्धतास्ते न्यगृह्णन् ।।35।।

There was a city called Apurva Sarasvati on the banks of Sarasvati river, which flowed close to river Sindhu. The warring people took the surya sansthana under their control.

सोऽहं कुत्सोऽन्ये च राजान आर्या एवं भूयो दस्युभिः पीड्यमानाः ।
स्वत्राणार्थं स्वर्गराजं भवन्तं प्राप्ता नत्वाऽभ्यर्थयामः शरण्यम् ।।36।।

I'm that Kutsa. Similarly, all the Arya rulers, terrorized by the asuras, have come to you for protection, bow before you and make humble requests.

कुरुते च घोषणामिह मानुष्येषा प्रजा परितः ।
अवधीत् पुरा पणीन् यो मानस्थानं प्रभुः स इन्द्रो नः ।।37।।

The human subjects announce from all quarters that Indra, who had come to their rescue in ancient times, is their lord.

यत्पाञ्जन्यया विशेन्द्रे घोषा असृक्षत ।
असतृणाद् बर्हणा विपोर्यो मानस्य सक्षयः ।।

(ऋग्वेदः, 8.52.7)

When the Panchajana sing hymns in praise of Indra, then that Indra slaughters all the enemies with his might. May that knowledgeable Indra, master of all, be revered.

दस्युनिग्रहार्थम् इन्द्रस्य अभिक्रमणम् ।

Indra's assault to subdue dasyus.

इत्थं कुत्साभ्यर्थनातो दयार्द्रः प्रौढो रक्षां संप्रतिश्रुत्य तेषाम् ।
कुत्सं सख्येनाभ्युपेत्य प्रतस्थे मारुत्येन्द्रः सेनयाऽभिक्रमार्थी ।।38।।

Moved by the earnest requests of Kutsa, Indra made Kutsa his friend and after vowing to protect the Arya, Indra departed from Dyauloka to attack the asuras.

आश्रितदीनजनार्थं स्वार्थमयैवाभिन्यते यो हि ।
स सखा सख्यं त्वाहुः पक्षग्रहणं सहायकत्वेन ।।39।।

The one who empathises with the poor is a true friend, and taking a stand to help is called friendship.

कुत्समुखेन श्रुत्वा दस्यूनामुग्रतामयं घोराम् ।
तन्निग्रहाय बुद्धिं चक्रे जनताभिरक्षार्थम् ।।40।।

After hearing the extreme and merciless attacks of asuras, Indra used his wisdom to subdue them.

सद्यः स हि प्रतस्थे सह कुत्सेनाश्वमारुह्य ।
दस्युकुलं प्रतिकर्तुं यानायादिश्य मारुतीं सेनाम् ।।41।।

After that Indra rode away on his horse and asked his army to assault and destroy the asuras.

4.4.1. निषधपर्वताभिज्ञानम्

4.4.1. Introduction to Nishadh mountain

वेगेनाविश्रान्तैरहर्निशं धावमानैस्तौ ।
इन्द्राकुत्सावश्वैस्त्र्यहेण हिमगिरिमुपाययतुः ।।42।।

Indra and Kutsa, riding their horses non-stop and at full speed, reached the Himalayas in three days.

कुत्सस्तस्येन्द्रस्य हि निषधिगिरौ विश्रमस्थानम् ।
प्रागेव कल्पयित्वा तमुपेतं त्र सादयन्नाह ।।43।।

Kutsa, who had already fixed Nishadh mountains as the halting place for Indra, took him there and said:

योनिष्ट इन्द्र निषदे अकारि तमा निषीद स्वानोर्नावा ।
विमुच्यावयोऽवसायाश्वान् दोषाविस्तोर्वहीयसः प्रपित्वे ॥
(ऋग्वेदः, 1.104.1)

'O Indra! This place has been made for you to sit. Therefore, unbridle your tired neighing horses and take your seat.'

दोषावस्तोरश्वान् वहीयसो यदवदत् स कुत्स इह ।
तेन ज्ञायत इन्द्रस्यागमने मार्ग विश्रमो नासीत् ॥44॥

Kutsa's request to give rest to the horses, who were running non-stop for three days, means that Indra didn't halt anywhere during the journey.

इन्द्रस्य निषधपर्वते स्कन्धावारम् ।

Indra camping his army on Nishadh Mountain.

गान्धारेऽस्मिन्देशे श्वेतगिरिप्रान्तमागत्य ।
निषधे स्कन्धावारं कृत्वेन्द्रो व्यश्रमयत् तत्र ॥45॥

Indra camped his army on the Nishadh mountain in the Shvetagiri province of Gandhara. Since this is the place where Indra took rest, it came to be known as Nishadh. Nishadh means encampment. This is a Vaidik term and over years became distorted.

इन्द्रो न्यषीददस्मिन्निषदनतो निषद् इत्यभूत्प्रथितः ।
निषदेति वैदिकाख्या तदपभ्रंशात्तु 'निषध' संज्ञाऽभूत् ॥46॥

This place got its name because Indra had halted here and took rest.

अद्यत्वे यो देशः पामीरः कथ्यते स पुरा ।
मेरू कदाचिदासीत्तेन प्राग् मेरुरुक्तः सः ॥47॥

The region known today as Pamir was once called Meru Parvat. That is why it has been called Pragmeru.

काश्मीरादुत्तरतोऽष्टत्रिंशे तूत्तराक्षांशे ।
सार्धात्सप्तत्यंशाद् 'ग्रिनविच' देशान्तरात् पूर्वात् ॥48॥

It is located at 38° latitude north of Kashmir and 71.5° east of Greenwich prime meridian.

तन्मध्यादिषु वेदव्यासार्द्धं मण्डलं यत् स्यात् ।
द्वीपानामन्तःस्थं जम्बूद्वीपं तमाह सप्तानाम् ।।49।।

The sphere of 45 radius that is formed between them, that place is called Jambudvipa among the seven land masses.

दक्षिणातः प्राग् मेरोर्या प्रथते पर्वतश्रेणी ।
पूर्वापरायताद्रिस्तस्या भागास्त्रयो भाव्याः ।।50।।

The mountains running from east to west of the mountain ranges extending to the south of Pragmeru should be considered in three parts.

भारतवर्षादुत्तरदिशि यः पूर्वापरो महाशैलः ।
पूर्वाब्धेराक्रोञ्चात्सिन्धुनदान्तो हिमालयः सोऽस्ति ।।51।।

The mountains running from east to west to the north of India are the Himalayas, extending from the East Sea to Kronch mountains across Sindhu.

'अफगानस्थानस्य' प्रत्यक् सीमान्तविस्तृतो योऽद्रिः ।
स हि हेमकूट उक्तस्तत्पश्चान्निषध आयवनात् ।।52।।

The huge mountain ranges extending to the western frontier of Afghanistan are the Hemakut mountains, which ends in the Nishadh mountains towards the west across the Yavana country.

अपि चाष्टोत्तरशतकाद् 'ग्रिनविच' पूर्वांशतः समारभ्य ।
आषट् सप्तत्यंशं योऽद्रिः स हिमालयो नाम ।।53।।

The mountain ranges which are on the 108° east and 76 ansh of Greenwich are the Himalayas.

तस्मादुत्तरतो यो विंशशतांशात्तु पूर्वतः प्रभृति ।
द्वापञ्चाशं यावद् विततोऽसौ हेमकूटोऽस्ति ।।54।।

Hemakut lies further north, extending from 120° east longitude to 52° east longitude.

तस्मादुदक् तु सप्तत्यंशात् त्रिंशांशकं यावत् ।
नानापर्वतनिचितः कुलपर्वत एष निषधोऽस्ति ।।55।।

The Nishadh mountains are a chain of mountains further north of the Hemakut mountains and they extend from 70° to 30° longitude.

अपि च 'स्याम' समुद्रात् पारस्याख्यातगः स हेमाद्रिः ।
'चीन' समुद्रा'ल्लोहित' सिन्ध्वन्तो हेमकूटोऽस्ति ॥56॥

The mountains from Black Sea to a place called Paras are the Himalayas. The Hemakut mountains extend from the 'Chinese Sea' to the Red Sea.

सिन्धुनदादिनिषधः प्रथते भूमध्यसागरं यावत् ।
इत्थं पर्वतमाला त्रिविधा प्राग्मेरुदक्षिणे ख्याता ॥57॥

The Nishadh mountains extend from Indus River to the Mediterranean Sea. Thus, there are three mountain ranges running to the south of Pragmeru.

एते कुलाचलाः स्युस्त्रयोऽपि ताः श्रेणयस्तिस्रः ।
एकैकस्यां श्रेण्यां शाखापादाद्रयोऽसंख्याः ॥58॥

These three mountain chains have three ranges each and each range has numerous peaks.

गान्धारोत्तरसीम्नि प्रथते या हेमकूटाद्रेः ।
कृष्णगिरिः शाखाद्रिर्भवति चतुस्त्रिंशकेऽक्षांशे ॥59॥

The mountain lying at 24° latitude north of Hemakut on the northern frontier of Gandhara is called Krishnagiri.

तत उत्तरतोर्द्धांशे 'श्वेतगिरि'स्तस्य शाखाद्रिः ।
स च पेशावरगजनीमध्यस्था 'च्छ्वेतगिरि' तोऽन्यः ॥60॥

A branch of Krishnagiri called the Shvetagiri lies further north. This Shvetagiri differs from the Shvetagiri lying between Peshawar and Ghajani.

श्वेतोदरः स नाम्ना गजनी यस्यान्तिके नगरी ।
कृष्णगिरेरुत्तरतः श्वेतगिरिः पाण्डुरो नाम्ना ॥61॥

The mountain close to the Ghajani city is called Shvetodar. Shvetagiri is also known as Pandur.

तस्माच्छ्वेतगिरेरपि योंऽशेनैकेन तूत्तरस्थोऽद्रिः ।
मधुपर्वतः स उक्तः स च निषधस्यास्ति शाखाद्रिः ॥62॥

One degree north of Shvetagiri is another branch of the Nishadh mountains called the Madhu mountains.

सार्धे पञ्चत्रिंशेऽक्षांशे मुरुघावनद्यान्यम् ।
युक्तो मधुस्त्रिषष्टिप्राये देशान्तरे पूर्व्ये ॥63॥

'योवकडिया' प्रदेशान्नैर्ऋत्येऽवस्थितो यो वा ।
याम्येऽस्ति 'मार्गियाना' प्रदेशतः पर्वतः समधुः ॥64॥

The Madhu mountains are conjoined with Murughav river at 35.5° latitude which is located in the *nairritya* (corner of east and south triangle) in the Yovakadiya province situated at 63° east longitude in the south. The Samadu mountains lie in the Maghriana province.

अपि पश्चिमोत्तरेऽस्मादस्ति 'गुलिस्तान' पर्वतो विततः ।
भारतवर्षीयार्या यं 'पुष्पक'पर्वतं ब्रुवते ॥65॥

A mountain named Gulistan extends further north-westwards. The Arya called it the Pushpaka mountains.

एषोऽस्ति 'मार्गियाना' प्रदेशतः पश्चिमे न्यस्तः ।
पूर्वोऽस्ति कश्यपाब्धेः पुष्पकगिरिरुत्तरः 'खुरासानात्' ॥66॥

This Pushpaka mountain lies to the west of Margiana province, east of Caspian Sea and north of Khurasan.

षट्त्रिंशादक्षांशादंशत्रयमस्ति पश्चिमोत्तरतः ।
पुष्पकगिरिस्ततोऽन्यो दक्षिणतः पर्वतः कपिलः ॥67॥

षट्त्रिंशादक्षांशात् सप्तत्रिंशांशकं यावत् ।
आरभ्य सप्तपञ्चाशांशाद्देशान्तरोनषष्ट्यन्ते ॥68॥

कपिलोऽपि पर्वतोऽसावैशान्यां 'पार्थिया' प्रान्तात् ।
पुष्पकगिरितो याम्ये सौम्ये देशात् खुरासानात् ॥69॥

There is another Pushpaka mountain lying 3° to 36° latitude. To its south lies Kapila mountain. This Kapila mountain is located between 57° and 59° longitude to the south of Pushpaka mountain and north of Khurasan at the Ishana *kona* [angle] from Parthian territory.

मधुपुष्पककपिलेषु त्रिषु शाखा गिरिषु निषधस्य ।
ऐन्द्रः स्कन्धावारः कुत्सेनासीद् विनिर्दिष्टः ॥70॥

Kutsa had ordered for the arrangement of Indra's rest over all the three mountain ranges of Nishadh—Madhu, Pushpaka, and Kapila.

मधुपर्वते तु शिविरो देवेन्द्रस्याथ 'मारुती' सेना ।
पुष्पकगिरौ सहायकसेनानिहिता तु कपिलाद्रौ ॥71॥

Devendra took rest on the Madhu mountain while the 'maruti' army and associate armies camped on the Pushpaka and Kapila mountains.

निषिधगिरौ विश्रान्तायेन्द्राय कुत्सस्तत्कालेतिकर्तव्यताम् अनुमन्त्रयामास ।

Discussion about the immediate duty of Kutsa for Indra resting on the Nishadh mountain.

इन्द्रागमनं श्रुत्वा भूयस्युपसर्पतीह जनतेयम् ।
निज निकार्यपथान् प्रतिगमयैतां कार्यसंसिद्धयै ॥72॥

A huge number of people came to see Indra. All those people were given their respective duties to perform.

देवाश्च दासजनता क्रोधं प्रतिकृत्यनः प्राग्वत् ।
संपादयन्तु वर्णं कुत्सः प्रोचे तदित्थमिन्द्राय ॥73॥

Kutsa said taking into account the anger of people, the devas, without fear, should restore order.

ओत्येनर इन्द्रमूतये गुर्नूचित्तान्त्सद्यो अध्वनो जगम्यात् ।
देवासो मन्युं दासस्य श्वम्नन्ते न आवक्षन्त्सुविताय वर्णनम्॥ (ऋग्वेदः, 1.104.2)

Those human beings have come to Indra for protection. Indra made them take the best possible path. The devas should bring an end to the wrath of the asuras and bring the venerable Indra to the divine yajna.

स्वागतीयसभां प्रस्तुत्य नाभाककृता इन्द्राग्न्योः स्वागतप्रशस्तयः ।

Nabhaka praises Indra and Agni during his welcoming remarks at the assembly.

अथ नाभाकः काण्वो निषधगिराविन्द्रमेतमुपगम्य ।
युतमग्निना मनुष्येश्वरेण तत्स्वागतं चक्रे ॥74॥

Next, sage Nabhaka Kanva goes to the Nishadh mountain and welcomes Indra and King Agni.

अपि शुष्णपीडितोऽयं शुष्णं प्रति वर्द्धितं निजक्रोधम् ।
आवेदयन् सहैव च तद्वधमुद्वेगतोऽर्थयामास ॥75॥

Nabhaka expresses his anger against Shushna's oppression and requests for his slaughter.

इन्द्राग्नी युवं सुनः सहन्ता दासथो रयिम् ।
येन दृह्ला समत्वा वीलु चित्साहिषीमह्यग्निर्वनेववात इन्नभन्तामन्यके समे ॥
(ऋग्वेदः, 8.40.1)

In the fortieth sukta of eighth mandala of Rigveda, Sage Nabhaka Kanva submits: O Indra and Agni, destroyers of enemy, give us supreme wealth so that we can destroy a huge army in the battlefield as wind and fire wipe out the forests. May our other enemies be destroyed in the same manner.

नहि वां वव्रयामहेऽथेन्द्रमिद्यजामहे। शविष्ठं नृणां नरम् ।
सनः कदाचिदर्वता गमदावाजसातये गमदा मेधसातये नभन्ता मन्यके समे ॥
(ऋग्वेदः, 8.40.2)

O Indra and Agni! We revere you both; we worship Indra, the supreme and the most powerful. When will that great Indra visit us for food and horses? All our other enemies will be wiped out naturally.

ताहि मध्यं भराणामिन्द्राग्नी अधिक्षितः ।
ता उ कवित्वना कवीपृच्छ्यमाना सखीयते। संधीतमश्नुतं नरा नभन्ता मन्यके समे ॥
(ऋग्वेदः, 8.40.3)

Indra and Agni live in the midst of battle. O Heroes! You both are omniscient and omnipresent, bless us with your friendship and destroy all our enemies.

अभ्यर्च नभाकवदिन्द्राग्नी यजसागिरा ।
ययोर्विश्वमिदं जगदियं द्यौः पृथिवीमह्युपस्थे विभृतोवसु। नभन्ता मन्यके समे ॥
(ऋग्वेदः, 8.40.4)

O Man! Worship the omnipresent Indra and Agni like sage Nabhaka. Indra and Agni are the lords of wealth. Other enemies will be destroyed naturally through their support.

प्रब्रह्माणि नाभाकवदिन्द्राग्निभ्यामिरज्यत ।

Humans worship Indra and Agni like sage Nabhaka.

या सप्तबुध्नमर्णवं जिह्मवारमपोर्णुत। इन्द्र ईशान ओजसा। नभन्ता मन्यके समे ॥
(ऋग्वेदः, 8.40.5)

Men! Worship Indra and Agni like sage Nabhaka. They opened the seven-layered gates of ocean [the clouds]. Indra rules with his splendour and glory. Thus, other enemies are destroyed naturally.

स्वागतमिन्द्राग्निभ्यामित्थं कृत्वा स नाभाकः ।
शुष्णवधाय विशेषादिन्द्रं प्रोवाच तत्प्रवक्ष्यामि ॥76॥

Now, I will state the way Nabhaka, welcoming Indra and Agni warmly, requested Indra to kill Shushna.

इन्द्रस्य आतिथ्यपरिचर्या ।

Providing hospitality to Indra.

इन्द्रः स्वाराण्निषधे तिष्ठन्नासीत्सा कुत्सस्य ।
अतिथिस्तेन सकुत्सः पर्यचरत् तं हि सर्वतोभावैः ॥77॥

Indra was staying at the Nishadh mountain in Kutsa's hospitality. Kutsa attended to Indra with complete devotion.

देवानामविशेषात् प्राशनसमयास्त्रयो दिवा नियताः ।
प्रातः सवनं माध्यन्दिनसवनं वा तृतीयसवनं वा ॥78॥

The deities took their meals three times in a day.

कुत्सो विश्वामित्रं न्ययोजयत् तस्य भोजनाद्यर्थे ।
प्रातःसवने मध्यन्दिनसवनेऽथो तृतीयसवने च ॥79॥

Kutsa appointed sage Vishvamitra to take care of the three meals of Indra.

ऋभुरथ विभ्वावाजः पूषा वैतस्य देवराजस्य ।
सहभोजने नियुक्ताः पर्वतहर्यश्वपूर्वकाश्चान्ये ॥80॥

Ribhu, Vibhva, Vaj, and Pusha were appointed to have meal with the king of deities. Besides, Parvat, Haryashva, and others were also appointed.

पूषा पशुशालानामध्यक्षः किन्तु सोऽस्ति हर्यश्वः ।
देवेन्द्रः प्रियवाहनहर्यश्वान् यो विशेषतोऽधीष्टे ॥81॥

Generally, the deity named Pusha was the chief of the *pashushala* (cattle shed); but Haryashva was the one who used to take care of the favourite vehicle Haryashvas of Indra.

इन्द्राय यत्र धानास्तृतीयसवने प्रदीयन्ते ।
तत्रभवे च वाजायेन्द्रहरिभ्यां च दीयन्ते ॥82॥

If Indra was served rice in the third meal, then Indra's horses, Vaj and Ribhu, were also offered the same.

इन्द्रस्य पानभोजनसमये तत्र च मरुद्गणः सर्वः ।
पिबति च सोमममपूपं भुङ्क्ते चानुग्रहादैन्द्रात् ।।83।।

During Indra's drinking and dining, all marudganas used to drink Soma and eat *apupa* (a small round cake of flour) with Indra's blessing.

भोजनसामग्र्या ये धर्त्तारस्ते जनाः प्रयस्वन्तः ।
सोमादिपानदाने परिचरितारस्तु जरितारः ।।84।।

Those who used to manage food-items were known as *prayasvana*. Those who used to serve Soma and other drinks were known as *jarita*.

सर्वेषां सोऽध्यक्षो विश्वामित्रो महर्षिरिन्द्रं तम् ।
आमन्त्र्य सूक्तवाकैर्मधुवाकैश्चोपचरति स्म ।।85।।

Maharshi Vishvamitra was the head of all those who were invited to offer prayers to Indra.

तत्र विश्वामित्रकृतो देवेन्द्राय भोजनसमये मधुवाकः ।

Lyrical speech composed by Vishvamitra for Indra during the meal.

धानावन्तं करम्भिणमपूपवन्तमुक्थिनम् ।
इन्द्र प्रातर्जुषस्व नः ।।

(ऋग्वेदः, 3.52.1)

In the fifty-second sukta of third mandala of Rigveda, sage Vishvamitra praises Indra: O Indra! Kindly drink the Soma-rasa prepared by us from rice, curd, and pua in the morning.

पुरोडाशं पचत्यं जुषस्वेन्द्रा गुरस्व च ।
तुभ्यं हव्यानि सिस्रते ।।

(ऋग्वेदः, 3.52.2)

O Indra! These havyas are offered to you so that you may become powerful by eating these thoroughly baked *purodash* (an offering made with grounded rice).

पुरोडाशं च नोघसो जोषयासे गिरश्च नः ।
वधूयुरिव योषणाम् ।।

(ऋग्वेदः, 3.52.3)

पुरोडाशं सनश्रुत प्रातः सावे जुषस्व नः ।
इन्द्रक्रतुर्हि ते बृहन् ॥

(ऋग्वेदः, 3.52.4)

O Indra! Since your deeds are great, you must eat our famous purodash in the morning meal. O Indra! As the one who gets what one desires by eating our purodash, please enjoy our praises. O Indra! Since your deeds are great, you must eat our purodash in the morning meal.

माध्यन्दिनस्य सवनस्य धानाः पुरोडाशमिन्द्रकृष्वेह चारुम् ।
प्रयत्स्तोता जरिता तूर्ण्यर्थो वृषायमाण उपगीर्भिरीट्टे ॥

(ऋग्वेदः, 3.52.5)

O Indra! Since the one whose oration is powerful and who inspires yajna, praises you in his own voice, you must eat rice and purodash in this sacrifice you must eat rice and purodash offered in the midday yajna.

तृतीये धानाः सवने पुरुष्टुत पुरोडाशमाहुतं मामहस्व नः ।
ऋभुमन्तं वाजवन्तं त्वा कवे प्रयस्वन्त उपशिक्षेम धीतिभिः ॥

(ऋग्वेदः, 3.52.6)

O poet Indra! In the evening meal you must eat the purodash prepared from the special rice. We, who long for food, praise you.

पूषण्वते च कृमा करम्भं हरिवते हर्यश्वाय धानाः ।
अपूपमद्धि सगणो मरुद्‌भिः सोमं पिब वृत्रहाशूर विद्वान् ॥

(ऋग्वेदः, 3.52.7)

O Indra! You give prosperity, ward off pain, and own horses named Hari. For you, we have prepared Soma with rice and curd. O valiant and learned Indra, the destroyer of Vritra! Bring marudganas along, and drink Soma and eat apupa.

प्रतिधाना भरत तूयमस्मै पुरोडाशं वीरतमाय नृणाम् ।
दिवे दिवे सदृशोरिन्द्र तुभ्यं वर्धन्तु त्वा सोमपेयाय धृष्णो ॥

(ऋग्वेदः, 3.52.8)

O Indra, offer sufficient parched grain and purodash to the mightiest of men. O Indra, the slayer of enemies! Accept the libation of those who sit together and worship you everyday.

विश्वामित्रकृतस्तृतीयसवने ऋभुत्रयपरितोषार्थः प्राशनीयो मधुवाकः ।

For the satisfaction of ribhus during the evening meal, Vishvamitra composed a melodious speech suitable for the meal. In the third mandala of Rigveda, sage Vishvamitra says:

इहेह वो मनसा वन्दुता नर उशिजो जग्मुरभि तानि वेदसा ।
याभिर्मायाभिः प्रतिजूति वर्पसः सौधन्वना यज्ञियं भागमानश ॥
(ऋग्वेद:, 3.60.1)

O Ribhus! You, who possess superior bow, attack the enemy to exhibit your glory. You are bound here with the men who praise those grand deeds of yours because of which you are entitled to your portion in the yajna.

याभिः शचीभिश्चमसाँ अपिंशत यया धिया गामरिणीति चर्मणः ।
येन हरी मनसा निरतक्षत तेन देवत्वमृभवः समानश ॥
(ऋग्वेद:, 3.60.2)

O Ribhus! The dexterity with which you have given a beautiful shape to chamasa, the intellect with which you crafted a cow, the mind with which you made the horses powerful, for all these reasons you have been raised to the status of divinity.

इन्द्रस्य सख्यमृभवः समानशुर्मनोर्नपातो अपसोदधन्विरे ।
सौधन्वनासो अमृतत्वमेरिरे विष्ट्वी शमीभिः सुकृतः सुकृत्यया ॥
(ऋग्वेद:, 3.60.3)

Ribhus have won and possessed Indra's friendship. They perform superior deeds and keep the spirits high. Possessors of bow and performers of good deeds, the ribhus have attained immortality with their powers and superior deeds.

इन्द्रेण याथ सरथं सुते सचाँ अथो वशानां भवथा सहश्रिया ।
नवः प्रतिमै सुकृतानि वाघतः सौधन्वना ऋभवो वीर्याणि च ॥
(ऋग्वेद:, 3.60.4)

O Ribhus, possessors of superior bow and intellect! You accompany Indra in his chariot to the Somayajna. The one who seeks you, you bless him with wealth and affluence. Your deeds and valour are unparalleled.

इन्द्र ऋभुभिर्वाजवद्भिः समुक्षितं सुतं सोममा वृषस्वा गभस्तयोः ।
धियेषितो मघवन्दाशुषो गृहे सौधन्वनेभिः सह मत्स्वानृभिः ।।
(ऋग्वेदः, 3.60.5)

O Indra! Take the well-blended Soma in your hands. O Maghavan! May you rejoice and visit donator's place along with intellectually motivated and supreme archers.

इन्द्र ऋभुमान्वाजवान्मत्स्वेह नोऽस्मिन्त्सवने शच्या पुरुष्टुत ।
इमानि तुभ्यं स्वसराणि येमिरे व्रता देवानां मनुषश्च धर्मभिः ।।
(ऋग्वेदः, 3.60.6)

O Indra, praised by many great men! Rejoice here in this sacrifice of ours in the company of mighty and powerful ribhus. You dictate the days and the deeds and the rules for men and gods.

इन्द्र ऋभुभिर्वाजिभिर्वाजयन्निह स्तोमं जरितुरुपयाहि यज्ञियम् ।
शतं केतेभिरिषिरेभिरायवे सहस्रणीथो अध्वरस्य होमनि ।।
(ऋग्वेदः, 3.60.7)

O Indra! Come with mighty Ribhus, strengthen all, and come to this praiseworthy sacrifice. O Indra! You know thousand supreme ways. Come on a hundred supremely fast horses to this non-violent sacrifice and bless us.

देवमेदेन सोमपानसमयभेदः ।

Timing of the Soma consumption according to the hierarchy of devas.

समयः पृथगिव नियतो देवानां सोमपानाय ।
आसीदित्यावेदितमाथर्वणनवमकाण्डेऽपि। ।।86।।

For drinking Soma, different times were fixed for the gods; it has been so mentioned in the ninth section of Atharvaveda.

यथा सोमः प्रातः सवने अश्विनोर्भवति प्रियः ।
एवा मे अश्विनावर्च आत्मनि ध्रियताम् ।।
(अथर्ववेदः 9.2.11)

As Ashvi gods enjoy Soma drink in the morning, thus those Ashvi gods accept my offering.

यथा सोमो द्वितीये सवन इन्द्राग्न्योर्भवति प्रियः । (अथर्ववेदः, 9.2.12)
यथा सोमस्तृतीये सवन ऋभूणां भवन्ति प्रियः ।। (अथर्ववेदः, 9.2.13)

Indra and Agni enjoy Soma drink in the second meal [afternoon meal] and the ribhus enjoy Soma in the third meal [evening meal].

4.5 निषधगिरौ प्रमहाख्यः सोमाभिषव

4.5 FESTIVAL OF SOMA ON NISHADH MOUNTAIN

तत्रेन्द्रस्य प्रीत्यै सम्मानार्थं महोत्सवं कुत्सः ।
सोमाभिषवं नामाऽऽतेनेऽत्युत्साहसम्भारैः ।।87।।

Then, Kutsa organized a festival named somabhishava with intense fervour to please and honour Indra.

युद्धात्पूर्वं पश्चादासीन्नियतं तु वीरपानं प्राक् ।
उद्दिश्य वीरपानं कुत्सेनायं महोत्सवः क्लृप्तः ।।88।।

In ancient times, the Soma drink was taken before and after the battle to boost morale. Therefore, Kutsa organized this festival named *veer-paan* (drink of valour).

धानापूपकरम्भामिक्षादध्याशिरादयो भोज्याः ।
सोमाग्रपेयपूर्वा गुणकीर्तनभक्तिसूक्तान्ताः ।।89।।

At first, there used to be Soma-drink with eatables such as *dhaan* (unhusked rice), apupa, *karambha* (flour mixed with curd), *amiksha* (curd of milk and whey), and *dadhyashir* (curd). After this, there were glorification of virtues and devotional hymns.

महतो यो माहात्म्यं दर्शयितुं क्रियत उत्सवस्तं हि ।
प्रमहं मह इति चाहुः सूनृतवाङ्महसि पानमशनं च ।।90।।

This festival was organized to celebrate the grandeur of great men. This festival was known as Maha. This Maha used to have drink, food and auspicious recitation.

तत्रानेकसहस्राण्यासन्निन्द्राय सोमकुम्भानाम्
विनिमयनार्था गावः प्रणयवचांसि च निवेदनीयानि ।।91।।

Several thousand jars filled with Soma [Soma kumbhas] and cows were offered to Indra along with appeals to befriend him.

विनिमयनव्यवहाराज्जस्यार्थं राजशासनप्रख्यम् ।
अद्य यथा पश्यामस्ताम्रपणं रौप्यणं स्वर्णम् ।।92 ।।

एवं देवयुगे प्रागासीद्गोनाम विनिमयद्रव्यम् ।
तद्गौरेव हिरण्यं वान्यद्वेत्येवमनुचिन्त्यम् ।।93।।

As copper and gold, and other currencies are used today, similarly there used to be a currency named gau that was used for exchange during the devayuga. It is doubtful, nevertheless, whether cow, gold, or any other substance were used for actual exchange.

अद्येव पूर्वकाले क्रयविक्रयवत्प्रभूपहारेऽपि ।
विनिमयनीयद्रव्याण्यावेद्यन्ते स्म ता गाव: ।।94।।

In fact, gau was the currency that was used in ancient times for sale and purchase and also to honour great men.

आराध्या: सम्भ्रान्ता: संभावितसज्जनाश्च समवेत्य ।
प्रणयप्रदेयमर्थं स्वै: स्वै: काव्यै: सहार्पयामासु: ।।95।।

Adored, respected, honoured and virtuous men gathered and presented the substances to be offered with love with their respective hymns.

येयं प्रथते वैदिकमन्त्राणां संहितात्रितयी ।
काव्यानि तान्यृषीणामित्युक्तं शतपथेऽष्टमे काण्डे ।।96।।

The three famous collections of Vedic hymns were the poetry of sages, it has been mentioned in the eighth section of Shatapatha Brahmana.

तत्र च कुत्सुनियुक्तो विश्वामित्रो महर्षिरुत्थाय ।
दस्युवधायेन्द्रायावदेयदभ्यर्थनासूक्तम् ।।97 ।।

शुष्मिन्तरमं च वनुते दस्युभ्य: स्वगृहराष्ट्ररक्षार्थम् ।
भोज्यान्नलाभहेतोर्द्युम्निनियुक्ति न स्रोऽर्शते सोमम् ।।98।।

There, as appointed by Kutsa, Vishvamitra stood up and chanted the hymn of petition for Indra for the destruction of the asuras. He requested the enlightened Indra to protect their homeland from the asuras and requested him to partake Soma.

4.6 विश्वामित्रकृतो दस्युवधाभ्यर्थनासूक्तपाठः

4.6 VISHVAMITRA'S PLEA TO DESTROY DASYUS

वीरपानप्रमहे विश्वामित्रकृतो दस्युवधाभ्यर्थनासूक्तपाठः ।

Hymn composed by Vishvamitra urging for the destruction of dasyus in the *veer-paan* (drinking of Soma) festival.

विश्वामित्रो भोजनादिप्रबन्धाध्यक्षः क्लृप्तस्तेन पानोत्सवस्य ।
अध्यध्यक्षः सोऽभवत् तत्सभायां सग्धेरन्तेऽभ्यर्थनां सोऽध्यवोचत् ।।99।।

Vishvamitra was appointed as the chief organizer of food and drink in that festival. He was the chairperson of that meeting and offered benediction at the end of the function.

वार्त्रहत्याय शवसे पृतनाषाह्याय च ।
इन्द्रत्वा वर्तयामसि ।।

(ऋग्वेदः, 3.37.1)

In the thirty-seventh sukta of third mandala of Rigveda, Vishvamitra states: O Indra! We request you for strength, destruction of enemies and to slay Vritra.

अर्वाचीनं सुते मन उत चक्षुः शतक्रतो ।
इन्द्र कृण्वन्तु वाघतः ।।

(ऋग्वेदः, 3.37.2)

O Shatakrato Indra! May these worshippers stimulate your spirit and eyes.

नामानि ते शतक्रतो विश्वाभिर्गीर्भिरीमहे ।
इन्द्राभिमातिषाह्ये ।।

(ऋग्वेदः, 3.37.3)

O Shatakrato Indra! We attain your strengths in the battle through petition-hymns.

पुरुष्टुतस्य धामभिः शतेन महयामसि ।
इन्द्रस्य चर्षणीधृतः ।।

(ऋग्वेदः, 3.37.4)

We worship Indra, the one worshipped by many, full of myriad glory and supporter of mankind.

इन्द्रं वृत्राय हन्तवे पुरुहूतमुपब्रुवे ।
भरेषु वाज सातये ॥

(ऋग्वेद:, 3.37.5)

I invoke Indra, the one invoked by many, for gaining nourishment and for destroying Vritra.

वाजेषु सासहिर्भव त्वामी महे शतक्रतो ।
इन्द्रवृत्राय हन्तवे ॥

(ऋग्वेद:, 3.37.6)

O Shatakrato Indra! You are the destroyer of enemies in the battles. I invoke you to slain Vritra.

द्युम्नेषु पृतनाज्ये पृत्सुतूर्षु श्रवःसु च ।
इन्द्र साक्ष्वामि मातिषु ॥

(ऋग्वेद:, 3.37.7)

O Indra! Destroy enemies and be a victor in the battle for food.

शुष्मिन्तमं न ऊतये द्युम्निनं पाहि जागृविम् ।
इन्द्रसोमं शतक्रतो ॥

(ऋग्वेद:, 3.37.8)

O Shatakrato Indra! For our protection drink Soma that makes one bright, vigilant and strong.

इन्द्रियाणि शतक्रतो याते जनेषु पञ्चसु ।
इन्द्र तानि त आ वृणे ॥

(ऋग्वेद:, 3.37.9)

O Shatakrato Indra! I bow before you for the power that you have over the five classes of beings [deva, manushya, Gandharva, Apasara, Naga, and Pitra].

अगन्निन्द्रश्रवो बृहद् द्युम्नं दधिष्व दुष्टरम् ।
उत्ते शुष्मं तिरामसि ॥

(ऋग्वेद:, 3.37.10)

O Indra! We praise your strength, may you get this supreme food and drink this glorious Soma, that is, unattainable by enemies.

अर्वावतो न आ गह्यथो शक्रं परावतः ।
ऊलोको यस्ते अद्रिव इन्द्रेह तत आ गहि ॥

(ऋग्वेदः, 3.37.11)

O thunder-bearing Indra! Come to us from the nearest as well as the farthest place, or come to us from the place where you reside.

4.7 नाभाककाण्वकृतो दस्युवधाभ्यर्थनासूक्तपाठः

4.7 PLEA BY NABHAKA KANVA TO DESTROY DASYUS

अपि वृश्च पुराणवद् व्रततेरिव गुष्पितमोजो दासस्य दम्भय ।
वयं तदस्य सम्भृतं वस्विन्द्रेण विभजेमहि नभन्तामन्यके समे ॥
(ऋग्वेदः, 8.40.6)

In the fortieth sukta of eighth mandala of Rigveda, Nabhaka Kanva has composed the petition-hymn: O Indra! Cut the enemies as the trunk of a tree wrapped in vines is slashed. Destroy the glory of asuras. May we attain the hidden wealth of enemy with the blessings of Indra. May all our enemies be destroyed on their own.

यदिन्द्राग्नी जना इमे विह्वयन्ते तना गिरा ।
अस्माकेभिर्नृभिर्वयं सासह्याम पृतन्यतो वनुयामं वनुष्यतो नभन्ता मन्यके समे ॥
(ऋग्वेदः, 8.40.7)

At the time when these men invite Indra and Agni with their songs and prayers. May we with our great heroes conquer enemy's army. Let's praise them, who praise us. May all our enemies be destroyed on their own.

या नु श्वेताववो दिव उच्चरात उप द्युभिः ।
इन्द्राग्न्योरनु व्रतमुहाना यन्ति सिन्धवो यान्त्सी वन्धादमुञ्चतां न भन्ता मन्यके समे॥
(ऋग्वेदः, 8.40.8)

Indra and Agni are by nature powerful, with their radiance they wander below, near and even above the sky. They release rivers from their fetters and help those who offer sacrifices. May all our enemies be destroyed on their own.

पूर्वीष्ट इन्द्रोपमातयः पूर्वीरुत प्रशस्तयः सूनो हिन्वस्य हरिवः ।
वस्वो वीरस्यापृचो यानु साधन्त नो धियो नभन्तामन्यके समे ॥
(ऋग्वेदः, 8.40.9)

O thunder-bearing Indra who creates all! Bless those with wealth who please you. Many are your aliases and praises; these praises have only sharpened our intellect. May all our enemies be destroyed on their own.

तं शिशीता सुवृक्तिभिस्त्वेषं सत्वानमृग्मियम् ।
उतो नु चिद्य ओजसा शुष्णस्याण्डानि भेदति जेषत्स्वर्वतीरपो नभन्तामन्यके समे ।।
(ऋग्वेद:, 8.40.10)

Glorify with supreme hymns and means that Indra who killed the progenies of asura Shushna, contained the frolicking rivers, and is worshipped with glorious and powerful hymns. May all our enemies be destroyed on their own.

तं शिशीता स्वध्वरं सत्यं सत्वानमृत्वियम् ।
उतो नु चिद्य ओहत आण्डा शुष्णस्य भेदत्यजैः स्वर्वतीरपो नभन्तामन्यके समे ।।
(ऋग्वेद:, 8.40.11)

The one who travels in all the directions and slays Shushna's progenies, who has contained the frolicking rivers, who leads us to the supreme path, glorify that indestructible, powerful and praiseworthy Indra.

एवेन्द्राग्निभ्यां पितृवन्नवीयो मन्धातृवदङ्गिरस्वदवाचि ।
त्रिधातुना शर्म्मणा पातमस्मान्वयं स्याम पतयो रयीणम् ।।
(ऋग्वेद:, 8.40.12)

Thus, like Mandhata [a king of the solar dynasty] and Angiras [a celebrated sage to whom many hymns of Rigveda are ascribed], I offer prayers to Indra and Agni anew, may these two, fortified with three metals [gold, silver, and copper] protect us and become the master of riches.

4.8 दस्युनिग्रहणार्थं कुत्सेनोपायप्रदर्शनं तत्प्रदर्शितमार्गाश्रयणं च

4.8 KUTSA'S PLEA FOR DESTROYING DASYUS

अथ सुप्रसन्न इन्द्रो दस्यूनामभिजनस्थितिप्रचारादि ।
अपि तद्दमनोपायाद्यध्यवसातुं परामृक्षत् ॥100॥

Afterwards, a pleased Indra considered the lineage of the asuras [clan, race, habitation, and origin], natural conducts [travels and wanderings] and the matters related to their destruction.

व्यज्ञपयत्तु स कुत्सो निषधादस्मात्तु पूर्वतः सरिताम् ।
पारेऽञ्जस्यादीनां प्रस्यासन्ने 'शिफा' नद्याः ॥101॥
कुयवग्रामं जाने किन्त्वञ्जस्यादयोतिदुष्पाराः ।
बलवज्जलसंवेगाः सन्ति पथि प्राणहारिणः ॥102॥

Kutsa informed that he knew about an asura village named Kuyava situated near river Shipha. This river flowed closer to Anjasi and other rivers east of the Nishadh mountain. But this river, Anjasi, is extremely treacherous to cross. The flow of these rivers is so rapid that it is fatal to cross them mid-stream.

यद्यपि सरित्प्रवाहो हस्तद्विशतीमितोस्ति विस्तारे ।
किन्तु तथापि न नौभिर्गन्तुं शक्योन्तरश्मभिर्घातात् ॥103॥

Since the river is enormously wide and full of stones, it is not even possible to cross the river in boats.

जलवेगप्राबल्यादुच्चावचभूमिसञ्चारात् ।
सरितां पारं गन्तुं न बाहुतरणात्समर्थन्ते ॥104॥

Also, because of the tremendous flow of water in the river, one cannot even cross it by swimming.

दस्यव एते निपुणा गिरिशिखरप्रोतदोलवर्तन्याः ।
शिक्याभिर्मशकैर्वा यातायातं प्रकुर्वन्ति ॥105॥

These asuras are very smart and they used rope bridges and leather bags to cross these rivers and travel across the mountains.

दासातिरिक्तजनता त्वासां पारं समर्थते नैतुम् ।
तत्कृतदोलनिपातादवहनतो मशकशिक्यानाम् ॥106॥

Since other dasas did not have leather bags and skills to use rope-bridges, only the asuras managed to cross these rivers.

दोलाद्यारूढा अपि बहवो नद्यां निपातिता द्वेषात् ।
तस्मात्तेषां ग्रामाः सहसा द्रष्टुं न शक्यन्ते ।।107।।

There is hardly anyone who could see the asura villages. In fact, the asuras dared any intruder to cross the river by rope-bridges and they would toss into rivers any intruder who was caught.

मध्ये च बहवो दासा मार्गं च सन्ति रुन्धानाः ।
तस्मात्तेषां ग्रामा दुरधिगमा दुर्गमाः सन्ति ।।108।।

They guard the route to their villages and thus these villages are unattainable and unreachable.

आसां ततो नदीनां निस्तारार्थं नियुज्यन्ताम् ।
आहूय राष्ट्रशूराः आर्या वनरक्षिणः कुशलाः ।।109।।

Thus, to cross these rivers, great heroes and skilled forest-guards are required.

दासानां पथि चरतां व्यामोहार्थं नियुज्यन्ताम् ।
कृतदासवेषभूषास्तद्भाषायां च शिक्षिता मरुतः ।।110।।

To confuse, disturb, and entrap the wandering asuras, marutas, who know the asura language, should be dressed as the asuras.

ततो दस्युनिग्रहार्थं कुत्सप्रदर्शितमार्गाश्रयणम् ।

Pursuing Kutsa's plan to destroy dasyus.

इत्थं कुत्सादिष्टमार्गं स इन्द्रः सम्यग् मत्वा तत्तथैवादिदेश ।
दस्यूनेतान् संनिगृह्य स्वराज्ये भूयोऽप्यार्यान् धातुमाधात् प्रतिज्ञाम् ।।111।।

Accepting the request of Kutsa, Indra imprisoned those asuras and permitted the Arya to once again become superior in their own region.

सिन्धोः पारे नैषधोऽद्रौ स इन्द्रः स्कन्धावारं विश्रमाय प्रकल्प्य ।
गूढं दस्युस्थानमादौ विचेतुं विज्ञान् द्रोण्यां प्रेषयामास चारान् ।।112।।

काले भूयस्यप्यनिश्चित्य तेषां शैलद्रोणीगह्वरस्थान्निकेतान् ।
प्रत्यावृत्तास्ते चरा आयुराजप्रेष्यारण्याभिज्ञवेशानकुर्वन् ।।113।।

At first, Indra established a detachment across Indus on the Nishadh mountain to set up a base and sent emissaries into the valley to identify the hidden abodes of the asuras. After a long time, when these emissaries returned without any information about the whereabouts of the asuras, then he sent King Ayu's men, who were trained in travelling through the forests, and used to dress like the savages, to investigate.

आसीदायुः प्राक् प्रतिष्ठानराजो हेमाद्रिस्थे पञ्चगौरप्रयागे ।
ये तद्भृत्याः केऽप्यटव्यां नियुक्तास्ते खल्वासन् दस्युजातीयजीवाः ।।114।।

In ancient times, Ayu was the king of the state Pratishtan, which was situated in Panchgaurprayaga in the Himalayas. Some of his men, who were deployed in the forests, belonged to the asura clan.

आयुराजस्य प्रतिष्ठानं पुराधिष्ठातुः परिचयः ।

Pratishthanpur King Ayu's introduction.

गन्धर्वराजपौत्रो बुधपुत्रो यः पुरूरवा राजा ।
तत्पुत्र आयुरासीद् गन्धर्वेशः प्रतिष्ठाने ।।115।।

Ayu was the son of the king named Pururava who was the grandson of Gandharvaraja. He was the king of Gandharvas in Pratishtan.

'गौरी' नदीसमीपे मूजवतः पर्वतादर्वाग्देशे ।
गान्धारे प्रागासीदिदं प्रतिष्ठानमायुपुरम् ।।116।।

King Ayu's kingdom Pratishtan was located in the Gandhara state behind the Munjavana mountain near river Gauri.

अधुना केचिद्ब्रुवते भारतवर्षीयमध्यरेखाप्राक् ।
'झूसी'-'प्रायाग'-सन्निभे पुरं प्रतिष्ठानमित्यलीकं तत् ।।117।।

Many people believe that Pratishtan is located before Bharatavarsha's 'madhya rekha' near 'Jhusi' and Prayaga; however, it is untrue to say so.

राजा ययातिरवसद् वार्धक्ये तं प्रयागमभ्येत्य ।
तस्य निवासस्थानं विदुः 'प्रतिष्ठान' मित्यन्यत् ।।118।।

Prayaga, where the king stayed during his old age, was called as Pratishtan, but that was another city.

अस्मिन् भारतवर्षे सन्ति हि 'बाह्लीक' 'वैतुला'दीनि ।
बाह्लीक-वैतुलादि-प्रतिकृतिरूपाणि तद्वदन्यत्तत् ।।119।।

In Bharatavarsha, there have been different cities with the same names, as in the case of Bahlika and Vaitula; similarly, Pratishtan is also a different city.

जाह्नवदेशप्रथिता 'जाह्नवी' नाम या गङ्गा ।
तस्याः कूले मुख्यं पुरं प्रतिष्ठानमासीत्तत् ।।120।।

It was situated on the bank of Ganges famously called Jahanvi in the state of Jahnva.

अत्र प्रमाणजातं निदर्शितं पौरवख्यातौ ।
आयुः पौरूरवसो दासानपि कांश्चिदीष्टे स्म ।।121।।

Paurava-Khyati mentions that Pururava's son Ayu used to rule the asuras.

इन्द्रस्तस्मादायुराड्वन्यवर्गात्तेषां भाषावेशभूषादि साम्यम् ।
संपाद्य स्वांस्तत्र वर्गे स्थानं तेषामध्यवास्यत् क्रमेण ।।122।।

Because of the similarity in language and dress with Ayu's subjects, Indra made them enter his own city and stayed at their places.

अप्रतिरथमहोवाकः ।

Aprathirath's war cry.

अथ तत्र देवसेना मारुत्या सेनया सयुक् सज्जा ।
समराङ्गणेऽवतरितुं प्रतीक्षते स्म प्रभोराज्ञाम् ।।123।।

Afterwards, fully prepared armies of devas and marutas waited for the order to enter the battlefield.

अथ समराय मरुद्भिः सयुजं निषधात् प्रतिष्ठमानं तम् ।
प्रोत्साहयितुं चैन्द्रौऽप्रतिरथ उपासते स्म ।।124।।

Next, while marching out of the Nishadh state with the marutas, the unrivalled warrior Indra motivated them with prayers.

आभिक्रमिकः सुभटः प्रास्थानिकसमयमालक्ष्य ।
राजनियत्याऽभ्यूचेऽप्रतिरथ ऐन्द्रो महोवाकम् ।।125।।

Before the war, the warriors, with the permission of their king, repeated Indra's war cry.

4.9 युद्धयात्रारम्भे अप्रतिरथसूक्तपाठः

4.9 A WAR SONG FOR INDRA

"आशुः" शिशानो वृषभो न भीमो घनाघनः क्षोभणश्चर्षणीनाम् ।
संक्रन्दनोऽनिमिष एक वीरः शतं सेना अजयत्साकमिन्द्रः ॥
(ऋग्वेदः, 10.103.1)

In the one hundred and third sukta of tenth mandala of Rigveda, sages worship Indra: Sharp striker, omnipresent, fierce like a bull, powerful, tormentor of men, enemy's destructor, always vigilant, and great warrior Indra overpowers hundreds of armies at once.

संक्रन्दनेनानिमिषेण जिष्णुना युत्कारेण दुश्च्यवनेन धृष्णुना ।
तदिन्द्रेण जयत तत्सहध्वं युधो नर इषुहस्तेन वृष्णा ॥
(ऋग्वेदः, 10.103.2)

Indra is the one who is invincible, destroys enemies, remains vigilant, seeks victory and us skilled in war. May we conquer with Indra's help. O battle-loving men! That Indra is powerful and bears a bow in his hand.

स इषुहस्तैः स निषङ्गिभिर्वशी संस्रष्टा स युध इन्द्रो गणेन ।
संसृष्टजित्सोमपा बाहुशर्ध्युग्रधन्वा प्रतिहिताभिरस्ता ॥
(ऋग्वेदः, 10.103.3)

Indra accompanies the marutas who bear bow and sword. Indra is about to enter the enemy's group for combat. That conqueror, Soma drinker, strongly-armed, fierce-archer destroys enemies with his arrows.

बृहस्पते परि दीया रथेन रक्षोहामित्राँ अप बाधमानः ।
प्रभञ्जन्त्सेनाः प्रमृणो युधा जयन्नस्माकमेध्यविता रथानाम् ॥
(ऋग्वेदः, 10.103.4)

O Brihaspati! March ahead with your chariot. You are the slayer of demons, destroyer of enemies, destructor of enemy's army and victor in battle. May you protect our chariots.

बलविज्ञायः स्थविरः प्रवीरः सहस्वान्वाजी सहमान उग्रः ।
अभिवीरो अभिसत्वा सहोजा जैत्रमिन्द्र रथमातिष्ठ गोवित् ॥
(ऋग्वेदः, 10.103.5)

O Indra! You are the epitome of energy, foundation of everyone's life, great warrior, mighty, aggressive, endowed with nourishment, slayer of fierce enemy, surrounded with warriors, followed by many and full of energy and cows. Mount your conquering chariot.

गोत्रभिदं गोविदं बज्रबाहुं जयन्तमज्म प्रमृणन्तमोजसा ।
इमं सजाता अनुवीरयध्वमिन्द्रं सखायो अनुसंरभध्वम् ।।
(ऋग्वेदः, 10.103.6)

O gathered warriors! Follow the greatness of Indra who rips clouds, explodes mountains, bears thunder, conqueror and slayer of all enemies. O Friends! Follow Indra, and perform your duty.

अभि गोत्राणि सहसा गाहमानोऽदयो वीरः शतमन्युरिन्द्रः ।
दुश्च्यवनः पृतनाषाळयुध्योस्माकं सेना अवतु प्र युत्सु ।।
(ऋग्वेदः, 10.103.7)

Powerful Indra penetrates clouds. May Indra, the one who is pitiless, a warrior, aggressive, unshakeable, destroyer of enemy and invincible, protect our army in the battle.

इन्द्र आसां नेता बृहस्पतिर्दक्षिणा यज्ञः षुर एतु सोमः ।
देवसेनानामभिभञ्जतीनां जयन्तीनां मरुतो यन्त्वग्रम् ।।
(ऋग्वेदः, 10.103.108)

Indra is the leader of all these armies. Thus, Brihaspati, his skilled army, sacrifice and Soma must precede Indra and he should lead the maruta army, the destroyer of enemies.

इन्द्रस्य वृष्णो वरुणस्य राज्ञ आदित्यानां मरुतां शर्द्ध उग्रम् ।
महामनसा भुवनच्यवानाङ्घोषो देवानाञ्जयतामुदस्थात् ।।
(ऋग्वेदः, 10.103.9)

May we get the support and strength of powerful Indra, King Varuna, adityas and marutas. The victory roars of victorious devas, of the supreme warrior, of the ruler of the whole world, makes the whole universe tremble.

उद्धर्षय मघवन्नायुधान्युत्सत्वनां मामकानां मनांसि ।
उद्वृत्रहन्वाजिनां वाजिनान्युद्रथानां जयतां यन्तु घोषाः ।।
(ऋग्वेदः, 10.103.10)

O Maghavan! Activate our weapons. Encourage the spirits of my soldiers. O *Vritaghana* (the slayer of Vritra)! Strengthen our horses. Let the roar of our victorious chariots echoes.

अस्माकमिन्द्रः समृतेषु ध्वजेष्वस्माकं या इषवस्ता जयन्तु ।
अस्माकं वीरा उत्तरे भवन्त्वस्माँ उ देवा अवता हवेषु ॥
(ऋग्वेदः, 10.103.11)

May Indra protect us when we gather under our flags. May our armed soldiers be victorious. May our army be of superior class. O devas! Protect us in the battle.

अमीषां चित्तं प्रतिलोभयन्ती गृहाणाङ्गान्यप्वे परेहि ।
अभिप्रेहि निर्दह हृत्सु शोकैरन्धेनामित्रास्तमसा सचन्ताम् ॥
(ऋग्वेदः, 10.103.12)

O Apva! Trap and seize these enemies. Travel a long distance with the enemies, march with them and burn the fire of sorrow in their hearts and make them suffer in utter darkness.

अवसृष्टा परा पत शरव्ये ब्रह्मसंशिते ।
गच्छामित्रान्प्रपद्यस्व मीमीषां कञ्चनोच्छिषः ॥
(ऋग्वेदः, 6.75.16)

O sharp arrow! You have been sharpened with wisdom. Thus, once shot, may you slay all the enemies.

प्रेता जयता नर इन्द्रो वः शर्म्म यच्छतु ।
उग्रा वः सन्तु बाहवोऽनाधृष्या यथासथ ॥
(ऋग्वेदः, 10.103.13)

O men [warriors]! March on and be victorious. May Indra please us. May you be aggressive so that you never get defeated.

असौ या सेना मरुतः परेषामभ्यैति न ओजसा स्पर्द्धमाना।
ताङ्गूहत तमसापव्रतेन यथामी अन्यो अन्यन्नजानन् ॥
(यजुर्वेदः 17.47)

Let the marutas, fighting fiercely with the enemy army, be taken away from darkness and the enemies be put in such houses that they would not identify each other.

यत्र बाणाः सम्पतन्ति कुमारा विशिखा इव ।
तत्रा नो ब्रह्मणस्पतिरदितिः शर्म्म यच्छतु विश्वाहा शर्म्म यच्छतु ।।
(ऋग्वेदः, 6.75.17)

May Indra, Brihaspati and Aditi protect us from arrows in the battlefield.

मर्म्माणि ते वर्मणा छादयामि सोमस्त्वा राजामृतेनानु वस्ताम् ।
उरोर्वरीयो वरुणस्ते कृणोतु जयन्तं त्वानु देवा मदन्तु ।।
(ऋग्वेदः, 6.75.18)

May your vital parts be covered with armour. King Soma immortalizes you. Varuna showers supreme wealth on you. May the victory delight all devas.

4.10 नृमेधपुरुमेधाभ्यां गीतं बृहद्गानम्

4.10 INVOCATIONS BY NRIMEDHA AND PURUMEDHA

नृमेधपुरुमेधौ बृहद्गानेन देवेन्द्रम् अभिष्टोतुं देवेन्द्रसहचारिणं प्रधानामात्यम् इन्द्रतनूनपातं मरुद्गणं तावदभ्यर्थयेते ।

Sages Nrimedha and Purumedha request the marudgana, the companions of Indra and the protectors of body power, to sing '*brihad gana*' (long poem) to worship Indra.

बृहदिन्द्राय गायत मरुतो वृत्रहन्तमम् ।
येन ज्योतिरजनयन्नृतावृधो देवं देवाय जागृवि ।।

(ऋग्वेदः, 8.78.1)

In the eighty-ninth sukta of eighth mandala of Rigveda, sage Dvaya states:
O Marutas! Sing the *samagana* (songs of Samaveda) songs of praise for Indra, the slayer of enemies, that you sang to kindle eternal light.

अपाधमदभिशस्तीरशस्ति हाथेन्द्रो द्युम्न्याभवत्।
देवास्त इन्द्र सख्याय येमिरे बृहद्भानो मरुद्गण ।।

(ऋग्वेदः, 8.78.2)

O Marudaganas! Indra, the slayer of enemies has slaughtered all enemies. O Indra! Everyone longs for your friendship.

प्र व इन्द्राय बृहते मरुतो ब्रह्मार्चत ।
वृत्रं हनति वृत्रहा शतक्रतुर्वज्रेण शतपर्वणा ।।

(ऋग्वेदः, 8.78.3)

O Marutas! Sing hymns for the great Indra. Indra is the doer of myriad deeds and slayer of Vritra. Indra slays enemies with a sharp thunder.

अथेन्द्राय तौ बृहद्गानं गायतः ।

Afterwards, they render brihad gana for Indra.

अप्रतिरथे प्रयुक्ते मारुत्या सेनयेन्द्रमासक्तम् ।
उपतस्थाते तु बृहद्गानं गातुं नृमेधपुरुमेधौ ।।126।।

Then, Nrimedha and Purumedha came forward to render their long songs of praise.

अभिप्रभर धृषता धृषन्मनः श्रवश्चित्ते असद्बृहत् ।
अर्षन्त्वापो जवसा वि मातरो हनो वृत्रं जया स्वः ।।

(ऋग्वेदः, 8.78.4)

The hymn sung by these two sages is recorded in the eighty-ninth sukta of eighth mandala of Rigveda: O Strong-hearted Indra! Bless us with the superior nourishment you have. O Indra! After killing Vritra, you released the waters,which nourished us like a mother; let them flow with force.

यज्जायथा अपूर्व्य मघवन्वृत्रहत्याय ।
तत्पृथिवीमप्रथयस्तदस्तभ्ना उत द्याम् ।।

(ऋग्वेदः, 8.78.5)

O, exremely affluent Indra! The valour that you displayed to kill Vritra, the same valour you have displayed to expand Prithviloka, and stabilize Dyauloka.

तत्ते यज्ञो अजायत तदर्क उत हस्कृतिः ।
तद्विश्वमभिभूरसि यज्जातं यच्च जन्त्वम् ।।

(ऋग्वेदः, 8.78.6)

O Indra! This sacrifice has been performed for you, and those fervent mantras have also been chanted for you. O Indra! Everything that has happened, and yet to happen in this universe, happen according to you.

आमासु पक्वमैरय आ सूर्यं रोहयो दिवि ।
धमं न सामन्तपता सुवृक्तिभिर्जुष्टं गिर्वणसे बृहत् ।।

(ऋग्वेदः, 8.78.7)

O Indra! You gave nutritious milk to cows, established the sun in the heaven. O Men! The manner in which oblation *pravagya* [a ceremony preliminary to the Soma sacrifice] is initiated, similarly, praise Indra with pleasing paens and finest hymns.

आनो विश्वासु हव्य इन्द्रः समत्सु भूषतु ।
उप ब्रह्माणि सवनानि वृत्रहा परमज्या ऋचीषमः ।।

(ऋग्वेदः, 8.79.1)

May Indra, the slayer of Vritra, possessor of bowstring, supreme Soma-drinker and praiseworthy, adorn sacrifices and incantations named Brahma.

त्वं दाता प्रथमो राधसामस्यसि सत्य ईशानकृत् ।
तुविद्युम्नस्य युज्या वृणीमहे पुत्रस्य शवसो महः ।।
(ऋग्वेदः, 8.79.2)

O Indra! You are the donator of supreme wealth. You are truthful and a great ruler. We desire wealth from tremendously affluent, mighty, powerful, and great Indra.

ब्रह्मा त इन्द्र गिर्वणः क्रियन्ते अनतिभ्दुता ।
इमा जुषस्व हर्यश्व योजनेन्द्र या ते अमन्महि ।।
(ऋग्वेदः, 8.79.3)

O praiseworthy Indra and the lord of horses! We religiously sing those songs which invoke Brahma.

त्वं हि सत्यो मघवन्ननानतो वृत्रा भूरि न्यृञ्जसे ।
स त्वं शविष्ठ वज्रहस्त दाशुषेऽर्वाञ्चं रयिमा कृधि ।।
(ऋग्वेदः, 8.79.4)

O affluent Indra! You are truthful and invincible. You slay several Vritras with your supreme strength. O warrior and thunder-bearing Indra! You make him prosperous who donates.

त्वमिन्द्र यशा अस्यृजीषी शवसस्पते ।
त्वं वृत्राणि हंस्यप्रतीन्येक इदनुत्ता चर्षणीधृता ।। (ऋग्वेदः, 8.79.5)

O Indra, the lord of devas! You are mighty and a Soma drinker. Single-handedly, you slay fierce and brave enemies with your thunderbolt.

तमु त्वा नूनमसुर प्रचेतसं राधो भागमिवेमहे ।
महीव कृत्तिः शरणा त इन्द्र प्रते सुम्ना नो अश्नवन् ।।
(ऋग्वेदः, 8.79.6)

O Saviour Indra! Kindly give us our share of wealth. O Indra! Kindly give us all your joys. Take us under your protection; your protection acts like a great armour.

4.11 इन्द्रेण सरयुपारस्थमार्यराजद्वयं निहननम्

4.11 INDRA SLAYS TWO ARYAS LIVING ACROSS SARAYU

निषधाद्रिगिरे: प्रतस्थे मारुत्या देवसेनया च सह ।
महतोत्साहेनेन्द्रोऽश्विविष्णुयुक् कुत्सयुग् बृहस्पतियुक् ।।127।।

After staying on the Nishadh mountain, Indra enthusiastically moved ahead with the marutas, Ashvi, Vishnu, Kutsa, and Brihaspati.

दस्यूनिन्द्रो हन्तुं शैलानेवाभियातुकमोऽपि ।
मध्ये मार्गं प्रथमं द्वावार्यौ प्रतिययौ हन्तुम् ।।128।।

आर्याविमौ नरेशावार्यकुलध्वंसनोपायान् ।
परिदर्शयतस्तेषां दासानां प्रेमवशभूतौ ।।129।।

इत्याकर्ण्य स इन्द्र: प्रथमं तावेव धर्षितुं चकमे ।
रुग्भैषज्यात्पूर्वं रुक्प्रभवोत्सादनं श्रेय: ।।130।।

Although he was keen on marching towards the mountains to kill the asuras, Indra returned to slay two Arya kings who were supporters of the asuras. Fearing that these two Aryas would help the asuras in their attack against the Arya, Indra decided to kill these two Aryas first.

सरयो: सरित: पारे क्वचिदार्यावर्णचित्ररथौ ।
भूपो वसत: स्मैतौ दाससखौ तद्धितप्रवणौ ।।131।।

Arna and Chitraratha were the two Arya kings who used to live across the river Sarayu. They were supporters and well-wishers of the asuras.

4.4.1 सरयूनदीपरिचय:

4.4.1 Introduction to river Sarayu

आत्रेय: श्यावश्व: सरयुं सह पठति सिन्धुना कुभया ।
क्रुम्वाथगय: प्लातोऽपि सिन्धुनापि च सरस्वत्या ।।132।।

Atreya Shyavashva describes Sarayu along with the river Kubha. Two mountain springs named Krumu and Gaya have been described along with the rivers Sindhu and Sarasvati.

मावोरसाऽनितभा कुभा क्रुमुर्मावः सिन्धुर्निरीरमत ।
मावः परिष्ठात् सरयुः पुरीषिण्यस्मे इत् सुम्नमस्तुवः।।
(ऋग्वेदः, 5.53.9)

The fifty-third sukta of fifth mandala of Rigveda states: O great marutas! May you be not harmed by the dirty river Rasa, nor obstructed by violent streams of Sindhu, or besieged by the flooded Sarayu. May us alone experience your presence.

सरस्वती सरयुः सिन्धुरुर्मिभिर्महो महीरवसा यन्तु वक्षणीः ।
देवीरापो मातरः सूदयित्न्वो घृतवत्पयो मधुमन्नो अर्चत ।।
(ऋग्वेदः, 10.64.9)

May the twenty-one mighty, honoured and rhythmic rivers such as Sarayu, Sarasvati, and Sindhu come to protect us and these motherly and stimulating rivers bless us with sweet and nutritious water like clarified butter.

एतेनेयं सरयुः सिन्धुगता काचिदन्तरिक्षेऽस्ति ।
न तु साऽयोध्याप्रान्तस्थिता श्रुता कुत्रचिद्वेदे ।।133।।

In the antariksha, the river Sarayu was somewhere closer to river Sindhu. In the Vedas, however, there is no reference to Sarayu being in the region of Ayodhya.

तक्षशिलानगरी तलवहना या सिन्धुसंगमना ।
सा सरयुरिति सत्यव्रताख्यासामश्रमी प्राह ।।134।।

According to Satyavrata Samashrami (well-known commentator of Vedas), Sarayu is the river that flows through the city of Takshashila and flows into river Sindhu.

अपरे त्वेतां सरयुं हिन्दुकुशपर्वतप्रभवाम् ।
प्राहुस्तथाहि तस्याः परिचयमित्थं विजानीयात् ।।135।।

But others have referred to Sarayu as the river that originates from the Hindukush mountains. Therefore, it should be regarded as such.

वेदे यक्षुर्योक्ता चक्षर्जम्बूश्च सा पुराणोक्ता ।
'अक्सस'-इति तां म्लेच्छा आहु 'रमू' इति च तामाहुः ।।136।।

The river referred to as Yaksu in the Vedas has been referred to as Chaksu and Jambu in the Puranas. The mlecchas referred to it as Aksasa and Ramu.

तस्या दक्षिणकूले यक्षः पू 'रोक्सियाना' ख्या ।
तद्देशस्था उक्ता यक्षव इति वेदमन्त्रे प्राक् ॥136॥

एतानेव तुपश्चान्म्लेच्छा विदु 'रोक्सियानी' ति ।
यक्षव आर्या आसन् पश्चान्म्लेच्छा बभूवुस्ते ॥137॥

The city of Yakshapu, situated on the southern bank of this river, has been known as Roxiyano. These Yakshus were Arya, who became mlecchas later.

यक्षुष उदक् तु शिग्रुर्नदी 'सुगद' स उच्यते म्लेच्छैः ।
यक्षुषि सैति च सुगदप्रान्तोऽयं 'सुगदियाना' ख्या ॥138॥

In the north of Yakshu was the river Shigru that had been named as Sugadha by the mlecchas. This river was in the city of Yakshu, and the region of Sugadha was known as Sugadhiyana.

सुगदनदी यद्गिरितः प्रवहति 'सुगदी' स पर्वतः कथितः ।
तद्गिरिशिखरे स ऋषिर्मार्कण्डेयः पुरायुगे न्यवसत् ॥139॥

The mountain from which Sugadha originates is known as Sugadhi. It was the mountain where sage Markandeya used to live.

अथ 'हिन्दुकुश'–'सुगदानिया' न्तरे यक्षुषोऽवाच्याम् ।
प्रान्तोऽस्ति वक्ट्रियाना हिन्दूकुशजा नदीह 'दर्गिदुसा' ॥140॥

In the south of Yakshu, in between Hindukush and Sugadhiyana, lies the region named Vaktriyana and the river Dargidusa that originates from Hindukush also flows through the same region.

बाह्लीक एव 'वक्ट्रा' नाम्नाख्यातः पुरा म्लेच्छैः ।
स च बाह्लीकप्रान्तस्तैरुक्तो 'वक्ट्रिया' नाम्ना ॥141॥

In ancient times, Bahlika was referred to as Vaktra by the mlecchas and later on it came to be called as Vaktriya [Bactria] in Bahlika region.

शैलद्वयान्तराले प्रवहन्त्युत्तरमुखी तु 'दर्गिदुसा' ।
तृत्सुः सा तत्प्रान्ते 'जरियस्या' सैव 'वक्ट्रा' पूः ॥142॥

The northward flowing river that flows between two mountains is known as Dargidusa; in fact, it is the same river that is named as Tritsu. The city of Jariyasya is also located in the same region which is also known as Vaktra.

प्रान्तोऽस्ति 'मार्गियाना' पश्चिमतो 'वक्ट्रिया' प्रान्तात् ।
तत्र च हिन्दूकुशजा 'मरग्युसो' दङ्मुखी नदी वहति ॥143॥

Margiyana is the region located to the west of Vaktriya; the northward flowing river named Margyusa, which originates from Hindukush, flows in that region.

योऽर्वाक् तु मार्गियानाप्रान्ताद् हिन्दूकुशोऽस्य दक्षिणतः ।
उद्भूय पश्चिमां प्रागथोत्तरामनु तु या नदी वहति ॥144॥

From the southern part of Hindukush, which lies before the region Margiyana, originates a river that flows westward and towards north-east. [In ancient times, people of Bharatavarsha used to live there.]

प्राक्सीम्नि 'हरसियाना' प्रान्तस्यौ 'च्छुस' नदीन्तु यान्वेति ।
या च 'सरीफी' पर्वतपश्चिमपार्श्वानुगोत्तरां याति ॥145॥

'अरियुस' नदी तु सोक्ता सरयुः स्यात् सा नदी वेदे ।
दक्षिणतोऽस्याः प्रान्तः प्रथते वा एरियानेति ॥146॥

River Chus is the one that flows in the eastern border of the region Harsiyana and the one that flows through the western side is known as Ariyusa. In the Vedas, this river is referred to as Sarayu and the southern part of this region is famous as Ariyana.

प्रागेतदेरियानाप्रान्तात् प्रत्यक्तटे सुलेमानात् ।
प्रान्तो य इण्डियाख्यस्तत्र वसन्ति स्म भारतीयाः प्राक् ॥147॥

The region situated on the eastern side of Ariyana and the western side of the Suleman mountain is known as 'India' and in ancient times, people of Bharatavarsha used to live there.

फरहनदीनिर्गमने पारस्यानां तु 'पर्सिया' नगरी ।
तस्या उत्तरतः सा सरयुर्या 'मरियुसं' प्राह ॥148॥

The city Parsia of the Parsis was situated on the bank of river Faraha. Sarayu used to flow to the north of this river and was known as Mariyus.

अर्णचित्ररथयोः स्वजातिविद्वेषो वधे हेतुः ।

Caste-animosity was the reason behind the killing of Arna and Chitraratha.

तस्या सरयोः परितस्तावार्यावर्णचित्ररथौ ।
कुत्साद्यार्यगृहाणां परिस्थितिं दस्युषु स्म सूचयतः ॥149॥

तस्मादार्यावेव तु समूलघातं जघान स प्रथमम् ।
इति वामदेव ऊचे तुर्यस्य त्रिंशके सूक्ते ॥150॥

The Arya kings, Arna and Chitraratha, used to live across the river Sarayu. They used to spy on the Arya for the dasyus. In the thirtieth sukta of fourth mandala of Rigveda, Vamadeva states that these two were the first to be destroyed.

उत त्या सद्य आर्या सरयोरिन्द्र पारतः ।
अर्णाचित्ररथावधीः ॥

(ऋग्वेदः, 4.30.18)

O Indra! Those arya kings immediately killed Arna and Chitraratha who lived across river Sarayu.

सरस्वतीप्रान्तवासिचित्रराजापेक्षया सरयुप्रान्तवासिनः चित्ररथस्य भिन्नत्वम् ।

Chitraraja [inhabitant of Sarasvati region] vis-à-vis Chitraratha [inhabitant of Sarayu region].

यं सोभरिस्तु काण्वो दातारं भूरि तुष्टाव ।
सोऽन्यश्चित्रे राजा सरस्वतीतटेऽवसन्नृपप्रवरः ॥151॥

Chitraraja and Chitraratha were two different kings. Chitraraja was the one who used to live on the banks of Sarasvati. He has been highly praised by the descendent of Kanva Sobhari.

इन्द्रो वा घेदयन्मघं सरस्वती वा सुभगा ददिर्वसु ।
त्वां वा चित्र दाशुषे ॥

(ऋग्वेदः, 8.21.17)

'Kings who live on the bank of river Sarasvati are enlightened and praiseworthy rulers.'

चित्र इद् राजा राजका इदन्यके यके सरस्वतीमनु ।
पर्जन्य इव ततनद्धि वृष्ट्या सहस्रमयुता ददत् ॥

(ऋग्वेदः, 8.21.18)

'Ritvija, who offered havya to Indra, was blessed with wealth by him. Indra's disciple Sarasvati showered valuable gifts on him.'

अर्णचित्ररथयोः गन्धर्वत्वम् ।

Arna and Chitraratha being gandharvas.

अर्णश्चित्ररथो वा मन्ये स्यातामिमौ तु गन्धर्वौ ।
मन्ये तद्वधमेव त्वकीर्तयत्कुरुसुतिः काण्वः ॥

अभि गन्धर्वमतृणदबुध्नेषु रजःस्वा ।
इन्द्रो ब्रह्माभ्य इदवृधे ॥

(ऋग्वेदः, 8.66.5)

Both Arna and Chitraratha were Gandharvas. According to me, they were the two Gandharvas whose killings have been mentioned by Kanva's son Kurusuti in Rigveda: 'Indra removed these Gandharvas for the prosperity of sages.'

4.12 सप्तदस्युराजराष्ट्राभिक्रमणम्

4.12 ATTACK ON SEVEN DASYU RULERS

अञ्जस्याद्या दुस्तरा आपगाया आसंस्तासां पारमासाद्य कष्टात् ।
दस्युग्रामान् वीर आक्रम्य हत्वा कांश्चित् कांश्चिज्जीवतोऽपि न्यगृह्णत् ॥152॥

Anjasi and others went across the rivers and slaughtered and captured various groups of dasyus there.

सप्तभ्योऽशत्रुभ्यः शत्रुरभूदिन्द्र एष यानवधीत् ।
कुयवं शुष्णं शंबरमहिबंगृदरौहिणान् कृष्णम् ॥153॥

Indra killed seven of his ferocious dasyu enemies, namely Kuyava, Shushna, Shambar, Ahi, Bangrida, Rauhina, and Krishna.

एषां भुवनान्यासन् सप्तानां सप्तभिन्नतन्त्राणि ।
गणनागासुरभेदादेते सङ्कीर्णजातिका दासाः ॥154॥

All these dasyus used to rule over seven different regions. They belonged to the naga and asura races.

अहिरत्र नाग आसीदसुराः कृष्णश्च रौहिणो नमुचिः ।
अपरेऽपगणा वृत्त्या दस्यव एतेऽसुरानुगा अभवन् ॥155॥

Ahi was a naga. Krishna and Rauhina were *namuchi-asuras* (the demons) and other dasyus belonged to an inferior caste. These dasyus had instincts like the asuras and imitated them.

पर्वतयात्रायां रासभरथादयः परिकराः ।

Description of chariots pulled by donkeys on the mountain tracks.

रासभरथेन चेन्द्रो दस्युविदासाय पर्वतप्रान्ते ।
अचरद् विष्णुसहायः स बृहस्पतिरन्वितोऽश्विभ्याम् ॥156॥

Indra used chariots pulled by donkeys to slaughter the dasyus in the mountains. Vishnu's ally Brihaspati travelled on the ashvis.

हरयः पृष्ठानुचरा दश तु शतानीन्द्रमेतमनुचेरुः ।
मारुत्या सेनया भागत्रयमत्र सह भेजे ॥157॥

Indra was accompanied by three divisions of the maruta army, and was followed by thousand horse-riders.

हरिभिः सहस्रसंख्यैर्हरिवानुक्तः सहस्राक्षः ।
स मरुद्भिस्तु मरुत्वान् न विना हरिभिर्मरुद्भिः सः ।।158।।

Since he was escorted by thousand horses, Indra came to be known as Sahastraksa. He is also known by the name Vahamarutvana since he was accompanied by the marutas.

द्वौ तु हरी इन्द्राश्वौ खे भुवि चाभ्यामयं चरति ।
याति गिरीणां विषमं शृङ्गाच्छृङ्गान्तरं ताभ्याम् ।।159।।

Indra had two horses named Hari. He used to ride them through the mountains.

रौहिणासुरनिपातः ।

Fall of asura Rohina.

दस्युकुलध्वंसायाभिक्रममाणं निशम्य देवेन्द्रम् ।
स्वर्गं रिक्तं मत्वा तं जेतुं रौहिणश्चक्रमे ।।160।।

Rohina came to know about Indra's attack on the dasyus and decided to conquer svarga.

तं द्यामारोहन्तं सत्वरमाक्रम्य रौहिणं परितः ।
निजघान वज्रहस्तो देवेन्द्रः कम्पयन् दासान् ।।161।।

But before he could attack, the thunder-bearing Indra attacked Rohina mid-way and slaughtered all the dasyus.

4.13 अहिनिर्यातनम्

4.13 KILLING OF AHI

आसन् केचित् पर्वतास्तत्र दस्युग्रामो वासाऽध्वादि निर्गूहतेऽलम् ।
तेषामन्तः क्वापि शैलस्य गर्भे दासग्र्योऽहिर्नागवंशोऽध्यवात्सीत् ।।162।।

There were hills where groups of dasyus used to hide. The dasyu king, Ahi, used to live in the core of one of those mountains.

अहिरयमसुरः कुयवप्रभृतीनां दासमुख्यानाम् ।
साहाय्येन कदाचित् सिन्धोः स्रोतोऽवरोधनं चक्रे ।।163।।

He had blocked the flow of Sindhu with the help of Kuyava and other powerful dasyus.

सिन्धोः सप्तस्रोतांस्यन्यान्यग्रावगह्वरोद्भेदात् ।
तेषां यमदिग्वाहीन्ययनान्युपरोधयाञ्चक्रे ।।164।।

He had blocked one of the seven sources of Sindhu that used to flow southward.

शैलद्रोण्यामद्रिद्वययोगेन पथि संकीर्णे ।
स्थूलोपलैः प्रपातैः प्रचितैः स्रोतांसि रुद्धानि ।।165।।

The flow of Sindhu was blocked by placing massive stones in the steep valley of the mountain.

गिरिकुलगह्वरभागाः सर्वेऽप्यभवन् पयोभिराकीर्णाः ।
ओघः समुद्रवद्भूद्दुर्गैः कूटैरितस्ततः प्रचितः ।।166।।

The whole valley got inundated with water and was transformed into an ocean.

वंक्षण्यो याः सरितामद्रीणां याश्च वंक्षणा आसन् ।
तत्रापां बिलमखिलं प्रस्तरखण्डैर्निरोधयामासुः ।।167।।

The dasyus used to place huge stones in the caves of rivers and mountains and block all the routes of the water-flow.

स्रोतःसृत्यवरोधो रक्षार्थं दासपत्न्योऽग्र्याः ।
आसंस्तत्र नियुक्ता निरीक्षका यामिका बहवः ।।168।।

The dasyu women and several guards used to be deployed to protect the barricades of those sources.

तत्र च पयःप्रसारेऽन्तरीपदेशे विशालशैलस्य ।
अधरशिलाविस्फोटात् तिर्यग्विवरं चकार दूरतरम् ।।169।।

Overflowing water and the stone blasts created a slanting trench in the lower region of that mountain.

जलमयमन्तर्विवरं प्लवगम्यं तत्परं तमसा ।
छन्नं वर्त्म ततस्तद्विशति गिरेरुदरमत्यजिरम् ।।170।।

The water-filled inner outlet had to be crossed by swimming first and then an utterly dark route used to lead to the central part of that mountain.

तत्र च विविधाः शाला राजगृहाण्यपि, गृहाणि भृत्यानाम् ।
दृषदुत्किरणात् सिद्धान्यत्र च भाः शिखरविवरेभ्यः ।।171।।

Various shelters, residences and rest-houses for soldiers were built there by cutting stones. It used to get light through the crevices of the mountain.

इत्थं पर्वतगर्भे दृषदुद्धरणान्महाजिरे जाते ।
सिद्धेष्वनेकसदनेष्वहिरण्यमाशेत संवृतोऽम्भोभिः ।।172।।

Thus, Ahi used to live in this palatial complex of stone buildings, surrounded by water, in the heart of the mountain.

अम्भसि पर्वतगर्भे तमसाक्रान्ते बिलेशयः सोऽहिः ।
लोकान् दृष्ट्वा दृष्ट्वा गिरिकुहरेह्नोष्ट दुष्ट आत्मानम् ।।173।।

The cruel Ahi used to hide himself in the caves of the mountain to stay away from people; he stayed in a dark cave covered with water in the core of the mountain.

समुद्रे अन्तः शयत उद्ना वज्रो अभीवृतः ।
भरन्त्यस्मै संयतः पुरःप्रस्रवणा बलिम् ।।

(ऋग्वेदः, 8.89.9)

The eighty-ninth sukta of eighth mandala of Rigveda states: Indra places his thunderbolt in the middle of the ocean. Panic-stricken enemies retreat and offer sacrifices for Indra or for his thunderbolt.

इन्द्रस्तेषां पर्वतानां च पक्षांश्छित्वाक्रम्योद्बोधयामास सुप्तम् ।
अत्युग्राहिं तं जघानाद्रिभेदात्तस्मादापोऽगु: समुद्रं सरस्त: ।।174।।

Indra cuts the corners of mountains, awakens brutal Ahi and slaughters him. With mountains breaking apart, water drained into the ocean.

शैलद्रोण्यां वंक्षणाख्या अपां ये बन्धा आसन् दासपत्नीप्रगुप्ता: ।
ते च ध्वस्ता: शैलपक्षावभेदादाप: सर्वा: सप्तसिन्धुष्वगुस्ता: ।।175।।

The reservoirs, built in the valley and protected by the dasyu women, were devastated by the demolition of the mountain and water stored in them flowed into Saptasindhu (seven sources of river Indus).

सगरो नामस्थानं तदन्तरिक्षं यतो मूलात् ।
सिन्धो: सप्तस्रोतांस्युन्मोच्यावाहयत् सिन्धौ ।।176।।

The water of Sindhu flowed into the ocean after breaking its seven sources at the base of the place named Sagara.

तत्र प्रान्ते पर्वतश्रेणिबन्धे संरुद्धानां तह्र्यपां भूयसीनाम् ।
शैलोद्भेदात् स्रोतसाऽभूद् 'वितस्ता' भूमिप्रान्ते सिन्धुवारां प्रसार: ।।177।।

People were confounded by this and could not figure out the origin, the middle, and the end of water stored in the dams in the mountain ranges.

तत्रैकहेलयाऽपामोघविसारे पुराऽवरुद्धानाम् ।
क्वासां गूलं गध्यं वाऽन्तो वेत्यवगमे जना मुमुहु: ।।178।।

The previously contained water was so vast that it was difficult to see its origin, middle, and the end. People were bewildered.

4.14 शम्बरहत्यम्

4.14 KILLING OF SHAMBAR

प्रस्तोकाख्यः सृञ्जयपुत्रः कथितो दिवोदासः ।
'अतिथिग्व'श्व स एवाश्वथ उक्तो गर्गयजमानः ॥179॥

Srinjaya's son named Prastoka is known as Divodasa. He is also called Atithigva and Ashvatha. He was the patron of sage Garga.

'अतिथिग्वं तु 'कशोजुव' मपीडयच्छम्बरो दिवोदासम् ।
अश्विभ्यां मयमिन्द्रस्तमरक्षच्छम्बरं हत्वा ॥180॥

One dasyu, Shambar used to harass this Divodasa. This dasyu of the Maya class was killed by Indra with the help of ashvis.

अतिथिग्वशत्रुशम्बरनिग्रहणायेन्द्र आदिशत् पूर्वम् ।
तद्भयतो गिरिगह्वरतमसि पयःसंवृतः सोऽस्थात् ॥181॥

Indra ordered the slaying of Shambar, the enemy of Atithigva. Shambar got scared and hid himself in the dark trenches of the mountains.

अत्युच्चपर्वतोपरि गृहमासीत् किञ्चिदस्यान्तः ।
अवरोहणसोपानेऽभूदवतरितं तु कन्दरद्वारम् ॥182॥

Shambar had constructed a house on the top of a mountain. The stairs of that house led to a secret door.

उत्कीर्णाश्मकृताजिरमासीदुदरं गिरेस्तत्र ।
अन्तर्विविधाः शाला आसन् वर्त्मानि चत्वराणि सरः ॥183॥

A complex was built in the core of that mountain that had numerous shelters, routes, roundabouts, and lakes.

आरुह्यादौ शिखरं गृहान्तरद्वारमासाद्य ।
अवरोहणसोपानेनावतरन् विंशति गह्वारायतने ॥184॥

Shambar used to climb the mountain to reach the inner-door of the house and go down through the stairs to the secret complex.

इत्थं सोतिनिगूढं सुरक्षितं दुर्गमाश्रित्य ।
इन्द्रनियुक्तैश्चारैरलक्षितः शम्बरोऽजीवत् ॥185॥

He thus remained safe from Indra's emissaries in these safe and secret hill forts.

चत्वारिंशद्वर्षाण्यात्मानं निह्नुवानः सः ।
शुष्णनिबर्हाभिक्रमकालेऽकस्मादयं ददृशे ।।186।।

He managed to thus hide for almost forty years. But, suddenly, one day he appeared during the battle with Shushna.

पर्वतशिखरस्योपरि शम्बर एत्य स्थितो रिपुं द्रष्टुम् ।
शृङ्गान्निपात्य भूमौ तमश्विनौ जघ्नतुः क्रूरम् ।।187।।

When he came and stood on top of the mountain to search for the enemy, ashvis threw him down and killed him.

याभिर्महामतिथिग्वं कशोजुवं दिवोदासं शम्बरहत्य आवतम् ।
याभिः पूर्भिद्ये त्रसदस्युमावतं ताभिरूषु ऊतिभिरश्विना गतम् ।।
(ऋग्वेदः, 1.112.14)

The 112th sukta of first mandala of Rigveda states: O Ashvi devas! Come to us with the same strength that you exercised to protect Atithigva, Kashojuva, and Divodasa and to kill Shambar, and the one that you exhibited in the battle to devastate the cities of enemies.

शतमश्ममय्य आसन् शम्बरपुर्यो दृढाऽऽसु या मुख्या ।
आयस्येका शम्बरदस्योः सा राजधान्यासीत् ।।१८८।।

Shambar had a hundred stone cities. *Ayasi* [the iron-city] was his capital and the most popular city.

नवनवतिर्याः पुर्यस्तासामीशाश्च नवनवतिः ।
बाहव इव ते चासन् वशंवदाः शम्बरस्यास्य ।।189।।

The other ninety-nine cities were ruled by same number of leaders. They were followers of Shambar and strong like him.

निर्हत्य शम्बरं प्रागतिथिग्वायाददात्पुरीं मुख्याम् ।
नवनवतिं तु पुरीस्ताः सर्वा विध्वंसयामास ।।190।।

Indra gave Ayasi to Atithigva after killing Shambar. The other ninety-nine cities were devastated.

मध्ये मध्ये श्रान्तः स्थगितः समरे बभूव यर्हीन्द्रः ।
तर्हि भरद्वाजः सहकाले तत्रार्पयत्सोमम् ॥191॥

During the battle, rishi Bharadvaja would offer Soma to Indra whenever he paused fighting.

यस्य त्यच्छम्बरं मदे दिवोदासाय रन्धयः ।
अयं स सोम इन्द्र ते सुतः पिब ॥

(ऋग्वेदः, 6.4.31)

The fourth sukta of sixth mandala of Rigveda states: O Indra! Kindly drink the Soma prepared exclusively for you that encouraged you to kill Shambhar to favour Divodasa.

यत्सानोः सानुमारुहद् भूर्यस्पष्ट कर्त्वम् ।
तदिन्द्रो अर्थं चेतति यूथेन वृष्णिरेजति ॥

(ऋग्वेदः, 1.10.2)

You travel through mountains and ascertain the intention and quickly support the one who performs several deeds.

शम्बरपुरी विभेदनकर्मणि राजा तु यो नियुक्तोऽभूत् ।
त्रसदस्युन्तं दासैः प्रहण्यमानं ररक्षतुर्दस्रौ ॥192॥

The king who was appointed to destroy Shambarpuri was named Trasadasyu. He was protected by ashvis from the attack of dasyus.

'वर्ची' शम्बरसेनापतिरसुरस्तस्य वीरान् सः ।
इन्द्रो विष्णुसहायः शतं सहस्रं न्यवधीत् ॥193॥

With the help of Vishnu, Indra killed several thousand soldiers of Shambar's commander Varchi. Ninety-nine dasyu cities were destroyed and several thousand soldiers were killed along with Shambhar.

सखे विष्णो वितरं विक्रमस्व द्यौर्देहि लोकं वज्राय विष्कभे ।
हनाव वृत्रं रिणचाव सिन्धूनिन्द्रस्य यन्तु प्रसवे विसृष्टाः ॥

(ऋग्वेदः, 8.89.12)

In the eighty-ninth sukta of eighth mandala of Rigveda, it is stated: O friend Vishnu! Exhibit immense valour. O Deva! Give enough space for our thunderbolt. O Vishnu! Let us kill Vritra together and release water. Make the water flow straight to Indra.

शम्बरहत्ये नवति नव च पुरीरासुरीस्तु यद् व्यधमत् ।
यद्वा शतं सहस्रं वीरान् भूमौ न्यपातयत्साकम् ।।194।।

Ninety-nine dasyu cities were destroyed and several thousand soldiers were killed along with Shambar.

पर्वतभेदाच्चक्रे मार्गं सेनाभियानाय ।
कतिपयपर्वतपक्षानशातयत् सप्तसिन्धुषु यत् ।।195।।

स्रोतांसि दासरुद्धान्यचारयत्सागरं यावत् ।
महदिदमैन्द्रं वीर्यं प्रभाव उग्रोऽद्भुतं कर्म ।।196।।

A route for the movement of troops was carved out of the mountains. The water blocked by the dasyus was released to flow into the ocean. Indra's valour was full of aggression and extraordinary action.

पुरां भिन्दुर्युवा कविरमितौजा अजायत ।
इन्द्रो विश्वस्य कर्मणो धर्ता वज्री पुरुष्टुतः।।

(ऋग्वेदः, 1.11.4)

The eleventh sukta of first mandala of Rigveda states: When the thunder-armed Indra, the great destroyer of cities of enemy, doer of all actions, appeared, he was praised by all.

इन्द्रो मानुष आसीदमानुषं कर्म यच्चक्रे ।
तत्सर्वं व्याचष्टे गृत्समदो वज्रिणं स्तुत्वा ।।197।।

Indra performed humanly deeds, and was a simple human. Gritsamada [rishi] states it while praising Indra.

अहिशम्बरयोर्युद्धे पर्वतपक्षावभेदनादिन्द्रः ।
लेभे गोत्रभिदाख्यां पुरन्दराख्यां तु पुरशतोद्भेदात् ।।198।।

Indra has been famously named as Gotrabhida for cutting the sides of mountains and Purandar for devastating hundred cities.

यच्छम्बरसमकालो राजाऽऽसीद् भारते दिवोदासः ।
तदतो दस्युनियुद्धात्प्रागपि सभ्यस्थितिं विजानेऽत्र ।।199।।

Devodasa and Shambar were contemporaries in ancient Bharatavarsha. It is likely that civilized people used to live there even before the war with the dasyus.

4.15 कृष्णासुरत्वगुत्कर्तनम्

4.15 SKINNING OF ASURA KRISHNA

अंशुमती तु नदी या तस्यास्तीरेऽसुरस्तु कृष्णाख्यः ।
अयुतानुचरोपेतस्तत्प्रान्ते नृन् प्रपीडयन्नासीत् ।।200।।

The asura Krishna used to live on the banks of a river named Anshumati. He, along with his ten thousand followers, used to exploit the inhabitants of that region.

पश्चिमतो दक्षिणतश्चोत्तरतस्तं बृहस्पतिर्न्यरुणत् ।
इन्द्रः पूर्वत इत्वा मध्ये सन्तं तमाक्रामत् ।।201।।

He was blocked on the west, north and south by Brihaspati and Indra attacked him from the east.

सर्वाजय्यात्माभिमानेन दासस्तुच्छं जानन् सर्वमन्यं युयुत्सुम् ।
अभ्यायान्तं वीरमिन्द्रं प्रशंसन् हास्ये कृष्णः कौतुकादाजुहाव ।।202।।

The arrogant and self-proclaimed invincible Krishna disrespected all other warriors. However, he eulogized and invoked Indra.

स्तुतिमुखनिन्दां कुर्वन् राज्ञः पत्युः स्फुटं ब्रुवन् दोषान् ।
सन्धिं चेच्छन् रक्षां चार्थयते योद्धुमाह्वयति ।।203।।

Krishna invoked and taunted Indra, called him weak and yet sought protection from him, and thus he called out to Indra for a battle.

अस्तेव सुप्रतरं लायमस्यन्भूषन्निव प्रभरा स्तोममस्मै ।
वाचा विप्रास्तरत वाचमर्यो निरामय जरितः सोम इन्द्रम् ।।
(ऋग्वेदः, 10.42.1)

This battle is described in the forty-second sukta of tenth mandala of Rigveda: As an able archer shoots right on the target; O Vipra! Compose hymns for Indra and use them against your enemy. O worshipper! Win the favour of Indra.

दोहेन गामुप शिक्षा सखायं प्रबोधय जरितर्जारमिन्द्रम् ।
कोशं न पूर्णं वसुना न्यृष्टमा च्यावय मघदेयाय शूरम् ।।

किमङ्ग त्वा मघवन्भोजमाहुः शिशीहि मा शिशयं त्वा शृणोमि ।
अप्नस्वती मम धीरस्तु शक्र वसुविदं भगमिन्द्रा भरा नः ॥
(ऋग्वेदः, 10.42.2-3)

O worshipper! Please Indra for the fulfillment of desires, as a cow is milked. Invoke mighty Indra with your hymns to gain wealth. O Maghavan! Why are you called a benefactor? Bless me with wealth. You are famous for showering prosperity. May we become wise and blessed with supreme wealth.

त्वां जना ममसत्येष्विन्द्र सन्तस्थाना विह्वयन्ते समीके ।
अत्रा युजं कृणुते यो हविष्मान्नासुन्वता सख्यं वष्टि शूरः ॥
(ऋग्वेदः, 10.42.4)

O Indra! Invoked with reverence by all in battles, while invading, Indra befriends only those who offer havya, and and not the ones who do not partake Soma.

धनं न स्पन्द्रं बहुलं यो अस्मै तीव्रान्त्सोमाँ आसुनोति प्रयस्वान् ।
तस्मै शत्रून्त्सुतुकान्प्रातरह्नो नि स्वष्ट्रान्युवति हन्ति वृत्रम् ॥
(ऋग्वेदः, 10.42.5)

Indra kills Vritra and destroys enemies and blesses sons of the patron who offers Soma to him.

यस्मिन्वयं दधिमा शंसमिन्द्रे यः शिश्राय मघवा काममस्मे ।
आराच्चित् सन्भयतामस्य शत्रुर्न्यस्मै द्युम्ना जन्या नमन्ताम् ॥
(ऋग्वेदः, 10.42.6)

Indra fulfils their desire to gain supreme wealth who worship him. Indra's enemies get destroyed and he wins their wealth.

आराच्छत्रुमपबाधस्व दूरमुग्रो यः शम्बः पुरुहूत तेन ।
अस्मे धेहि यवमद्गोमदिन्द्र कृधी धियं जरित्रे वाजरत्नाम् ॥
(ऋग्वेदः, 10.42.7)

O *Puruhuta* (the one who vanquished the Purus) Indra! Destroy our enemies with your thunderbolt. Bless us with millet and cows. O Indra! Bless us with wealth and gems.

प्र यमन्तर्वृषसवासो अग्मन्तीव्राः सोमा बहुलान्तास इन्द्रम् ।
नाह दामानं मघवा नियंसन्नि सुन्वते वहति भूरि वामम् ॥
(ऋग्वेदः, 10.42.8)

Indra drinks strong and appetizing Soma. Indra never counters the patron who offers sacrifices. Indra makes him prosperous who offers him sufficient Soma.

उत प्रहामतिदीव्या जयाति कृतं नश्वघ्नी विचिनोति काले ।
यो देवकामो न धना रुणद्धि समित्तं राया सृजति स्वधावान् ।।
(ऋग्वेदः, 10.42.9)

As a true gambler beats the one who had defeated him earlier, so also, Indra attacks and slays the sinner.

गोभिष्टरेमामतिं दुरेवां यवेन क्षुधं पुरुहूत विश्वाम् ।
वयं राजभिः प्रथमा धनान्यस्माकेन वृजनेना जयेम ।।
(ऋग्वेदः, 10.42.10)

O Puruhuta! May we overcome ignorance with cows and hunger with millets. May we get superior wealth from kings and be victorious.

बृहस्पतिर्नः परिपातु पश्चादुतोत्तरस्त्मादधरादघायोः ।
इन्द्रः पुरस्तादुत मध्यतो नः सखा सखिभ्यो वरिवः कृणोतु ।।
(ऋग्वेदः, 10.42.11)

May Brihaspati protects us from three sides and Indra defends us from the east and centre. May our friend Indra bless us with supreme wealth.

अच्छा म इन्द्रं मतयः स्वर्विदः सध्रीचीर्विश्वा उशतीरनूषत ।
परिष्वजन्ते जनयो यथा पतिं मर्यं न शुन्ध्युं मघवानमूतये ।।
(ऋग्वेदः, 10.43.1)

My heart longs for omnipresence, friendship, fulfilment of all kinds of desires and worships Indra. Like women who embrace husbands to please them, we sing hymns for Indra.

न घा त्वद्रिगपवेति मे मनस्त्वे इत्कामं पुरुहूत शिश्रय।
राजेव दस्म निषदोभि बर्हिष्यस्मिन्त्सु सोमेऽवपानमस्तु ते ।।
(ऋग्वेदः, 10.43.2)

O Puruhuta, my heart seeks only you, and no one else. Only you I desire. O beautiful Indra! Sit like a king sitting on a throne and drink Soma.

विषूवृदिन्द्रो अमतेरुत क्षुधः स इन्द्रायो मघवा वस्व ईशते ।
तस्येदिमे प्रवणे सप्त सिन्धवो वयो वर्धन्ति वृषभस्य शुष्मिणः ।।
(ऋग्वेदः, 10.43.3)

May Indra stay with us to protect us from ignorance and hunger. Indra is the lord of wealth and all glory. May seven rivers of Sindhu produce grains of excellent quality.

वयो न वृक्षं सुपलाशमासदन्त्सोमास इन्द्रं मन्दिनश्चमूषदः ।
प्रैषामनीकं शवसा दविद्युतद्विदत्स्वर्मनवे ज्योतिरार्यम् ।।

(ऋग्वेदः, 10.43.4)

May Indra drink a chamas full of entrancing Soma. May Soma vitalise Indra and he blesses men with glory.

कृतं न श्वघ्नी विचिनोति देवने संवर्गं यन्मघवा सूर्यं जयत् ।
न तत्ते अन्यो अनु वीर्यं शकन्न पुराणो मघवन्नोत नूतनः ।।

(ऋग्वेदः, 10.43.5)

The way a gambler finds another gambler, similarly, Indra wins over the sun that obstructs rain. O Maghavan! There is no parallel to your strength and valour.

विशं विशं मघवा पर्यशायत जनानां धेना अवचाकशद्वृषा ।
यस्याह शक्रः सवनेषु रण्यति स तीव्रैः सोमैः सहते पृतन्यतः ।।

(ऋग्वेदः, 10.43.6)

Mighty Indra resides in all and answers their prayers. He who pleases Indra manages to defeats all his enemies with Soma.

आपो न सिन्धुमभि यत्समक्षरन्त्सोमास इन्द्रं कुल्या इव ह्रदम् ।
वर्धन्ति विप्रा महो अस्य सादने यवं न वृष्टिर्दिव्येन दानुना ।।

(ऋग्वेदः, 10.43.7)

The way rivers flow into ocean, channels flow into lake, similarly, Soma flows into Indra. The sages augment Indra's prominence as divine rain augments millet.

वृषा न क्रुद्धः पतयद्रजस्वा यो अर्यपत्नीरकृणोदिमा अपः ।
न सुन्वते मघवा जीरदानवेऽविन्दज्ज्योतिर्मनवे हविष्मते ।।

(ऋग्वेदः, 10.43.8)

Indra runs like an angry bull, rips clouds and releases water. Indra drinks Soma and enlightens the donor and worshipper.

उज्जायतां परशुर्ज्योतिषा सह भूया ऋतस्य सुदुघा पुराणवत् ।
विरोचतामरुषो भानुना शुचिः स्वर्णशुक्रं शुशुचीत सत्पतिः ।।
(ऋग्वेदः, 10.43.9)

May Indra rise with the lightning. May rita [the voice that gave birth to the cosmic order] be revived. And, may Indra, the protector of all, be illuminated like a sun.

गोभिष्टरेमामतिं दुरेवां यवेन क्षुधां पुरुहूत विश्वाम् ।
वयं राजभिः प्रथमा धानान्यस्माकेन वृजनेना जयेम ।। (ऋग्वेदः, 10.43.10)

O Puruhuta! May we overcome ignorance with cows and hunger with millets. May we get supreme wealth from kings and be victorious.

बृहस्पतिर्नः परिपातु पश्चादुतोत्तरस्मादधारादघायोः ।
इन्द्र पुरस्तादुत मधयतो नः सखा सखिभ्यो वरिवः कृणोतु ।। (ऋग्वेदः, 10.43.1)

May Brihaspati protect us from three sides and Indra defend us from the east and centre. May our friend Indra bless us with supreme wealth.

आयात्विन्द्रः स्वपतिर्मदाय यो धर्मणा तूतुजानस्तुविष्मान् ।
प्रत्वक्षाणो अति विश्वा सहांस्यपारेण महता वृष्ण्येन ।।
(ऋग्वेदः, 10.44.1)

May Indra, the lord of wealth, come for our happiness. Filled with energy and strength, Indra destroys all enemies. May he come to this sacrifice.

सुष्ठामा रथः सुयमा हरी ते मिम्यक्ष वज्रो नृपते गभस्तौ ।
शीभं राजन्त्सुपथा याह्यर्वाङ् वर्धाम ते पपुषो वृष्ण्यानि ।।
(ऋग्वेदः, 10.44.2)

O Indra, the lord of all! Owner of an elegant chariot, well-mannered horses and a thunderbolt, come to us and allow us to enhance your strength with Soma.

एन्द्रवाहो नृपतिं वज्रबाहुमुग्रमुग्रासस्तविषास एनम् ।
प्रत्वक्षसं वृषभं सत्यशुष्ममेमत्स्मत्रा सधमादो वहन्तु ।।
(ऋग्वेदः, 10.44.3)

May these horses bring the truthful, warrior, valiant, and cheerful Indra to us.

एवा पतिं द्रोणसाचं सचेतसमूर्जः स्कम्भं धरुण आ वृषायसे ।
ओजः कृष्व सङ्गृभाय त्वे अप्यसो यथा केनिपानामिनो वृधे ॥
(ऋग्वेदः, 10.44.4)

O Indra! Drink a vessel full of vitalising Soma and strengthen us. Be our guardian, because you give wisdom to learned and wise.

गमन्नस्मे वसून्या हि शंसिषं स्वाशिषं भरमायाहि सोमिनः ।
त्वमीशिषे सास्मिन्ना सत्सि वर्हिष्यनाधृष्या तव पात्राणि धर्मणा ॥
(ऋग्वेदः, 10.44.5)

O Indra! Since we worship you, bless us with supreme wealth. O Indra! Since you are the lord of all, come to our Soma yajna and bless us. Chaste and decorated are your Soma-pitchers. Thus, you come and bless us in this sacrifice.

पृथक् प्रायन् प्रथमा देवहूतयोऽकृण्वत श्रवस्यानि दुष्टरा ।
न ये शेकुर्यज्ञियां नावमारुहमीर्मैव ते न्यविशन्त केपयः ॥
(ऋग्वेदः, 10.44.6)

O Indra! Since ancient times, those who worship the devas gain passage to different devalokas; they are able to perform extremely difficult and glorious tasks. And those who do not ride the boat of yajna and are engaged in sins attain inferior status.

एवैवापागपरे सन्तु दूढयोश्वा येषां दुर्युज आयुयुज्रे ।
इत्था ये प्रागुपरे सन्ति दावने पुरूणि यत्र वयुनानि भोजना ॥
(ऋग्वेदः, 10.44.7)

Thus, the chariots of those who commit sinsare pulled by spoilt horses and such people are of inferior status. On the contrary, one who performs yajna attains high status [heaven], and is blessed with enormous wealth and food.

गिरीँरज्रान्रेजमानाँ अधारयद्द्यौः क्रन्ददन्तरिक्षाणि कोपयत् ।
समीचीने धिषणे विष्कभायति वृष्णः पीत्वा मद उक्थानि शंसति ॥
(ऋग्वेदः, 10.44.8)

Indra has stabilized charming but crumbling mountains. He roars in the sky, shakes the space, rules the space as well as the earth, drinks Soma and delightfully proclaims supreme words.

इमं बिभर्मि सुकृतं ते अङ्कुशं येनारुजासि मघवञ्छफारुजः ।
अस्मिन्त्सु ते सवने अस्त्वोक्यं सुत इष्टौ मघवन्बोध्याभगः ।।
(ऋग्वेदः, 10.44.9)

O Maghavan! Possessor of *ankush* [a defensive weapon], destroyer of sinners, may this sacrifice please you. O glorious Indra! Kindly accept our beautiful hymns offered to you through proper rituals in this Soma yajna.

गोभिष्टरेमामतिं दुरेवां यवेन क्षुधं पुरुहूत विश्वाम् ।
वयं राजभिः प्रथमा धानान्यस्माकेन वृजनेना जयेम ।।
(ऋग्वेदः, 10.44.10)

O Puruhut Indra! May we overcome ignorance with gau and hunger with millets. May we get supreme wealth from kings and be victorious.

बृहस्पतिर्नः परिपातु पश्चादुतोत्तरस्मादधरादघायोः ।
इन्द्रः पुरस्तादुत मध्यतो नः सखा सखिभ्यो वरिवः कृणोतु ।।
(ऋग्वेदः, 10.44.11)

May Brihaspati protect us from three sides and Indra defend us from the east and centre. May our friend Indra bless us with supreme wealth.

4.16 बङ्गृदादिदस्युग्रामाणां निर्मूलनम्

4.16 DESTRUCTION OF DASYU VILLAGES

पौरूरवसस्यायोः शत्रुं वेशं तु नम्रतामनयत् ।
षड्गृभिमरन्धयत् तं यः सव्यायादर्दयत्पूर्वम् ।।204।।

Pururava's son Ayu's enemy Vesha and Shadgrabhi, who harassed Savya, were slayed.

स्मदिभं तूग्रं कुत्सद्विषं श्रुतर्वद्विषं न्यहन् मृगयुम् ।
अश्मं चार्बुदमुरणं बलं दृभीकं रुधिक्रां च ।।205।।

Kutsa's immensely ferocious enemy Smadhibh and Shrutarva's enemies Mrigayu, Urana, Bala, Dribhik and Rudhikra were slaughtered.

सुश्रवसः पुनरार्यस्यासन् विद्रोहिणो दासाः ।
बङ्गृदकरञ्जपर्णमुख्याः क्रूराश्च निःषपिनः ।।206।।

The Arya king Sushruva's adversaries, the dasyus named Badagridh, Karanj and Parnay, were of cruel and wicked nature.

बङ्गृद एष ऋजिश्व द्वेषी पर्णयकरञ्जौ तु ।
अप्यर्बुदोऽतिथिग्वस्यायोर्वेशः सपत्नोऽभूत् ।।207।।

They were the enemies of Riji, Parnay, Karanj and Abrud Atithigva and a dasyu named Vesha was the enemy of King Ayu.

शम्बरवदस्य बङ्गृदनाम्नो दस्योः शतं पुर्यः ।
आसंस्ता अपि सर्वा मरुतो विध्वंसयामासुः ।।208।।

Like Shambar, Badagridh was also the ruler of hundred cities. The marutas destroyed all of them.

बङ्गृदप्रमुखानामभिमर्दे निर्हता दासाः ।
षष्टिसहस्राणीति प्रोचे सव्यस्त्रिपञ्चाशे ।।209।।

Almost 6,000 dasyus were killed in the battle against Badagridh, it has been mentioned by sage Savya in the fifty-third sukta of Rigveda.

4.17 शुष्णस्य निगडबन्धनं कुत्सकुवीयहननं च

4.17 CAPTURE OF SHUSHNA AND DEFENCE OF KUTSA

यो वा शुष्णः सर्वतः पूर्वमागात्सूर्यस्थानं तेऽत्र पुत्री दिवो यः ।
धृष्टोऽबध्नात् प्रेमपाशेऽथ तस्यै यातायातं भूयसा योऽत्रचक्रे ।।210।।

Initially, Shushna had come to surya sansthana. That insolent asura had allured a dasyu's daughter with his love, and used to visit regularly to meet her.

सर्वाशान्तेर्हेतुरासीत् स तस्माज्जीवन्तं तं तर्जयामास दण्डैः ।
दाम्नाबध्नाच्चाऽऽयसेन प्रगाढं कारागारे चाऽऽयसे तं न्यगृह्णात् ।।211।।

He was the root cause of all disturbances therefore he was beaten with sticks. He was bound with an iron chain and put in an iron cage.

सूर्यस्याधिष्ठाने शुष्णस्य निगडबन्धनं श्रुत्वा ।
कुयवः सहस्रसुभटैराक्रामीच्छुष्णन्तमुद्धर्तुम् ।।212।।

Shushna's imprisonment at the surya sansthana infuriated Kuyava. He attacked the site to free Shushna.

कुयवाक्रमणं रोद्धुं कुत्सः प्रतिचक्रमे सुभटैः ।
कुयवप्रबलाक्रमणात् कुत्सो विजितः पराभवं चापत् ।।213।।

Kutsa counter-attacked with his men to encounter Kuyava. But he could not thwart the fierce attack of Kuyava, and was defeated and humiliated.

विद्वान् प्रतूर्णिरिन्द्रः सहसाऽकस्मादुपस्थाय ।
कुयवाक्रमणात् कुत्सं परितत्रेऽन्याँश्च तत्रार्यान् ।।214।।

Indra rushed to Kutsa's rescue and saved him from Kuyava's attack and protected the Arya.

आक्रममाणं कुयवं प्रत्याक्रम्येन्द्र एष आहत्य ।
भूमौ निपात्य तरसा तस्य शिरश्छेदयामास ।।215।।

Indra counter-attacked and threw Kuyava down on the earth and pierced his head with immense force.

उन्नताधरधराधरस्थली स्यन्दनादिव शिफाग्र्यनिर्झरे ।
कृत्रिमोत्समुखसंपतत्पयः क्षीररवद्भवति शुभ्रमुज्ज्वलम् ।।216।।

Kuyava was a philanderer and used to bathe his two wives in the milky waters of Shipha river which looked like a spring of milk.

क्षीरवद्धवलधारया तया कौतुकात् कुयव एव नित्यशः ।
स्नापयत्युदकमध्यगः स्वयं स्वे स्त्रियौ जलविहारहर्षितः ।।217।।

स्त्रैण एष कुयवः स्वभार्ययोः प्रेमपाशहतविक्रमो हतः ।
दासराजवधजातविस्मया दस्यवो व्यपगता इतस्ततः ।।218।।

Every day, in the middle of those milky waters, Kuyava playfully bathed with his wives and enjoyed himself in frolicking. This Kuyava, entrapped in the passion of his two wives, was killed ingloriously. His death sent the dasyus helter skelter in fear and confusion.

क्षुब्धदासकुलमाकलय्य ते योषितौ च कुयवस्य तत्क्षणात् ।
स्वामिनं तमनुगन्तुमुद्यते योद्धुमेत्य निहते बभूवतुः ।।219।।

Two of Kuyava's wives, who had followed their husband into the battlefield, attacked with an army of angry dasyus but were killed.

निहते तु दस्युराजे कुयवे शुष्णे च शम्बरे चाहौ ।
सर्वेऽपि कान्दिशीकाः शेषा भेजुर्दिशो दासाः ।।220।।

The dasyus were directionless after the death of Kuyava, Shushna and Shambar, and had lost strength and action. All of them thereafter dispersed.

4.18 पञ्चाशत्सहस्रदस्युनिग्रहणम्

4.18 CAPTURE OF FIFTY-THOUSAND DASYUS

सप्तापीत्थं दासराजान् हिमाद्रिद्रोणीसंस्थानुग्रवीर्यन्निगृह्य ।
हत्वा चैषां सैनिकानां सहस्राण्युग्राण्यन्यानानयामास बध्वा ।।221।।

After slaughtering these seven dasyu kings, thousands of their soldiers were taken into confinement.

इन्द्रः पञ्चाशत्सहस्राणि तेषां नीत्वा प्राधाच्चायुराट् पारवश्ये ।
सम्यक् तेषा सभ्यताशिक्षणार्थं सोऽनेनाभूदायुराजो नियुक्तः ।।222।।

Indra directed King Ayu to enslave 50,000 dasyus and decreed him to 'civilize' them.

इत्थं प्राप्तो निग्रहं दस्युसङ्घः प्रतिष्ठोऽपि प्राक् प्रतिष्ठानराष्ट्रे ।
सोऽयं सभ्यः शिक्षितो वीरयोद्धा प्रातिष्ठानोऽभूत्प्रसिद्धः पुरात्वे ।।223।।

Thus, this famous dasyu race of the region Pratishtan was incarcerated. They were civilized and educated. In ancient times, the state of Pratishtan was famous for mighty warriors.

ये चेदानीं म्लेच्छवर्गे पठाना इत्याख्याता आयुराट्शिक्षितास्ते ।
प्रातिष्ठानाः क्षत्रियत्वे पुराऽऽसन् पश्चान्म्लेच्छैर्म्लेच्छतां प्रापितास्ते ।।224।।

The dasyus educated by King Ayu are known as 'Pathan' today. As they lived in Pratishtan they achieved the status of kshatriyas. But when they went with the mlecchas, they ceased to be kshatriyas and were known as mlecchas.

पूर्वे म्लेच्छा आहुरेके 'पतान' स्यापभ्रंशात्तं पठानेति शब्दम् ।
किन्त्वेकस्यासीत्पतानत्वमिष्टं नैते सर्वे तस्य वंशे प्रसूताः ।।225।।

In ancient times, the word 'Pathan' was considered as a distorted version of the word 'Patan'. Indeed, one Pathan dynasty could be related to Patan, but not all Pathans.

4.19 अपहृतराजेभ्यः कुत्सादिभ्यः इन्द्रकर्तृकं प्राग्वद् स्वस्वविभागदानम्

4.19 INDRA DISTRIBUTES SEIZED PROPERTY TO KUTSA AND OTHER KINGS

यद्यत् क्षेत्रं यद्धयपां स्रोत आसीदन्नानां वा स्तूपसामीत्तृणानाम् ।
दस्युक्लिष्टं सूर्यधामापि तत्तत् प्राग् यस्यासीत्तस्य तत्तस्ससान ।।226।।

All the resources of water, heaps of grain, heaps of grass and the suryadhams, forcibly taken by the dasyus, were returned to their original owners.

इत्थं निगृह्य दस्यूनिन्द्रो राज्ञां स्वकं धनं प्राग्वत् ।
कुत्सादिभ्यो विभजन् व्यभजत्सूर्यं च तद्वद्देवैभ्यः ।।227।।

Thus, Indra confined the dasyus and distributed their wealth among Kutsa and other kings and handed over the surya sansthana to the devas.

भूमेर्जलाशयानां सूर्यस्य च दस्युभिर्गृहीतानाम् ।
तेभ्यो विभागदानं यदभूद् वर्षागिरास्तदेवाहुः ।।228।।

The donation of land among kings after the defeat of the dasyus has been mentioned by Varshagirs [Varshagira's sons] in the Rigveda.

एतत् त्यत् त इन्द्र वृष्ण उक्थं वार्षागिरा अभिगृणन्ति राधः ।
ऋज्राश्वः प्रष्टिभिरम्बरीषः सहदेवो भयमानः सुराधाः ।।
(ऋग्वेदः, 1.100.17)

In the hundredth sukta of the first mandala, sage Varshagira states:

Along with other sages, we sons of Varshagira, namely, Rijrashva, Ambarisha, Sahadeva, Bhayaman, and Suradha, sing praises for the mighty Indra.

दस्यूञ्छिम्यूँश्च पुरुहूत एवैर्हत्वा पृथिव्यां शर्वा निबर्हीत् ।
सनत्क्षेत्रं सखिभिः श्वित्न्येभिः सनत्सूर्यं सनदपः सुवज्रः ।।
(ऋग्वेदः, 1.100.18)

The Puruhuta Indra and his warriors destroyed the cruel and violent, and rooted out their entire race with his thunderbolt. Thunder-bearing and brightly dressed Indra and his friends won back the earth, the sun and the ocean.

स मन्युमीः समदनस्य कर्ताऽस्माकेभिर्नृभिः सूर्य सनत् ।
अस्मिन्नहन्त्सत्पतिः पुरुहूतो मरुत्वान्नो भवत्विन्द्र ऊती ।।
(ऋग्वेदः, 1.100.6)

Indra is the destroyer of enemies, the cause of war that can be celebrated, lord of benign beings and praised by all. May we all be protected by Indra and the marutas.

इति मधुसूदनविद्यावाचस्पतिप्रणीतस्य ब्रह्मविज्ञान शास्त्रसंबन्धिनो ।
भारतवर्षीयार्यो पाख्याने दस्युसंहाराख्य श्चतुर्थः प्रसङ्गः संपूर्णः ।।4।।

Thus the translation of the fourth chapter, namely, destruction of dasyus, in the Bharatavarshiyaryopakhyan related to Brahmavijnanashastra of Madhusudan Ojha is concluded.

प्रक्रमः पञ्चमः

इन्द्रविजयाभिनन्दनम्

CHAPTER FIFTH

FELICITATION OF VICTORIOUS INDRA

5.1 विज्ञानशालायां विजयोत्सवः

5.1 VICTORY CELEBRATIONS

विज्ञानशालायां भारतीयार्यैः कृतः कृतज्ञतासूचको विजयमहोत्सवः ।
सारस्वते सूर्यसदने विजयाभिनन्दनमहोत्सवः प्रमहाख्यः ।

The conclusion of the celebration of victory organized by the Arya as a mark of gratitude. The conclusion of the grand celebration called Pramah at the surya-sadhana in the city of Sarasvati.

दस्यूनां निग्रहणादार्याणां च स्वराज्यसंप्राप्तेः ।
सुस्थेऽत्र सर्वलोके स्वार्गायेन्द्रः स गन्तुमभ्यैच्छत् ॥1॥

Having subjugated the enemies and having gained the independence for the superior beings, having also established the rule of law and order, Indra was ready to set upon his sojourn to the heaven.

आर्याणामधिवक्तुर्देवेन्द्रस्याद्य सम्मानम् ।
कर्तुं स कुत्स ऐच्छज्जनतास्तत्राभ्यमन्त्रयत् प्रमहे ॥2॥

In such an atmosphere of gaiety, sage Kutsa wanted to honour Indra. He consulted those present on how to celebrate Indra's victory and felicitate the saviour of the devas.

निषधगिरिस्थस्कन्धावारे शिविरेऽभवन् महः प्रथमम् ।
अद्य तु सूर्यस्थाने सोमाभिषवोत्सवं पुनर्व्यतनोत् ॥3॥

First of such events took place at the encampment on the Nishadh mountain with a drink of Soma and the celebrations were once again held in the city of sun.

सूर्यस्यायं सदने प्रमहो विजयाभिनन्दनीयो यः ।
तत्रेन्द्रमस्तुवन्निति विश्वामित्रश्च वक्ति सव्यश्च ।।4।।

In the celebrations held at the surya-sadana, Indra was showered with eulogies by the sages present there. Sages Vishvamitra and Savya said:

युधेन्द्रो मह्ना वरिवश्चकार देवेभ्यः सत्पतिश्चर्षणिप्राः ।
विवस्वतः सदने अस्य तानि विप्रा उक्थेभिः कवयो गृणन्ति।।
(ऋग्वेदः, 3.34.7)

The one who fulfils the wishes of mortal beings and is the guardian of those who are upright, has defeated the enemies by the sheer force of his might and acquired the wealth of the conquered for the sake of the gods. The learned men thus praise Indra with mantras.

न्यू षु वाचं प्रमहे भरामहे गिर इन्द्राय सदने विवस्वतः ।
नू चिद्धि रत्नं ससतामिवाविदन्न दुष्टुतिर्द्रविणोदेषु शस्यते ।।
(ऋग्वेदः, 1.53.1)

In the yajna being performed in the *ashram* [abode] of Vivasvan, Indra is being worshipped and praised in exceptional terms. Indra acquires and annexes property and everything else with the dexterity of a thief who steals the riches of those who have fallen asleep. Thus those who are defeated cannot fall upon the excuse of having been unfairly conquered.

उपकर्तृकृतोपकृतिं कीर्तयितुं यो महोत्सवः क्रियते।
उत्तरमहस्तदुक्तं तत्र च पानाशने गुणाख्यानम् ।।5।।

These celebrations of victory are known as *uttarmah* (beyond victory), accordingly described as valediction and contains mention of offerings including food.

बहुभिः सयुङ्नृपालैः कृतज्ञतां दर्शयंस्तदेन्द्राय ।
प्रमहे चक्रे हर्षात् तस्मिन् विजयोत्सवे कुत्सः ।।6।।

Sage Kutsa and a long list of kings expressed their gratitude for participating in the victory celebrations.

5.2 विश्वामित्रेण कृतं इन्द्राभिनन्दनसूक्तम्

5.2 EULOGY OF INDRA BY VISHVAMITRA

वीरपानप्रमहाध्यक्षो विश्वामित्रो दस्युवधं कीर्तयन् इन्द्रम् अभिनन्दयामास ।

On the occasion of celebrating victory with soma-pana, Vishvamitra eulogizing Indra while narrating the account of the killing of dasyus.

इन्द्रस्य कर्म सुकृता पुरूणि व्रतानि देवा न मिनन्ति विश्वे ।
दाधार यः पृथिवीं द्यामुतेमां जजान सूर्यमुषसं सुदंसाः ॥
(ऋग्वेदः, 3.32.8)

Thus said sage Vishvamitra, in the thirty-second sukta of third mandala of Rigveda: By the virtue of having accomplished noble deeds, he has encompassed both the heaven and earth through his magnificence and also created sun and moon. The virtue, noblity and deeds of Indra so named cannot just be rendered insignificant even by the devas of this world.

त्वमपो यद्ध वृत्रं जघन्वाँ अत्याँ इव प्रासृजः सर्तवाजौ ।
शयानमिन्द्र चरता वधेन वव्रिवांसं परिदेवीरदेवम् ॥
(ऋग्वेदः, 3.32.6)

O Indra! You are the one who killed the wretched Vritra, who had stopped the flow of water, by the force of a mighty arm moving with a redoubled force and freed the waters to flow freely like horses.

अहन्नहिं परिशयानमर्ण ओजायमानं तुविजात तव्यान् ।
न ते महित्वमनु भूदध द्यौर्यदन्यया स्फिग्या क्षामवस्थाः ॥
(ऋग्वेदः, 3.32.11)

O Indra! The creator of space and matter. O! The mightiest of all, you had slain the ferocious Ahi who had contained the waters of the earth. You were the one who held the earth in your powerful hand and yet no one knew about you in Dyauloka.

यज्ञो हि त इन्द्र वर्धनो भूदुत प्रियः सुतसोमो मियेधः ।
यज्ञेन यज्ञमव यज्ञियः सन् यज्ञस्ते वज्रमहिहत्य आवत् ॥
(ऋग्वेदः, 3.32.12)

O Indra! Yajna is performed for your success and the soma-rasa made for the yajna has become your favourite. Protect the holy fires of this yajna so that it can protect your vajra in the battle in which Ahi is to be killed.

मखस्य ते तविषस्य प्र जूतिमियर्मि वाचममृताय भूषन् ।
इन्द्र क्षितीनामसि मानुषीणां विशां दैवीनामुत पूर्वयावा ॥

(ऋग्वेद:, 3.34.2)

O Indra! I adore you, I worship you, and I sing the hymns in your praise so as to gain amrita. O Indra, you are the first among the devas and men.

महो महानि पनयन्त्यस्येन्द्रस्य कर्म सुकृता पुरूणि ।
वृजनेन वृजिनान्त्सं पिपेष मायाभिर्दस्यूँरभिभूत्योजा: ॥

(ऋग्वेद:, 3.34.6)

The deeds of you, the great Indra, are heroic and grand, and thus full of praise. Carrying the supreme force of his might, Indra has killed and defeated our arch enemies.

सत्रासाहं वरेण्यं सहोदां ससवांसं स्वरपश्च देवी: ।
ससान य: पृथिवीं द्यामुतेमामिन्द्रं मदन्त्यनु धीरणास: ॥

(ऋग्वेद:, 3.34.8)

O Indra! The one who has bequeathed a spiritual solemnity to both Dyauloka and Prithviloka; the slayer of the slain; the lovable of the loved; the mightier of the mightiest, and the nobler of the noblest. O! Indra, you bestow the wise ones with grace and fortitude.

ससानात्याँ उत सूर्यं ससानेन्द्र: ससान पुरुभोजसं गाम् ।
हिरण्ययमुत भोगं ससान हत्वी दस्यून्प्रार्यं वर्णमावत् ॥

(ऋग्वेद:, 3.34.9)

As alms, Indra gave horses, cow, sun, jewellery, and clothings made with gold. By destroying the fiends, Indra has saved the good people.

इन्द्र ओषधीरसनोदहानि वनस्पतीं रसनोदन्तरिक्षम् ।
बिभेद बलं नुनुदे विवाचोऽथाभवद्दमिताभिक्रतूनाम् ॥

(ऋग्वेद:, 3.34.10)

O Indra! You have given us medicinal herbs, vegetation, the day and antariksha. You vanquished Balasur and wiped out the arrogant and insensible. May your virtue protect us and remove pride and ignorance of the meaner ones.

सखा ह यत्र स सखिभिर्नवग्वैरभिज्ञ्वा सत्वभिर्गा अनुग्मन् ।
सत्यं तदिन्द्रो दशभिर्दशग्वैः सूर्यं विवेद तमसि क्षियन्तम् ॥
(ऋग्वेदः, 3.39.5)

Having gained the wisdom of material things, Indra proceeded to seek the inner light with the help of nine faithful [five vital breath, mind, conscience, intellect and ego] and ten other friends [five sensory organs and their five cognitions like touch, taste, smell, colour and sound] and ultimately found the true light, the sun, in the realm of darkness.

5.3 कुत्सेन कृतम् इन्द्राभिनन्दनसूक्तम्

5.3 KUTSA'S EULOGY FOR INDRA

अथ शान्तिकवीरपानानन्तरं प्रमहप्रमुखेन कुत्सेन कृतम् इन्द्रविजयाभिनन्दनसूक्तम् ।

Hymns sung by Sage Kutsa in praise of Indra after the ceremonial intake of Soma by the warriors.

प्र मन्दिने पितुमदर्चता वचो यः कृष्णगर्भा निरहन्नृजिश्वना ।
अवस्यवो वृषणं वज्रदक्षिणं मरुत्वन्तं सख्याय हवामहे ॥
(ऋग्वेदः, 1.101.1)

O mortals! Praise and adore Indra—the one who is radiant with the fervor and embodies wisdom at the tip of his tongue and has vanquished, accompanied by King Rijrashva, the remote and unknown citadels of arch-fiends. We, who desire protection from the enemies, invoke Indra, who carries the weapon of destruction in his right hand and is endowed with the ferocity of the great wind, to be our saviour.

यो व्यंसं जाहृषाणेन मन्युना यः शम्बरं यो अहन्पिप्रुमव्रतम् ।
इन्द्रो यः शुष्णमशुषं न्यावृणङ्मरुत्वन्तं सख्याय हवामहे ॥
(ऋग्वेदः, 1.101.2)

Indra, the one who killed a shoulder-less demon, the one who annihilated Shambar, the one who imprisoned the reckless Pipru and, above all, the one who destroyed the greatest of enemies Shushna. We supplicate before such Indra, to bless and protect us.

यस्य द्यावापृथिवी पौंस्यं महद्यस्य व्रते वरुणो यस्य सूर्यः ।
यस्येन्द्रस्य सिन्धवः सश्चति व्रतं मरुत्वन्तं सख्याय हवामहे ॥
(ऋग्वेदः, 1.101.3)

Indra, whose power compels admiration and recognition in Dyauloka and Prithviloka in equal measure and one who causes Varuna, Surya, and Sindhu to commence and cease. We invoke him to come and bless us.

यो अश्वानां यो गवां गोपतिर्वशी य आरितः कर्मणि कर्मणि स्थिरः ।
वीळोश्चिदिन्द्रो यो असुवन्तो वधो मरुत्वन्तं सख्याय हवामहे ॥
(ऋग्वेदः, 1.101.4)

Indra, the one who can restrain unbridled power and is thus the master of horses; the one who has compassion in him and is thus the master of the cows and one who is unaffected by changes, the one who slays those who do not abide by the ethics of yajna; we invoke such one to appear and bless us.

यो विश्वस्य जगतः प्राणतस्पतिर्यो ब्रह्मणे प्रथमो गा अविन्दत् ।
इन्द्रो यो दस्यूँरधराँ अवातिरन् मरुत्वन्तं सख्याय हवामहे ॥
(ऋग्वेदः, 1.101.5)

Indra, the one who is the creator of all organic beings, the one who obtained cows for the brahmins for the first time, the one who defeated and slayed the enemies. We invoke such one to appear and bless us.

य शूरेभिर्हव्यो यश्च भीरुभिर्यो धावद्भिर्हूयते यश्च जिग्युभिः ।
इन्द्रं यं विश्वा भुवनाभिसंदधुर्मरुत्वन्तं सख्याय हवामहे ॥
(ऋग्वेदः, 1.101.6)

Indra, the one who could be invoked both by those who are mighty and weak; the victor and vanquished, and the one who is thought to be the best and supreme among all. We invoke him to come and bless us.

रुद्राणामेति प्रदिशा विचक्षणो रुद्रेभिर्योषा तनुते पृथु ज्रयः ।
इन्द्रं मनीषा अभ्यर्चति श्रुतं मरुत्वन्तं सख्याय हवामहे ॥
(ऋग्वेदः, 1.101.7)

Indra, the one who is prudent and preserves the wind, spreads aura all across by bringing wind and the sun to Dyauloka. The one who is blessed by the gratitude of the mortals. We invoke him to come and bless us.

यद्वा मरुत्वः परमे सधस्थे यद्वावमे वृजने मादयासे ।
अत आयाह्यध्वरं नो अच्छा त्वाया हविश्चकृमा सत्यराधः ॥
(ऋग्वेदः, 1.101.8)

O Indra! Energized by wind! You are liked and admired by the poor and rich alike, charge forward and become an embodiment unto our yajna. O steadfast and radiant Indra! We, your devotees, are now offering this order of sacrifice to you.

त्वायेन्द्र सोमं सुषुमा सुदक्ष त्वा या हविश्चकृमा ब्रह्मवाहः ।
अधा नियुत्वः सगणो मरुद्भिरस्मिन्यज्ञे बर्हिषि मादयस्व ॥
(ऋग्वेदः, 1.101.9)

O Indra! The mightiest of warriors! We desire to seek your blessing thus we prepare the holy nectar [Soma-rasa]. O Indra! The one who could be pleased by hymns. We are offering this sacrifice to seek your blessings. O the protector of the horses! Come along with the train of wind and bless us.

मादयस्व हरिभिर्ये त इन्द्र विष्यस्व शिप्रे विसृजस्व धेने ।
आ त्वा सुशिप्र हरयो वहन्तूशन्हव्यानि प्रति नो जुषस्व ।।
(ऋग्वेद:, 1.101.10)

O Indra! You, who have tamed the horses with pleasure, utter blissful words. O the one with beautiful forehead! May the horses bring you unto us. O adorable Indra! May you grant us your bounty at yajna.

मरुत्स्तोत्रस्य वृजनस्य गोपा वयमिन्द्रेण सनुयाम वाजम् ।
तन्नो मित्रो वरुणो मामहन्तामदितिः सिन्धुः पृथिवी उत द्यौः ।।
(ऋग्वेद:, 1.101.11)

O Indra! The one who is adored by the wind and one who slays the fiends and protects us. May we obtain meaning and significance of life by adoring you. O Mitra, Varuna, Aditi, Sindhu, and Dyauloka, we supplicate and seek your help.

इमां ते धियं प्रभरे महो महीमस्य स्तोत्रे धिषणा यत्त आनजे ।
तमुत्सवे च प्रसवे च सासहिमिन्द्रं देवासः शवसा मदन्ननु ।।
(ऋग्वेद:, 1.102.1)

O Indra! The force of whose divinity is invigorated by the hymns we offer, so we supplicate to the supreme of devas. Indra, the one who has amassed infinite riches, and defeated the enemies, is adored even by the devas.

अस्य श्रवो नद्यः सप्त विभ्रति द्यावाक्षामा पृथिवी दर्शतं वपुः ।
अस्मे सूर्याचन्द्रमसाभिचक्षे श्रद्धे कमिन्द्र चरतो वितर्तुरम् ।।
(ऋग्वेद:, 1.102.2)

The grace of Indra abound in the seven rivers and his divine form is manifest in Dyauloka, prithvi, and antariksha. O Indra! You who give us light and to adore your bounty, both the sun and moon revolve and rotate.

तं स्मा रथं मघवन् प्राव सातये जैत्रं यं ते अनुमदाम संगमे ।
आजा न इन्द्र मनसा पुरुष्टुत त्वायद्भ्यो मघवञ्छर्म यच्छ नः ।।
(ऋग्वेद:, 1.102.3)

O Indra! The one who makes the hymns graceful. Your victories makes us jubilant. O! Make your chariot turn towards us and protect us! O, we your worshippers, seek you blessings and supplicate you to grant us peace.

वयं जयेम त्वया युजा वृतमस्माकमंशमुदवा भरे भरे ।
अस्मभ्यमिन्द्र वरिवः सुगं कृधि प्रशत्रूणां मघवन्वृष्ण्या रुज ।।
(ऋग्वेदः, 1.102.4)

O Indra! The wealthy one! May we win our enemies on account of your help! May you protect us, acquire wealth, and kill our enemies.

नाना हि त्वा हवमाना जना इमे धनानां धार्तरवसा विपन्यवः ।
अस्माकं स्मा रथमातिष्ठ सातये जैत्रं हीन्द्र निभृतं मनस्तव ।।
(ऋग्वेदः, 1.102.5)

O Indra! The one who is resplendent with wealth, who multitudes of mortals supplicate and worship. O! May you appear before us as you bask in the glory of victory.

गोजिता बाहू अमितक्रतुः सिमः कर्मन्कर्मपञ्छतमूतिः खजङ्करः ।
अकल्प इन्द्रः प्रतिमानमोजसाथा जना वि ह्वयन्ते सिषासवः ।।
(ऋग्वेदः, 1.102.6)

O Indra! The one whose arms have acquired the compassion of cows and the one who himself is endowed with incomparable power; the one who is the cause of every effect and the one who is an eternal warrior whose prowess is supreme. We, who desire to procure similar wealth of virtue, invoke him.

उत्ते शतान्मघवन्नुच्च भूयस उत्सहस्राद्रिरिचे कृष्टिषु श्रवः ।
अमात्रं त्वां धिषणा तित्विषे मह्यधा वृत्राणि जिघ्नसे पुरन्दर ।।
(ऋग्वेदः, 1.102.7)

O Indra! The one who is capable of having myriads of forms and thus begets fame and renown beyond these. The hymns sung in praise of Indra multiplies in intensity as he charges forward to vanquish the enemies and annihilate the dwellings of fiends.

त्रिविष्टिधातु प्रतिमानमोजसस्तिस्रो भूमिर्नृपते त्रीणि रोचना ।
अतीदं विश्वं भुवनं ववक्षिथा शत्रुरिन्द्र जनुषा सनादसि ।।
(ऋग्वेदः, 1.102.8)

O Indra! The guardian of the mortals, your might does not call for any proof as such. O you! The one who rules over the three realms, the three auras, and extends his authority all across the universe, as you have vanquished all enemies since times immemorial.

त्वां देवेषु प्रथमं हवामहे त्वं बभूथ पृतनासु सासहिः ।
सेमं नः कारुमुपमन्युमुद्भिदमिन्द्रः कृणोतु प्रसवे रथं पुरः ॥
(ऋग्वेदः, 1.102.9)

O Indra! Gods call upon you since you slay the enemies. May the one charge forward and move through chariot so that we can win this eternal war.

त्वं जिगेथ न धना रुरोधिथार्भेष्वाजा मघवन्महत्सु च ।
त्वामुग्रमवसे सं शिशीमस्यथा न इन्द्र हवनेषु चोदय ॥
(ऋग्वेदः, 1.102.10)

O Indra! The one who prevails upon the enemies and blesses everybody with the wealth acquired. We, the rich and small alike, call upon you to protect us in war and prompt us towards victory in the war.

विश्वाहेन्द्रो अधिवक्ता नो अस्त्वपरिह्वताः सनुयाम वाजम् ।
तन्नो मित्रो वरुणो मामहन्तामदितिः सिन्धुः पृथिवी उत द्यौः ॥
(ऋग्वेदः, 1.102.11)

O Indra! You are the one who always favours us and inculcates the wisdom of compassion in ourselves. May mitra, Varuna, aditi, Sindhu, prithvi, and Dyauloka grant us enough virtue.

तत् त इन्द्रियं परमं पराचैरधारयन्त कवयः पुरेदम् ।
क्षमेदमन्यद्दिव्यन्यदस्य समी पृच्यते समनेव केतुः ॥
(ऋग्वेदः, 1.103.1)

Sage Kutra Angirasa said: O Indra! One whose immense power has been praised and one who has been hailed as the vanquisher of enemies by the learned on prithvi and in the Dyauloka.

स धारयत्पृथिवीं पप्रथच्च वज्रेण हत्वा निरपः ससर्ज ।
अहन्नहिमभिनद्रौहिणं व्यहन्व्यंसं मघवा शचीभिः ॥
(ऋग्वेदः, 1.103.2)

O Indra! The one who has embodied prithvi and extended it. The one who has slayed Vritra with his mighty arms and freed the flow of water. The one who has killed Ahir, Ahivasur, and Vyanasur.

स जातूभर्मा श्रद्दधान ओजः पुरो विभिन्दन्नचरद्वि दासीः ।
विद्वान्वज्रिन्दस्यवे हेतिमस्यार्यं सहो वर्धया द्युम्नमिन्द्र ।।
(ऋग्वेदः, 1.103.3)

O Indra! O the mighty one,who carries weapons as swift as the force of lightning and one who has pleased the gods of war. The one who has fiercely destroyed the enemy dwellings. O, the wise and mighty Indra! Kill the enemies of your devotees and bless us with fame and renown.

तदूचुषे मानुषेमा युगानि कीर्तेन्यं मघवा नाम बिभ्रत् ।
उपप्रयन्दस्युहत्याय वज्री यद्ध सूनुः श्रवसे नाम दधे ।।
(ऋग्वेदः, 1.103.4)

The one, who carried the mighty arms and the one who slained the enemies and the one who became famous on this account shall be worshipped and adored till times immemorial.

तदस्येदं पश्यता भूरिपुष्टं श्रदिन्द्रस्य धत्तन वीर्याय ।
स गा अविन्दत्सो अविन्ददश्वान्त्स ओषधीः सो अपः स वनानि ।।
(ऋग्वेदः, 1.103.5)

O Indra! The one who obtained supreme forms of wealth in cows, horses, waters, and the like. May you, the mighty warrior Indra, be adored by the mortals.

भूरिकर्मणे वृषभाय वृष्णे सत्यशुष्माय सुनवाम सोमम् ।
य आदृत्या परिपन्थीव शूरोऽऽयज्वनो विभजन्नेति वेदः ।।
(ऋग्वेदः, 1.103.6)

O Indra! You are the one who is a warrior par excellence, blesses the wise ones and punishes those who hoard money and do not perform yajna and those who are demons. He is the one who blesses the wise ones and does noble deeds like giving alms and protecting the truth. May we thus drink this Soma to the health of truthful, noble, mighty, and alms giver.

तदिन्द्र प्रेव वीर्यं चकर्थ यत्ससन्तं वज्रेणाबोधयोऽहिम् ।
अनु त्वा पत्नीर्हृषितं वयश्च विश्वे देवासो अमदन्ननु त्वा ।।
(ऋग्वेदः, 1.103.7)

O Indra! You are the one who prevailed upon the slumbrous Ahi by the force of your mighty arm and caused the nymphs around to worship you and thus made the wind and all the gods adore you. O! You are the one who proved the might of your prowess.

शुष्णं पिप्रुं कुयवं वृत्रमिन्द्र यदावधीर्विपुरः शम्बरस्य ।
तन्नो मित्रो वरुणो मामहन्तामदितिः सिन्धुः पृथिवी उत द्यौः ॥
(ऋग्वेदः, 1.103.8)

O Indra! While you slained Shushna, Pipru, Kuvaya, and Vrithva, you also plundered the dwellings of Samerasur. May thus mitra, Varuna, aditi, Sindhu, prithvi and Dyauloka bless us.

योनिष्ट इन्द्र निषदे अकारि तमा निषीद स्वानो नार्वा ।
विमुच्या वयोऽवसायाश्वान्दोषा वस्तोर्वहीयसः प्रपित्वे ॥
(ऋग्वेदः, 1.104.1)

O Indra! We have received this place to be, thus, fit for your abode. We invoke you to bless and receive the sacrificial rites just like the horses who have been freed from a day's labour.

ओ त्ये नर इन्द्रमूतये गुर्नू चित्तान्त्सद्यो अध्वनो जगम्यात् ।
देवासो मन्युं दासस्य श्चम्नन्ते न आवक्षन्त्सुविताय वर्णम् ॥
(ऋग्वेदः, 1.104.2)

When the yearning mortals came forth and supplicated before Indra, he guided them to tread upon the right path and thus strengthened the devas to annihilate the demons and facilitate the performance of yajna. May Indra come unto us.

अव त्मना भरते केतवेदा अव त्मना भरते फेनमुदन् ।
क्षीरेण स्नातः कुयवस्य योषे हते ते स्यातां प्रवणे शिफायाः ॥
(ऋग्वेदः, 1.104.3)

Kuyasur, the one who is the knower of the hidden riches of the earth, is himself the one who steals the wealth of others and makes the water of rivers get diverted towards his dwelling to facilitate his wives to bathe. O Indra! May you come and destroy them both, by drowning them in river Shipha.

युयोप नाभिरुपरस्यायोः प्र पूर्वाभिस्तरते राष्टि शूरः ।
अञ्जसी कुलिशी वीरपत्नी पयो हिन्वाना उदभिर्भरन्ते ॥
(ऋग्वेदः, 1.104.4)

The dwelling of the demons is behind the skies and their power comes from the mighty waters of the rivers; they are thus blessed by the waters of the river.

प्रति यत् स्या नीथादर्शि दस्योरोको नाच्छा सदनं जानती गात् ।
अधस्मा नो मघवञ्चर्कृतादिन्मा नो मघेव निष्षपी परादाः ॥
(ऋग्वेदः, 1.104.5)

O Indra! We have seen the place where demons abound and the path that leads us to the house of demons. O! Bounteous Indra! Protect us from the demons and don't abandon us; be with us.

स त्वं न इन्द्र सूर्ये सो अप्स्वनागास्त्व आ भज जीवशंसे ।
मान्तरां भुजमां रीरिषो नः श्रद्धितं ते महत इन्द्रियाय ॥
(ऋग्वेदः, 1.104.6)

O Indra! Illumine us with the light of the sun, shower us with the waters of seas and rivers and engage us in deeds noble and pure. O Indra! Don't pity us, the subjects, as we have truthfully adored the might of your prowess.

अधा मन्ये श्रत्ते अस्मा अधायि वृषा चोदस्व महते धनाय ।
गा नो अकृते पुरुहूत योनाविन्द्र क्षुध्यद्भ्यो वय आसुतिं दाः ॥
(ऋग्वेदः, 1.104.7)

O the mighty and rich, I honour you, I adore you for your might. Lead us to the path of virtue, enrich us with virtues and make the bounties fall upon those who are poor.

मा नो वधीरिन्द्रमा परादा मा नः प्रिया भोजनानि प्रमोषीः ।
आण्डा मा नो मघवञ्छक्र निर्भेन्मा नः पात्रा भेत्सहजानुषाणि ॥
(ऋग्वेदः, 1.104.8)

O! The virtuous and noble Indra! Don't despise us, don't abandon us, don't deflect our sacrificial rites, and don't deprive the already born and newly born of your love and compassion.

अर्वाङेहि सोमकामं त्वाहुरयं सुतस्तस्य पिबा मदाय ।
उरुव्यचा जठर आवृषस्व पितेव न शृणुहि हूयमानः ॥
(ऋग्वेदः, 1.104.9)

O Indra! You, who are fond of Soma, appear before us. This Soma that we have made for you to drink, to become content and blissful. May you grant our prayers like a patriarch.

5.4 इन्द्रविजयाभिनन्दने वार्षागिराणां कुत्ससहयोगित्वम् आत्मसमर्पणम् च

5.4 HYMNS PRAISING INDRA OFFERED BY SONS OF KUTSA

इन्द्रविजयाभिनन्दसूक्ते वार्षागिराणां राज्ञां कुत्ससहयोगित्वम् ।

Hymns hailing the support of Varshagir's sons, who were kings, to Kutsa.

ऋज्राश्वाद्याः पञ्च वार्षागिराख्या राजानः प्रागिन्द्रतो नष्टकष्टाः ।
दस्युध्वंसेऽत्युग्रमैन्द्रं चरित्रं संसद्युक्त्वाऽख्यापयन् सर्वलोके ॥7॥

Of those whom Indra had rescued—Rijrashva and the other kings of Vrishagiri thus gathered to sing hymns in praise of the mighty and great Indra, who had vanquished the enemies.

पञ्चदशर्क्षु न्यास्थन् संस्तविकं त्वं वृषागिरः पुत्राः ।
चतसृष्वन्ते कौत्सात् संस्तविकाच्च सहयोगिताऽत्रास्य ॥8॥
संरक्षकतामेते याचन्ते तेन करदानम् ।
अभ्युपगम्यात्मानं न्यवेदयन्निन्द्रपारतन्त्र्येऽपि ॥9॥

Of the five compositions to supplicate Indra, the kings of Vrishagiri, in the last four compositions, seek the protection of Indra by offering him taxes and surrendering to him.

वार्षागिराणाम् आत्मसमर्पणम् ।

The surrender of Varshagirs.

इन्द्रविजयाभिनन्दने वार्षागिराणां कुत्ससहयोगेन आत्मसमर्पणं सूक्तम् ।

Clear description of the surrender of Varshagiri kings with the help of Kutsa in the hymn explaining the surrender.

स यो वृषा वृष्ण्येभिः समोका महो दिवः पृथिव्याश्च सम्राट् ।
सतीनसत्वा हव्यो भरेषु मरुत्वान्नो भवत्विन्द्र ऊती ॥
(ऋग्वेदः, 1.100.1)

The kings of Varshagiri offered the following hymns in the victory celebration of Indra: 'O Indra! The one who is mighty and seeks the company of those who are rich and wealthy, the one who is the king of heaven and earth. The one who makes the waters flow and thus is indispensable for victory in the wars. May Indra, endowed with the power of wind, protect us.

यस्यानाप्तः सूर्यस्येव यामो भरे भरे वृत्रहा शुष्मो अस्ति ।
वृषन्तमः सखिभिः स्वेभिरेवैर्मरुत्वान्नो भवत्विन्द्र ऊती ।।
(ऋग्वेदः, 1.100.2)

O Indra! The one whose power is as incomprehensible as the heat of sun and none could be more ferocious than him. The one who kills Vritra and thus becomes invincible. And the one who combines the power of winds to become deadly and mighty. May Indra, carrying the force of wind, protect us.

दिवो न यस्य रेतसो दुघानाः पन्थासो यन्ति शवसापरीताः ।
तरद्द्वेषाः सासहिः पौंस्येभिर्मरुत्वान्नो भवत्विन्द्र ऊती ।।
(ऋग्वेदः, 1.100.3)

O Indra! The blessing of one whose grace could create fertility all around, and the one who could always be marching ahead is also the one who could kill all the enemies within and beyond. May Indra, the friend of wind, protect us.

सो अङ्गिरोभिरङ्गिरस्तमो भूद्वृषा वृषभिः सखिभिः सखा सन् ।
ऋग्मिभिर्ऋग्मी गातुभिर्ज्येष्ठो मरुत्वान्नो भवत्विन्द्र ऊती ।।
(ऋग्वेदः, 1.100.4)

The one who is adorable amongst all sages, best among all friends and mightiest among all mighty and supplicable among all the supplicates and desirable among all the desired. May Indra, the one who is equal to wind, protect us.

स सूनुभिर्न रुद्रेभिर्ऋभ्वा नृषाह्ये सासह्वाँ अमित्रान् ।
सनीळेभिः श्रवस्यानि तूर्वन् मरुत्वान्नो भवत्विन्द्र ऊती ।।
(ऋग्वेदः, 1.100.5)

Indra! The one who is affectionate like the sun and the one who has defeated the enemies in the wars with the powers of wind. May Indra, the one who controls the wind, the one who causes plants to grow and waters to fall down, protect us.

स मन्युमीः समदनस्य कर्ताऽस्माकेभिर्नृभिः सूर्यं सनत् ।
अस्मिन्नहन्त्सत्पतिः पुरुहूतो मरुत्वान्नो भवत्विन्द्र ऊती ।।
(ऋग्वेदः, 1.100.6)

The one whose radiance scares the enemies and the one who attends to the joy of victory with heroic heart, and the one who goes upon the war and protects the compassionate. Indra, whom everybody adores, shall bring the light back to us from the demons. May Indra protect us.

तमूतयो रणयञ्छूरसातौ तं क्षेमस्य क्षितयः कृण्वत त्राम् ।
स विश्वस्य करुणस्येश एको मरुत्वान्नो भवत्विन्द्र ऊती ।।
(ऋग्वेदः, 1.100.7)

The warriors have pleased Indra by heroic deeds in the wars in which so much of wealth is acquired and the subjects have made him the protector of everything. The one who is an embodiment of wisdom and virtue of everything; may Indra, the friend of winds, protect us.

तमप्सन्त शवस उत्सवेषु नरो नरमवसे तं धनाय।
सो अन्धे चित्तमसि ज्योतिर्विदन्मरुत्वान्नो भवत्विन्द्र ऊती ।।
(ऋग्वेदः, 1.100.8)

O Indra! The one who is pleased on account of war and victory celebrations; The one who has brought light to the darkness; may he be our protector.

स सव्येन यमति व्राधतश्चित्स दक्षिणे संगृभीता कृतानि ।
स कीरिणा चित्सनिता धनानि मरुत्वान्नो भवत्विन्द्र ऊती ।।
(ऋग्वेदः, 1.100.9)

The one in whose left hand lies the power to vanquish enemies and in his right hand is hidden all the virtues of the time and the one who is pleased just by the hymns and grants wealth. May he be our guardian.

स ग्रामेभिः सनिता स रथेभिर्विदे विश्वाभिः कृष्टिभिर्न्वद्य ।
स पौंस्येभिरभिभूरशस्तीर्मरुत्वान्नो भवत्विन्द्र ऊती ।।
(ऋग्वेदः, 1.100.10)

That Indra grants wealth from the association of marutas and by chariots. He is known even today by one and all, and he vanquishes the detractable enemies with his powers. May that powerful Indra be our guardian.

स जामिभिर्यत्समजाति मीह्लेऽजामिभिर्वा पुरुहूत एवैः ।
अपां तोकस्य तनयस्य जेषे मरुत्वान्नो भवत्विन्द्र ऊती ।।
(ऋग्वेदः, 1.100.11)

The one who is supplicated by many, and the one who goes equally well with those who like him and also those who don't. Still, like a protector, he brings victory for them. May he, in whom the wind is embodied, be our guardian.

स वज्रभृद्दस्युहा भीम उग्रः सहस्रचेताः शतनीथ ऋभ्वा ।
चम्रीषो न शवसा पाञ्चजन्यो मरुत्वान्नो भवत्विन्द्र ऊती ॥
(ऋग्वेदः, 1.100.12)

O Indra! The one who carries the arms, kills the fiends, becomes ferocious, mighty, wise and shrewd. The one who is incomparable and is also the inheritor of five principal forces and thus, protects five kinds of mortals. May Indra, the carrier of wind, be our guardian.

तस्य वज्रः कन्दति स्मत्स्वर्षा दिवो न त्वेषो रवथः शिमीवान् ।
तं सचन्ते सनयस्तं धनानि मरुत्वान्नो भवत्विन्द्र ऊती ॥
(ऋग्वेदः, 1.100.13)

The one whose arms fall like thunder, the one who protects heaven and is radiant, prudent, and virtuous in all deeds—in wealth and alms. May he be our guardian.

यस्याजस्रं शवसा मानुमुक्थं परिभुजद्रोदसी विश्वतः सीम् ।
स पारिषत्क्रतुभिर्मन्दसानो मरुत्वान्नो भवत्विन्द्र ऊती ॥
(ऋग्वेदः, 1.100.14)

O Indra! The one whose valour protects both the domains of existence. The one whose brave deeds should make us free from all worries. May he be our guardian.

न यस्य देवा देवता न मर्त्ता आपश्चन शवसो अन्तमापुः ।
स प्ररिक्वा त्वक्षसा क्ष्मो दिवश्च मरुत्वान्नो भवत्विन्द्र ऊती ॥
(ऋग्वेदः, 1.100.15)

O Indra! The one whose secret of might, wisdom, prudence, and virtue is not to be known, even by the gods, mortals, and the waters. The one who is the most prized on earth and heaven on account of his great powers. May he be our guardian.

रोहिच्छ्यावा सुमदंशुर्ललामीर्द्युक्षा राय ऋज्राश्वस्य ।
वृषण्वन्तं बिभ्रती धूर्षु रथं मन्द्रा चिकेत नाहुषीषु विक्षु ॥
(ऋग्वेदः, 1.100.16)

Embellished with red and black ornaments, Manushi is driving the chariot with powerful Indra in the seat, to protect sage Rijrashva.

एतत्त्यत्त इन्द्र वृष्ण उक्थं वार्षागिरा अभिगृणन्ति राधः ।
ऋज्राश्वः प्रष्टिभिरम्बरीषः सहदेवो भयमानः सुराधाः ।।
(ऋग्वेदः, 1.100.17)

O Indra! The sages who live in your neighbourhood—Rijrashva, Ambarisha, Sahadeva, Bhayaman and Suradha—all of them, sons of Varshagira supplicate you from the heart of their hearts.

दस्यूञ्छिम्यूँश्च पुरुहूत एवैर्हत्वा पृथिव्यां शर्वा निबर्हीत् ।
सनत्क्षेत्रं सखिभिः श्वित्न्येभिः सनत्सूर्यं सनदपः सुवज्रः ।।
(ऋग्वेदः, 1.100.18)

The one who has killed fiends and enemies by the force of his mighty arms. The one who carries the most powerful of weapons, has subjugated everything accompanied by his peers and and freed the sun and water. May he be our guardian.

विश्वाहेन्द्रो अधिवक्ता नो अस्त्वपरिह्वताः सनुयाम वाजम् ।
तन्नो मित्रो वरुणो मामहन्तामदितिः सिन्धुः पृथिवी उत द्यौः ।।
(ऋग्वेदः, 1.100.19)

O Indra! Grant us wisdom, grant us kindness and grant us life. O mitra, Varuna, aditi, Sindhu, prithvi and Dyauloka be our companion and bless us.

5.5 अन्यैः कृताः सूक्तवाकाः

5.5 THANKSGIVING BY OTHER ARYA

इतः परं कुत्सवत् अन्येषाम् अपि आर्याणां यत्र प्रमहे धन्यवादरूपाः सूक्तवाकाः ।

Thereupon, like Kutsa, thanksgiving hymns by other Arya.

कुत्सवदन्येषामप्यार्याणामूतिरिन्द्रेण।
काले काले बहुधा कृतेति तेऽप्यागमन् प्रमहे ॥10॥

Thereupon, like Kutsa, other Arya offered hymns in honour of Indra. Like Kutsa, Indra has granted protection to other superior beings from time to time and they too wanted to join the celebration.

किन्त्वेषामखिलानां ये यावन्तः प्रतिष्ठिताः प्रवराः ।
आसन् त एव सूक्तान्यावेदयितुं नियोजिता अभवन् ॥11॥

Yet only those who were best among them were ordained to render hymns.

तत्र हिरण्यस्तूपः सव्यभरद्वाजवामदेवाश्च ।
अपि दुर्मित्रः कौत्सो बहदुक्थो वामदेव्यश्च ॥12॥

वत्सश्रुष्टिगुमेध्यागर्गसुहोत्रौ च शुनहोत्रः ।
गौतमनोधः कक्षीवन्तस्तद्वत् परुच्छेपः ॥13॥

गृत्समदोऽथावस्युर्बभ्रुर्गातुस्तथाऽगस्त्यः ।
विश्वामित्रो विमदः संवरणो वा प्रजापतेः पुत्र ॥14॥

अपि च वसिष्ठो वसुकृद् वासुक्रो गौरिवीतिश्च।
अष्टादंष्ट्रोऽन्योऽन्यः शतप्रभेदन इमौ तु वै रूपौ ॥15॥

वैखानसस्तु वभ्रो मरुत् तिरश्चीर्द्युतानो वा ।
एषां पश्चादिन्द्रः किञ्चिदुवाचेह वामदेवाय ॥16॥

The following were selected to praise the son of Prajapati, Indra—Hiranyastupa, Savya, Bharadvaja, Vamadeva, Durmitra [son of Kutsa], Vrihaduktha, the son of Vamadeva, Vatsa, Shrushtigu, Medhya, Garga, Suhotra, Shunhotra, Gautam's son Nodha, Kakshivan, Paruchep, Gritsamada, Avasyu. Babhra, Gathu, Agastya, Vishvamitra, Vimada, and Samvaran. Similarly Vasishta, Vasukrida, Vasukra, Gauriviti, Virupa [Ashtadanshtra and Shathprabhedan], Vabra [son of Vivashvan], Maruta, Tirashchi and

Dhyuthana came forward to praise and appeal to Indra.

इत्थं तत्र सभायामार्यनृपाः सप्तगोत्रजा ऋषयः ।
असुरा मरुतो देवाः सर्वे भक्त्या सभाजयामासुः ।।17।।

Thus each of the Arya kings, the sages related by blood, asuras, marutas and devganas supplicated Indra.

एते तत्र तदानीं घटान् सहस्राणि सोमानाम् ।
गाश्चोपायनविधया सर्वस्वं च न्यवेदयन्तास्मै ।।18।।

Following the tradition of offering gifts, each one of the kings offered one thousand casks of Soma, cows and themselves.

विनिमयनव्यवहाराञ्जस्यार्थं राजशासनात् सिद्धम् ।
अद्य यथा पश्यामस्ताम्रपणं रौप्यकं स्वर्णम् ।।19।।

एवं देवयुगे प्राग् 'गो' नाम विनिमयद्रव्यम् ।
गौर्वा तच्च हिरण्यं वाऽन्यद् वेत्येवमनुभाव्यम् ।।20।।

As in the present, silver, gold, and bronze are considered lawful modes of exchange in the trade, in the devayuga, the gau was the instrument of exchange. The cow was thus equivalent to gold or any other precious object.

अद्येव पूर्वकाले क्रयविक्रयवत् प्रभूपहारेऽपि ।
विनिमयनीयद्रव्याण्यावेद्यन्ते स्म ता गावः ।।21।।

Similar to the practice in the present, in antiquity, the offering that was made to the kings intended and entailed its prospective utility in exchange. Thus gau was the medium of exchange.

कवयोऽमी खलु तस्मै चक्रुर्विजयाभिनन्दनं हर्षात् ।
प्रत्यक्षं च परोक्षं चक्रुर्गुणकीर्तनं तस्य ।।22।।

These sages, in the joy of victory, sang hymns in praise of Indra and adored him for the virtues he encompassed.

यद्वत् कुत्सस्तद्वदन्येऽपि भूपाः काले काले स्वस्वरक्षोपलक्षे ।
आहूयेन्द्रं सोमयज्ञोत्सवेऽस्मै सोमं सुत्वाऽवेदयन् भक्तिसूक्तम् ।।23।।

On account of his being saved by Indra, Kutsa like other kings praised Indra and sang hymns and drank Soma.

यद्वत् कुत्सोऽयं स्वसूक्ते परेषां राज्ञामिन्द्राद्रक्षणं विब्रवीति ।
अन्येप्येवं कुत्सरक्षां ब्रुवाणा दस्योर्युद्धं चक्षते स्वस्वकाव्ये ।।24।।

Like Kutsa, other kings also praised Indra on account of his having protected Kutsa in his war with the demons.

यद्यत्पूर्वं यच्च दस्युप्रबाधे कर्मार्याणामिन्द्र उत्या अकार्षीत् ।
सर्वं तत्तद्वर्णयामासुरार्याः स्मारं स्मारं सव्यमुख्याः स्वसूक्ते ।।25।।

Having remembered the deeds of Indra in saving and protecting each of them from arch-fiends and demons, each recollected such an account and sang hymns in praise of Indra.

बार्हस्पत्या गाव आसन् कदाचिद्दुष्टैश्चोरैर्दस्युभिर्लुण्ठिताः प्राक् ।
तच्च श्रुत्वा देवराजः सवीरो दस्यून् हत्वा प्रापयद् ब्रह्मणे ताः ।।26।।

In the yore, Brihaspati's cows were forcibly taken away by the demons and when Indra came to know of the theft, he killed the demons and brought back the cows to Brihaspati.

एवं ये ये चोपकाराः कृताः प्राग् देवेन्द्रणानेन तानत्र सर्वान् ।
स्मारं स्मारं कीर्तयन्तः स्वकाव्यैरार्याः प्रोचुः स्वं कृतज्ञत्वमस्मै ।।27।।

Remembering the deeds of Indra in the yore of chivalry of nobility and of warfare, each recollected the bravery of Indra and thus expressed gratitude for the same.

दस्योर्युद्धादल्पकालेन पूर्वे भूयोऽप्यासंश्चोरिता गाव एतैः ।
तासां भूयोन्वेषितानामलाभात्केचिद्देवा विह्वलास्तत्र चासन् ।।28।।

While thus engaged before the war with demons, the cows of these superior beings were stolen by the demons and despite repeated efforts, nothing could be known of them. The devas then had fallen into despair and hopelessness.

दस्युग्रामध्वंसनादिन्द्रवीर्यं प्राशस्त्यार्थेऽत्युत्सवेऽस्मिन् प्रवृत्ते ।
गोरक्षार्थं दैवतैः प्रार्थनापि स्तुत्यैवोपस्थापिताऽस्मै तदानीम् ।।29।।

The hymns sung by the devas in praise of Indra in killing the demons turns into worship itself.

तेषां काव्ये दस्युयुद्धप्रसङ्गो दृष्टो यावानुल्वणो यत्र वाक्ये ।
तावद्वाक्यं दर्श्यते संगृहीतं सर्वं सूक्तं तावतैवोपलक्ष्यम् ।।30।।

In this part of epic, the account of a war with demons appears to be in excess yet it is uniformly described all along.

Despite losing limbs, Vritra rose to challenge the supreme Indra, but fell again on the ground by mighty Indra's fatal blows.

नदं न भिन्नममुया शयानं मनो रुहाणा अतियन्त्याप: ।
याश्चिद्वृत्रो महिना पर्यतिष्ठत्तासामहि: पत्सुत:शीर्बभूव ।।
(ऋग्वेद:, 1.32.8)

Springs on the earth, rescued from the captivity of Vritra, started flowing fast. Vritra, the one who blocked the flowing water, was now lying on the ground, bereft of sense and motion, like Ahi.

नीचावया अभवद्वृत्रेन्द्रो अस्या अव वधर्जभार ।
उत्तरा सूरधर: पुत्र आसीद्दानु: शये सहवत्सा न धेनु: ।।
(ऋग्वेद:, 1.32.9)

The dying Vritra begins whimpering and cries out for his mother; the mother covers her lost warrior son with her body to protect him but Indra forcibly rolls him over and strikes him with blows and weapons of light.

अतिष्ठन्तीनामनिवेशनानां काष्ठानां मध्ये निहितं शरीरम् ।
वृत्रस्य निण्यं विचरन्त्यापो दीर्घं तम आशयदिन्द्रशत्रु: ।।
(ऋग्वेद:, 1.32.10)

Vritra was hidden in the constantly moving and restless waters and water flowed over him. Indra's enemy Vritra had made it dark every where.

दासपत्नीरहिगोपा अतिष्ठन्निरुद्धा आप: पणिनेव गाव: ।
अपां बिलमपिहितं यदासीद्वृत्रं जघन्वाँ अप तद्ववार ।।
(ऋग्वेद:, 1.32.11)

Like panis, the ones who hide cows in remote locations, the demons Vritra and Ahi stopped the flow of water. It was only after Vritra was killed by Indra that waters began to flow again.

अश्व्यो वारो अभवस्तदिन्द्र सृके यत्त्वा प्रत्यहन् देव एक: ।
अजयो गा अजय: शूर सोममवासृज: सर्तवे सप्तसिन्धून् ।।
(ऋग्वेद:, 1.32.12)

Clever Vritra had attacked the weapon of Indra but Indra dodged the blow as a horse would shake its tail. O mighty Indra! You rescued cows, you obtained Soma and you brought life back upon the seas by releasing the flow of water.

नास्मै विद्युन्न तन्युतः सिषेध न यां मिहमकिरद् ध्रादुनिं च ।
इन्द्रश्च यद्युयुधाते अहिश्चोतापरीभ्यो मघवा विजिग्ये ।।
(ऋग्वेदः, 1.32.13)

When the mighty Indra fought, nothing—thunder, lightning, rain and flood—detered him. When the great Indra went on to clash with Ahi, he could overpower every conceivable obstacle brought forth by the enemy and thus became worthier.

अहेर्यातारं कमपश्य इन्द्र हृदि यत्ते जध्नुषो भीरगच्छत् ।
नव च यन्नवतिं च स्रवन्ती श्येनो न भीतो अतरो रजांसि ।।
(ऋग्वेदः, 1.32.14)

O Indra! You are the one who retained the calm of mind while clashing with Ahi and thus you became victorious. O! The mightier of the mightiest! You scaled the roaring seas of this universe unlike the falcon that moves away from the moaning seas.

इन्द्रो यातोऽवसितस्य राजा शमस्य च शृङ्गिणो वज्रबाहुः ।
सेदु राजा क्षयति चर्षणीनामरान्न नेमिः परि ता बभूव ।।
(ऋग्वेदः, 1.32.15)

O Indra! You who are the embodiment of deadly arms and rules over all those who move, the one who bears horses on his head and is the king of all the mortals.

एतायामोप गन्तव्य इन्द्रमस्माकं सुप्रमतिं वावृधाति ।
अनामृणः कुविदादस्य रायो गवां केतं परमावर्जते नः ।।
(ऋग्वेदः, 1.33.1)

In the thirty-third sukta of first mandala of Rigveda, sage Hiranyastupa says: Let us come together to seek cows from Indra.Indra will grant us knowledge that is invincible. By worshipping him, Indra will certainly grant us knowledge, wisdom, wealth, and cows.

उपदेहं धनदामप्रतीतं जुष्टां न श्येनो वसतिं पतामि ।
इन्द्रं नमस्यन्नुपमेभिरर्कैर्यः स्तोतृभ्यो हव्यो अस्ति यामन् ।।
(ऋग्वेदः, 1.33.2)

The one who is desirous of wealth and wisdom and strives to be mighty must please Indra with divine hymns to seek his blessings. O Indra! The one who always protects those who are unto him.

नि सर्वसने इषुधीँरसक्त समर्यो गा अजति यस्य वष्टि ।
चोष्कूयमाण इन्द्र भूरि वामं मा पणिर्भूरस्मदधि प्रवृद्ध ॥
(ऋग्वेद:, 1.33.3)

O the chief of mighty armies—the one who carries arms on his back. O Indra, the ruler of all, the one who gifts cows to those who supplicate him. O Indra! The fairest of fair, make us wealthy.

वधीर्हि दस्युं धनिनं घनेनँ एकश्चरन्नुपशाकेभिरिन्द्र ।
धनोरधि विषुणक्ते व्यायन्नयज्वानः सनकाः प्रेतमीयुः ॥
(ऋग्वेद:, 1.33.4)

While you went to the battle with the demons along with your army, yet you alone slained bold Vritra by your strength and powerful vajra. When the demons surrounded you, without fear you killed each of those who had obstructed the yajna.

परा चिच्छीर्षा ववृजुस्त इन्द्राऽयज्वानो यज्वभिः स्पर्धमानाः ।
प्र यद्दिवो हरिवः स्थातरुग्र निरव्रताँ अधमो रोदस्योः ॥
(ऋग्वेद:, 1.33.5)

O Indra! Those enemies, who did not perform yajna, took to their heels when they could not cope with those performing the yajna. O victor of horses, a force in the battle field and valiant Indra! You drove away the followers of improper dharma from this prithvi, Dyauloka, and antariksha.

अयुयुत्सन्ननवद्यस्य सेनामयातयन्त क्षितयो नवग्वाः ।
वृषायुधो न वध्रयो निरष्टाः प्रवद्भिरिन्द्राच्चितयन्त आयन् ॥
(ऋग्वेद:, 1.33.6)

The holy and mighty legion of Indra's warriors subdued and annihilated those who fought with them. The enemies fled like cowards and showed no intention to fight with the high and mighty.

त्वमेतान्रुदतो जक्षतश्चायोधयो रजस इन्द्र पारे ।
अवादहो दिव आ दस्युमुच्चा प्र सुन्वतः स्तुवतः शंसमावः ॥
(ऋग्वेद:, 1.33.7)

O Indra! You have driven the enemy to the ground. O, you the one who has granted protection to the performers of this Soma-yajna.

चक्राणासः परीणहं पृथिव्या हिरण्येन मणिना शुम्भमानाः ।
न हिन्वानासस्तितिरुस्तं इन्द्रं परि स्पशो अदधात्सूर्येण ॥
(ऋग्वेदः, 1.33.8)

The enemies adorned themselves with gold and diamonds and gained control over earth. They were growing in numbers. O Indra! You defeated them [enemies] with the radiance of the sun contained in you.

परि यदिन्द्र रोदसी उभे अबुभोजीर्महिना विश्वतः सीम् ।
अमन्यमानाँ अभिमन्यमानैर्निर्ब्रह्मभिरधमो दस्युमिन्द्र ॥
(ऋग्वेदः, 1.33.9)

O Indra! You have full control of prithvi and Dyauloka and you are the one who helped the believers in defeating the non-believers.

न ये दिवः पृथिव्या अन्तमापुर्न मायाभिर्धनदां पर्यभूवन् ।
युजं वज्रं वृषभश्चक्र इन्द्रो निर्ज्योतिषा तमसो गा अदुक्षत् ॥
(ऋग्वेदः, 1.33.10)

O Indra! Those who could not fathom the depths of Dyauloka, Prithviloka and Antariskhaloka; they could not defeat the munificient Indra with any of their tricks; the brave Indra then held his vajra and rescued the cows from the prison of darkness.

अनु स्वधामक्षरन्नापो अस्याऽवर्धतमध्या नाव्यानाम् ।
सध्रीचीनेन मनसा तमिन्द्र ओजिष्ठेन हन्माऽहन्नभि द्यून् ॥
(ऋग्वेदः, 1.33.11)

When the waters were flowing to enrich the land, Vritra came in his boat to stop the flow of the water. A tolerant Indra killed the enemy in just few days.

न्याविध्यादिलीबिशस्य दृह्ला वि शृङ्गिणमभिनच्छुष्णमिन्द्रः ।
यावत्तरो मघवन्यावदोजो वज्रेण शत्रुमवधीः पृतन्युम् ॥
(ऋग्वेदः, 1.33.12)

O Indra! The one who has plundered the enemy citadels and uprooted them from their forceful occupation of the land, O Indra! You have mutilated the horn-headed Vritra and fought with might unheard of in these realms.

अभि सिध्मो अजिगादस्य शत्रून्वि तिग्मेन वृषभेणा पुरोऽभेत् ।
सं वज्रेणाऽसृजद्वृवमिन्द्रः प्र स्वां मतिमतिरच्छाशदानः ।।
(ऋग्वेदः, 1.33.13)

O Indra! The one whose weapons fell upon and destroyed the enemies, annihilated the cities of foes. O! The one who moves with the force measured and vanquishes the foes, the one who is wise and prudent.

आवः कुत्समिन्द्र यस्मिञ्चाकन्प्रावो युध्यन्तं वृषभं दशद्युम् ।
शफच्युतो रेणुर्नक्षत द्यामुच्छ्वैत्रेयो नृषाह्याय तस्थौ ।।
(ऋग्वेदः, 1.33.14)

O Indra! The one who extended the force of his mighty arms to save Kutsa; the one who protected the performers of yajna. O! The one whose galloping horses raised dust that rose and extended all across Dyauloka. Shvayshraiya, who sought greatness, too was blessed by you.

आवः शमं वृषभं तुग्र्यासु क्षेत्रजेषे मघवञ्छ्वित्र्यं गाम् ।
ज्योक् चिदत्र तस्थवांसो अक्रञ्छत्रूयतामधरा वेदनाकः ।।
(ऋग्वेदः, 1.33.15)

O virtuous Indra! You are the one, who, having won the war, had saved the stout but marooned Shivatraiya. The foes fought for long but you made them eat dust.

5.7 सव्यकृतम् इन्द्राभिनन्दनसूक्तम्

5.7 PRAYERS OFFERED BY SAVYA ANGIRASA

सव्यो नामाङ्गिरसो राजर्षिरार्योपकारिणे स्वराजे कृतज्ञतासूक्तम् आवेदयितुं कवयामास ।

The composition of hymns expressing gratefulness to Devendra, the protector of Arya, by sage Savya, son of Angirasa.

पुत्रो मे स्यादिन्द्रतुल्यो मनीषीत्येवंकामोऽतप्यतैषोऽङ्गराः प्राक् ।
तस्मात्पुत्रः सोऽयमिन्द्रावतारः सव्यो जज्ञे तं स इन्द्रं स्तवीति ॥34॥

Sage Angirasa, long time ago, went into a penance with a desire to beget a son as mighty and as prolific as Indra. As a result, Savya was born, and, now, he thus prays to Indra.

ऋग्वेदाद्ये मण्डले कामसूक्तादिन्द्रं सव्यः सामसूक्तान्तमस्तौत् ।
तेभ्यो दासायोधनं रूपयन्तीः संदर्श्यन्ते काश्चिदत्रर्च एताः ॥35॥

In the first mandala of Rigveda, Savya has eulogized Indra from Kama sukta to Sama sukta. Some compositions [in the fifty-first sukta and first mandala of Rigveda] narrating Indra's battle are presented here:

त्वमपामपिधानाऽवृणोरपाधारयः पर्वते दानुमद्वसु ।
वृत्रं यदिन्द्र शवसाऽवधीरहिमादित्सूर्यं दिव्यारोहयो दृशे ॥
(ऋग्वेदः, 1.51.4)

O Indra! You are the one who caused rains to fall, and dispossessed Vritra and acquired his wealth, and by the might incomparable killed Vritra and Ahi. Victorious, you made the sun to brighten the whole universe.

त्वं मायाभिरप मायिनोऽधमः स्वधाभिर्ये अधि शुप्तावजुह्वत ।
त्वं पिप्रोर्नृमणः प्रारुजः पुरः प्र ऋजिश्वानं दस्युहत्येष्वाविथ ॥
(ऋग्वेदः, 1.51.5)

O! The one who killed the wretched demons who played mischief with sacred offerings. O Indra! We thus accord praise on you, the one who killed Pipru, plundered his citadel and saved sage Rijrashva.

त्वं कुत्सं शुष्णहत्येष्वाविथारन्धयोऽतिथिग्वाय शम्बरम् ।
महान्तं चिदर्बुदं निक्रमीः पदा सनादेव दस्युहत्याय जज्ञिषे ॥
(ऋग्वेदः, 1.51.6)

O Indra! The one who killed demon Shushna and saved sage Kutsa. To protect the performers of yajna, you wiped out Shambar and to vanquish Arbud, you stood on top of him and tore apart his body. O! The one who, since times immemorial, has been the main slayer of the demons.

विजानीह्यार्यान्ये च दस्यवो बर्हिष्मते रन्धया शासदव्रतान् ।
शाकी भव यजमानस्य चोदिता विश्वेत्ता ते सधमादेषु चाकन ।।
(ऋग्वेद:, 1.51.8)

O Indra! The one who knows both the prudent and meaner ones, come towards us to protect the performance of the rites and vanquish the non-believers and heathen and subjugate them and destroy them. O invincible Indra, I supplicate you to embolden the believers for the performance of the rites, so much so that they rise in praise and honour. May you thus grant us grace and fortitude.

अनुव्रताय रन्धयन्नपव्रतानाभूमिरिन्द्र: श्नथयन्ननोभुव: ।
वृद्धस्य चिद्वर्धतो द्यामिनक्षत: स्तवानो वम्रो विजघान संदिह: ।।
(ऋग्वेद:, 1.51.9)

'You are the one who slays non-believers and blesses those who are eternally upright and just,' having thus supplicated Indra, sage Vabhra slaughtered the demons transgressing Dyauloka.

तक्षद्यत्त उशना सहसा सहो वि रोदसी मज्मना वाधते शव: ।
आ त्वा वातस्य नृमणो मनोयुज आ पूर्यमाणमवहन्नभि श्रव: ।।
(ऋग्वेद:, 1.51.10)

O Indra! Sage Ushna has magnified your power and glory and you have become invincible in both Dyauloka and Prithviloka. You are the one supplicated by mortals; may you achieve grace and fortitude like the incomparable riches of the universe and like the horses galloping with the wildness of the wind.

मन्दिष्ट यदुशने काव्ये सचाँ इन्द्रो वङ्कू वङ्कुतराऽधितिष्ठति ।
उग्रो ययि निरप: स्रोतसाऽसृजद्वि शुष्णस्य दृंहिता ऐरयत्पुर: ।।
(ऋग्वेद:, 1.51.11)

While, thus pleased on account of the supplications of Ushna, you ruled over the demons. O mighty Indra, you are the one who had made the waters flow by bringing down the skies and who had plundered the magnificent citadels of Shushna.

इदं नमो वृषभाय स्वराजे सत्यशुष्माय तवसेऽवाचि ।
अस्मिन्निन्द्र वृजने सर्ववीरास्मत्सूरिभिस्तव शर्मन्त्स्याम।।
(ऋग्वेदः, 1.51.15)

We, thus rise in prayer of the great, the high, the mighty, and the invincible Indra. O Indra, may we and our progeny live in your abode with fortitude.

स पर्वतो न धरुणेष्वच्युतः सहस्रमूतिस्तविषीषु वावृधे ।
इन्द्रो यद्वृत्रमवधीन्नदीवृतमुब्जन्नर्णांसि जर्हृषाणो अन्धसा ।।
(ऋग्वेदः, 1.52.2)

Sage Angirasa thus speaks, You have acquired a variety of wealth of the universe and killed Vritra and caused waters to flow. O, the one who had caused the mighty and renowned to seek shelter like the steadfast mountain quietly brooding over the waters passing by.

जघन्वाँ उ हरिभिः संभृतक्रतविन्द्र वृत्रं मनुषे गातुयन्नपः ।
अयच्छथा बाह्वोर्वज्रमायसमधारयो दिव्या सूर्यं दृशे ।।
(ऋग्वेदः, 1.52.8)

O the noble and virtuous Indra, you slew Vritra and carried the deadliest of weapons in your arms and caused the sun to illumine the whole universe by implanting it there in the sky. O, the one who rode on the mighty horses and saved the mortal progenies from annihilation and brought waters upon the land.

बृहत्स्वश्चन्द्रममवद्यदुक्थ्यमकृण्वत भियसा रोहणं दिवः ।
यन्मानुषप्रधना इन्द्रमूतयः स्वर्नृषाचो मरुतोऽमदन्ननु ।।
(ऋग्वेदः, 1.52.9)

Having had a glimpse of Indra's fame, the mortals supplicated before him with a desire to be blessed. O, mighty, and full of wisdom, and being thus pleased with the supplications, noble Indra charged forth to protect the mortals and other living beings. Save us, O! Indra.

द्यौश्चिदस्यामवाँ अहेः स्वनादयोयवीद्भियसा वज्र इन्द्र ते ।
वृत्रस्य यद्बद्बधानस्य रोदसी मदे सुतस्य शवसाऽभिनच्छिरः ।।
(ऋग्वेदः, 1.52.10)

O Indra! The one who, invigorated with Soma, killed Vritra who was tormenting Dyauloka and Prithviloka. Enraged by the mighty blows of Indra, Vritra's loud cries frightened even the brave ones in Dyauloka.

न्यूषु वाचं प्र महे भरामहे गिर इन्द्राय सदने विवस्वतः ।
नू चिद्धि रत्नं ससता मिवाविदन्न दुष्टुतिर्द्रविणोदेषु शस्यते ।।
(ऋग्वेदः, 1.53.1)

Thus prays sage Angirasa, we the Vivasvans, pray and supplicate before Indra with a pure conscience and graceful devotion. O Indra! The one who conquers as swiftly as a thief who steals in the blink of an eye and the one who is not swayed by the false and perfidious.

एभिर्द्युभिः सुमना एभिरिन्दुभिर्निरुन्धानो अमतिं गोभिरश्विना ।
इन्द्रेण दस्युं दरयन्त इन्दुभिर्युतद्वेषसः समिषा रभेमहि ।।
(ऋग्वेदः, 1.53.4)

O Indra! You are the one who removed our poverty by giving us gifts of cows and horses blessed with Soma and your power. May thus we please, O, you Indra! With offerings of Soma, and may you be our sole protector.

त्वं करञ्जमुत पर्णयं वधोस्तेजिष्ठयाऽतिथिग्वस्य वर्तनी ।
त्वं शता वङ्गृदस्याभिनत्पुरोऽनानुदः परिषूता ऋजिश्वना ।।
(ऋग्वेदः, 1.53.8)

O Indra! The one who decimated Karanja and Parnaya, those who troubled and threatened Atithigva. O, the one who took on demon Bangrida who had harassed Rijrashva and plundered his dwellings.

त्वमेताञ्जनराज्ञो द्विर्दशाबन्धुना सुश्रवसोपजग्मुषः ।
षष्टिं सहस्रा नवतिं नव श्रुतो नि चक्रेण रथ्या दुष्पदावृणक् ।।
(ऋग्वेदः, 1.53.9)

O eternal Indra! You are the one who, single handedly, killed those twenty kings and their six hundred thousand troops who had come to attack King Susrava.

त्वमाविथ सुश्रवसं तवोतिभिस्तव त्रामभिरिन्द्र तूर्वयाणम् ।
त्वमस्मै कुत्समतिथिग्वमायुं महे राज्ञे यूने अरन्धनायः ।।
(ऋग्वेदः, 1.53.10)

O Indra! The one who had granted protection to Susrava and Turvyana and from them you brought under control Kutsa, Atithigva and Ayu.

य उदृचीन्द्र देवगोपाः सखायस्ते शिवतमा असाम ।
त्वां स्तोषाम त्वया सुवीरा द्राघीय आयुः प्रतरं दधानाः ॥
(ऋग्वेदः, 1.53.11)

O Indra! May we be devoted to you and live with fortitude. May grace, peace, happiness, and prosperity shower on us and we live long to enjoy your care and protection.

त्वं दिवो बृहतः सानु कोपयोऽव त्मना धृषता शम्बरं भिनत् ।
यन्मायिनो व्रन्दिनो मन्दिना धृषच्छितां गभस्तिमशनिं पृतन्यसि ॥
(ऋग्वेदः, 1.54.4)

Thus said sage Savya Angirasa: Armed with a sharpened vajra, when you kill the demons with such a force that it seems as if you are angry with the entire Dyauloka. O Indra! You are the one who killed Shambar with amazing might.

नियद्वृणक्षि श्वसनस्य मूर्धनि शुष्णस्य चिद्व्रन्दिनो रोरुवद्वना ।
प्राचीनेन मनसा बर्हणावता यदद्याचित्कृण्वः कस्त्वा परि ॥
(ऋग्वेदः, 1.54.5)

O Indra! you are the one who, with a force of your mighty hand,smashed the head of Shushna, and left him roaring with pain. You, with your power embodied in your arms and mind, have been destroying demons for eons. You have devastated the demons; thus there is no one superior to you, Indra.

त्वमाविथ नर्यं तुर्वशं यदुं त्वं तुर्वीतिं वय्यं शतक्रतो ।
त्वं रथमेतशं कृत्व्ये धने त्वं पुरो नवतिं दम्भयो नव ॥
(ऋग्वेदः, 1.54.6)

O Indra! You are the virtuous and upright. Ever since the beginning of this war, you granted solemn protection to the mortals as various as *narya* (progenitor), *turvasha* (genitor) and *yadu* (proto-genitor). Along with Ratha and Aitasha, you also rescued Urviti of the clan of Vayya and plundered ninety-nine cities of the asuras.

अपामतिष्ठद्धरुणह्वरं तमोऽन्तर्वृत्रस्य जठरेषु पर्वतः ।
अभिमिन्द्रो नद्यो वव्रिणा हिता विश्वा अनुष्ठाः प्रवणेषु जिघ्नते ॥
(ऋग्वेदः, 1.54.7)

When Vritra the demon contained all the waters of the universe in his body, the mighty Indra rescued and released these waters and made them flow perennially.

स तुर्वणिर्महाँ अरेणु पौंस्ये गिरेर्भृष्टिर्न भ्राजते तुजा शवः ।
येन शुष्णं मायिनमायसो मदे दुध्र आभूषु रामयन्नि दामनि ।।
(ऋग्वेदः, 1.56.3)

Thus said Savya Angirasa: O Indra! The one who slays the demons, the one who captures the mystical Shushna and makes him a prisoner, the one who puts on an invincible shield, is the one who is supreme. O Indra, you shine with a sparkle as brilliant as the first rays of the sun falling on the highest peak of a mountain.

त्वं तमिन्द्र पर्वतं महामुरुं वज्रेण वज्रिन्पर्वशश्चकर्तिथ ।
अवासृजो निवृताः सर्तवा अपः सत्रा विश्वं दधिषे केवलं सहः ।।
(ऋग्वेदः, 1.57.6)

O Indra! The carrier of mighty weapons, the blow that you gave to Megha fragmented it and from the ruins of the skies you caused waters of the universe to flow. O! You are the one in whom whole strength of the universe is contained.

5.8 गृत्समदकृतम् इन्द्राभिनन्दनसूक्तम्

5.8 PRAYER BY GRITSAMADA

गृत्समदो दस्युवधं कीर्तयन् इन्द्रं महयति ।

Praise of Indra by Gritsamada for killing dasyus.

सृजो महीरिन्द्र या अपिन्वः परिष्ठिता अहिना शूर पूर्वीः ।
अमर्त्यं चिद्दासं मन्यमानमवाभिनदुक्थैर्वावृधानः ।।

(ऋग्वेदः, 2.11.2)

O mighty Indra! The one who has freed the waters from the clutches of Ahi and thus created the seas. You are the one who vanquished invincible demons and tore into pieces the powerful Ahi by assuming the form of lightening. Waters thus released became holy and blissful with the sun shining on them.

शुभ्रं नु ते शुष्मं वर्धयन्तः शुभ्रं वज्रं बाह्वोर्दधानाः ।
शुभ्रस्त्वमिन्द्र वावृधानो अस्मे दासीर्विशः सूर्येण सह्याः ।।

(ऋग्वेदः, 2.11.4)

O Indra! May we strengthen your grace and renown, and empower you to destroy the demons and help us prosper.

गुहा हितं गुह्यं गूह्‌लमप्स्वपीवृतं मायिनं क्षियन्तम् ।
उतो अपो द्यां तस्तभ्वांसमहन्नहिं शूर वीर्येण ।।

(ऋग्वेदः, 2.11.5)

O Indra! May you slay Ahi the demon, the one who contains the waters both that is visible and invisible, destroy the one who, by the force of his enchantment, ceases the flowing waters in Dyauloka.

इन्द्रो महाँ सिन्धुमाशयानं मायाविनं वृत्रमस्फुरन्निः ।
अरेजेतां रोदसी भियाने कनिक्रदतो वृष्णो अस्य वज्रात् ।।

(ऋग्वेदः, 2.11.9)

Indra killed the mammoth, treacherous, wicked yet clever Vritra who had blocked the flow of water; both Dyauloka and Prithviloka trembled with the din of their clashing weapons.

अरोरवीद्वृष्णो अस्य वज्रोऽमानुषं यन्मानुषो निजूर्वीत् ।
नि मायिनो दानवस्य माया अपादयत्पपिवान्त्सुतस्य ।।
(ऋग्वेद:, 2.11.10)

You are the saviour, O Indra! You are the one who slew Vritra, the mortal fiend, in the midst of terrible noises made by their clashing weapons; Indra, imbued with Soma, has rid us of the impious deeds of Vritra.

धिष्वा शवः शूर येन वृत्रमवाभिनद्दानुमौर्णवाभम् ।
आपवृणोर्ज्योतिरार्याय नि सव्यतः सादि दस्युरिन्द्र ।।
(ऋग्वेद:, 2.1.18)

O mighty Indra! May you embody the same power with which you killed Vritra who had spread his tentacles all across. Having killed Vritra, you illuminated the whole world. May you, with the same power, protect us.

सनेम ये त ऊतिभिस्तरन्तो विश्वाः स्पृध आर्येण दस्यून् ।
अस्मभ्यं तत्त्वाष्ट्रं विश्वरूपमरन्धयः साख्यस्य त्रिताय ।।
(ऋग्वेद:, 2.1.19)

O Indra! May we the devotees acquire virtues of this life and world by overpowering and overcoming the troubles given by the demons. O, you are the one who subjugated Vishvarupa, the son of Tvashta, just to enter into an alliance with Trith.

यो हत्वाहिमरिणात्सप्तसिन्धून्यो गा उदाजदपधा वलस्य ।
यो अश्मनोरन्तरग्निं जजान संवृक् समत्सु स जनास इन्द्रः ।।
(ऋग्वेद:, 2.12.3)

O mortals! You are the one who, with triumphant force, killed the demons and rescued the cows, vanquished Ahi and released the waters and replenished the seven rivers and brought fire by rubbing two stones together and the one who kills the demons by the sheer strength of arms is also none other than Indra.

येनेमा विश्वा च्यवना कृतानि यो दासं वर्णमधरं गुहाकः ।
श्वघ्नीव यो जिगीवां लक्षमाददर्यः पुष्टानि स जनास इन्द्रः ।।
(ऋग्वेद:, 2.12.4)

O mortals! The one who has made the three lokas active, made the demons inferior amongst the races by subjugating them, achieved the objectives by prudence and manoeuvre, and who has snatched the nourishment of the enemies like the hunter who snatches the prey from the dogs hunting with him, such one is Indra.

यः शश्वतो मह्येनो दधानानमन्यमानाञ्छर्वा जघान ।
यः शर्धते नानुदाति शृध्यां यो दस्योर्हन्ता स जनास इन्द्रः ॥
(ऋग्वेदः, 2.12.10)

O mortals! The one who has destroyed mightiest of the fiends with the unconquerable array of astounding weapons and vanquished those who are full of arrogance and ego, such one is Indra.

यः शम्बरं पर्वतेषु क्षियन्तं चत्वारिंश्यां शरद्यन्वविन्दत् ।
ओजायमानं यो अहिं जघान दानुं शयानं स जनास इन्द्रः ॥
(ऋग्वेदः, 2.12.11)

O mortals! The one who hunted Shambar for forty years and found him hiding in the mountains, and who decimated the powerful Ahi, such one is Indra.

यः सप्तरश्मिर्वृषभस्तुविष्मानवासृजत्सर्तवे सप्त सिन्धून् ।
यो रौहिणमस्फुरद्वज्रबाहुर्द्यामारोहन्तं स जनास इन्द्रः ॥
(ऋग्वेदः, 2.12.12)

O mortals! The one who has contained in him the seven rays of the sun, is also the one who is mighty, wise and the one who has caused the rivers to flow. The one, with his powerful weapons, who vanquished demon Rauhina, who was planning to attack the heaven, such one is Indra.

यः शम्बरं पर्यतरत् कसीभिर्यो चारुकास्नापिबत् सुतस्य ।
अन्तर्गिरौर्यजमानं बहुं जनं यस्मिन्नामूर्च्छत् स जनास इन्द्रः ॥
(अथर्ववेदः, 20.34.12)

The one who has defeated Shambar, the one who appears embodied with aura and powered with invincible weapons, the one who has drunk the Soma and the one who always blesses those who are unto him. O mortals! Such one is Indra.

यः सोमकामो हर्यश्वः सूरिर्यदस्माद् रेजन्ते भुवनानि विश्वा ।
यो जघान शम्बरं यश्च शुष्णं य एकवीरः स जनास इन्द्रः ॥
(अथर्ववेदः, 20.34.17)

The one who is the cause of this creation and always ready to drink Soma, the one who rides on invisible horses and travels beyond the bounds of the universe. The one who is adored and admired in the whole universe. The one who slew Shambar and Shushna and the one who is the mightiest of all, such one is Indra.

अध्वर्यवो यो अपो वव्रिसांसं वृत्रं जघानाशन्येव वृक्षम् ।
तस्मा एतं भरत तद्वशायँ एष इन्द्रो अर्हति पीतिमस्य ॥
(ऋग्वेद:, 2.14.2)

O mortals! The one who struck down Vritra with vajra, like the lightning that uproots a tree. O this Indra, he is the one who deserves Soma and is always keen on being offered Soma.

अध्वर्यवो यो दृभीकं जघान यो गा उदाजदप हि बलं व: ।
तस्मा एतमन्तरिक्षे न वातमिन्द्रं सौमैरोर्णुत जूर्न वस्त्रै: ॥
(ऋग्वेद:, 2.14.3)

O mortals! Indra is the one who has freed the cows by killing the demons Dhurbhika and Val. Like Vayu is established in the sky, establish Soma for Indra. May you cover him with Soma as a weak person protects his body with a cloth.

अध्वर्यवो य उरणं जघान नव चख्वांसं नवतिं च बाहून् ।
यो अर्बुदमव नीचा बबाधे तमिन्द्रं सोमस्य भृथे हिनोत ॥
(ऋग्वेद:, 2.14.4)

O mortals! Indra, the one who slew Urana by taking out his nine eyes and severing his ninety arms and eyes, and who killed Arbuda by throwing him to the ground. May you please him by offering Soma.

अध्वर्यवो य: स्वश्नं जघान य: शुष्णमशुषं यो व्यंसम् ।
व: पिप्रुं नमुचिं यो रुधिक्रां तस्मा इन्द्रायान्धसो जुहोत ॥
(ऋग्वेद:, 2.14.5)

O mortals! The one who vanquished Ashna, invincible Shushna, an armless Ahi, Pipru, Nanudhi and Rudhrika. May you offer Indra with a product of grain in sacrificial fire.

अध्वर्यवो य: शतं शम्बरस्य पुरो विभेदाश्मनेव पूर्वी: ।
यो वर्चिन: शतमिन्द्र: सहस्रमपावपद्भरता सोममस्मै ॥
(ऋग्वेद:, 2.14.6)

O mortals! The one who slew the dreaded armies of the arch fiend Ghor Varchi and plundered the dwellings of Shambar by the fierce blow of his stone-like vajra. May you offer Soma unto Indra.

अध्वर्यवो यः शतमा सहस्रं भूम्या उपस्थेऽवपज्जघन्वान् ।
कुत्सस्यायोरतिथिग्वस्य वीरान्न्यवृणग्भरता सोममस्मै ॥

(ऋग्वेदः, 2.14.7)

O mortals! Indra is the one who killed demons and warriors of Kutsa, Atithigva and Ayu and dispersed them all around. May you offer Soma to such an Indra.

प्र धा न्वस्य महतो महानि सत्या सत्यस्य करणानि वोचम् ।
त्रिकद्रुकेष्वपिबत्सुतस्यास्य मदे अहिमिन्द्रो जघान ॥

(ऋग्वेदः, 2.15.1)

Of whom I speak is the one who realizes truth and is absolute on account of his virtues. This Indra drank Soma from three containers and then killed Ahi with great enthusiasm.

स्वप्नेनाभ्युप्या चुमुरिं धुनिं च जघन्थ दस्युं प्रदभीतिमावः ।
रम्भी चिदत्र विविदे हिरण्यं सोमस्य ता मद इन्द्रश्चकार ॥

(ऋग्वेदः, 2.15.9)

O Indra! You made the two demons Chumuri and Dhuni swoon first and then killed them to protect Dabhiti and won riches from Rambhi. Indra performed all these acts in enthusiasm gained from Soma.

स सुन्वत इन्द्रः सूर्यमा देवो रिणङ्मर्त्याय स्तवान् ।
आ यद्रयिं गुहदवद्यमस्मै भरदंश नैतशो दशस्यन् ॥

(ऋग्वेदः, 2.19.5)

As a father bequeaths hidden wealth to his son, so is Indra bestowed with wealth by Aitasha. Pleased by this, Indra makes the world radiant with the light of the sun and blesses the performers of yajna.

स रन्धयत्सदिवः सारथये शुष्णमशुषं कुयवं कुत्साय ।
दिवोदासाय नवतिं च नवेन्द्रः पुरो व्यैरच्छम्बरस्य ॥

(ऋग्वेदः, 2.19.6)

Thus to save his own charioteer Kutsa, Indra killed Shushna, Ashusha,

Kuyava and and to save Divodasa, Indra killed Shambar and plundered his ninety-nine cities.

सो अङ्गिरसामुचथा जुजुष्वान्ब्रह्मा तूतोदिन्द्रो गातु मिष्णन् ।
मुष्णन्नुषसः सूर्येण स्तवानश्नस्य चिच्छश्नथत्पूर्व्याणि ॥
(ऋग्वेदः, 2.20.5)

O Indra! The one who grants prayers of the devotees and solemnises them with strength to be virtuous, extolls devotees with wisdom and prudence, makes the earth radiant with the light of the sun.

स ह श्रुत इन्द्रो नाम देव ऊर्ध्वो भुवन्मनुषे दस्मतमः ।
अव प्रियमर्शसानस्य साह्वाञ्छिरो भरद्दासस्य स्वधावान् ॥
(ऋग्वेदः, 2.20.6)

O Indra! The one who is prudent, solemn, graceful, and noble is always forthcoming to protect the mortals. He is the one who slays the demons by dismantling the crown.

स वृत्रहेन्द्रः कृष्णयोनीः पुरन्दरो दासीरैरयद्वि ।
अजनयन्मनवे क्षामपश्च सत्रा शंसं यजमानस्य तूतोत् ॥
(ऋग्वेदः, 2.20.7)

O the one who killed Vritra, plundered the dwellings of enemies, overcome desire and acquired water and land for the mortals. May thus he blesses us.

तस्मै तवस्य मनु दायि सत्रेन्द्राय देवेभिरर्णसातौ ।
प्रति यदस्य वज्रं बाह्वोर्धुर्हत्वी दस्यून्पुर आयसीर्नितारीत् ॥
(ऋग्वेदः, 2.20.8)

O Indra! The one, blessed by the gods with redoubled power, fell on the fiends and plundered their magnificent cities.

5.9 वामदेवकृतम् इन्द्राभिनन्दनसूक्तम्

5.9 PRAYER BY VAMADEVA

वामदेवो दस्युवधम् अनुकीर्तयन् इन्द्रम् अभिनन्दयामास ।

Vamadeva praises Indra for killing dasyus.

आदस्युघ्ना मनसा याह्यस्तं भुवत्ते कुत्सः सख्ये निकामः ।
स्वे योनौ निषदतं सरूपावि वां चिकित्सदृतचिद्ध नारी ॥
(ऋग्वेदः, 4.16.10)

O Indra! May you come to us and slay the demons, may you cast an eye of solemnity on Kutsa. May you bless us, and may thus knowledge and truth prevail on account of you.

यासि कुत्सेन सरथमवस्युस्तोदो वातस्य हर्योरीशानः ।
ऋज्रा वाजं न गध्यं युयूषन्कविर्यदहन्पार्याय भूषात् ॥
(ऋग्वेदः, 4.16.11)

O Indra! The one who walks in equal measure with Kutsa so that the wise Kutsa embodies the strength and overcomes the odds by driving the horses with amazing speed.

कुत्साय शुष्णमशुषं निबर्हीः प्रपित्वे अह्नः कुयवं सहस्रा ।
सद्यो दस्यून्प्रमृण कुत्स्येन प्रसुरश्चक्रं वृहतादभीके ॥
(ऋग्वेदः, 4.16.12)

O Indra! The one who had killed the arch fiend Shushna at twilight. The one who had killed tens of thousands of warriors of Kuyava and dismantled the ferocious weapons of the enemies.

त्वं पिप्रुं मृगयं शूशुवांसमृजिश्वने वैदथिनाय रन्धीः ।
पञ्चाशत्कृष्णा नि वपः सहस्रात्कं न पुरो जरिमा विदर्दः ॥
(ऋग्वेदः, 4.16.13)

O Indra! The one who had vanquished the demon Pipru just to save Rijrashva, the son of Vitithi, and decimated demon Mrigya. O you are the one, who had destroyed millions of demons and their cities like some one tearing away old clothes.

त्वं महाँ इन्द्र तुभ्यं ह क्षा अनु क्षत्रं मंहना मन्यत द्यौः ।
त्वं वृत्रं शवसा जघन्वान्त्सृजः सिन्धूँरहिना जग्रसानान् ॥
(ऋग्वेदः, 4.17.1)

O Indra! The one who is invincible, the one who caused the earth to move; the one before which the grand heaven bows down. You are the one, who had killed Ahi and made the waters flow freely.

त्वमध प्रथमं जायमानोऽमे विश्वा अधिया इन्द्र कृष्टीः ।
त्वं प्रति प्रवत आशयानमहिं वज्रेण मघवन्वि वृश्चः ॥
(ऋग्वेदः, 4.17.7)

O Indra! You the one who had inspired a breath of life in the progenies of the earth and thus defeated demon Ahitya, who had confined the waters of the world.

अयं चक्रमिषणत् सूर्यस्य न्येतशं रीरमत्ससृमाणम् ।
आ कृष्ण ईं जुहुराणो जिघर्ति त्वचो बुध्ने रजसो अस्य योनौ ॥
(ऋग्वेदः, 4.17.14)

O Indra! The one who had thwarted and killed demon Aitasha by ferociously mounting the wheel of the sun around your finger. O, you are the one, who had made the whole universe radiant, and you made the sky and waters your abode and sojourn.

ममच्चन ते मघवन्व्यंसो निविविध्वाँ अप हनू जघान ।
अधा निविद्ध उत्तरो बभूवाञ्छिरो दासस्य संपिणग्वधेन ॥
(ऋग्वेदः, 4.18.9)

O the noble Indra! The one who had beheaded demon Vyandha, who dared to challenge your supremacy by hitting on your chin with force. Thus on such an account you became the mightiest and fell upon the fleeing armies of the demons.

अतृप्णुवन्तं वियतमबुध्यमानं सुषुपाणमिन्द्र।
सप्त प्रति प्रवत आशयानमहिं वज्रेण विरिणा अप्रवन् ॥
(ऋग्वेदः, 4.19.3)

O Indra! The one who is insatiable, unyeilding, invincible and also the one who had vanquished Ahi, the demon who had blocked the passage of waters, by smashing his head. Thus Indra shook the bounds of heaven and earth like a strong breeze thunderously makes the waters roar. The mighty Indra thus slew the arch enemies and plundered the dwellings of fiends in the mountains.

अक्षोदयच्छवसा क्षाम बुध्नं वार्ण वातस्तविषीभिरिन्द्रः ।
दृह्लान्यौभ्नादुशमान ओजोऽवाभिनत्ककुभः पर्वतानाम् ।।
(ऋग्वेदः, 4.19.4)

Indra shook the Dyauloka and Prithviloka in the same way as the wind causes turbulence in the water. The powerful Indra slew even the most powerful enemies with ease and pruned the wings of the mountains.

अभि प्र दद्रुर्जनयो न गर्भं रथा इव प्रययुः साकमद्रयः ।
अतर्पयो विसृत उब्ज ऊर्मीन्त्वं वृताँ अरिणा इन्द्र सिन्धून् ।।
(ऋग्वेदः, 4.19.5)

O Indra! The one who is blessed by the ferocity of his weapons; the weapons you carry are deadlier than the most ferocious wind. O Indra! The one who had brought forth the rains from the depth of the sky and thus made the rivers resplendent with water.

त्वं महीमवनिं विश्वधेनां तुर्वीतये वय्याय क्षरन्तीम् ।
अरमयो नमसैजदर्णः सुतरणाँ अकृणोरिन्द्र सिन्धून् ।।
(ऋग्वेदः, 4.19.6)

O Indra! The one who thus granted fortitude to Vritti and Vayyay by making this magnificent earth rich and fertile. O Indra! The one who had contained the waters of the rivers making them navigable.

इन्द्रस्य वामदेवः प्रियतम आसीदयं हि देवस्य ।
इन्द्रस्य मूर्तिपूजां प्रचारयामास लोकेऽस्मिन् ।।36।।

Indra was fond of Vamadeva and the same Vamadeva brought in vogue the idol worship of Indra in these realms.

ऋक्संहितातुरीयकमण्डलसूक्ते चतुर्विंशे ।
दशमच्यैन्द्रप्रतिमां व्यक्रीणाद् धेनुभिर्दशभिः ।।37।।

In the twenty-fourth sukta and fourth mandala of Rigveda, there is a description of an exchange of an idol of Indra for ten cows.

सर्वप्रथमं मन्ये देवयुगे वामदेव एवायम् ।
देवप्रतिमापूजां प्रचारयामास मानुषे लोके ।।38।।

I firmly believe that the same Vamadeva had made idol worship prevalent among the people of this land.

यद्यपि ततोऽपि पूर्वं सारस्वतसूर्यसदनेऽभूत् ।
अपि सूर्यचक्रमूर्त्तेरुपासनारम्भ इत्याहुः ।।39।।

Nevertheless, the authority of idol worship of the sun god by the inhabitants of the same city also holds ground.

विज्ञानार्था सेयं किन्त्वासीत् सूर्यचक्रस्य ।
दृष्टिपरीक्षोपासा देवप्रतिमार्चना नैवम् ।।40।।

This worship of the sun god was, however, primarily to gain knowledge of the solar system. It was certainly not to canonize the idol worship of the sun.

योगस्त्रिधा क्रियाया भक्तेर्ज्ञानस्य भेदेन ।
भक्तेस्ते चत्वारो हठलयसन्मन्त्रराजयोगाख्याः ।।41।।

The yoga has three divisions—*kriya* (action), *bhakti* (devotion) and *jnana* (knowledge). Bhakti is of four kinds—*hatha* (through force), *laya* (concentrated), *sanmantra* (through chanting) and rajayoga.

देवप्रतिमोपासा प्रकल्पिता मन्त्रयोगविधा ।
मन्त्राराधितदेवः प्रत्यासन्नोऽवति प्रायः ।।42।।

Chanting of mantras is a specific mode of worshipping the gods. By chanting the mantra, the gods are aroused and awakened, and thus bless the devotees.

देवानामिदवो महत् तदावृणीमहे वयम् ।
वृष्णामस्मभ्यमूतये ।।

(ऋग्वेदः, 8.72.1)

It is also mentioned in the Vedas that this Agni is definitely the greatest among the gods. That is why, of all the gods, we choose him only. Like a powerful being, this Agni is always prompt in our defence.

उत्कृष्टं बहुमूल्यं विक्रीणन् द्रव्यमल्पमूल्येन ।
पूजाफलोपलब्धौ समयं प्रत्यर्पणाय चक्रे सः ।।43।।

He sold the costly idol for a low price and vowed to return the idol after being blessed for his worship.

अत एवेन्द्रस्तमृषिं महयितुमिव वामदेवस्य ।
प्रमहोत्सवेऽभिगरमनु वक्तुं प्रतिगरमिहान्तरोत्तस्थौ ।।44।।

Therefore, to enhance the importance of sage Vamadeva, Indra stood up in a thanksgiving gesture after the prayer in that pramoha ceremony.

वामदेवं प्रतीन्द्रः स्वं चरितम् अनुवर्णयति ।

Indra describing his nature to Vamadeva.

अहं मनुरभवं सूर्यश्चाहं कक्षीवाँ ऋषिरस्मि विप्रः ।
अहं कुत्समार्जुनेयन्यृञ्जेऽहं कविरुशना पश्यता मा ।।
(ऋग्वेदः, 4.26.1)

I am, Indra that is atma, Manu, I am the sun, I am the wise sage Kakshivan; I energised Arjuna's son Kutsa, I am the far-sighted poet Ushana—see me.

अहं भूमिमददामार्यायाऽहं वृष्टिं दाशुषे मर्त्याय ।
अहमपो अनयं वावशाना मम देवासो अनु केतमायन् ।।
(ऋग्वेदः, 4.26.2)

I made available land for the elevated human beings, rained water for the charitable ones, I am the sound that inspires the waters to flow and may all gods act in harmony with my will.

अहं पुरो मन्दसानो व्यैरं नवसाकं नवतीः शम्बरस्य ।
शततमं वेश्यं सर्वताता दिवोदासमतिथिग्वं यदावम् ।।
(ऋग्वेदः, 4.26.3)

I destroyed the asura Shambar with ease, destroyed in one effort his ninety-nine towns and when I granted protection to Divodasa, the one who gave cows as alm to the people, I built the hundredth city for his abode.

अथवा देवेन्द्रस्य व्याहतिमयमेव वामदेव ऋषिः ।
प्रतिनिधितयेन्द्रभावं स्वस्मिन्नारोप्य वक्ति स्म ।।45।।

It may be thus that these words had been uttered by sage Vamadeva on behalf of Indra by assuming the form of Indra himself.

पुनः वामदेवः अनुकीर्तयन् इन्द्रं महयति ।

Vamadeva again praises Indra.

त्वा युजा तव तत्सोम सख्य इन्द्रो अपो मनवे सस्रुतस्कः ।
अहन्नहिमरिणात्सप्त सिन्धूनपावृणोदपिहितेव खानि ।।

(ऋग्वेदः, 4.28.1)

In the Rigveda, sage Vamadeva thus speaks, O Soma! Having become your compeer, Indra sought your help and brought forth the waters for the mortals.

त्वा युजा नि खिदत्सूर्यस्येन्द्रश्चक्रं सहसा सद्य इन्द्रो ।
अधिष्णुना बृहता वर्तमानं महो द्रुहो अप विश्वायु धायि ।।

(ऋग्वेदः, 4.28.2)

O Soma! On account of your help, Indra extended his reign to the whole solar domain and became active in the Dyauloka. You are the one who held the wheel of the sun to your captivity.

अहन्निन्द्रो अदहदग्निरिन्दो पुरा दस्यून्मध्यन्दिनादभीके ।
दुर्गे दुरोणे क्रत्वा न यातां पुरू सहस्रा शर्वा नि बर्हीत् ।।

(ऋग्पेदः, 4.28.3)

O Soma! Even before the first quarter of the war, Indra had killed the fiends and consigned them to the flames. The one who destroyed the citadels inaccessible and with his might vanquished tens and thousands of dwellings of the demons.

विश्वस्मात्सीमधमाँ इन्द्र दस्यून्विशो दासीरकृणोरप्रशस्ताः ।
अबाधेशाममृणतं नि शत्रूनविन्देशामपचितिं वधत्नैः ।।

(ऋग्वेदः, 4.28.4)

O Indra! You are the one who freed the beings from subjugation, and having killed the fiends relegated them to their places. O Indra and Soma! Both of you who have killed the enemies by the might of your weapons. May thus we supplicate both of you.

नकिरिन्द्र त्वदुत्तरो न ज्यायाँ अस्ति वृत्रहन् ।
नकिरेवा यथा त्वम् ।।

(ऋग्वेदः, 4.30.1)

In the thirtieth sukta of fourth mandala of Rigveda, Vamadeva thus supplicates Indra: O Indra! O the slayer of Vritra, the one who does not have a compeer nor does have one above him. O you! The one who is peerless.

सत्रा ते अनु कृष्टयो विश्वा चक्रेव वावृतुः ।
सत्रा महाँ असि श्रुतः ।।

(ऋग्वेदः, 4.30.2)

O Indra! Your subjects thrive at your behest and like the wheel of the chariot they move in unison at your will. On such an account, you are not only great but famous as well.

विश्वे चनेदना त्वा देवास इन्द्र युयुधुः ।
यदहा नक्तमातिरः ।।

(ऋग्वेदः, 4.30.3)

O Indra! The gods of heaven proceed to war at the instance of your might. You killed the fiends even when it was dark.

यत्रोत बाधितेभ्यश्चक्रं कुत्साय युध्यते ।
मुषाय इन्द्र सूर्यम् ।।

(ऋग्वेदः, 4.30.4)

O Indra! The one who had raised the wheel of the sun to save Kutsa who fought with the enemies and thus granted solemnity to your devotees.

यत्र देवाँ ऋघायतो विश्वाँ अयुध्य एक इत् ।
त्वमिन्द्र वनूँरहन् ।।

(ऋग्वेदः, 4.30.5)

O Indra! You are the one who went all alone to decimate the demons who were harassing the devas and killed them all.

यत्रोत मर्त्याय कमरिणा इन्द्र सूर्यम् ।
प्रावः शचीभिरेतशम् ।।

(ऋग्वेदः, 4.30.6)

O Indra! The one who had created the sun to make your progenies happy and with your manoeuvre granted protection to Aitasha.

किमादुतासि वृत्रहन् मघवन् मन्युमत्तमः ।
अत्राह दानुमातिरः ।।

(ऋग्वेदः, 4.30.7)

O Indra! The slayer of Vritra! The one who rages on the fiends and the one who killed all the demons with pleasure.

एतद्घेदुत वीर्यमिन्द्र चकर्थ पौस्यम् ।
स्त्रियं यद्दुर्हणायुवं वधीर्दुहितरं दिवः ।।

(ऋग्वेदः, 4.30.8)

O Indra! The one whose mortal deeds are beyond praise. You who had contained usha in that you made the sun to rise and vanquished remnants of darkness in the morning.

दिवश्चिद्घा दुहितरं महान्महीयमानाम् ।
उषासमिन्द्र सम्पिणक् ।।

(ऋग्वेदः, 4.30.9)

O Indra! The one who is great and also the one who has destroyed the chariot of usha, the virtuous progeny of the heaven.

अपोषा अनसः सरत्सम्पिष्टादह बिभ्युषी ।
नि यत् सीं शिश्नथद्वृषा ।।

(ऋग्वेदः, 4.30.10)

While you broke the chariot into pieces, usha fled in sheer apprehension.

एतदस्या अनः शये सुसम्पिष्टं विपाश्या ।
ससार सीं परावतः ।।

(ऋग्वेदः, 4.30.11)

The ruins of the chariot of usha was found near the Vipasha river and usha fled to a far off place.

उत सिन्धुं विबाल्यं वितस्थानामधि क्षमि ।
परि ष्ठा इन्द्र मायया ।।

(ऋग्वेदः, 4.30.12)

O Indra! The one who had contained the mighty waters of river Sindhu and thus made Sindhu to come to the earth.

उत शुष्णस्य धृष्णुया प्र मृक्षो अभि वेदनम् ।
पुरो यदस्य सम्पिणक् ।।

(ऋग्वेदः, 4.30.13)

O Indra! The one who had ruined and plundered the dwellings of Shushna and captured all his wealth.

उत दासं कौलितरं बृहतः पर्वतादधि ।
अवाहन्निन्द्र शम्बरम् ॥

(ऋग्वेदः, 4.30.14)

O Indra! The one who threw Shambar, the son of slave Kulitar, from the height of a mountain.

उत दासस्य वर्चिनः सहस्राणि शताऽवधीः ।
अधि पञ्च प्रधीँरिव ॥

(ऋग्वेदः, 4.30.15)

O Indra! The one who had vanquished the mighty army of the fiends which was five lakh in number. The ones who were obliterated like grooves under the wheel.

उत त्या सद्य आर्य्या सरयोरिन्द्र पारतः ।
अर्णाचित्ररथावधीः ॥

(ऋग्वेदः, 4.30.18)

O Indra! The Arya had killed Arna and Chitraratha who dwelt beyond Sarayu.

शतमश्मन्मयीनां पुरामिन्द्रो व्यास्यत् ।
दिवोदासाय दाशुषे ॥

(ऋग्वेदः, 4.30.20)

Indra honoured Divodasa by granting him the reign of the city of the enemy which had hundred magnificent citadels.

अस्वापयद्दभीतये सहस्रा त्रिंशतं हथैः ।
दासानामिन्द्रो मायया ॥

(ऋग्वेदः, 4.30.21)

To save Dabhiti, Indra killed thirty-thousand mighty fiends.

प्र ते वोचाम वीर्या या मन्दसान आरुजः ।
पुरो दासीरभीत्य ॥

(ऋग्वेदः, 4.32.10)

In the thirty-second sukta of fifth mandala of Rigveda, Vamadeva Gautam thus speaks: O Indra! The one who, in the celebration of warfare, vanquished and uprooted the cities of warring enemies. We thus render the following description to the magnificence of your power.

ता ते गृणन्ति वेधसो यानि चकर्थ पौंस्या ।
सुतेष्विन्द्र गिर्वणः ॥

(ऋग्वेदः, 4.32.11)

O the supplicated one, O Indra! The learned ones thus accord praise to your bounties.

सहस्रं व्यतीनां युक्तानामिन्द्रमीमहे ।
शतं सोमस्य खार्यः ॥

(ऋग्वेदः, 4.32.17)

O Indra! We thus supplicate you to bestow on us thousands of mighty and agile horses to uproot the enemies.

सहस्रा ते शता वयं गवामा च्यावयामसि ।
अस्मत्रा राध एतु ते ॥

(ऋग्वेदः, 4.32.18)

O Indra! We thus pray to you, bestow on us tens of thousands of holy cows so that we could imbibe your fame.

दश ते कलशानां हिरण्यानामधीमहि ।
भूरिदा असि वृत्रहन् ॥

(ऋग्वेदः, 4.32.19)

O Indra! We thus enjoin upon ourselves ten casks of gold, O the slayer of Vritra! You are the one who proffers alms unto us.

भूरिदा भूरि देहि नो मा दभ्रं भूर्या भर ।
भूरि घेदिन्द्र दित्ससि ॥

(ऋग्वेदः, 4.32.20)

O the bounteous Indra! May thus you lavish unto us immense wealth! O the one who desires to make us resplendent with riches, do bless us.

5.10 मधुच्छन्दःकृता इन्द्रस्तुतिः

5.10 PRAYERS OF MADHUCHANDAS

जेता माधुच्छन्दसः स्तौति ।

The prayers of the triumphant Madhuchandas.

पुरां भिन्दुर्युवा कविरमितौजा अजायत ।
इन्द्रो विश्वस्य कर्म्मणो धर्ता वज्री पुरुष्टुतः ।।

(ऋग्वेदः, 1.11.14)

O Indra! The one who is mighty, bold, prolific, radiant, young and endowed with weapons, the harbinger of good sense and the one who is supplicated by all. O, the one who is born to vanquish the enemies.

मायाभिरिन्द्र मायिनं त्वं शुष्णमवातिरः ।
विदुष्टे तस्य मेधिरास्तेषां श्रवांस्युत्तिर ।।

(ऋग्वेदः, 1.11.7)

O Indra! The one who killed the deceptive Shushna with greater deception. The wise ones thus know the power of your wisdom. May you thus grant courage and conviction to them.

5.11 सुमित्रकृता इन्द्रस्तुतिः

5.11 EULOGY BY SUMITRA (SON OF KUTSA)

शतं वा यदसुर्य प्रति त्वा सुमित्र इत्थास्तौद्दुर्मित्र इत्थास्तौत् ।
आवो यद्दस्युहत्ये कुत्सपुत्रं प्रावो यद्दस्युहत्ये कुत्सवत्सम् ।।

(ऋग्वेदः, 10.105.11)

The son of Kutsa prays to Indra in the 105th sukta of tenth mandala of Rigveda: O brave Indra! When you protected me, Sumitra or Durmitra, son of Kutsa, at the time of the slaughter of dasyus, I pray to you to bestow riches upon me.

5.12 वभ्रुकृतम् इन्द्राभिनन्दनम्

5.12 EULOGY BY VABHRU [SON OF ATI]

परो यत्त्वं परम आजनिष्ठाः परावति श्रुत्यं नाम बिभ्रत् ।
अतिश्चिदिन्द्रादभयन्त देवा विश्वा अपो अजयद्दासपत्नीः ॥
(ऋग्वेदः, 5.30.5)

O mighty Indra! Your glory is known to the dasyus despite living in distant lands. You were born with inherent glory and you are feared by the devas ever since. You have freed the waters blocked by the dasyus.

तुभ्येदेते मरुतः सुशेवा अर्चन्त्यर्कं सुन्वन्त्यन्धः ।
अहिमोहानमप आशयानं प्र मायाभिर्मायिनं सक्षदिन्द्रः ॥
(ऋग्वेदः, 5.30.6)

These marutas, capable of performing supreme deeds, drink Soma in your name. Indra killed the asura named Ahi, who had troubled the devas and blocked the rivers.

वि षू मृधो जनुषा दानमिन्वन्नहन्गवा मघवन्त्सञ्चकानः ।
अत्रा दासस्य नमुचेः शिरो यदवर्तयो मनवे गातुमिच्छन् ॥
(ऋग्वेदः, 5.30.7)

O munificent one! Immediately after your birth, you killed Danasura with your divine thunderbolt. You are worthy of eulogy. You slit the throats of Dasa and Namuchi with your thunderbolt to clear the way for Manu.

युजं हि मामकृथा आदिदिन्द्र शिरो दासस्य नमुचेर्मथायन् ।
अश्मानं चित्स्वर्यं वर्तमान प्र चक्रियेव रोदसी मरुद्भ्यः ॥
(ऋग्वेदः, 5.30.8)

O Indra! You slit the throats of Dasa and Namuchi, who stood thundering like the clouds. Thereafter, you befriended the marutas and divided the earth into two parts for their sake.

स्त्रियो हि दास आयुधानि चक्रे किं मा करन्नबला अस्य सेनाः ।
अन्तर्ह्यख्यदुभे अस्य धेने अथोप प्रैद्युधये दस्युमिन्द्रः ॥
(ऋग्वेदः, 5.30.9)

In due course, the dasyus, fearing Indra, gathered an army of females.

Indra knew that the weak dasyu army was not capable of harming him. He attacked the dasyus and imprisoned two beautiful women, after which the whole army took to their heels.

5.13 अवस्युकृतम् इन्द्राभिनन्दनम्

5.13 EULOGIES BY AVASYU

इन्द्रो रथाय प्रवतं कृणोति यमध्यस्थानमघवा वाजयन्तम् ।
यूथेव पश्वो व्युनोति गोपा अरिष्टो याति प्रथमः सिषासन् ।।
(ऋग्वेदः, 5.31.1)

It is mentioned in the thirty-first sukta of fifth mandala of Rigveda: This powerful Indra instills amazing speed in whichever chariot he rides. Like a cowherdsman who mobilizes his herd of cows, Indra offers wealth and encouragement to his army, making them invincible.

अनवस्ते रथमश्वाय तक्षन् त्वष्टा वज्रं पुरुहूत द्युमन्तम् ।
ब्रह्माण इन्द्रं महयन्तो अर्कैरवर्द्धयन्नहये हन्तवा उ ।।
(ऋग्वेदः, 5.31.4)

O Indra! The craftsmen designed these chariots to harness your horses, sage Tvashta created your weapon, vajra and your worshippers pleaded with you to kill Ahi.

वृष्णे यत्ते वृषणो अर्कमर्चानिन्द्र ग्रावाणो अदितिः सजोषाः ।
अनश्वासो ये पवयोऽरथा इन्द्रेषिता अभ्यवर्तन्त दस्यून् ।।
(ऋग्वेदः, 5.31.5)

O Indra! By your grace, the marutas slaughtered the dasyus on chariots bereft of horses. Then they crushed with hard stones to drink Soma.

प्र ते पूर्वाणि करणानि वोचं प्र नूतना मघवन्या चकर्थ ।
शक्तीवो यद्विभरा रोदसी उभे जयन्नपो मनवे दानुचित्राः ।।
(ऋग्वेदः, 5.31.6)

O powerful, glorious Indra! I will narrate all your deeds old and new when you won over the earth and obliged the human beings by offering water to them.

तदिन्नु ते करणं दस्म विप्राहिं यद् घ्नन्नोजो अत्रामिमीथाः ।
शुष्णस्य चित्परि माया अगृभ्णाः प्रपित्वं यन्नप दस्यूँरसेधः ।।
(ऋग्वेदः, 5.31.7)

O adorable and wise Indra! All those great deeds of yours, that is, slaughter of the asuras, Ahi and the magical Shushna, are worthy of praise.

त्वमपो यदवे तुर्वशायारमय: सुदुघा: पार इन्द्र ।
उग्रमयातमवहो ह कुत्सं सं ह यद्वामुशनाऽरन्त देवा: ।।
(ऋग्वेद:, 5.31.8)

O Indra! You made the water run for the plants of Yadu and Turvasa to grow. You end sorrow. You protected Kutsa from the aggressive and powerful enemy and then Ushana, and the gods prayed to you.

इन्द्राकुत्सा वहमाना रथेना वामत्या अपि कर्णे वहन्तु ।
नि:षीमद्भ्यो धमथो नि: षधस्थान्मघोनो हृदो वरथस्तमांसि ।।
(ऋग्वेद:, 5.31.9)

O Kutsa and Indra! Both of you take these extremely swift horses to the battlefield. You slaughtered the asura who was hiding in water and you, the kind-hearted and rich one, drove sin and fear out of the hearts of human beings.

5.14 गातुकृतम् इन्द्राभिनन्दनम्

5.14 EULOGY OF INDRA BY GATHU

अदर्दरुत्समसृजो वि खानि त्वमर्णवान्बद्बधानाँ अरम्णाः ।
महान्तमिन्द्रपर्वतं वियद्वः सृजो वि धारा अव दानवं हन् ।।
(ऋग्वेदः, 5.32.1)

O Indra! You slaughtered the demons and tore clouds to bring rains. You liberated the captive waters. You ripped huge mountains for the streams of water to flow.

त्वमुत्साँ ऋतुभिर्वद्बधानाँ अरंह ऊधः पर्वतस्य वज्रिन् ।
अहिं चिदुग्र प्रयुतं शयानं जघन्वाँ इन्द्र तविषीमधत्थाः ।।
(ऋग्वेदः, 5.32.2)

O Indra! You tore the rainy clouds, who were angry. O wielder of thunderbolt! After demolishing the strength of asura Megha, you woke up the sleeping asura Ahi and killed him too. O brave one, you are so powerful.

त्यं चिदेषां स्वधया मदन्तं मिहो नपातं सुवृधं तमोगाम् ।
वृषप्रभर्मा दानवस्य भामं वज्रेण वज्री निजघान शुष्णम् ।।
(ऋग्वेदः, 5.32.4)

The propitiator of rain bearing clouds and wielder of thunderbolt, Indra slew asura Shushna, who lived on the grains offered by living beings and in return he had blocked their water.

त्यं चिदस्य क्रतुभिर्निषत्तममर्मणो विददिदस्य मर्म ।
यदीं सुक्षत्र प्रभृता मदस्य युयुत्सन्तं तमसि हर्म्ये धाः ।।
(ऋग्वेदः, 5.32.5)

O Indra! You have discovered the mystery of Vritrasura, which no one else could find out. O masculine Indra! With the magic of Soma, you captured Vritrasura in a dark place.

त्यं चिदित्था कत्पयं शयानमसूर्ये तमसि वावृधानम् ।
तं चिन्मन्दानो वृषभः सुतस्योच्चैरिन्द्रो अपगूर्या जघान ।।
(ऋग्वेदः, 5.32.6)

After drinking Soma, Indra hit Vritrasura with his thunderbolt, who was sleeping hidden in a dark place, having blocked the life giving waters.

त्यं चिदर्णं मधुपं शयानमसिन्वं वव्रं मह्यादुग्रः ।
अपादमत्रं महता वधेन नि दुर्योण आवृणङ्मृध्रवाचम् ॥

(ऋग्वेदः, 5.32.8)

The brave Indra killed Vritrasura, who told untrue things, drank wine and slept, attacked despited being orthopaedically disabled, defeated the enemies. Indra killed this asura with his thunderbolt.

5.15 संवरणकृतम् इन्द्राभिनन्दनम्

5.15 REVERANCE OF INDRA BY SAMVARANA

पुरू यत्त इन्द्र सन्त्युक्था गवे चकर्थोर्वरासु युध्यन् ।
ततक्षे सूर्याय चिदोकसि स्वे वृषा समत्सु दासस्य नाम चित् ।।
(ऋग्वेदः, 5.34.4)

O Indra! It has been said about you in hymns in your praise that you released water to make the land fertile, established the sun in Dyauloka and exterminated the asura Dasa in the battlefield.

न पञ्चभिर्दशभिर्वष्ट्यारभं नासुन्वता सचते पुष्यता चन ।
जिनाति वेदमुया हन्ति वा धुनिरा देवयुं भजति गोमति व्रजे ।।
(ऋग्वेदः, 5.34.5)

This Indra is all powerful. He does not need any enforcement even while fighting several enemies. Despite being rich, he does not befriend those who do not do Soma yajna. This Indra, who instills fear in the enemies, fights and kills those not performing sacrifices and offers cows to those who adore him.

वित्वक्षणः समृतौ चक्रमासजोऽसुन्वतो विषुणः सुन्वतो वृधः ।
इन्द्रो विश्वस्य दमिता विभीषणो यथावशं नयति दासमार्यः ।।
(ऋग्वेदः, 5.34.6)

Indra, the valiant and wielder of discus standing on the chariot, the destroyer of those performing the Soma yajna and whom the enemies dread, pervades the whole world and captures his enemies.

5.16 ऐन्द्रविमदवसुकृतम् इन्द्राभिनन्दनम्

5.16 EULOGY OF INDRA BY AINDRA

विमद ऐन्द्रः प्राजापत्यो वा वसुकृद् वासुक्रो वा अभिनन्दयति ।

Veneration of Indra by Aindra or Prajapatya Vimada or Vasukrida or Vasukra.

आ न इन्द्र पृक्षसेऽस्माकं ब्रह्मोद्यतम् ।
तत्त्वा याचामहेऽवः शुष्णं यद्धन्नामानुषम् ॥

(ऋग्वेदः, 10.22.7)

In the twenty-second sukta of tenth mandala of Rigveda, more paens are sung for Indra: O Devendra! Take care of us from all sides. We offer our prayers and offerings of yajna for you only. We aspire for your care and the divine power with which you have killed asura Shushna.

अकर्मा दस्युरभि नो अमन्तुरन्यत्रतो अमानुषः ।
त्वं तस्या मित्रहन्वधर्दासस्य दम्भय ॥

(ऋग्वेदः, 10.22.8)

O Indra, the destroyer of Ahi! The asuras who do nothing, insult everyone, do not perform any yajna, full of demonic activities, are all around us. Destroy them in punishment.

मक्षू ता त इन्द्र दानाप्नस आक्षाणे शूर वज्रिवः ।
यद्ध शुष्णस्य दम्भयो जातं विश्वं सयावभिः ॥

(ऋग्वेदः, 10.22.11)

O mighty Indra! With great confidence, with the marutas, you killed asura Shushna and even in the battlefield all your deeds with grace and generosity soon became fruitful.

अहस्ता यदपदी वर्धत क्षाः शचीभिर्वेद्यानाम् ।
शुष्णं परि प्रदक्षिणिद्विश्वायवे नि शिश्नथः ॥

(ऋग्वेदः, 10.22.14)

This earth gets empowered by the yajna performed by sages and for the good of the entire world, you takes care of us from all sides, with this good intention you killed rogue Shushna.

5.17 वासुक्राष्टादंष्ट्रकृतम् इन्द्राभिनन्दनम्

5.17 EULOGY OF INDRA BY VASUKRASHTADANSHTRA

प्र ते अस्या उषसः प्रापरस्या नृतौ स्याम नृतमस्य नृणाम् ।
अनु त्रिशोकः शतमावहन्नुन्कुत्सेन रथो यो असत्ससवान् ॥
(ऋग्वेदः, 10.29.2)

O Indra! You are supreme among the human beings. May we better ourselves by praying to you at the dawn. O Indra! Sage Trishoka prayed to you and got help from hundred human beings. It was because of you that Kutsa got the chariot.

इन्द्रो दिवः प्रतिमानं पृथिव्या विश्वा वेद सवना हन्ति शुष्णम् ।
महीं चिद्यामातनोत्सूर्य्येण चास्कम्भ चित्कम्भनेन स्कभीयान् ॥
(ऋग्वेदः, 10.111.5)

The sage says in the one-hundred-eleventh sukta of tenth mandala of Rigveda: Indra has the knowledge of all the sacrifices because he is the representative of Dyau and prithvi. Indra slays Shushna and illuminates the vast earth and space with the sun. Indra bestows grains on the earth by causing rains. The supreme one among the founders of the world, Indra pervades the whole world.

वज्रेण हि वृत्रहा वृत्रमस्तरदेवस्य शूशुवानस्य मायाः ।
वि धृष्णो अत्र धृषता जघन्थाथाभवो मघवन्बाह्वोजाः ॥
(ऋग्वेदः, 10.111.6)

O Indra! You killed Vritra with a stroke of your thunderbolt. O fighting Indra! You destroyed the dark and deceitful illusion of Vritra. O Indra! The strength of your arms grew with time.

सचन्त यदुषसः सूर्येण चित्रामस्य केतवो रामविन्दन् ।
आ यन्नक्षत्रं ददृशे दिवो न पुनर्यतो न किरद्धानु वेद ॥
(ऋग्वेदः, 10.111.7)

When the rays of the sun becomes visible in the early morning dawn, a splendid array of colours is produced. And, when the sun goes higher in the sky during daytime and the stars are no longer visible, the rays of sun lose their value.

दूरं किल प्रथमा जग्मुरासामिन्द्रस्य याः प्रसवे सस्रुरापः ।
क्व स्विदग्रं क्व बुध्न आसामापो मध्यं क्व वो नूनमन्तः ।।
(ऋग्वेदः, 10.111.8)

O water! The primordial water which flowed by the grace of Indra, had gone a long distance, but there is no trace of the origin, middle, root or destination of the remaining water. [In other words, everything holds its existence solely due to Indra.]

सृजः सिन्धूँरहिना जग्रसानाँ आदिदेताः प्रविविज्रे जवेन ।
मुमुक्षमाणा उत या मुमुच्रेऽधेदेता न रमन्ते नितिक्ताः ।।
(ऋग्वेदः, 10.112.9)

O Indra! When you released the water blocked by Vritrasura, it gushed forth with great speed. The stream of water released by Indra does not stay at a place because of its velocity and is pure as well.

सध्रीचीः सिन्धुमुशतीरिवायन्त्सनाज्जार आरितः पूर्भिदासाम् ।
अस्तमा ते पार्थिवा वसून्यस्मे जग्मूः सुनृता इन्द्र पूर्वीः ।।
(ऋग्वेदः, 10.112.10

The fast flowing streams of water flowing to dyau reach out to the ocean in the same way as a desirous woman reaches out to her husband. The slayer of enemies and destroyer of enemy forts, Indra has always been the lord of water. O Indra! Bless us with glory, wealth and abode in this world.

5.18 शतप्रभेदनवैरूपकृतम् इन्द्राभिनन्दनम्

5.18 EULOGY OF INDRA BY SHATPRABEDHNA VAIRUPA

वृत्रेण यदहिना बिभ्रदायुधा समस्थिथा युधये शंसमाविदे ।
विश्वे ते अत्र मरुतः सह त्मनावर्धन्नुग्र महिमानमिन्द्रियम् ॥
(ऋग्वेदः, 10.113.3)

In the battlefield, when Indra fights Vritra, who is rushing forth towards him, with his weapons, I sing in praise of him to enhance his glory. O dreadful Indra! All the marutas enhance your might.

भूरि दक्षेभिर्वचनेभिर्ऋक्वभिः सख्येभिः सख्यानि प्रवोचत ।
इन्द्रो धुनिं च चुमुरिं च दम्भयञ्छ्रद्धामनस्या शृणुते दभीतये ॥
(ऋग्वेदः, 10.113.9)

O praying one! Pray to Indra with hymns, delightful voice, loving speech and your mind. This very Indra had slain asuras named Dhuni and Chumuri to protect king Dabhiti. That Indra listens to those who pray to him.

5.19 बृहदुक्थवामदेव्यकृतम् इन्द्राभिनन्दनम्

5.19 EULOGY OF INDRA BY BRIHADUKTHA VAMADEVA

तां सु ते कीर्तिं मघवन्महित्वा यत्वा भीते रोदसी अह्वयेताम् ।
प्रावो देवां आतिरो दासमोजः प्रजायै त्वस्यै यदशिक्ष इन्द्र ॥
(ऋग्वेदः, 10.54.1)

It is thus said in the fifty-fourth sukta of fifth mandala of Rigveda: O munificent one! We sing beautifully in praise of all those great acts of yours which enhance your glory. This heaven and earth, too, calls for your help in fear of the demons. I sing in praise of your acts of protection of the devas, killing the asuras tormenting the devas and eliminating fear from the hearts of your subjects.

यदचरस्तन्वा वावृधानो बलानीन्द्र प्रबुवाणो जनेषु ।
मायेत्सा ते यानि युद्धान्याहुर्नाद्य शत्रुं ननु पुरा विवित्से ॥
(ऋग्वेदः, 10.54.2)

O Indra! You grow in strength by the prayers of people and roam about amid chants of your praise. This act of yours is not illusion. The ancient sages narrate your battles during those days, but you have no enemies of your own.

क उ नु ते महिमनः समस्यास्मत्पूर्व ऋषयोऽन्तमापुः ।
यन्मातरं च पितरं च साकमजनयथास्तन्वः स्वायाः ॥
(ऋग्वेदः, 10.54.3)

O Indra! No one is qualified enough to sing your glory in its full, because this heaven and earth has originated from your body itself.

5.20 वत्सादिकृतम् इन्द्राभिनन्दनम्

5.20 EULOGY OF INDRA BY VATSA

वत्सः काण्वः अभिनन्दयति ।

Veneration of Indra by Vatsa, son of Kanva.

विचिद्वृत्रस्य दोधतो वज्रेण शतपर्वणा ।
शिरो बिभेदवृष्णिना ।।

(ऋग्वेदः, 8.6.6)

Vatsa says in the sixth sukta of eighth mandala of Rigveda: Indra slit the throat of trembling Vritrasura with his divine thunderbolt with sharp edges.

नि शुष्ण इन्द्र धर्णसिं वज्रं जघन्थ दस्यवि ।
वृषा ह्युग्र शृण्विषे ।।

(ऋग्वेदः, 8.6.14)

O Indra! You killed the asura named Shushna with your hundred-edged thunderbolt, which made you famous in the world.

श्रुष्टिगुः काण्वः अभिनन्दयति ।

Adoration of Indra by Shrustigu, son of Kanva.

प्र यो ननक्षे अभ्योजसा क्रिविं वधैः शुष्णं निघोषयन् ।
यदेदस्तम्भीत्प्रथयन्नमूं दिवमादिज्जनिष्ट पार्थिवः ।।

(ऋग्वेदः, 8.53.8)

When the asuras had stopped this Dyauloka, the thundering Indra killed Shushna by his dreadful weapons and liberated the earth.

यस्यायं विश्व आर्यो दासः शेवधिपा अरिः ।
तिरश्चिदर्ये रुशमे पवीरवि तुभ्येत्सो अज्यते रयिः ।।

(ऋग्वेदः, 8.53.9)

That Indra whose treasury is guarded by all the Aryas and dasas, is the lord of all. O Indra! It was because of you that the secret wealth of sages Rusham and Paviru was created.

मेध्यः काण्वः अभिष्टौति ।

Reverence of Indra by Medhya, son of Kanva.

य आयुं कुत्समतिथिग्वमर्दयो वावृधानो दिवेदिवे ।
तं त्वां वयं हर्यश्वं शतक्रतुं वाजयन्तो हवामहे ।।

(ऋग्वेदः, 8.53.2)

O Indra! You have helped Ayu, Kutsa, and Atithigva rise. O Indra! You possess horse namely Hari and perform hundreds of good acts, hence we pray to you to provide us with strength.

गोषूक्त्यश्वसूक्तिनौ काण्वायनावभिनन्दयतः ।

Reverence of Indra by grandsons of Kanva, Goshukti and Ashvasukti,

अपां फेनेन नमुचेः शिर इन्द्रोदवर्तयः ।
विश्वा यदजयः स्पृधः ।।

(ऋग्वेदः, 8.14.13)

The fourteenth sukta of eighth mandala of Rigveda says: O Indra! You won over the whole army and slit the throat of the asura Namuchi with the foam of water.

मायाभिरुत् सिसृप्सत इन्द्र द्यामारुरुक्षतः ।
अवदस्यूँरधूनुथाः ।।

(ऋग्वेदः, 8.14.14)

O Indra! You instilled fear in all those demons who aspired to attack the Dyauloka and conquer the whole world.

5.21 नोधा-गौतमाङ्गौरवकृतम् इन्द्राभिनन्दनम्

5.21 EULOGY OF INDRA BY NODHA GAUTAMA

नोधा गौतमः अभिनन्दयति ।

Reverence of Indra by Nodha Gautama.

अस्मा इदु त्यदनु दाय्येषामेको यद्वब्ने भूरेरीशानः ।
प्रैतशं सूर्ये पस्पृधानं सौवश्व्ये सुष्विमावदिन्द्रः ।।
(ऋग्वेदः, 1.61.15)

This Indra possesses many riches. The devotees sing only those hymns which he desires to listen. Indra had fought with Surya, son of Sauvashva, to protect Aitasha.

त्वं सत्य इन्द्र धृष्णुरेतान्त्वमृभुक्षा नर्यस्त्वं षाट् ।
त्वं शुष्णं वृजने पृक्ष आणौ यूने कुत्साय द्युमते सचाहन् ।।
(ऋग्वेदः, 1.63.3)

O Indra! You are the protector of truth, killer of enemies, lord of the three worlds, leader and tolerating. You killed Shushna to protect the young Kutsa in the battlefield.

अङ्ग औरवः अभिनन्दयति ।

Reverence of Indra by Aurava, son of Uru.

तव त्य इन्द्र सख्येषु वह्नय ऋतं मन्वाना व्यदर्दिरुर्वलम् ।
यत्र दशस्यन्नुषसो रिणन्नपः कुत्साय मन्मन्नह्यश्च दंसयः ।।
(ऋग्वेदः, 10.138.1)

Your devotees, blessed with the power of your friendship, killed the demon Bala. O Indra! With your blessing, Kutsa saw the dawn singing hymns in your praise and liberated water, as a result of which all the bad deeds of Vritra were automatically annulled.

अवासृजः प्रश्वः श्वञ्चयो गिरीनुदाज उस्रा अपिबो मधु प्रियम् ।
अवर्धयो वनिनो अस्य दंससा शुशोच सूर्य ऋतजातया गिरा ।।
(ऋग्वेदः, 10.138.2)

O Indra! You created water from cloud, freed the cows hidden by Balasura in the caves and drank Soma after this. The trees of the forest were propagated by the rains. At the time of yajna, when Indra was worshiped with the worthy hymns of Veda, then the sun shone forth due to the glory of Indra.

वि सूर्यो मध्ये अमुचद्रथं दिवो विदद्दासाय प्रतिमानमार्यः ।
दृह्लानि पिप्रोरसुरस्य मायिन इन्द्रो व्यास्यच्चकृवाँ ऋजिश्वना ।।
(ऋग्वेदः, 10.138.3)

Indra disowned the dasas, then the sun started moving his chariot in Dyauloka. Indra, by befriending rajrishi Rijrashva, destroyed the vast and remote cities of the illusory asura named Pipru.

अनाधृष्टानि धृषितो व्यास्यन्निधीँरदेवाँ अमृणदयास्यः ।
मासेव सूर्यो वसु पुर्यमाददे गृणानः शत्रूँरशृणाद्विरुक्मता ।।
(ऋग्वेदः, 10.138.4)

The invincible Indra destroyed the enemies; he killed the powerful and mighty asuras on the prayer of sage Vyasa. As the sun in a particular month draws water from the soil, in the same way Indra acquires wealth of the enemies. You kill the enemies with your lightning thunderbolt.

अयुद्धसेनो विभ्वा विभिन्दता दाशद्वृत्रहा तुज्यानि तेजते ।
इन्द्रस्य वज्रादिबिभेदभिश्नथः प्राक्रामच्छुन्ध्यूरजहादुषा अनः ।।
(ऋग्वेदः, 10.138.5)

This Indra, without making the soldiers fight, kills his enemies with his vajra, kills Vritrasura and bestows wealth upon his loved ones. The asuras get frightened by his vajra. When Indra gives light to the sun, then usha runs her chariot.

एता त्या ते श्रुत्यानि केवला यदेक एकमकृणोरयज्ञम् ।
मासां विधानमदधा अधि द्यवि त्वया विभिन्नं भरति प्रधिं पिता ।।
(ऋग्वेदः, 10.138.6)

O Indra! You have killed those who disturb the sacrifices, your acts of bravery are worth listening. The sun, the creator of months, was established in the Dyauloka by you and this Dyauloka is powered by you to hold the chakra.

5.22 इन्द्रेण कुत्साय प्रीतिप्रसादानम्

5.22 KUTSA'S HYMNS OF GRATITUDE FOR INDRA

कृतज्ञतास्तुतिसूक्तपाठानन्तरम् इन्द्रेण कुत्साय वेशभूषापरिच्छदैः स्वसारूप्यं सोमसग्धिश्चेति द्विविधं प्रीतिप्रसाददानम् ।

In gratitude, Indra offers two gifts to Kutsa—making him look like him, with his dress and ornaments, and making him a partner in drinking Soma amidst the chanting of hymns.

इत्थं तत्र सभायां सभासदै राजभिर्मनुष्यैश्च ।
ऋषिभिर्देवैरसुरैः सभाजितोऽभून्महोत्सवे स्वाराट् ।।46।।

Thus that mighty Indra was honoured by all the kings, devas, human beings, sages, and the asuras gathered in that ceremony.

आराध्याः संभ्रान्ताः संभावितसज्जनाश्च समवेत्य ।
सप्रश्रयं सविनयं न्यवेदयन् श्रद्धया कृतज्ञत्वम् ।।47।।

The adorable, rich, honourable and noble men gathered to offer their gratitude to Indra with humility and gaiety.

तेषां कृतज्ञतां तामभिनन्द्य हृदा स्वभक्तिभावम् ।
प्रतिपद्य च सौहार्द्यं दर्शयितुं समयमनुमेने ।।48।।

All of them vowed to show their gratitude by praying, adoring and showing respect towards Indra.

महसि च मघवानिन्द्रो महसा परितोषितः प्रददौ ।
कुत्साय तत्र तस्मै सोमे सग्धिं स्वसारूप्यम् ।।49।।

In that festival, the glorious Indra, satisfied with the festive ceremony, offered sage Kutsa his company in consuming Soma and bestowed upon him a form like his own.

तत इन्द्राकुत्साभ्यां सहभावं सह च सोमसवम् ।
भूषावेषपरिच्छदपरिचरसाम्यं च तत्राभूत् ।।50।।

In this way, Indra and Kutsa acquired identical forms, including their guise, jewellery and their attendants; they looked equal in every way.

इत्थं महः समाप्तौ विश्वामित्रः सभां विसर्जयितुम् ।
मन्त्रं विसर्जनीयं प्रत्युत्थायेन्द्रमन्वाख्यत् ॥51॥

In this way, after the end of the ceremony, sage Vishvamitra stood up after Indra and chanted the hymn of completion.

इन्द्रेण कृतो यावानुपकारस्तं पुनः प्रथयन् ।
स्वीयां कृतज्ञतां च प्रदर्शयन्निन्द्रमस्तौत्सः ॥52॥

He eulogized Indra and expressed once again his reverence for Indra while describing the favours done for him.

5.23 देवेन्द्रस्य स्वर्गगमनम्

5.23 INDRA RETURNING TO HEAVEN

सभाविसर्जनावसरे जिगमिषुं देवेन्द्रं प्रति विश्वामित्रस्य प्रणयवचनम् ।

Vishvamitra's thanksgiving at the conclusion of the ceremony and before the departure of Indra.

इन्द्रापर्वता बृहता रथेन वामीरिष आ वहतं सुवीराः ।
वीतं हव्यान्यध्वरेषु देवा वर्धेथां गीर्भिरिळया मदन्ता ॥
(ऋग्वेदः, 3.53.1)

In the fifty-third sukta of third mandala of Rigveda, Vishvamitra says: O Indra who is a like a mountain! Come on your mighty chariot and bless us with most excellent offspring and huge amount of wealth desired by us. O devas! Attain growth by our prayers and accept our oblations. Gain bliss from the food that we offer to you.

तिष्ठा सु कं मघवन्मा परागाः सोमस्य नु त्वा सुषुतस्य यक्षि ।
पितुर्न पुत्रः सिचमा रभे त इन्द्र स्वादिष्ठया गिरा शचीवः ॥
(ऋग्वेदः, 3.53.2)

O Maghavan (munificent) Indra! Come and sit close to us and don't move away. I'll perform a yajna of well-prepared Soma for you. O powerful Indra! I seek refuge in you through my eulogizing prayers in the same way as a son seeks support from his father.

शंसावाध्वर्यो प्रति मे गृणीहीन्द्राय वाहः कृणावाव जुष्टम् ।
एदं बर्हिर्यजमानस्य सीदाऽथा च भूदुक्थमिन्द्राय शस्तम् ॥
(ऋग्वेदः, 3.53.3)

O Adhvaryo! Inspire me, thereafter both of us [Adhvaryo and Ritvig] will pray to Indra. Sit down on the seat of yajamana, so that the two of us can sing hymns in praise of Indra.

जायेदस्तं मघवन्त्सेदु योनिस्तदित्त्वा युक्ता हरयो वहन्तु ।
यदा कदा च सुनवाम सोममग्निष्ट्वा दूतो धन्वात्यच्छ ॥
(ऋग्वेदः, 3.53.4)

O wealthy Indra! Home is where your beloved is. Therefore, O Indra!

Command the horses pulling your chariot to take you to that place of abode. Like an envoy, Agni will carry the soma-rasa prepared by us to you.

परा याहि मघवन्ना च याहीन्द्र भ्रातरुभयत्र ते अर्थम् ।
यत्रा रथस्य बृहतो निधानं विमोचनं वाजिनो रासभस्य ।।

(ऋग्वेद:, 3.53.5)

O Maghavan! O Brother! Either you stay close to us or go to your place of abode. You are important at both the places. Therefore, wherever you go, unbridle the neighing horses of your chariot and take complete rest.

अपा: सोममस्तमिन्द्र प्रयाहि कल्याणीर्जाया सुरणं गृहे ते ।
यत्रा रथस्य बृहतो निधानं विमोचनं वाजिनो दक्षिणावत् ।।

(ऋग्वेद:, 3.53.6)

O Indra! Go back to your abode after drinking the Soma-rasa,because your well-wishing and auspicious wife waits for you at your home. You will be happy there. O Indra! Wherever you stop your chariot, unbridle the horses with compassion and take complete rest.

इमे भोजा अङ्गरसो विरूपा दिवस्पुत्रासो असुरस्य वीरा: ।
विश्वामित्राय ददतो मघानि सहस्रसावे प्रतिरन्त आयु: ।।

(ऋग्वेद:, 3.53.7)

The sons of energetic and brave Indra and Bhoj, Angiras and Virusas, increased my lifespan in order to perform the yajna by bestowing many riches upon me [Vishvamitra].

रूपं रूपं मघवा बोभवीति माया: कृण्वानस्तन्वं परि स्वाम् ।
त्रिर्यद्दिव: परि मुहूर्तमागात्स्वैर्मन्त्रैरनृतुपा ऋतावा ।।

(ऋग्वेद:, 3.53.8)

This Indra, replete with divine majesty and coming from Dyauloka, uses his wondrous powers to pervade the three lokas instantaneously. This Soma-drinking Indra, who regulates karmas in accordance with the seasons, adopts several forms while performing astonishing deeds.

महाँ ऋषिर्देवजा देवजूतोऽस्तभ्नात् सिन्धुमर्णवं नृचक्षा: ।
विश्वामित्रो यदवहत्सुदासमप्रियायत कुशिकेभिरिन्द्र: ।।

(ऋग्वेद:, 3.53.9)

He is a well-wisher of the world, born of great devas, endowed with divine qualities and is great. That Vishvamitra halted the flooded river and went to the yajna of Sudas to ensure a place of affection for Indra by the Kushikas.

हंसा इव कृणुथ श्लोकमद्रिभिर्मदन्तो गीर्भिरध्वरे सुते सचा ।
देवेभिर्विप्रा ऋषयो नृचक्षसो वि पिबध्वं कुशिकाः सोम्यं मधु ॥
(ऋग्वेदः, 3.53.10)

O wise, foresighted and well-wishers of humanity Kushikas! Drink the sweet Soma-rasa after extracting it from the yajna [by grinding with stones] and chant the hymn in tune and unison like a goose.

उप प्रेत कुशिकाश्चेतयध्वमश्वं राये प्रमुञ्चता सुदासः ।
राजा वृत्रं जङ्घनत्प्रागपागुदगथा यजाते वर आ पृथिव्याः ॥
(ऋग्वेदः, 3.53.11)

O Kushikas! Come closer in ecstasy and unbridle the horses of Sudas in order to attain divine majesty. The gifted Indra has destroyed the enemies in all directions and he performs yajna seated at the prime location on the earth after killing the enemies.

य इमे रोदसी उभे अहमिन्द्रमतुष्टवम् ।
विश्वामित्रस्य रक्षति ब्रह्मेदं भारतं जनम् ॥
(ऋग्वेदः, 3.53.12)

I prayed to heaven and earth, and Indra. This prayer performed by me [Vishvamitra] protects and helps the *bharatavasis* [descendents of king Bharata] prosper.

विश्वामित्रा अरासत ब्रह्मेन्द्राय वज्रिणे ।
करदिन्नः सुराधसः ॥
(ऋग्वेदः, 3.53.13)

The friends of the world [that is, those who love the world] composed hymns in praise of Indra, the wielder of vajra. Therefore, Indra helps us gain supreme wealth.

किं ते कृण्वन्ति कीकटेषु गावो नाशिरं दुह्रे न तपन्ति घर्मम् ।
आ नो भर प्रमगन्दस्य वेदो नैचाशाखं मघवन्नन्धया नः ॥
(ऋग्वेदः, 3.53.14)

O Maghavan! The cows living in the Kikat [anarya] lands neither provide milk to Indra nor do they provide fuel to kindle the fire of yajna, hence they are useless. O Indra! Bring to us the wealth of the usurpers and subjugate the anaryas for us.

5.24 इन्द्रकुत्सयोः स्वर्गाय सह प्रस्थानम्

5.24 INDRA AND KUTSA GOING TOGETHER TO HEAVEN

कुत्सः सहानुगन्तुं मनो दधे शक्रसत्कृत्यै ।
इन्द्रोपि तत्र कुत्सं सत्कर्तुं पथि पुरश्चक्रे ।।53।।

Kutsa decided to go with Indra in order to show hospitability to him. Indra, too, put Kutsa ahead of himself in the journey to show respect to him.

इन्द्रसमानैर्मानैः कुत्सस्याभूत् पुरो यानम् ।
तत्पश्चात् पथि शक्रः स्वपरिकरैर्यानमारेभे ।।54।।

By receiving hospitability equal to that of Indra, the cavalcade of Kutsa moved in front and Indra followed him in the company of his attendants.

अस्ति सहस्रास्वीने पथि लोकः स्वर्ग इत्येवम् ।
व्याचष्ट ऐतरेयः सहस्रमेतत्त्वनेकार्थम् ।।55।।

According to Aitareya Brahmana, the svargaloka is located on the Sahastrasvin Marga. The word sahastra has many meanings.

इन्द्राकुत्सौ त्वश्वैस्त्रिभिर्दिनैर्जग्मतुः स्वर्गम् ।
सह च सहस्रं किञ्चित् पश्चात्तु मारुती सेना ।।56।।

Indra and Kutsa reached svargaloka on their horses in three days, accompanied by a thousand horses, with the divine army following them at some distance.

अमरावत्यां देवाः श्रुत्वा वैकुण्ठमागमिष्यन्तम् ।
पुरतः कृत्वेन्द्राणीमुपह्वरे स्वागतायागुः ।।57।।

On hearing about the arrival of Baikuntha Indra in Amaravati, the devas put Indrani in front and took him to a private place to welcome him.

अभ्यायान्तौ दूराद् दृष्ट्वेन्द्रौ द्वौ शचीन्द्राणी ।
चकितातिविस्मिता सा प्रोषितपत्यर्चने च संमुमुहे ।।58।।

On seeing two Indras coming from a distance, Indrani was astonished and bewildered but she was happy that her husband was returning home.

मरुदुद्बोधितवृत्ता स्वामिनमवधार्य्य पूजयामास ।
सारूप्यदानविषये संवादं केन्द्रतश्चक्रे ॥59॥

After listening to the story of the lord from the devas, Indrani performed the worship with the lord in her mind and conversed with Indra about *Sarupyadana* (blessing someone with the likeness of Indra).

5.25 स्वर्गे विजयाभिनन्दनोत्सवः

5.25 FELICITATION OF INDRA IN HEAVEN

अमरावत्यामिन्द्रः स्वीयं सदनं समासाद्य ।
सत्कारदानमानैः कुत्सं संभावयामास ।।60।।

After reaching his palace in Amaravati, Indra honoured Kutsa with hospitality, gifts and respect.

मानुषलोके कुत्सप्रस्थानं दस्युसंहारम् ।
इन्द्रविजयमुपलक्ष्य च महोत्सवः कल्पितो देवैः ।।61।।

The devas organized this festival keeping in mind the departure of Kutsa to the human world, destruction of the dasyus and victory for Indra.

तत्र बृहस्पतिनुन्नः सप्तगुरिन्द्रं महोत्सवे प्रमुखः ।
विजयितमभितुष्टाव प्रोच्य विजयसिद्धमेतदुत्कर्षम् ।।62।।

In this grand festival, inspired by Brihaspati, Saptagu sang in praise of the victorious Indra and his rise.

आर्यं वर्णं दस्युभिरुपद्रुतं यो द्रुतं समाश्वास्य ।
उदजापयत् तमिन्द्रं सप्तगुमुखतः सुरास्तदाऽभ्यगृणन् ।।63।।

Indra gave assurance to the Arya tormented by the rebellious dasyus that he would free them from this trouble soon. Thus, the devas honoured Indra through the medium of Saptagu.

5.26 नृमेधपुरुमेधकृता इन्द्रस्तुतिः

5.26 NRIMEDHA AND PURUMEDHA PRAISING INDRA

तत्रेन्द्रस्तुतिविधानाय नृमेधपुरुमेधौ देवेन्द्रसातेयं मरुद्‌गणम् अभिलक्ष्य मन्त्रयतः ।

There, Nrimedha and Purumedha, while singing in praise of Indra, chanted mantras invoking all the gods together with Devendra.

बृहदिन्द्राय गायत मरुतो वृत्रहन्तमम् ।
येन ज्योतिरजनयन्नृतावृधो देवं देवाय जागृवि ॥

(ऋग्वेदः, 8.78.1)

In the eighty-ninth sukta of eighth mandala of Rigveda, Nrimedha and Purumedha say this about Indra: O propagators of yajna, marutganas! By the formula with which you have produced the light with divine splendour, utter that hymn namely brihat for Indra, the destroyer of Vritra.

अपाधमदभिशस्तीरशस्तिहाथेन्द्रो द्युम्न्याभवत् ।
देवास्त इन्द्र सख्याय येमिरे बृहद्‌भानो मरुद्‌गण ॥

(ऋग्वेदः, 8.78.2)

O illuminated Marutganas! Indra has killed all those violent enemies who were bad. This act has made Indra so energetic and gifted. Everyone goes to Indra to earn his friendship.

प्र व इन्द्राय बृहते मरुतो ब्रह्मार्चत ।
वृत्रं हनति वृत्रहा शतक्रतुर्वज्रेण शतपर्वणा ॥

(ऋग्वेदः, 8.78.3)

O Marutganas! That Indra has slaughtered Vritra with his divine thunderbolt. He has performed hundreds of pious acts and has killed the enemies. All of you should sing hymns in praise of that Indra.

अभि प्र भर धृषता धृषन्मनः श्रवश्चित्ते असद् बृहत् ।
अर्षन्त्वापो जवसा वि मातरो हनो वृत्रं जया स्वः ॥

(ऋग्वेदः, 8.78.4)

O strong-willed Indra! Provide us that supreme food in abundance with your firm and powerful mind. O Indra! Win over the water bodies by killing Vritra and encourage the fast-flowing rivers to flow with all their might.

अथैतौ नृमेधपुरुमेधौ देवेन्द्रम् एव अभिलक्ष्य महयतः स्म ।

Thereupon, Nrimedha and Purumedha sang in praise of Devaraja Indra.

यज्जायथ अपूर्व्य मघन्वृत्रहत्याय ।
तत्पृथिवीमप्रथयस्तदस्तभ्ना उत द्याम् ॥

(ऋग्वेदः, 8.78.5)

O Indra, gifted with divine majesty and performer of extraordinary acts! The power with which you destroyed Vritra, with the same divine power you expanded the realms of the world and stabilized heaven and earth.

तत्ते यज्ञो अजायत तदर्क उत हस्कृतिः ।
तद्विश्वमभिभूरसि यज्जातं यच्च जन्त्वम् ॥

(ऋग्वेदः, 8.78.6)

O Indra! All of this is yours in entirety. The yajnas that were performed, the mantras that were chanted, even the *vushatkara* [exclamation uttered at the end of the sacrificial verse, svaha] is for you only. All those things that originated in this world are all yours.

आमासु पक्वमैरय आ सूर्यं रोहयो देवि ।
धर्मं न सामन्तपता सुवृक्तिभिर्जुष्टं गिर्वणसे बृहत् ॥

(ऋग्वेदः, 8.78.7)

O Indra! The nourishing milk was implanted in the cows by your grace and you put the sun in Dyauloka. O human beings! Make Indra grow with supreme hymns of praise in the same way as the *pravargya* [a ceremony at which fresh milk is poured into a heated vessel] is the first step in the Soma sacrifice. Sing the brihat sama for the revered Indra.

पुनरेतौ नृमेधापुरुमेधौ देवेन्द्रम् अभिवर्णयतः ।

Nrimedha and Purumedha singing again in praise of Devendra.

आ नो विश्वासु हव्य इन्द्रः समत्सु भूषतु ।
उप ब्रह्माणि सवनानि वृत्रहा परमज्या ऋचीषमः ॥

(ऋग्वेदः, 8.79.1)

This Indra, who is the destroyer of Vritra, mightiest among the drinkers of Soma, the one who possesses the supreme bowstring of the divine bow, and the one who is sought for help in battles, that Indra should adorn our mantra and yajnas.

त्वं दाता प्रथमो राधसामस्यसि सत्य ईशानकृत् ।
तुविद्युम्नस्य युज्या वृणीमहे पुत्रस्य शवसो महः ॥

(ऋग्वेदः, 8.79.2)

O Indra! You are the greatest giver of gifts and you have complete command over truth. We aspire for wealth worthy of the brilliant Indra.

ब्रह्मा त इन्द्र गिर्वणः क्रियन्ते अनतिद्भुता ।
इमा जुषस्व हर्यश्व योजनेन्द्र या ते अमन्महि ॥

(ऋग्वेदः, 8.79.3)

O Indra, the possessor of the finest horses! Be kind enough to accept the hymns in your praise that we sing to narrate your real [divine] form and the same hymns which we encourage others to chant.

त्वं हि सत्यो मघवन्ननानतो वृत्रा भूरि न्यृञ्जसे ।
स त्वं शविष्ठ वज्रहस्त दाशुषेऽर्वाञ्चं रयिमा कृधि ॥

(ऋग्वेदः, 8.79.4)

O Maghavan! You are the destroyer of several Vritras, speaker of truth and you never succumb to anyone. O destroyer of Vritras, powerful Indra! Provide more wealth to the giver of gifts.

त्वमिन्द्र यशा अस्यृजीषी शवसस्पते ।
त्वं वृत्राणि हंस्यप्रतीन्येक इदनुत्ता चर्षणीधृता ॥

(ऋग्वेदः, 8.79.5)

O lord of powers! You are glorious, drinker of Soma and you protect the human beings with your vajra from the Vritras, who are otherwise indomitable.

तमु त्वा नूनमसुर प्रचेतसं राधो भागमिवेमहे ।
महीव कृत्तिः शरणा त इन्द्र प्र ते सुम्ना नो अश्नवन् ॥

(ऋग्वेदः, 8.79.6)

O wise Indra! We want to cherish you. We ask for wealth from Indra in the same way as a son asks for wealth from his father. O Indra! You are the protector of lives, your shelter is like an armour for us; we request you to give us wealth.

5.27 मारुतकृता इन्द्रस्तुतिः

5.27 EULOGY OF INDRA BY MARUTA

अव द्रप्सो अंशुमतीमतिष्ठदियानः कृष्णो दशभिः सहस्रैः ।
आवत्तमिन्द्रः शच्या धामन्तमप स्नेहितीर्नृमणा अधत्त ।।
(ऋग्वेदः, 8.85.13)

The fast-moving Krishnasura halted at the banks of the Anshumati river with an army of 10,000 and Indra, proud of his immense power, confronted Krishnasura and totally destroyed the enemy camp.

द्रप्समपश्यं विषुणे चरन्तमुपह्वरे नद्यो अंशुमत्याः ।
नभो न कृष्णमवतस्थिवांसमिष्यामि वो वृषणो युध्यताजौ ।।
(ऋग्वेदः, 8.85.14)

I have seen Krishnasura, facing me like a beaming sun, and Drapsa wandering in the cave on the banks of Anshumati river. O Indra! I need your help, fight them.

अध द्रप्सो अंशुमत्या उपस्थेऽधारयत्तन्वं तित्विषाणः ।
विशो अदेवीरभ्या चरन्तीर्बृहस्पतिना युजेन्द्रः ससाहे ।।
(ऋग्वेदः, 8.85.15)

Thereafter Drapsa assumed an irradiating form on the bank of Anshumati river. With Brihaspati's help, Indra defeated the enemies, who were attacking from all sides.

त्वं ह त्यत्सप्तभ्यो जायमानोऽशत्रुभ्यो अभवः शत्रुरिन्द्र ।
गूह्ले द्यावापृथिवी अन्वविन्दो विभुमद्भ्यो भुवनेभ्यो रणं धाः ।।
(ऋग्वेदः, 8.85.16)

त्वं ह त्यदप्रतिमानमोजो वज्रेण वज्रिन्धृषितो जघन्थ ।
त्वं शुष्णस्यावातिरो वधत्रैस्त्वं गा इन्द्रशच्येदविन्दः ।।
(ऋग्वेदः, 8.85.17)

O thunderbolt-wielding Indra! You killed Vritra, possessing unequalled power, with your thunderbolt. You slaughtered the asura named Shushna with your weapons to release the cows from their bondage.

त्वं ह त्यद् वृषभ चर्षणीनाङ्घनो वृत्राणां तविषो वभूथ ।
त्वं सिन्धूँरसृजस्तस्तभानान् त्वमपो अजयो दासपत्नीः ॥
(ऋग्वेदः, 8.85.18)

O Indra, the most powerful one among the humans! It is you who became all powerful by killing the Vritras, you were the one who caused the blocked rivers to flow. You defeated the dasa to release the flow of all those stagnated rivers.

5.28 वैखानसवभ्रकृता इन्द्रस्तुतिः

5.28 ADULATION OF INDRA BY SAGE VABHRA

स द्रुह्वणे मनुष ऊर्ध्वसान आ साविषदर्शसानाय शरुम् ।
स नृतमो नहुषोऽस्मत्सुजातः पुरोऽभिनदर्हन् दस्युहत्ये ॥
(ऋग्वेदः, 10.99.7)

That most excellent Indra uses vajra to annihilate the wicked and violent ones. He is the best among men, born in a highly respected family; he will slaughter our enemies in fierce battles to punish the wicked ones and to demolish their strong forts.

सो अभ्रियो न यवस उदन्यन्क्षयाय गातुं विदन्नो अस्मे ।
उप यत्सीददिन्दुं शरीरैः श्येनोऽयोपाष्टिर्हन्ति दस्यून् ॥
(ऋग्वेदः, 10.99.8)

Like clouds, he causes rains for our crops to grow and he showers our places of abode. That Indra gets hold of the enemies like the Shyen bird clutching its prey in its sharp and strong claws. When he goes to Soma in his complete form, he destroys the enemies.

स व्राधतः शवसानेभिरस्य कुत्साय शुष्णं कृपणे परादात् ।
अयं कविमनयच्छस्यमानमत्कं यो अस्य सनितोत नृणाम् ॥
(ऋग्वेदः, 10.99.9)

That Indra vanquishes the powerful enemies with his potent weapons. This Indra slaughtered the asura named Shushna for his devotee Kutsa, who prayed to him. He also curbed the enemies of poet Ushna. This poet Ushna knew about the all-pervasive form of the rain god, Indra, as well as his follower marutas.

अस्य स्तोमेभिरौशिज ऋजिश्वा व्रजं दरयद्वृषभेण पिप्रोः ।
सुत्वा यद्यजतो दीदयद्गीः पुर इयानो अभि वर्षसा भूत् ॥
(ऋग्वेदः, 10.99.11)

Rijrashva, son of Usija, who gained strength by praying to Indra, tore apart the vital organs of an asura named Pipru. When worshipping, Aushija uttered hymns while offering Soma in the yajna, he destroyed the enemies in the process of destroying their cities.

5.29 सप्तगुवर्णितः इन्द्रमहिमा

5.29 HYMNS IN PRAISE OF INDRA SUNG BY SAPTAGU

अथ प्रमहप्रमुखः सप्तगुः स्वर्णरः प्राधान्येनेन्द्रं महयति ।

Thereupon, hymns, mostly in praise of Indra, were sung by Saptagu.

जगृभ्मा ते दक्षिणमिन्द्र हस्तं वसूयवो वसुपते वसूनाम् ।
विद्मा हि त्वा गोपतिं शूर गोनामस्मभ्यं चित्रं वृषणं रयिं दाः ।।
(ऋग्वेदः, 10.47.1)

It is said in praise of Indra in the forty-seventh sukta of tenth mandala of Rigveda: O lord of wealth, Indra! We who aspire for wealth hold your right hand [because the right hand is used to gift things]. O Indra! We know you as the lord of the cows. Offer us astonishing and desired wealth.

स्वायुधं स्ववसं सुनीथं चतुःसमुद्रं धरुणं रयीणाम् ।
चर्कृत्यं शंस्यं भूरिवारमस्मभ्यं चित्रं वृषणं रयिं दाः ।।
(ऋग्वेदः, 10.47.2)

Indra is the possessor of magnificent weapons like vajra, the one who controls every one, has beautiful eyes, offers glory to all the four oceans, is producer of wealth and relieves us from pain and misery. He is worthy of praise. We know, you can offer us awesome wealth.

सुब्रह्माणं देववन्तं बृहन्तमुरुं गभीरं पृथुबुध्नमिन्द्र ।
श्रुतऋषिमुग्रमभिमातिषाहमस्मभ्यं चित्रं वृषणं रयिं दाः ।।
(ऋग्वेदः, 10.47.3)

O Indra! We know you. You are great, loyal to the god, worthy of praise, all-pervasive, possessing deep, extensive, and serious knowledge, majestic and destroyer of enemies. Therefore, O Indra! Bless us with an adorable and powerful son.

सनद्वाजं विप्रवीरं तरुत्रं धनस्पृतं शूशुवांसं सुदक्षम् ।
दस्युहनं पूर्भिदमिन्द्र सत्यमस्मभ्यं चित्रं वृषणं रयिं दाः ।।
(ऋग्वेदः, 10.47.4)

O Indra, the producer of food, most excellent, all powerful, provider of wealth, destroyer of enemies and their forts and symbol of truth! Gift us with our desired strong son.

अश्वावन्तं रथिनं वीरवन्तं सहस्रिणं शतिनं वाजमिन्द्र ।
भद्रव्रातं विप्रवीरं स्वर्षामस्मभ्यं चित्रं वृषणं रयिं दाः ॥
(ऋग्वेदः, 10.47.5)

O Indra! Endowed with horses, chariots and warriors, possessing hundreds and thousands of servants, accomplished with auspicious attendants, most excellent warrior and giver of joy, bless us with the wealth of our desired powerful son.

प्र सप्तगुमृतधीतिं सुमेधां बृहस्पतिं मतिरच्छा जिगाति ।
य आङ्गिरसो नमसोपसद्योऽस्मभ्यं चित्रं वृषणं रयिं दाः ॥
(ऋग्वेदः, 10.47.6)

Give me [Saptagu] excellent and knowledgeable wisdom. I'm Brihaspati, the performer of acts of truth and possessing great wisdom. I've been born in the lineage of Angiras, I saluted the gods and was close to them, therefore bless me with the wealth of an exceptional and powerful son.

वनीवानो मम दूतास इन्द्रं स्तोमाश्चरन्ति सुमतीरियानाः ।
हृदिस्पृशो मनसा वच्यमाना अस्मभ्यं चित्रं वृषणं रयिं दाः ॥
(ऋग्वेदः, 10.47.7)

May Indra receive our affectionate requests made in earnest and friendly disposition! These hymns are heart-touching and are uttered from the conscious mind. Therefore, I wish to be blessed with an extraordinary wealth of a son.

यत्त्वा यामि दद्धि तन्न इन्द्र बृहन्तं क्षयमसमं जनानाम् ।
अभि तद् द्यावापृथिवी गृणीतामस्मभ्यं चित्रं वृषणं रयिं दाः ॥
(ऋग्वेदः, 10.47.8)

O Indra! Bless me with all that I desire from you. Give me the best abode and an exceptionally good home which will be praised in the heaven and on earth. O Indra! Bless us with astonishing and opulent wealth.

अभिगरप्रतिगरनियमः ।

Law of argument and counter argument.

सदसि पुरातनसमये संवादेऽभ्यर्थनासु वा महताम् ।
प्रथमं यद्वक्तव्यं सोऽभिगरः प्रतिगरस्तु तत्र परः ।।64।।

In ancient times, the first statement uttered in assemblies, conversation or praise of great people was called *abhigara* and the statement given in response was termed as *pratigara.*

यं प्रत्यभिगर उक्तः सोऽभ्युपयन् प्रतिगरं कुरुते ।
सोऽपगरोऽभिगरं चेदाक्षिपति त्रुटिमुदाहरँस्तस्य ।।65।।

In case, the one towards whom the abhigara been aimed at finds fault with the statement and he objects, the speaker has to do pratigara.

स्वर्गे विजयमहोत्सव-संसदि सप्तगुकृतेऽर्थनाऽभिगरे ।
प्रतिगरतया महेन्द्रोऽभ्युपयन्नूचे पुराकृतं त्राणम् ।।66।।

In the forty-eighth sukta of tenth mandala of Rigveda, Indra responds [pratigara] to the pronunciation of request [abhigara] by sage Saptagu in the assembly convened in the heavens to celebrate his victory.

सप्तगुमुखेन देवानामभिगरे देवेन्द्रस्य प्रतिगरः ।

Indra's response to the prayers of devas.

अहं भुवं वसुनः पूर्व्यस्पतिरहं धनानि सं जयामि शश्वतः ।
मां हवन्ते पितरं न जन्तवोऽहं दाशुषे विभजामि भोजनम् ।।
(ऋग्वेदः, 10.48.1)

I'm the owner of all the wealth; I always win over my enemies along with their wealth. All the living beings call upon me in the same way as a child calls his father respectfully. I'm the donor and I provide grains and other accomplishments to the subjects.

अहमिन्द्रो रोधो वक्षो अथर्वणस्त्रिताय गा अजनयमहेरधि ।
अहं दस्युभ्यः परि नृम्णमा ददे गोत्रा शिक्षन् दधीचे मातरिश्वने ।।
(ऋग्वेदः, 10.48.2)

I slit the head of Dadhichi, son of Atharva; I had produced water from the clouds to replenish Trita, I had obtained wealth from the dasyus, and I made the clouds pour down water for Dadhichi, the son of Matharishva.

मह्यं त्वष्टा वज्रमतक्षदायसं मयि देवासोऽवृजन्नपि क्रतुम् ।
ममानीकं सूर्यस्येव दुष्टरं मामार्यन्ति कृतेन कर्त्वेन च ॥
(ऋग्वेदः, 10.48.3)

Tvashta made vajra for me, which is as hard as iron; the devas perform yajnas for me, my army is invincible like the sun, and people attain me only through their good acts.

अहमेतं गव्ययमश्व्यं पशुं पुरीषिणं सायकेना हिरण्ययम् ।
पुरू सहस्रा निशिशामि दाशुषे यन्मा सोमास उक्थिनो अमन्दिषुः ॥
(ऋग्वेदः, 10.48.4)

When the devotees please me with chanting of hymns and Soma, I sharpen the edges of my thousand weapons. Then I win all the cows, horses, gold, and milk from the enemies with my weapons.

अहमिन्द्रो न परा जिग्य इद्धनं न मृत्यवे व्रतस्थे कदाचन ।
सोममिन्मा सुन्वन्तो याचता वसु न मे पूरवः सख्ये रिषाथन ॥
(ऋग्वेदः, 10.48.5)

I, Indra, can never lose my wealth; I never let death overcome me. Therefore, O Soma-drinking yajamanas! Ask for wealth from me only. O human beings, never give up your friendship with me.

अहमेतापञ्छाश्वसतो द्वाद्वेन्द्रं ये वज्रं युधयेऽकृण्वत ।
आह्वयमानाँ अव हन्मनाहनं दृह्ला वदन्ननमस्युर्नमस्विनः ॥
(ऋग्वेदः, 10.48.6)

I, Indra, kill two of those living enemies at a time who challenge me; Indra, armed with vajra, is the destroyer of enemies. I skillfully slaughter those who challenge me for battle by making them powerless and I never succumb before those who thunder before me.

अभीदमेकमेको अस्मि निष्षाळभी द्वा किमु त्रयः करन्ति ।
खले न पर्षान् प्रति हन्मि भूरि किं मा निन्दन्ति शत्रवोऽनिन्द्राः ॥
(ऋग्वेदः, 10.48.7)

I can defeat one enemy or two at a time, and even three of them, all alone, they can hardly do any harm to me. I slaughter them in the same way as a farmer rips the spikes of wheat with his sickle. How can those enemies of Indra weaken me?

अहं गुङ्गुभ्यो अतिथिग्वमिष्करमिषं न वृत्रतुरं विक्षु धारयम् ।
यत्पर्णयघ्न उत वा करञ्जहे प्राहं महे वृत्रहत्ये अशुश्रवि ॥
(ऋग्वेद:, 10.48.8)

I, the producer of grains and destroyer of enemies, made Divodasa, son of Atithigva, honored among the subjects to protect the kingdom of Gungus in the same way as the grain is honoured. I became famous in the battlefield by defeating two rivals namely Karanja and Parnaya.

प्र मे नमी साप्य इषे भुजे भूद्गवामेषे सख्या कृणुत द्विता ।
दिद्युं यदस्य समिथेषु मंहयमादिदेनं शंस्यमुक्थ्यं करम् ॥
(ऋग्वेद:, 10.48.9)

The one who sings hymns in my praise is welcomed by everyone, his granary is always full, and he gives food in charity. People welcome them to donate cows and make friends with them.

प्र नेमस्मिन्ददृशे सोमो अन्तर्गोपा नेममाविरस्था कृणोति ।
स तिग्मशृङ्गं वृषभं युयुत्सन् द्रुहस्तस्थौ बहुले बद्धो अन्तः ॥
(ऋग्वेद:, 10.48.10)

Indra sees Soma in either of his two devotees. This protecting Indra appears with his vajra in front of his devotees. That Indra has stood in stark darkness like a sharp-horned bull in front of enemies desirous of war.

आदित्यानां वसूनां रुद्रियाणां देवो देवानां न मिनामि धाम ।
ते मा भद्राय शवसे ततक्षुरपराजितमस्तृतमषाह्लम् ॥
(ऋग्वेद:, 10.48.11)

That Indra does not destroy the homes of aditya, vasu, rudra, and other devas. May all these devas be pleased to give me strength and well-being. I'm invincible, enthusiastic and powerful.

स्वर्गप्रमहेण दस्युविजयनीयेन्द्रचरितपूर्णताख्यानम् ।

Conclusion of the ceremony to thank Indra for his victory over dasyus.

इत्थं स्वाराड् दस्युनाशं व्यधात् प्राग् वैकुण्ठेन्द्रो नैषधेऽद्रौ स्थितः सन् ।
कुत्सं राज्ये स्थापयित्वा स दस्यूनार्यो राष्ट्रे तान्निगृह्य स्वरागात् ॥67॥

Thus, the *Vaikuntpati* [lord of paradise] Indra, while staying on the Nishadh mountain, first slaughtered the dasyus and then coronated Kutsa as the king before returning to the heaven.

कुत्सो राजाऽन्ये च राजान एते सिन्धोः प्रत्यग् नीवृति प्राग् यथाऽऽसन् ।
सर्वे सभ्या आर्यराजास्त एते स्वं स्वं राज्यं प्राग्वदत्राध्यतिष्ठन् ।।68।।

Kutsa and the other kings ruled over the country west of the Indus. They were Arya rulers and regained their earlier glory.

परिशिष्टाख्यानम्

Additional narratives.

5.30 दस्युभिः सारस्वतसूर्यापहरणम्

5.30 ABDUCTION OF SURYA BY DASYUS

इत्थं देवस्वाराट् प्रतापतः सर्वरूपायाम् ।
विहितायामपि शान्तौ नातिष्ठत् सा चिरं शान्तिः ॥69॥

Thus, the king of devas, Indra established peace in all quarters by his prowess. But peace could not be sustained for long.

धृष्टा उद्धतहृदयाः कुर्वाणाः पुनरुपद्रवं भूयः ।
आक्रममाणाः सूर्यस्थाने पुनरप्यशान्तिमातेनुः ॥70॥

The insolent and rowdy ones resorted to violence by attacking the place of sun and causing disturbance.

वैकुण्ठद्विषि हन्तुं देवकुलं प्रस्थितेऽसुराधीशे ।
प्रह्लादे त्वार्याणां क्षोभाद् दस्युभिरयं हतः सूर्यः ॥71॥

This sun was abducted in response to the displeasure shown by the Arya against Prahlada, the king of asuras, who had marched to demolish the dynasty of devas because of his anger against Indra.

गान्धारस्थं सूर्यं विद्वेषाद् ध्वंसयन्तोऽन्ये ।
असुरा यवनप्रान्ते पुनरैच्छन् तं निधापयितुम् ॥72॥

The remaining jealous asuras demolished the sun located in the Gandhara country and tried to re-establish themselves in the Yavana region.

5.31 सीरियादेशे बालवकभवननिर्माणम्

5.31 CONSTRUCTION OF BALVAKA BHAVAN IN SYRIA

शामो रोमकतनयस्तद्दाय: शामदेशो य: ।
स च पश्चादवरुद्ध: सुरैस्तत: सीरिया नाम ।।73।।

Sham was the son of Romak and his share of kingdom was called Shamdesha or Sam. In ancient times, this country was captured by the devas and, hence, it came to be known as Syria.

तस्मिन् देशे हेलि: पौलस्त्यो निर्ममे सौरम् ।
भवनं बालवकाख्यं तस्मिन् शालाऽद्भुतस्कम्भा ।।74।।

In that land of Syria, Heli, the son of Pulastya, got a surya-bhavan constructed, which had a shala with unique pillars.

अद्याप्येक: स्कम्भ: श्वेताश्ममयोऽत्र दृश्यते भुग्न: ।
चत्वारिंशत् सप्त च हस्ता ऊर्ध्वे परिस्तृतौ तु नव ।।75।।

Even to this day, remnants of a decaying pillar made of white stone can be seen here. This pillar is roughly forty-seven feet in height and nine feet in circumference.

तैरिदमद्भुतमासीत् सुदृढविशालै: शिलास्तम्भै: ।
भवनं तत्र च शाला विहितासीत् पूर्वसाम्येन ।।76।।

That palace, made of massive and awe-inspiring stone pillars, was marvelous and several shala-s, identical to that of the surya-bhavan in the east, were constructed within that palace.

नासीत्तत्र तु चक्रं शालैवासीद्विशालैषा ।
चक्राभावात् तस्मिन् प्रतिबिम्बार्थं च न द्युरन्ध्राणि ।।77।।

Though these shala-s were big, it had no chakra and had no holes in the roof either to capture the reflection of the sun.

अचरन् देवाश्चक्रं शालं त्वसुरा: समाश्रिता आसन् ।
इत्थं शतपथ उक्तं काण्डे षष्ठेऽष्टमाध्याये ।।78।।

As has been said in the eighth chapter of the sixth khanda of Shatapatha Brahamana, the devas took shelter in the chakra whereas the asuras relied only on the shala.

सैषाऽस्ति हि परिभाषा सर्वत्रैवोपनीयते तस्मात् ।
चक्रमनस्तच्छालं कुम्भीत्येवं हविर्ग्रहणे ।।79।।

Therefore, this definition is accepted everywhere—chakra refers to *shakata* (vehicle) and shal is the earthen pot which is used to accept havya.

चक्रं त्वश्मा पृश्निः शालं यन्त्रं तु सूर्यविज्ञाने ।
चक्रं परित्यजन्तः शालामेवाऽसुरा व्यदधुः ।।80।।

In solar science, chakra refers to *ashma* (unique stone) and *shal yantra* refers to *prishni* (domain of the light or gau). The asuras abolished the chakra to construct the shalas.

5.32 अब्राह्मीसूर्यप्रतिष्ठापना

5.32 ESTABLISHMENT OF ABRAHMI SURYA

सरस्वत्याख्यब्राह्मीसूर्यप्रातिनिधेन अब्राह्मीसूर्यप्रतिष्ठापना ।

Establishment of abrahmi surya (linked to the *asuras*) as a representative of *surya* namely Sarasvati (related to Brahma).

सिन्धुसरस्वत्योः प्राक्कूलात् प्राच्यां पुरा स्थितः सूर्यः ।
सिन्धोरब्राह्मया अपि नद्याः प्राच्यां प्रतिष्ठितः पश्चात् ।।81।।

In ancient times, this sun was placed on the eastern side of the eastern bank of Sindhu and Sarasvati; it was also established east of Abrahmi river in latter times.

भूमध्यसागरस्य प्राक्कूले वहित या नाम्ना ।
इवरिम नदीयमेवाब्राह्मी तां क्वचिदडोनिसं चाहुः ।।82।।

The river Ivarim, flowing across the eastern margin of the Mediterranean Sea, which has also been known as Odonis, is the Abrahmi river.

संवत्सरे कदाचिज्जलमब्राह्मया भवत्यस्याः ।
नद्या लोहितमचिरात् तत्र न जानन्ति कारणं केचित् ।।83।।

For a part of the year, the water of this river turns red for unknown reasons.

अब्राह्मी तु नदी या बालवकं नाम यद् भवनम् ।
क्रोशा विंशतिरनयोरन्तरमस्तीह पश्चिमेऽस्ति नदी ।।84।।

The river Brahmi is separated from the surya-bhavan by a distance of approximately forty miles, with the river flowing to the west of this building.

उज्जयनमध्यरेखापश्चिमदेशान्तरे स्थितं तदिदम् ।
चत्वारिंशप्राये धाम चतुस्त्रिंशकेऽक्षांशे ।।85।।

This *dham* (pilgrimage) is situated at approximately 34° latitude west of the mid-meridian of Ujjaini.

ऊनचत्वारिंशकेंऽशे, सप्तविंशतिसाधिके ।
उज्जायिन्याः पश्चिमतः स्थानं बालवकं स्थितम् ।।86।।

At 39° latitude and 27 kala west of Ujjaini on the Indian western longitude, is a placed called Balavak.

तद् ग्रीनवीचस्तु प्राच्यां षट्त्रिंशके सपादेंऽशे ।
बालवकाख्यं सौरं सद्माद्भुतमसुरनिर्मितं रेजे ॥87॥

Here, the asuras constructed a wonderful building called saur balavaka; it was at 36° latitude and 15 kala east of Greenwich.

तत्र च बालवकाख्ये भवने यं स्थापयामासुः ।
सूर्यमदेवाः सोऽपि च तत्रागारे तमोमये विबभौ ॥88॥

In this dark house in Balavak, the asuras established the sun in all its splendour.

पूर्वभारतस्य पश्चिमसीम्नि सूर्येऽस्तमिते पश्चिमभारतस्य पश्चिमसीम्नि किञ्चित्कालं सूर्यदर्शनम् ।

The western frontier of western India witnessing sunlight briefly after the sunset on the western boundary of eastern India.

सूर्योऽस्ति यत्र दिशि तत्र भवन्ति देवास्तत्पृष्ठदिश्युपनमन्त्यसुराः पृथिव्याम् ।
सूर्येऽसुराक्रमणतोऽस्तमितेऽथ पश्चात् तामासुरीं दिशमनूदयते स सूर्यः ॥89॥

The devas reside in the direction of the sun on this earth and the asuras live on the opposite side. After the sun sets on the deva side, because of the attacks by the asuras, the sun rises on their side.

इयं वैज्ञानिकी संस्था नित्यं दृष्टाऽधिदैवतम् ।
साम्यं तथाधिभूतं च प्रकृतेहानुवर्तते ॥90॥

असुरैः प्रत्याक्रमणात् सूर्यः सारस्वतो जगामास्तम् ।
भूमध्यसागरस्य प्राचीकूले पुन स उदियाय ॥91॥

स्वभावतः सूर्य उदेति पूर्वतः प्रातः प्रतीचीं स इतोऽस्तमेति ।
पुनः पुरस्तात् स उदेति चक्रवत् क्रमात् पुनर्भारतमेव एष्यति ॥92॥

This scientific process is seen every day in adhidaivat. Since adhibhuta is similar to adhidaivat, therefore adhibhuta follows adhidaivat naturally. After the sarasvat surya sets because of the attacks of the asuras, it rises again on the eastern coast of Mediterranean Sea. The sun rises naturally in the east every morning and thereafter sets on the western horizon. It again rises in the east next day and thus returns to Bharatavarsha.

5.33 वैदिकधर्मस्योत्थानपतनविचारः

5.33 DECLINE OF VEDIC DHARMA

भारतवर्षीयवैदिकधर्मस्य उत्थानपतनयोः दैवो हेतुः ।

The divine cause of rise and fall of bharatiya Vaidika Dharma.

नाकस्थविष्णोः परितस्तु वेददृग्व्यासार्द्धजे संचरति ध्रुवं ध्रुवः ।
वृत्ते ततः क्वापि पुरा युगे स हि प्राग् मेरुखस्वस्तिकगोऽभिजित्यभूत् ।।93।।

This Dhruva [Pole Star] circulates on a radius of 24° around Vishnu [this multi-circular location of Vishnu has been called 'tad Vishno paramam padam'] located on the *naka bindu* [the point of circle which is at the centre of the revolutionary path of the pole and on whose axis this pole moves]. Therefore, in ancient times, that Dhruva was a lunar asterism falling on the kha-svastika of Pamir.

प्राग्मेरुस्थे हंसपृष्ठेऽभिजिद्भागे ब्रह्मण्यासीत् सा ध्रुवो यत्र काले ।
ब्रह्मादिष्टो वेदधर्मस्तदासीत् सर्वप्रीतो हृद्गतः प्रोन्नतश्च ।।94।

When Dhruva was placed on the lunar asterism (Abhijit) and Brahma was settled on the back of a swan in the abode of temporal Brahma on the Pamir, at that point of time the *vaidikadharma* [a living code enunciated by the Vedas], postulated by Brahma, was accepted by all.

तर्ह्येवासीद् भारते सोऽपि सूर्यो विज्ञानेनोच्छ्राययन् भारतीयान् ।
अस्तं यातो भारतस्यैष सूर्यः क्लिश्यन्त्यार्य्यास्तेन बुद्ध्यन्धकारात् ।।95।।

At that point of time, the people of Bharatavarsha were enlightened through surya-vijnana. Now this sun has set on Bharat, as a result of which the Arya are living in intellectual darkness.

प्राग्मेरुखस्वस्तिकमेष हित्वोत्तरस्य खस्वस्तिकमर्णवस्य ।
गतो ध्रुवः कर्षति वेदधर्मविपर्ययेणाद्य विपर्ययस्थः ।।96।।

Since this Dhruva has now shifted to the kha-svastika of the northern ocean from the kha-svastika of Pamir, the vaidikadharma has been degenerating rapidly.

तारावशादपि फलं ध्रुव एषदत्ते तेनाभिजित्परिगतः स हि वैदिकानाम् ।
प्रागुन्नतिं बहु चकार स चाधुनैषां वेदद्विषां सततमुन्नतिमातनोति ।।97।।

This Dhruva offered bounties even under the influence of the stars, therefore, when it was located on the conquered lunar asterism, the vaidika people [people living in the Vedic times] prospered. Today, it is helping the enemies of the Vedas to prosper.

कालेन केन च परिक्रममाण एष प्राचीमुपेत्य पुनरेष्यति दक्षिणाशाम् ।
तेन ध्रुवं ध्रुवं इहाभिजिति प्रपन्नो भूयः करिष्यति स भारतधर्मवृत्तिम् ।।98।।

After some time, when this star reaches east before coming to south, it will align with abhijit nakshatra to revive the bharat dharma.

5.34 पूर्वदिशार्यसूर्योदयः

5.34 SUN WILL AGAIN RISE IN EAST

पश्चिमदेशीयसूर्योदयानन्तरं पुनः पूर्वदिशार्यसूर्योदयः ।

After the western *suryodaya* (sunrise), there will be an arya suryodaya in the east again.

अथ गान्धारे देशे क्षोभणतः क्षोभणादित्यम् ।
आर्याः क्षोभस्मृत्यै मार्त्तण्डं स्थापयामासुः ।।99।।

The Arya established a sun namely kshobhanaditya in memory of the losses (*kshobh* means anguish) suffered in the war at a place called Kshobhana in Gandhara [the venue of the deva-dasyu war].

स्कान्दे प्रभासखण्डे कथितोऽयं शीलाध्याये ।
चित्रादित्यस्तवने गान्धारे क्षोभणादित्यः ।।100।।

This sun called kshobhanaditya in Gandhara finds mention in the hymns to Chitraditya in the 130th chapter of Prabhasa Khand of Skanda Purana.

गान्धारे चित्रपथा चित्रा वा ब्रह्मकुण्डसंनिहिता ।
नद्यस्ति सुप्रसिद्धा प्रावृट्काले वहत्येषा ।।101।।

There is a river called Chitrapatha or Chitra in Gandhara, which flows close to Brahmakunda. This rivers flows only during the rainy season.

चित्रादित्य इहासीच्चित्रेण स्थापितः सोऽयम् ।
चत्वारिंशशतेऽस्मिन्नध्याये वर्णितः स्कान्दे ।।102।।

It was set up here by Chitraditya Chitra. It finds mention in the 140th chapter of Skanda Purana.

कश्मीरे श्रीनगरादग्निदिशि काप्यदूरवद्देशे ।
मट्टनसाहिबनाम्ना कुण्डः कोऽप्यस्ति तीर्थमार्य्याणाम् ।।103।।

There is a ko-kund namely Mattan Sahib in Agnikon near Srinagar in Kashmir which is a pilgrimage for the Arya.

तत्रैव पूर्वमासीदन्यन्मार्त्तण्डमन्दिरं तस्य ।
भग्नावशेषमद्य तु कौरवपाण्डवमिति प्राहुः ।।104।।

In ancient times, there was a sun temple in that Mattan Sahib, the relics of which are now called Kaurava-Pandava.

अर्च्चामन्दिरमेतन्न तु तद्विज्ञानमन्दिरं सौरम् ।
अनृषिभिरेव च जुष्टं तदपि यशःशेषतां यातम् ।।105।।

This sun temple was used for worshipping and not for scientific research. It was served by sages and hermits, and today even that act of worshipping has become a formality.

अन्तर्हितोऽत्र सूर्योऽप्यभवत् काले स दस्युनिकृतत्वात् ।
स यथा राहुग्रस्तो दिवि सूर्योऽन्तर्हितो भवति ।।106।।

With the passage of time, that sun has vanished due to the dasyu attacks in the same way as the sun, wary of rahu, vanished from the Dyauloka.

विज्ञानकूप आसीत् तमिदानीं चाह वाविलेत्याख्यम् ।
म्लेच्छा विदुरिह निगडबद्धौ हारूतमारूतौ ।।107।।

There was once a *vijnana-kupa* (*kupa* means a well) which in now called Vavil. The mlecchas say that two men called Harut and Marut were chained there.

विज्ञानकुण्डमपि तं मटनेत्याख्यं वदन्ति ते म्लेच्छाः ।
वैज्ञानिकी व्यवस्था सर्वा विध्वंसिताऽनार्यैः ।।108।।

Those mlecchas call this vijnana kund too as Mattan. The anaryas destroyed all of these scientific structures.

नीचप्रकृतिर्दस्युः परकीर्तिध्वंसकृद् भवति ।
प्रतिपन्थी जगतामयमकारणं द्वेषमाचरति ।।109।।

The wicked dasyus are destroyers of others' glory, they are anti-world and they are spiteful for no reason.

5.35 स्वदेशीयानां भारतीयानां विजयः

5.35 VICTORY FOR THE PEOPLE OF BHARATAVARSHA

देशिकदस्युभिः परिपीडितानां भारतीयानां स्वदेशीयानाम् अन्ततो विजयः ।

Victory for the oppressed Indians over the alien dasyus in the end.

त्रेधा लोकः कल्पितोऽयं यदासीदिन्द्रः स्वर्गे पूर्वकाले तदासीत् ।
आसन्नस्मिन् भारते तर्हि विद्याः शौर्यं लक्ष्म्यः सिद्धयश्चानवद्याः ॥110॥

When this world was divided into three domains, at that time Indra used to live in svarga. At that point of time, knowledge, valour, opulence, and all kinds of uncorrupted siddhis used to exist in India.

ब्रह्मवीर्यपरिवृद्धिहेतवः सूर्यसोमरसयज्ञधेनवः ।
क्लेशसिन्धुतरणाय सेतवः संहृता अथ विधिर्दधे नवम् ॥111॥

The main reasons for the overall growth of brahmavirya are—surya, Somarasa, yajna and gau. These served as the bridge to cross the ocean of suffering, and Brahma had to create a new bridge after their end.

क्षत्रियाय इह सूर्यसोमजा ब्राह्मणाय इह यज्ञसूत्रिणः ।
विड्व्रजा य इह धेनुपालकास्तेषु सन्ति विजया धियः श्रियः ॥112॥

The powers originating from surya and Soma are meant for the kshatriyas and the powers originating from yajna are meant for the brahmins. The vaishyas used to rear cows. The ones possessing these powers are endowed with victory, wisdom, and radiance.

5.36 ग्रन्थसम्पूर्तिः

5.36 COMPLETION OF THIS TREATISE

इतिवृत्तं सदसद्वा रजस्तथाऽऽकाशमपरं च ।
आवरणं च तथाम्भोऽथामृतमृत्यू अहोरात्रौ ॥113॥

दैवः संशयवादः सिद्धान्तश्च श्रुतावुदिताः ।
द्वादशवादा विहिताः शास्त्रेऽस्मिन् ब्रह्मविज्ञाने ॥114॥

Twelve *vadha*-s (ism-s) have been propounded in this Brahmavijnana-shastra, which include: Itivrittvadh, Sadasdvadh, Rajovadh, Vyomvadh, Aparvadh, Avaranvadh, Ambhovadh, Amrtivadh, Mrityuvadh, Ahoratravadh, Devavadh, Samshayvadh and other theories mentioned in the Shrutis.

तेष्वाद्ये विज्ञानेतिवृत्तवादे प्रकरणानि ।
ब्राह्मं दैवं भारतमार्षं विज्ञानसूत्रं च ॥115॥

These treatises on vijnana has five sections namely—brahma, daiyva, bharata, arsha, and vijnana-shastra.

तत्र च भारतवृत्ते पञ्च निरुक्ताः परिच्छेदाः ।
भारतपरिचय आद्यस्तथार्यदासीय इत्यन्यः ॥116॥

विज्ञानभवनसंज्ञो दस्युवधो विजयकीर्तनप्रमहः ।
पञ्चप्रसङ्गमित्थं भारतवृत्तं शुभायास्तु ॥117॥

The section dealing with Bharat has five chapters in it; the first two of them being 'bharatparichaya' and 'aryadasiya' respectively. The third, fourth, and fifth chapters are 'vijnana bhavan', 'dasyuvadh' and 'vijay-kirtanapramah' respectively. May this Bharatvarshiyaryopakhyan [discourse on Bharatavarsha] comprising five chapters be auspicious.

इति मधुसूदनविद्यावाचस्पतिप्रणीतस्य ब्रह्मविज्ञानशास्त्रसम्बन्धिनो भारतवर्षीयार्योपाख्याने इन्द्रविजयाभिनन्दनं नाम पञ्चमः प्रक्रमः सम्पूर्णः ।

Thus the translation of the fifth chapter namely Indravijayabhinandan in the Bharatavarshiyaryopakhyan related to Brahmavijnanashastra of Madhusudan Ojha is concluded.

Glossary

adhibhautika entire material world

adhidaivika world of supraphysical energies

adhyatma spiritual (in the sense of comprising both the material and energy components of an individual)

aditya sun; one of the numerous supraphysical energies emanating from sun; one of the many suns referred to in the Vedas

agama vidya refers to one of the two principal types of knowledge or vidya—agama vidya and nigama vidya; both exist (and are not created); agama vidya emanates from Shiva and nigama vidya from Brahma.

agastya a supraphysical energy; and the seer-scientist who discovered it and is known by that name

agneya produced from agni; full of agni

agni fire; a supraphysical energy

agnihotra a vedic ritual of making oblations to fire

agni somayajna the interaction or fusion of agni and soma which transforms into supraphysical energies like agni.

akasha space, one of the five *mahabhuta*-s (gross elements); space generated by antariksha (the separation of heaven and earth), the principal space being a continuous, unbounded extension in every direction.

amrita immortal; imperishable. In the technical sense, this term is used for the unchanging principle in an individual as distinguished from the ever-changing principles/factors.

angira the supraphysical energy from which agni, vayu and aditya stem.

anirukta not articulated; not explained (because of being self-evident).

annada which consumes anna (fire in relation to fuel).

antariksha (loka) the space between heaven and earth; also translated as 'interspace'.

antaryami that which determines the innate nature of every individual.

anumana inference; one of the three distinct instruments of knowledge—the other two being perception (dhrishta) and reliable testimony (aptavachana)

apa (apah) supraphysical variant of the physical entity, commonly known as water; also called ambha and jal.

apara vidya the knowledge (science) of all affairs pertaining to the cosmos (as distinct from 'para', the knowledge of the undifferentiated homogenous source from which the cosmos evolves).

arka a ray; a flash of lightning; a specific state of sun.

Aranyaka every Veda has two parts—mantra and Brahmana; Aranyaka is a part of Brahmana.

ashvin kumars generally identified as the father of the founder of Ayurveda. In vedic usage, there are two ashvin kumar-s among the thirty-three devas.

asura generally translated as demons or opponents of the devas; a class of supraphysical energy. There are different types of asuras, namely dasyus, daityas, danavas, and panis.

atma indivisible; unlimited; the all-pervasive and indestructible substratum of every individual, erroneously translated as 'spirit'; the real self.

atmabala inner strength

atmonnati self evolution

atri a supraphysical energy, and the name of one of the seven seer-scientists (rishis) who discovered other supraphysical energies.

bala the first formation in the process of creation when rasa, the vast limitless stillness, is stirred and a unifying principle begins to divide itself into separate and diverse units of supraphysical energy.

bhuvah earth; second of the seven vyahritis which are deeply meaningful utterances signifying seven 'worlds': Bhu, Bhuva, Sva, Maha, Jana, Tapa and Satya.

bindu pure existence; the point of departure for the coming into being of the cosmos.

Brahma the foundation or basis of the totality of the created universe. This universe is another manifestation of Brahma.

Brahmagni the subtlest state of agni.

Brahma kalpa a unit to measure the immeasurable span of time.

Brahmana a portion of the texts of the Vedas which elucidates the application of yajna vijnana (scientific principles).

brihati the location of the sun in the cosmic matrix; a metre of thirty-six syllables.

chhanda metre; one of the six branches of the Vedangas.

devagni a supraphysical energy called agni.

devata a specific class of supraphysical energies, as distinct from asura which emerges from the same source.

dharana	concentration of mind; retention; holding.
dharma	this is a comprehensive term that reflects the blending of ethics, duty, characteristics and properties of an individual; merit.
dhatu	layer; stratum; ingredient; matter (generally used for metals); root (language).
divya yuga	the period related to the Partial Collapse (one year in the human time-scale is one-day night unit in the divya time-scale)
drashta	seer; observer.
gandharva	a class of entities; a species different from human beings, generally regarded as celestial musicians or singers.
garhpatya	one of the three sacred fires in the house. It belongs to the the master of the household and must be kept burning in the garhpatya mound, which is circular in shape. No offerings are made directly into this fire.
gau	generally translated as 'cow'; in the technical sense; it is the rays emanating from the sun, and also a unit for measuring supraphysical energy.
gayatri	the incoming supraphysical energy of prana returning and passing through the earth.
ghari	a measure of time; one ghari is equal to twenty-four minutes.
hari	supraphysical energy radiating out from the centre.
hiranyagarbha	a golden foetus; the seed of elemental existence from which creation followed; a name of Brahma.
hiranyagarbha prajapati	the initial manifestation of prajapati, the first individual to manifest in the creative process.
Ishwara	the supreme principle which regulates the universe, comprising all disparate individuals (jeeva regulates individuals and Ishwara regulates jeevas).
itihasa	historical episodes illustrating and explaining supraphysical forces and their functioning.
jamadagni	one of the twelve creative supraphysical energies (ignorance being burnt to ashes in the fire).
jnana	consciousness; knowledge; awareness; faculty of judgement; knowing how diversity ultimately coalesces into unity.
kalpa	one of the six Vedangas; a measure of time; a specified period; the Vedic auxiliary science dealing with the practical applications, rites and rituals of everyday life.
kshatriya	one of the four sections in which ancient society was organized.
kundakshetra	a designated place of yajna.
madhyama	between the two levels of speech (vaikharee and pashyanti)

there is a middle level known as madhyama vak—the level of thought. Its association is chiefly with buddhi (the mind or intellect); sustenance.

mahima space around a pinda, the 'sphere of radiance' of an individual.

mana one of three components of atma, the other two being prana and vak; also translated as 'mind' or 'heart'.

mantra a verse in the Vedas; the words in which the seer-scientists articulated their discoveries of the processes of nature, the cosmos and beyond.

mareechi a particle of light; a shining mote or speck in the air.

matra a measure of any kind; quantity; size; duration; number; degree; the duration of time required to pronounce a short vowel.

maya an extraordinary power which emanates from the infinite and makes possible the interplay of finite phenomena.

mleccha outsider, inferior, language other than Sanskrit.

nigamana inference identical with initial assertion (in the intellect's logical process of reasoning); conclusion that assists the hypothesis as proved; incidental cause.

nirukta this term is related to the linguistic analysis of words to derive their correct meaning within the context. Nirukta emphasises the derivation of difficult and apparently unanalysable terms. It is the auxiliary science of etymology in the Vedas. Nirukta vak means sound which conveys meaning; one of the six Vedangas.

nyaya one of the six darshanas, a system of ancient Indian philosophy propounded by seer-scientist Gautama.

parameshti the prajapati which orbits around Brahma and is filled with apa; also one dimension of the five-dimensional universe, the other four being svayambhu, surya, chandra, and prithvi.

pathyasvasti the language of the Vedas (Pandit Madhusudan Ojha has written a book with the same name).

pitra 'ancestors' or 'forefathers'. Technically, it stands for one of the several unchangeable supraphysical energies.

praja all created entities.

pramana means or process of valid cognition.

prana supraphysical energy; breath.

pranonnati elevation of life

purusha the ultimate manifested ocean of energy, which is observable as differentiated variegated nature.

rajas the second of the three gunas or qualities (the other two

	being satva—the most positive quality signifying goodness or peace—and tamas—the most negative quality signifying darkness or inertia). Rajas comes in-between these two and signifies vigour or activity.
rasa	a supraphysical essence.
rik	the fundamental tatva from which all forms evolve; one of the four Vedas.
rishi	a supraphysical energy which comes into motion spontaneously; a seer-scientist who discovers a specific supraphysical energy.
rita	That tatva, or portion of a tatva, which has no body and no centre or navel.
rodasi	of the three triple worlds comprising the earth, the sun and interspace between the two, one is called rodasi, and the other two are krandasi and samyati.
rudra	the agni (supraphysical energy) emanating from vayu (there are eleven rudras); this supraphysical energy maintains a special relationship with soma and yama; also called rudra devata.
sama	the extent to which an individual or an entity can be seen; one of the four Vedas.
samkhya	a school of ancient Indian philosophy or darshana; theory derived from knowledge; the yoga of knowledge (as compared to the theory of yoga of action).
samskara	knowledge-impression; cognition residue
sanvatsara	a year; the annual cycle; the aggregate of the seasons; the yajna from where the triadic worlds of prithvi, antariksha and dyau emanate.
satya	truth; eternal; unchanging.
savita	the direct luminosity of the sun; luminous rays radiating from the mass of every individual. Also known as 'savitra' and 'savitri'.
Shatapatha Brahmana	One of the Brahmana texts which has 100 chapters related to Yajurveda.
shiksha	the first among the six limbs of the Vedas, this science deals with the character of Vedic syllables and determines their true nature; phonetics as applied to the Vedas.
shruti	another term for the Vedas (literally meaning 'that which has been transmitted orally and heard by a disciple of the guru'); a direct statement.
shoonya	nothingness; the symbol zero; void; empty.
smarthvidya	what is not vedic vidya; it is one of the two vidyas, the other being shrouta vidya.

soma the material cause of the universe; a specific category of supraphysical energy.

sphota the sentence taken as an integral symbol.

stoma a layer or 'stack' of supraphysical energy.

svaha one of the seven regions of the universe

svastika one of the four divisions (90 degree each) of brihati chhanda (a metre of thirty-six syllables).

svayambhu that which comes into being on its own. This is the name given to the yajna which occurs at the very outset in the entire process of creation.

tapa intense endeavour, heat.

tatva essence; the fundamental factor from which something evolves.

vak the substance in an object; the matter within the shell; speech.

Veda the fundamental tatva which goes into the evolution of the cosmos; the Vedas are the texts which elucidate and explain veda tatva.

Veda mantra aphorisms in which the seer-scientists have articulated the principles of the Vedic sciences. These mantras cause vibration in the channels and help a seeker to realize the experienced reality.

vedanga a 'limb' of the Vedas. There are six of these, namely phonetics, etymology, grammar, prosody, astronomy and rituals.

virya creative vitality.

vijnana knowledge of how the variegated universe evolves from a unified, single harmonious tatva; science.

vishvadeva a supraphysical energy situated in the north of parameshti.

vivasvan one of the twelve states of the sun; one of the early recipient of the knowledge elucidated in Srimad Bhagavad Gita.

vrata the leading prana in a cluster of supraphysical energy.

vyakarana a manner of linguistic analysis which determines the exact form of words; the science of grammar; one of the six Vedangas.

vak prana the supraphysical energy that pulsates in matter.

yajna the interaction and fusion of supraphysical energies and/or material substances; the process of the acculturation of agni; the refinement and embellishment of agni.

yama generally understood as the 'god of death'; ferocious wind.

yoga etymologically means 'to yoke together' and to concentrate upon a discipline. One of the six darshanas propounded by Patanjali.

उद्धृतग्रन्थ

Cited Works

अथर्ववेदः Atharvaveda
अग्निपुराणम् Agni Purana
अमरकोशः Amarakosha
ऋग्वेदः Rigveda
ऐतरेयब्राह्मणम् Aitareyabrahmana
कौषीतकिब्राह्मणम् Kaushitaki Brahmana
पद्मपुराणम् Padma Purana
पाणिनीयशिक्षा Paniniyashiksha
बृहत्संहिता Brihatsamhita
बृहदारण्यकोपनिषद् Brihadaranyakopanishad
ब्रह्मपुराणम् Brahma Purana
भविष्यपुराणम् Bhavishya Purana
भागवतपुराणम् Bhagavata Purana
महाभाष्यम् Mahabhashya
महाभारतम् Mahabharata
मत्स्यपुराणम् Matysa Purana
मनुस्मृतिः Manusmriti
मन्त्रमहोदधिः Mantramahodadhi
मार्कण्डेयपुराणम् Markandeya Purana
यजुर्वेदः Yajurveda
योगसूत्रम् Yogasutram
रामायणम् Ramayana
वामनपुराणम् Vamana Purana
वाक्यपदीयम् Vakyapadhiyam
विष्णुपुराणम् Vishnu Purana
विष्णुस्मृतिः Vishnu Smriti
शतपथब्राह्मणम् Shatapatha Brahmana
श्रीमद्भगवद्गीता Srimad Bhagvad Gita
सामवेदः Samaveda
सिद्धान्तशिरोमणिः Siddhanthshiromani
सुश्रुतसंहिता Sushrusamhita
सूर्यसिद्धान्तः Surya Siddhantha
स्कन्दपुराणम् Skanda Purana

सन्दर्भग्रन्थ सूची

Bibliography

साक्षात् स्रोत

Primary Sources

अग्निपुराण, नाग पब्लिशर्स, दिल्ली, 1985.

Agnipurana, Nag Publishers, New Delhi, 1985.

अत्रिख्याति, पण्डित मधुसूदन ओझा, (सम्पा.) सत्य प्रकाश दुबे, (हि.अनु.) अनन्त शर्मा, मधुसूदन ओझा शोध प्रकोष्ठ, जोधपुर, 1997.

Atrikhyati, Pandit Madhusudan Ojha, edited by Satya Prakash Dubey and translated by Anant Sharma, Madhusudan Ojha Shodh Prakosht, Jai Narain Vyas University, Jodhpur, 1997.

अत्रिख्याति, पण्डित मधुसूदन ओझा, (सम्पा.) कैलाश चतुर्वेदी, (हि.अनु.) रामदेव, मधुसूदन ओझा वैदिक अध्ययन शोधपीठ संस्थान, जयपुर, 2010.

Atrikhyati, Pandit Madhusudan Ojha, edited by Kailash Chaturvedi and translated by Ramdev, Madhusudan Ojha Vaidik Adhyayan Shodhpeeth Sansthan, Jaipur, 2010.

अथर्ववेदसंहिता (भाग 1-4), (सम्पा. एवं अनु.) श्रीपाद दामोदर सातवलेकर, स्वाध्याय मण्डल पारडी, 1985.

Atharvaveda samhita (parts 1-4), edited and translated by Sripad Damodar Satvalekar, Swadhyay Mandal, Paradi, 1985.

अपरवाद, पण्डित मधुसूदन ओझा, (सम्पा.) दयानन्दभार्गव, (हि.अनु.) अनन्त शर्मा,
मधुसूदन ओझा शोध प्रकोष्ठ, जोधपुर, 1992.

Aparavad, Pandit Madhusudan Ojha, edited by Dayanand Bhargava and translated by Anant Sharma, Madhusudan Ojha Shodh Prakosht, Jai Narain Vyas University, Jodhpur, 1992.

अमरकोश, अमरसिंह, सुधाटीका सहित, (सं) शिवदत्त वासुदेव लक्ष्मण शास्त्री, राष्ट्रीय संस्कृत संस्थान, पुनर्मुद्रित संस्करण, नई दिल्ली, 2003.

Amarakosha (with Amarsingh, sudhateeka), edited by Shivdutt Vasudev and Lakshman Shastri, Rashtriya Sanskrit Sansthan, New Delhi, 2003.

अम्भोवाद, पण्डित मधुसूदन ओझा, (सम्पा.) दयानन्दभार्गव, (हि.अनु.) अनन्त शर्मा, मधुसूदन ओझा शोध प्रकोष्ठ, जोधपुर, 2002.

Ambhovad, Pandit Madhusudan Ojha, edited by Dayanand Bhargav, translated by Anant Sharma, Madhusudan Ojha Shodh Prakosht, Jai Narain Vyas University,

Jodhpur, 2002.

अहोरात्रवाद, पण्डित मधुसूदन ओझा, (सम्पा.) आद्यादत्त ठाकुर, लखनऊ, 1926.

Ahoratravada, Pandit Madhusudan Ojha, edited by Adyadutt Thakur, Lucknow, 1926.

आधिदैविकाध्याय, पण्डित मधुसूदन ओझा, (सम्पा.) सुरजनदास स्वामी, वि.सं. 2007.

Adhidaivikadhyaya, Pandit Madhusudan Ojha, edited by Surjandas Swami, Published by Pradhyumn Sharma Ojha, Jaipur, 1950.

आवरणवाद, पण्डित मधुसूदन ओझा, (सम्पा.) दयानन्दभार्गव, (हि.अनु.) अनन्त शर्मा, मधुसूदन ओझा शोध प्रकोष्ठ, जोधपुर, 1993.

Avaranvad, Pandit Madhusudan Ojha, edited by Dayanand Bhargav and translated by Anant Sharma, Madhusudan Ojha Shodh Prakosht, Jodhpur, 1993.

आशौचपञ्जिका, पण्डित मधुसूदन ओझा, (सम्पा.) सुरजनदास स्वामी, वि.सं. 2007.

Ashauchpanchika, Pandit Madhusudan Ojha, edited by Surjandas Swami, Published by Pradhyumn Sharma Ojha, Jaipur, 1950.

उपनिषत्संग्रह, (सम्पा.) पं. जगदीश शास्त्री, मोतीलालबनारसीदास, दिल्ली, 1984.

Upanishatsangraha, edited by Pandit Jagdish Shastri, Motilal Banarsidass, Delhi, 1984.

ऋग्वेदसंहिता (भाग 1-2) सायणभाष्यसहित (हि.अनु.) पं. रामगोविन्द त्रिवेदी, चौखम्भा विद्याभवन, वाराणसी, पुनर्मुद्रित संस्करण, 1997.

Rigveda Samhita (parts 1-9), translated by Pandit Ramgovind Trivedi, Chaukhamba Vidyabhavan, Varanasi, 1997.

ऐतरेयब्राह्मण, (सम्पा. एवं हि. अनु.) सुधाकर मालवीय, तारा बुक एजेन्सी, वाराणसी, 2015.

Aiterayabrahmana, edited and translated by Sudhakar Malaviya, Tara Book Agency, Varanasi, 2015.

कादम्बिनी, पण्डित मधुसूदन ओझा, (सम्पा.) गणेशीलालसुथार, मधुसूदन ओझा शोध प्रकोष्ठ, जोधपुर, 2003.

Kadambini, Pandit Madhusudan Ojha, edited by Ganeshilal Suthar, Madhusudan Ojha Shodh Prakosht, Jodhpur, 2003.

कौषीतकि ब्राह्मण, (सम्पा.) बी. लिण्डर, जेना, हेर्मान, कोस्टेनोबल, 1887.

Kaushitaki Brahmana, edited by Bruno Lindner, Hermann Costenoble, 1887.

गोपथब्राह्मण, (सम्पा.) प्रज्ञा देवी एवं मेधा देवी, चौखम्भा संस्कृत प्रतिष्ठान, दिल्ली, 2008.

Gopathabrahmana, edited by Pragya Devi and Medha Devi, Chaukhamba Sanskrit Pratishtan, Delhi, 2008.

छन्दोभ्यस्ता, पण्डित मधुसूदन ओझा, (सम्पा.) प्रद्युम्न शर्मा, दी प्रिन्टर्स एण्ड पब्लिशर्स लि. जयपुर.

Chhandobhyastha, Pandit Madhusudan Ojha, edited by Pradhyumn Sharma, The Printers and Publishers Ltd, Jaipur.

छन्दः समीक्षा, पण्डित मधुसूदन ओझा, (सम्पा.) सुरजनदास स्वामी, राजस्थान संस्कृत अकादमी, 1991.

Chhandhsamiksha, Pandit Madhusudan Ojha, edited by Surjandas Swami, Rajasthan Sanskrit Akademi, 1991.

जगद्गुरुवैभवम्, पण्डित मधुसूदन ओझा, (सम्पा.) प्रद्युम्न शर्मा, वि.सं. 1991.

Jagadguruvaibhavam, Pandit Madhusudan Ojha, edited and published by Pradhyumn Sharma, 1934.
तैत्तिरीयब्राह्मण (सायणभाष्य सहित), (सम्पा.) गणेश उमाकान्तथिटे, न्यू भारतीय बुक कारपोरेशन, दिल्ली, 2012.
Taittiriyabrahmana, edited by Ganesh Umakant Thite, New Bharatiya Book Corporation, Delhi, 2012.
दशवादरहस्य, पण्डित मधुसूदन ओझा, (सम्पा.) अनन्त शर्मा, (हि.अनु.) लक्ष्मी शर्मा, मधुसूदन ओझा शोध प्रकोष्ठ, जोधपुर, 1997.
Dashvadarhrahsya, Pandit Madhusudan Ojha, edited by Anant Sharma and translated by Lakshmi Sharma, Madhusudan Ojha Shodh Prakosht, Jai Narain Vyas University, Jodhpur, 1997.
देवतानिवित, पण्डित मधुसूदन ओझा, (सम्पा.) आद्यादत्त ठाकुर.
Devatanivith, Pandit Madhusudan Ojha, edited and published by Adhyadutt Thakur, Lucknow.
पञ्चभूतसमीक्षा, पण्डित मधुसूदन ओझा, (सम्पा.) प्रद्युम्न शर्मा, जयपुर 1947
Panchabhuthasamiksha, Pandit Madhusudan Ojha, edited and published by Pradhyumn Sharma Ojha, Jaipur, 1947.
पथ्यास्वस्ति, पण्डित मधुसूदन ओझा, (सम्पा.) सुरजनदास स्वामी, राजस्थान प्राच्य प्रतिष्ठान, जोधपुर, 1969.
Pathyasvasthi, Pandit Madhusudan Ojha, edited by Surjandas Swami, Rajasthan Prachya Prathishtan, Jodhpur, 1969.
पद्मपुराणम् (भाग 1.4), नाग पब्लिशर्स, दिल्ली, 1984.
Padmapurana (part 1-4), Nag Publishers, Delhi, 1984.
पाणिनीयव्याकरणमहाभाष्य, पतञ्जलि, (कैयटप्रणीत-प्रदीप-नागेशभट्टविरचित-उद्योत-सहित) (सम्पा.) श्रीभार्गवशास्त्री, चौखम्भा संस्कृत प्रतिष्ठान, दिल्ली, पुनर्मुद्रित संस्करण, 2000.
Paninivyakaranmahabashya, edited by Bhargav Shastri, Chaukhamba Sanskrit Pratishtan, Delhi, 2000.
पातञ्जलयोगसूत्र, (सम्पा.) रामशंकर भट्टाचार्य, (हि.अनु.) स्वामी हरिहरानन्द, मोतीलाल बनारसीदास, दिल्ली, 1987.
Patanjali Yogasutra, edited by Ramshankar Bhattacharya, translated by Swami Hariharanand, Motilal Banarsidass, Delhi, 1987.
पितृसमीक्षा, पण्डित मधुसूदन ओझा, (सम्पा.) देवीदत्त शर्मा चतुर्वेदी, मधुसूदन ओझा शोध प्रकोष्ठ, जोधपुर, 1991.
Pitrasamiksha, Pandit Madhusudan Ojha, edited by Devidutt Sharma Chaturvedi, Madhusudan Ojha Shodh Prakosht, Jai Narain Vyas University, Jodhpur, 1991.
पुराणनिर्माणाधिकरण, पण्डित मधुसूदन ओझा, (सम्पा.) पद्मलोचन शर्मा, वि.सं. 2009.
Purananirmanadhikarana, Pandit Madhusudan Ojha, edited by Padmalochan Sharma, Published by Pandit Yogeshchandra, Jaipur, 1952.
प्रत्यन्तप्रस्थानमीमांसा, पण्डित मधुसूदन ओझा, (सम्पा.) विनोद शास्त्री, (हि.अनु.) रामप्रपन्न शर्मा, राजस्थान संस्कृत अकादमी, जयपुर, 2003.
Pratyanthprasthanmimamsa, Pandit Madhusudan Ojha, edited by Vinod Shastri

and translated by Ramprapanna Sharma, Rajasthan Sanskrit Akademi, Jaipur, 2003.
ब्रह्मपुराण, नाग पब्लिशर्स, दिल्ली, 1985.
Brahmapurana, Nag Publishers, Delhi, 1985.
बृहत्संहिता, वराहमिहिर, (भाग 1-2) (हि.व्या.) पं. अच्युतानन्दझा, चौखम्भा विद्याभवन, वाराणसी, 2010.
Brihatsamhita (parts 1-2), Varahmihir, translated by Pandit Achyutanand Jha, Chaukhamba Vidyabhavan, Varanasi, 2010.
बृहदारण्यकोपनिषद्, (शाङ्करभाष्यसहित), गीताप्रेस, गोरखपुर, पुनर्मुद्रित संस्करण, 2014.
Brihadarynakopanishad, Gita Press, Gorakhpur, 2014.
ब्रह्मचतुष्पदी, पण्डित मधुसूदन ओझा, (सम्पा.) प्रद्युम्न शर्मा, वि.सं. 2009.
Brahmachatushpadi, Pandit Madhusudan Ojha, edited and published by Pradhyumn Sharma Ojha, Jaipur, 1952.
ब्रह्मविनय, पण्डित मधुसूदन ओझा, (सम्पा.) वासुदेव शरण अग्रवाल, पृथिवी प्रकाशन, वाराणसी, 1964.
Brahmavinaya, Pandit Madhusudan Ojha, edited by Vasudev Sharan Aggarwal, Prithvi Prakashan, Varanasi, 1964.
ब्रह्मसमन्वय, पण्डित मधुसूदन ओझा, (सम्पा.) प्रद्युम्न शर्मा, जयपुर, वि.सं. 2001.
Brahmsamanvaya, Pandit Madhusudan Ojha, edited and published by Pradhyumn Sharma Ojha, Jaipur, 1952.
ब्रह्मसिद्धान्त, पण्डित मधुसूदन ओझा, (सम्पा.) वासुदेव शरण अग्रवाल, (सं.टीका) गिरिधर शर्मा चतुर्वेदी, काशी हिन्दू विश्वविद्यालय, वाराणसी, 1961.
Brahmasiddhanta, Pandit Madhusudan Ojha, edited by Vasudev Sharan Aggarwal with commentary by Giridhar Sharma Chaturvedi, Banaras Hindu University, Varanasi, 1961.
ब्रह्मसिद्धान्तपण्डित मधुसूदन ओझा, (हि.अनु.) देवीदत्त शर्मा चतुर्वेदी, राजस्थान पत्रिका प्रकाशन, जयपुर, 2005.
Brahmasidhantha, Pandit Madhusudan Ojha, translated by Devidutt Sharma Chaturvedi, Rajasthan Patrika Prakashan, Jaipur, 2005.
ब्रह्मविज्ञान, पण्डित मधुसूदन ओझा, (सम्पा.) प्रद्युम्न शर्मा ओझा, राजस्थान पत्रिका प्रकाशन, वि.सं. 2044.
Brahmavijnana, Pandit Madhusudan Ojha, edited by Pradhyumn Sharma Ojha, Rajasthan Patrika Prakashan, 1987.
भविष्यपुराण (भाग 1-3), नाग पब्लिशर्स, दिल्ली, 1984.
Bhavishyapurana (parts 1-3), Nag Publishers, Delhi, 1984.
मत्स्यपुराण, मेहरचन्द लछमनदास, दिल्ली, 1984.
Matsyapurana, Meherchand Lachmandas, Delhi, 1984.
मनुस्मृति, (सम्पा. एवं हि.अनु.) पं. रामेश्वर भट्ट, चौखम्भा संस्कृत प्रतिष्ठान, दिल्ली, 2011.
Manusmriti, edited and translated by Pandit Rameshwar Bhatt, Chaukhamba Sanskrit Pratishtan, Delhi, 2011.
मन्त्रमहोदधि, महीधर, (सम्पा. एवं व्या.) सुधाकर मालवीय, चौखम्भा संस्कृत प्रतिष्ठान, दिल्ली, 2015.
Mantramahodhati, edited and translated by Sudhakar Malviya, Chaukhamba Sanskrit Prathishtan, Delhi, 2014.

महाभारत (भाग 1-18), वेदव्यास, (सम्पा.) विष्णु एस. सुक्थंकर, भण्डारकर ओरियण्टल रिसर्च इंस्टीट्यूट, पूना, 1998.

Mahabharata (parts 1-18), Veda Vyasa, edited by Vishnu S. Sukthankar, Bhandarkar Oriental Research Institute, Pune, 1998.

महाभारत (भाग 1-6), वेदव्यास, (हि.अनु.) रामनारायणदत्त शास्त्री, गीता प्रेस गोरखपुर, पुनर्मुद्रित संस्करण, 2006.

Mahabharata (parts 1-6), Veda Vyasa, translated by Ramnarayan Shastri, Gita Press, Gorakhpur, 2006.

मार्कण्डेयपुराण, चौखम्भा विद्याभवन, वाराणसी, 1995.

Markandeya purana, Chaukhamba Vidyabhavan, Varanasi, 1995.

महर्षिकुलवैभव, पण्डित मधुसूदन ओझा, (सं.टीका) गिरिधर शर्मा चतुर्वेदी, (हि.अनु.) देवीदत्त शर्मा, राजस्थान प्राच्य प्रतिष्ठान, जयपुर, 1994.

Maharshikulavaibhava, Pandit Madhusudan Ojha, commentary by Giridhar Sharma Chaturvedi, translated by Devidutt Sharma, Rajasthan Prachya Prathishtan, Jaipur, 1994.

यज्ञसरस्वती, पण्डित मधुसूदन ओझा, (सम्पा.) प्रद्युम्न शर्मा ओझा

Yagyasaraswati, Pandit Madhusudan Ojha, edited and published by Pradhyumn Sharma Ojha, 1946.

रजोवाद, पण्डित मधुसूदन ओझा, (सम्पा.) वी.एस. अग्रवाल, बनारस हिन्दू विश्वविद्यालय, वाराणसी, 1964.

Rajovada, Pandit Madhusudan Ojha, edited by V.S. Aggrawal, Banaras Hindu University, Varanasi, 1964.

रामायण, वाल्मीकि, (भाग 1-8), (सम्पा.) शास्त्री श्रीनिवासकट्टिमुधोल्कर,परिमल पब्लिकेशन, दिल्ली, 1983.

Valmiki Ramayana (parts 1-8), edited by Shastri Srinivas Katti Mudhvolkar, Parimal Publication, Delhi, 1983.

वर्णसमीक्षा, पण्डित मधुसूदन ओझा, (सम्पा.) दयानन्दभार्गव, (हि.अनु.) शिवदत्त शर्मा चतुर्वेदी, मधुसूदन ओझा शोध प्रकोष्ठ, जोधपुर.

Varnasamiksha, Pandit Madhusudan Ojha, edited by Dayanand Bhargav, translated by Shivdutt Sharma Chaturvedi, Madhusudan Ojha Shodh Prakosht, Jodhpur,1991.

वायुपुराण, (हि.व्या.) शिवजीत सिंह, चौखम्भा विद्याभवन, वाराणसी, 2013.

Vayupurana, translated by Shivjit Singh, Chaukhamba Vidyabhavan, Varanasi, 2013.

वामनपुराण, (सम्पा.) आनन्दस्वरूप गुप्त, (हि.अनु.) गोपालचन्द्र वेदान्तशास्त्री एवं नारायण सिंह, सर्वभारतीय काशीराज न्यास दुर्ग, रामनगर, वाराणसी, 1938.

Vamanpurana, edited by Anandswarup Gupt and translated by Gopalchand Vedantashastri and Narayan Singh, Sarvabharatiya Kashiraj Nyas Durg, Ramnagar, Varanasi, 1968.

विज्ञानविद्युत्, पण्डित मधुसूदन ओझा, (हि.अनु.) शिवदत्त शर्मा चतुर्वेदी, राजस्थान पत्रिकाप्रकाशन, 1990.

Vigyanvidyutha, Pandit Madhusudan Ojha, translated by Shivdutt Sharma Chaturvedi, Rajasthan Patrika Prakashan, 1990.

विष्णुपुराण, नाग पब्लिशर्स, दिल्ली, 1985.

Vishnupurana, Nag Publishers, Delhi, 1985.

विष्णुस्मृति, (सम्पा.) जूलियसजॉली, चौखम्भा अमरभारती प्रकाशन, वाराणसी, 2010.

Vishnusmriti, edited by Julius Jolly, Chaukhamba Amarbharati Prakashan, Varanasi, 2010.

वेदधर्मव्याख्यान, पण्डित मधुसूदन ओझा, (सम्पा.) दयानन्दभार्गव, (हि.अनु.) सत्यप्रकाशदुबे, मधुसूदन ओझा शोध प्रकोष्ठ, जोधपुर, 1999.

Vedadharmavyakhyan, Pandit Madhusudan Ojha, edited by Dayanand Bhargav and translated by Satyaprakash Dubey, Madhusudan Ojha Shodh Prakosht, Jodhpur, 1999.

वैज्ञानिकोपाख्यान एवं वैदिकोपाख्यान, पण्डित मधुसूदन ओझा, (सम्पा.) सुरजनदास स्वामी, वि.सं. 2007.

Vaigyanikopakhyan and *vaidikopakhyan*, Pandit Madhusudan Ojha, edited by Surjandas Swami, published by Pradhyumn Sharma Ojha, Jaipur, 1950.

व्योमवाद, पण्डित मधुसूदन ओझा, (सम्पा.) दयानन्दभार्गव, (हि.अनु.) अनन्त शर्मा, मधुसूदन ओझा शोध प्रकोष्ठ, जोधपुर, 1993.

Vyomavada, Pandit Madhusudan Ojha, edited by Dayanand Bhargav, translated by Anant Sharma, Madhusudan Ojha Shodh Prakosht, Jodhpur, 1993.

शतपथब्राह्मण (भाग 1-2), (सम्पा.) विद्याधर शर्मा, भारतीय विद्या प्रकाशन, दिल्ली, 1994.

Shatapatha Brahmana (parts 1-2), edited by Vidyadhar Sharma, Bharatiya Vidya Prakashan, Delhi, 1994.

शारीरकविज्ञान, पण्डित मधुसूदन ओझा, (हि. अनु.) शिवदत्त शर्मा चतुर्वेदी, राजस्थान पत्रिका प्रकाशन, 1990.

Sharirikavigyana, Pandit Madhusudan Ojha, translated by Shivdutt Sharma Chaturvedi, Rajasthan Patrika Prakashan, 1990.

शारीरकविमर्श, पण्डित मधुसूदन ओझा, (सम्पा.) आद्यादत्त ठाकुर, वि.सं. 2001.

Sharirikavimarsha, Pandit Madhusudan Ojha, edited by Giridhar Sharma Chaturvedi, Jaipur, 1943.

शुक्लयजुर्वेदसंहिता (महीधरभाष्यसहित), (हि. व्या.) रामकृष्ण शास्त्री, चौखम्भा विद्याभवन, वाराणसी, पुनर्मुद्रित संस्करण, 1996.

Shuklayajurvedasamhita, translated by Ramakrishna Shastri, Chaukhamba Vidyabhavan, Varanasi, 1996.

श्रीमद्भगवद्गीता विज्ञानभाष्य, पण्डित मधुसूदन ओझा, (हि.अनु.) गणेशी लाल सुथार, मधुसूदन ओझा शोध प्रकोष्ठ, जयनारायण विश्वविद्यालय, जोधपुर, 2006.

Shrimadbhagwadgitavigyanabhashya, Pandit Madhusudan Ojha, translated by Ganeshi Lal Suthar, Madhusudan Ojha Shodh Prakosht, Jodhpur, 2006.

श्रीमद्भगवद्गीता विज्ञानभाष्य, पण्डित मधुसूदन ओझा, (सम्पा.) नरेन्द्रअवस्थी, (हि.अनु.) आर. टी. व्यास, मधुसूदन ओझा शोध प्रकोष्ठ, जयनारायण विश्वविद्यालय, जोधपुर, 2009.

श्रीमद्भागवपुराण (भाग 1-2), गीताप्रेसगोरखपुर, 1992.

Shrimadbhagwadgitavigyanabhashya, Pandit Madhusudan Ojha, edited by Narendra Awasthi, translated by R.T Vyas, Madhusudan Ojha Shodh Prakosht, Jodhpur, 1991.

श्रीमद्भगवतगीता, (सम्पा.) वासुदेव लक्ष्मण शास्त्री पणशीकर, चौखम्भा संस्कृत प्रतिष्ठान, दिल्ली, 1992.

Shrimadbhagwadgita, edited by Vasudev Lakshman Shastri, Chaukhamba Sanskrit Pratishtan, Delhi, 1992.

सदसद्वाद, पण्डित मधुसूदन ओझा, (सम्पा.) पद्मलोचन शर्मा.

Sadasdvadh, Pandit Madhusudan Ojha, edited by Padmalochan Sharma (publisher and year of publication not known).

सन्ध्योपासन रहस्य, पण्डित मधुसूदन ओझा, (सम्पा.) प्रद्युम्न शर्मा, वि.सं. 2021.

Sandhyopasana rahasya, Pandit Madhusudan Ojha, translated by Surjandas Swami, published by Pradhyumn Sharma Ojha, 1964.

सामवेदसंहिता (सायणभाष्यसहित), (सम्पा. एवं व्या.) पं. रामस्वरूप शर्मा गौड, चौखम्भा विद्याभवन, वाराणसी, पुनर्मुद्रित संस्करण, 1994.

Samvedasamhita, edited and translated by Pandit Ramswarup Sharma Gaur, Chaukhamba Vidyabhavan, Varanasi, 1994.

स्कन्दपुराण (भाग 1-7), नाग पब्लिशर्स, दिल्ली, 1983.

Skandapurana (parts 1-7), Nag Publishers, Delhi, 1986.

सिद्धान्तशिरोमणि, भास्कराचार्य, (भाग 1-2), (सम्पा. एवं व्या.) सत्यदेव शर्मा, चौखम्भा सुरभारती प्रकाशन, वाराणसी, 2016.

Sidhanthashiromani, Bhaskaracharya (Parts 1-2), edited and translated by Satyadev Sharma, Chaukhamba Surbharati Prakashan, Varanasi, 2016.

सुश्रुत संहिता, सुश्रुत, (भाग 1-3) (सम्पा. एवं व्या.) अनन्तराम शर्मा, चौखम्भा सुरभारती प्रकाशन, वाराणसी, 2013.

Susruth Samhita, *Susruth* (parts 1-3), edited and translated by Anantram Sharma, Chaukhamba Surbharati Prakashan, Varanasi, 2013.

सूर्यसिद्धान्त, (सम्पा. एवं व्या.) रामचन्द्रपाण्डेय, चौखम्भा सुरभारती प्रकाशन, वाराणसी, 2014.

Suryasidhanta, edited and translated by Ramchandra Pandey, Chaukhamba Surbharati Prakashan, Varanasi, 2014.

संशयतदुच्छेदवाद, पण्डित मधुसूदन ओझा, (हि.भाष्य) मोतीलाल शास्त्री, राजस्थान पत्रिका प्रकाशन, जयपुर, वि.सं. 2050.

Sanshayataduchedvada, Pandit Madhusudan Ojha, translated by Pandit Motilal Shastri, Rajasthan Patrika Prakashan, Jaipur, 1993.

स्मार्तकुण्डसमीक्षाध्याय, पण्डित मधुसूदन ओझा, (सम्पा.) रामकृष्ण व्यास, (हि.अनु.) रामप्रपन्न शास्त्री, राजस्थान पत्रिका प्रकाशन, जयपुर, वि.सं. 2044.

Smarthkundsamikshadyaya, Pandit Madhusudan Ojha, edited by Ramkrishna Vyas and translated by Ramprapanna Shastri, Rajasthan Patrika Prakashan, Jaipur, 1987.

असाक्षत् स्रोत

Secondary Sources

ईशावास्योपनिषद्, हिन्दी विज्ञान भाष्य, मोतीलाल शास्त्री, राजस्थान, वि. सं. 1990.

Ishwasyopanishad, Pandit Motilal Shastri, Rajasthan, 1933.

कठोपनिषद्, हिन्दी विज्ञान भाष्य, मोतीलाल शास्त्री, राजस्थान पत्रिका प्रकाशन, जयपुर, 1997.

Katopanishad, Pandit Motilal Shastri, Rajasthan Patrika Prakashan, Jaipur, 1997.

दिग्देशकालस्वरूपमीमांसा, मोतीलाल शास्त्री, राजस्थान वैदिकशोध संस्थान प्रकाशन, जयपुर, सं 2015

Digdeshkalaswarupamimamsa, Pandit Motilal Shastri, Rajasthan Vaidikshod Sansthan Prakashan, Jaipur, 1958.

पुराण परिशीलन, गिरिधर शर्मा चतुर्वेदी, बिहार राष्ट्रभाषा परिषद्, पटना, द्वितीय संस्करण 1998.

Purana Parisheelan, Giridhar Sharma Chaturvedi, Bihar Rashtrabhasha Parishad, Patna, 1998.

प्रश्नोपनिषद्, हिन्दी विज्ञान भाष्य, मोतीलाल शास्त्री, राजस्थान पत्रिका प्रकाशन, जयपुर 1995.

Prasnopanishad, Pandit Motilal Shastri, Rajasthan Patrika Prakashan, Jaipur, 1995.

भारती मानव और उसकी भावुकता हिन्दी विज्ञान भाष्य, मोतीलाल शास्त्री, राजस्थान वैदिकशोध संस्थान प्रकाशन, जयपुर, सं 2012.

Bharati Manav aur uski bhavukta, Pandit Motilal Shastri, Rajasthan Vaidikshodh Sansthan Prakashan, Jaipur, 1955.

मुण्डकोपनिषद्, हिन्दी विज्ञान भाष्य, मोतीलाल शास्त्री, राजस्थान पत्रिका प्रकाशन, जयपुर, वि. सं. 2049.

Mundakopanishad, Pandit Motilal Shastri, Rajasthan Patrika Prakashan, Jaipur, 1992.

वैदिक विज्ञान और भारतीय संस्कृति, गिरिधर शर्मा चतुर्वेदी, बिहार राष्ट्रभाषा परिषद्, पटना, द्वितीय संस्करण 1972.

Vaidik Vijnana and Bharatiya Sanskriti, Giridhar Sharma Chaturvedi, Bihar Rashtrabhasha Parishad, Patna, 1972.

वैदिकविज्ञान, गिरिधर शर्मा चतुर्वेदी, श्रीलालबहादुरशास्त्री राष्ट्रीय संस्कृत विद्यापीठ, नई दिल्ली, द्वितीय संस्करण, 2005.

Vaidik Vijnana, Giridhar Sharma Chaturvedi, Shri Lal Bahadur Shastri Rashtriya Sanskrit Vidyapeeth, New Delhi, 2005.

शतपथब्राह्मण, हिन्दी विज्ञान भाष्य, (छह भाग) मोतीलाल शास्त्री, मानवाश्रम, जयपुर, 1959.

Shatapatha Brahmana (parts 1-6), Pandit Motilal Shastri, Manavashram, Jaipur, 1959.

सत्तानिरपेक्ष संस्कृति एवं सत्तासापेक्ष सभ्यता शब्द, मोतीलाल शास्त्री, राजस्थान वैदिकशोध संस्थान प्रकाशन, जयपुर, सं 2015.

Sattanirapeksha Sanskriti avam Sattasapeksha Sabhyata Shabd, Pandit Motilal Shastri, Rajasthan Vaidikshodh Sansthan Prakashan, Jaipur, 1958.

सांस्कृतिक व्याख्यान पञ्चकम्, मोतीलाल शास्त्री, राजस्थान पत्रिका प्रकाशन, जयपुर, 1994.

Sanskritikavyakhyanpanchakam, Pandit Motilal Shastri, Rajasthan Patrika Prakashan, Jaipur, 1994.

गीताविज्ञानभाष्य, मोतीलाल शास्त्री, जयपुर, 1939

Gitavigyanabhashya, Pandit Motilal Shastri, Jaipur, 1939.

Before the Beginning and After the End, Rishi Kumar Mishra, Rupa & Co, Delhi 2000.

The Cosmic Matrix, Rishi Kumar Mishra, Rupa & Co, Delhi 2001.

The Realm of Supraphysics, Rishi Kumar Mishra, Rupa & Co, Delhi 2003.

The Ultimate Dialogue, Rishi Kumar Mishra, Rupa & Co, Delhi 2007.
The Whole Being, Rishi Kumar Mishra, Rupa & Co, Delhi 2011.

कोशग्रन्थ
Dictionaries

अंग्रेजी-हिन्दी शब्दकोश-कामिलबुल्के; कैथोलिक प्रेस, राँची, 1972.
English-Hindi Dictionary, Camil Bulke, Catholic Press, Ranchi, 1972.
पारिजातकोश, सम्पादक- पं. ईश्वरचन्द्र, परिमल पब्लिकेशन, दिल्ली, 2005.
Parijatakosha, edited by Pandit Ishwarchand, Parimal Publication, Delhi, 2005.
भारतीय दर्शन बृहत्कोश - बच्चुलाल अवस्थी; शारदा पब्लिशिंग हाउस; 2004.
Bharatiya Darshan Brihatkosh, Bacchulal Awasti, Sharada Publishing House, 2004.
भारतीय दर्शनपरिभाषा कोश - दीनानाथ शुक्ला, प्रतिभा प्रकाशन, दिल्ली, 1993.
Bharatiya Darshan Paribhasha Kosha, Dinanath Shukla, Pratibha Prakashan, Delhi, 1993.
मीमांसाकोश -केवलानन्द सरस्वती, श्री सतुगुरूपब्लिकेशन्स, इण्डियन बुक सेंटर, दिल्ली, 1992.
Mimamsakosha, Kewalanand Saraswati, Sri Satguru Publications, Indian Book Centre, Delhi, 1992.
न्यायकोश-भीमाचार्य झलकीकर, भण्डारकर ओरिएन्टल रिसर्च इंस्टीच्यूट, पूना, 1978.
Nyayakosha, Bhimacharya Jhalkikar, Bhandarkar Oriental Research Institute, Pune, 1978.
वाचस्पत्यम्, सङ्कलनकर्त्ता-तारानाथवाचस्पति, राष्ट्रीय संस्कृत संस्थान, नई दिल्ली, पुनमुद्रित संस्करण, 2002.
Vachaspathyam, Taranath Vachaspati, Rashtriya Sanskrit Sansthan, New Delhi, 2002.
शब्दकल्पद्रुम, राजाराधकान्त देव, राष्ट्रीय संस्कृत संस्थान, नई दिल्ली, पुनमुद्रित संस्करण, 2002.
Shabdkalpdvam, Raja Radhakant Dev, Rashtriya Sanskrit Sansthan, New Delhi, 2002.
संस्कृत वाङ्मयकोश (परिभाषा-खण्ड), (सम्पा) श्रीधर भास्कर वर्णेकर, भारतीय भाषा परिषद् कलकत्ता, 1932.
Sanskrit Vakya Kosh, edited by Sridhar Bhaskar Varnokar, Bharatiya Bhasha Parishad, Calcutta, 1932.
संस्कृत-हिन्दी शब्दकोश, वामन शिवरामआप्टे, (सम्पा.) उमा प्रसाद पाण्डेय, कमल प्रकाशन, नई दिल्ली; 1999.
Sanskrit-Hindi Shabdkosh, Vaman Shivram Apte, edited by Uma Prasad Pandey, Kamal Prakashan, Delhi, 1997.
Encyclopedia of Indian Philosophies, (Ed.) Karl H. Potter, Vol. 1-2, Motilal Banarsidass, Delhi, 1995
Oxford English-English Hindi Dictionary, (Ed.) Dr Suresh Kumar & Dr Ramanath Sahai, Oxford University Press, 2008.

श्लोकानुक्रमणिका

Verse Index

आ

ऐ

ओ

औ

द

ह

Index

Pandit Madhusudan Ojha

Vidyavachaspati Pandit Madhusudan Ojha (1866–1939) was an illustrious scholar of the Vedas. His lifelong devotion and profound scholarship in pursuing Veda Vijnana led not only to the revival of the Vedic studies in its true spirit, but also cleared many myths and misleading theories surrounding the ancient texts.

His outstanding command over Sanskrit was matched in equal measure by his profound knowledge and insights into the Vedas. Under the guidance and advice of his guru, Pandit Shiv Kumar Shastri, Pandit Ojha dedicated most of his life to understand the mysteries of Veda Vijnana and explain it to a wider audience of seekers. Pandit Madhusudan Ojha wrote 288 volumes in all, many of which were lost through neglect. Only sixty of them have so far seen the light of the day; *Indravijayah* is one of them. Most of his works were comprehensive in content and volume, running over 500 pages. He was a good illustrator and illustrated many of his works himself.

His writing was prolific and illuminating. His oration was equally inspirational and incisive. From the royal courts of Jaipur to the learning centres of Kashi, Pandit Ojha's name was taken with reverence. He continues to be a torchbearer of Vedic wisdom even today with countless *acharyas* (teachers) and scholars across the world pursuing the path of learning which he chose—to explore the boundless wisdom of the Vedas.

About Shri Shankar Shikshayatan

For thousands of years, the oldest repository of mankind's understanding of the mysteries of Creation, the Vedas, remained buried in the dark recesses of time and history. It was only a little more than a hundred years ago that an exceptional scholar and teacher, Pandit Madhusudan Ojha, rescued these lost treasures of wisdom from the debris of ignorance, distortion and misrepresentation.

For Pandit Madhusudan Ojha, the Vedas represented the ultimate knowledge, Veda Vijnana, of how everything in the universe owes its creation to one source and how that source multiplies in diverse and variegated forms. He devoted his whole life in pursuit of Veda Vijnana.

Realizing that the task he had undertaken would need more than a lifetime, Pandit Ojha took Motilal Shastriji as his disciple and found him to be an illustrious student who could take forward this unparalleled work of rediscovering Veda Vijnana.

Following the footsteps of his guru, Pandit Motilal Shastri wrote extensively on the wisdom contained in the Vedas with remarkable clarity and assurance. Subsequently, Shastriji, in turn, found a gifted disciple and torchbearer of Veda Vijnana in Rishi Kumar Mishra.

Shri Shankar Shikshayatan, set up by Rishi Kumar Mishra at the beginning of the millennium, embodies the spirit, purpose and wisdom of Pandit Madhusudan Ojha, and seeks to generate awareness about the invaluable treasures contained within the Vedas as enunciated by him.

Bharatavarsha: The India Narrative, an English translation of Pandit Ojha's work *Indravijayah*, is the first book to be published by Shri Shankar Shikshayatan.

In addition, Shri Shikshayatan has hosted several published works of Pandit Ojha, Pandit Motilal Shastri and Rishi Kumar Mishra on www.shankarshikshayatan.org

Translator's Acknowledgements

On the publication of the translation of Madhusudan Ojha's extraordinary *Indravijayah*, I recall with deep gratitude the affection and trust that revered Shri R.K. Mishra ji bestowed on me. I recall his great goodness and commitment to the cause of India's Vedic knowledge systems and the need to relocate the Indian mind in that intellectual heritage. Towards that end, Mishra ji decided on having this book translated and gave me this great opportunity to translate it and, thereby, serve, in a small way, the cause that was so dear to him. Shri Shankar Shikshayatan, the Trust founded by Mishra ji to promote the study and dissemination of Vedic Vijnana, entrusted the task to me and supported it generously, for which I am deeply obliged to the Trust.

Through all this, from the very beginning, Mrs Renuka Mishra, affectionately addressed by us as Renuka ji, inspired and guided this endeavour. To me personally, Renuka ji has ever been very considerate and generous.

I acknowledge with deep gratitude the help extended in this complex translation of a profound text by the following friend-professors and students who adorn faculty positions now. Their invaluable help came in many forms—academic and technical advice, etymological and referential research and often even draft translation of difficult portions.

Whatever merit and honour comes to be attached to this work is theirs as well, equally:

Professors:
Jagbir Singh
Shrawan Kumar Sharma
D.R. Purohit
Rajnish Kumar Mishra

Student-professors:
Ms Garima
Dr Chetan Katoch
Dr Avinash